Dear Noelani

THE ROAD TO
BANDIDON SERIES

Book One

A Prince of a King

by

Gene Abravaya

For a lunch break
or a rainy day.
Thanks for reading.

Gene

Ocean of
No Boating
This Way to
the Edge of
the World
Castle Bandidon
Bandidon
Land of the
Woolly-Bullies
Noel's
Shoals
Cumberland
Cumberland Gap
Gonad
Uncharted Lands
Pyorrhea
The Tanta Mounts
Jasperland
Hyperbole
Upper
Thorax
Land of
The
Gravelings
Thalamus
The Entrance
The Sea
of
Ill Luck
Lower
Thorax
Badlands
Very
Badlands
Appen-Dectia

PROLOGUE

I, Ayland Downing, being the last of the noble order of Gudi-Gudi Bowmen, too aged and bent now to lift my bow against the evil I swore to oppose upon joining the order as a young man, take pen in trembling hand while there is still strength in me to do so, and record this story in the hope that some traveler, lost and bewildered as I once was, might stumble upon it and - unless he or she is completely witless - publish it and live comfortably on the profits.

Some fifty-odd years have passed since I first became a Gudi-Gudi and embarked upon the arduous road of self-denial and discovery. During all that time my body and mind were sharply honed and quick to respond. But lately a fog has settled on my eyes; my strength is failing; and I have suddenly developed bladder problems.

Admittedly, my greatest failing has always been my vanity. Not wishing to suffer ridicule like one of those old men who, oblivious of his surroundings, passes wind or wets himself, I have parted company with civilization and moved to the caves where I first encountered the spirit of my predecessor. Aye, a spirit I say, the master of all Gudi-Gudis, who passed on to me his powerful bow then possessed me when I was not looking.

I can still recall the terror I felt as he settled in among my organs. My heart raced at the gallop and carried my breath away; my head began to spin. But I quickly realized he was there to teach me the ways of the Gudi-Gudi as well as offer an occasional suggestion when I could not decide what to wear for the day or what to eat for lunch.

Though it is over fifty years since he took up residence inside my body, which, I should note, made me feel very bloated at times, I think of him almost every day. I can still hear his deep, resonant voice, coming from a point half-way between my ears. "A Gudi-Gudi does not tremble in the face of the enemy! He does not shrink away! Lock your knees! Lock them! Not knock them!"

I was a slow learner then, and in those early days before I was even a novice, I would hit my head in frustration and cry, "Help me! Please! I'm troubled and confused!" But people began to give me strange looks; so I stopped doing that.

Imagine what would have happened if I had told them I was addressing a spirit within me, that of an ancient bowman who was encouraging me to fight evil-doers. Why, I'd have been gagged instantly and taken to the nearest asylum.

Even now, after so many years of silence, I will often pause and call to him softly, "Oh, Spirit – Are you with me?" And then I will wait, hoping that the movement within me is not just nature calling.

But there is never a reply. He is gone.

Circumstances being what they were, I did not even have the chance to say goodbye. Though he left me feeling most uncertain of my future, I have always been grateful to him for the knowledge and skills he imparted to me, not to mention the two inches that he somehow added to my height.

So, I have spent my life as he would have had me spend it, traveling to the limits of civilization, fighting injustice wherever I have happened upon it. And I have come to learn one thing: there are lots of nasty people out there.

I have known many defeats (a Gudi-Gudi can only do so much,) but I have also known many triumphs for which I was rewarded with much kindness and good fellowship.

Money would have been nice, too, but nothing substantial was ever offered.

Except once I should note. I was given property and a

title by the King of Bandidon, Bryand the first, for helping to restore him to his throne. The house, I'm told, for I have never seen it, overlooks the sea near the town of Port Lansia, the place of my birth. It is infested with insects whose diet consists solely of wood and costs me a fortune each year in upkeep and taxes. I would sell it but then I would lose my title and, being as vain as I am, I would no longer have anything to brag about to the other hermits in the area.

I mention the King of Bandidon and joy immediately fills my heart. Also sadness; for he is gone now along with so many of my other friends. Much of this story is about him and his struggle to become King. Were it not for Bryand I might still be a simple scribe and mapmaker, working in the same shop as had my father and his father before him.

Were it not for Bryand, I might never have traveled beyond the end of my street, let alone to the farthest reaches of civilization. Were it not for Bryand, I might never have known a woman's love, one I might add that has sustained me throughout years of hardship and deprivation.

However, were it not for Bryand, I might never have been chased by soldiers bent on cutting out my innards. I might never have experienced camping in mosquito infested woods with only a rock for a pillow, or learned the ins and outs of foraging spores and roots to satisfy my gnawing hunger.

Can you imagine it!? Spores and roots!

Were it not for Bryand, I might never have risked drowning while fording a swollen river, nor risked plummeting to my death along a hazardous mountain trail. Nor might I have risked strangulation at the hands of a savage beast, nor the countless other things that left me driveling like a village idiot when I wasn't completely frozen with fear!

THANK YOU, MY LORD, FOR ALL THOSE THINGS I AM CERTAIN I COULD NOT HAVE LIVED WITHOUT...!!!

Forgive me, but that's been pent up inside me for many years.

Yet, strangely enough, by voicing my anger, I have just discovered something I never realized before. True, I could have lived my whole life without experiencing any of those things and not have regretted a single day. But then again, if I had not lived through each and every one, I might never have discovered the bow nor understood its worth.

But I have gotten far ahead of myself, which is something I tend often to do these days. It seems my mind travels faster than my fingers. My fingers travel faster than my legs, and my legs travel faster than my urine. I can stand at my favorite spot, oh, mayhaps three, four minutes at a time, waiting to release, concerned, should I happen to be discovered, that I might be taken for an exhibitionist...

Alas, there I go getting ahead of myself again.

Anyway...

I did not find the bow and encounter the master of all Gudi-Gudis until much had already occurred to change the quiet life I pursued. A life that consisted mostly of copying books and legal documents for the nobility of Port Lansia or charting maps for the sea captains whenever they dropped anchor in the harbor. It was an orderly life, made more so by the little lists I scribbled for myself. (Lists have always been important to me.)

Even the arguments with my clerk, Rolfo, who I will describe in detail later on, were so commonplace that a day - make that an hour - without one would have proven out of the ordinary.

I will say this much about him. He has been with me many years (I am looking at him now as I write this,) and in all that time he has never learned to use a handkerchief. I would be loathe to ever touch his right sleeve.

Looking back at those routine days in my shop, I can honestly say we had no idea of the drama that was unfolding around us. Had anyone suggested then that I would take up a bow in the service of my King, or that Rolfo - who was a bigger coward than I - would be declared a national hero, I would have laughed myself silly and called the person daft. But how could I have known? The future is something always just around the corner and out of sight, like the ruffian who once beaned me on the head. To know what will become of us, let alone the next man, is not within our power.

This brings to mind something that Nap, the rug maker from down the street, once said upon waylaying me as he was want to do whenever I made the mistake of passing his shop. He was forever expounding on the most ridiculous topics, but this one remark struck me as being, for him, quite profound.

I remember he was untying a knot in some thread when, suddenly, he looked up and said, "It occurs to me, Ayland, that each man's destiny is but a single skein feeding an enormous loom; and on that loom must be a tapestry of grand design."

I admit that, at the time, I was thinking more about the shoddy rug he had sold me than what he was saying, but it must have impressed me or I would not have been able to recall it today.

So, I begin this story not at the time of my own entrance, nor King Bryand's, nor at the time of our births. For destiny was already at work on its 'grand design' long before either of us were born. I must begin earlier still - forty eight years to be precise - so that you, the discoverer of this work, will know the whole story.

Why you might ask? The answer is quite simple. History demands it. Truth demands it. And most important of all - I've been waiting a long time to tell it.

CHAPTER ONE

Times being dark as they were, most men lived their whole lives untouched by the outside world; except, of course, for those unlucky few who were cleaved in two by rampaging knights or devoured by foraging beasts. However, glamorous ends like these did not happen very often. One was more likely to be felled by a falling tree or a persistent cough or a bad piece of meat. In fact, there were so many ordinary things in the world that were potentially lethal anyone who reached the age of twelve was considered lucky. Anyone who reached the age of twenty was considered ancient, and anyone older than that was looked on with suspicion, as if he were in league with an evil agent.

With the recent advances in medicine, and by this, I mean the wondrous new poultices that physicians use instead of those slimy blood-sucking leeches, the average person can now expect to live a long and prosperous life of anywhere from thirty-five to forty years. In some cases, even longer depending on one's physical condition.

Aye, a strong and healthy body is essential in weathering the challenges of life, and especially helpful when attempting to outrun a conquering horde bent on murder and destruction.

I, for one, am over seventy. But mine is a special case. I have never been an outstanding physical specimen. Even after becoming a Gudi-Gudi and being possessed by the Master Gudi-Gudi's spirit, I cannot say there was much difference in my physical appearance. True, he added two inches to my height, but for the most part I was still the lanky, nondescript weakling that the town bully mercilessly pelted with rocks whenever she happened upon me.

Oh, she made my life hell! The dirty little trollop! May the dogs of the underworld be forever biting her on...

Pardon me. I digress. Again.

Where was I?

Oh, yes.

The land was tilled by peasants, a dreary lot, who believed the edge of the world lay just beyond the next rise. So firmly entrenched was this belief that anyone who was foolish enough to venture beyond the next rise, was looked on as something inhuman by the people he encountered there and immediately burned at the stake.

Superstitions abounded, and out of ignorance and fear, Gods with tempestuous dispositions were created to bear answer to the misfortunes of a seemingly unalterable existence.

There were Gods for everything; for making the crops grow; the winds blow; the rain and the snow.

There was a God for war, a God for peace, and a God for temporary armistices. There was a God for love, for child bearing, and there was a God for potency who was greatly revered.

There was a God for pleasure and debauchery; he was popular too. And there was a God for penitence, but he was seldom called upon. And ruling all these Gods was a God who might, at any moment, countermand anything the lesser Gods had done.

He was known by many names. Oygut; Watchitdare. But Himagain was the one most often used.

"But why should the crops have failed?!" a peasant might cry. "Did we not give proper sacrifice to Humus, God of Vegetation?"

And then someone might reply, "Uh-oh, it must

have been Him again!"

Now men were not the only creatures inhabiting the land at this time. There were others as well; even some with keen intelligence such as elves and dwarves and forest sprites. But these races kept far away from human settlements. For they were hounded by men, who believed they were magical beings and, therefore, capable of providing them with unearned income.

Though most elves and dwarves did indeed have a crock of gold stashed away, there was nothing magical about this. Most elves and dwarves simply knew how to manage their money. It was not their fault that men were spendthrifts; nor was it their fault that men were volatile creatures who tended to go unwashed for long periods of time. That was just the way of things.

To be fair, I must say we humans have many redeeming qualities as well. One that comes to mind at once is the affection we show to our young. There are some creatures about, namely goblins and trolls, that look upon their offspring as their next meal.

This was a time of overwhelming ignorance. Men were slaves to their passions, often killing one another over a throw of the dice or the attention of a woman. Not even the very rich understood the importance of knowledge; although the rich were smart enough to hire poor men to do their fighting for them.

Lovemaking they did for themselves, except for the Earl of Gimmimore who, it is said, enjoyed watching others.

Despite this abundant ignorance, there were still some men who sought to make something better of themselves; men who were born with higher intelligence, inasmuch as they instinctively knew how to utilize all their fingers when counting. Knowledge such as this gave them power over other men, especially at droving time.

One such man was Armadon, Overlord of all the

Bandidonian Kingdoms. Yet he was not always of royal station; in fact, he was not even of noble birth. At the time of his emergence, Bandidon was nothing more than a handful of minor Kingdoms, warring endlessly over boundary lines that had never been clearly drawn.

Out of this disorder came Armadon, a simple man and a smithy by trade, who, with cunning and skill, united his people by fulfilling an ancient prophecy.

Once a year, on what had come to be known as Knock-Knock Day, which was always the fourteenth day after the first full moon after the first thaw, the strongest men of the country would travel to the wooded hills of Bandidon.

There they would gather in a mossy glade in whose center stood a large rectangular boulder about six feet tall and four feet wide. It was called the Headstone, and upon it was inscribed:

Who So Breaketh This Stone with His Head,
Shall Be .... King .. This ... . Day .. ..

After years of studying ancient texts and manuscripts, I have come to learn that this was only part of the engraving, the rest having been obliterated over the ages by the crash of many heads. The original inscription was:

Who So Breaketh This Stone with His Head,
Shall Be Treated as a King on This His Last Day of Life.

Now Armadon was a very crafty fellow. Not wishing to have his head smashed in like so many of the other candidates before him, he fashioned a skull cap of iron and covered it with the skin of a long-haired goat that he had dyed with pitch to match the color of his own woolly hair. When next came the annual ritual and his name was called, he stepped over the bodies of the candidates who had preceded him and charged the stone like an angry bull.

Once; twice; three times. The crowd was amazed at his fortitude. By now, even with the iron cap, Armadon was dazed.

His next attempt failed but this was because he charged - instead of the stone - a very stout friar with no neck who was dressed in gray robes. Luckily the friar was a congenial fellow who didn't mind being rammed in the chest. After a few dry heaves, he regained his breath and pointed Armadon in the right direction.

Most grateful, the smithy lowered his head and charged once more, this time cracking the stone in half upon impact. The crowd went wild and fell upon him, tossing him into the air again and again; and just two days later, when he had regained consciousness, Armadon was proclaimed King.

To understand a man like Armadon, it is important to keep in mind the time in which he lived. This was a barbarous age. Disputes between countries were settled on the battlefield. Arguments on a personal level were handled in much the same way.

Most men kept in mind the old adage, "Run him through or he'll do it to you." Armadon, though a man of insight, was no different.

To insure the safety of his newly acquired throne, he swiftly overwhelmed his enemies and confiscated their property. When the last of his enemies had fallen, he turned upon his allies, eliminating all but three friends he had known since childhood, bestowing upon them the fertile provinces of Willowbrook, Pepperill and Torklestone.

I must note that these three names, Willowbrook, Pepperill and Torklestone, will appear again in this story, so careful attention should be paid to them.

Not even the members of Armadon's family were spared, though in their case, he did the world a favor, for they were despicable people; and rather than execute some and thus create hard feelings amongst the rest, he decided it best to execute them all. All save his brother's wife, Herminie, whom he had long coveted.

And so he married his sister-in-law, which was not out of keeping with Bandidonian Law. Indeed, it is written:

He who takes his brother's life,
Must also take his brother's wife.

The next four years were dedicated to the conquering of other Kingdoms and the slaughtering of innocent peoples until Armadon had carved for himself a vast Empire. However, having already put thousands of men to the sword, there were not many left to subjugate, at least not for the first eighteen years or so. So during that time, he turned his attention to the betterment of his own land, building a mighty castle on the same spot as the Headstone. Armadon hired quarriers, stone masons, mortar makers, carpenters, plumbers, diggers, and other laborers. Blacksmiths, however, were overlooked, but only because Armadon still enjoyed doing his own smithing.

Within a scant ten years the castle was completed. During that time, a town, which had started as the barracks for the troops and laborers, grew up around it. Armadon named the town. Henceforth it would be called Bandidon. He proclaimed Bandidon (*the town*) the capital of Bandidon (*the land.*) The castle itself, he named Castle Bandidon.

Though a great warrior, Armadon was not very imaginative.

Then came the day the heralds were dispatched to every village and hamlet of the Empire. Queen Herminie had borne the King a son.

They named him Audanot, and it is he who is thought of as being the greatest of Bandidon's Kings.

Of course, we've only had three thus far, but nevertheless, the man was truly enlightened.

Upon the death of Armadon, who it is said, never fully recovered from the beating his head took on that long ago Knock-Knock Day, young Audanot assumed his place as King.

He was fourteen.

In three years' time, with the help of his father's friends, the Lords Willowbrook, Pepperill and Torkelstone, (*See? There are those important names again.*) Audanot rid the land of an army of robber trolls, stamped out the remaining grogre population *(the largest and most corpulent of the ogre species, also the most slovenly,)* and slew the last of the flagon dragons that was plundering the royal wineries.

The King was now seventeen, and it was long past the time for him to produce an heir. So he married the lady Benethia, who was of true noble birth, and, due chiefly to her influence, the King learned to rule wisely and benevolently.

A summer palace was built upon the shore of Lake Imakidagen, whose waters were known to have wondrous restorative powers. One drink and most people felt their aches and pains disappear.

Some even said it was capable of increasing one's sexual prowess, though I cannot endorse this claim, having drunk gallons of it myself with little or no effect.

The palace itself was an impressive structure made from stone and cut timbers. It was two stories, with a terrace that ran the entire length of its perimeter, and it was surrounded by breastworks and a moat that had been dug into the side of the lake.

Upon its completion, Audanot invited all the neighboring Kings and Queens - no matter what their net worth - to the palace for tournaments and feasts and other frolics that lasted past the summer, past the falling of the leaves, and well into the rainy season. In fact, Audanot seemed content to stay at the summer palace forever.

For these were happy days, crowned by the joyous news that Queen Benethia *(Queen Bee to her closest friends)* was with child. So they danced, and feasted, and partook of Lake Imakidagen's waters, unaware that their lives were about to change forever.

Aye, seven and a half months later, on a hot, cloying summer day, Queen Benethia felt a sudden rush inside her and, looking down, found her kirtle stained. At first, the King thought his wife was merely sweating, but when she screamed in pain and grabbed him by his bottom lip, he realized the birthing process had begun.

The Queen was quickly bound and gagged, and carried to her chamber. *(The reason for this, I can only assume, was to preserve her dignity before the masses)*. The royal midwife was summoned at once. She was a tall woman, with muscular arms and a rutty complexion. When not attending pregnant royals, she was out by the lake, coaching the ladies-in-waiting syncronized swimming team.

It is said, hearing of the Queen's condition excited her so, that she leaped from her coaching station and did handsprings across the castle lawn and through the rear gate.

In the meantime, shaken by his wife's display, King Audonot went to the palace chapel, where he placed a basket of chicken eggs upon the family alter and prayed to Placenta, the Goddess of childbirth, to favor his wife with a successful delivery.

The Goddess must have heard his prayers, for eighteen hours later, the king emerged onto the terrace, holding not one son, but two. Twins, they were, identical to the last wrinkle, and were it not for the different markings on their swaddling, no one could tell them apart.

Before the children were an hour old, Audanot had gathered his friends in the Great Hall of the palace to witness the proclaiming of the heir to his throne. The child who had emerged from his mother's womb first was named Bryand, after Benethia's father, and it was he who was to be the next King of Bandidon. The second child was named Daron, after the Queen's favorite uncle, despite the fact that he had fallen out of favor with the rest of her family.

It is said he had a brief indiscretion. In my research, I have discovered that the indiscretion was not brief but lasted more than ten years. This seems likely as it is also known that Daron's wife, the lady Nocum-Nierme, was devoutly religious, insisting often that she intended saving herself for the gods themselves after ascending to the heavens.

Trumpets blared in triumph, cymbals crashed, rainbows of garlands flew everywhere, yet the ceremony was not complete until Augor, the King's wizard, was summoned to the Great Hall.

Though enlightened in many ways, King Audanot was still a man of his times and believed in the power of magic only slightly less than he believed in the power of the Gods. Therefore, he always paid his wizard much courtesy and went out of his way to keep him happily employed.

Bursting with pride and expectation, the King said, "Speak to us, man. Tell us what greatness lies ahead for my sons."

So charged, Augor, being a master of the dark arts and a doctor of peptic fizzes, faced the King and, in a low, determined voice, replied, "Ten gold pieces, please. You know my oracles aren't free."

"Ten gold pieces?" said the King, surprised. "Isn't

your fee usually five?"

"How many princes do you see here, your majesty? Two, right? Two princes; two fees."

"Still, ten gold pieces--"

"All right, make it eight. But I'm not making much of a profit on this."

With the fee paid, his body went rigid; his face grew taut and sallow. A cold wind swept across the hall, dimming the torches, yet the room remained alight from an eerie glow that emanated from the wizard. Then, in tones that seemed to rise from the depths of the dark world itself, Augor chanted:

"He who is,
Is he who is not.
And he shall reap,
The other's lot.
Until such time,
In his brother's name,
The rightful heir,
His throne doth claim."

This profound declaration was followed by a lengthy pause during which Audanot and his friends glanced at one another with baffled looks upon their faces. But no one dared to utter a word because Augor was most fussy when interrupted in the middle of an incantation. Only after the wizard's eyes had uncrossed and the color had returned to his cheeks did the King venture to speak.

"Is that it?"

Augor glared at him.

"What I mean is," added the King with a tentative smile, "What does it mean?"

"How should I know," replied the wizard. "I'm not responsible for the things I say."

"But Augor--"

"Look, you get what you get. No refunds. Especially not after a discount."

At this, Augor clapped his hands and vanished in a blast of flames that knocked the King and his nobles off their feet. Unfortunately, the blast also set the furnishings in the room afire. In an instant, the ceiling rafters were ablaze as well, and then the apartments above. Thus the summer palace was burned to the ground and Audanot, in a terrible rage, went searching for the wizard with sword in hand. But Augor had seen everything in a prior vision and had already removed himself - as well as all of his belongings - far from Audanot's reach.

Things went from bad to worse. In the rush to protect the Princes from the flames, their swaddling was lost as they were handed from servant to servant, yeoman to yeoman, along the corridors, down the stairwell, through the main gate and across the drawbridge, until at last they were well beyond the moat and out of danger. However - being identical twins - without their swaddling, no one could tell them apart. Consequently, no one could say which of them was the first born.

Queen Benethia was not yet coherent from a labor that had lasted almost eighteen hours. The queen's mother had cataracts therefore her judgement was as clouded as her vision. Only the midwife could identify the children.

Distraught, Audanot went searching for her. But inasmuch as the fire had consumed her along with the princelings' swaddling, the king was prevented from pursuing the matter any further.

(I should note the ladies-in-waiting synchronized swim team suffered greatly from this development, too.)

A heated discussion with his friends ensued.

But no one could provide him with an answer to his dilemma. It was finally decided to consult the most learned man they could find at such short notice.

His name was Bertold, and he had been a priest in the service of Charisma, the God of politicians, until he had been caught skimming from the tithing box. While in prison he had written a book about his experiences that had won him minor acclaim. Since his release he had been touring the kingdom giving lectures.

"In my opinion," said the ex-priest. "And please remember, sire, this is just my opinion - any actions you take shall be solely your own-- ."

"Yes, yes, go on," said the King impatiently.

"Well, were I in your position, I would simply give the children the names you had planned and pretend that nothing happened."

"But what about the first born?"

"Perhaps you can say they came out at the same time."

Audanot's first impulse was to cut off the man's head. But maintaining his composure, he said, "And then what? Who would be the rightful heir?"

"In my opinion - and please remember, sire, this is just my opinion - I would leave the decision up to the Gods. Surely by their signs you will know which child deserves to rule in your place."

So, it was that Audanot held his sons in each of his arms, and deeming the child on his left, Bryand, and the child on his right, Daron, the decision was made to wait and see which of the two the Gods would favor.

For some time, the King thought himself cursed, for the babies did naught but spit up or suck their toes. Though Queen Benethia insisted this was normal behavior, Audanot remained unconvinced. He became so desperate that he even had the babies' fouled swaddling examined by a seer for any auspices.

"What is that?!" the King cried hopefully.

"Undigested corn, sire."

"Are you sure?"

"Quite, sire. I passed some myself the other day."

Finally, Queen Benethia - having had her fill of his dark mood - took him by the arms and shook him.

"Enough of this, my husband. Stop hovering over the children and go do something worthwhile. Is there not a province you could conquer or a town you could sack?"

"Do you really think I should?"

"Absolutely. Was it not you who said, nothing clears a man's head faster than lopping off another?"

"Not exactly. What I said was, nothing clears a man's head faster than having it lopped off."

"Even so. I'm sure you could find some new land to conquer if you set your mind to it."

"Well, there is that one northeast of here with all those mad highland clans."

"You see?"

"However, they're known to be quite reluctant about being put to the sword."

"Since when has that stopped you?"

"That's true. I suppose it wouldn't take much longer than six or seven months. A year at most. We could start out next week."

"Why wait a week? You could issue the command to your personal guard today and be on your way tomorrow."

"You know, you're right. Anything I lack I could commandeer along the way or have Lord Willowbrook bring up with the auxiliaries."

"There you have it. Feeling better now?

"Much. I think you're right, my dear. I think it's time we had another war."

Had Audanot known then that it would take

him not six or seven months, not a year, not two, but five long, bitter, arduous years to subdue the clans, he would not have started out at all. He would have left them alone and, thus, never made such a treacherous enemy.

He soon learned why they were called the 'mad' highland clans. Centuries of incestuous breeding had left them bereft of any intelligence, and because they were too stupid to know better, they were truly fearless warriors. The conflict might have continued even longer had not their leader, MacBrutish, been captured.

He had been found raving by the shore of a small mountain lake. Apparently, he had mistaken his own reflection for another clansman, whom he thought was mimicking him. He was quickly subdued and brought before the King still cursing his image for insubordination.

To the surprise of everyone, including MacBrutish, Audanot spared his life. Despite his friends' efforts to change his mind, five years of bloody conflict had made the King sick of war.

So, instead, MacBrutish was set free upon his pledge to recognize Audanot as his overlord, after which the highlander scampered off, stopping only once at the top of a distant hill to raise his shift and expose himself. But Audanot was not offended by this, for he considered the highlander to be much like an animal and it was well known that animals exposed their genitals as a sign of trust and submission.

Upon his return to the capital, Audanot was met by a most endearing sight. He had carried away with him the image of his infant sons as they suckled upon their wet nurse. How it warmed his weary heart to see them five years older now and still suckling. Tears came to his bloodshot eyes, and he vowed that - no matter which of his sons became heir - they would share his love equally.

But as the years passed and the children grew, his vow was all but forgotten. It seemed the Gods did indeed favor one child over the other, for while Prince Bryand spent his time studying mathematics, the sciences, Bandidonian lore, and courtly graces, Prince Daron collected insects for his fiendish enjoyment and forced scullery maids to undress with threats of execution.

It became quite plain to everyone that Bryand was the King's favorite. They would spend hours together discussing the rulings of the day, sharing ideas for the betterment of the Kingdom, and generally enjoying each other's company. There seemed to be nothing lacking in the boy; though one small thing about him did trouble the King. He was always getting lost. It was as if he had no sense of direction.

The most famous example of this is the time - about ten years before his death - King Bryand insisted upon leading his troops in pursuit of a fleeing enemy. And marching his army in what turned out to be a large circle, he proceeded to attack the rear of his own column. Sadly enough, even at his funeral, the hearse drawing his body turned left when the rest of the procession turned right.

I suppose if he had had a sense of direction he might never have required my services as a mapmaker and my life would have taken a more normal course. Not that I regret one moment of it. Though there are some times when I think I should have listened to my mother and joined my uncle's olive pressing concern.

There was something else about his favorite son that Audanot found disturbing. The King was an emotional man, meaning he had always been guided by what he felt in his heart or gut. Bryand seemed not to have the same instincts. There was a remoteness about him. Not that he was aloof or unloving; he was a dutiful son. Yet he always kept close guard on his feelings and weighed questions that were presented to him almost too carefully before making a particular decision or judgement.

Daron, on the other hand, seemed not to have any judgement at all and was forever getting into trouble. If a sudden scream or crash erupted, it was a certainty that someone had been victimized by one of his pranks.

"Why does he do those things?!" the King would ultimately demand of his wife.

"Who dear?"

"You know, what's his name."

"Daron?"

"Aye."

"Perhaps he wouldn't act that way if you paid him more attention. You seem only to have time for one of your sons."

"Nonsense. He accompanies me every day to the executions. He just hasn't shown an interest in anything else."

As the years passed, the rift between them grew wider and wider. It was as though the boy went out of his way to provoke his father's anger.

For instance, there was the time he set loose a pair of skunks in the main hall while the King was receiving some visiting dignitaries, and the time he doctored the chutney - a popular condiment with the court - in such a way as to send everyone at the feasting tables rushing for a chamber pot.

But no one was more routinely the recipient of Daron's cruelty than his brother. Yet, no matter how deceitful the sleight, Bryand never asked their father to intervene. For this loyalty, Daron hated him.

There seemed a shred of hope for Daron when the young men added warfare to their princely training. Each became a master of the sword and could unhorse many veteran knights in a joust. By their eighteenth birthday, Bryand was champion of the Kingdom and Daron second only to his brother (*who he longed to thrash*).

As a reward for their achievements, Bryand was appointed commander of all the armies, and Daron was appointed his first general. But instead of using strategy to win battles as his tutor, Lord Crushmore, the Master at Arms, had instructed, Daron would send his ranks charging straight into the enemy's spears. He often found himself out-flanked and in need of reinforcements. Were it not for Bryand counter-attacking and turning the tide of the battle, Daron would have been captured or killed more than once.

Ultimately, after it was decided that Daron had slain more of his own men than the enemy, he was relieved of his command and sent back to the court where he proceeded to drink heavily and cheat at dice.

It was about this time that King Jasper, the wealthiest and most powerful of Audanot's vassals, presented his two daughters to the court. Immediately upon seeing MeAnne, the fairest daughter, Audanot was determined to have their two bloodlines merged.

He sought out his son, which was not difficult to do, as Bryand spent most of his time training with his soldiers on the lists between the tournament stands.

"Marry, father?" asked the Prince, busy sharpening his sword with a honing stone. "Pray, tell me why?"

"Why, to preserve the house, lad."

"What has marriage to do with the house?" Bryand replied absently. "Was it not renovated this past spring?

It was then Audanot realized, though he was an effective King, he had been remiss in his duties as a parent. "Sit down, my son. We've much to talk about."

And so, Bryand became betrothed to MeAnne.

She was a comely lass with hair the color of harvest wheat and piercing green eyes that always traveled in the same direction unlike her mother and older sister who were walleyed.

Bryand liked her well enough for someone whom he had only recently met. So, adhering strictly to the rules of courtship, he arranged for a chaperon to accompany them at all times, which was hardly necessary, for he was always careful not to act in any way that might compromise the lady's virtue.

Daron - who had been romping in the maid's quarters since the age of eleven - would observe his brother with incredulity and mock him whenever the chance arose. But inwardly he burned with jealousy.

That his father had chosen MeAnne for Bryand left no doubt he was the favored son. And were it not enough to provoke Daron's wrath, as part of the marriage bargain, he had been plighted to MeAnne's older sister, Blindella. She might have been a pretty lass had she not inherited her mother's affliction. Though she tried earnestly to please him, he found it most disturbing to have someone stare at both his ears at the same time.

He was jealous for another reason, and this he kept a closely guarded secret. The moment he had set eyes upon MeAnne, he had felt something stir, for the first time, not in his loins but in his heart.

Suddenly everything about his life seemed changed. The women he could have, he did not want any more. Those he had primed to seduce, he all but brushed aside.

Thoughts of MeAnne filled his day and drove his sleep away at night. He would pace the room, stopping occasionally at his window to gaze at the moon, his breathing labored, his body bathed in sweat. Yet the more he dwelled on her loveliness, on the glow of her skin and the warmth of her smile, the less comfort he received. For he knew she would never be his.

Never, he thought, one night as he lay awake, frustrated, perplexed. How can that be?! Am I not every bit as good-looking as-- . (*He did not want to say his name.*) As him? Am I not just as smart? Am I not as convivial? Why, I'm smarter than he. And I'm certainly much more entertaining at parties.

Why would she want him, when she could have me?

At first, the thought rankled him. But then - after considering it more carefully - his eyes went wide and he bolted upright in his bed.

"Could it be?" he muttered, throwing off the covers.

He hurried across the cold floor to the full-length mirror by his dressing table. He studied his reflection. It was no different from what he had always seen save for a pimple or two. But - and this was the crux of the matter - did not Bryand always see the very same reflection when gazing in his own mirror?

How often had they been mistaken for each other? Even his mother had trouble telling them apart. For this very reason Daron had grown up hating his looks. *(Being someone who would not even share his toys, you can imagine how he felt about sharing his appearance.)*

At one time, he had contemplated sneaking into his brother's room and shaving Bryand's head as he slept. But when he realized it would have to be done every three months or so, he had abandoned the idea.

Yet now, despite the years of wanting an identity all his own, he was nothing less than overjoyed to be his brother's double. The answer to his troubles was literally staring him in the face.

If MeAnne was pledged to his brother, then he would be his brother. Aye, he would become Bryand, only not quite so dull.

Oh, the genius of it! And so simply achieved! He would shed his identity - if just for one night - step into his brother's shoes *(no pun intended)*, and woo the girl without her ever knowing it.

What happened next was related to me many years later, fifty-six to be precise, by Queen MeAnne herself. Unfortunately, old age was upon her, and she suffered from what many people thought was a delusion. I will say only this for now: in my travels I have seen many strange things, including some that defy not just understanding but the laws of nature as well.

There was one other source, that being Daron's diary. But this was filled with such a lewd interpretation that I doubt it was true. So I have gleaned a little from both and have come up with something as close to the truth as anyone will ever get.

The garden was dark. No moonlight shone. Daron stood among some tall bushes, nervous energy coursing through him, heightening his awareness and his desire.

In Bryand's name he had sent MeAnne a note beseeching her to join him after the court had retired. He chuckled at his own cleverness, recalling how she had cast those adoring glances at his brother. And Bryand, the fool, not knowing what they were about, had stiffly inquired if she were feeling poorly.

Oh, what sport! What mischief! Surely, he thought, pleased as punch with himself, this is the greatest of my schemes.

An hour passed. He heard the watch change upon the battlement. One by one the lights that burned through the castle embrasures were extinguished. His legs ached from standing in place and his hands were stiff from the cold. I should have taken one of Bryand's cloaks, he thought, annoyed. The brown one. Aye, I like that one.

He looked down at the tunic and hose he had stolen from his brother's wardrobe. Now that I think about it, I like all of his clothes better than mine. And this struck him as odd, for when it came to dressing, Bryand had no flair.

Just then there came the sound of the latch turning on the garden door. He tensed and sank deeper into the shadows. He heard the door creak open, then close again with a soft thud. His heart quickened and suddenly the chill was gone. He knew she had come; and it took all his strength to remember that he was supposed to be his brother.

MeAnne peered into the darkness. She was nervous. She was excited. She was afraid. The cold air trapped between the high castle walls sent a shiver racing through her, and she pulled her mantle tighter around her.

Since the day they had been pledged before the court she had yearned for this moment, imagining it over and over again in her mind. But then her conscience chided her. No woman of her lofty station would have locked her handmaiden in her room and answered such a brazen request as this. But she did not care. There were words she longed to hear; the words he might have whispered despite the presence of an escort but, as yet, had not.

She had observed the way other couples shared their secret smiles; how they engaged in repartee, leaning close, enjoying the nearness of one another. Why then was it different for her? Before receiving Bryand's note he had acted so formal, so distant. Was it because he was a prince of the realm and felt it his duty to act that way?

She recalled the ceremony and how he had stood before the throne so handsome and erect. She had fallen in love with him then and there. It mattered not that he was wearing last year's fashion.

And when he pledged himself to her, she thought her heart would crack from its hammering. Calling upon an ancient custom of her people, she had pledged to embroider him the tapestry of his choosing as a token of her devotion.

"This I shall do for you, my lord," she had proclaimed before the court. "And on the day that it is complete I shall be your bride. What then shall I make for you?" she had said, averting her eyes. "Some simple scene of pastoral beauty to hang above our bed?"

After pausing to consider, he had replied, "How about something for the Great Hall? We could use a tapestry along that balcony there."

She had never been inside the Great Hall. So, when she turned and saw what he was suggesting, the smile on her face collapsed at once. "But that must be fifty feet long and almost as high -- !"

"What about a mural?" he had said, his voice building with enthusiasm. "Aye, a mural depicting the major historical events of the Kingdom. Don't you think that would look impressive?"

Why, a tapestry that size might take her ten years to complete. Perhaps even longer! Tears had come to her eyes, and had not control and dignity been stressed during all her years of training she might have cried in front of him. But she did not.

Though a storm raged inside her, she presented him with a polite smile and curtsied to signify her compliance. Then, with all the dignity she could muster, she had stepped to his side and received the salutations of the court.

But it was a joyless occasion for her. A life that seemed so promising had, with the utterance of one request, soured like milk left standing for three days.

But now, from out of her bitter disappointment, hope had arisen, hope that the ten years to come would not be barren, loveless years; that, despite the delay, she had found some romance to keep her warm during those long cold nights she would lie alone.

She leaned against the garden gate and, in a soft, tremulous voice, said, "Dearest Amorus, God of love and pre-marital overtures, grant me this one encounter. Let his words of devotion flow like water from an urn. Let me drink so, that I might sleep tonight with my thirst quenched."

She started down the flagstone path, her heart dancing with joy, her head dizzy with anticipation. Tonight she was a young maiden trysting with her lover and not a woman of noble birth who was expected to be above such passion.

She peered into the darkness. "Bryand?" called MeAnne softly, her voice trembling. "Are you here?"

"Aye," came an abrupt reply.

She peered around the garden. "Where are you?"

"Here. Behind the bushes."

"Why do you hide from me? Am I not alone as you requested?"

"That I am hidden is but my way of being close to you."

"How is that to be achieved?" said MeAnne somewhat peevishly. In all the ways she had imagined their assignation, she had not once pictured herself talking to the shrubbery.

"The darkness, it is like a cloak that covers us

both."

It was then she realized he was attempting to woo her. He cares! she thought, ecstatic. He really cares!

Her first impulse was to rush into his arms and shower him with kisses. But then she remembered how he had so casually sentenced her to ten years hard labor at her loom.

Keeping the sobering thought in mind, she took a deep breath to steady herself and answered as indifferently as she could. "A cloak, you say, that covers us both. But in what way? Like two strangers caught in a sudden downpour? Making polite conversation until they can go their separate ways?"

"No, my lady, nothing quite so impersonal."

"Then perhaps like an old married couple about to retire, their heads filled with thoughts of sleep and nothing more."

"Not so complacent, either."

"Then how?"

"Like the friend it is to lovers." He stepped onto the path and came face to face with her. "For that is what we are and what we will always be."

Though the darkness was all about them, she could feel his eyes upon her, an intense stare that pierced her facade and lodged in her heart. "Are we lovers?"

"Nothing more, nothing less," replied the Prince, leaning closer. "But in that simplicity lies all the worth there is to possess."

"Yet you are a man of obvious wealth and power," retorted MeAnne quickly, attempting to regain the upper hand. "Surely those things are more important to you than something as intangible as love."

Smart girl, thought Daron. "For all my worldly goods, until the day I met you, I was the poorest man alive. Say the word and I will give away all of my possessions - my lands, my fortune, even my good name. I need naught else but you to be as rich as any King."

"You flatter well, my lord. It strikes me that you've had much practice."

"You think me insincere?"

"No, my lord. I trust you believe every word you say - each time you say it."

"Aye, I've said these words before. Over and over again inside my head as I'd lie awake thinking of the joyous moment when I could declare my love to you. But now, having allowed them to escape my lips, they seem so trivial, so paltry compared to the torrent that rages in my breast. I fear mere words may never suffice." He took her hand and pressed it hard against his chest. "Oh, the agony, the torment. To have such love inside with no means to set it free! I am like a jailer locked in his own keep. And the only person near enough to hear his cries is the one person to whom he cannot speak!"

Oh, how she wished she could see him better. "These things you say -- I never dreamed you were so troubled."

"I hold a lot inside."

Suddenly she felt ashamed. She had wanted him to shower her with endless words of devotion as did the lovers in the epic poems she had read. Instead he had offered her something much more eloquent and profound - the simple truth (o*r so she believed.)*

Thus moved, she abandoned all thoughts of courtship and pretense. She wanted only to be as honest with him. "I, too, have suffered, my lord. You've been so distant until now; I was afraid you did not want me for your wife."

"Not want you?! Dearest lady, you are the beacon that lights my way. When we are apart I am plunged into darkness and hopelessly lost. I wander among the shadows calling your name. MeAnne! MeAnne! My life!

My love! My salvation!"

Tears collected in her eyes. "Then wander no more, dearest one. I am here now, and I will never stray."

"Thank the Gods!" cried Daron, drawing her to him and burying his face in her neck.

The suddenness of the move made her gasp for breath. The feel of his body as it pressed against hers sent her blood racing through her veins at breakneck speed. She quivered from an excitement she had never known. And she might have succumbed to it had he not at that moment nuzzled her neck.

An alarm went off inside her, for even though she had abandoned the repartee there were still certain rules of courtship that needed to be observed. Fawning was allowed, but only by way of a casual brush of the arm or a light touch of the hand.

Nuzzling was definitely out of the question.

"My lord," said the Princess, breaking away. "You forget yourself!"

"If I do, it is because I am intoxicated by your presence."

"Then I shall quit this place."

She tried to leave but he held her hand tightly against his chest. "Can you not feel how my heart pounds? And each beat is a renewal of my love for you."

She let her hand linger as she considered what to do. Was a nuzzle so terrible a breach of conduct that it warranted ending this glorious encounter? After all, were they not already pledged to be married?

"It must be so," conceded MeAnne; and then, looking away, she admitted, "For my heart beats the same way."

"Really? Let me feel."

For a moment, she was so shocked that she could do naught but stare at his hand upon her breast.

"Hmmm," said Daron boldly. "Methinks It's just

stepped up its pace."

Outraged, MeAnne slapped his hand away and exclaimed, "Sir! You go too far! I am not a piece of chattel to be handled whenever you so choose. You will do well to remember that, even after we are married!"

Though he called and called, she refused to acknowledge him, and she marched straight for the garden door, slamming it shut behind her.

"Hang them all!" shouted Daron *(it was his favorite expression.)* He had not expected her to be so strong-willed. Any of the other women he had known would be playing plant the cucumber with him right now.

He was angry. Not just because she had refused his advances but because he knew she would never consent to meet him again in such an intimate way. From here on out, she would make herself available to him only if there were other people about or if she was accompanied by an escort.

Cursing, he went about deflowering the rose bushes. But he found them to be a poor substitute for the lady.

Unable to ease the ache in his heart or, for that matter, the ache in his loins, he vaulted the garden wall and headed for the town brothel where he intended to stay until at least one of his problems was solved.

MeAnne's outrage propelled her down a series of corridors before she realized she was heading the wrong way. She retraced her steps and found the Great Hall, empty now.

The feast had been cleared, the tables cleaned. The raucous laughter that earlier filled the room had been replaced by an eerie silence. Even the fire that had blazed in the massive hearth had slowed to a mere showing.

No one was there save the stone mason repairing the floor where the acrobat who performed that evening, had landed after a breathtaking but nevertheless overambitious leap from the second story balcony; the very same balcony she was expected to decorate with an enormous tapestry.

She stared at it, miserable; already feeling the ache in her hands from the weight of the fabric.

She entered the central turret and proceeded to climb the stairs to the second level where her apartment was located. There she paused and leaned against the stone arch, thinking of the Prince once more.

He said he loved her. But if he loved her, would he have acted so outrageously?

Perhaps he had acted that way *because* he loved her. She was very confused. It was then she recalled something her mother had said just before the betrothal announcement.

"Men, my dear, Me, are obsessed with sex. It's amazing they can accomplish anything. Even after all these years, your father still can't keep his hands off me. Though his hands are not as troublesome as that beastly thing in his codspiece."

Well, Bryand, for all his merits, had proven to be as typical a man as her father. And this annoyed her. Did he expect her to be receptive to these advances? Had she no choice, no say in the matter? She was not like the women of her mother's day who were content to be the object of a man's desire and nothing more. She had learned to read and write. She had studied history and science and philosophy. Aye, she could think as well as any man! Except when it came to mathematics - for some reason she had no head for numbers.

It was very likely that Bryand would rule one day. She had hoped he would think of her as his partner in all things, seek her council, even implement some of her ideas. She would be most unhappy if all he wanted was her body - enticing as it was - and not her mind as well.

Feeling troubled and confused, she stepped to her door and was about to enter when Bryand (*the real Bryand*) appeared at the end of the corridor.

"There you are," said the Prince. "I've been searching for you everywhere." In his hand was a small frame.

"It appears you have found me," replied MeAnne coolly.

"So I have." He approached, avoiding her eyes, and stood for a moment, shifting his weight from side to side. "You left so abruptly," he said after clearing his throat.

Though he meant the feast, she thought he was referring to their encounter in the garden. "Yes, I did."

"I was concerned-- . I mean-- ." He gazed at her. "Did I do something to displease you?"

She shot him an incredulous look.

"I did, didn't I? I knew it!" He struck the wall with his fist. "I'm such a dolt!"

"My lord," said MeAnne, somewhat taken aback. "You need not punish yourself on my account."

"But I must. You see, I wouldn't want to displease you."

"Really?" said the Princess. Though she wanted to remain cool and detached, she found herself weakening.

"Certainly not." Again, he paused and squirmed a bit. "I'm not very good at this, as you can tell. Anyway, I wanted you to know that-- . That-- . Well, here." He thrust the wood frame toward her.

"What is this?" asked MeAnne, confused.

"The frame for your tapestry."

"But you asked for one the length of the balustrade in the Great Hall."

"Yes, I know. But I've changed my mind."

(*Actually, it was his father who had changed his mind - after another of their enlightening talks.*)

He cleared his throat again; something he did often when he felt awkward or uncomfortable. "I didn't realize it then that I was postponing my own happiness."

She could not help but smile. Apparently, he loved her enough to swallow his pride and apologize. For that was what she took this clumsy overture to mean. Suddenly, all her worries were gone. Joy filled her heart, and she leaned close and kissed him lightly on the cheek.

"You have pleased me very much."

"I have?" said Bryand, surprised.

She took the frame. "I will work on this day and night. Nothing will keep me from my task."

"Well, I wouldn't want you to over-tax yourself."

"But the sooner I complete it, the sooner we can be wed. And the sooner we are wed, the sooner we can-- ." She lowered her eyes and smiled demurely. "I think you know my meaning.

"I think I do," replied the Prince, having not the slightest inkling of what she meant.

"Hold on, dearest one."

"To what?" replied Bryand, looking about the corridor.

Thinking his remark somewhat suggestive, she smiled in spite of herself and cuffed him lightly on the cheek. "You are a rogue! I think it best I leave now, before you get into trouble again."

She bid him a tender good night and entered her apartment, pausing long enough to smile at him before shutting the door. She leaned against it, still smiling. Oh, what a wonderous evening, she thought. Thank you, Amorus. I asked for a morsel and, out of your boundless generosity, you provided a ten-course feast.

She practically danced across the room, enraptured, and unlocked the door to her inner chamber, setting free her handmaiden, Jona, who was very disgruntled and pouty.

Ignoring the girl's protests, MeAnne pulled her to the bed and sat her down beside her, then proceeded to relate the entire evening's events.

"How romantic," sighed Jona. She was a sweet girl, with a pleasant face and long auburn hair, which she wore plaited down her back.

"Is it not so?" said MeAnne, beaming as she clutched the frame to her breast. Suddenly she leaped to her feet and ran about the room. "Quickly, Jona, where is my sewing basket?"

"Oh, my lady, you're not going to start that now, are you? It's so late."

"I don't care," answered MeAnne. She found her basket and a bolt of cloth and went directly to her table. "I'll work day and night. I'll allow naught to distract me. Neither hunger, nor thirst, nor sleep will keep me from my task."

"But what about-- . You know; going tee-tee?"

MeAnne's eyes fell upon a vase. "Empty that and bring it here. It should do for about a week."

Bryand, in the meantime, was still lingering outside in the corridor, trying to make some sense of what had just transpired between them. But finding it all too confusing, he finally shrugged and started off for his apartment.

Yet as he went, he found himself feeling more and more elated. So much so, that, by the time the Prince had entered his room, he was whistling a merry tune. He slapped Cower, the family retainer, squarely on the back and leaped onto his bed, placing his arms behind his head.

Cower, who was not used to seeing his prince so unrestrained, eyed him carefully. "Are you feeling well, my lord?"

"Quite well, as a matter of fact." Bryand raised himself onto his elbows. "You know something, Cower?"

Cower stared down his long, hawk-like nose, and with a hint of a smile, asked, "What, my lord?"

"I think I'm going to like being married." He paused, a thoughtful expression upon his face. "Father says copulation is most enjoyable. Have you not found it to be so?"

Furrowing his brow, the retainer considered the question, then said in a straightforward manner, "Well, my lord, I've enjoyed myself the few times I've indulged. But keep in mind marriage between royalty is more than just copulation. There are picnics as well and state functions to attend."

He considered what Cower had said. As a prince of the realm, he had always understood that his life would never really be his own. State functions would always dictate his behavior and the kingdom's needs would always come before his.

But even royals had their private moments; at night; once the bedroom door was closed, and as he thought of this, a smile stretched across the Prince's face, complimenting his strong, good looks. "Aye," he said, more to himself than to Cower. "I think I'll like being married. I think I’ll like it very much."

CHAPTER TWO

The ways of the Gods are strange at times; how they can reward one with happiness one moment only to revoke it the next is perplexing indeed. What comes to mind at once is the image of a delicious red apple, the first of the season, biting into it... and finding a worm. Ask me not why I thought of this. I really do not know. Except, of course, that fruit rarely comes my way in these mountains. And the fruit that I can buy is usually as old and as leathery as I.

King Audanot sat at the center of the dais. He wore his finest tunic, one of yellow and orange velvet embroidered with his family crest, a hammer and tongs crisscrossed above a blacksmith's anvil. Covering his legs were bright green hose the color of new sod with other smithy tools embroidered on them in yellow, white and rose gold thread. Fastened to his shoulders by a pair of gold hinges, a purple and orange cape stretched to the floor and atop his head was a gold circlet at the center of which, resting in the middle of his brow, was a bronze horseshoe.

King Audanot was very proud of his heritage and wanted others to know it, too, an honest emotion in spite of the fact that he was a garish dresser. Queen Bee had tried her best to refine his tastes and gentle his manners, though he would only go so far. He had agreed to bathe regularly and use the knife on the dining table to stab his food instead of anyone who might be vexing him at the time.

But when it came to his wardrobe he refused all suggestions.

Flanking him on both sides of the dais were the rulers of all the other countries that comprised the newly formed Council of the United Kingdoms. This Audanot considered his finest achievement. Unlike his father who had conquered his neighbors without a care for their welfare, Audanot wanted to reach out to his vassals in friendship, to make them an active part of a rich and prosperous empire that would, with abundant trade and rapidly growing industry, fatten their treasuries as well as their bellies. "A fully stocked larder and a coffer laden with riches did much to keep an ally loyal", was what Prince Bryand had said. For this new Council was also a new idea, one which his son had convinced him to try after many hours of serious discussion and many goblets of wine.

Forty tables, each twenty feet of solid wood hewn from the trunks of ancient clobbernut trees, stood upon the council chamber floor. They were divided into two equal groups by a wide aisle that ran the length of the room. At these tables sat the hundreds of noblemen and knights who had sworn allegiance to the Council.

Their banners and pennants hung from the rafters overhead, a colorful array of sigils, among them the willow and brook of House Willowbrook, the peppercorn of House Pepperill, the rocky crag of House Torkelstone, the strutting peacock of House Egotist, the loping stag of House Fleemore, and the prostrate opossum of House Roadkill.

Weapons were not allowed in the chamber, but ceremonial swords representing each of the houses, had been suspended from pegs upon the walls, forming row upon row of glistening steel. Above each sword, sitting upon a long shelf that ran the length of the wall, were the half-helms of every man in attendance and the claim check ticket that corresponded with the number they had received from the castle steward upon entering the room.

Audanot stood and raised his hands and the hall customarily quieted. The king peered across the room, locating Pomp, the court chamberlain, and signaled to him to begin the day's ceremony. Pomp, an arrogant man who prided himself on being the third generation of his family to serve the kings of Bandidon, responded in his usual manner by nodding with bored disdain. King or serf it did not matter, Pomp treated everyone with the same contempt.

He strode across the hall with a regimented gate, stood before the dais and scowled at the council lest they think him intimidated by their wealth and power. "Hear ye! Hear ye!" he said, pivoting to face the room. He tapped his staff of office thrice upon the stone floor. "All food and drink to be put away! All bad jokes and off-color stories to cease! This council is now in session. The honorable Audanot, King of Bandidon and Overlord of all the lands between the Tanta Mounts and the Spreading Bottoms, presiding."

"Proceed," said Audanot from his chair.

Pomp tossed him a condescending look and muttered, "Well, of course I'll proceed. What else would I do?" Reaching into his pocket, he produced a scroll and unrolled it. "First case. A dispute between the Lords Ikenfloss and Gallstone over the rights to the Gentleflow river."

"Your Grace," said Ikenfloss, leaping to his feet and addressing Audanot. "That river has belonged to the Ikenflosses for a hundred years. It is Gonad's traditional borderline."

"*Was* the traditional borderline," Gallstone responded angrily, standing and addressing Audanot. "Until last year when it changed course and traveled close to thirteen miles further south onto my family lands in Upper Thorax."

Audanot peered at King Mitashmeer, who was Gallstone's closest neighbor. "Is that true, my lord?"

"Aye, your grace," Mitashmeer replied. "What once was green pasture is now ten feet under water. Mygut, what a soggy mess."

Ikenfloss strode to the center aisle. "Rivers change course, your grace. How can that have anything to do with ownership rights?"

Gallstone joined him, his face flushed with anger. "No one disputes your ownership of the river. It's the land now on its other side. What of the low-folk that have lived there as citizens of Upper Thorax for all these years? What of the crops they will produce next growing season, what of the harvest I have lost? What of the taxes due me by my landowners?"

The two men faced each other, their arguments growing louder and more severe. But their words grew steadily fainter in Audanot's ears until he stared at their moving mouths, their erratic gestures, hearing nothing at all.

The king looked down at his hands. They were tingling, and the more he gripped the arms of his chair the more intense the tingling became. Something is wrong, he thought. Something is happening to me. His head felt light, his chest heavy as a stone. And his throat. His throat was on fire!

Audanot pulled himself to his feet. "Hold!" he cried, although he could not hear his own words save for a distant droning that echoed in his skull. "The court will recess for a moment..."

Pomp turned to the king and sneered. "What? So soon?"

But Audanot did not hear him either, and collapsed where he stood.

The court physician, whose name was Lystillus,

was summoned immediately upon the realization that Audanot was seriously unconscious and not just temporarily unconscious from the excessive drinking he had done the night before.

Arriving on the scene, Lystillus, a lean man with a gaunt face and skin the color of a taper, quickly determined malicious vapors from the hall had gathered about the king. Four strong knights rushed forward to carry Audanot upstairs to his room. Once there, Lystillus determined that the malicious vapors were still present. He ordered the room cleared save for Cower, then together they fanned the entire chamber, shouting, "Be gone vapors. Be gone!"

Still Audanot did not respond.

Queen Bee burst into the room, her eyes wide with fear and glistening with tears. She had been down in the gardens, speaking with the gardener. Someone had purposely torn all the blossoms from her rose bushes. "How is my husband? Tell me the truth, Lystillus."

"Grave," he said, mincing not his words. He guided her toward the door. "Please, your majesty, you mustn't linger. There are malicious vapors at work here."

"But I want to be near my husband."

"I fear contagion, majesty. You must away."

She stared at Audanot as he lay upon his bed, praying silently to herself. Dearest Gods, protect my husband. It is true he is descended from common stock, but nevertheless he is a good man and a good king. "Very well then. Send Cower to my apartment with news of any change."

Immediately upon the Queen's exit, the physician commanded Cower to remove all of Audanot's clothing, believing the vapors had saturated them. Cower stripped the King naked, then, holding his breath, ran to the kitchen with the clothes to boil them in the castle caldron. The physician was now satisfied Audanot would regain consciousness soon. Yet after a turn of the hourglass, the king still had not improved. At length, the physician determined vapors were not the cause at all. Perplexed, frustrated, he began to probe the King's orifices, all of them, spreading each one wide in an attempt to discover what had felled him.

An hour later Bryand arrived and padded softly to the physician's side. He had been conducting an inspection of the city's sewer system when the news reached him, and rather than retrace his steps to the main drainage ditch on the outskirts of town, he had jumped the railing and slogged through the muck in search of the nearest portal.

"What's wrong with him?" asked Bryand, gazing at his father with alarm. The King was still unconscious and there were dark circles around his eyes. His breathing came in short labored spurts.

"I must admit, my lord, I am quite baffled by your father's symptoms. So I have taken some precautionary measures."

"What measures?"

"Well, on the off-chance the King's heart was manufacturing too much blood, I decided to relieve him of some of it."

"How much?"

"About five pints."

"Why is he so pale?"

"That is probably caused by the collar."

"What collar?"

"The one I placed around his neck to keep the excess blood from getting to his head."

Bryand eyed his father anxiously. "Will he live?"

"That, I'm afraid, is up to the Gods. I've done all that I can to save him."

It was then Daron arrived, slightly inebriated. He had been tapping the larder ale when the word reached him, and after one more tankard, he had headed directly for his father's chambers, pausing only briefly to relieve himself at the garderobe just across the hall.

He came abreast of Bryand, sniffed once, and immediately wrinkled up his nose. "Lord, you smell worse than I do, and I haven't bathed in a fortnight."

"I've been in the sewers."

Daron studied him a moment. "You've an odd sense of fun, brother, do you know that?"

Ignoring the remark, Bryand turned to Lystillus and thanked him for his efforts.

"Well," replied the physician. "I always try to do my best." He finished collecting his probes and headed for the door, stopping there to say, "If he grows uncomfortable just tighten the collar a notch or two. That will quiet him."

Daron stared at his father and said, "He looks terrible." Noticing the angry expression upon his brother's face, he quickly added, "I didn't mean terrible... He looks *dead.*"

The Prince approached the bed. "So, the old boy's finally passing on."

"Not yet," said Bryand scornfully.

"Don't get your hackles up, brother dear. I don't want to see him go, either." Daron smiled shamelessly. "At least not until he's proclaimed one of us the next King."

Bryand shook his head and sneered. "Naturally, that would be the first thing on your mind."

"Please!" Daron retorted. "Spare me your noble airs. You want to rule as much as I do."

"Not at father's expense."

"Then you're a bigger fool than I thought."

Bryand closed on Daron. He might have been

staring in a mirror so identical were they. "I have never raised my hand to you no matter how you have mistreated me. But don't presume that I will always look the other way. One day you'll go too far."

"And what?" Daron challenged, undaunted.

"I'll strike you."

Daron burst out laughing.

"Hard," added Bryand, but this only made his brother laugh more uproariously.

"I'm glad to see you boys getting along for a change," came their father's voice.

Bryand pushed past his brother. "Save your strength, father."

Taking a short, labored breath, the King replied hoarsely, "It doesn't matter. I'm a dead man."

"No, father," said Daron in a consoling tone. "You only look like a dead man." Bryand glared at him. Responding, Daron explained, "I'm just trying to comfort the man."

With a feeble gesture, Audanot waved them closer. Flanking the bed, the Princes knelt and waited for their father to speak, and for a moment the only sound in the room was the King's labored breathing.

"I know I have not been the best of fathers," he said at last. "I've neglected you; been absent when perhaps you needed me. But a King, a good King, must place his people over everything; even his own family."

Audanot looked at Bryand and smiled tenderly. "Despite that, you have always given me joy." Then, he turned to Daron and his smile faded. "While you have always given me gas."

Suddenly Audanot's face screwed up with pain.

"You must rest now, father," said Bryand.

"No! Can't rest. The end's too near!"

A tear ran down Bryand's cheek.

"Never cry, my son," rasped the King. "Never cry,

never run from a fight, never eat pork that's not fully cooked -- ."

Frowning, Bryand addressed his brother. "He's delirious."

Daron shrugged. "I think he makes good sense."

"Bryand," said the King urgently, gripping his son's arm. "I've decided you are to succeed me. You shall be Bandidon's next King."

"You're right," said Daron quickly. "He's delirious."

Audanot struggled to sit up and shot Daron a hard look. "I know exactly what I say, do you hear?! 'Tis my will; Bryand shall rule after me. Bryand is the next King!" He stared about the room with a wild look in his eyes. "Why is the light so dim? And the air-- . The air is so thick and foul; like that of the underworld!" He frowned. "Wait a minute." The King sniffed and sniffed until his nose led him to Bryand, and with a grimace, he said, "It's you."

"I've been inspecting the sewers, father."

Audanot nodded, relieved if not pleased. "Just remember to change before you see your mother." Suddenly he convulsed, and when the pain had subsided enough so that he could speak, the King said, "Rule well, my son. But not just with your head. Try listening to your heart every now and then." He winced and sucked in a labored breath. Then peering past his son to the chamber door, he shouted, "Come in, blast you! It's open!"

But no one had even knocked.

"So, you've come for me, eh?" growled the King. "Very well then. Bryand, pay him for my passage."

"Who, father?" asked the Prince, perplexed.

"Why, death's envoy, of course. By the door. The one with no face."

Though he saw no one, Bryand approached the

door.

"Make sure I get a First-Class seat."

"Aye, father," said Bryand, playing along. He removed two gold pieces from his purse and proffered them to the empty air.

"Won't you be surprised if he makes change," said Daron snootily.

I find it interesting to note that throughout all the lands I have traveled, and as a Gudi-Gudi I have been chased to quite a few, death's envoy is depicted exactly in the same way in each of the tapestries and etchings I have come across. He is always dressed in a hooded black robe, wearing sandals upon his withered brown feet. His skeletal fingers are tipped with long talon-like nails, and from his belt hangs a coin purse for collecting passage to the underworld. Sometimes this purse is leather, sometimes it is plain cloth, and sometimes it is not a purse but a ditty bag. In one etching, there was no purse at all, but a cash box instead.

"Is it done?" asked the King.

"Aye, father."

"Good. Well, then, I'm off--- "

Indeed, it was as if death's envoy had been there. For no sooner had Audanot spoken his last word than his head slumped upon his chest and he fell backwards onto his pillow. The king was dead.

Bryand returned to the bed and, with his heart aching, closed his father's unseeing eyes and placed the coins on his lids. "We'll miss you," said the young man sadly.

"Speak for yourself," muttered Daron.

Bryand gently folded Audanot's hands across his chest, making a mental note to have his father's fingernails trimmed before the funeral service. "We must go to mother."

"Sure, sure," said Daron, but he made no attempt to move. "I suppose you realize it's your word against mine."

"What is?" replied Bryand absently.

"With no witnesses, who's to say he chose you to be King."

"But he did. You heard him say so yourself."

"I'll deny it. I'll say he died before he could make his decision. No, wait; forget that; I'll say he proclaimed *me* King."

"You?!" said Bryand, abashed.

"Aye. I'll say he called you too weak and indecisive to rule. And though we've had our differences in the past, he knew I would make the better King."

"But that's a lie."

Daron laughed tauntingly. "You really are a fool." He sobered abruptly and eyed his brother with contempt. "Do you actually think you have the makings of a King?"

"And do you actually think you'd make a better one?" said Bryand, his face flushed with rage. "You who have done naught but indulge your own selfish needs? Why there's nary a maid between here and the Spreading Bottoms who isn't nursing thanks to you. Nor a barman without an overdue account."

"So I've been a little unruly; that's all in the past now. With a wave of my hand, I bid my old life and my old ways goodbye. Well, mostly, anyway."

"Very well, then," said Bryand boldly, an unexpected grin upon his face. "Call the guards. Call the pages. Call anyone you please."

Daron cast him a wary glance.

"Go on. Summon the court and the Council, and proclaim yourself King. Then it will be my turn to laugh, as will everyone else, at your absurdity. Then who will be the fool?" It was Bryand's turn to gloat. "Tell me, Daron? Who will be the fool? Certainly not I."

Daron's eyes narrowed, his lips curled downward

into a hard frown, and being one to act rashly whenever he could rely on nothing else, he reached for the dagger at his belt and unsheathed the blade. "Hang them all! How I hate it when you're right!"

"Hold!" said Bryand firmly. "Would you dare to fight me in father's presence?"

Daron kicked the bed. "What does he care? He's dead!"

Outraged, Bryand uttered a savage cry and reached for the hilt of his dagger.

"How impetuous of you, brother," goaded Daron, bracing himself for an attack. "I didn't think it in you."

But to Daron's surprise, Bryand stayed his hand, and in a tone dripping with malice, he said, "Though nothing would please me more than to best you here and now, I will not defile the sanctity of this chamber."

"Then choose another; it matters not to me!"

Bryand took a bold step forward, his eyes locked upon his brother's. "Upon the lists. Before the entire court. Before all the people of the land. Well, as many of them that can squeeze into the tournament grounds. You know, I was thinking we should expand it. Maybe double the size..."

"Get on with it, will you?!" cried Daron, exasperated.

Bryand, back on track now, said, "We can settle this matter between us and at the same time determine which of us will become King."

"That suits me fine," spat Daron. "I'll dispatch the pages to gather the court right now."

"Wait," said Bryand quickly. Daron looked at him, curious. "We must see to father first."

"Still the dutiful son," mocked Daron. "Ever mindful of protocol and good taste. I'm surprised you never tire of it."

"Say what you will, I'll not fight you until father's

ashes have been scattered by the wind."

Daron glanced at his father and then back at Bryand. "Agreed," said the Prince, relaxing his stance. He replaced the dagger in its scabbard with a loud snap. "What a marvelous idea," he sneered. "A funeral, a joust, and then another funeral. All on the same day." He strode to the door and flung it open. "Oh," said the Prince, turning back to his brother. "I hope you'll give my best to father when next you meet him in the underworld." And with that he disappeared from sight, the sound of his laughter echoing in the corridor.

But Daron had not gone very far before he faltered in his stride, the laughter, which had seemed so delicious at first, now sticking in his throat. For it occurred to him that he had been outmaneuvered; by his brother of all people; someone whom he had always considered to be a bore and a fool. Of course, Bryand would want to compete upon the lists. Bryand was the better jouster! Out of all the times they had tilted lances, Daron had beaten him only twice. "Hang them all!" he raged. "How could I have been so stupid?!" His hands clenched into fists and, striking out at the first thing he saw, he swung at a passing steward.

But his blows were unwieldy and the steward escaped.

Daron stood for a moment, out of breath, his anger shriveling and rapidly turning to fear. I've done it this time, he thought, chewing on his bottom lip. Now what am I going to do? He was not about to tilt with his brother and lose. Not with a wealthy Kingdom at stake.

What to do? What to do?! he thought, aware of the panic that was taking hold of him. He began to pace. Pacing sometimes soothed his nerves and helped him think. There has to be some way of turning this to my advantage; but how?

Think, man, think! Dig into that bag of tricks of

yours. There must be something in there you can use! You can't kill him outright. The court would never stand for that. And if you had an assassin kill him, the finger of guilt would still point to you.

So...

If you can't kill him, and if you can't beat him fairly, then you must find a way to beat him unfairly.

But how?

He strolled to an embrasure and stared at the courtyard below. A man with twisted legs hobbled by.

If only Bryand were as crippled, he thought, sighing deeply. Picturing him thusly, cheered him a little. Perhaps I could have his legs broken. But then his brow knitted and he frowned. No. Still too obvious. It's got to be something that will handicap Bryand without implicating me.

Something subtle; something undetectable. He perked up. Undetectable! And then the answer was as clear to him as the gin he had consumed only hours before.

Of course! Why didn't I think of it right away!? Poison! Poison would do the trick! Not a large dose; just enough to blur his vision and unsettle his wits.

"That's it! That's it!" he shouted gleefully, and he hugged himself. "Oh, I'm such a clever fellow!"

Convinced he had found the way to defeat his brother and make himself King, he started down the corridor with a jaunty bounce to his step. And as he went, he began to hum, and as he hummed he began to dance, and as he danced he ultimately began to sing:

"Poison! Poison!
But just a little bit;
Aye, just enough,
To cross his eyes,
And give the man a fit!"

CHAPTER THREE

However, concocting a poison that would be potent enough to incapacitate his brother, yet not so potent that it would kill him on the spot, was something well beyond Daron's capabilities. Although he had 'dabbled' in the past, he had never come up with anything more sinister than a potion that would give a man the runs (*as in the chutney affair;*) and even that had failed upon occasion.

The stakes were too high this time. He needed something guaranteed to work. And for that, he needed an expert.

But he was not concerned. He knew exactly who to approach. In those days there was no one more adept than the Earl of Nightshade. Indeed, with him, poisoning was more than just a skill, it was an art.

Only a handful of brigands knew of his preoccupation. Yet even hardened men such as these, spoke of the Earl in hushed and wary tones. Loose tongues had been known to suddenly turn black and swell in a man's throat. If Daron had not spent half his life at the Slaughter House, a seedy tavern on the outskirts of the city, he might never have heard of the Earl and his duplicitous talent.

Dressed in a plain homespun shirt and wool leggings and a long, hooded cape, Daron arrived at the tavern two hours past sunset. Arranging the meeting had been a simple task. The Earl of Nightshade frequented the Slaughter House almost as often as Daron. As a go-between, he had charged Snips, a local cutpurse who owed him money, with the task of approaching the Earl. He was a wiry man who looked much like a sewing needle. His fingers were as long as the knives he carried on his belt. At first, Snips emphatically refused. Few parted from the Earl's company without parting from life as well. But when Daron offered to cancel his debt and pay for a week's romp at the town brothel, Snips had finally agreed.

The moon was hidden behind a bank of dense clouds, and with the darkness so complete, the roads were empty. Daron fingered the sword at his belt, then adjusted the dagger he had hidden in his boot. It was always a good idea to enter The Slaughter House well armed.

But instead of opening the door in the normal way, Daron flattened against the adjacent wall, reached around, pushed open the door, then quickly drew back his arm. A dim yellow light spilled onto the ground followed by a storm of bottles, flagons, knives, and cudgels. It was the traditional way of greeting unsuspecting travelers. Anyone who had been there before knew never to stand in the open doorway.

In my many travels, I once made the mistake of stopping at the Slaughter House. After being pelted by a score of objects, my indignation got the better of me. I marched to the center of the room, placed my arms akimbo, and announced in a loud voice that I was a Gudi-Gudi. I will not elaborate on what happened next. Suffice it to say it was the worst defeat I have ever suffered.

Though he had often come with the intention of starting a fight, tonight Daron wanted no such distraction. He scanned the room. Save for one or two unfamiliar faces, the usual scum were there.

The present owner - for the tavern changed hands almost nightly - was a burly man with a deep gash that ran from under his left ear, across his left cheek, over the bridge of his nose, and up the right side of his forehead. He was often referred to as rut-face, but never when he was present. Anyone who was interested in living, addressed him only by his given name, Alf.

"Evenin', Daron."

"Evening, Alf."

"You'll be wantin' the back room tonight."

Daron cast him a wary look. "How did you know I was expecting someone?"

"Already there," replied the barman with a quick nod toward a door half hidden in shadows.

Daron removed the dagger in his boot. It was a throwing knife, well-balanced and with no cross guard. He slid the blade up his left sleeve and palmed the hilt in such a way that it was almost invisible in his hand. He tossed a quick glance behind him to see if he had aroused anyone's suspicions, but no one had looked his way.

He opened the door and entered the room and was immediately pleased to see the Earl of Nightshade sitting at a grimy table with his back to the wall. He was a rotund man with a head shaped like a brown onion. When he smiled at the Prince his eyes all but disappeared behind his fleshy cheeks. Not the sort one expected, but he was a villain all the same.

"Welcome, my lord," said the Earl graciously, attempting to stand.

"Don't get up," replied Daron, joining him at the table and sitting. "I trust you are well."

"Never better, sire. I somehow feel lighter on my feet everyday, despite the fact that everyday I have to punch a new hole in my belt. One could say, a punch for a spreading paunch."

Daron chuckled heartily, wanting very much to put the man at ease. Acting rude or condescending would only put him off, and Daron needed him just then; needed his knowledge, which was vast.

He had learned everything from his mother, the Lady Belladonna, an enchantress from the Wayward Woods. Lady Belladonna had, without any need for concealment, placed a spell on Nightshade's father, who subsequently married her and signed over all of his wealth and property to her right before his death one week later. In addition to his acquisitions, he left the lady something else; something she had not expected. He left her pregnant, which also left the lady puffy and irritable until the day she gave birth to a large boy child.

She did not enjoy being a mother. For someone who saw people merely as test subjects, it surprised even her that she allowed the child to live. But as the years went by, as the boy developed skills in a matter of weeks that, for her, had taken decades, she grew to tolerate him; even like him.

Under her tutelage he quickly learned to distinguish the various roots and herbs and berries that - when combined in the right proportions - could kill the healthiest person in a matter of seconds. His talent had finally surpassed even that of his mother when he developed a mixture to which even she was not immune.

"You've done me proud, my son," she had said. "You've also done me in."

"And how are you, sire?" asked the Earl, pouring a goblet of wine and offering it to him.

"Oh, fine. Just fine," said Daron absently, accepting the goblet. In addition to the one he held and the one Nightshade was filling for himself, there were two others upon the table.

"My condolences, my lord, on the loss of your father. He was a great man and a great King." Nightshade raised his cup and smacked his lips. "To his memory!"

But Daron hesitated. It occurred to him he did not know the Earl that well, and in the presence of a man so practiced in the art of poisoning, he was reluctant to drink anything offered by his hand.

Nightshade noticed his hesitation. "Is that not a proper toast, my lord?"

"Well-- . Yes, but-- ." Daron stared at his wine and frowned.

"Oh!" exclaimed the Earl, catching on. "You think I've poisoned your drink!"

"Well-- . Yes," said Daron bluntly.

Nightshade laughed heartily, his chin sinking into his thick neck, his rotund belly shaking up and down. "I quite understand your suspicions and take no offense." He rolled forward. "You know, my wife used to have a servant taste everything before she'd eat or drink."

"Used to? What happened?"

"We ran out of servants."

"And where is she now?" asked Daron, feeling less sure about drinking his wine with each new thing the Earl said.

"Dead, I'm afraid."

"Really?" Daron said it so tentatively that Nightshade looked up from his goblet and gazed at him. "Dead, you say."

Once again, the Earl burst out laughing. "Of natural causes. Here," he said, motioning for Daron to hand him his wine. "Give it here."

Daron obliged and watched the man drain both goblets.

"Not bad," said Nightshade, after a loud contented belch. "Now what can I do for you, my lord?"

Suddenly Daron felt awkward. "I'm in need of your... services," said the Prince with some difficulty.

"Well, that much I assumed. But what is it exactly that you need?"

Though they were the only people in the room, Daron instinctively lowered his voice. "Something fast acting. Yet not so strong that it will kill my-- ." He checked himself. "My intended victim. I wish only to slow his hand."

"I see," reflected the Earl, weighing the requirements against a list of ingredients in his head. "An inhibitor, so to speak."

"Exactly," said Daron eagerly. "Is that possible?"

"Of course, my lord," replied Nightshade, chafing.

"There must be no other ill effects."

"Still possible, my lord."

"Excellent," said Daron, growing excited. Things were progressing far better than he had hoped.

"But I'll need some specifics."

Not quite sure where the Earl was leading, Daron straightened in his chair and said cautiously, "Like what?"

"How tall is the man?"

"My height. *About* my height."

"How much does he weigh?"

"About as much as I."

"Is he right or left handed?"

"Right." Daron frowned. "What has that to do with anything?"

"Much, my lord. I've things to deaden all parts of the body. It may sound like bragging, but I can deprive a man the use of a single finger."

"That's extraordinary," said Daron, genuinely awed.

"Well, I've had a great deal of practice." Nightshade poured himself another goblet of wine and emptied it. "Now then, when will you need this?"

"I must have it within two days." But then Daron

thought of something that had not previously occurred to him, and growing immediately concerned, he asked, "Will that give you enough time?"

"Oh, there's no problem with that, my lord. No problem at all." Nightshade grinned and, in a provocative tone, said, "Two days, eh? Would that be before or after your father's funeral?"

Daron's eyes narrowed. "After."

Nightshade's grin broadened into a toothy smile. His eyes disappeared, and he said, "But before the joust, I'll wager."

Daron said nothing.

"You've a way to administer the poison?"

The Prince frowned. "No. I haven't yet worked that out." And it worried him. It was one thing to acquire the poison, but getting it into Bryand's system was something altogether different.

His brother was naive, but he was not stupid. Anything Daron offered him to eat or drink would be regarded as suspicious. And rightly so. Had he not at one time handed his brother a plum pudding laced with tacks? And then there was the jewel-encrusted goblet he had presented him on his birthday; the one with tiny holes in its rim so that anything Bryand drank would dribble down his chin.

At that moment Daron regretted all the pranks he had ever played on him... Well, not all of them. But certainly, most of them.

Seeing the concern on Daron's face, Nightshade said, "Fear not. I can help there, too."

"But how -- ?"

"T'is better for both of us if you don't know." Nightshade saw that Daron was not convinced. He leaned closer and gripped the Prince's arm. "Trust me, my lord. I know your game. And the time and place. I promise you that your-- ." He checked himself and grinned once more. "Your *victim* will never know what hit him. Apart from your lance, of course."

Daron's eyes blazed as he pictured himself thundering down the list, his weapon leveled at his brother's heart. He heard the screams and shouts from the crowd as he tore Bryand from his saddle and sent him sprawling to the ground. And lastly he heard his brother, with his dying breath, admit defeat and call him King. "Very well then," he said, coming out of his reverie. "I'll leave it in your hands."

"Good!" exclaimed the Earl. He poured more wine into his cup. "Now let's drink to our success."

Things were moving a bit too fast for Daron. "But we've still one thing more to discuss."

Nightshade drained his goblet and wiped his mouth with the back of his hand. "And what is that, my lord?"

"Payment for your services."

The Earl chuckled. "Let us discuss payment upon completion of the job. For after that, my lord, you will be - shall we say - very well off indeed." They shared a conspiratorial smile.

"One thing before you go," said Nightshade, reaching into his purse. "Take this tonight before you go to bed." He handed Daron a small glass vile that contained a muddy colored liquid. "It tastes awful and it will make you sick for about a day. But after that you'll start feeling better again. More important, you'll be immune to just about any poison there is. Certainly all the ones I know."

Daron jiggled the vile and frowned. "Why must I take this?"

"If no one is to suspect foul play you must be able to drink from the same cup as-- ." He prodded Daron with his elbow. "You know who."

Daron realized he meant the ceremonial cup of

wine that would be offered before the joust. But though he understood the need, Daron relished not the idea of making himself sick. "Will there be any pain?"

"I'm afraid so, my lord. In this case, the cure is almost as deadly as the poison itself." The Prince went pale. "But think of the outcome, my lord. Or should I say... Your Majesty?"

Daron accepted the Earl's flattery with a wan smile and, after giving the contents of the vile one last dubious look, placed it in his purse.

"Now would you care for some wine, my lord? It might restore your spirits."

"No, thank you," replied Daron half-heartedly. "The sooner I return to the castle, the sooner I can get this over with." He rose, shook the Earl's hand, and crossed to the door. But just as he was about to leave, he hesitated and said, "There's no chance that-- ." He shivered. "That it could kill me, is there?"

"None whatsoever!" said the Earl with conviction. "You can trust in that." But after the Prince had gone, he added under his breath, "More's the pity."

Now, had Daron been less preoccupied with arranging his brother's fate and more astute about the man with whom he was dealing, he might have questioned why there were four wine goblets on the table instead of only two. But the fact is it never crossed his mind. So he had no idea that as he left by his door, two men would enter the back room by another.

"How interesting," said one. He was tall and gaunt, with light brown hair that hung to his shoulders, blue remorseless eyes, and a hawk-like nose. Though he wore a tunic and hose, the garb of a nobleman, there was no crest upon his chest, for he had been stripped of it long ago by Daron's father along with his land and estate.

His name was Cunninghim, previously the Duke of

Cunninghim, and he had no love for either of Audanot's sons. "So, Daron intends to be King at Bryand's expense. I like that. I like that well indeed."

"I could still poison him if you wanted me to," said Nightshade eagerly.

"No. Let him rid us of Bryand first. Then we'll rid the world of him."

The other, who had been staring at the door through which Daron had exited, was as tall as Cunninghim but huskier. He was darkly complected, with dark eyes and dark hair as well. He wore a full but neatly trimmed beard and a small gold ring in his left ear.

His name was Mortamour, which, in the language of the ancient Bandidonians, meant 'lover of death,' and he was Cunninghim's henchman. "I wonder what he'd do if he knew we'd poisoned his father?" said the man in a harsh, gravelly voice.

Cunninghim sneered. "Probably congratulate us."

The henchman approached the table and poured himself some wine.

But just as he was about to drink, Nightshade waved his hand and said, "Don't."

Mortamour looked at him, then at the wine. "You mean it's-- . It's-- !?"

With a shrug, Nightshade confessed, "I do it out of habit."

CHAPTER FOUR

On the day of the funeral, the wind - which had been blowing swiftly from off shore for almost a week – ceased abruptly, leaving out of deference to the King a death-like stillness to the air. And though the streets were packed with citizens and pilgrims who had traveled to the capital for the funeral, all was silent. Even the market place, usually a tumult of colors and a cacophony of sounds, was empty save for a few scrawny dogs in search of food.

At dawn, the castle doors were parted, and the vaulted hearse bearing Audanot's body creaked across the lowered drawbridge and down the main street of the city. It was drawn by twenty and six horses, each caparisoned in black with Audanot's crest emblazoned in gold on the sides.

Following closely behind the hearse, marched the Queen, the two Princes, the Council of Kings, and the members of the court and their attendants, all carefully avoiding the droppings left behind by the horses. The populace came next, unmindful of the droppings as they were accustomed to slogging through the very thing day after day.

The procession passed through the Southern gate of the city and emerged onto the clearing just beyond the wall, where a massive pyre had been erected. There, the royal family took their place upon a viewing stand that had been constructed a short distance from the pyre and draped in flowing black silks.

Unfortunately, the Funeral Director had not taken into account the lay of the land, for one end of the stand was somewhat higher than the other, causing the royal family to list to one side. Seeing this, everyone else who had gathered around the stand and the field, leaned to one side as well.

The King's body was lifted from the hearse and placed on a long wooden pallet that had been sanded smooth and polished to a brilliant sheen for the occasion. But having it made in such a fashion was yet another mistake on the Funeral Director's part. Each time the pallbearers attempted to climb the pyre, the King's body would slide off the pallet. After the third try, the wood slab was discarded, and Audanot was hauled up by a block and tackle.

The Funeral Director, much embarrassed by all that had transpired, decided not to trust anything more to anyone else, and started the fire himself. But in his distraction, he had forgotten to climb down the pyre before igniting it.

Luckily, he was wearing a loose robe and, discarding it quickly, jumped to the ground, dressed only in his loin cloth. Thus, he barely, or almost barely, escaped becoming the first human sacrifice in the history of Bandidon.

Though he was quite distressed and apologized to the Queen and the assembled nobility over and over again, everyone agreed that he had only added to the spectacle. So, from then on, jumping from a burning pyre, dressed only in a loin cloth, was included in the ritual.

Bryand stared at the flames as they rose into the sky. Even from fifty feet away, he could feel their heat on his face. He stared at his father's body and frowned. Oh, look, they placed him upside down. That is not as it should be. But there was no time to correct the mistake.

The flames had crept too close.

Goodbye Father, he thought, feeling his heart tug. May you find a place of honor waiting for you in the Heavenly Halls. I pray I can accomplish all that you expected of me. Perhaps you'll watch over me from your lofty height in the heavens. I would like that. Hopefully you'll have an apartment with an eastern view.

Queen Bee stared in silence, her teary eyes reflecting the flames. So many memories, she thought. A lifetime of serving others. Being served. Go forward to your afterlife, my husband, with an untroubled mind. You leave behind a mighty empire. One that your sons will protect. And as for me, despite all the proposals I have received the past few days, I will not marry ever again. It is flattering, though.

Daron stood by his mother's side, staring as well. Who is that saucy thing on the far side of the pyre? Must be she's new in town or I would have seen her before. I wonder if she's Sir Bragalot's intended? I heard she was a redhead. His thoughts were interrupted by the loud gurgle that came from his stomach and the resulting pain that gripped his bowels. His mother looked at him. "Nerves," he said, and that was all.

But inside he was cringing. Since an hour after he had downed Nightshade's so-called antidote he had been suffering from excruciating pains that lingered on and on, one wave after another.

They had kept him awake the whole first night, ultimately driving him into a corner of the room, clutching his knees to his chest and gnashing his teeth. Had not Cower, the royal retainer, seen him like this before - most often when Daron had lost a large sum of money at dice - he might have thought something was urgently wrong.

The next day had crawled by at a snail's pace, the pains just as intense and just as frequent. Convinced he was going to die, Daron had prayed and prayed to each and every God he could think of, promising them that he would mend his ways and forfeit the joust if only they would let him live.

By evening it appeared the Gods had heard his prayers, for the pains were farther apart and less intense. Though awakened by a few short spasms, he had been able to sleep most of the next night. And now, the pains were all but gone - the last spasm being the first since dawn. But this he blamed on himself. Not only had he awakened with a ravenous appetite and had stuffed himself, but he had also recanted his promise to the Gods to forfeit the joust.

His one fear was that the pain would return during the contest.

The sun was at the peak of its arc when the fire had at last burned itself out. An urn containing the King's ashes was handed to the Queen who, crying out stridently, handed it to Bryand who, in turn, wailed and handed it to Daron. Daron snorted grudgingly and handed it back to Bryand who wailed again and returned it to his mother.

This too was a ritual.

In my studies, I have learned that the 'passing of the ashes' began centuries ago and has remained unchanged except for one small detail. In earlier times the urn was not used. Mourners, having hot ashes dumped onto their naked palms, would cry out from pain and try to pass them on to anyone else they could find.

Queen Bee held the urn at arm's length, presenting it to the crowd, which parted for her as she walked slowly toward the city. Be strong, she said to herself. Do not let the masses see you hurting. My, this urn is heavy. Who would have thought a handful of ashes could weigh so much.

Once beyond the gate, she ascended the stone

steps that led to the top of the battlements. There she leaned out over a crenelation in the wall and turned the urn upside down. With the air as still as it was, the ashes floated toward the ground, gently coming to rest on a blind beggar who, unaware of his good fortune, was then pelted by hundreds of coins for having been thus blessed.

The ceremony was now complete, and the crowd - which had been so solemn up till then - seemed suddenly charged with excitement. A thousand voices broke the silence at once, everyone talking about the same thing, everyone wondering who would be the new King.

The blare of trumpets rose above the din, announcing the coming tournament. And like an ocean, the crowd surged toward the grandstands that flanked the jousting field, filling every seat.

Those who were slow to arrive found themselves shut out. Even the battlements that overlooked the lists were packed with people. For this was something no one wanted to miss. This was history in the making. Many Kingdoms had been usurped, many had been won or lost in war, but never had two men faced each other on the field of honor and competed for a throne.

Though I was many leagues away in Port Lansia, my thoughts were also on the joust. So too the entire town.

Everywhere I went people were chattering about the competition between the two Princes. Everyone seemed quite thrilled; but I, in truth, felt only trepidation.

I have always been high-strung by nature, meaning that most things, no matter how inconsequential, tended to upset my constitution. When the royal messenger rode into the town square and announced King Audanot's death, my stomach felt like it had dropped to my shoes and I immediately began to perspire.

I remember rushing to the temple of Broodus, God

of worrywarts and malcontents, and asking his scowling image, "What will become of us?" After all, King Audanot had ruled Bandidon and the neighboring Kingdoms for my entire life, which at that time was a total of twenty-two years; and, though I had never even seen him, nor had any of his doings ever really effected my daily routine, I immediately assumed that everything that was familiar to me was about to change.

The moment Queen Bee turned the ceremonial urn upside down, Daron tossed his brother a flippant wave and started for the north end of the jousting field where his tent had been pitched. Once inside, however, he stumbled to a lounge and collapsed upon it, clutching his stomach.

No more, he thought. It's not fair. I've suffered enough already. A stabbing pain gripped his midsection. He coiled his legs beneath him and huddled in a tight ball. Blast you Nightshade. Blast your villainy. When I'm King, I'll shove a spit up your blubbery ass and roast you over a low flame!

The room began to spin. His heart ran lunatic in his chest. A chorus of gurgles rose up from his bowels, followed by a wave of icy chills. He broke wind, long and noxiously, trumpeting a whole octave before he was through. And then, to his great surprise, upon the expulsion of his gas, the pain disappeared.

He waited for a moment, expecting it to rear its ugly head once more. A minute went by, two, and when the pain did not return, he uncurled himself and rose slowly to his feet. He took a deep breath to steady himself. Well, that was interesting, he thought, relieved.

He held out his hands. They trembled. He shook them, then went to his table where Cower had placed his chain mail, gloves, and helmet. Somehow, with the end of the pain, he knew the ordeal was over. He had lived through it, and now, as he donned his armor slowly, methodically, he was ready to taste the sweetness of victory.

If it were possible to be in two places at once, one might have been able to observe Bryand preparing in much the same way as his brother. But Bryand was not alone. Along with Cower, there were three young men within the tent.

Their names were Niles Willowbrook, Dwayne Pepperill, and Dillin Torkelstone, and they were the sons of Audanot's closest friends. As boys, they had been Bryand and Daron's playmates. But as the years had passed, they had grown closer to Bryand - whose demeanor was more in keeping with their own - and further away from Daron.

Though they had often quarreled, their loyalty to each other and to Bryand had remained unshakable through the years.

"I hope you won't take too long at this," Niles griped. He was of average height and build, with a long face and dark brown eyes that flashed often with impatience. His hair hung to his shoulders, unkempt and thick as a destrier's mane. "I'm hungry for my noon feast." He hefted Bryand's sword and swung it from side to side.

"Watch it, will you?" snapped Dwayne, hopping out of the sword's path. "You almost nicked my nethermost end."

"Your what?!" chortled Niles.

"You know what I mean."

Dwayne was far from portly. He was the tallest and the huskiest of them, with a massive chest, thighs as thick as young trees, and, unfortunately, buttocks that were proportionately as big.

"Well," said Niles with a shrug. "If your bum weren't so large, I might be inclined to admit I was wrong. I might even apologize. But the fact is, your bum's enormous. Therefore, I feel no need to do either."

"Quiet you two," chided Dillin. He was the oldest and most serious-minded of the three. "You'll break Bryand's concentration."

Niles snorted. "He doesn't need concentration to beat Daron. Can we please get on with this? I'm hungry!"

"Take back what you said," growled Dwayne.

"Very well then. I'm not hungry."

"I meant about my bum!"

"Enough!" cried Dillin, gathering each of them by an arm and leading them to the entrance of the tent. "Get out of here before I crack your heads open."

"You see what you did?" said Niles as he and Dwayne were exiting. "You made him mad."

"*I* did?!"

"Of course. Now he'll be peevish all day."

When they had gone, Dillin shook his head and muttered, "Addle-brained fools."

Bryand grinned but made no reply. Cower handed him his belt and waited for him to buckle it before presenting him with his sword. Though the retainer spoke not a word, Bryand knew he was troubled by the dour look upon his face. The Prince had seen it many times before, most often when the retainer was returning from his brother's chamber.

"Thank you, Cower," he said with a reassuring smile, hoping he might coax him into a better mood.

"Your welcome, my lord," said Cower in a brittle tone.

Bryand did not like to see Cower upset nor did he like the idea that it was he who was responsible for upsetting him. When Cower had learned about the joust, all the color had drained from his face and his mouth had screwed up into a knot. Since then he had been very polite to the Prince and very efficient. Bryand knew he was furious with him.

Dillin grabbed the Prince's helmet and held it under the crook of his arm. "Remember, keep your shield up. He rides high in his saddle."

"Aye," said Bryand.

"Don't couch your lance too soon or he'll know where you intend to strike."

"Aye," said Bryand again.

"And remember to throw your weight behind your thrust."

"Dil, have you ever beaten me in a joust?"

"No."

"Then stop giving me advice."

Dillin snorted at the rebuke and faced him squarely. "Just keep your wits about you."

"And if I don't?" replied Bryand. "If I should lose, what then? Would you follow me into exile?"

Dillin, who had never possessed a sense of humor in all his twenty-six years, gave Bryand a stern look. "Exile? Why, give Daron half the chance and he'll dispatch you to the underworld." But then, upon seeing the Prince's grin, he realized Bryand was mocking him. "Ach!" he scowled. "You're as bad as Niles and Dwayne sometimes."

Bryand grinned. If he had been given his choice of brothers out of all the men in the Kingdom, he would have chosen Dillin first, for there was no man he liked or respected more. Though he was ofttimes long-winded and overbearing - especially when he considered himself in the right - he was also honest and straightforward. Beneath the stolid bearing he presented to the world, lay a kind and generous soul. He was a man who - regardless of the consequences - would give anything of himself, anything he owned, to help a friend in need. "Have no fear," said Bryand, gripping Dillin's shoulder. "I'm up for the fight."

"Your gloves, my lord," said Cower, handing them

to the Prince.

"And you!" said Bryand, cuffing the retainer lightly on the arm. "Stop walking around with that frown upon your face. You look like an old fishwife."

"My lord," replied Cower soberly. "If I wish to frown, that is my business. Perhaps if you had tended to your business, I might not feel it necessary to frown."

"Well said," commented Dillin.

"And when have I been remiss?" asked Bryand, indulging the retainer.

"I like it not," said Cower, growing even bolder, "that the fate of your father's Kingdom rests on a single joust. Why - and I shudder at the thought - what if something went amiss for you out there. Your brother would be King. Think of that, my lord. Your brother! Though I've cared for him all these years as I have for you, there is something very odd about him. And the thought of him as our next King, sends a shudder up my spine."

Bryand eyed the retainer kindly. Often as a boy, Bryand had been troubled by thoughts he was unable to express. Cower, by a word or two, or a simple gesture, had always found a way to help him understand his feelings. Certainly, there was no one who knew him better, his likes, his dislikes, even something as inconsequential as his favorite color (*which happened to be brown.*)

"I thank you both for your concern," said the Prince. "No man could ask for a more loyal pair of mother hens." He chuckled at their disapproving looks. Then, having had his fun, he sobered. "But you worry needlessly. I have been preparing for this day for as long as I can remember. I am the rightful King of Bandidon. And no one - least of all my brother - will keep me from my purpose."

"May the Gods see it done," Cower muttered.

He waited for Dillin to comment. When he did not, Bryand pulled on his gloves, flexing his fingers, warming the leather into a second skin. His words had been bold. They were the words of a ruler. But they meant nothing without the confidence he had hoped to find inside himself. He turned away from them, wondering. Am I ready? Am I fully prepared? He thought of his father. His stature alone commanded the respect of his peers. Would he be as good a king?

"Excuse me, my lord."

Bryand turned to the entrance of the tent. Niles had poked his head inside.

"There's someone here to see you."

Dwayne poked his head in just above Niles'. "A very pretty someone."

They stepped back and pulled the tent flaps with them, revealing MeAnne. She wore a simple, unadorned kirtle. Over her shoulder was draped a shawl; the green and red colors of her clan. Her hair was plaited with a gold ribbon and coiled atop her head. The ribbon shimmered in the light, casting a glow above her face.

At the sight of her, Bryand's heart quickened, and he stood for a moment, speechless. Though they were betrothed, they were still strangers, and he had always been shy around women.

"Try asking her to come in," said Niles with a smirk. "Unless you want all this space between you."

Bryand extended his hand. "Please."

MeAnne entered the tent. "My lord," she said, taking his hand and curtseying. With Cower and his friends present, she addressed him in a formal manner. "The crowd is so thick. The grandstands are full and the entrances are packed with those who were tardy finding seats. I feared the joust would begin before I could see you." A different thought struck her. "Unless, of course, you prefer to be alone."

"No," he blurted, pleased. "You are... You are..."

"A welcome distraction," Dwayne supplied, smiling.

Bryand nodded. "Yes. What he said."

She placed a green silk kerchief in his hand. It was the color of a meadow after a spring rain, with gold and silver threads woven through it. "It would please me if you carried this with you today."

"It would please me to carry it," replied the Prince. He tucked the kerchief between his tunic and the suit of chain mail he wore.

There was so much she wanted to tell him. She was terrified he would be hurt, perhaps killed, and she did not want to face life without him. "You'll be careful, won't you?" said MeAnne, her voice quivering. "Please, my lord; be careful."

"I will," replied the Prince, gripping her hand tighter. He stared deep into her eyes, searching for words, elusive words. Speak fool! Speak you dunderhead!

MeAnne saw the cloud pass over his face. "You are troubled. I can tell."

"No, my lady," he replied.

"Then, what is it?"

He smiled and shrugged. "I only wonder why-- Not why. How. I mean, how you. As nice as you are. Not nice. I don't mean nice. I mean, I do mean nice, but you're also much more--"

"That was lovely," said Niles, smirking. "Very lovely. And here I thought you a hem-and-haw when it came to women."

Dillin cuffed him on the arm. "Quiet, lout! You intrude where you don't belong."

Bryand led her to the opening, and they lingered there for a moment in silence. He wanted to take her in his arms, to tell her about all the new and wondrous feelings she had awakened in him. But with his friends present, he contented himself with a kiss upon her palm and said, "I'll look for you in the grandstand."

He watched her cross the field, and it occurred to him that he wanted to be king now more than ever, a great king, and he wanted to do great things, all for her.

"It is time, Bryand," said Dillin.

Bryand reached for the kerchief under his tunic, then with a nod to Dillin that signified his readiness, the two young men strode into the daylight.

The crowd immediately began to cheer.

The Prince gazed at the royal box situated in the center of the grandstand to his left. The Queen was sitting in the front row, Lord Willowbrook, Niles' father, on her left and Lord Torklestone, Dillin's father, on her right. She tossed him a dignified wave, then turned toward the other end of the field and did the same for Daron who had appeared almost exactly at the same time. Bryand could not see his eyes, but he could feel his brother's hatred even with the length of the field between them.

The Prince turned his attention to the grandstand on his right. At the center, directly opposite the royal box, sat the council. Behind them was MeAnne with Blindella and their mother the lady Inoya. MeAnne was gazing at him, while Blindella looked off at Daron, or somewhere in between. He acknowledged MeAnne's look with a touch of his hand to his heart and felt the kerchief once more beneath his tunic. She grabbed her sister's scarf, the same color as the one at his breast and waved to him.

The royal trumpeters blew a long fanfare signaling the start of the commencement ceremony. The crowd fell silent. Even the vendors, who up until that moment were busy selling pennants and roasted nuts, tossed what was left of their wares into the crowd and went running to their seats.

The two princes marched to the center of the

field, then turned and stood before Lord Crushmore, the Master at Arms, who had ridden up to them upon a war horse caparisoned in black.

He was very old. (*Lord Crushmore, that is, though the horse was also getting on in years.*)

He had, in fact, not only been the Princes' instructor, but their father's as well. Strapped to his chest was the same boiled leather breastplate he had worn as a young warrior, only now it was cracked and moldy and seemed three times too big for him. Upon his head was a rusty flat-topped helmet that covered his ears, and poking out from beneath it were the thin silvery wisps of what remained of his hair.

"You have entered upon the field of honor," said the Master at Arms in a raspy but formal voice. He carried a ceremonial baton, which he touched to his helmet in salute. He paused and squinted first at Bryand and then at Daron. A puzzled look came over his face. "Don't I know you boys?"

"Aye, Master," said Bryand in a discreet tone, conscious that this was a breach of ceremony. "It is I, Bryand."

"Who?!"

"Bryand, Master," said the Prince louder, remembering Crushmore was hard of hearing.

"Oh, of course. Then you must be what's his name."

"Daron," said Daron through gritted teeth, making a mental note to have the man executed the moment he was proclaimed King.

"Have you come to see the fight?"

The Princes glanced at each other awkwardly, then Bryand said, "No, Master, we *are* the fight."

"You?!" said Crushmore, taken aback. "Does your father know about this?"

"The King is dead," said Daron impatiently.

"Don't you remember?"

Crushmore's eyes narrowed as he scratched his chin with the baton. "Let's see now. Let's see. Was he the one we burned this morning?"

Daron rolled his eyes. "Aye!"

"Well then, if the King is dead, which of you is to rule in his place?"

"The winner of this joust!" shouted Daron angrily.

A look of understanding dawned upon Crushmore's face. "Ohhh! So that's why they dressed me up. Very well. State your names for all to hear."

And they were back in the ceremony.

In a voice filled with strength and pride, Bryand said, "Bryand, son of Audanot, supreme ruler of Bandidon and Overlord of all the lands between the Spreading Bottoms and the mad highland clans."

Daron sneered at his brother and, in a voice just as powerful, exclaimed, "Daron. Ditto."

"Sons of Audanot, why are you met here on the field of honor?"

The Princes replied in unison, "To determine which of us will rule."

"Do you swear to give quarter should one of you yield?"

"Aye," answered Bryand without hesitation.

Daron, on the other hand, was silent, the muscles at his jaw bulging.

Crushmore waited for his reply, then scowled and leaned forward in his saddle. "Have you drifted off again, boy, the way you used to?"

"I heard you," replied the Prince irascibly.

"Then will you give quarter?!"

Daron turned to his brother and glared at him. "No."

Cries and jeers erupted from the crowd in the

grandstands. Many jumped to their feet and shook their fists in protest. Daron swept the stands with his eyes, a hard frown curling his lips.

"Silence!" shouted the Master at Arms. The crowd obeyed. He peered at Daron with a cocked eyebrow. "You wish to duel to the death?"

"Aye! To the death!"

Crushmore looked at Bryand. "And do you agree?"

Bryand said nothing. He glanced toward his mother, wondering what she must be thinking. She was crying, and knowing that he was the cause of her pain made his heart ache. But the time had come for him to take his rightful place upon the throne. He did not want to end things with Daron this way. But his brother had spoken first. To the death. So that was what it would be.

"Aye," he said grimly and nothing more.

"It has been agreed. The duel shall be to the death."

Upon hearing the announcement, MeAnne gasped aloud. Those around her looked her way. But she cared little just then about appearing dignified. She tore at the scarf in her hands, twisting it again and again until it was coiled like a rope between her fingers. Dearest Gods, she prayed. I've only just met him. Please don't take him from me now. Things have been so promising. He's even starting to talk.

Though she tried not to think the worst, she could not keep the thoughts from invading her mind. What would happen if he were killed? How could she stay in Bandidon, widowed even before she had become a bride. Foolish girl! she said, chiding herself. Think of *him* now. Not yourself! Tears came to her eyes, not the tears of a silly girl, but the tears of a woman in love.

She turned to her sister, looking for some comfort. But when she saw Blindella's one eye upon her, while the other observed the field, MeAnne realized she was not the only one in pain. Even though Blindella had hardly spent a moment with Daron, she was still his betrothed. "Poor sister," MeAnne sobbed, hugging her. 'One of us will have her hopes crushed this day."

"I can't look," said Blindella.

"Yes. I know."

A royal steward approached the two princes bearing a large chalice of polished silver with rubies and emeralds adorning the sides. It had been filled with a dark red wine, the finest from the royal cellar, crushed from grapes harvested from the fertile valleys of Corkin.

Catching sight of the cup, Daron's eyes began to blaze; his heart leaped in his chest; and a wicked smile played at the corners of his mouth. For he knew it had been poisoned. And suddenly all the pain he had suffered for the past two days was forgotten; and he felt more invigorated and more elated than he had ever felt before. A few sips, that's all, he thought triumphantly. And the throne is mine.

But just as suddenly all his joy turned to horror as he saw Lord Crushmore lean down from his horse and grab the ceremonial cup.

"I'm sure you boys won't mind sharing a drink with your old instructor," said the Master at Arms, eyeing the wine with relish. "Here's to a long life! For the winner, that is." And he brought the cup to his lips and drank.

Daron's eyes went wide and his mouth fell agape. He wanted to scream and tear the cup from Crushmore's hands. But he knew he could not. For such an action would appear peculiar or, far worse, indicate he knew something was amiss with the wine. So he stood there helplessly, his hands clenched into tight fists and watched the Master at Arms drink his fill.

"Ahhhhh!" exclaimed Crushmore contentedly.

"Now there's a brew to raise a dead man!" He handed the cup back to the steward who presented it to the Princes with an embarrassed look.

Daron grabbed the goblet and stared at the wine. Half the cup was empty. Only two decent swallows left, he thought.

"Drink to the victor," proclaimed Crushmore ceremoniously. "Drink to the vanquished. And may the Gods protect our future King."

Presenting a wan smile to the Master at Arms, Daron brought the cup to his mouth and, not wanting to waste a single drop, barely let the wine wet his lips. He handed the cup to Bryand and watched intently as his twin drained the remainder, hoping he had drunk enough to produce an effect.

The steward retrieved the cup, bowed, and hastened toward the grandstand.

Lord Crushmore leaned forward in his saddle and pointed his baton at Daron. "Do you swear to fight cleanly?"

Daron eyed him askance. "That all depends on what you mean by cleanly?"

Crushmore bristled. "Let no man strike at horse lest he be declared craven."

"All's fair on the rider, though, correct?"

"That is correct."

"I swear," said Daron.

"I swear," said Bryand.

Crushmore raised his baton high. "Let the joust begin!"

The Master at Arms wheeled his horse around and cantered off toward the side of the grandstand. But he traveled no more than twenty yards before he fell to the ground with a loud thud. Bryand, who had been walking to his tent, rushed to him, motioning to several guards along the way.

"Blast it if my right leg's not gone to sleep," said Crushmore, replacing his helmet on his head. They stood him on his feet but he crumpled like a child's rag doll. He tried to raise himself. "And now my right arm's numb, too."

"Let me help you," said the Prince, lifting him, and he carried him to where the court physician was stationed.

After a cursory examination, Lystillus turned to Bryand and said, "He's probably manufacturing too much blood." The physician directed his two attendants to place the Master at Arms upon a stretcher and bid them hasten to his chambers.

"How thwange," said Crushmore as he was being carried off. "It theemth the wight thide of my faith ith altho athweep."

"Fear not," said Lystillus. "I've a collar that will fix that."

And they were gone.

Bryand stared after them, only barely conscious of the tingling sensation in his right hand. He rubbed it as he watched Lystillus and the others disappear from sight around the city wall. Then, his mind once again on the joust, he turned and proceeded to his tent where Niles, Dwayne, and Dillin stood waiting.

"How is the old coot?" asked Niles. "Will he be all right?"

"Aye," said Bryand absently, for the tingling had spread up his arm.

"What's wrong?" asked Dillin, noticing the concerned look on the prince's face.

Bryand tried to smile, but it was clear to all that he was shaken. "My hand-- It's numb."

From his seat at the top of the Grandstand, Nightshade watched the Master at Arms drink from the ceremonial cup. "Oh, dear," he fretted. "I didn't plan for that." He suddenly felt queasy which was rare for a man with his acquired knowledge. He had taken a remedy or an antidote for every poison that existed. Nothing could take his life let alone irritate his stomach. Nothing except fear. Perspiration beaded his brow as he glanced first at the Duke of Cunninghim seated on his left and then at Mortamour seated on his right. "I think I'll find myself some wine," he said, starting to get up.

But he had not risen far before Cunninghim's hand was on his shoulder and pressing him down once again to his seat. "You're not going anywhere."

"Roast his liver," growled Mortamour, grinding to pulp the nuts that were in his hand. "The meddlesome old fool's fouled everything."

"Not so loud," chided Cunninghim. He looked around to see if the henchman's remark had drawn attention. Satisfied it had gone unheard, Cunninghim turned to Nightshade. "Well?" asked the Duke in a hushed but sharp tone. "What of Bryand?"

Nightshade gave him a weak smile and fidgeted with his purse. "I don't know if he got enough."

Just then Lord Crushmore fell from his horse.

Cunninghim looked on, the muscles in his jaw bulging. "You'd better pray that he did."

"Take my hand as if you're wishing me good fortune," said Bryand to Dillin. He obeyed. "Squeeze. Hard. Hard, I say."

"I'm using as much strength as I dare. I don't want to break your hand."

Bryand shook his head ominously. "I can't feel a thing."

"What sorcery is this?!" said Dillin, confounded.

"Not sorcery," said Bryand, rubbing his hand. He cast a glance at Crushmore's horse as it grazed unattended by the side of the grandstand, then faced the opposite end of the field, where his brother was making his final preparations. 'Tis another sort of treachery."

"Whatever it is," said Dwayne in an urgent tone, "You must postpone the joust."

"No."

"Bryand, you can't fight a duel to the death without the use of your good arm."

It was then Niles chimed in. "You might as well just stand there and let Daron lop off your head."

"There's no alternative," said Dillin gravely.

Dwayne turned on his heels. "To having his head cut off?! How can you say that, Dil!"

"What Dillin means," said Bryand. "Is that a postponement in the case of a duel such as this, is tantamount to a forfeit. The crown would go to Daron. And I'll not let that happen. At least, not without a fight."

"But he intends to kill you," Dwayne implored.

"He can try."

"I know what we can do," said Niles excitedly. "We'll go back inside the tent, then you and I will exchange clothes. I'll come out wearing your helmet and tunic and everyone will think I'm you."

Dwayne was first to comment. "That is, by far, the stupidest thing you've ever said."

"How so? I'm the best jouster of the three of us. I can beat Daron."

Dwayne shoved him aside. "You're also a full head shorter than the Prince. Don't you think people will notice?"

"I'll walk on my toes."

"You'll look like the fool that you are."

"Have you any better ideas!?"

"Enough," stated Bryand firmly. "I won't hear anything more. This is my fight, and I'm going to see it through." He gazed across the field at his brother, who appeared to be in the best of health. Daron must have had an antidote prepared for him, Bryand determined. Something that would prevent him from feeling the poison's effects.

Suddenly the Prince felt very depressed. When will I learn, he thought, chiding himself for having fallen into yet another of his brother's traps. I should have seen this coming. I should have been prepared. But the damage was already done, time was running short and still he lacked a way to even the sides.

"You've got to forfeit," said Dillin. "Those words are hateful to me, but if truth be told, I'd rather have you alive and about than dead and buried."

"Let them declare him King," said Dwayne. "We'll raise an army."

"We'll crush him before his bum warms up the throne," added Niles.

Bryand presented him with a weak grin, for he was bitterly disappointed. The tingling sensation had grown more intense. His hand was withering, on the verge of paralysis, and now even the right side of his face felt thick and unresponsive. Is this the way of it?! Am I to be halted in my reign before I can even begin?

"What's it to be, Bryand?" asked Niles.

The Prince turned to his friend, torn, confused, and then, from out of nowhere he remembered the card game Niles had once taught him.

It was late at night. Dwayne and Dillin had long since fallen asleep.

"No, no," Niles had said from across the table. "Don't fold your hand outright. I might have one that's worse than yours."

"Then what should I do?" he had asked, perplexed.

"Bluff. Make me think you're holding four of a kind."

"How do I do that?"

"Be bold. Bet high.

He had removed his pouch full of coins and thrown it on the table.

"Good. Now smile like you can't lose. That's right. Now you're catching on. All right, what have you got?"

"A pair of threes."

"You lose."

Sometimes it worked, sometimes it didn't. He hoped this was one time it would work. So he turned abruptly on his heels and addressed the others.

"Laugh!" he said with a broad smile. They stared at him, one as puzzled as the other.

"Laugh! Pretend I've said something amusing!" Though they had not a clue regarding his intentions, they obeyed.

At the sudden outburst, Daron looked up and gazed across the field. They're laughing, he thought. They're having a good time. He watched with growing concern as Bryand stood away from the others and began to stretch vigorously. But this demonstration did not disturb Daron half as much as the smile he could see upon his brother's face. Damn Nightshade! The poison didn't work. He didn't get enough! Fear surged inside him, his stomach churned, and his confidence dried up like a worm that had been out too long in the hot sun. Perspiring, he eyed the crowd, hoping to catch a glimpse of Nightshade and receive from him a reassuring glance. But he could not locate him.

"Squire me," said Bryand to Dillin, who snorted and shook his head disapprovingly. "Please," added the Prince. "I know what I'm doing."

"This is madness, Bryand." But Dillin knew there was nothing he could say that would change the Prince's mind. He untied the reins to the Prince's horse and led it to him. Once Bryand was in the saddle, Dillin fitted the Prince's shield onto his left arm, then went around to his other side and placed the blunt end of Bryand's lance in the leather receptacle by his stirrup.

"Come close," said Bryand, leaning over. Dillin obeyed. "Take MeAnne's kerchief out of my tunic. Carefully. Don't let Daron see you. Good. Now tie my hand securely to the lance." Dillin hesitated. "Do it, Dillin."

"Madness. Utter madness," grumbled Dillin, looping the kerchief between Bryand's fingers.

"Well that's what comes from playing cards too much," replied the Prince.

When Dillin had finished securing his hand to the lance, Bryand leaned down to receive his helmet. Once Dillin had placed it firmly on his head, the Prince smiled and said, "Now pretend I've told you something funny. But don't laugh too hard. Everyone knows you've no sense of humor."

The trumpets blared, announcing the salute of the combatants. Bryand waved his shield at his friends and spurred his horse forward at a fast trot. When Daron was almost opposite him, the Prince smiled boldly at his brother and tipped his lance. But just a little, for, in reality, he did not have much control of the weapon. Though the poison had numbed only his hand, the tingling sensation it produced had severely limited the use of his arm. He knew he could tilt the lance but once and that was all. If he judged the distance right, and his timing was perfect, he could still unhorse his brother. After that, his fate was up to the Gods.

Daron returned Bryand's salute with a scowl. In a moment, they had wheeled their mounts about and were headed back to their respective sides, only this time neither twin acknowledged the other. There came a short pause, during which Bryand adjusted his position and lowered his visor with his good hand. The crowd hushed, and Queen Bee, acting as temporary monarch, stood with her kerchief in her hand.

She hesitated, not to increase the tension, which increased nevertheless, but because she knew by dropping the kerchief she was signaling the death of one of her sons.

Though her manner remained regal and poised, her heart was breaking. She let the kerchief go and sank to her chair, and would not look upon the field as her sons came thundering toward each other.

Bryand kept his eyes locked upon his brother, studying his posture, his balance, the height at which he held his shield, all the while hoping he could find an opening for the tip of his lance. Not yet, he thought, his weapon still pointing to the sky. Daron drew nearer, his lance already couched and in striking position. "Not yet," Bryand muttered aloud as his horse chewed up the distance between them. Sweat poured down his forehead and stung his eyes, yet he dared not even blink. But then the lance was tipping. "No," he thought, panicky. "Not yet. Not now!!"

His arm had failed. His strength was gone. "Is this what you want?" he railed at the Gods. "Is this how it ends?!" The lance continued to drop, lower, lower, past striking level, downward toward the ground until its tip drove deep into the soft earth. Before he could stop himself, Bryand was torn from his saddle and thrown into the air. He heard the lance snap, felt the vibrations of the splintering wood travel up his limp arm into his shoulder. The world was a blur, first sky then grass, sky then grass. And then, as if from out of nowhere, Daron was directly in front of him, dropping his weapon, covering his face. Bryand felt the impact, heard the smack of armor crashing. Suddenly his helmet was no longer on his head and his shield had been ripped from his good hand.

He hit the ground with a groan and skidded, felt pain streak through his entire frame. For a moment, he lay upon the grass, dazed, aware of nothing save the sound of his own heart beating. But then there came a voice, faint at first, then louder. "Get up", it said over and over again through the fog that had settled on his mind. "Get up and see this through!" At first he thought it was his brother taunting him, but then he realized it was his own voice - the one inside his head - prodding him on. He shook away the last of the fog, and ignoring the sharp pain in his side, pulled himself onto his feet.

He eyed the field, searching for Daron, and there he was, sprawled upon the ground. Seeing his brother in such a state amazed him. Not a blow had been struck; at least, not a blow with his lance. His mind was awhirl. Apparently, when the weapon's point drove into the ground, it had vaulted him into the air...

...and into Daron.

Bryand staggered to his brother, his right hand still tied to the splintered shaft of his lance. He reached down with his other hand and drew his brother's sword from its scabbard. Then he rested the point at Daron's throat and waited for him to regain consciousness.

Daron awoke with a start. He attempted to rise, but when he felt the sword's point bite into his flesh, he froze. He raised his visor slowly, and when he saw Bryand above him, he groaned.

"I know what you tried to do," said Bryand, his voice hoarse with rage.

"So, kill me and be done with it."

"By the Gods, I should. And I'd be done with all your treachery."

"So, do it, then. Don't let decency stop you. Were

the situation reversed and I the one holding the sword you'd be dead already."

Bryand's lips curled into a snarl, and he raised the blade above his head. But just as he was about to strike, he heard his mother scream. He looked up, and saw her clutching the railing, tears streaming down her cheeks. He looked at Daron, the all too familiar sneer upon his lips. And with a vengeance that had been building inside him for years, a savage cry escaped from Bryand's lips and he swung the sword in a downward arc, slicing the earth just an inch away from his brother's ear. Daron, who had gone very pale, stared at his brother in disbelief.

"And *that*," shouted Bryand in Daron's face, "is the difference between us!"

He flung the weapon far across the field, and stepping back, for the first time, became conscious of the tumultuous cheers from the grandstands. He raised his hand. After a moment, the crowd became silent. "I, Bryand, regent of Bandidon by my right as champion this day, hereby grant quarter to my brother Daron. But be it known throughout the Empire he is proclaimed outlaw and henceforth banished from Bandidon and all the lands under its sovereignty for a period no less than that of my lifetime." Then in a voice only his brother could hear, he said, "Pack your things and go. If by next week you're still within my reach, I'll have your head."

Bryand called for the Captain of The Guard. "Escort the Prince to his chambers. Keep men posted outside his door until he is ready to depart, then give him horse and provisions and see him safely to the city gate. There you are to watch until he has ridden out of sight. If he tries to return, beat him off as you would a marauding army."

And with that said, Bryand turned on his heels and stumbled for the grandstand, where MeAnne stood, weeping, reaching out to him.

"Your kindness will be your undoing!" called Daron to his brother's back. He scrambled to his feet. "I tell you your kindness will be your undoing. You're weak! Do you hear?! Too weak to ever be a King!"

But his words were lost beneath the cheers of the crowd.

CHAPTER FIVE

"Curse him!" Daron shouted to the heavens. "Curse him and his name."

He looked around for something to break, found his chamber pot, and sent it crashing against his apartment wall.

"May his insides rot and drain from every hole in his body!"

He kicked his night table over, scooped it up by the legs, and dashed it against the floor again and again until it broke apart in his hands. And still his anger was not vented, so he rushed to his window, yanked down the curtains, and ripped them to shreds with his teeth.

At length, his strength spent and his jaws aching, he lumbered to his bed and collapsed upon it.

"How I hate him," he droned wearily. "Thoroughly; completely; anything more than that, too."

He was exhausted, but sleep eluded him like the buxom chambermaid in the east wing. His thoughts kept returning to the events of the day. In his mind's eye he saw his brother standing over him, triumphant in spite of his efforts, Bandidon's regent, Bandidon's next king.

Anger surged in him once more, and he struck his mattress repeatedly with his fists. "How I hate him. How I hate him, hate him, hate him, hate him!"

By now he was quite out of breath. He lay without moving for a long time, staring at the ceiling, lost between the present and the past.

This can't be, he said to himself. I don't believe it. I'm not supposed to suffer such humiliation, I'm a prince for heaven's sake.

He grabbed his pillow and hugged it. The satin cover felt cool and smooth against his cheek.

This prompted him to gaze at all the other lush appointments about the room; at least the ones he had not yet destroyed; and it occurred to him that - even though he had spent most of his life in his brother's shadow - being a prince had had its advantages.

What will become of me now? he thought. I'm no good at providing for myself. I need someone to dress me, feed me, pull my covers down at night.

Suddenly, he saw himself cast adrift in the outside world, among peasants and other dreary sorts. He saw himself eating gruel and stale bread, and washing them down with dishwater.

He saw himself huddled upon the cold hard ground, his only company being the lice he carried with him; his only protection against the elements being his tattered cape that once was trimmed with gold.

"I can't let that happen!" said Daron, bolting upright, his eyes wide with fear. "Why, I won't last two weeks out there!"

He began to gnaw on his pillow, racking his brain for a solution. But nothing came to him, and in a tormented rage, he threw the pillow across the room with all his might and leapt to his feet.

"Exile me, will he? He ravaged the immediate area, tearing his sheets, his feather mattress.

"Kick me out, will he?"

He rushed to a chair and lifted it above his head, and was about to smash it upon the floor when something caught his eye. He stood for a moment completely arrested, the chair poised above his head.

What is that? He dropped the chair and crossed

to the fireplace, kicking the pillow out of his path. He stared at the empty hearth and his eyes widened somewhat with interest.

The back wall of the hearth was slightly ajar.

He bent low and stepped inside the fireplace, his head directly beneath the flue. He touched the wall and it swung open easily, noiselessly, revealing darkness behind.

"Of course," he said. "The passageway." Apparently, when he had thrown the pillow against the fireplace mantle, it had tripped the locking mechanism.

He had not thought of it in years. Built as an escape route for the Royal Family against the castle being stormed, it ran behind the royal chambers and tunneled under the city wall. As a boy he had often used it late at night to sneak into Bryand's room while he was asleep and short sheet his brother's bed.

He stepped back, bumping his head on the edge of the flue.

"Ouch!" he said, annoyed. "That hurt."

He sat upon his haunches rubbing the base of his skull. It was then his eyes went wide and his mouth fell open.

For the bump had inspired an idea. And the more he examined it, the more convinced he became that it was a brilliant idea.

Not just brilliant, it was devious and cunning, too, and worthy of all his wretchedness.

He hastened to his mirror, which was the first thing he smashed upon entering the room. Though it was now ribboned with many cracks, he could still see his reflection, and presently this made him smile.

Had he not successfully impersonated Bryand once before? What was to stop him from doing it again? This time permanently!

Daron stood a moment, turning the plot over in

his mind. Was not Bryand always reserved before the court? Who could say they really knew him? Other than his friends, of course, and as far as Dillin, Niles and Dwayne were concerned, any differences they might see in him, he could blame upon the stresses of ruling the kingdom.

He went to the embrasure and took the chill night air deep into his lungs, feeling powerful again; invigorated. Oh, how he loved it when inspiration struck him unaware. Was anything more thrilling?

A devious smile curled his lips. All that was necessary for the plan to succeed was for the real Bryand to be eliminated.

"That's it!" he cried as loudly as he dared. "That's the solution!"

He danced about the room, clicking his heels in mid air. He slowed, as a new thought struck him, and a lean, hungry look fell across his face.

"And when I'm King, MeAnne will be my Queen."

He waited long past the changing of the guard and the watchman's early morning inspection of the royal corridor. He waited long past the castle steward and the scullery maid had rotated new torches in the wall sconces and placed clean rushes upon the hallway floor. He waited long past their hushed and heated groping, long past their departure, and long past the newness of the silence that had followed.

It was the hardest thing he had ever done. But he knew the wait was worth it. And when at last, the time was right, he grabbed a lighted candlestick and his dagger and entered the passageway.

The air within was stale. Cobwebs laced the ceiling where it joined the walls. He padded softly, though he knew he was surrounded by thick stone and could not be heard. He shivered, but it was more from excitement than from the cold.

There were times when he knew his schemes would work, even before they had actually succeeded. So bold were they that no one thought to suspect foul play. Like the time he relieved himself in the wine vat that was to supply his father's birthday celebration.

He could still see the distaste on everyone's face after the first toast. Yet no one wished to offend the King so they drank to his health until they were sick.

Killing his brother and stealing his identity went so far beyond the realm of decency it could not fail. No one would think him capable of such deceit. But of course, there was no level to which he could not sink when it came to his own gratification.

He located the entrance to Bryand's room, slipped his dagger through his belt, and blew out the candle. The smell of melted paraffin wafted under his nose. The darkness was absolute now, save for the tiny glow from the candle's wick, and were this any other time he would have been screaming. (*Daron hated the dark.*)

Feeling along the rough stone, he found the edge and, holding his breath, pulled the secret door open. Thanks to the architect, it moved silently in his hands.

The hearth was now in front of him, deep in shadow, well-swept. A cool draft from the chimney above him brushed his cheek.

Daron peeked inside. Directly across from the fireplace stood Bryand's empty bed. But where was Bryand?

He swung the wall inward, widening the crack, and he was about to take a bolder look when, without warning, Bryand strolled past the fireplace. Responding instinctively, Daron swung the wall shut, nipping his fingertips.

Hang them all! He's awake!

This was not how he had imagined things would go. At this late hour, his dullard brother was supposed to be in bed, his head full of dull, unimaginative dreams.

He waited for what seemed an eternity, hoping Bryand had at last fallen asleep. He stole another careful look.

This time, upon pulling the stone inward, he spied his brother on the far side of the room standing on his balcony.

Hang them all a second time! Wasn't the man ever going to sleep?!

Daron sat back on his haunches. He had hoped to strike a quick and easy blow, but now it seemed no longer possible. In fact, it seemed more likely there would be a struggle.

Daron knitted his brow. Could he handle a struggle? Bryand was strong, and Nightshade's antidote had put him through quite an ordeal; instead of his brother, he himself might be killed.

Daron frowned. Dying was not what he had in mind.

Yet-- .

He thought of his future; saw it as a storm-tossed sea, washing over him, dragging him down into its dark and frigid depths.

Anger surged in him once again, anger fused with wild abandon. So, what if he were killed! If he allowed himself to be banished, he would surely die any number of ways be it villainy along the road, exposure to the elements or, worse still, as the main course for some forest beast!

Well, then, brother, if that is the case, I have nothing to lose and everything to gain. Hang caution. Hang convention. And as the herdsmen say, let the chips fall where they may.

His determination renewed, he opened the secret door.

Bryand stared at the kerchief in his hands. MeAnne's kerchief. Without it, he would never have won the joust.

Much had happened afterward; a tumult of sights and sounds. Subjects bowing before him, advisors rushing to his sides, lords and knights swearing their allegiance or pledging him their swords, and all the while he wanted only to find MeAnne.

He saw her on the fringe of the confusion, waving, trying earnestly to catch his attention. He waved back, his heart quickening at the sight of her. He fought against the advancing crowd, getting close enough to touch her fingertips before being swept along by the human tide.

A procession followed, courtly duties, and then a council session that had lasted long into the night. The watch had already changed when they had adjourned, too late to see her.

He had considered knocking on her door, but trusting that she was already asleep, he did not want to disturb her. Besides, the words he wanted to say were so difficult to speak. He knew them. He heard himself saying each and every one. But speaking them in her presence seemed harder than standing alone against an entire enemy army.

Bryand massaged his right hand. The feeling had returned and now only a slight tingling lingered.

He looked out at the slumbering city that stretched before him. It had grown since he was a boy, acres beyond the old stone walls. A cool breeze, pungent with the smell of roasted meat, drifted up from the ward below. He knew the kitchen workers would already be hard at work, preparing food for the next day's feast. He heard a soldier humming atop the battlement, like as not to keep awake, and somewhere in the city a hungry infant cried.

It occurred to him that as King he had the opportunity to accomplish many things for his people. The Council of Kings was the first step. Together they would establish trade and develop industry. Perhaps there might even be time for finer things as well, he mused, such as art and music.

Enlightenment! That was the key to longevity. He had studied the history of other Kingdoms. Steeped in violence and ignorance, they had withered just as quickly as they had bloomed. Their walls were the dust beneath his feet.

But that would not be Bandidon's fate. It would withstand the test of time; its walls would remain straight and well braced against the eroding winds.

The night sky was clear and studded with a myriad of stars. He gazed at the sky feeling a sense of peace, ready to take on the challenge of creating a new age. Yet there was one thing that still plagued his mind and wearied him - Daron.

He wondered if he had done the right thing by granting him his life. His father would have executed him on the spot, kin or no kin.

But he was not his father. He could not begin his reign with his brother's blood upon his hands.

He was glad he had been merciful; for his mother's sake as well as for his own. But more than anything else, he wanted to think that, by granting Daron his life, he had taken the first step towards enlightenment.

Thus occupied, he was unaware that someone stood behind him, the one person able to slip into his shadow without distorting it. He heard a muffled thump and quickly associated it with the pain sweeping up the back of his head. And the last thing he saw was the stars bursting in a dazzling conflagration, before the sky went black.

Daron stood over his brother, looking down at his dagger. Not a drop of blood blemished the blade.

At the last moment, to his own surprise, he had turned the dagger around and knocked Bryand unconscious with the hilt. Why he had allowed such a perfect opportunity to escape him was something he himself did not understand.

Perhaps-- . No, don't even think such a thing!

But he could not shake the thought.

Perhaps - being his twin - there was a little bit of Bryand in him.

He shuddered and stared at his brother. Hate surged in him renewed, but this time it was not so much for Bryand as it was for the weakness he saw in himself. He raised the dagger over his head.

"I'll do it," he said aloud. "I will!"

But seeing Bryand below him, his face the mirror image of his own, he could not go through with the deed. He lowered the dagger, backed up against the wall and sank to the floor. He ran his hand through his hair, forlorn.

What kind of villain am I? he asked himself. It must be true, then; there must be some of Bryand in me after all.

He had never felt so depressed, so weary. His life had never looked so bleak.

He was trudging off to his room, ready to start packing, when a new thought struck him and made him pause.

Even if he had killed Bryand, would that have made up for all the years of living in his shadow? And he realized the answer was, no.

He wanted Bryand to suffer more than just death. He wanted Bryand's suffering to be endless. Would it not be sweeter revenge to keep him alive, assume his identity, and banish Bryand in his stead?

But no, he thought, there was no logic in that. Bryand would never be silent. Knowing him, he would raise an army with the help of his friends and be back upon the throne within a fortnight.

The Prince shook his head, depressed once more. No, for a plan like that to work, Bryand would have to be kept under lock and key.

Daron perked up at the thought.

So, what's wrong with that? he asked himself, taking an immediate liking to the idea; especially when he pictured his brother chained to a wall surrounded by vermin and decay.

"That's it!" said Daron aloud. "That's the answer."

He would have his brother thrown into the darkest, deepest hole in the ground. He was sure the dungeon had a lower level!

He began to pace, excited now. Just think of all the years he would suffer! This was much better than killing him. Much better indeed!

He would steal everything that belonged to Bryand - his identity, his throne, MeAnne - and the best part of the plan was that he would have the pleasure of flaunting it all in Bryand's face whenever he was of the mind to visit him in his cell.

He jumped to his feet, knowing he had to work fast. He hastened to the chamber door and bolted it as quietly as he dared. Then, returning to the balcony, Daron dragged his brother into the room.

He stripped Bryand naked; chuckling; so very

pleased with himself.

He removed his own clothes. During this, Bryand groaned and sat up on his knees. But another blow to the back of the head returned him to oblivion.

Dressed once more, only now in Bryand's clothes, Daron stood before his brother's mirror. The tailoring was exact, every seam lay in the proper place, but in spite of his looks, in spite of his daring, he knew there was something wrong about the plan (*apart from it being unethical.*)

He stared at his reflection and then beyond it at the dagger on the floor. And then it came to him.

He took up the dagger, staring at the blade, noting its length and the way it tapered to a needle-like point. He cast a look at his brother and his mouth stretched downward into a hard frown.

But he no longer intended to use the dagger on Bryand. Now he intended to use it upon himself. Though he relished not the idea, he knew it was exactly what the plan needed for it to succeed.

He was about to make an outrageous claim, one that would be disputed by his brother even from as far away as his dungeon cell. People would hear things. They always did. What better way to establish his innocence, and thus galvanize the court's support, than by suffering a grievous wound.

He knew he had to act fast, before the voice inside his head tried to convince him otherwise and stay his hand. The words "dumb idea" had already come to mind.

He went to Bryand's wardrobe and removed a handkerchief. Dumb idea rang out again even louder.

No one's arguing the point, he whispered aloud, and then stuffed the handkerchief into his mouth lest he scream too loud from the pain. He turned the dagger's blade inward. His hand trembled. He felt squeamish, and he cringed.

Do it! he thought. You've got to do it! So he shut his eyes tightly, bit down on the cloth, and stabbed himself just above his left breast.

His face contorted as pain streaked down his arm and across his chest. He felt like he was going to faint.

Boy, he thought. The things I do to get attention.

He stumbled to his brother's table and clung to it. He sucked in his breath, bit down on the cloth once more, and pulled the dagger out.

He crumpled to his knees, tears running down his cheeks. When the cramping in his shoulder subsided, he spit out the handkerchief.

"Well then," he muttered. "It's time for the pain to go away. Go away pain......Pain you're not going away!"

He rose, clutching his arm, then staggered to Bryand and collapsed by his side with a grimace. He placed the dagger in his brother's hand.

"That was a terrible thing you just did," said Daron as he curled Bryand's fingers around the hilt. "I'm surprised at you. Actually, I'm surprised at me."

He got to his feet, then proceeded to kick over the furniture and make as much noise as possible.

"Help!" cried Daron. "Guards! Guards! Help me!"

He heard them approaching.

"Put down that knife, Daron!" he yelled as he sank against his brother's footboard. "You don't know what you're doing!"

By this time the guards were smashing against the door again and again. At last, the bolt gave way, and four yeomen, members of the King's personal guard, burst into the room. Daron pointed limply at his brother.

"The Prince--. He tried to kill me." He indicated the secret passageway. "He came from there."

"What's going on here?" said Bryand, dazed. He found himself being pulled to his feet by his guards.

"What is it? What has happened?" But they did not respond.

Just then, he heard his own voice say, "See you, he holds the dagger even still."

Something was knocked out of his hand and clattered on the floor. He looked up, and saw his brother's face before him. "Daron. What-- ?"

"Take him to the dungeon," said his brother. "And be quick about it. I do not wish to look upon him anymore."

Still dazed, his head pounding, Bryand took in the scene. Suddenly terror gripped him. "Wait! You don't understand!" He struggled to break free, but the guards held him fast.

"Silence him," said Daron, frowning. "I will not hear another word uttered from his lips."

A gag of sorts was shoved into his mouth and he was led away through the crowd that had gathered in the hall.

The news of Daron's treachery had traveled fast. Bryand caught sight of the Queen, and he began to struggle more. But she would not look at him. Instead, she lowered her eyes - eyes filled with sorrow and regret - and began to weep.

King Jasper remained by his door and cast him a stony glance, while MeAnne, refusing to look at him, started for the royal chamber. Even Cower, loyal Cower, went by him without a word.

"My lord, my dearest," said MeAnne, kneeling by Daron's side. Her gaze fell upon his shoulder and she gasped.

"What?" said Daron weakly. He looked down and saw the crimson stain above his breast.

"Is that my blood?" he asked, genuinely awed.

"Aye, my lord," said MeAnne, choking back her tears.

"I thought so."

And with that, his eyes rolled up into his head and all things – sight, sound, pain - faded into nothingness.

CHAPTER SIX

The following events were pieced together through the use of several manuscripts that I have obtained over the last twenty years. The chief source was, again, Daron's diary, "Memoirs of A Mad Monarch." Though most of this is a shocking description of his sexual exploits, there were many passages that helped me in my attempt to reconstruct the events that transpired after Bryand's imprisonment.

Other sources included, "Tapestries - The Art of Love," by MeAnne, Queen of Bandidon; "Two-facedness - A Second Point of View," by the Duke of Cunninghim; and "Poison and Other Remedies," by the Earl of Nightshade.

MeAnne sat by the side of the bed, watching the Prince's face intently for any sign of discomfort. Though he was alive and out of danger, her heart remained lodged in her throat and tears pooled in her eyes.

For she had known the terror of that breathless moment when her lover, the one dearest to her heart, had stood upon the brink of death. And in that moment, when no one could determine the outcome, her life had hung in the balance along with his.

Such irony, she had thought in growing rage. To be separated from him by life itself, a life that would be no better than death. How cruel the Gods were at times.

"Take me with him!" she had cried to the heavens, shocking Lystillus and the other physicians in the room. "For he bears my soul with his!"

Silence had fallen instantly, and all eyes had turned to MeAnne expecting her to fall to the floor in a lifeless heap (*The Gods were very accommodating about granting death requests. It was the least of their miracles and an effective reminder of their omnipotence.*)

But nothing had happened to the Princess.

Instead, the Prince's chest had heaved violently, and an instant later he had bolted upright in his bed, his eyes wide and alert, and he had said, "Could I have some water, please? I feel like I've swallowed a sock."

There had been much rejoicing among the physicians, and MeAnne had wept openly on Cower's shoulder, who had wept as well while shouting praises to the Gods for their generosity. The Prince was lavished with water until he had quenched his thirst and his eyes had fluttered shut, and he had fallen into a contented sleep.

Twelve hours had passed, and still he had not stirred. "Rest comfortably, my lord," said MeAnne softly, though she knew he could not hear her. "Dream peaceful dreams." And to herself she added, I wonder if he snores?

Under normal circumstances, she would never have been allowed beyond the threshold of his apartment, let alone inside his private chamber. Custom dictated that a lady of noble character hide her eyes before a man's nakedness, but in the urgency of the moment she had helped strip him down to his bloomers. And now, with the danger past, she allowed a slight grin to curl her lips. He looked adorable in bloomers, especially the way they crept up between his cheeks.

She lingered on his buttocks for as long as she could before the shocking events of the previous night came tumbling back to mind. I almost lost him, she reflected, and she started to tear up again.

She cast an imploring look to the heavens. Please, please no more scares. All I ask is that you keep him alive long enough for us to wed. I'd prefer longer, of course, much longer, but I don't want you to think I'm greedy.

In just three or four months her tapestry, the symbol of her maidenhood and the direct cause of their lengthy courtship, would be complete. Frowning, she recalled the cursed day when, in her blissful ignorance, she had embraced the tradition of 'The Wall Hanging' as a means of pleasing her betrothed.

Sparing not one minute more, she intended the nuptials be performed upon the final stitch, before she had tied the final knot. No one in his right mind could accuse her of being impatient. Not after almost losing him in such a horrid fashion. And if perchance someone did think her indiscreet, she would not use her exalted station as a means of obtaining satisfaction. She would use her fists instead.

Days passed and with each visit the fear of losing him became more and more remote until the reason for his bed rest was practically forgotten.

She spent hours by his side, reading to him, fluffing his pillows, experimenting with new hairstyles (*he was so patient.)* He had changed much since their late-night meeting in the castle garden. The adoring glances he gave her and the gentle, almost shy, things he said worked upon her heart, causing her to ache with joyous rapture.

Her private fantasies had all come true, life was complete, and she faced the future, their future, with eager anticipation.

So, it was that, two months to the day after being attacked by his brother, her dearest love, her liege and lord, her husband to be, was crowned King.

Or so she believed.

For he looked like Bryand; he talked like Bryand; he walked like Bryand; in fact, everything about him was like Bryand except for one minor detail.

He was Daron.

On the day of the coronation, the sun, a dazzling yellow jewel, reigned like an overlord above the capital. The sky, not to be outdone, was a deep and lustrous blue and presented itself uncluttered save for a feathery strand of white clouds that drifted in the shape of a heavenly bower.

The surrounding hills were crowded with lush green vegetation. The trees stood taller still. It seemed like the whole world had taken notice and dusted itself off in time for the celebration.

Daron paused at the entrance of the Great Hall. Before him, dressed in their finest array, were MeAnne and the Queen Mother, the Council of Kings, lords and ladies of the court, knights of the realm, leaders of the provincial clans and tradesmen of influence from every corner of the Empire.

Squires stood along the walls, holding aloft their banners, and behind them, freshly bathed, men at arms clad in tunics bearing the royal sigil.

Pomp, the castle chamberlain strode forward. He wore his finest robe, the one his father had passed down to him, and being thusly dressed, his look was of rare contempt this day.

Harumphing loud enough for even Daron to hear, who was at the opposite end of the hall, Pomp rapped his staff of office upon the floor and proclaimed, "Approach ye, Bryand, son of Audanot, Prince of Bandidon and Regent of the land. Approach ye and be crowned King."

Twelve military drummers struck up a ceremonial beat. A score of trumpeters sounded a magnificent fanfare, and all present bowed as Daron, his shoulders back and head held high, marched into the room.

Almost done, he thought. In spite of the pageantry and the overflowing goodwill, he was wary. After all, he was not fooling himself. He was an impostor, a villain, and he knew of no story where the villain, in spite of all his plotting, ever triumphed. He gazed from side to side, expecting Bryand to burst into the room and accuse him of his treachery.

That would be just like him to spoil my fun.

He checked the exits for a fast escape, noting Sir Hefta, King Mitashmeer's eldest son, stood closest to the back door. Built like his father, he was very large and had an enormous chest. I could use him as a shield and a door jam if things go haywire.

But the upset never came. His brother never appeared. The crown was placed upon his head, the oath of honor sworn, the pledge of faithful service to the court and to the people spoken.

It was done. The ceremony was complete. He was King, and though he was composed and acted in a regal fashion, inside he was shouting, "I did it! I've won! I've won-I've-won-I've-won-I've-won!"

Pomp rapped his staff upon the floor. "His most royal Highness, Bryand, King of Bandidon."

"Hail to the King," people cheered. "Hail to King Bryand."

"That's me," thought Daron. He gave the room a placid look, a benevolent look, a look that befitted a King. Then he climbed the steps to the throne and sat upon it, noting how well it framed his rump.

This is such fun. And it's just the first day!

He cleared his throat, paused for effect, and said, "It is time for a new beginning." He scanned the room, saw the encouraging smiles and the eager acceptance on people's faces.

That was a good opening, he thought. Of course, he had stolen it from his brother, who was always talking about some sort of new this or that.

"Aye, a new beginning."

He paused again, this time not just for the effect. Hmmmm, mayhaps I should have written a speech after all.

"Uh... For what is a beginning if not something that is new." Think fool, think. What would Bryand say. "We, uh... We are different peoples... uh... come together... as one. The differences of the past, the things that separated us... are ended now. We face the challenges of today and all the days to follow as kin... as brethren... nobleman and commoner... for the, uh, common good. We have seen terrible tragedy in the past few months. The death of my father, and the treachery of my brother."

He fell silent. Odd, he thought. Passing judgement on myself.

"I have wrestled long and hard over the question of my brother, deciding whether or not he should be executed. It weighs heavily upon my mind even still. Naturally, anyone who harms the King's person must be punished. But, though he did me a grave injustice, I cannot bear to see him die. After all, he is my brother and save for some minor flaws, Prince Daron is a good person at heart."

There came a low but startled murmur from the court.

"Say what you will, Prince Daron has worked hard for the Kingdom. Did he not construct the new aqueduct and bring water to the southern provinces?"

Shouts rose up from the crowd; protests.

"It swamped six towns!" someone cried.

"Who said that?!" snapped Daron. "I want that

man's name!" But he immediately regained his composure. "He, uh, he should be commended for his observation and his courage. It must be hard to speak your mind in the presence of your king."

Returning to the question at hand, Daron proclaimed. "Henceforth, Prince Daron, for his crimes of treason and attempted murder, shall remain in the castle dungeon for the remainder of his life."

This mollified all save those upon whom Daron had played nasty tricks. Yet it left Daron brooding. It's nice to know what people really think about you when you're not around.

"At any rate," he continued. "I bid you accept my decision. Let this simple act usher in a new era of acceptance; of justice; and mercy for all men born high or low."

What came next surprised him to such an extent that he burst out laughing with relief. For after he finished speaking, there followed a long pause, during which not a word was spoken, not a cough or a sneeze were heard; a silence so complete that it felt like a living presence. And then, just as he started to doubt himself, the hall erupted in what seemed like a thousand cheers that went on and on and on.

So exuberant was the crowd, that MeAnne laughed through tears of joy. King Jasper smiled and nodded approvingly, and from his place at the side of the hall, Cower put his hands on his heart and gushed with pride.

"Places, please," Pomp announced, trying to regain order. "Places! Places for the Grand Procession."

Daron tossed him a quizzical look. "Grand Procession?"

Pomp raised an eyebrow. "As I explained to his majesty yesterday, you shall lead the entire court down the main street of the city, whereupon you shall proceed to the House of the Gods and beg them to look kindly upon your reign from the heavens."

Daron felt his stomach churn. "Give thanks to the Gods?"

"But of course," Pomp replied. "Did his majesty not read the pamphlet I sent over? Sir Robert's Rules of Chivalric Order?"

"Rules of order, yes, I glanced through them."

"Then shall we proceed?"

Daron hardly relished approaching the Gods. Being Gods, they were omniscient, which meant they were well aware of his deception. Why they had not yet intervened was a mystery to him. Surely asking for their blessing would only provoke them.

Yet any break in ceremony would appear odd to the court and he did not want to give anyone the slightest reason to question his behavior.

"Certainly," said Daron, wanting his relationship with the man to start off on the right foot. "On to the House of the Gods. We don't want to keep them waiting, do we?"

Pomp gave him an effete smile before rolling his eyes. "No, sire, we do not."

The court reassembled in the inner ward, where scores of horses caparisoned in a cavalcade of colors stood saddled and waiting. In the sparkling sunlight, every bridle bit glinted, every belt buckle shined.

Here and there, already mounted, standard bearers from each of the United Kingdoms held their flags unfurled, and these waved in the breeze in a chaotic dance, smacking anyone who happened by at the wrong time, dislodging helmets and headdresses alike.

Daron located Groom, the royal groom, and started toward him. But when he realized the man had prepared not his usual mount but Bryand's, Daron halted in his tracks. It had not occurred to him until just then that he would be riding his brother's horse.

Of course, he thought. You're Bryand. Naturally you must ride Bryand's horse. But would the horse let him? Would it sense something amiss? How intuitive was a horse, anyway?

He was still ten feet away when the steed whickered. Five feet away and it bobbed its head vigorously. Two feet away and it skittered backward almost breaking free.

"Dunno what's botherin' 'im, yer grace," said Groom, tightening his grip on the reins. He was a large man with rock-hard muscles that bulged beneath his grimy shirt. "He be skittish fer weeks now."

Nervous as he was, Daron was not about to let a horse undo him. He smiled and took the reins from Groom, then gently stroked the horse's withers until it calmed.

"He'll be fine. We just need a few minutes to get acquainted." He saw the quizzical look on Groom's face. "He's never been ridden by a King."

It took a moment for the remark to sink in. But when Groom finally grasped its meaning, he grinned, mostly gums and a few broken stumps that were once his front teeth. Over the years Groom had been kicked in the head many times, costing him not only his teeth but a large measure of his intelligence.

"Ho! Ya! Never been ridden by a King! That's a good one, yer grace!"

As Groom retreated, Daron leaned close to the horse's ear and cooed, "You don't know what to make of me, do you? Am I Bryand or not? I look like him, don't I. Even smell like him, too, thanks to his clothes. But something's different, isn't it?"

The horse snorted and bobbed its head.

"Now listen carefully. You let me ride you and I'll give you all the carrots and apples you can eat. But give me any trouble and I'll turn you into a gelding on the spot."

The horse seemed to understand. He allowed Daron to mount without any trouble.

The procession formed ranks and started down the main street of the city, Daron acknowledging the cheering crowd with a regal wave. By midway, he was feeling most at ease, and leaning forward to pat the horse's neck, he said, "It's good to see you know who's boss. I was thinking I might have to ship you off to a glue factory, but now I think I'll wait."

Once again it was as if the horse had understood. Only this time its ears went back and it snorted.

Picking up its pace, it veered to the left, heading for a low hanging sign. Were Daron not an expert rider, he might have found himself unhorsed. But using spurs, knees and reins, he managed to avoid the sign and steer the animal back to the center of the street.

"Do that again," Daron growled behind a frozen smile, "And you'll be a horse-hair blanket by nightfall."

The horse seemed to understand this as well.

The procession ended at Soothsayer Square in the center of the city. It was there upon the steps of the House of the Gods, the men and women gifted with prescience congregated each morning, revealing to one another what was in store over a hot beverage and a sweet roll.

This day, however, they were nowhere to be found, knowing full well for at least a week that the square would be jammed with citizens trying to catch a glimpse of the new King. (*This, I should mention, had nothing to do with their ability to see into the future. They simply read the decrees that had been posted by the royal heralds.*)

The House of the Gods was a very large, very grandiose two-story edifice of polished stone. Except for the priests' quarters at the rear of the structure, there were no interior walls, only a series of slender alabaster columns forming a large square. In the center of the square was a beautiful atrium full of lush green herb plants and ferns dedicated to the Goddess Rhododendron, *(who, according to the Ancient Book, is caretaker of the Heavenly Halls' gardens. It is written she enjoys mulching very much and irrigating but is not too fond of pruning.)*

Beside each column was a tall pedestal. Upon each pedestal sat a marble bust of one of the one hundred eighty three major deities worshipped by the Bandidonians. This did not include the several dozen minor deities and demigods whose statuary were across town in a more moderate rent district.

Daron dismounted and led the court into the temple. The interior was surprisingly cool and smelled of spices and moist earth.

He shivered. But it was not from the chill in the air. The time had come to see just how much the Gods would tolerate.

For Daron had plans. Roaming the city's streets as often as he did, he knew certain things about the people that would boost his popularity with them straight away.

Bread and cheese, the staples of the lower class, were always in short supply. He would build two new granaries on the outskirts of the city, and give land away to anyone willing to farm the outlying provinces. He would build lumber mills in Gonad by damming the gentleflow river, construct new peers in Port Lansia and build a fleet that would fish the uncharted waters of the Ocean of No Boating.

He would pay for all this using funds from the treasury, which he knew would run out quickly. But he was prepared for this.

He was already considering a new source of income, a yearly levy on the people, one he had already named the Cost of Living Tax. It's premise was simple - if you were alive you had to pay. Nobleman and commoner alike; there were no exceptions.

Well, actually, there were two. Those persons close to death could avoid payment by speeding up their departure. Those persons already dead were exempt.

He would wait, however, to introduce the new tax. He needed time to put in place certain safeguards, and by this he quite literally meant safe guards. Men of certain talents who were capable of collecting the tax and enforcing all of its provisions.

These he would find among the inexhaustible supply of cutthroats that frequented the Slaughter House. True, not one of them had done an honest day's work in his life. But this was not going to be honest work.

He would deploy them to every local garrison in the kingdom. Once these were under his control, he could demand anything from the rest of the United Kingdoms. And he intended to demand a lot.

Oh, the misfortune he would heap upon those who had ridiculed him! The only thing that kept his revenge from being complete was that all his subsequent actions would be done in Bryand's name and not his own.

A cruel smile curled his lips, and he wondered if his brother was enjoying his new accommodations. He had not seen him since the castle guards had dragged him off to the dungeons. Perhaps, Daron thought with a smirk, it's time for my first visit.

Impatient suddenly for the temple service to end, he barely paused at the remaining twenty-seven Gods and went directly to the foot of Himagain's statue. There he knelt and bowed his head, and recited the prayer he had been taught as a boy:

"Himagain, Himagain,

Praised, be ye.
I come most humbly,
On bended knee.
My chief protector,
Your servant still;
Oh, Himagain, Himagain,
Don't do me ill."

He glanced at the statue's face and realized it looked very much like his father's. Of course, he thought, scowling. It had been commissioned only a few years ago.

Stone, he found himself thinking. That's all you are. And an inferior grade, too. Well, Most Highest, if you are indeed in there, here's your chance to strike me dead. I've blasphemed. I've cheated. I've... Why name them all. Suffice it to say I've been a very bad boy.

He waited. But nothing happened.

It was then, the head priest, whose name was Sanctimonius, approached the King. He was a tall, gaunt man, with a narrow face, and large piercing brown eyes that Daron found unnerving almost at once.

He wore a white homespun robe and a floor-length stole embroidered with pearls and tourmaline gemstones. Draped from his arms, which were folded in front of him, voluminous sleeves covered all but his fingertips. Upon his head he wore a tall conical-shaped turban that tapered to a crooked point.

"Good morrow to your grace," he said, smiling unctuously. "And may the Gods protect your reign."

"I thank you, Sanctimonius," Daron replied.

"I trust that, on this most blessed of days, your grace is well?"

"Aye. Well, indeed." Those eyes, Daron thought, trying not to grimace. Doesn't he ever blink?

"Then your grace is, of course, ready to give thanks to our most highest of lords, Himagain, God of unexpected interventions?"

Daron glanced at the statue, glad for an excuse to break eye contact with the man. "Aye."

"Splendid. And I assume his grace has brought the offerings?"

Traditionally, one did not enter the temple empty-handed. According to the priests, such forgetfulness was looked down upon by the Gods.

Daron motioned for his pages to carry forward the numerous platters of cooked meats and trimmings brought from the castle.

"What? No rum torts?" asked Sanctimonius, eyeing the offerings as they were placed at the statue's base. "He that is Most Awesome is very fond of rum torts."

"Sorry," said Daron meekly. "But I did bring a fruit cake."

"He still has one from last year. Any jelly rolls?"

"Aye," Daron replied brightly. "Two platters full."

"You know, He was telling me just the other day that He was in the mood for raisin brandy."

"I'll have some brought over."

"And a cask of ale."

"Consider it done."

"Also some taffy, and a few good cigars."

"Cigars?"

"Those new things folks are smoking instead of pipes."

"Very well. Anything else?"

Taking advantage of Daron's offer, Sancitimonius turned and huddled with three associate priests. They whispered back and forth, glancing at Daron from time to time until the head priest straightened and resumed a dignified air. "Sixteen pounds of butter, twelve crates of eggs, one hundred gallons of milk - cow's preferably

- twenty five cheese logs, and ten bushels each of corn, broccoli, and onions."

"Also turnips," one of the associate priests chimed in.

Daron blinked. "Turnips?"

The priest nodded and said with conviction, "He likes turnips."

Daron scanned their expectant faces. "Then He shall have a wagon load."

A moment passed, during which no one spoke. Then, without warning, Sanctimonius convulsed and proclaimed, "Ooo-yea, ooo-yea, ooo-yea. I'm receiving a message from the All Mighty."

The other priests quickly genuflected and bowed their heads. Daron felt obliged to do the same.

Sanctimonious' eyes went wider. "Aye, Lord, aye. I will tell him." He looked at Daron. "He wants you to know He's very pleased. You should have no troubles in the foreseeable future."

"But what about after that?" asked Daron, concerned.

Sanctimonius glanced at the other priests then back at Daron, and with a grin he replied, "well, let's see how long the food holds out."

Daron emerged from the temple into the crystal sunlight. Before he had raised his hands, he was met with a thousand cheers. So apparent was the crowd's love for him, that a genuine smile broke across his face.

He stood at the top of the steps, filled with an unaccustomed feeling; the confidence that came from knowing he was loved. How strange, he reflected, delving inwardly. This just might outweigh the pleasure I get from being devious.

But, then again, no. For the thought of his brother, lying in his own waste, gave him goose bumps.

Eager now to taunt him, Daron hastened to the bottom of the temple steps where he gave MeAnne a perfunctory kiss upon her hand and tossed a wave to the dozens of nobles and dignitaries who had gathered to wish him well.

Yet, before he could escape, the Duke of Cunningham and the Earl of Nightshade blocked his path.

"Greetings, your Majesty," said Cunninghim with a fluid bow. "A word with you if I might."

"Aye," Daron replied absently, for at the moment he was thinking, "I wonder how often they change Bryand's straw?"

"I offer you my services, my lord," Cunninghim continued. "And my sword, should you ever need a good strong arm. Day or night, call upon me whenever you will."

Daron studied his face. "Cunninghim, is it not?"

"Aye, Majesty," he replied with a proud smile.

"My father never liked you." This was delivered not as a slight but as a statement of fact.

Cunninghim's smile weakened. "True, sire. Though he had no cause. I have never been anything but loyal to the crown."

"I seem to recall an attempted rebellion two years ago--."

"My uncle's doing. It was I who exposed the plot."

The child of a second son, Cunninghim was born with noble blood in his veins but very little wealth. Though an intelligent lad, he grew up feeling discontented and jealous of other people's possessions.

Fate seemed to further conspire against him when a fire destroyed his house and claimed the lives of his parents. Cunninghim inherited only what the flames had spared - an empty wardrobe. Though perfect for keeping his clothes pressed, he had naught but what was on his back.

His uncle, however, being the first born of the family, had inherited its wealth and its title, and lived upon a large estate just outside the capital. After traveling many leagues with the wardrobe on his back, Cunninghim presented himself to the man. Impressed by the boy's tenacity, and in need of a solid wardrobe, the uncle welcomed Cunninghim into his household.

The uncle was a reckless and self-indulgent man, who gave Cunninghim neither harsh nor kind treatment, but looked upon him with casual indifference. Though he had a roof over his head and food to satisfy his hunger, Cunninghim grew up alone and followed no one's rules but his own. When he did think of other people it was to control them or to exploit their labors, and from this he decided he would make an excellent king.

Toward this end, he strove with single-mindedness. He took control of his uncle's affairs, which were in great disorder. Too much of the manor's acreage had been left fallow, and the storehouses were now almost empty.

Determined to make the estate profitable, Cunninghim divided it into small farms and hired serfs to work the soil. He bought a mill and charged his tenants and the neighboring manors a stiff fee for grinding their wheat.

In just three years, he had settled his uncle's debts, in three more, the estate was turning a profit, and by three more after that, he had made his uncle the wealthiest suzerain of his shire.

For this, the uncle, who was childless and a bachelor, adopted him and proclaimed Cunninghim the family heir.

Even though life in his uncle's household had

lacked all warmth or caring, Cunninghim was grateful to the man. As a Duke, the uncle had access to the King's court, and being the Duke's newly proclaimed heir, Cunninghim now had access to it as well.

For six months he sent cards and favors to the King. But despite these efforts, Audanot remained unimpressed by him.

And because Audanot did not favor him, many of the King's lords withheld their friendship, and being not as young or as handsome as the Princes, even the ladies paid him little heed.

A year passed and still his dinner placard was most often found at the table farthest from the royal dais, the one reserved for distant relatives and the evening's entertainment. When tournaments came round and sides were chosen for the joust, he was always chosen last.

In this case, however, it was not because he was disliked, but because he was simply a poor jouster.

Nor could he wield a sword with any prowess or loose an arrow toward a given mark. All told, the only things at which he showed any talent were plotting and creating discord.

So skillful was he at deception that no one ever suspected the rumors he spread were of his own making. He sought out others who were also discontent with their standing, and playing upon their particular vanities, he quickly became their confidante and ultimately their leader in a clever plot to assassinate the King.

Cunninghim convinced his uncle - who was by now a quarrelsome drunk - to perform the deed the next time the King went riding.

But the plot was never meant to succeed. For Cunninghim himself set the trap that caught his uncle, then led a detachment to the other conspirators and looked on as they were put to the sword.

Cunninghim returned to the castle expecting accolades for his loyalty. But instead he found himself stripped of his lands and banished, escorted from the capital in disgrace.

He had not stepped foot in the kingdom until he fell in with Nightshade and - through the use of the man's talents - discovered the way to take revenge upon the King.

But even if Daron had known the whole truth about Cunninghim's past, he still would have found it of no concern. What mattered now was that his father had disliked the man, and anyone his father had disliked, Daron intended to embrace as a brother.

"I believe you," he said amiably. "In fact, allow me to make amends for any injustices done you in the past. Dine with me tonight. I am in need of good council."

"As you wish, sire," said Cunninghim, surprised.

Nightshade took this opportunity to clear his throat and step closer. "Your highness," he said with a stunted bow. "Long life to you."

In response to this statement, Daron laughed aloud - his first good laugh in a month - while the two nobles passed baffled looks between them.

"Nightshade, aye, long life indeed. Sorry things didn't work out the way you expected."

Nightshade's face turned white, then red, then green. "Beg pardon, sire?"

"Better luck next time, eh?" said Daron playfully, and he pantomimed drinking a glass of wine.

At first, when facing exile, the prince had wanted to skewer the man and roast him over a low flame. But now that Daron was on the throne, his anger had subsided.

Nightshade could serve him well in the future. Especially now that he was immune to any deadly surprises the man might have in store.

"Come, my lord," said Daron in a most congenial way. "Dine with Cunninghim and me tonight, and we will explore all the ways you can serve me."

"It would be an honor, sire," said Nightshade, flustered. "To think that you would-- . After I tried to-- ."

"Aye," said Daron, cutting him short. "Now if you'll excuse me, I want to see how the Prince is faring in the dungeon."

He stepped past them and up to Bryand's horse. But the look it gave him was so plainly belligerent (*if a horse can look belligerently*) that he decided to walk.

This seemed to the crowd a magnificent gesture. The King had come down to their level and was passing among them. Were Daron to have tried this in six month's time, he would have been attacked.

"He knows!" said Nightshade, panicky. "We must act quickly. Send for Mortamour!"

"No," said Cunninghim calmly. "Let's play the game a while longer and see what this new King is about."

"But what if it's a trap? What if he's got soldiers waiting for us when we get there?"

"He doesn't strike me as the cagey type. Let's hold off and hear what he has to say."

"Perhaps I could bring him some homemade wine."

Cunninghim gave him a withering look. "Under the present circumstances, I doubt if he'd accept it."

By the time Daron reached the castle ward, he had been sufficiently pawed by the exuberant crowds. Though he had nodded benevolently and presented them with an endearing smile, inwardly it made him cringe as he shook their calloused hands and watched the dust rise into the air when he patted their shoulders.

A bath was an absolute must, and most definitely a change of clothing. He wanted to look his very best when he visited Bryand in the dungeon. Not just for his own peace of mind but because he knew it would torment his brother.

So instead of heading directly for the dungeon he vaulted the steps of the main turret and proceeded toward the royal apartment, singing to himself:

"I'm King now,
I'm King now,
I wear the crown,
Upon my brow.
When Bryand hears,
I know not how,
But he shall have a cow!
Oh-h-h-h-h-h!
I'm King now,
I'm King now..."

He was about to enter his room when the door to his mother's chamber opened, and he saw her lean into the hallway.

"My son," she said with a pained smile. "May I speak with you?"

"Of course, mother."

He entered her apartment. He was surprised to find it cold and dark.

"Mother," he said, shivering. "You should have a fire going. It's freezing in here. And open your curtains. Let some light in."

His mother had seemed very withdrawn since his father's death, shunning the court, keeping to herself. This morning, after the coronation, instead of joining the royal procession, she had opted to return to her room.

"It is cold because your father is no longer here to

fill it with his warmth. It is dark to remind me of where your brother now resides."

"Aye, well, if you find it comforting... Now if you'll excuse me-- ."

"I want you to set him free."

"Beg your pardon," he said, stopping abruptly and turning to her.

"It hurts me to think of him in that dark smelly place."

"He deserves no better," said Daron stonily.

"But he's your own flesh and blood. Mark me, Bryand. You will suffer his pain more than you know. He is you. You are he. It must be so or the Gods would never have made you twins."

"Mother, he tried to kill me."

"I don't believe it. Aye, the dagger was in his hand but when it came to the blow it was not leveled at your heart."

"Are you saying I should forgive him for only wounding me?"

"Yes."

"That's asking a lot."

"There is goodness in him, Bryand. I know there is. If your father had been a different man, he might have recognized it too. You never needed me the way your brother did."

She paused a moment, staring off into space. When next she spoke, her voice sounded very far away.

"Had I been there for Daron more, perhaps he'd never have become so wretched." She looked at him, her eyes filled with tears. "Set him free, Bryand, so I might show him he is loved even now after doing such a terrible thing."

"You-- . You love him?" asked Daron, rocked.

"Of course I love him. He's my son. The same as you. Each time I see your face I will be reminded of him.

Were he dead and gone, I might someday recover from this pain. But to know he is wasting away beneath us, never again to see the light of day, is just too much for me to bear."

A breeze parted the curtains and daylight spilled into the room, a sure sign that Daron might have mocked at any other time. But now, with his mother's confession, he felt compassion and forgiveness, and the sun only confirmed his change of heart. Apparently, all those years of nice boy, now run along, she was really saying, I love you!

He felt weak; almost giddy.

"Mother," he said, aware of his own tears welling up. "I never knew you felt this way."

"Aye."

"And no matter what he did, nothing would turn you from him?

"Nothing."

"No matter how base or offensive it was? No matter how duplicitous? You would still love him?"

"Aye."

"How about wicked or downright dastardly?"

"All that and more. It matters not. He is part of me - as you are - body and soul."

So swept up was he by the flood of his newly acquired emotion that Daron, unable to control himself, blurted before thinking, "Mother! It is I!"

"Yes, Bryand, dear. I know, it is you."

"No, Mother. I am not Bryand."

"You are not you? What can you possibly mean by that? Is the pressure of ruling the kingdom already distorting your thinking?"

"Mother, I know exactly what I'm saying. I am not Bryand! I am Daron!"

"What?"

"Truly, mother."

"Bryand, this is a cruel jest -- "

"I'm not jesting; I've taken Bryand's place. He's the one in the dungeon. A moment ago, I felt very good about it, but now... Now that I know how terrible you feel, I think it best to make a full confession of the deed. Of course, I won't give up the crown or the throne, but it must surely count for something, my telling you the truth about things."

She gazed into his eyes and saw the same look she had seen there countless times before; and upon the realization that he was indeed Daron, and that he had been crowned King in place of his brother, terror rose up inside her and she began to scream.

This was not the reaction he had expected.

Startled, Daron grabbed her and placed his hand over her face. "You seem upset, Mother."

She screamed again and struggled to break free.

"Mother, calm down. Let's discuss this."

He dragged her to the apartment door, his hand still firmly covering her face. He peered up and down the hall, hoping they had not been overheard. The hall was empty.

He dragged her inside her apartment and shut the door with his foot. Quite suddenly she stiffened in his arms; then, just as suddenly she went limp.

"Well, now; that's better. If you promise not to scream again, I'll remove my hand. Promise?"

He waited for a nod, a sign, anything.

"Mother?"

He let her go, and she collapsed upon the floor in a heap. Daron looked at her, shaken.

"Was it something I said?"

CHAPTER SEVEN

"I'm warning you," shouted MeAnne, struggling to free herself from Bryand's embrace. "If you try that again, I'll bite your ear off!"

Bryand laughed aloud and tickled her. The girl howled and protested at the same time. "Would you now, my lovely?" replied Bryand. "Perhaps I should tickle you more!"

"Hee-hee! Stop it! Haw-haw! I swear it, you loon. Stay away from me! Hee-hee-haw-haw-haw! Guard! Guard! Hee-hee! Come quick, he's at it again!"

"Call for help if you will," chortled Bryand. "Maybe this will stop you."

He nuzzled her neck. But suddenly, finding her skin unexpectedly rough and hairy, he bounded back with a start.

He shook his head violently, hoping the hammering pain behind his eyes would cease. He squinted into the gloom, searching for the girl, but she was no longer there. Instead, chained to the wall, was the wizened old prisoner who shared his cell.

"Unnatural, that's what you are!" said he.

Bryand stumbled backward in shock. "I'm-- I'm, sorry. I don't know what came over me. I must be having visions."

"That's not all you've been havin'. You keep your hands to yourself, you hear?!"

"Aye," said Bryand, confused, embarrassed. "I will. I swear."

"That's what you said the last time. A person's not safe anywhere these days. Can't even waste away in peace."

Bryand's head felt like it would burst. "What's happening to me?!" he bellowed toward the heavens. He gazed at his fellow prisoner. "What's happening?! I've got to know!"

"Don't ask me," answered the old man scornfully. "I've been here almost fifteen years, and I ain't never seen the likes of you."

Just then the cell door swung open with a harsh squeal, and a blazing torch was thrust into the room, compelling them to shield their eyes from the unaccustomed light.

"All right, what's goin' on in here?" came a gruff voice.

"The looney's off again," said the old man, jerking his head toward Bryand.

A potbellied jailer with a scraggly beard that looked like it was host to any number of living creatures stepped up to Bryand and grabbed him roughly by his blouse. "Look here," he snarled, his breath reeking of garlic. "I've had just about enough of you."

"*You* have!" blurted the old man. "Try sharin' a cell with him for a month or two."

"Quiet, baggage," barked the jailer.

"I won't! I tell you I'm at my wits' end. I can't sleep at night fearin' what he might do."

"Well, old man," replied the jailer, releasing Bryand with a shove. "You can always room with Nagar the barbarian."

The old man's eyes went wide with fear. "Whaduya mean? He's already got a mate."

"Not any more. Nagar ate him last night."

The jailer laughed sardonically then turned to Bryand with a scornful frown. "Now you listen good," he said in a voice dripping with malice. "I don't want no more trouble from you, understand? I've orders not to harm you. Why, I don't know. But if you so much as utter one more peep, I'll beat your head so far in, you'll be starin' out yer bum. Ya got that?!"

"Oh, dear," chirped a voice from behind him. "Has our prisoner been giving you trouble?"

The jailer turned on his heels, and the scowl on his face changed to a look of awe. Before him, halfway in the shadows, stood Daron, the crown of Bandidon upon his head. "Curl my toes, it's the King!"

"No!" Bryand protested.

"Of course it's the King!" snapped the jailer, glowering at him. "Can't you tell royalty when you sees it?!"

A mocking grin stretched across Daron's face. "Aye, don't you recognize your King?"

Bryand's eyes smoldered. "I see only a fraud."

This remark shocked the jailer. "Why, of all the insolent-- ." He raised his hand to strike the Prince.

"Stop!" commanded Daron, stepping fully into the torchlight.

The jailer paused, his hand still raised, and turned with a puzzled expression. Seeing Daron's face now unhampered by the shadows, his jaw dropped. He looked again at the prisoner. But for the filth that streaked his face and the fouled clothing, he bore the same countenance as the King.

Of course! he thought, gazing at Bryand. This one's Prince Daron. Why, I'll be hanged, he really is crazy.

"Leave us, jailer," said Daron with a casual wave of his hand.

The man bowed and took a step, then hesitated. "Beg pardon, your majesty, but do you think that's wise?" He jerked his head toward Bryand and shot him a wary glance. "You never know what they're likely to do."

Daron could not keep from smirking. "I'll be safe." He nodded toward the old man. "Put this one in another cell for now. And leave the torch."

The jailer placed the torch in a sconce by the door then unlocked the old man's manacles. "Let's go you," he grunted as he dragged him to his feet.

"Anyone but Nagar," pleaded the prisoner, his eyes alive with fear. "I'd rather marry loony here, than be someone else's lunch."

The cell door clanged shut, and the twins faced each other, Daron looking his regal best, Bryand looking lousy.

"Well," said Daron cheerfully. "I see your stay here hasn't disagreed with you completely. You're still alive."

"Spare me your concern," spat Bryand.

"Now, brother. Is that anyway to behave?"

Anger surged in him. "Remove these chains and I'll show you how I can behave."

"My, my, my, how cross you are today. This is not at all like you."

"How else would you have me act toward the villain who stole my throne?"

Daron's eyes glinted with mirth. "Try being a good sport; that sort of thing."

"Why have you done this?!" Bryand raged, struggling with his chains. "Why have you jailed me in my own dungeon?"

"*My* dungeon, you mean."

The response only made Bryand angrier and he strained against his chains even more, trying desperately to pull them out of the wall. But soon his strength failed him and he fell to the floor. "Why, brother?" he said, breathless. "Tell me why?"

Daron, having watched his twin's display of temper, was somewhat unsure now of his own feelings. And not knowing how best to answer the question, he simply shrugged and said, "I wanted to be King."

Bryand stared at his brother in disbelief. "You must be mad. I never thought so in the past. But now..."

Daron knitted his brow. "I prefer to think of it as unpredictable."

Bryand struggled to his feet. "How long do you think you can maintain this deception before someone realizes you're not me? You'll be discovered in no time."

"Oh, I wouldn't be so sure about that," said Daron with a confident smile. "Actually, you yourself have been most helpful in that respect; I mean, being as tight-lipped as you are, not many people out there really know you. So it hasn't been too difficult. I've fooled the council, and the court suspects nothing. Everyone thinks I'm you."

Strong as it may appear, an earthen dam will begin to crumble when the waters behind it are swollen from the melting winter snow. So it was with Bryand's defenses upon hearing such discouraging news. He began to perspire; his stomach churned, and it took all his will to keep his knees from buckling.

"There are some you'll never convince," he said, his voice betraying his growing fear. "Our mother, for one."

Daron sighed wistfully, recalling their earlier confrontation. "Ah, yes, mother. Dear, dear, mother. For the time being, she's discreetly packed away in the north tower."

"She's sequestered?!"

"No, dead. I don't think she liked my idea."

For a moment, Bryand stared at his brother, stunned. "You murdered your own mother!?"

Daron frowned. "Of course not. What kind of a person do you think I am? Her heart failed when she learned what I was up to."

Bryand's knees collapsed beneath him and he fell

to the ground. "Mother is gone?"

"Fear not, I'll give her a decent funeral just as soon as the time is right."

Bryand fought down the urge to vomit. "This can't be happening."

Suddenly a thought struck him. "Surely MeAnne has guessed the truth. Surely she knows you're an imposter."

Daron shook his head. "Sorry to disappoint. Truth is, she's never liked you more. As a matter of fact, she's working harder than ever on her tapestry."

He smiled triumphantly, his revenge sweet. "You see, brother, I've even found ways to improve you."

His hope failing, Bryand stared at the cell walls. In the rippling torchlight they seemed to be closing in on him. He felt like he was tottering on the brink of insanity; one slip and he would be a raving madman forever more.

But just when he was about to surrender to the tempest in his head, a light as clear and clean as the sun's rays pierced through the maelstrom. "What of Dillin, and Niles, and Dwayne? You'll never fool them."

"Aye, well, they don't like you very much right now. I've managed to quarrel with each of them over the past month. They think being King has gone to your head. They've quit the court until you come to your senses. They don't know it yet, but they'll soon be arrested on some false charge and hanged before anyone is the wiser."

Bryand stared at him, beaten, speechless.

"You find it inconceivable that I could act so deceitfully, don't you?"

"Aye," muttered Bryand, dazed.

Daron's eyes narrowed and he stepped closer to his brother. "I wonder if you can imagine what it's been like living all these years in your shadow, watching as you were lavished by father's praises, knowing he had none for me. There was a time when I foolishly thought that if I could be like you, he might care for me a little. So I studied everything about you, the way you walked, the way you talked; everything. I used to sneak into your room at night to observe the way you slept. You never knew I was there, watching you drool onto your pillow. But nothing I did was ever good enough for him. So I stopped trying to be you and did my best to be my worst me."

"You've certainly succeeded at that."

"Unfortunately, everything I wanted was still yours for the taking. Therefore, I had to become you and--. Well, you know the rest."

"So why not just kill me?" asked Bryand bitterly.

"Oh, no. That would only give me a moment's pleasure. Knowing you are here, rotting slowly away, while I indulge myself in what's rightfully yours, will provide me with enough satisfaction to last the rest of my life."

He strolled to the door. "Here is your Kingdom, brother. And there are your subjects." He pointed to two rats in the corner of the cell. "Rule them well."

Daron called for the jailer. A moment later the cell door was opened and, tossing his brother one last mocking grin, the man who called himself King disappeared within the shadows of the dungeon corridor.

Bryand watched him leave, already aware of the awful droning sound that silence could produce. His heart stepped up its beat, his insides began to quiver, and he felt his reason slipping away.

"Where's the old man?" Bryand asked, though his voice sounded distant and no longer his own. "What's happened to him?"

The jailer grabbed the torch and went to the door, where he paused and turned to face the Prince. "I understand he's delicious," he said, and he slammed the cell door shut, his laughter echoing in the hall.

"My lord," said Cower, slipping into the King's private chamber. There was a confused look upon the retainer's face.

"What is it, Cower?" asked Daron, donning a brown sash.

"My lord, the Earl of Nightshade awaits you in the outer chamber. He-- . He comes with Cunninghim, sire."

"Good, good. Is the food prepared?"

"Aye, my lord. But-- . But-- ." Cower hesitated, reluctant to proceed. In the past few weeks, the King had become very testy.

"But, but, what?" said Daron, knitting his brow.

"My lord," said the retainer, lowering his voice. "Cunninghim was banished from the Kingdom by your father."

"My father is dead," said Daron simply. "I am King now." He went to his mirror and studied his appearance with a frown. "Brown, brown, brown; everything in my wardrobe is brown. Or beige. I'm sick of brown and beige."

This surprised Cower.

"I think I need a change. I know," he said, brightening. "Have my brother's clothes brought to me. I always liked the way he dressed." Then, pulling at the bloomers that had ridden up between his buttocks, Daron grumbled, "We've also got to do something about these shorts."

As Daron preened, the Earl of Nightshade and the Duke of Cunninghim awaited the King's presence in the outer chamber. Nightshade, who was very nervous, rocked back and forth on his heels, his fingers meshed before him and his thumbs drumming on his corpulent stomach.

Cunninghim, on the other hand, despite his apprehension, remained controlled as he gazed about the royal apartment, taking in the lavish appointments with a look that went from envy to contempt.

He eyed the dining table, crowded with platters of roasted mutton, fowl, and boar, and his stomach growled. It had been a long time since he had eaten this well.

Blast Audanot for banishing him! For confiscating his home and his family lands! He was not meant for such a life as he had led these past two years, hopping from one inn to the next, running up tabs for food and lodging, then sneaking off during the night once the bill came due.

The only good that had come out of it was his alliance with Nightshade. Though, if truth were told, he thought the man an incompetent fool and a hindrance to his long term plans.

Nightshade chose that particular moment to glance at him and Cunninghim gave him a reassuring grin. Aye, someday Nightshade will have an accident, thought the Duke. A fatal accident.

His grin widened somewhat. Mortamour will like that. A good man, that Mortamour. Strange interests, though, all those blood sports of his, but a loyal henchman nevertheless. Such a pity even he will have to be eliminated someday.

The Duke of Cunninghim did not like anyone knowing his business.

Finding the silence almost as unbearable as the wait, Nightshade said in a hushed voice, "I think our coming here was a mistake."

Sweat poured down his face in tiny streams. His voice grew more and more strained.

"He could be toying with us, prolonging the kill, so to speak. Why should he accommodate us like this? Especially since he knows I tried to poison him? It makes no sense, I tell you. No sense at all."

"Calm down," whispered Cunninghim, eyeing him coldly. "You sound like a squealing pig."

Nightshade scowled at the rebuke but said nothing more. He sighed, and having nothing better to do, he drifted to the dining table where his eyes fell upon a pitcher of wine.

He stared at it, licking his lips. Then, tossing a quick glance at the King's door, he reached into his purse.

"Stay away from that wine," hissed Cunninghim.

Nightshade quickly removed his hand. "I beg your pardon?"

"I said stay away from that wine. You're much too weak-willed when it comes to your little pleasures."

"I wasn't going to do anything," said Nightshade defensively.

"Of course you were. Now stop being so silly. I tell you, if he wanted to arrest us, he could have done so this afternoon." Cunninghim gazed at the King's door. "He wants something from us. I'm sure of it."

"And what do you suppose that could be?"

"I wish I knew," replied Cunninghim, annoyed. He had never liked surprises. Walking into situations like this, without knowing what to expect, always made him edgy. "But I'll wager it's not our heads."

Nightshade remained dubious, and he gazed at the wine and sighed. "I could do it so easily."

Just then the chamber door opened, and the King appeared with a gracious smile upon his face. "Ahhh, my lords, forgive me for keeping you. I'm sure you are hungry."

They bowed.

Daron took his seat at the table and, with an ingratiating smile, gestured for them to join him. They hesitated, then sat in silence, while Daron, appearing totally unaware of the awkwardness of the situation, unfolded a napkin and tucked it under his chin.

During this silence Cower stepped to the table, picked up the pitcher of wine and proceeded to pour each of them a cup.

"Thank you, Cower," said Daron. "You may go now."

Though Cower would have liked to stay, he knew he could not disobey the King. Frowning, he replaced the pitcher on the table and headed toward the door.

Daron waited until the retainer was gone, then raised his goblet in toast. "To Bandidon."

"To Bandidon," his guests repeated, and they drank.

Actually, Daron and Nightshade drank. Cunninghim took the smallest of sips.

"And to you, my lord," said Cunninghim. "May your reign be long and prosperous."

"Thank you, my dear Duke."

Cunninghim could not tell if he was being purposely insulted. "I beg your pardon, your grace. But that title no longer pertains to me. I was stripped of it some time ago."

"Aye, so I've been told. But that was my father's doing." Daron paused, mostly for affect, then said, "It is my will to restore your good name."

Cunninghim stared at him in disbelief and said in a somewhat guarded tone, "You're majesty is too kind."

Daron chuckled. "I don't blame you for being suspicious. But I speak the truth. Tomorrow, before the entire court, you shall be reinstated among the ranks of the Bandidonian nobility; your manor and lands shall be returned to you; then you, and you, my dear Nightshade, will take your places in the council chamber as my newest advisors."

Nightshade was so overwhelmed that he could do naught but stare at the King with mouth agape.

"Your majesty has done us a great service," said Cunninghim, taken aback; then, choosing his words carefully, he went on, "But I cannot help but wonder why. I was an outcast during your father's reign. You and I are no better than strangers, and Nightshade here-- . Well, we all know what Nightshade tried to do. Yet, rather than clap us in irons and send us to the block, you lavish us with positions of great importance. Frankly, my liege, your motives are beyond my understanding."

Nightshade, believing Cunninghim had ruined not only the evening but their chances of surviving the evening, tried his best to salvage what he could. "Nevertheless, I am certain you have the noblest of intentions. Pure even. Almost God-like."

Daron laughed heartily. "I am most flattered, my lord. Most flattered indeed." He paused to look at them both. "I have great plans for the future, gentlemen. New granaries, lumber mills, bridges, dams; even paved roads, if we can. These improvements are long overdo. But much as I would like to accomplish them, I must also recognize the fact that my father, may he rest in peace, left almost nothing in the treasury. I have enough to support the guard for six months; that is all. After that, we are a kingdom without a regular army, on the verge of ruin."

He leaned in closer. "I must admit, I am at a loss for ideas and, therefore, at my wits' end. Can you think of anything I could do to rectify the situation?"

Cunninghim gave him a long look, then leaned in closer as well. "I can, your grace. If you will permit me."

"Go on," Daron urged amiably. "I welcome your advice."

Cunninghim straightened in his seat. "I've always found taxes to be a burden. But then again, I have never been on the receiving end. What would the King think about raising taxes?"

Daron sat for a moment in silence, staring at the table. The Duke was making things easy. "I like the idea. It is time for an increase. If I recall correctly, the kingdom has not seen one in at least ten years."

"Eleven," said the Duke. "The increase would certainly stave off the coming crisis. But in order to begin the improvements his majesty has mentioned, he will need a great deal more than what an increase could yield. What would you think of a brand new tax?"

"Hmmmmm," Daron responded, acting most intrigued. He decided to play along. "A brand new tax. Not a bad idea. Perhaps one payable by everyone in the kingdom?"

"Surely not the nobles," said Nightshade, somewhat piqued.

"Most certainly the nobles," answered Cunninghim, eyeing him askance.

"And how could we justify such a tax?" Nightshade retorted.

Cunninghim turned and stared at him. "By making known exactly what it is intended for. Keeping the army strong and planning the improvements the King has mentioned."

"I like it," said Daron.

"And so do I," Nightshade agreed quickly. "But how, if you don't mind my asking, shall the King enforce it?"

Daron's mouth curled up slightly on one side of his face. "I know just the right men for the job." He reached for the pitcher of wine and proffered it to the nobles. "Gentlemen?"

"Thank you, but no, your grace," said Cunninghim politely.

Nightshade licked his lips, but when he saw the Duke's disapproving look, he begged off as well.

Daron poured a cup for himself. "You inspire me, Gentlemen. We will call it the Cost of Living Tax, and we will hire all the right men to help collect it."

"We, Sire?" said Cunninghim.

"Certainly. You, my lords, will be in charge of organizing the collection." Once again he paused so that his words would have their fullest effect. "And when the King's coffers are full, so, too, will be yours."

Cunninghim and Nightshade could not help but grin, for the King had appealed to the most basic part of their natures - their greed.

"At your service, my lord!" exclaimed Nightshade, pouring himself a cup despite Cunninghim's scowl.

"At your service, indeed," echoed Cunninghim. But though he paid close attention to the King for the remainder of the evening, agreeing with his points of view, laughing at his jests, inwardly he was already thinking of the ways he could turn this good fortune even more to his advantage.

The news of Prince Daron's attempt to kill the King and his subsequent imprisonment spread like wildfire across the country. In Port Lansia life seemed far removed from the intrigues of the court but we were shocked by the events nevertheless. However, people were far too busy in those days to dwell upon anything for very long. The day to day business of supporting a family and making ends meet took precedence over everything. So, by the end of a week, the Prince's betrayal was hardly mentioned, and all was back to normal.

Or so we thought.

Three weeks after the King's official coronation new

troops arrived to replace the garrison. They were ugly brutes with missing teeth and cauliflower ears who enjoyed showing off their scars to one another and extorting coins from little children and old women.

They roamed the streets, terrorizing the populace. Each day the number of people on crutches increased. Their favorite ploy was to approach some unsuspecting citizen and, without any provocation, state, "I don't like the way you look," then poke him or her in the eyes.

One outraged citizen, disregarding the threats to his life, brought a guard before the town magistrate.

"Is this the man who beat you senseless?" asked the official.

"I think so," the citizen replied.

"Think so? Don't you know?"

"Well, you see, there were these fingers in my eyes-- ."

The magistrate clapped his gavel upon his bench. "Case dismissed."

However, almost in the same breath, he turned to the guard, who was smirking, and said in a harsh, remonstrative tone, "But don't let me catch you in this court again."

The following morning the citizen was found in an alley, his arms and legs tied together in a knot. The following day, the magistrate was ousted from his seat. Unfortunately, it was from a third story window.

Things went from bad to worse when the King's chief administrator, the Duke of Cunninghim, arrived to collect the new tax that had been imposed. At first, there was strong opposition among the elders of the town.

The mayor of Port Lansia dedicated the new gallows in the main square and all too soon found it his final campaign platform. The town elders, despite their years of experience and accumulated wisdom, ceased their aging at the end of a rope.

And so it progressed until my name and address tablet was covered with thick black ink scratches. Each night, with the shutters closed and the shop door barred, I would update it with my clerk, Rolfo, starting at the top of the alphabet and working down. Within three months all A's, B's, and half the C's had been eliminated.

Each night was the same, my pen and ink ready to scratch away a life, and each night I would begin with the first of the names that had remained unscratched.

"Cuttle, the fisherman?"

"Oh, he's dead."

Scratch.

"Dimm, the miller."

"Him, too."

Scratch.

"Farley, the carpenter's son?"

"Saw him hung just an hour ago."

"Oh, dear! I wonder how the carpenter is taking it?"

"Not well, I image. He was swingin' next to Farley."

Scratch. Scratch.

And during all this time the one question on my mind was, why is the King doing these hateful things? Why?!

The sun, a fiery crimson orb, was touching the horizon, bidding the land farewell till its resurgence on the morrow, when Daron emerged onto the balcony of the King's apartment, carrying the royal house cat in his arms. He eyed the scene before him with a deep sense of peace, though he could still hear the drunken revelry of his guards here and there, mixed with the screams and shouts of irate citizens. All's well, he thought, and a contented smile stretched across his face.

Being King was such fun. Knowing that, at any moment, upon any whim, he could order a person's death or spare a person's life set his toes curling inside his slippers.

It was such a shame his mother had died on the spot. She would have been amazed at the changes he had made.

Well, perhaps not amazed. He frowned. Actually, now that I think of it, she probably would have hated every one.

His mother had always thought right and wrong were two separate things. While he had always viewed them as being right and not-quite-right.

But she was packed away in a crate in the north tower where no one ever went and, as far as everyone else was concerned, off on an extended holiday to the baths at Tapwater.

No one but Cower had even questioned her sudden disappearance, and he was certain no one would. At least not until the summer heat when she began to stink.

He made a mental note to announce her death no later than the spring thaw.

So much to do, some much to do, he mused, stroking the cat vigorously. He would see Bryand's name live forever in the hearts and minds of the people even if he had to brand it there with a hot iron.

Bryand; the name had always appealed to him more than his own. And now that it was finally his, he felt as though he had slipped into an old suit that was soft and worn in all the right places.

And yet, as much as this pleased him, there were moments when he missed being Daron and missed the pranks he used to play. The inflated pig's bladder under a seat cushion, raising the drawbridge during a religious procession, spiking high tea, tricks such as these only made life more flavorful.

Impersonating Bryand was such a bore sometimes. Every day the same routine; smile and be pleasant; wave to the crowd. He sneered contemptuously.

The crowd! What had they to do with being King? With court balls and archery contests and heavy petting in the garden?

His hand came up filled with fur and he peered at the cat lying still in his arms, noting how good-natured it had become since he had had it stuffed.

A pensive look came over his face. There were some people he'd like to stuff as well, starting with the council.

First there was King Blunderon, by the Gods he was inept. Then there was King Fallacius with all his deceptions, and King Mittashmeer with all his complaints.

But worse of all was King Jasper and his stony looks. The man knew not how lucky he was, being MeAnne's father. He had endured the man's countless objections thus far, but any more discord and even she could not save him from the block.

"How dare they oppose my decisions and question my commands," he grumbled to himself. "They're lucky I don't send them all to the block."

But enough of that, he thought with a flouncing gesture that made the cat's head bob up and down. He was not going to let anything upset him tonight.

The Duke of Cunninghim had returned from Port Lansia and Nightshade from the northern shires, and with them was the first installment of the new tax.

He had ordered a feast prepared in their honor with all the finest foods and wines from his larder. Entertainers had been summoned from every corner of the land, jugglers, jesters, minstrels even an exotic dancer named Lulu. It was sure to be the finest evening the court had ever spent.

Aye, being King was truly a wonderful thing, thought Daron, filled with a deep sense of satisfaction.

Casting one last look at the setting sun, he walked into his room and tossed the cat onto his bed. Then he strolled to the full-length mirror that stood next to the fireplace and studied his reflection.

He enjoyed gazing at himself these days, even if his looks were still not completely his own. For each time he thought of his brother now, it was in the way he had last seen him, with grime on his face and bugs in his hair and straw sticking out of his ears.

The fire on the hearth reflected in his eyes and cast a faint orange glow across his face. Everything about him now was kingly, his robe, his tunic, his jeweled belt and sword. Even his bloomers bore the royal seal.

You certainly cut a dashing figure he thought, well pleased. No wonder the single women of the court are always flirting with you.

But then he thought of MeAnne.

The gleam in his eyes faded, and the countenance staring back at him in the mirror wore a hungry look. For MeAnne was, quite possibly, the one woman left in the Kingdom whose delights he had not yet sampled. And this made her all the more desirable.

The anticipation of their union was driving him to distraction. But since that night in the garden she was as unmoved by his predicament as was a promontory in the face of a flood.

Yet though she filled him with frustration, he knew of no other woman that was as perfect a mate as she. Certainly a namby-pamby like Bryand had never deserved a woman with such vitality, nor had she deserved such a cruel fate as his brother would have supplied.

Why, she would have perished from boredom in a fortnight. He could see it now, lectured into a state of melancholia, languished of all peak experiences, until finally - broken of her spirit - she took to her bed and died.

Aye, MeAnne was meant for him, for he knew how

best to please her. He would respect her wishes and wait until the wedding. But after that, her body would be his playground, and when it came to playing he knew lots of games.

Best think of something else right now, he decided. For he did not want to appear in public with his pride showing.

"My lord," came a timorous voice.

Daron scowled and turned toward the door where Cower stood. "I thought I told you not to disturb me."

"My lord left instructions to be informed the moment the Duke of Cunninghim and the Earl of Nightshade had arrived."

"When did I tell you that?" asked Daron, eyeing him askance.

"Just before you told me not to disturb you, my lord."

"Aha! And by telling you not to disturb me, I countermanded my previous command. Therefore you have deliberately disobeyed me."

Daron chuckled inside. Tormenting Cower was such fun.

"Now help me on with my ceremonial cape while I determine what sort of punishment you deserve."

"Aye, my lord," droned Cower, removing the cape from the royal wardrobe. "Whatever you deem fitting."

He pictured his body stretched across a rack, manacles biting into his flesh, salt stinging his wounds. Perhaps it's for the best, he thought, sighing as he joined the King at the mirror.

These past few months had been exhausting, always walking on egg shells, barely daring to breathe lest the King berate him for some trifle. Up until now he had been treated like a member of the family, respected, even loved. Yet suddenly everything he did, everything he said, displeased the King.

He gazed at himself over the King's shoulder and was saddened by what he saw. Once he had been a vital specimen; now an old man with sunken eyes and hollow cheeks stared back at him.

Oh such torture! Such pain! And for no apparent reason.

"I beg your pardon, my lord," he ventured. "But are you feeling well?"

"Of course, I'm feeling well," replied the King irritably. But being one who never trusted his good health, Daron immediately thought the retainer had observed something new about his pallor.

"Why?" he asked, studying his reflection. "Do you think I look sick?"

"No, no, my lord, you look very well indeed. It's just that-- . I'd swear these past few months you've had something troublesome on your mind."

Daron's eyes narrowed and a muscle in his cheek began to twitch. "What do you mean?"

"Just that you've not been yourself." And with a tentative laugh, he added, "And more like your brother Daron instead."

At the very least he had hoped to evoke a grin, a nod, a glimmer of the camaraderie they had once shared. Instead, he received a look so filled with malice and contempt that he stood back from the king at once.

He knew immediately he had said the wrong thing. Not just the wrong thing, but the very worst thing he could have said.

"I beg your pardon, my lord. Please forgive me." Words began to spill from his mouth as he desperately tried to remedy the situation. "It was a jest, a very poor jest. How could I have said such a thing."

Daron recovered quickly and put his Bryand face on, which meant, he presented Cower with a limp smile and let his eyes wander aimlessly. "Of course. I see now it was said in fun. And you are right. I have not been myself. Affairs of state and all. Perhaps we can share a draft or two sometime soon. Like we did before life became so complicated." What rot, thought Daron, but if it mollified the old coot then he was glad to say it.

"Yes, absolutely. I would very much like that," said Cower, as he straightened the King's robe. "And you may rest assured, my lord, I will never say anything like that again."

But, of course, as soon as he said those words, a thought flashed across his mind. The King was definitely not acting like himself and, what's more, he was indeed acting more like his brother.

What if the man standing before him was not Bryand but really Daron?

He tried to dismiss the thought, horrified by what it implied. But no matter how hard he tried, he could not shake it from his mind.

What if he were Daron? What if he'd taken his brother's place on the night of the stabbing? And based upon that assumption, came the sudden realization - which was far more horrible than the supposition - that he had stumbled upon the truth.

Cower's mouth fell open. He froze in terror. No wonder Bryand had been acting so strangely. He wasn't Bryand at all!

"You've guessed; haven't you?" said Daron, staring at Cower in the mirror. He turned and looked directly at the retainer. "Haven't you?"

"Daron," uttered Cower, shuddering. "It is you."

"I should've known I couldn't fool you for long."

The calmness of Daron's voice only intensified Cower's terror. "My lord, I-- . I-- . "

But nothing more would come, so shocked was he, so filled with loathing and fear.

"Well, now you've sealed your fate."

At last, Cower found his voice. "But, my lord, all the years of faithful service-- ."

"Will be taken into consideration when choosing the method of your execution."

Daron walked to the door, opened it, and beckoned to the guards in the hall. He faced Cower and said, "Would you mind going with these two gentlemen? They'll show you to your cell."

Cower quaked as he was flanked by the guards. He gazed from one to the other, then at the man who pretended to be the King. "How can you do this? How?"

Daron shrugged. "I don't know. It just comes naturally, I suppose."

And addressing to the officer in charge of the detail, he said, "Alert Cleave, the executioner, will you? Tell him I've a job for him tonight. Nothing flashy. No spectators. Not even the professional mourners."

CHAPTER EIGHT

"Look, mistress," said Jona, MeAnne's lady in waiting. In her hands was a package wrapped in crinkled parchment. "A present has arrived for you."

"Is it from my lord?" cried MeAnne excitedly, bouncing to her. "Is it from the King?"

"No. The Weavers Guild, my lady; local three."

"Let me undo it, please. I love presents."

MeAnne tore away the wrapping and found a beautiful kirtle of heather colored wool. "Oh, is it not exquisite? So luxurious to the touch. I will wear it tonight. Quickly, help me put it on."

She removed her lounging robe and slipped the dress over her head. "What do you think?" asked the Princess, smoothing her hair.

Jona eyed her appraisingly. "I don't think it's quite right for your skin coloring. You're more a winter person."

"Really?" said MeAnne, surprised.

"Perhaps if you dressed it up a bit and wore your gold arm bands."

"The pair with rubies, or with pearls?"

"Oh, the one with pearls, by all means."

It was then MeAnne's father, King Jasper, first ruler under Bryand and Council Majority Leader, entered the room, paying the girls' protests no heed.

"Are ya not ready yet, lass?" scowled Jasper, and he slapped his gauntlets against his thigh.

He was a stout man, made stouter by the gambeson and chain mail he wore beneath his tunic, with hazel eyes and bushy blonde hair that looked like straw. Between a bulbous nose and a thick upper lip he bore a woolly mustache that reached to the sides of his square chin.

"You women astound me. You've a corset an' a dress ta don. If ya had to wear the layers that I carry 'round, we'd n'er see ya at all."

"Hush," said MeAnne, ignoring him. Jona slipped the wide gold bands onto her arms. "I'm almost ready. Don't you want me to look my best for the King and his advisors?"

"Ach," scoffed Jasper with a wave of his hand. "Now there's three stooges for ya."

"Father," chided the Princess mildly. "I'll not have you mock my betrothed that way."

"If a man insists on acting like a fool, he should be prepared for others ta mock him."

"Father!" she said, her patience slipping.

"Never have I seen a nobleman so lacking in noble spirit. Noble airs he has plenty of, that I'll say for him. He makes a grand show of things with his banquets and his entertainments. But underneath it all, there's no humility. Not an ounce. He's quite easily the most conceited man I've ever met."

She whirled on him, her eyes ablaze. "He is your King and overlord – ." She paused intentionally and gave Jona a look which the handmaiden knew instantly meant for her to leave the room.

When they were alone, MeAnne continued purposefully. "And as your King and overlord, he deserves your respect no less than your loyalty. This way in which you speak of him is beneath you, and dangerously close to treason."

"Let him kill me then," answered Jasper bluntly. "Better that than to stand by and watch him ruin the country. In but a few months' time he's brought the economy to near collapse."

"I'll not listen to this--. " said MeAnne, striding past him.

"You will," he said, grabbing her arm. "We live in an ordered society, lass. We order, an' the peasants provide. It's as basic as that. But soon he'll have tortured or killed every decent, hard-workin' serf in the country. Scores of fiefs have shut down for lack of laborers. Scores more have been confiscated by those hoodlums he calls his guards."

"This country has never known such wealth and prosperity," she retorted, pulling away. "While you were content to war against your own people, he aspired to unite them all."

"That was his father's dream you may recall. One which I helped to build. And now the son does all that he can to destroy it!"

He saw the tears well in her eyes, and his heart wrenched in his chest. "MeAnne, darlin', I know my words are hateful to ya, but can ya not see what he's become? I tell ya he's a madman; worse than his brother ever was. An' were that not disastrous enough, he's allied himself with two of the lowest scoundrels I have ere had the cursed luck to meet."

"Cunninghim is a gentleman," she protested, her lower lip beginning to tremble.

"Cunninghim is a villain. A demon. Why, the man's had designs to rule long before Bryand ascended the throne. Everything he does is a calculated effort to steal power from the King and freedom from the people. And Nightshade, the poor misguided fool, will say anything, do anything that Cunninghim tells him. I swear, he'd slap himself silly were Cunninghim of such a mind."

"I cannot believe what I hear! You spout treason as easily as you would order a gooseberry pie."

"Not so," denied Jasper. "I've n'er cared for gooseberry pie."

She stared at him in disbelief. "Could I have been so wrong about you? Has the man I've worshipped all these years been nothing more than a traitor?"

Jasper stepped back, hurt as he had hurt his daughter, and he cast his gaze to the floor. "Ya must search your heart for the answer to that one, lass. I can only say that my love for ya is as strong today as it was when they first brought ya to me in a swaddlin' cloth. And my love for my country is as steadfast as the day I swore allegiance to Audanot. But I also swore to protect the country from its enemies, those within as well as those without. And from that purpose, I will never be swayed."

"Everything you stand for is a threat to the man I love," said MeAnne, shaking her head regretfully. "I cannot honor you, and honor him as well."

He looked at her, the seed of his loins, the issue of the woman that he loved, and with sadness filling his heart, he said, "Then this is quite a pickle."

He strode to the door, but stopped and turned back to her. "Ya must make your own choice, MeAnne. You're of age now and can marry whomsoever ya please. But I'll not stay here another day. I leave tonight for home right after the banquet. And I'm taking your mother with me, and your sister, too. Poor Blindella. I've never seen someone so broken-hearted. She can hardly see straight."

MeAnne nodded. "Yes, I know."

"You're welcome to join us if ya want. Tis your decision."

She lowered her gaze. "My place is here."

She watched him leave the room, wanting to call him back. But she could not find the words.

At length, she called to her lady in waiting, her

dearest friend and confidante. "Oh, Jona!" she said, distraught, "I don't know what to do. Please tell me? Tell me, Jona, what would you do?!"

And after studying her a moment, Jona nodded her head and said, "I would definitely wear the pearls."

Cleave, the executioner, had finished his supper and had just lit his favorite pipe, when the royal guards came knocking at his door bearing a new order from the King.

"What? Another? Does the king know what time it is? I punched out over two hours ago."

"Doesn't matter," said the officer in charge. "He wants it done immediately."

"Where's the warrant?"

"No warrant."

"And the order of execution. Where's that?

"No order of execution."

Receiving just one of the two required documents was not completely unusual. It happened from time to time - a shortage of staff or errors processing the paperwork, those sorts of things. It was an irregularity and frowned upon by the guild but not an actual breach of guild rules.

But to be handed no documentation at all was not only a breach of guild rules but a breach of law as well. "Hold on there. You have no warrant and no order of execution. Who's to say the accused should be beheaded?"

"The king, of course," said the officer churlishly.

Well, he has a point, thought the executioner. But the rules and regulations-- .

"Now wait a minute," said Cleave. "The king should know there's procedure involved. I can't go cuttin' someone's head off with no back-up documents. If it ever were disputed, you know, down the road, I could be held responsible. It could mean my head on the chopping block."

"And what about me?" the guard protested. "Do you think I like operating outside legalities? I'm an officer in the king's service, not just some unfeeling brute with no respect for the order of things. If you only knew what I have to wrestle with these days. The havoc I reap in the king's name. Why, it strains my sense of decency, it undermines everything they taught me in public school. Now are you coming?"

"What about my gratuity?"

"Seriously?"

"So no tip, either?"

"No tip. No frills. And no gabbing about this at the pub afterward."

"I don't drink."

"I do. Let's go."

Disgruntled, Cleave, doffed his nightcap and threw it to the floor, then sighed and motioned to the officer that he would follow shortly.

Another job, he scowled, pulling on his doublet. When's a fellow to relax a bit and enjoy the pleasures of his family. He was no shirker by the most ambitious man's standards and a staunchly loyal subject, but something had to be done about the increasing length of his workday.

Enough was enough! Executions had multiplied tenfold in just three months. Perhaps if he started charging a higher rate after a certain number of heads, the King might not call upon him quite so readily.

But then again, he had never been so well off as now. And with the tips he collected for prime cuts, he was earning a very handsome wage.

And then there were Malady and the boys to consider. She was a loving wife and mother, yet she was a sickly lass by nature, frail and peaked.

What she needed was to be gone from this foul-smelling, garbage-rotting city and living in the countryside where the air was always fresh and the sun shined unencumbered. If he continued to be as busy as he had been these past few months, he could earn enough money to buy a little cottage somewhere, a quiet place that had its own well, clean rushes on the floor, a stick or two of furniture, and a fireplace.

Aye, a fireplace made of stone and a privy just a few short paces from the back door. His family deserved the finer things in life, and he intended to provide them.

Oh well, he thought, pulling on his leggings and lacing them up, another job, another swish of the blade. That reminds me, I have to sharpen my axe; felt like it was sticking a bit that last time.

"Here ya go, luv," said Malady, crossing the room with his hood. She might have been a pretty woman had not her face been so drawn and sallow. There were dark circles under her eyes and she wheezed with each breath.

Childbearing had not been easy for her. Like her mother she was built narrow in the hips.

Her first delivery had lasted twenty hours; her second nearly killed her. But she cared deeply for her husband and would have consented to bear more children had not the fates stepped in on her behalf.

For on a rainy day some time back, Cleave's axe had slipped from his hands and had come close to rendering him a eunuch. When the wound had healed and they could once again make love, they discovered that he was no longer capable of issuing his seed, therefore pregnancy was no longer a concern.

"Don't want no man o' mine goin' out in public half dressed." She handed him the hood and frowned.

"What's wrong, puddin'?" asked Cleave, thinking she was ill.

"Shave yer head t'day, luv?"

"Aye," he replied, running his hand across his scalp. "That's just me five o'clock shadow. Feelin' right, puddin'?"

"O' course! Just the same old thing."

The same old thing, as she described it, was actually a pain that ran from her right shoulder to her right leg. At times it kept her in such agony that she could do naught but walk in a tight circle like a dog chasing its tail.

"Now come over here ya brute, an' I'll put some oil on that arm o' yours."

He followed her to the hearth where she dipped her fingers into a pan of cooled chicken fat, then watched her as she massaged it into his skin. With the increased workload, he had recently developed a minor case of 'axe elbow.'

"That's nice," said Cleave in a suggestive tone, and he ticked his eyebrows up and down. She responded with a smirk and a light slap upon his breast.

He looked around. "Where've the kids gone off to so late?"

"To berate the prisoners what's due for beheadin' tomorrow."

"Aw, the little dears," chuckled the man. "Bet they'll be followin' in their dad's footsteps before long."

When she was done, Malady walked him to the door.

"Ta, luv," he said, grabbing his ax.

"Ta," she replied, offering her cheek for him to peck.

She stood at the threshold and watched him until he had reached the end of their street and had rounded the corner of the main thoroughfare. He was a good man, she thought, stepping back into their hovel. A bit of a dullard sometimes, but considerate of her needs and affectionate to the children.

All in all she had a good life; food in her stomach; thatch over her head, and two fine young sons to do her proud when she was gone. For she knew her time was short. The brightest flame did not alter the dimness of her sight. Thank the Gods she had set to memory everything in the place or she'd be forever running into the furniture. And the ache in her joints! And her feet! Her feet were killing her!

Cower sat in a shadowy corner, his knees drawn up tightly against his chest, his back against cold stone. He was confused, hurt, but mostly he was afraid. He had always been loyal to the royal family. He had always done his best to please them, right down to the little things like drawing back the covers on their beds each night and leaving them little sprigs of mint on their pillows.

It had never been just a job to him, in at seven, gone by eleven. These people had been his life.

He scanned his cell yet another time, hoping to find something different about it, something that would expose it as a delusion. But nothing, not the slimy walls not the smelly straw not the creepy crawly things, had changed.

This was no dream. Reality itself had become a nightmare. What could he have done to deserve so horrible a fate? Why had the Gods suddenly abandoned him and brought him to such ruin?

I'll wager it was because I cheated last tithing day and didn't declare enough of my income, he thought, chewing on a hangnail. Aye, that must be it!

Well, I guess it's true what they say, "You can fool

some of the Gods some of the time..."

And then his thoughts drifted to the two princes he had helped to raise - so remarkably alike on the outside yet so different on the inside. He remembered how he had held them during thunderstorms, and how he had played with them, and how one of them had often tied him to a tree and plied him with sharp sticks.

Poor Daron, he reflected. So evil. No, not evil, he decided. Hopelessly deranged, but not evil. Even there, in the bowels of the castle, surrounded by decay and the odor of sweaty bodies and oily hair, he remained loyal.

Cower rose to his feet and wandered to the small barred window opposite the cell door. Between the bars he could see a limited portion of the heavens.

The heavens, he reflected. Home of the Gods. And addressing them, he called, "All this over a few undeclared copper pieces? Don't you think the penalty is rather stiff?"

In response to his query, there came a high-pitched, angelic voice, not from the heavens as he had hoped, but from the corridor just outside his cell.

"Nope. It's what ya d'serves."

Squeals of laughter cruel and shrill poured through the tiny portal in the middle of the door as Cower, burdened by his chains, struggled across the room.

"Who's out there? Is this your idea of a jest? Eavesdropping on a man as he makes his peace with the Gods?"

"Now, now, mustn't waste our last minutes gettin' angry," responded a slightly deeper voice that cracked once uncontrollably.

"Me dad's gonna spruce ya up for yer trip," taunted the angelic voice. "Yesirree, he's gonna shave ya real close, he is - right down ta yer shoulders!"

Cower peered into the gloom. "Show yourselves. Let me see your faces, if you dare."

"I'll show ya me bum, is all," rejoined the deeper voice, accompanying the remark with a vulgar sound.

"So, there you are, kids!" came still a third voice, one that belonged to an older man and was vaguely familiar to the retainer. "Who've we here?"

"A new one, dad. Just come in this evenin' fer 'mmediate execution. We was makin' him feel right at home, we was. Gettin' him oriented so ta speak."

"That's my good lads. Well, let's have at it then."

Cower heard the jingle of keys; heard the lock click and the door groan on its hinges as it swung inward. He gasped and stumbled backwards, struck to the very core of his being by a terror he had never known.

For it was a terror that men felt only upon the verge of their death, when the light that was life grew faint about them and threatened to merge with the infinite darkness. This can't be happening to me, he told himself. Any second now I'll wake up from this nightmare! But again, he knew he was not dreaming.

The door fully open now, Cleave entered the cell flanked by his two sons. And to Cower, in his present state of mind, this was an utterly absurd and revolting sight - the executioner, the merciless instrument of death, accompanied by his children, the essence of life and all that was innocent.

"Me dad's gonna slice ya into pieces now," said the little one, his large brown eyes filled with mirth.

The older boy, who was pimple-faced and awkward in his movements *(the telltale sign that manhood was imminent and that soon he would be excited by milkmaids, tavern girls, and riding atop a wagon on a bumpy road,)* leaned around his father and cuffed his brother playfully on the head, croaking, "Here now, Donoim. Mustn't badger a man what's about ta be made so much shorter than he is." He chuckled at his own jest, revealing crooked, yellowish brown teeth.

"That's enough, Noim," chided Cleave gently as he gazed at the prisoner. There was something about the man that bothered him. And when he stepped closer for a better look, he understood why. "Is that you, Master Cower?"

"Aye," the retainer replied, still gripped with fear.

Much to his children's amazement, Cleave removed his hood, approached the prisoner, and extended his hand. "You remember me, don't you? Cleave?"

Cower cringed and shied away. "Remember you...?"

"Aye. That terrible stormy night two years ago when my wife was ailing and the court physician refused to come and see her. It was you who brought some potions. Your very own, as I recall."

With this simple remark, Cower was granted a brief reprieve from his torment. He stared at the executioner, warily at first, but when he recognized the man, he began to breathe again more easily.

"Aye. My aunt had sent them from the swamps by her home. They were supposed to have wondrous restorative powers."

"'Tis true," said Cleave, exuberant, shaking Cower's hand. "I can attest to it. Why if it weren't for you my wife would be moldering today."

"Then she's better?"

"Well, you know how long these things can hang on sometimes. But she's no worse."

"Please give her my best regards."

"I will, and thank you." It was then Cleave knitted his brow and said in a concerned tone, "Tell me, Master Cower, what brings you to this sorry state?"

Reminded of what had taken place in the last few hours, Cower stooped, drained of his strength, and began to weep. "A monstrous thing has happened. Pity me; pity you; pity the world."

The executioner gathered up Cower's chains and guided him to the wall, where they sat. "There now," said the man, trying to comfort him.

Cleave motioned for the boys to leave the cell, who, after a surly protest or two, obeyed their father and departed. "Why don't you tell Cleave all about it?"

Cower looked at him through bloodshot eyes. "I go to my death because I possess a knowledge that is disastrous to the Kingdom. A secret so horrible that if the world knew of it, order would crumble, panic would ensue, and the days of chaos would be upon us once more."

"Really." replied the executioner, trying to be a polite listener. "Chaos, you say?"

"Utter ruination. And worse."

"What could be worse than utter ruination?" asked the executioner, his curiosity aroused.

Cower's words had spilled out like a flood, unintentionally but incautiously as well, and now, with this having dawned upon him, he gave Cleave a guarded look.

Should I trust him? What will he do with the information? Or should such a secret ever be revealed.

For what was more disastrous, he pondered, to have Daron ruling in Bryand's stead with no one the wiser, or to expose the impostor without heed to the calamity that would follow?

And then there was the simple question of whether or not the executioner would believe him. Even now, though stuck in a dungeon with manacles about his wrists, he hardly believed it himself.

Yet, he thought. That does not make it any less the truth; Daron has committed a heinous crime; he has usurped his brother's throne. He must be stopped.

Cower sat upon his knees, energized now. "What

I'm about to tell you will seem far fetched, preposterous even, but it is the truth just the same. You must believe me."

"I will, Master Cower," said Cleave earnestly. "I have always thought of you as a good and honest man."

"But know this. Once you hear what I have to say, your life will be forever changed."

"Forever changed," Cleave repeated.

"Well, maybe not forever, but at least until the situation has been rectified. Shall I continue?"

"Yes," Cleave replied.

"Very well then." Cower took a deep breath, leaned closer, and in a voice just above a whisper, he said, "The King is not who he claims to be."

"And who is that?" asked Cleave, intrigued.

"The King."

"Aye, but who does he claim to be?"

"The King does not claim to be anyone else but the King."

"But you said--. "

"Never mind what I said. The King is not the King!"

"Well, if the King's not the King, then who is he?"

"The Prince."

"The King's the Prince?"

"Aye."

"I thought the Prince is the Prince."

"He is."

"You've lost me."

"Look, it's really very simple. The King is not the King, but the Prince instead pretending to be the King."

"All right then, where's the King?"

"The Prince wants everyone to believe he's the Prince."

"I thought you said the Prince wants everyone to believe he's the King."

"He does."

"I still don't know where the King is."

"In prison."

"Why is he in prison?"

"Because everyone thinks he's the Prince!"

Cleave rubbed his brow, hoping to alleviate the sudden pain that had developed there. "I'm sorry, Master Cower, but I'm still not with you."

"Let me start over."

"Must you?"

"I'll put it another way. The person you think is Bryand is really Daron. The person you think is Daron is really Bryand. Daron has been crowned King and Bryand is a prisoner because everyone thinks he's Daron."

"Ahhhh, now I understand," said Cleave, and he fell silent, his brow knitting once again. In that time, Cower watched him carefully, holding his breath. Was he truly convinced? Had he won his first alley?

At length, Cleave sighed and rose to his feet, whereupon he produced a small key from his purse and unlocked the manacles around Cower's wrists.

"You believe me!" said the retainer, and tears sprang to his eyes.

"Aye, I believe you," said the executioner, donning his black hood. "'Tis so fantastical that it must be true."

"Dear friend!" Cower blurted, shaking with relief. "I was afraid you'd think me mad!"

"Oh, no, I could never think that. Not of you, master Cower. Well, time to go."

"Yes, yes. We must away. And quickly. Where to then?"

"The courtyard."

"Good!" But once they were in the hallway, the retainer paused. "The courtyard?"

"Aye."

"What's in the courtyard?"

"The block, of course."

"What?!" cried Cower, falling against the wall. "After all I've told you, you're going to execute me anyway?!"

"What has that to do with us?" asked Cleave simply.

"I think you're being a little shortsighted, my friend. You've got to look further than the chopping block. Prince Daron has usurped his brother's throne and is posing as Bryand."

"Yes, you said that."

"And it means nothing to you?"

"I'm sorry, but I try to steer clear of politics." From the blank look on Cower's face, the executioner felt compelled to continue. "When you're a member of my class, the poor working class, that is, you tend not to get involved in such things. It doesn't matter who sits on the throne as long as it doesn't interfere with your efforts to put food on the table and clean straw on the floor."

"Don't you understand?! There's a madman ruling the country. An impostor. And it's our duty to stop him."

"Look," said Cleave, growing annoyed. "I know my duty. I don't need you to tell me about my duty. And right now my duty is to execute you. Now, I'd appreciate it if we could end the discussion. I've got a powerful headache, and I'm having a hard-enough time going through with this as it is. You want a hood?"

"A hood?"

"A blindfold then? I'll let you know beforehand when we come to any steps."

The retainer shook his head, no.

"Very well then, off we go."

Knowing he was just moments from his death, the last of Cower's hopes came crashing down. He felt miserable and puny and forsaken by the Gods.

"To the block," he muttered as he followed the

executioner. "And that is how things end. I should have bought that life insurance policy last year when I had the chance. I don't suppose we could stop along the way-- ."

"Sorry, friend," said Cleave, sympathetically. "Wish I could allow it but it's against guild rules. And besides, now that you've been condemned, the insurance company would consider it a preexisting condition."

CHAPTER NINE

The banquet hall was choked with ladies and gentlemen of the court when the trumpeters sounded the familiar fanfare that preceded the King's entrance. All voices hushed instantly, all eyes turned to the massive doors as they were swung apart, revealing the King who, at that precise moment, was trying to adjust the bloomers that had ridden up between his buttocks.

"Blast these shorts," he muttered.

Embarrassed by this very personal display yet not knowing what else they should do, the entire assemblage applauded.

Daron assumed a regal pose and marched into the room, acknowledging the well wishes of the lords and ladies he passed. When he reached the royal armchair behind the royal dais, he sat, and very benignly raised his hand as a signal for everyone else to do the same.

There ensued a madcap scramble for seats as many tried to sit as close to the King as possible. While dozens pushed and shoved and crammed together at tables nearer the dais, others sat contentedly, or alone, at tables farther away.

"Please, please," said the impostor benevolently. "There's room for all."

Once again the court applauded.

But when the last person in the room had found a seat, and the King discovered the chair to his left and the two chairs to his right unoccupied, a dark and brooding look fell across his face.

"Where is the Princess MeAnne?" asked the King. "And my two advisors? Where are the Duke of Cunninghim and the Earl of Nightshade?"

Pomp approached the dais in a regimented step and, in a voice filled with practiced disdain, said, "My lord, they are being placed in the vestibule at this very moment."

Daron gripped the arms of his chair. "Why were they not admitted before me?"

Unruffled, Pomp replied, "Sire, protocol demands that your guests be received by you. Surely my lord does not wish to break from years of ceremony and be greeted by the very men he wishes to honor."

Daron gazed at the expectant faces about him. "No. Certainly not," he said, relinquishing. "Very well then, bring them in."

Pomp turned on his heels, a smug look upon his face, and, in the same regimented step, he proceeded to the doors, rapped the floor with his long baton and announced, "With your Majesty's permission: the Duke of Cunninghim and the Earl of Nightshade."

The trumpeters sounded another fanfare and the doors were swung open, revealing an empty hallway.

The King shifted irritably in his seat. Seeing this, Pomp ignored the muttering of the crowd and quickly directed the court attendants to shut the doors.

He, cleared his throat to silence the hall, and with a staid expression, announced, "With your Majesty's permission: the Duke of Cunninghim and the Earl of Nightshade."

Once again the trumpeters sounded their fanfare, and once again the doors were swung open, revealing an empty hallway.

"Well, chamberlain?" Daron asked with growing impatience. "Where are they?"

◆ ◆ ◆

At the far end of the corridor leading to the banquet room, just a few paces beyond the corner of the connecting hall, stood the gentlemen in question. Cunninghim peered down the corridor, preoccupied. Nightshade rocked as usual, his hands meshed and thumbs drumming upon his belly.

"We're overdue, you know," said the Earl a bit frostily, breaking the silence. "I've heard them call our names twice already."

"I'm not deaf," said Cunninghim, without looking at him. "Do you want to go in there without knowing if Mortamour took care of things? I, for one, do not."

They had decided it was time for the King to meet his unexpected demise. The taxes they had collected amounted to what was probably the largest fortune anyone had ever amassed, and rather than turn it over to the King, they had decided to use the money to buy Cunninghim's way to the throne.

So Nightshade's talents were employed once more. The King's chalice was painted with poison.

It was a subtle mixture. One that was designed to make everyone think the King had died of natural causes, specifically, the swelling shut of his throat and nasal passages. Since the beginning of the rainy season, minor bouts with clogged lung syndrome had popped up here and there among members of the court. It was an easy way to disguise an assassination.

"The ingredients I've used are of a very interesting nature," Nightshade had offered as he and the Duke made their way to the banquet.

He was particularly proud of this concoction. After administering it to his servant, (*he went through many,*) the man had died exactly as Nightshade expected.

"You see, by themselves, they would do nothing more than give a man a slight case of the runs, but when mixed in the right proportion-- ."

"Why don't you say that a bit more loudly," Cunninghim had whispered with a sudden flash of temper. "Better yet, why don't you just announce it at the banquet!"

Nightshade had said nothing more about it but had brooded the rest of way to the hall.

The echo of rapid footfalls reached their ears and, in a moment, Mortamour appeared around the far corner of the passageway. Seeing the two lords, the henchman broke into a fast trot and came to a halt before them.

"Well?" asked Cunninghim with bated breath. "Is it done?"

"Aye," growled Mortamour. One could never tell the man's true disposition, growling the way he did all the time. "It's on the dais right in front of him."

In the early morning hours, Mortamour had stolen into the servants' quarters, slipped into the silver pantry and have painted the chalice himself.

"Good," said Cunninghim, and turning to Nightshade, he added, "Now remember, you must offer a toast."

"Why can't you do it?" said Nightshade petulantly. "You know how I hate speaking in front of crowds."

"It would look rather suspicious, don't you think?" said the Duke, trying to control his temper. "Especially since I don't drink!"

"I suppose so," said the Earl grudgingly. "But what am I going to say?"

"Anything. Toast the Kingdom."

"Now wait a minute," Nightshade protested. "In front of all those people? I think I should say something a little more eloquent than here's to the Kingdom."

"What's the difference -- !" Cunninghim exclaimed as loudly as he dared. "The important thing is to get the King to drink."

Why I continue to associate with such a fool is beyond me, thought the Duke. A child has more guile!

"Nevertheless," said Nightshade, resolute. "I've an image to maintain." And he began to compose his oration.

"I, I can't understand the delay, your majesty," said Pomp in a most uncharacteristic manner, for he had dropped to one knee with his hands clasped before him so tightly that they were shaking.

"This has never happened before. I don't know what to say. I-- . I-- . "

"Find them immediately," said the impostor, the muscles at his jaw bulging. "Search every inch of the palace, the entire city if you must, but find them and bring them to me." When it came to tax money, Daron had no sense of humor. Or trust.

Humiliated, shaking with terror, the chamberlain scurried to the rear of the hall where two attendants, underlings whom he had always looked down upon, mocked him as they swung open the doors.

To Pomp's considerable surprise, as well as everyone else's, there stood the Duke of Cunninghim and the Earl of Nightshade just outside, waiting patiently to be announced.

"Gods be praised!" exclaimed Pomp. "I thought I'd lost you for good."

Ignoring their curious looks, the chamberlain smoothed his hair, straightened his tunic, and turned back to the room. "They're here!"

Daron felt his heart quicken with anticipation as the two nobles headed toward the dais.

"Ahhh, my lords, my friends," he called buoyantly. "With this simple state function we welcome you home again after your long, arduous journey. Come. Take your places at my side and share with me some food, some drink, some pleasant diversion, all to show our gratitude for your undertaking."

"I thank you, my lord, for this tribute tonight," said Cunninghim in a voice that filled the hall. "We are your humble servants."

"Then let us partake of this fare," said Daron, delighted. "And we shall discuss your journey afterwards."

Course after course was served. Trays overflowing with honeyed pork roasted to perfection, peppered mutton marinated in brandy wine, brown sugar yams on a bed of millet.

Nightshade was in heaven and had seconds of everything. Being thus occupied, he would have forgotten about the toast completely had not Cunninghim given him a swift kick to the shin under the table.

"Oh!" Nightshade blurted, realizing his moment had come. It was a struggle, trying to stand without taking the chair with him, but eventually, after a steward had helped him, the Earl was on his feet.

"I wish to thank his majesty for-- . For the honor he has bestowed upon us. Uh, how about a toast?" And without waiting for the King's permission, he swept up his goblet and raised it high. "Here's to the Kingdom!"

"The Kingdom!" the hall resounded and goblets were raised in salute.

Nightshade watched intently as the King sipped from the royal vessel. Better get him to drink the whole glass, he thought. Just in case the film has evaporated. "Uh--- Here's to the lady MeAnne!"

"MeAnne!" the hall responded and everyone drank.

"The Queen Mother!"

"The Queen Mother!"

"To tonight! Isn't it a lovely evening?!"

"A lovely evening!"

Nightshade watched the King drain the last of his cup. Then, satisfied that the job was done, he took his seat and wiped his brow, deliberately ignoring Cunninghim's scornful look.

"Boys, it's past your bedtime. Go home to your mother," said Cleave, placing Cower comfortably before the block.

"Aw, dad, can't we stay," whined Donoim. "We want ta see how far his blood spurts. Last guy came nowhere near breakin' the record."

"I said, go home to your mother. Now. Or It'll be time out for the both of you." (*Time out meaning time knocked out and thoroughly unconscious.*)

Angry, Donoim kicked the dirt and pouted. But Noim obeyed and, grabbing his brother by the arm, led him out of the small courtyard.

Cleave followed after them a few paces to make sure they had gone as very often they would double back to watch the beheadings.

"I'm sorry about that," he said, returning to the block. "They get a bit too exuberant at times."

"Think nothing of it," replied Cower. "They're nice kids. You should be proud of them."

"I am," said Cleave with fatherly pride. "I'm hoping they'll follow in my footsteps someday. You know, start a family tradition."

He grabbed his axe, hefted it a few times then took a practice swing. "All right, Master Cower, if you'll place your head down please?"

"Like so?" said Cower, complying.

"Yes. that's good. You might want to turn your collar down. It could grab the blade and keep it from slicing clean through."

"Of course. Wouldn't want sloppy."

He adjusted his collar, then rested his head upon the polished wood. Nice grain, he thought, birds-eye maple I'd guess. And this surprised him.

By now, he had expected to be overcome with fear. But instead, a strange peace had come over him, ushering with it, memories long past that rose to the surface of his mind with stunning clarity.

So this was how the Gods prepared a man for death, he marveled; by distracting him. Bless me, if it isn't that little peasant girl I knew as a young man. My she was pretty. That is, until she met with the black death. I wonder if I'll be seeing her again? I don't suppose one can catch the plague after one is dead.

The executioner raised his axe. Higher. Higher still, until it was at the peak of its arc. He took a long, slow breath; the breath he normally used to sustain the control he needed to bring the axe down swiftly and accurately.

But then, he paused, and to his own surprise, he lowered the axe to the ground.

It took him a moment to collect his thoughts, for he had not used his mind very often to consider weighty things. And what Master Cower had presented to him was definitely a most weighty thing.

From what he had understood, or thought he had understood, the Prince was the King and the King was the Prince.

And that's not right, he determined. And if that's not right, then shouldn't I let Master Cower go?

But then the practical side of his nature spoke up. Now wait a minute, that's not very good business. I've a reputation to maintain in the community, and orders from the King no less.

But wait! he thought. He's not the King. He's an impostor! He has no right to order anyone's death.

"Could you please hurry things up a bit?" asked Cower without moving his head. "My life has been flashing before me and I'm getting pretty close to the present."

Cleave was sweating, and for the first time in his career, his hands shook. His hood felt suffocating and he tore it from his head. He was about to tell the retainer to stand up when he was struck by yet another thought.

True, he may be an impostor, but as long as everyone thinks he's the King, he has the right to do as he pleases. If I disobey him, I might find myself in the same position as Master Cower. And then who would take care of Malady and the kids?

I've got to buy that cottage in the country and get her out of here or she'll not last much longer. But then he remembered, that had it not been for Master Cower and his potions, she would have already passed on.

So much to consider. So much he truly did not understand and, oh, how his head was throbbing.

"Stand up, Master Cower. I'll not take your life."

The retainer tossed him a dubious look. "This wouldn't be a sample of executioner humor, would it?"

"No," replied Cleave with a slight grin, and helping the retainer to his feet, he added, "this time I'll just have to take the loss."

But then he sobered. "Master Cower, do you think the King, I mean, the Prince, I mean, whoever's down there in the dungeon, would help me and my family?"

"I'm sure of it," replied Cower, encouraged.

Cleave nodded thoughtfully. "Then I suggest we act quickly."

They made their plans and departed, Cower for the

castle kitchen to do his part and Cleave for home to prepare Malady and the boys.

But when he confronted her and told her what he had done, she stared at him in disbelief. In an angry tone, she said, "Ya let him go?! How could ya do such a foolish thing?!"

"Cause I owed him somethin' more than loppin' off his head," he tried to explain.

She burst into tears and made a gurgling sound. The same sound she always made when phlegm collected in her throat.

Cleave, however, was not too alarmed at this; he knew just how to attend her. Taking his wife by the shoulders and turning her around, the executioner whacked her squarely on the back two or three times to break up her sudden congestion.

"Look," he said patiently, turning her to him. "He saved your life. If it weren't for Master Cower's kindness you wouldn't be here now."

She gazed at him, her nose dripping. "I understand that. But there's things what come b'fore gratitude. Cash, fer instance. I suppose ya even returned his tip."

"He never gave me one."

"Oh!" she exclaimed, exasperated, then she clutched her breasts. "We've kids ta feed, ya know. An' these dried up years ago!"

Suddenly a new thought struck her. She walked to the threshold of their hovel, opened the door a crack, and peered down the street. "Supposin' the King finds out?" she asked in a fearful tone. "What then?"

Cleave glanced at the floor sheepishly. "Well-- . Speakin' of the King; there's somethin' else you should know."

Malady closed the door and faced him. "What've ya done?"

His head began to ache again. The information

Master Cower had confided in him was spawning new ideas that, even in their infancy, were more complex and provoking than anything he had ever thought. They were confusing, unsettling, and made his stomach churn. Yet he could not dismiss them.

He tried his best to explain to Malady exactly what he was feeling. Malady, however, after hearing him out, flew into a rage.

"Of all the addle-pated...! What's gotten into ya, Cleave?! You've gone an' ruined us!"

"Have you heard nothin'?!" shouted the man. She stared at him in shock. This was the first time he had ever raised his voice to her. "There's things what come up sometimes that are more important than just gettin' by. An' this is one of 'em. Now wake the kids an' start packin' while I scare up a wagon."

"Aw right," she said contritely. "But ya don't have ta snap."

He looked at her, and the hard expression upon his face softened to one of tenderness. He went to her and put his arms around her. "I'm sorry, puddin'. I should have consulted with you first."

He ran his hand over her hair, noting how gray and dull it was. Is that another bald spot? he thought, his brow knitting.

Anguished, he pressed her face tightly against his chest. "But what's done is done. We've always wanted to get away from here and have that cottage of our own. Well, now's our chance. The Prince will reward us; you'll see. And then you and the kids can have the life you deserve. Whaduya say, puddin'; are you with me on this one?"

"Aye, luv," came her smothered reply. "Now I could do with some air."

CHAPTER TEN

Cower stood before Bryand's jailer holding a platter of peppered mutton and yams that he had pilfered from the kitchen when Bisque, the castle chef, was not looking. "Nourishment for the Prince," said the retainer blandly, though inside he was quaking with fear.

What was I thinking?! he said to himself. Attempting a jailbreak! He was a manservant; a gentle manservant, who had not once in all his life picked up a sword other than to hand it to his noble charges.

Intrigues were made for men with steel running through their veins. Red blood ran through Cower's veins, and he preferred to keep it there.

Still, he told himself, you've come this far. You must see it through.

The jailer frowned and eyed Cower suspiciously. "On whose authority?"

"The King's, of course. I'm his retainer."

"No one told me about this."

"I wasn't aware the King consulted with you about anything," said the retainer, staring down his nose at him. Cower knew the hierarchy of the castle and knew he outranked the jailer. He only hoped the jailer knew it, too.

"Perhaps I should tell his Majesty you refused me admittance."

"Wait a minute," said the jailer. "No need gettin' your nose out of joint. Let's see what ya got there."

He hovered over the tray, eyeing the food. "Pretty

nice fare," said the man, lifting one of the mutton joints and peering at Cower from beneath his bushy brows.

The retainer sighed and rolled his eyes. "Take it. Now that you've touched it."

With a torch in one hand and the mutton in the other, the jailer led the way down the corridor. Cower's skin crawled as he eyed the slime upon the walls.

This section of the dungeon was separate from the rest. It had been deemed 'The Tombs' for it was reserved for those who were as good as dead.

They came to a pair of doors that stood side by side. Here the jailer halted and, realizing his hands were full, tried to put the mutton back on Cower's platter so he could retrieve his keys.

"Don't you dare," said Cower disdainfully, moving the platter quickly away.

"Let me help you there," said someone from behind them.

The jailer turned around and squinted into the gloom. "Cleave? Is that you?"

"Aye," said the executioner, joining them.

"What brings you to the Tombs?"

"Just this." He took the mutton leg from the jailer and, without a moment's pause, whacked him over the head with it.

The man crumpled to the floor.

"I doubt he'll be eating mutton after this," said Cower, watching Cleave remove the jailer's keys.

"I doubt he'll be eatin' anythin' after this," answered Cleave.

"You mean, he's-- ."

"Dead. I must've hit him too hard."

Cower had seen men killed before, upon the battlefield or upon the block. But never had he been directly or even indirectly responsible.

Yet, at that moment he could have cared less about

being an accessory to murder. Bryand was his first concern, and Cower was prepared to do anything - even rot in the underworld - in order to save the Prince's life.

Cleave chose the door closest to them and opened it. Cower did not even wait for the light, but plunged into the gloom, crying, "We're here, my lord! We've come to save you!"

And from somewhere in the shadows a shrill but polite voice rejoined, "Do we know each other?"

Sensing something amiss, Cleave picked up the torch that the jailer had dropped. He entered the cell.

Before them, bathed by the orange glow of the flame, was a little man chained to the wall, his feet dangling several inches from the floor.

"Come on in," said the prisoner cordially. "Grab a chain and hang around for a while." At that, he burst out laughing, and he did not stop until he was breathless and a tear ran down his cheek. "Ahhhhh!" he sighed, then he shook his head. "I've been waitin' to say that for an eternity."

"Uh-- . Pardon us," stammered Cleave.

"Oh, look, food," said the man, referring to the platter in Cower's hands. "Now that's something different for a change. It's not my birthday already, is it?"

"There's been a mix-up, you see," said Cower.

"Who knows any good songs? Aye, some songs! And then we'll play some party games. I love party games."

"We're in the wrong cell," explained Cleave.

"That's all right, I wasn't busy. Now, who'll go first? Don't be bashful. We're all friends here."

As they closed the door behind them, they heard the prisoner shout, "Pick up some ale, will you? We don't want to run out. All right then, it's my turn. What would everyone like to hear?"

Cleave unlocked the second door, whereupon Cower thrust the platter into the executioner's arms, grabbed the torch, and rushed inside. The stench was almost overpowering, and he would have vomited had it not been Bryand's stench.

"Dearest Gods!" gasped Cower, stricken. For there before him was the Prince, prostrate upon the floor, with rats scurrying over his arms and legs, and bugs nesting in his hair. "Oh, my lord; my dear, sweet boy!"

Cower fell to his knees and chased away the vermin, then rolled the Prince over and held him in his arms. "My lord, my lord, can you hear me?!"

Bryand's eyes opened, and staring at the retainer, he said in a voice weak from lack of use, "Cower? Is that you?"

"Aye, my lord," replied the retainer, tears running down his cheeks.

"Is it really you? Or am I having another vision?"

"It is really I, my lord. We've come to save you."

Bryand reached out with a trembling hand and touched the retainer's cheek. "Can it be true?"

"Aye, my lord."

"Cower!" cried Bryand. "You're really here! This is really your cheek! This is really your brow! This is really your nose!" It was then Cleave joined them. "But who are you?"

"The executioner, my lord."

Bryand stiffened with fear and clung to Cower. "Tell me he's a vision; please."

"No, no," said the retainer, repressing a smile. "He's real. And he's here to help you."

He had endured so much heartache, so much suffering without once breaking down in tears. But now, with the retainer holding him tight and the nightmare over at last, the Prince began to weep. "Oh, Cower, I was so close to despair. So close to losing my mind."

For a moment, the retainer did naught but rock the young man in his arms. Then, in a voice thick with emotion, he said, "The ordeal has ended, my lord. We've seen to that."

Cleave had been respectfully quiet. But he knew they did not have much time to waste. "We'd best be going," he said, unlocking the Prince's chains. "I'm not certain when the watch changes."

He dragged the jailer into the cell by his heels. "Come, m'lord," he said, lifting Bryand effortlessly. "I've got my wife waitin' at home with my kids and I found a wagon, too."

They entered the small anteroom. The jailer's seat sat empty by a rough-hewn table. Upon the table was a leather flask. Cower grabbed it instinctively and heard liquid swish inside.

They passed through an open archway, entered the stairwell behind and began to climb. The sound of their footfalls - leather scraping against stone - echoed all around them.

They were one turn away from the door that led to the upper cells when they heard it squeal on its hinges. They halted abruptly. The lyrics of a smutty song reached their ears. Someone was coming down the stairs, blocking their escape.

Cleave turned and motioned for Cower to retreat the way they had come. A moment later they were back in the jailer's room.

"What do we do?" asked Cower fearfully.

Cleave did not answer him. Instead, he stood Bryand by the wall adjacent to the stairwell. Then, leaving Cower to support him, the executioner stepped into the middle of the room.

The man coming down the stairs, who was the jailer's relief, saw the executioner at once and tossed him a congenial wave. "Evenin' Cleave."

"Is that you, Burly?" said Cleave, grinning.

"Aye." The jailer stepped onto the landing. "What're

you doin' down here in the-- ."

The guard saw Cower and the Prince immediately. He shot a look at Cleave and then back at them. His hand went for the dagger at his belt.

But before he could unsheathe the weapon, Cleave grabbed him by his shirt, spun him around, and leveled a blow to his face that sent him spilling over the table and crashing into the jailer's chair.

"Get the Prince away," said Cleave to the retainer, thrusting them both into the stairwell. "I'll join you right off."

He watched Cower struggle up the steps with the Prince in tow, and when they had disappeared from view, he turned to the guard once more. But in that brief pause, the man had recovered and removed his dagger.

Before Cleave could react, the blade sliced the air and penetrated his chest. He stumbled and hit the wall, then stood there for a moment, stunned. He looked down at the hilt, at his blood, and with a wince pulled the dagger out and threw it away.

"Now you've gone and done it, Burly," said Cleave in a menacing tone, and with a snarl he sprang toward the jailer.

"Help!" cried Burly, attempting to dodge the executioner and gain the stairs. But Cleave grabbed him and held him fast, then wrapped his massive arm around his throat.

"Sorry, Burly," said Cleave through gritted teeth as he snapped his neck. "But the man what kills me, dies in the tryin'."

He dragged the jailer's body down the corridor and into Bryand's cell, placing it next to the man Burly had come to relieve. He buried them both under the filthy straw, closed and locked the door, then dropped the key ring through the barred portal in the center of the door.

He had traveled only a short distance when a gripping pain took hold of him. Clutching his chest, he fell against the wall and slid into a heap.

He felt a chill spreading through his body, and this he found strange, for sweat ran freely down his cheeks. A thought ran over and over again in his head. Sleep. You need sleep. It's been an exhausting day.

He closed his eyes, and in the blackness behind his eyes he saw a shadowy curtain drawing shut.

But suddenly the executioner knew that if he waited until the curtain had closed, he would never see his wife and children again. So he forced his eyes open, and in doing so the pain returned with an even greater intensity.

This time, though, Cleave would not succumb to it, and with his teeth gnashed, he pulled himself onto his feet and staggered down the corridor toward the anteroom and the stairs.

He caught up to Cower on the upper landing and quickly relieved him of the Prince. The retainer took the lead, guiding them along a series of darkened corridors.

Soon they had found the door to the courtyard. Once outside, the shadow at the base of the wall made good cover, and they worked their way around the perimeter of the ward without attracting any further attention.

The doors to the castle gatehouse stood open and the portcullis was raised. There was nary a guard in sight, but nevertheless Cower cringed each time they passed by an arrow slit in the wall or beneath a murder hole in the ceiling.

"Where are they?" whispered the retainer, casting an edgy glance over his shoulder. "Why is there no one on duty?"

Cleave's voice came out strained and breathy. "The King sent two wagons of beer to the barracks in celebration of the Duke's return."

Of course, thought Cower, snorting. They're all out getting drunk.

Moments later, having crossed the drawbridge and descended the main ramp, they entered the town square. They were now in plain sight, *(had a single guard in the entire city been sober enough to see them,)* and it was then a man rushed toward them from the opposite side of the square. But he was just an ordinary citizen whose wife had found him cavorting at the town brothel and was in desperate need of a hiding place.

They started down the main thoroughfare, and when they reached the first cross street on their left, Cleave took the lead and headed down it a short way.

They approached a horse and wagon, rounded them and stopped at a heavy oak door. "Here it is," he said. "Not what you'd call grand, but home to me and mine." He put the Prince down, wiped his brow, then opened the door and bid the Prince and Cower to enter.

The executioner did not follow right away. Instead, he reached for a sack of potatoes that was by the door, emptied it into the wagon, then threw the sack over his shoulder to hide the dark stain on his doublet.

"There ya are," said Malady. She skirted the two men who had invaded her home and went to Cleave.

"All right, all right," he said with a wince as she placed her head against his chest. "Everything ready?"

"Everythin' 'cept the boys."

"Them bundles outside," he said, bringing her to the doorway. "Go throw 'em onto the wagon."

"Let me help," offered Cower.

"No," replied Malady flatly. "I'll do it."

When Malady had gone, Cleave pushed aside the curtain that separated the front room with the sleeping quarters. "What goes on here?"

"I ain't goin'," said Donoim, clutching a swagger

stick tightly. "Ya can't make me!"

"I'm not goin', either!" announced Noim, though he tried to sound defiant, his voice had taken that moment to crack.

Cleave frowned. "You'll do as yer told. Now get outside an' climb into that wagon."

"I won't!" cried the little one, brandishing his stick. "This is me home. I ain't gonna leave it!"

"Don't you threaten me with no stick. Why, I'll take that thing and put it across your you-know-what!"

"Says you!" sneered Donoim.

The executioner lunged at him, but the boy was fast and nimble. "Get over here, Donoim. An' you, Noim; don't test my patience."

During the chase, the sack fell from Cleave's shoulder. Though he was unaware of it, the boys saw the dark stain on his doublet and immediately froze. "That's better. Now drop that stick."

"Dad," said Noim, shocked. "What's happened to ya?"

Cleave looked down and saw that his wound was exposed. "Shhhhh!"

He found a shirt and packed in tightly between the doublet and his chest, then he threw the sack over his shoulder once more. He looked at the boys and saw the fear in their eyes. "It's nothin'. It's just a scratch."

Donoim started to cry. "But yer bleedin' somethin' awful."

"Stop that," said Cleave harshly, which only made the little one cry harder. He crouched before his sons and gathered them in his arms.

"Now we don't want to upset your mother about this. You know how sickly she is." He closed his eyes and his face screwed up with pain. "Look," said Cleave, when he could talk again. "I need you to be brave. Understand? What Dad did tonight was somethin' for the best of the country."

"Ya mean yer a hero?" asked Donoim, drying his tears with the back of his hand.

"Aye, ya might say that. Now listen to your dad a minute. If anythin' happens to me, Noim here is in charge. Ya got that Donoim? No back-talkin', no sassin', no nothin'."

"Aye, dad," said the little one with a disgruntled look to his brother.

"An' you," continued Cleave, clapping his older son on the shoulder. "Mind your mother while you're watchin' over her."

"But where'll you be, dad?" asked Noim, concerned.

"With you, of course. I'm just sayin' this in case somethin' happens an' we get separated for a while."

He hugged them, sniffing. "Blasted smoke," he said, releasing them and wiping his eyes. "Gets trapped in this room." He looked at them and nodded. "Well, we won't have ta worry no more about that no more. Now off ya go. Help yer mother."

Cower sat up front upon the flat board seat, holding the horse's reins tightly. The boys jumped into the back of the wagon and helped Malady aboard.

"What's with all the food 'n stuff?" asked Noim irritably, pushing aside some of the loose potatoes.

"Quiet, please," said the retainer a bit too harshly than he had intended.

"Says you," Donoim remarked at once. The boy lifted his head above the wagon wall. "Where's dad?"

No answer was needed, for just then Cleave exited the house with Byrand in his arms. He paused to look up and down the empty street. Then, with a groan, he lifted the Prince over the sidewall and rested a moment against the wagon.

"What's wrong?" said Malady to him.

When the pain had subsided, he smiled and said,

"Nothin', puddin'. Just a strain. Guess your Cleave's not as young as he used to be."

Malady watched him with growing concern. Though at night she could barely see a thing.

Cleave pulled himself onto the front seat next to the retainer. He coughed, and when he took his hand away from his mouth, he saw it was full of blood. Cower noticed it as well, but before he could speak, the executioner shot him a hard look and said, "Hand me the reins, Master Cower."

"But, Cleave-- ."

"Please, Master Cower," said the executioner firmly. "You'll have plenty of time to drive once we're out of danger."

Cower complied without saying another word, though his heart was wrenching in his chest.

"Tis not your fault," said Cleave as though he had read the retainer's mind.

"Not his fault for what?" asked Malady. By now, her intuition was telling her something was amiss.

Cleave spoke over his shoulder in a calm tone of voice. "That he never learned to drive, puddin'; that's all."

A flick of the reins and a click of his tongue, was all he needed to set the horse in motion. The wagon lumbered down the deserted street, the horse's hooves clomping on the cobbles and echoing between the canyon of mortar and stone.

They turned onto the main thoroughfare, which was also empty, and traveled past the House of the Gods, past the open marketplace, doorways cloaked in shadows and empty stalls, until at last they reached the South Gate and rolled through its gaping maw.

They crossed the clearing where the charred logs of Audanot's pyre still remained and soon were heading down the Southern road.

The wagon rocked gently as Cleave guided it along the ruts in the packed earth. A cool breeze wafted in his face and he took the air deep into his lungs.

The city was behind them now. Though he could not see very well, he knew the dark clumps on both sides of the road were trees and thickets. This was the first time in his whole life he had traveled beyond the city's walls, and already, he felt relieved, and reassured.

But not for himself. He knew he'd be dead before dawn. But at least Malady and the children would have a better life, and that was all he had every really wanted.

Suddenly a fight erupted between the boys.

"Cut it out!" snapped Noim, punching his brother in the arm.

"I had me legs there first!" insisted Donoim, whacking him back.

"Ya did not!"

"Did too!"

They exchanged blows once more.

"Malady, please," Cleave implored.

"Awright, that's it!" shouted Malady. "I've had enough o' this bickerin'. Donoim, you stay where ya are. An' you, Noim-- ." She sidled closer to the wall, making more room between herself and the Prince, then patted the open wagon boards between them. "You sits next ta me."

"I'm not sittin' anywhere near him," said Noim, nodding toward the Prince. "He smells worse 'n the garbage dump b'hind the house."

"Here you!" barked the executioner over his shoulder. "You mind your manners."

"Why? I ain't never had ta mind 'em b'fore?"

"Just do as yer father bids," said Malady with a brief, uneasy look at the Prince.

By this time, Bryand was more coherent. The night air was refreshing and knowing he was free was like a tonic to his spirits.

He was quickly becoming his old self again. His thoughts - so recently a jumble - came to him now in an orderly progression.

This, however, was not as comforting as he had hoped. For the very first thing that came to mind was the image of his brother sitting upon the throne.

Anger rose inside him. His hands curled into fists. But then another image came to him far worse than the first. He saw MeAnne in Daron's arms, and this filled him with such horror that he bolted upright and shouted, "Stop!"

Surprised by the Prince's outburst, Cower jumped, and Cleave pulled back hard on the reins.

"What is it?" asked the retainer, immediately concerned.

"I've got to go back," said the Prince. "I must see MeAnne."

"Who's MeAnne?" asked Malady.

"Now?" asked Cleave, somewhat vexed. "In the middle of escapin'?"

"She has to be told or she'll marry the wrong man."

"Who's MeAnne?" Malady asked again.

"My lord," said Cower indulgently. "We know not how long we have before someone discovers you've escaped. Surely you want to be as far away as you can when the alarm is sounded."

"Leave if you must. I'll understand. But I'm not going until I've seen her."

"But how -- ?" asked Cower, fretting.

"The same way Daron got to me on the night of the joust - by the secret passageway."

Cleave cast the retainer a dour look. "Yer sure we've got the right one here?"

"Of course!" replied Cower.

"Who's MeAnne?" asked Donoim to his mother.

"I don't know," said Malady, sternly. "I'm still tryin' ta find out!"

With a grunt, the Prince began to climb over the sidewall.

"Hang on," said Cleave.

"Good idea," replied Bryand in a strained voice.

"No, I mean, we'll take you."

"But why?" asked Malady, fretting.

"Because I'd do the same if it were you I was leaving behind." And without another word, he turned the wagon about.

"Who's MeAnne?" asked Donoim when the wagon was rolling again.

"Shut yer trap," said Noim, kicking his younger brother.

"I want ta know," said Donoim, kicking him back.

"A great lady," said Bryand to the boys. "A grand lady."

"What's the likes of you wantin' with a grand lady?" asked the older boy suspiciously.

But his only reply was the creaking of the wagon and the sounds of the night.

Bryand guided them around the outside of the city to where the castle wall and the city wall became one and the same.

"To the right now," Bryand pointed. "That grove on the far side of the clearing."

Cleave squinted into the darkness. "What grove? I can't see a thing."

Having spent three months in the dungeon, Bryand's eyes were as sharp as an owl's "Trust me. It's there."

They rolled across the field toward a dark splotch in the night sky, lurching from side to side each time the wagon hit a rock or a rut in the ground. At length, Cleave halted within a dense cluster of spruce trees.

The Prince gripped Cower's shoulder. "If I'm not back within the hour, make for Willowbrook. Niles will protect you with his life."

Bryand offered the executioner his hand. "In case this is goodbye, I thank you for what you've done."

Cleave shook it, then watched the Prince clamber over the side of the wagon and fall to the ground.

"Wait," said the executioner, frowning. He handed Cower the reins. "I'll take you."

"What?!" Malady blurted. "You can't do that!" She watched her husband climb down. "Cleave! Didja hear me?!"

"I've got to," said her husband. "He'll never make it by himself." Actually, the executioner was grateful for the opportunity, for he knew his time was short, and he did not want the boys to see him die.

He placed his hand over Malady's. "Stay with Master Cower. He'll look after you. And you kids? Remember what I said."

He helped Bryand onto his feet, then looked tenderly at his wife. "Take care of yourself, puddin'."

Malady watched her husband disappear into the darkness. Her hand came to rest on the sidewall of the wagon. It was moist. She looked closer and realized her hand was stained with blood. She knew it was Cleave's blood, and though her eyes filled with tears and her nose began to drain, she said nothing to the children. She would suffer as she always did, in silence during the lonesome hours of the night. Only this time, Cleave would not be snoring by her side. From this night forward, she would suffer alone.

Cleave and Bryand made their way deeper into the woods, skirting shrubs and thick bushes until they came to what seemed to be a large boil in the earth."Here it is," said Bryand.

They went around to the far side and halted before a copse of thorn bushes. Spreading back the limbs, they found the entrance to a tunnel that ran beneath the castle wall. Bryand slipped between the branches and entered, then Cleave did the same.

Once inside, however, the executioner stumbled and fell to his knees. Bryand went to him and tried to lift him, but he was too weak and was dragged to his knees as well. His hand came up covered with blood.

Astonished, he stared at the executioner. "You're hurt, man!"

"It's nothin'," said Cleave with a grimace as he leaned against the tunnel wall.

"But how-- . When-- . "

Cleave shut his eyes and sighed. "The jailer."

"You mean, all the time you were helping me, you were-- . Quickly, we must get you back to the wagon."

"I won't make it," said Cleave. He pulled out the blood-soaked shirt from under his doublet then looked at the Prince. "My family-- . Master Cower said you'd help them."

"I swear it," said Bryand. His throat grew thick and his eyes moistened with tears. "They'll never want for a thing."

Cleave nodded, shut his eyes once more, and after a pause, said, "You know, most folks think executioner's don't have feelin's. But we do."

"Aye," said Bryand.

"Oh, well. I suppose every job's got its drawbacks." His face twisted with pain. "Best go now, my lord. Never know when they'll discover you've escaped."

"I owe you my life."

"You owe me nothin'. Just keep your promise. Now go."

His legs shaking, using the wall for support, Bryand

raised himself up and started down the tunnel.

"By the way," said Cleave.

The Prince turned to him.

"You are Bryand, aren't you?"

"Aye."

"That's good."

And he was silent.

Bryand lumbered along in the darkness. He came to a steep flight of stairs and halted.

"Oh, no," he said to himself with dismay. "I forgot about these."

He took a deep breath and began to climb, crawl actually, using his hands and feet. By the time he reached the top of the stairs his whole body trembled, and he collapsed upon the stone floor, gasping for air.

This was a stupid idea, he told himself, staring at the cobwebs along the ceiling. I'll never make it. Someday, they'll find my skeleton here and they'll say, "So that's what happened to Daron."

The mere mention of his brother's name *(even if it was in thought,)* sent anger surging through him. No! It can't end like this. I won't let it.

Get up! he demanded of himself. This is me talking, do you hear?! You are not going to die in a forgotten hallway. Now get up, I say!

He rolled onto his stomach. He drew one knee up and then the other. He clawed at the wall, his joints cracking and his muscles screaming in pain.

At last he was on his feet. "Very good," he said aloud. "Now walk." He staggered to the first stone door.

This must be the royal apartment. At least, I think it is.

He gazed down the passageway, thankful that it ran only a short distance and in a straight line. Had it not, with his sense of direction, he might have wound up lost in the bowels of the castle forever.

He pressed on, locating the next entrance. It was slightly ajar and a candlestick stood next to it.

This must be my room, he thought, and he pulled the door open. He peered inside.

The chamber was dark and abandoned. He knew it was his, though at the same time it looked unfamiliar. He had endured such harshness in the past few months that all things of comfort appeared strange.

It was then a thought struck him, and his heart picked up its pace. Perhaps my sword is still inside!

"Please be there," he muttered as he crawled through the empty fireplace. He stood upright, grabbing the mantle for support as he surveyed the room. Everything stood in the same way as it had on the night he was arrested, even the furniture remained overturned.

He noticed his wardrobe was open. Drawing closer, he saw it was empty. At first he was confused, but then he understood. Daron's desperate scheme to impersonate him meant taking everything; even his clothes.

This worried Bryand, and he looked about quickly. Perhaps Daron had confiscated his sword as well.

And then he saw it, leaning in a shadowy corner, and he felt like shouting for joy. At first he found it strange that his brother had left it behind. But then it occurred to him that, upon being crowned King, Daron had inherited their father's sword, which was a much greater prize.

He took hold of it, drew it from its scabbard, saw how the blade reflected the moonlight that spilled in from the balcony. He closed his eyes, marveling at how such a simple thing could restore his strength.

Barbaric, perhaps. But there it was. As enlightened as he believed himself to be, he was still a man of his times. And thanks to Daron, it was now time for revenge.

He sheathed the blade and buckled it around his waist. He felt confident now, formidable, though in his present condition a toddler could have bested him in a duel.

He reentered the secret passageway, slipped past the door to his brother's chamber, and proceeded to the end. There he stopped and stared at the door before him and then at the one on his right. Think, he told himself. Try to picture the lay of the castle. MeAnne's room was around the corner from yours, therefore-- .

Crouching, he gripped the stone in front of him. It moved quickly in his hands, and he peered around the edge. His heart leaped in his chest, for across the room, staring as if lost in thought, was MeAnne.

He had no idea what time it was, what day it was, or how long he had been a prisoner in the dungeon. But he did remember the last time he saw her, standing in the corridor with tears spilling down her cheeks, and he found it odd that she was crying now, too.

MeAnne wiped her tears away with the back of her hand. The conversation with her father continued to weigh heavily on her mind. So much so, that she had delayed her appearance at the feast. The things he had said-- . Were they true?

She thought of Bryand. He was always gentle with her. Though lately, she was forced to admit, he had become a bit insistent, pawing her heedlessly and clutching her to him so tightly that she could feel his manliness upon her. But she attributed this behavior to his mounting need and, therefore, could excuse it. After all, she had her own yearnings too.

But the way he treated others; with so little concern. It bothered her. No. It did more than that. It went against everything she had been brought up to believe.

She thought of her fathers words to her long ago. "You can tell much about a powerful man by the way he speaks to those who have no power. Always treat the people serving you with the greatest respect and you'll never wind up with spit in your soup."

Thinking of her father, made her heart ache. She had loved him all her life, yet now they seemed more like adversaries than anything else. It was obvious he did not like Bryand. He had made that all too clear to everyone including the King himself.

She covered her face with her hands. She felt torn, confused, and thoroughly wretched. What to do? she lamented, her heart about to break.

It was then she became aware of another presence in the room. Jona, she assumed, as she took a deep breath to steady herself. But then it occurred to her that Jona had already left for the banquet.

She turned, annoyed now that someone had entered her private chamber without her permission. The last thing she expected to see was some filthy peasant.

"Don't be afraid," he said, holding his hands out in front of him.

"Who are you?" she demanded. He did not respond. She was about to chastise the fellow harshly for his audacity when she noticed the sword at his side. It was Bryand's sword. She recognized it immediately from the markings on the scabbard and the anvil-shaped pummel. What was a peasant doing with Bryand's sword?

She pointed to it. "Where did you get that?" she demanded. "Did you steal it?"

"No, my lady," he said. "This sword is mine."

"Yours," she said scornfully. "That sword belongs to the King."

"Aye, it does."

He took a step closer, into better light, and it was then she saw his eyes. They were Bryand's eyes. But how could that be? He was downstairs right now celebrating in the banquet hall. And she knew for a fact it was not a costume party.

But those eyes. There was only one other person in the whole world and he was-- .

Suddenly she understood. Daron had somehow escaped, and upon that realization, a shudder ran through her. "I know who you are," she said, backing up.

"I doubt that, my lady."

MeAnne found herself against her dressing table. He took another step closer. She tried to scream. But his hand was over her mouth before she could utter a sound.

"I know I must be an awful sight. Please don't be afraid. I won't harm you; I swear it." He spoke slowly; sincerely. "All I ask is that you let me speak with you."

MeAnne searched his eyes, looking for some sign of treachery or malice. She found none. Still she did not trust him.

"Please," he said. "Just a few words."

Against her better judgement, she nodded her consent. He removed his hand.

"I don't know how you managed it, but you'll never make it out of the castle."

"I think I will."

"There's a feast going on. I'm late already. Any minute now someone will arrive to escort me down there."

"I won't detain you long. If what I tell you does not sway you on my behalf, then I will let you go and never trouble you again."

MeAnne studied his face, not quite ready to trust him. But he looked and sounded so much like Bryand, that she felt moved to at least give him the chance to speak. "Go on. What is it you wish to tell me?"

Bryand took a deep breath to help collect his thoughts. Where to start? he wondered. How do I put this without sounding like a madman.

"You will no doubt think this preposterous, perhaps even insane." He saw her eyes fill with misgiving. "But I speak the truth nevertheless," he added quickly. "You must believe me."

"Go on," said the Princess, watching him carefully.

"The man downstairs at the feast, the man you call your King and future husband, is neither. I am Bryand. I am your betrothed." He paused, looking for some kind of reaction. He did not have long to wait.

"You were right," said MeAnne, scowling. "What you say is preposterous and insane." She tried to get past him but found herself imprisoned by his arms.

"Let go of me!" she snarled in his face.

"Please. You must believe me. The night of the joust my brother rendered me unconscious, and when I awoke, he had stolen not only my name and my crown, but the one person I hold most dear in the world."

She would not listen. "How ludicrous! How totally absurd!" She pressed her hands against his chest and pushed with all her strength. "That you would think I'd even consider such a fiendish lie!"

"Please!" he said, trying not to hurt her and, at the same time, to keep her restrained. "I beg of you."

MeAnne persisted until she realized she was not going anywhere. Finally, she relaxed in his arms and frowned. "Why should I believe you?"

He did something then she did not expect. He let her go and took a step back.

"Because if you don't, you'll marry the wrong man. And that would break my heart. Down there, in the dungeon; not knowing if I would ever see the sunlight again; the one thing that kept me from complete despair was the thought of you. You gave me hope."

He clutched the pummel of his sword. "I swear to you on this anvil sigil; the crest of my father and the symbol of our land; though I have no proof; no witnesses; nothing but my word, which I give to you now in complete truth; I am Bryand; I am your betrothed."

She stood for a moment, sorting things out in her head. The man downstairs at the banquet had indeed been acting odd lately. It was as if he had suddenly developed something she could only describe as a dark side to his personality. And it was during these moments that she felt he was a different person altogether.

What if the man before her was telling the truth? What if he was indeed Bryand?

MeAnne searched his face. But no, his looks could deceive her. She knew of only one way to be completely sure.

"I'm not saying I believe you. Not yet, at any rate. Not until you tell me something that only Bryand would know."

"Test me," said Bryand eagerly. "And I will set your mind at rest."

MeAnne thought a moment, and then it occurred to her. "That night we shared in the garden months ago. What did you say to me?"

Bryand frowned. "What night in the garden? We were never in the garden."

He knew immediately he had said the wrong thing, for her face became a stony mask.

"You are not Bryand," said MeAnne in a tone dripping with contempt.

"Wait," replied the Prince, flustered. "My mind's been such a war lately. Perhaps we were in the garden, but I just don't remember. I know I gave you a smaller frame for your tapestry. Is that good enough?"

"Daron could know that easily," said the Princess

unmoved.

"You told me I had pleased you. You kissed me on the cheek."

"Daron could have learned that as well. The only time Bryand and I were truly alone was in the garden."

There was that garden business again. "MeAnne, I-- ."

Footsteps in the hallway. An officer's command.

"You'd best leave before I go back on my word and scream."

"So you won't come with me?"

She sucked in her breath, making ready to cry out.

"All right, all right! I'll go!" He took a step toward the fireplace and stopped. "But take heed, and I tell you this for your own safety. One day my brother will reveal to you his true nature, and then you will believe me. By the Gods, I hope it's not too late."

There came a knock on the door and a voice called from outside. "My lady? Are you in there?"

He looked at her, knowing he might never see her again. "I love you, MeAnne. I'll think of you wherever I go." And then, casting aside all the conventions upon which he had structured his life, he swept the girl into his arms and kissed her.

There came another knock. "My lady? Are you well disposed?"

The last thing he wanted was to tear his lips from hers, but he did so.

"I'll be back someday," he said, looking deep into her eyes. He hastened to the fireplace, where he stopped and tossed her one last look. "And hopefully not as your brother-in-law!"

"My lady?" said the officer. "May I come in?"

She watched as he closed the secret door behind him, the taste of his kiss lingering on her lips. And then, struck by a sudden sense of urgency, she opened her chamber door and said to the officer standing there, "No need, good sir. I am coming."

He hastened down the passageway, falling twice. By the time he reached the stairwell he was shaking with fatigue.

He slid down the stairs on his stomach, crumpling into a heap at the bottom landing. He rested a moment. Then with a grunt, he gripped the wall, climbed to his feet, and started down the tunnel.

At length, he came upon the executioner. Cleave had rolled onto his side. His head lay upon his arm, and with his eyes closed, he looked like he was asleep.

"Goodbye," whispered Bryand sorrowfully. "The cost of this reckoning is already too dear."

Then, with quiet resolve, he crawled between the branches and made his way through the darkness until he was back with Cower and the others.

"Where's me dad?" asked Noim, frowning.

Bryand looked at him. "He's-- ."

The Prince looked at Malady, but it was plain she already knew the truth. So for the boy's sake, he said, "He's staying behind to protect our escape."

Noim's eyes grew wide with fear. "But he's just one man. He'll be-- . He'll be-- ." He could not say anything more, and bringing his knees up to his chest, he folded his arms over his head to hide his tears from the others.

Bryand climbed into the wagon. Cower, who felt quite desolate himself, slapped the reins on the horse's rump and they were off in the direction of the southern road.

"Hey, mum, did ya know Dad's a hero?" asked the little one, too young yet to grasp what his older brother already understood.

"Did ya know that, Mum?" He waited for her to answer. "Mum? Has your hearin' gone off again? I said Dad's a hero!"

"She heard you, lad," said Bryand gently. "And, aye, he surely is."

CHAPTER ELEVEN

It has been said that twins have a special link between them. One that is impossible for anyone else to perceive or completely understand. That being true, Daron might have felt some vague uneasiness while his brother was escaping or, at the very least, an annoying itch that would not go away. Yet he did not. As far as he knew, Bryand was locked in the dungeon forever, Cower had been beheaded, and there was no one left who could possibly expose him. So he was having a wonderful time at the feast, lavishing himself and his guests with food, wine and entertainment.

The only damper on the evening was MeAnne's queer absence. But even that was remedied when she appeared wearing a kirtle that clung to her in the most provocative places. So delighted was Daron to see her that he did not notice the troubled look upon her face as she rounded the dais and took her place beside him.

"Welcome, my lady," said the King with a flourish. "You look positively radiant tonight."

"Your pardon, Sire, for my tardiness, but-- . "

"No need, no need. Though you just missed a splendid food fight." He stood and raised his goblet and the hall fell silent.

"I drink to the Lady MeAnne. The beautiful Lady MeAnne. I count myself a lucky man simply being in her presence."

The court cheered his eloquence.

"And, in truth, I count myself luckier still that she

is my intended." More cheers and applause as Daron drained his goblet, sat down, a bit heavily, and leaned close to MeAnne. "Does that please you, my lady?"

"Aye, my lord," said the princess. "It pleases me very much."

He grinned and leaned closer. "That is our sincerest wish. To please you very much."

"Sire, there is something important I must tell you."

"And I, you," said Daron.

"My lord -- ."

"Wait," said Daron, squeezing her hand. The wine had finally reached his head, he could feel it; feel the sluggishness of his eyes and the thickening of his tongue. It was, perhaps, the first time in his life he regretted drinking too much. "I swear, my lady, I have never felt this way before."

MeAnne smiled endearingly. "Nor I, my dearest."

"No, really. I have never felt this way before. Is it hot in here?"

"A bit, my lord."

"I thought so. You truly care for me, don't you?"

"With all my heart."

"Yes. I can see it in your eye. I mean eyes. And I can see it in your face. I wish the room would stop spinning." Sobering, or trying to sober, he shook his head and took a deep breath. "You know, of course, you are the only one who could change me. "

"Change you, sire?"

"Change my ways."

"How so, my lord?" she asked.

"Before I met you, I was-- ."

He paused. He realized he had spoken carelessly.

"That was stupid," he remarked. When he saw the frown appear on MeAnne's face, he added, "did I just say that out loud?"

"Yes, sire."

"Not *that* was stupid; *I*, *I* was stupid. For not realizing just how much you meant to me from the first moment we met. I will chide myself forever for my stupidity. I will be penitent and contrite and make sacrifices to the gods twice a day until you forgive me for my foolishness."

"My dearest, you are already forgiven."

She bought it, thought Daron. "No, no," he said, aware now of the tightness in his throat. "I shall be grateful to you all the days of my life and I will devote myself to your happiness."

He paused to clear his throat, which silenced the hall immediately. "Anyone else think the air's a bit dry in here tonight?"

He was answered by a round of ayes. A few eager subjects rushed to the dais and offered him their snuff boxes or inhalers, which he politely refused.

"And now, my dear," he said, scooping up his goblet, "you must help me toast our guests of honor, for they have been most diligent collecting the new tax. My lords and ladies, join me, please, in toasting the Duke of Cunninghim and the Earl of Nightshade." He presented his cup to each of them. "Now, now, my lords, don't look so shocked. You are most deserving of this tribute."

Cunninghim smiled wanly, as did Nightshade. Neither one could believe the King was still upon his feet, for he had consumed three servings of wine from a poison-swabbed goblet and appeared only slightly inebriated instead of stone cold dead.

"To the Duke of Cunninghim and the Earl of Nightshade," Daron proclaimed. "May they continue to serve the crown well."

Distracted, MeAnne raised her cup and sipped. Even so, she was thinking of what the king had just disclosed to her. If she had not, only moments before, been confronted by his brother and forced to listen to his outlandish tale, the king's remark might have been dismissed as a less than sober comment at a less than sober moment. But to come so closely upon the heels of what she had learned-- .

Stop, she told herself. You make too much of it. Tis purely a coincidence. You saw his wound. You helped nurse him back to health. That smelly fellow in your apartment tonight was Daron. And with Daron at large, she decided, the king's life was in danger.

"My lord," she said, turning to him. "I really must speak with you."

"Ah, yes," Daron was saying in response to something she had not heard. "The new tax. How generous of the people to respond so quickly. We shall soon decide how best to distribute it." And as a way of punctuating his statement, he presented Cunninghim and Nightshade with a sly grin.

MeAnne saw that grin, it startled her, but more importantly, it planted even more doubt in her mind. Had the smelly fellow really been telling the truth? After all, he could have abducted me, she thought, and used me as a means to take revenge upon his brother. Yet he did not. And the way he took me in his arms-- . There was truly a gentleness about his touch. And his eyes-- .

"Now, my dear, what was it you wanted to tell me?" asked Daron as he sat down.

She looked into his eyes. Though they were the same as the man who had confronted her, there was something chilling about them now. Once again her intuition cautioned her. "Oh, nothing, really." She looked away, pretending to be embarrassed. "Just that I've made excellent progress on my tapestry."

"Hang the thing," he said, and he chuckled at his own jest. Then, with a slight edge to his voice, he added, "We'd be married by now were it not for that."

"Be patient, my lord. It is almost complete. Very soon now we'll be together."

For Daron, that was satisfying enough. He faced the hall, full of what he thought was complete triumph, and slapped his hand upon the dais. "It is time for some merriment! Where is the new jester, what's his name?"

"Feebus, my lord," said Cunninghim, pointing toward the back of the hall. He was not in the best of moods. Trust Nightshade to bungle things again. Now the tax would have to be handed over.

"Come jester Feebus! Perform for us!"

A mousy little man dressed in an ill fitting but brightly colored jester's costume sat upon the floor at the back of the hall, wrestling with a royal hound that was bent upon stealing his supper. Hearing his name, the jester looked up, giving the hound the opportunity to snatch the mutton chop from his hand and scurry off.

Aye, Feebus, came shouts from the crowd. Perform for us! Make us merry!

The jester gazed about the room, his heart pounding. Here he was, so young and already playing the Palace! Surely he would never get another chance like it; a success tonight could catapult his career. But was he ready?

Listen to them, Feebus, he told himself. They want you; they're clamoring for you. Now get out there and knock them dead!

He rose and marched to the center of the room, bowed to the King, and acknowledged the rest of the court.

"Thank you, thank you. It's an honor to be here tonight. I see we've got some folks from Lyre. Nice folks but you can't believe a word they say. And there's King Odius - why does everyone dislike you, Sire? And there's the Duke of Cunninghim. Hiya, Duke. You know, the Duke is so generous, I once saw him spare ten peasants.

Of course, if he hadn't thrown a gutter ball on his first try, he would've had a strike." The hall was silent. "Get it? Strike? As in lawn bowling?" A few people chuckled. "Thank you, you have good taste. I see the Princess MeAnne has arrived. You know, when they asked her if she had a hard time choosing between Daron and Bryand she said, 'not really. They both looked about the same to me!'"

When Feebus first started toward the dais, the hall had exploded with applause and cheers. Certainly, no one had paid much attention to Mortamour's arrival, which was always fine with him. Skirting the hall, he approached the dais. Though his face revealed nothing, Cunninghim knew something was wrong by the quickness of his gate. He whispered in the Duke's ear. Cunninghim frowned, shot him an angry look, and dismissed him.

"What is it?" asked Nightshade, but Cunninghim did not answer him. Instead, he turned to the King and, in a guarded voice, said, "Bad news, your majesty."

Daron looked at him, oblivious, smiling. "No! There will be no bad news tonight. You will keep it for the morrow!"

"Your brother has escaped."

It took a moment, but then the king's smile collapsed. "What!?"

Feebus, the jester, thinking the king had addressed him, said, "they both looked about the same to me! Get it? Because you're twins!"

"I want him taken and hanged!" cried Daron, his face crimson.

Thinking the King had referred to the jester, twenty soldiers and knights converged upon Feebus and wrestled him to the floor. "It was just a joke!" he screamed, panic-stricken.

"Not him!" shouted Daron. "My brother! The Prince

has escaped!" The King turned to Cunninghim with a murderous countenance. "Dispatch the royal spies and psycophants. Alert the local garrisons. Do whatever is necessary but I want him found."

"Aye, my lord," said Cunninghim, standing.

"And Cunninghim," said Daron, his eyes narrowing. "Fail at this, and I will not be so well-disposed toward you and Nightshade."

"He'll be dangling within the hour, sire," said Cunninghim.

As the advisors retreated, Daron called to a nearby captain. "You there." The guard snapped to attention. "Find me the executioner. I want whoever is responsible for this taken directly to the block! And call out the guard!"

"They are very drunk, your grace."

"What?!"

"From the ale and spirits your majesty provided."

It did not matter that it was his doing. Daron pounded his fist so hard that the cutlery and goblets around him lifted off the table and landed with a clatter. "Get them on their feet straight away! Do hear?!"

"Yes, your grace," said the officer, shaken.

"I want every castle gate and portal fully manned! I want all carts and wagons searched before leaving the city! And if I learn that my brother has escaped, there will be a hanging party for the entire guard. Do you understand my meaning?!"

"Yes, your majesty," said the guard. "Thank you, your majesty."

And he hurried out of the hall like a frightened dog with its tail between its legs.

MeAnne shrank in her seat, shocked at the King's fury; cringing at the accusations he spewed. There was nothing more she needed to know; nothing more she needed to see. A voice shouted inside her head. You are not my betrothed! You are not my Bryand!

She waited for the right moment, and without so much as a 'by your leave' she left the dais and made her way to the opposite side of the hall. She paused by the doors to see if he had noticed. But he was busy raving at several guards whom he had cornered.

She raced from one corridor to the next, skirting ladies in waiting and gentlemen of the court who were trying very discretely to disappear. Patrols roamed everywhere. Guards pounded on every door. The manhunt for Daron had begun.

She reached her apartment and slammed the door shut behind her. Wasting not a moment, she went directly to the exact spot where he had kissed her. It was also where she had turned him away. Sadness welled inside her. There could not be a more desolate place in all the world and a more pitiful person.

If only she had trusted him, they would be together now. "Why was I so foolish," she implored the heavens. She fell upon her bed and began to weep. No hope, she thought, no future save for marriage to a madman. That was what her father had called him, too.

"Father!" she said aloud, sitting upright. "Father will put things aright!"

She called Jona's name. But the girl did not answer-.When MeAnne went to her room and saw Jona's wardrobe empty, she remembered the girl was with her sister and parents and had already left the palace.

Fear took root inside her. If she allowed it to spred, she would soon be paralyzed by it.

But that was not going to happen. She refused to succumb to it. She was a Jasper; a warrior in heart and spirit. Her father was a king and her mother an ancestor of the ancient Citipati tribe, who, it was said, claimed the skys. Though she knew not what that meant specifically it still inspired her.

It's up to you, she told herself. No one else can help you now. She understood the urgency of the situation and the need to act quickly. She marched to her wardrobe and grabbed a pair of riding pants and a soft woolen shirt.

No, not that one, she thought. I don't like the neckline.

"What are you doing?!" she said aloud, chiding herself. Choose anything! Just get dressed!

When she had changed completely, she donned a pair of riding boots and threw a hooded cape over her shoulders.

Her mind had been working rapidly. She would steal a horse, ride as fast as she could and overtake her father's train on the road. Together they would make for home and raise an army, oust the impostor from the throne and hold it for Bryand no matter how long it took till he had been found.

She thought of him once more and of the way he had taken her into his arms. Oh, my dearest love, what you must think of me?!

But she would not forsake him a second time. He would know the extent of her love when he was safe again and restored to power.

She strode boldly across the chamber and pulled open the door. But standing before her, his hand ready to knock, was the King.

Startled, MeAnne fell back a step.

"My lady," said Daron, taking in her attire. "I did not see you leave the feast."

"I was not feeling well, my lord," replied the Princess awkwardly.

"I see." He chuckled. "Yet you feel fit enough to take some air. How is that?"

"I thought a stroll in the garden might help. The night air, so I'm told, has many restorative properties."

She hoped she had sounded convincing.

"Truly," the king agreed. He entered the room, his presence alone pushing her back. "And if this were a normal night, I would love to join you. But with my brother at large, it is not safe outside the keep. I think it better that we stay here."

"Here, my lord? In my private chamber?"

"It seems the safest place to me." He strolled past her, admiring the way she had made the room her own - the lace, the ribbons, the glass beads. "What is that?" he asked, intrigued as he pointed to a lantern on the fireplace mantle.

"Just something I picked up at the farmers' market," she answered. "A new type of lamp."

He examined it more closely. "What's this floating in the oil chamber?"

"I'm not certain, your grace, but the merchant called it lava."

"What makes the little globbish things go up and down like that?"

"I believe the heat from the lamp, your grace."

"The heat," he repeated to himself. "How ingenious." He glanced at the fireplace. "And speaking of heat, I'm surprised you have no fire going. There's a definite chill in the air."

"I am alone here, my lord. Jona, my handmaiden, left with my father and his train this evening."

"I see," said the king. Blast Jasper, he thought. I hope he catches his death upon the road. "Would you like me to do it?"

"Sire, you needn't go to the trouble -- . "

Kindling was already in his hands. "It's no trouble at all, my dearest."

It was then a breeze lifted some ashes from the grate, and he watched as they came to rest on his boots. Something about the swiftness of the breeze aroused his curiosity. He leaned down, and, at the back of the hearth, he saw the door to the secret passage was ajar. There was no direct link from the dungeon to the passage but he knew immediately Bryand had used it to mount his escape.

Daron dropped the kindling and faced MeAnne. "You wanted to say something earlier, but I selfishly insisted on speaking first. Please, my dear, tell me now. What was it you wished to say?"

"But I told you," she replied, a bit too insistently, watching Daron cross the room toward her loom. "I am almost done with -- ."

"Your tapestry?" said the king graciously, turning it gently in her direction. "It's quite lovely. But we obviously differ on what is nearly complete and what is not."

"I suppose I exaggerated a bit. I am so eager to have it done."

Ignoring her remark, he said, "Daron, was in here tonight. Wasn't he?"

"Here, my lord? Your brother? That is not possible."

"But it is, my dear. Quite possible. And I wonder why you decided not to tell me. Did he threaten you?

"Your brother would not harm me."

"And how do you know that?"

"Because he, at least, is an honorable man." It was indiscreet, yet she could not stop herself.

Her tone of voice pulled him up short. "Is that so?" said Daron, and from the steely look she gave him, he knew she had seen through his deception.

What to do? he thought. He truly did not know. Yearning for her as he did, he wanted to risk everything; admit everything. "Shall we move on with the conversation or shall I say out loud that which you suspect and I already know."

"No," she said with disdain. "I do not want to hear your name."

Her words all but crushed his hopes. "Does it matter so much to you that I am not really Bryand? Could you not be satisfied with someone who is every bit the same?"

"You are nothing like him at all," she sneered. "He's kind; he's gentle."

"He's a bore."

"He is worthy of being King. It is his rightful place."

For the first time in his life he spoke what was truly in his heart. "I could be all that and more. As I was about to say earlier, with your love I could be transformed."

"Never."

"There is so much we could do together."

"I say again; never."

"Do you think if you slept on it, you might change your mind?"

"Never, never, never, never!"

Sadness filled his heart. His throat - which was still very tight and scratchy - felt like he had swallowed a pomegranate whole. "I'm sorry you feel as strongly as you do, my dear. I could have given you great pleasure." In response to this, she stiffened, and he was filled with even greater sorrow. "But I can see now that it was never meant to be."

Yet there was more at stake here than just the love of a woman. He was King now, and he would never allow anyone to jeopardize that, not even MeAnne. "You've put me in a very awkward position. My feelings for you remain unchanged even now, yet I cannot have you going about convincing people of what you know."

"You would not dare to harm me. Only the King has the right to order my execution."

"You forget, my dear. To everyone else I am the King." He paused to allow his statement to have its full effect. "But fear not," said Daron, starting toward the door. "I have no desire to harm you." He stopped and looked back at her. "Even now, after suffering your rejection, I could not bear to think of you rotting in the dungeon."

MeAnne shivered. All those bugs!

"Still, I cannot risk having you at large. That wouldn't work at all. Therefore, you'll have to take an extended holiday with my mother while I think of what to do with you."

"To Tapwater?" said MeAnne, her mind already at work.

"Oh, no, no. I made that up. Mother never really left the castle. After she found me out I had to lock her in the north tower. You two should get along splendidly."

Cunninghim paced back and forth, while Nightshade sat at his worktable, going over the list of ingredients and their proportions for his latest lethal brew. "I don't understand it," he said finally, scratching his head. "I've mixed this twice now. It should have worked."

"Well, it didn't!" exploded Cunninghim, whirling on the man. "And thanks to your bungling, the taxes we collected are in the King's possession." He began to pace once more. "Oh, the men and arms I could have bought with that money!"

"I tell you, I didn't bungle the poison."

"Oh, stop it! Please! The man's alive. Or haven't you noticed?!"

"But he shouldn't be!"

"Achhhhh!" said the Duke with a wave of his hand. He was so furious that he could not find words to express it.

Nightshade usually acquiesced at times like this,

mostly to avoid being beaten. But he was so convinced he had done everything right that, with a deliberate stride, he crossed to his chamber door, opened it, and called to the man outside. "You there!"

"Aye, my lord," replied the man, snapping to attention.

"The new servant, right?"

"Yes, my lord."

"What's your name?"

"Salvardumi, my lord."

"Uh, fine. You've arrived just in time. Come in here."

The servant dropped his belongings, which were still bundled into a pack, then entered the Earl's private chamber.

"What are you doing?!" fumed Cunninghim.

"You'll see," rejoined Nightshade undaunted. "This is my new servant Salva... Salvar..."

"Salvardumi," supplied the man with a weak smile.

"Right. Meet the Duke of Cunninghim and his squire, Mortamour." Salvardumi greeted them humbly as the Earl dragged him to his worktable. There, Nightshade swabbed the rim of a goblet with a clear mixture, then filled the goblet with some wine. "Now sit you down and drink this." Salvardumi looked at the cup curiously. "Go on man," prompted the Earl. "Drink up."

"Thank you, my lord," said the servant, and he quaffed the brew.

Nightshade took the empty cup from him. "Now tell me a little bit about yourself."

"Like what, my lord?"

"Well, where do you come from? Do you have a family and if so, is there one person in particular I should contact in the event of your death?"

"Let's see now," said the man, finding nothing strange about the Earl's question. "I was born in Cumberland, in the county of Bentknee. My parents have passed on, but I have a sister who lives there still. Her name is Salvardimi. I suppose you could contact her. But better send a messanger 'cause she can't read. Not a word. Anyway, I arrived at the capital only this morning and went straight to the Groom's Guild. Who'd've thought there'd be an opening in the castle of all places, and for a manservant like -- ."

He said nothing more, probably because his throat took that moment to swell shut. And as he gasped for air, the Earl calmly led him to the door. "Thank you for coming. You don't happen to know if they took the notice down at the Groom's Guild?"

To that, Salvardumi shrugged.

"No matter if they have, I can always place another. Goodbye, Salva... Salva..."

"Salvardumi," supplied Mortamour with a wicked smile.

"That's right," said Nightshade, closing the door in Salvardumi's face.

Nightshade turned back to his cronies. "Three, two, one," whereupon there came a thud. Nightshade opened the door once more and there at the threshold, sprawled upon the floor, was the new servant, his eyes wide, mouth open, and altogether dead. Nightshade turned to the Duke with a smug grin. "I rest my case."

"That proves nothing," sneered Cunninghim. "So you mixed the batch right this time. I still say you bungled something."

"I followed that very recipe; down to the last grain," insisted Nightshade.

"Then why is the King not dead?!"

"I don't know. Perhaps he's immune to poison."

"Oh, don't be ridiculous," Cunninghim scoffed. He began to pace, muttering to himself. "Immune to poison; of all the lame excuses." He snorted contemptuously and shook his head. "How could the King be immune to poison?"

His feelings still bruised, Nightshade frowned and said with an edge, "Perhaps he had an antidote."

Cunninghim turned to him. "What do you mean an antidote!" It was not a question. "You mean like the one you gave -- ?"

Cunninghim fell silent suddenly.

Nightshade could see the Duke's mind at work. On what, though, he could not tell.

Mortamour smiled knowingly. "Of course!"

Nightshade shot him a quizzical look. "Of course what?"

Before Mortamour could say a word, Cunninghim burst out laughing. "Of course!! Why didn't I see it right off!"

Mortamour joined in with the Duke, laughing heartily. Nightshade gave them both a quizzical look, then, not wanting to be the odd man out, he began to laugh as well, though he had no idea why. "What? What didn't you see?"

"The King! The King!"

"You didn't see the King?"

Cunninghim went to Nightshade, who flinched, expecting to be struck. "I apologize," said the Duke with a short bow. "You were right. The poison was mixed correctly and it would have worked if the King were truly the King."

Nightshade smiled, though confused. "Isn't he?"

"Aye, he's the King all right. But he's not Bryand. He's Daron. And you yourself handed him the antidote that would make him immune to all your poisons."

"I did? I mean, I did."

Cunninghim turned away, elated for the moment, a schemer recognizing the brilliant work of another schemer. "Oh, the cleverness of it. And so simply achieved! Somehow he managed to take his brother's place. Probably just after the tournament." The thought made him chuckle out loud, something Cunninghim never did. "The way he courted us and took us into his confidence. I should have known Bryand would never have done that."

"So," said Nightshade, trying very hard to understand. "If that's Daron on the throne, then where's his brother?"

"On the run, of course," Mortamour answered with his usual sneer. "It was Bryand who escaped."

Cunninghim, feeling most pleased with himself, added simply, "that's why the King reacted so violently tonight when he learned of it. Do you think he wants his brother at large, convincing people he's the rightful heir?"

"But how does that effect us?" asked Nightshade, confused almost as much by Cunninghim's uncustomarily good mood as by the situation.

"Has not the King charged us with hunting him down?" said the Duke, spreading his arms wide. "We must do our very best then, mustn't we? We must arrest Prince Daron and anyone who helps him in his flight." He sobered abruptly and turned to Mortamour "Take as many men as you want. I'd suggest at least a company, that way you can take care of a few things along the way."

"Like what?"

Cunninghim strolled to the worktable, picked up a pestle, and played with it in his hands. "King Jasper has left for Jasperland. You must see to it that Bryand never catches up to him. He would be much too strong an ally should the Prince convince him of the truth."

"And how is he to accomplish that?" asked Nightshade.

"The trip from here to Jasperland is long and hard. Something could very easily happen to Jasper and his train along the way. There are many thieves about. I've even had reports of Woolly-Bullies raiding in the area."

"The mad clansmen?!" said Nightshade, aghast. "How horrible!"

Cunninghim shot him a withering look. "Not really, you fool. I just made it up."

"Ohhhh," replied Nightshade, relieved. "I see."

Cunninghim sighed and rubbed his temple. Suddenly he felt very fatigued. "Do you? Do you really?"

Nightshade knew there was no use in lying, the Duke could see right through him. "No," he said, embarrassed. "I'm afraid I still don't."

Thoroughly exasperated now, the Duke gestured for Mortamour to explain.

"Look. It's really quite simple," said the henchman slowly, deliberately, almost as if he were speaking to a child instead of a grown man. "We kill King Jasper and we make it look like he was attacked by Woolly-Bullies. That way, no one will think we did it. Understand now?"

"Aye," said Nightshade with a grateful smile.

Cunninghim led Mortamour to the door. "The King will want to know what measures I've taken to capture his brother. Leave just as soon as you can muster the troops. I'd wager Daron has already chewed his nails to the quick." They stepped over Salvardumi's body. "Once you've taken care of Jasper I want that tracker's nose of yours to the ground and sniffing out the Prince's trail. You can trust him to head straight for his friends unless, of course, we can get to them first. Make sure that you do, and see to it that the Masters of Willowbrook, Pepperill and Torkelstone, are in no condition to help him, either."

"Do I leave them breathing or not?"

"What do you think?"

Mortamour had his answer. "More Woolly-Bullies,

I suppose."

Cunninghim grinned. Such a pleasure, he thought, not having to explain things to at least one of his associates.

CHAPTER TWELVE

By dawn the next morning, Bryand and his companions found themselves well away from the capital. The fields and woods about them blazed with color and were fragrant with the odors of pinenut trees, wildflowers, and meadow grass.

A good meal consisting of boiled potatoes and salted venison and a halfway-decent night's sleep had done much to revitalize the Prince. His mind was clear now and his thoughts were focused, and he had already formed a plan of action.

Though he knew not how to get there, he intended to make for the small province of Willowbrook, where he hoped to find Niles alive.

From Willowbrook, he and Niles would link up with Dwayne at Pepperill, then move on to Torkelstone to locate Dillin. He would raise an army with the support of his three friends, rally the people against his brother, and take back what was rightfully his.

It was a good plan, perhaps a little sketchy, but with luck it could still succeed. Everything hinged upon whether or not Daron was telling the truth the day he visited him in the dungeon.

He thought of his friends. He feared for them. He knew now, his brother was capable of anything. Even murder.

About mid-day they came upon a peddler in the road, who, responding to their inquiry, told them they were indeed heading toward Willowbrook.

This surprised the Prince almost as much as it pleased him. He knew it had been chance alone that had guided them thus far.

Perhaps, he thought, the Gods will see us all the way to Nile's front door. Even Omnibus might decide to help, though I have never been in His favor. (*Omnibus: The God of travelers and wanderers. Also, supervisor of the Heavens' maintenance pool.*)

Using a few copper pieces from Cleave's savings, which Malady carefully noted, Cower purchased a new set of clothes for the Prince. Actually, they were not new. Actually, they were the clothes the peddler was wearing. But he did not mind, for he had charged the retainer thrice what they were worth when he had purchased them from their original owner.

Bryand donned them quickly, tossed the man his old shirt and leggings, and bid him good day. However, not more than half an hour later, he was wishing his new clothes had not been so well inhabited. By this he was referring not to the peddler, but to the peddler's fleas.

As the hours passed, the boys grew more and more curious about their fellow passengers and wanted to know why they had been dragged from their beds and spirited from the city.

"Where're we goin'?" asked Noim, eyeing Bryand coldly. There was no doubt that he blamed the Prince for his father's death.

"I told ya," said Malady, impatient with the boy. "Ta the country where we're gonna live."

"When're we gonna get there?" whined Donoim.

"Soon. Now be good lads n' shut yer traps. Mum's got an awful headache."

"Hey, mum," said Noim, observing the Prince. "Who is this guy, anyway?"

"I told ya already, didn't I? He's a friend o' yer dad's."

"Is that right. So how come I never seen 'im b'fore?"

"He's a very new friend." And turning to the Prince, she said, "I'm sorry 'bout this, m'lord."

"There ya go with that m'lord stuff again!" said Noim in an angry tone. "He ain't yer lord. Only Dad is. Or was. Were you boffin' this guy b'hind dad's back!?"

Seething, Malady cocked her arm and punched Noim in the face, sending him sprawling to the wagon floor. Donoim looked on, stunned.

"Ya want some o' the same?" growled Malady. The little one shook his head, no. "Then not a word out o' ya. You kids'll bring on one o' my seizures in a minute."

She found Bryand staring at her, his mouth open. "Gotta puts 'em in their place every now an' then," said the woman, rubbing her knuckles. "Don't want 'em turnin' out ta be brats."

Two days of hard riding brought them to the edge of a forest. Bryand could no longer tell if they were heading toward Willowbrook. They had come upon too many unmarked forks in the road where he could do naught but guess which way to take.

They were tired and hungry, their nerves were shot, and if the boys complained one more time, the Prince thought he would throw them into the road and run them over with the wagon.

And if he heard another word from their mother about the sorry state of her health-- ! Chivalry be hanged, he was going to put her out of her misery.

According to her, she had contracted every illness known, plus some the town physician could not diagnose. It was a wonder she was still alive.

From the way her eyes would roll up into her head and she would slump against him, he was sure she had died three times upon the journey thus far. And those convulsions! No normal human being could withstand such punishment!

The sun was overhead when they came to a river (*The Rapid River to be precise, though it had been anything but for decades.*) Here Cower turned the horse off the road and brought the wagon to a halt on the grassy bank. "I think we should rest for awhile," said the retainer, climbing down from the seat.

As Bryand was dragging himself over the sidewall, the boys leaped to the ground and ran to the water's edge. They stared at it with wonder on their faces. This was the first time they had seen a real river.

Every now and then they had waded into the main sewer channel by the city wall, but it was only a few inches deep and not at all the same color as the water before them.

"Careful there!" shouted Malady. They ignored her and waded further out. "You heed yer Mother or I'll box yer ears!"

Then, in a dainty voice she said, "Would his lordship be so kind as ta help me down? I'm afraid my legs have gone ta sleep."

The Prince sighed heavily and climbed aboard once more. He lifted her by the armpits.

"You have to help," he said to the woman.

"I can't," she replied. "Me legs are numb."

He struggled. "Just lift them a little."

"Sorry, m'lord. Once they're like this, there ain't nothin' I can do with 'em."

Eventually, he managed to hang her over the side of the wagon. Cower guided her feet to the ground. She rested against the retainer while Bryand climbed down, and together, they carried her to the bank and left her lying in the sun.

"Thank you," said Malady with a grateful smile. "I'm sure the blood'll work its way back into 'em now that they're straight."

"I'm sure," said the Prince with a wan smile.

"I should walk the horse," said Cower, starting for the animal.

"No, let me," insisted Bryand, leaving the woman rubbing her legs vigorously.

"But, my lord-- ."

Bryand looked at Malady and then at the boys. "Please. I've got to do something or I think I'll go mad."

The Prince unhitched the horse, walked it about for a few minutes then led it to the river to drink. Fighting sleep, he splashed some water on his face and watched the boys play. "Don't go out too far."

Donoim gave him a haughty look. "Says you!"

"Aye," added Noim in a spiteful tone. "You ain't me dad. So don't tell me what ta do."

He belched in Bryand's direction, which made the little one laugh, then he slapped the water calling, "Help, help, I can't swim."

Bryand glanced at Malady but she had fallen asleep. Nice boys, he thought, turning back to them. I wonder if the river is swift enough to carry them off?

When the horse had quenched its thirst, he led it up the bank and tethered it to a tree. He found a trunk for himself and sat with his back against it.

The breeze was cool on his face. Soon his eyes felt

heavy. Can't sleep, he told himself. Too far to go yet. Too dangerous.

By now, the sound of the boys frolicking in the water - their laughter; their vile curses - seemed very far away. A blanket of silence descended upon the forest. Slowly, his head drooped until his chin was resting on his chest. A moment later, he was asleep.

The horse's neigh startled him awake, and he rose stiffly to his feet. The sky was a purple hue over head, and deep crimson through a break in the trees where the sun had dipped below the horizon.

Confused, he turned to the wagon. He found Malady and the boys huddled by it.

"Why didn't you wake me," asked the Prince, annoyed.

"I didn't want ta disturb ya, m'lord. You was so weary. An' b'sides, it just started."

The Prince knitted his brow. "What's just started?"

A howl, long and loud, echoed in the woods in answer to his question and was joined by a chorus of the same. The horse neighed and stomped its hooves upon the ground and tugged at the rein tied about the tree.

Bryand frowned and scanned the trees around him. Then he ran to Cower and shook him vigorously. "Wake up. We're in trouble."

The retainer alerted instantly. "What is it?"

The Prince kept his eyes trained upon the woods. "Wolves."

Hearing this, Malady's face went more ashen than usual, and she began to gag and wheeze. Bryand started for her, thinking she had swallowed something and was choking on it.

But before he could reach her, Noim stood in his

way. He gave Bryand a stoney look, then, with a casualness that surprised the Prince, whacked his mother a few times upon the back and remedied the situation.

"What're we gonna do?" she blurted in a phlegmy voice.

For one horrible moment Bryand did not know what to do. He surveyed the area. "The tree branches are too high to reach, so climbing's out. And the river's no answer, either. Wolves can swim."

The howls came again, louder still. The horse shied and neighed in terror.

At a time like this most parents would keep their wits about them for the sake of their children. But not Malady.

She grabbed the boys and pinned them to her, screeching, "We're all gonna die! We're all gonna die!"

"We're not going to die!" snapped Bryand, resisting the urge to slap her. He scanned the area once again and his eyes fell upon the wagon.

When Cower had driven it off the road, he had not taken into acount the angle of the bank, and because of this, the wagon leaned sharply to one side.

"Come on," said the Prince, already on the run. "Help me push the wagon over."

The others joined him at the sidewall save for Noim, who stood his ground and folded his arms before him.

"What's that gonna do?" queried the boy antagonistically.

"Save your life," replied the Prince, straining against the wagon's weight. "Or would you rather stand there and be ripped apart by the wolves?"

Noim needed no further explanation and, wearing a sullen expression, hurried to the wagon.

"All right now-- ," said Bryand, pressing all his weight against the sidewall. "Heave! Come on; put your backs into it! Heave!" The wagon creaked, listed, and fell onto its side. "Again!"

There came a rustling sound in the bushes. Barks and growls quickly followed.

"Hurry!"

They gave the wagon one more push and it toppled belly up, creating a crate-like shelter with the ground. "Quickly, lads, crawl in," said the Prince as he unsheathed his sword.

"Looky at that knife!" said Donoim, awed.

"Get in there!" shrieked Malady, pushing the little one in ahead of her.

"Now you, Noim, and you, Cower. And plug those gaps on the side."

The retainer complied.

The horse screamed. In his haste Bryand had forgotten to untie it.

He started toward the animal, sword poised and ready to sever the rein. But he had not taken two strides before the wolves broke from the forest.

Too late, he thought, and he dove for the wagon. He scrambled inside, and had barely gotten a sack behind him when a pair of dripping jaws snapped at his fingers.

What happened next was a tumult of vicious growls and pounding sounds upon the ceiling above them; bared fangs chewing on wood planking; snouts poking through small gaps; and - louder than all the rest and heightening their terror - the screams of the beleaguered horse.

Given their cramped quarters, Bryand had not much room to use his sword. Despite the limitations, each time the light between the slats above him dimmed, he thrust the blade through, and in this way fended off at least one of their attackers.

Yelps. Growls. Gurgles. The sound of Noim whacking his mother's back and shouting "Breathe, mum, breathe!"

The attack broke off as quickly as it started. They sat perfectly still, sweat dripping down their faces, waiting for it to resume. But a second attack never came.

The wolves were still present, for they could hear them panting, sniffing. And then there was the sound of something heavy being dragged through the underbrush.

The sound continued for some time, growing fainter and fainter until all was silent. Though Bryand said nothing, he knew the horse was dead.

"They've gone," sighed the Prince. "Everyone all right?"

"Aye," chirped Donoim. He started to giggle. "Though, I think me mum peed on herself."

"Did not," replied the woman, cuffing him across the back of his head.

Bryand pulled the sack away and crawled out from beneath the wagon. He and Cower dragged Malady into the fresh air and leaned her against the sidewall. Noim and Donoim followed and eyed the carnage about them with boyish zeal.

One wolf lay dead upon the belly of the wagon, stabbed through the heart. Back by the treeline three more littered the ground, their heads crushed from the horse's hooves.

Bryand approached the tree where the horse had been tethered and, with a grim expression, lifted the piece of rein that still hung tied to the trunk. It had been gnawed through.

"Where's the horse?" asked the little one, perplexed.

Noim was first to answer. "He's dead." The lad turned to Bryand and, with an unmistakable note of scorn in his voice, said, "Ain't he, mister?"

Bryand eyed the trail of blood that led from the base of the tree into the underbrush. "I'm afraid so."

He saw Donoim's lip begin to quiver, and he knelt beside him. "But because of that we're still alive. Can you remember that?"

Donoim's eyes narrowed, and he cocked his head. "O' course I can. Whatta ya think I am, a dummy?"

He left the Prince to join his brother, who was poking a dead wolf with his toe. Bryand watched them for a moment, wondering if he still wanted to have children. Then, sighing deeply, he strode to Cower.

"We'd best put some distance between us and the wolves." He peered at the western sky. "I'd say we have about two hours left before it gets too dark to travel. Let's gather up what we can and be on our way."

However, they quickly discovered there was not much worth gathering. Everything that had landed outside the wagon when it flipped was now torn to shreds and scattered by the wolves. Their one sack of food had been ripped open, the meat devoured and potatoes well chewed.

"At least we've plenty of fresh water," said Cower, trying to remain cheerful.

"Swell. Instead o' dyin' o' thirst, we'll die o' hunger," grumbled Malady, retrieving her purse. "An' look at this!"

She held up a broken chamber pot. "This was a weddin' present from Cleave!" Her eyes filled with tears. "I still remember what he said the day he gave it ta me. Only the best for me puddin's puddin', he said."

She sank to the ground and began to weep. "Oh, my Cleave! My Cleave!"

Bryand knelt beside her. "I know this is hard for you. I know you feel lost without him. But now is not the time to grieve. You must stay strong, Malady. You must. And when we're out of danger you can tell me all about him."

She glanced at the Prince, her eyes red and bloodshot.

"I'd like that very much," he said, giving her a pained, sympathetic look. "For he could not have been a better friend had I known him my whole life." Bryand stood and offered his hand. "Ready?"

She rose, sniveling, and croaked, "Ready."

Cower and the boys had gathered some blankets and were tying them into individual bedrolls. They slung them over their shoulders and started across the river, first Noim and then Cower with the little one on his back.

"In you go," said Bryand to Malady.

She gave him a sheepish smile. "I-- . I can't swim. I been a city-dweller me whole life."

"Don't worry. It's only about waist deep."

"Even so, m'lord; water 'n me don't mix very well."

Bryand sighed, then lifted her in his arms and waded across.

They put nearly five miles between them and the river. And when the Prince informed the others of how far he believed they had traveled, a look of sheer surprise came over Malady's face and she promptly collapsed in the road.

Not again, thought Bryand, gazing at her supine body. He nudged her with his foot, but she did not stir.

"When she's out," offered Donoim, unperturbed. "She's out cold."

The light was fading fast now, dark shadows already stretched across the road, and they could hear the calls of hoop-hooper and dither birds in the distance, heralding the night.

The forest would soon be alive with the sounds of other night feeders, and not wanting to risk any more encounters, Bryand decided it was time for them to call an end to their march.

Hoisting Malady over his shoulder, he left the road and led Cower and the boys through the trees and up a gradual embankment.

When they reached the top, they found a small clearing from which they could observe the road. They halted and Bryand directed the boys to gather dry wood for a fire. Though it would be a beacon to anyone searching for them, it was also the best way to keep any hungry animals at bay.

Once the fire was crackling, the company felt somewhat cheered. Though Noim kept to himself, a dour look upon his face, Donoim was most talkative.

"That's a big knife ya got there," he said, eyeing the Prince's sword.

"Aye, lad. It is."

"I had a knife once, too."

"Really."

Donoim stared at the ground and pouted. "Me dad took it away after I killed me uncle with it."

Bryand did not know what to say. He glanced at Cower, who was also at a loss for words.

Noim laughed cruelly. "Donoim's a murderer, he is!"

Donoim glared at his brother. "You shut yer trap about that murderer stuff. I didn't do it on purpose, did I, mum?"

"'Course not," said Malady impatiently, waving him off. She turned to the Prince, saw his troubled look and offered him an explanation. "Mumble-the-peg. Bad throw."

Bryand was much relieved. "Certainly. Bad throw."

"Could happen to anyone," Cower added quickly.

Malady went on. "Landed in his uncle's foot. Deep. Tried keepin' it clean but it festered. After that, he died."

"Was he your brother?" asked Bryand, curious.

"No," said the woman. "Cleave's."

Speaking his name took her into her thoughts, for she fell silent after that, and stared with vacant eyes at the fire.

In the distance, hoop-hooper birds called and tiny night-feeding yacks barked. The night sky deepened to a cobalt blue and filled with countless stars.

Bryand scrutinized the shadows about them. "We'd best stand watch. I don't want anyone or anything surprising us during the night."

"An excellent idea, my lord. I'll take the first watch."

"Are you sure?"

Cower glanced at the others. The boys were tormenting a giant wood moth while Malady chewed on her fingernails.

"Quite."

Bryand left the retainer sitting with his back against a smooth rock and the sword resting across his lap. He returned to the fire, unfolded his bedroll and spread it on the ground a few feet from Malady.

Seeing this, Noim scowled and immediately positioned himself between them. Donoim, finding himself on the opposite side of the fire from everyone else, glanced about at the darkness and quickly joined his brother, wriggling between him and the Prince.

"'Scuse me," said the little one, shooting Bryand an arrogant look. "Could ya make some room?"

Bryand scooted over. "Terribly sorry. I should have known you'd want to sleep here."

The boy shrugged indifferently. "It's okay. Just don't do it again."

Bryand rolled over and closed his eyes. But he could not sleep; nor could he get comfortable. Something nagged at him, though he could not say what. At length he opened his eyes, and had his answer. He found Donoim wide awake and staring at him.

"What?" asked the Prince irritably.

"Is me dad dead?"

Bryand felt his stomach churn. "Aye, lad."

"I thought so."

Donoim looked up at the sky. After a moment a tear spilled down his cheek. Yet he said nothing, nor did he make any other sound. Instead, he wiped away the tear's track with his arm and rolled over again, this time with his back to the Prince.

Bryand watched him in silence, knowing there was nothing he could say that would comfort the boy. And thinking of his own parents, the Prince gazed at the heavens.

He had been lucky enough to say goodbye to his father, but not his mother. The last time he saw her was just after the joust. She had wept, something he had never seen her do before.

He felt quite low; and very much alone. Even with order restored, life would no longer be the same with both his parents gone.

He glanced once more at Donoim and sighed, envying the boy for the ease in which he could still cry and fall to sleep.

Cower gazed at the spherical moon as it rose above the treetops, and he noted the mass of clouds drifting toward it. Rain, he thought, scowling. Anything else you'd care to throw at us? This he directed at the Gods.

He knew they would not answer him. They never did. But that was because they wanted him always to find his own way through things.

He had been so desolate while serving Daron. All those weeks of abuse had bruised his spirit until it was good and sore.

But now, with Bryand free, it mattered not that they were outlaws. Serving the Prince while on the run was the same as serving him in the palace. Just not as comfortable.

As far as Cower was concerned, his life had returned to normal. Perhaps one day the world around them would return to normal, too.

It was then the bushes to his left rustled, and he heard what he thought were scampering feet. He tensed, gripped the hilt of the sword and sat trembling.

Surely the world would return to normal one day, he thought, staring wide-eyed into the darkness. But will I live that long?

Nothing charged him. After a while he relaxed again. Though, if he had been sleepy before, he was now fully awake; even after his shift had ended and Bryand had joined him.

Together, they listened to the shrill sound of dither birds calling to each other in the darkness.

"Cower," said the Prince. "There's something I've been meaning to say. My mind's been so clouded-- . And things have been so frantic -- . I just wanted you to know how grateful I am."

"My lord," replied the retainer, humbled. "I only wish I could have spared you all that suffering."

"How were you to know that Daron had stolen my identity. He's a very crafty fellow. Too crafty, I'm afraid." Bryand dug up some grass with the point of his sword. "I only hope there's a country left to rule by the time I've collected the arms and men to take it back."

It was then Donoim muttered something unintelligible, and rising to his feet, the boy proceeded to walk toward them at a methodical pace. Though he appeared to be awake, he spoke not a word, even after Bryand addressed him and asked where he was going.

"Don't worry 'bout him," came Noim's voice. They turned and saw the older boy leaning on his elbows. "He's sleep walkin'. Does it all the time."

Bryand furrowed his brow. "Shouldn't you go after him?"

"Naw. He'll come back. He always does."

And presently, the little one returned and settled again by his brother's side.

"See?" said Noim, with a haughty smirk. He put his head down and closed his eyes, taking no exception when his little brother snuggled closer to him and flopped an arm across his chest.

Bryand and Cower looked at each other.

"Strange family," said the retainer.

Bryand nodded in agreement. "Strange, indeed."

He was running, running for his life, over rocky open terrain, no cover but for a dense fog that clung to the ground turning all things a dismal gray. His lungs burned and the muscles in his legs screamed from overuse and with each breath that escaped his lips he whimpered like a frightened child. Suddenly in the distance he heard the royal dogs barking. He heard the huntsman's horn blaring:

Aaaaooooo!
Aaaaooooo!

They had found his trail.

"No!" he said, his throat on fire. He tossed a fearful glance over his shoulder and saw the hunting party through the dimness. "Dearest Gods, no!"

He pushed on, his entire frame rebelling, crying out for rest. Each labored stride claimed a bit more of his strength, a bit more of his courage, until at last, he stumbled and went crashing to the ground.

He lay panting, shuddering, a coward exposed, and then the dogs were upon him.

"Call them off," he cried, curling up into a ball. Teeth sank into his wrist, more into his thigh. "Please! I beg of you! Call them off!"

They tore at him, at his clothing and at his flesh. A syrupy wetness filled his mouth, welled in his throat, and he knew he was drowning in his own blood.

At length, he heard a voice from somewhere in the distance, somewhere through the pain. The dogs let go of him, whimpered and disappeared, and as his final breath hissed through his lips, before his vision faded completely to eternal blackness, his brother stood over him, the crown of Bandidon on his head.

"Noooo!" Daron shouted, bolting upright in his bed. Darkness was all around him. "A light! I must have a light!"

"Aye, your grace," came a frightened voice, and there was movement beside him.

"Quickly! Why is the fire out?!"

He heard the scratch of a flint, saw a brilliant spark, another, another, and soon a meager fire was crackling on the hearth. He watched in fear as a silhouette crossed the room holding a lit taper, and a moment later a candle glowed beside his bed. "I told you not to let the fire go out!"

Before him, completely naked, stood the kitchen girl he'd seduced earlier that evening, her raven black tresses cascading to her shoulders, her full round breasts illuminated by the candlelight. "I'm sorry, your grace. You've such a comfortable bed, I fell asleep."

Shivering, Daron pulled the blanket up to his neck. Since his brother's escape he had slept fitfully, plagued with bad dreams.

"Aye, well-- . I'm not partial to the dark." He realized she was staring at him. "I find the fire comforting."

"His grace had a bad dream."

Daron said nothing.

"Shall I leave now, your grace?"

He gazed at her. She was lovely. Quite lovely. So firm in all the right places, so soft in all the rest, and, if truth be told, he rather liked how she smelled of onions and fried pork fat. "No. I am in need of company. Return to bed."

The girl slid under the blanket and pressed herself against him. Shadows from the flickering light danced across her face; there, and there again. The height of her cheekbones, the angle of her nose, most everything about her reminded him of MeAnne.

His breathing deepened and his heart quickened in pace. He ran his hand along the gentle curve of her hip, across her buttocks, down to the back of her knee and then up along the inside of her thigh until he touched the soft flesh of her sex. She moaned, surrendering to his will, and he entered her.

But they were not joined for more than a few moments before his mind had wandered back to the dream, and even though he was awake now and occupied, it returned again with the same intensity. Running; running; growling; chewing; biting; crying; brother; crown. Would it never end?!

"Is there something wrong, your grace?"

Daron surfaced from his thoughts. "What?"

"Something wrong, your grace. You've gone soft."

"I've gone what?"

"Soft, your grace. The royal-- . You know."

Indeed it had. Daron shook his head attempting to clear his thoughts. "I believe we can remedy that."

He kissed her breasts, kissed her flat stomach trying hard to maintain his concentration.

But the dream came back, as vivid as before and his manhood remained just as shriveled. Frustrated, he rolled over and stared at the rafters. He felt her hand slide up his leg and touch his sex.

"Don't," he said.

She withdrew her hand immediately and lay there perfectly still. A moment of silence passed between them and then she yawned.

From the corner of his eye he watched her yawn, heard her sigh, and suddenly it was very important that he pleasure her. He threw himself upon her, kissing her lips, her breasts, her thighs, her sex. He heard her moans, watched her writhe with ecstasy, and grew hard in anticipation of their union.

There you are old friend, he thought, relieved. Now stay just as you are for a little while longer.

But the desire was not there; not really, and after a moment, he sat upon his haunches and stared at his sagging appendage.

The girl raised herself onto her elbows. "It's all right, your grace," she said kindly. "What with you bein' King and all, and needin' ta watch over a whole country, I imagine you've a lot on your mind."

He knew she meant to comfort him, but she had only succeeded in making him feel worse about himself. "You may go," he said unable to look at her.

"Very well, my lord." She gathered her things and went to the door, where she paused to slip into her kirtle. "We've some tasty roast pig and onions downstairs. Would you like me ta bring you some?"

"No," he replied.

"Made it m'self," she said, giving him a smile.

"Thank you, but no."

He did not look at her again until she was closing the door behind her.

Alone now, he dragged himself from the bed and pulled on a robe. He drifted to the embrasure and stared at the dark clouds that had collected in the sky.

He was sweating, and at the same time he had chills. He glanced down at his left hand and saw that it was trembling.

Take hold of yourself, man, he thought. You have nothing to fear. It matters not that Bryand has escaped.

Let him gather his friends. Let him rally whom he pleases. It's too late. You're King now. You're the one who wears the crown.

You've gathered more wealth in just a few months' time than father or grandfather did in their entire reigns combined. There is no one in all the United Kingdoms powerful enough to oppose you.

Feeling more confident now, he turned to the bed, only to find Bryand lying casually upon it, a broad smile on his face.

"Hello, brother," he said, with a flippant wave. "I hope the dogs haven't chewed you up too much."

Startled, Daron stumbled backwards, tripping over a small stool by the bed. He hit the floor hard, knocking the wind out of him. Great flashes of light exploded before his eyes, and then the room went dark.

The next thing he knew, he was staring at the raftered ceiling. Sunlight streamed through the embrasure and was bathing him in its warmth.

He lifted his head, and saw he was lying on the floor. At first, he thought it strange, but then he remembered the night before.

His heart picked up its pace. His face flushed with

anger.

"You are not there!" he said aloud. "And if you are, you'll wish you weren't!"

His muscles complained and his joints cracked, but he did not pay this any heed. He pulled himself to his feet, ready to confront his brother, only to find the bed empty.

He whirled around, expecting to see Bryand somewhere else. But he was no longer in the room.

Daron sat on the bed, perplexed (*he never was a morning person.*) He found himself thinking of the dream. In the daylight, it did not seem so terrifying. In fact, he felt refreshed.

It was then, he realized being unconscious, had allowed him to sleep the whole night through. Furthermore, it was the best night's sleep he had had in weeks, leaving him wondering if he should have someone knock him unconscious every night.

CHAPTER THIRTEEN

Cower awoke to find Noim and Donoim brawling, and Malady, shouting curses, struggling to pull them apart. Customarily, the manservant rose full of cheer, but this morning he was in no such mood. He had spent the night wrapped in a moldy horse blanket, his head lodged between two rocks. His back ached, his neck was stiff, and he was chilled to the bone.

"Madam!" he said sharply, enough for her to stop and look at him. "I don't suppose it too much to ask that you keep your children quiet and under control? There are others still trying to sleep."

"I'm doin' the best I can," she said as she struggled with the boys. "You try raisin' two upstarts an' see how good you do."

"I, for one can think of any number of ways to silence them. All it takes is a small measure of intelligence."

Nonplussed, Malady released her grip on the boys. "What right you got ta talk ta me like that? You ain't no better 'n me! I'm a sick woman, an' a widow, too, wiv two kids ta rear. If you was a gentleman, you'd treat me wiv respect instead o' lookin' down yer snooty nose at me an' sayin' all them nervy things."

"You tell 'im, mum," Noim chirped gleefully, shoving Donoim to the ground.

Donoim, his attention now on Cower, sat up and giggled. "Yeah, mum, tell mister fuss 'n strut ta bugger off 'n wipe his butt." He laughed harder, his brother joined in, and soon even Malady was chuckling too.

Gutter rats, Cower thought. Course, unruly, gutter rats. He rolled over, signaling he was done with the conversation.

But just then, something long, slimy and with pincers scurried up his pants leg. He screamed, leaped to his feet, and stomped the ground in a lunatic dance that made Malady and the boys laugh even harder.

Out fell the longest insect he had ever seen, slithering across his knobby ankle and onto the ground. Cower watched it disappear in the grass and shuddered aloud, which gave the others yet another reason to make fun of him.

Mustering what was left of his dignity, he strode to the edge of the clearing where Bryand sat keeping the watch. "Good morrow, my lord," he said, tossing a disgruntled look back in the boys' direction.

Bryand smiled. "How did you sleep for your first night under the stars?"

Unlike Malady, who seemed to complain constantly about one ill or another, Cower kept his aches and pains to himself. "It was... an experience."

"And one you will never forget, no doubt."

Cower snorted. "No doubt, my lord."

"Hey!" Donoim said, coming up to them. A glob of snot hung from his nose and his mouth was ringed with dirt. "Me mum's hungry and wants ta know what yer gonna do about food."

"I never said that," Malady called from where she stood.

Donoim looked at her and then at Cower and Bryand. "Yes she did," he said simply.

After a brief discussion between the two men, it was agreed that, were the Prince to go foraging, he might never find his way back to the campsite.

So, it fell to Cower to find something for them to

eat. He was by no means a woodsman or a hunter, but he was an expert horticulturist, having had his own garden in the castle ward. The forest was abundant with edible berries and roots. It just took knowing where to look and what to pick.

He had not gone very far when he discovered some wild clobbernut trees. Though their shells were hard and brittle, when boiled, clobbernuts cracked easily, and the meat was tender and delicious.

Not far from the clobbernut trees, the retainer found some ripe tickle berries. This was not their real name, but he had called them such since he was a child because of the way their fuzzy skin tickled the roof of his mouth.

Well, he thought, encouraged. The Gods are watching over us after all. Not only have they provided us with some tasty treats, but the very things to keep me regular on my journey.

Years ago, he had decided there was nothing more uncomfortable and more annoying while traveling long distances than becoming deaf to nature's call. It was a phenomenon not even Lystillus, the court physician, could explain.

But during all the years of traveling with King Audanot and his family, the moment he stepped foot outside the castle, his digestive system backed up like an old sieve and, no matter how hard he strained, he could not move a thing inside him for at least two days after he had returned.

However, recently and after much experimentation, he had discovered the magic of fruits and vegetables. For some reason they contained properties that helped unstop the sieve. Eating them every day he was able to maintain a regular schedule whether he traveled or not.

His foraging took him to the top of a wooded hill,

from which he could observe the road they had traveled the day before. There he found a copse of succum bushes growing near the crest - a flowering plant whose stamens issued nectar when plucked and squeezed.

Oh, goody, he thought, a smile curling his lips. This is becoming quite a delightful feast: clobber nuts, tickle berries and succum honey.

He had been picking stamens for about ten minutes, when he noticed some tiny glints of light in the distance. At first he thought it was the sun reflecting on the river they had crossed. But then he decided they had traveled much too far for that to be possible.

He stood for a moment, shielding his eyes with his hand, wondering what the flashes could be, until he realized they were closer now and heading his way.

He trotted along the hill, craning to get a better look. He found a large rock formation and, climbing to its top, discovered the answer to his question. Immediately his bowels turned to water and all thoughts of food disappeared. For in the distance, perhaps no more than a mile away, were mounted soldiers, their spears glistening in the sunlight.

Bryand stoked the fire, lost in thought. I'm sure Willowbrook is around here somewhere. I seem to remember it was surrounded by lots of trees.

He frowned and tossed his stick onto the fire. What a curse this is, having no sense of direction. I might as well be deaf and blind. At least then I'd have an excuse for stumbling about.

He was still considering this when Cower entered the clearing, berries spilling from his blanket. As soon as Bryand looked up he knew something was wrong.

"Put out the fire, my lord," said the retainer in a

frightened tone.

"What's wrong?"

Cower fell beside him. "Troops. Along the road."

As fast as he could, Bryand dug up dirt with his sword while Cower spread it on the flames.

"Is there gonna be a fight?" asked Noim excitedly.

"No," insisted the prince, fanning the air to disperse the smoke.

Donoim pounded the ground with his fist. "Ya mean, we don't get ta kill no one?"

"Shut yer trap an' keep it that way," growled Malady through gritted teeth. "Or I'll do some killin' o' me own!"

Bryand gestured for them to step in closer. Noim purposely folded his arms in front of him and stood his ground.

"We must keep ourselves hidden and pray their mission is something other than to hunt us down. Therefore, stay low and be quiet."

Donoim was about to make another of his sarcastic remarks, when Malady grabbed him to her and covered his mouth.

"That means keep yer trap shut," said the woman, staring down her nose at the boy.

He deposited them behind some bramble bushes on the far side of the clearing. He joined Cower by the edge of the embankment and crouched behind a fallen tree.

"Which direction?" asked the Prince in a hushed tone.

The retainer pointed to his left.

"This is just a guess," said Bryand. "But isn't that the same way we came last night?"

Cower nodded grimly.

"Then unless they're completely blind, they've seen our wagon. And if there's a good tracker among them, we're as good as dead."

The sound of galloping horses grew louder and louder until the ground beneath them began to tremble. This, in a way, was encouraging to the Prince.

For if the soldiers were tracking them, they would be traveling much slower, searching for prints in the road and other signs of their presence.

A moment later, the soldiers appeared from around a bend in the trail, a full company, riding hard. They were dressed in the green and purple colors of the Bandidonian Guard, the hammer, anvil and tongs sigil embroidered on their chests.

Each man carried a tall spear and bore full battle gear. But the man at the head of the column wore only a leather jerkin with no insignia on it.

I know him, thought the Prince, surprised. His name's Mortamour, and he's the Duke of Cunninghim's man. But what's he doing commanding the guard?

Eventually, the thundering of the horses' hooves diminished to a faint rumble. A moment or two more and it had disappeared completely, leaving behind an eerie silence that even the birds were wary to fill.

Bryand surfaced from his thoughts and turned to Cower. "How came the Duke of Cunninghim's henchman to command the King's personal guard? It makes no sense."

Cower looked away, uncomfortable now. He knew the answer to the Prince's question. He knew how deeply troubled it would make him. The Prince had suffered greatly at his brother's hands; the retainer did not wish to cause him any further pain. Even so, Cower thought it best to tell him the truth.

"Your brother has worked very hard these past few months to undo almost everything your father struggled to build. He's restored Cunninghim's title and given him back his lands. But worse still, he's taken the Duke into his confidence and proclaimed him Lord High Protector and Commander of the Guard."

Cower saw it on his face at once. The news had been devastating to the Prince.

"I'm sorry, my lord," said the retainer. "It pains me to be the bearer of such ill tidings. I would as lief rip my own tongue out than say anything that might cause you grief."

"You are not to blame."

"Perhaps, my lord. But neither are you."

They broke their fast on the tickle berries and succum honey that Cower had foraged. At first, Noim and Donoim were reluctant to try the make-do fare, but they were very hungry, and once they had tasted it and discovered it was sweet, they gobbled down handfuls of berries and sucked stamen after stamen dry.

Once their hunger was satisfied, Malady and the boys shook the leaves and grass from their blankets, rolled them length-wise and slipped them over their heads.

Cower worked at smothering the fire, watching the Prince while burying the coals. Bryand, lost in thought, stood by the edge of the clearing.

Since he was a young lad, it had been his way to go deep within himself before reckoning with his feelings. Cower knew Brynd would reveal his thoughts eventually, once he had time to sort them out.

"Everyone ready?" called Cower, dusting off his hands.

"Fer what?" replied Donoim in a surly tone.

The retainer was in no mood to bandy insults with a child. "For almost anything. Perhaps even a monster who eats little boys."

He glanced at the Prince. "My lord? The day awaits."

Bryand nodded and joined them. "The road is no longer safe to travel. Not with troops ahead of us. From now on we'll have to make our way through the forest."

"Very good, my lord," said Cower, though inwardly he was far less confident than he sounded. Knowing the Prince's sense of direction, he could easily lead them in circles for days.

They started off well enough, keeping the road in sight. But eventually this proved to be too difficult an undertaking.

The brush was dense and sinewy. In some places, it was so tangled the Prince was forced to use his sword to clear a path. But whenever he disturbed the foliage, a storm of tiny insects fell upon them, buzzing about their heads, landing in their eyes or up their noses.

There was no escaping them. Each time the band halted for Bryand to clear yet another two steps of ground, the wait became that much more intolerable.

Once the sun was above the trees, the air turned hot and cloying. There seemed no room to even breathe.

The boys began to fight. Malady began to grouse. Even Cower showed signs of stress by his virtual silence.

Bryand had spent much of his life in the woods. Though he had no sense of direction, he was a seasoned enough soldier to know he and the others were making little headway and wasting too much effort in the attempt. So, when they happened upon a narrow path, which was little more than a game trail, Bryand chose to follow it.

The trail bent right, then left, then right again, and after a while, the Prince could no longer tell if they were traveling parallel to the road. Cower suggested turning back but Bryand would not hear of it.

They had lost too much time, and time was precious. The guards they had spied that morning were on a different mission. But soon there would be more guards, and these would be hunting for them. Fearing this, Bryand pressed onward at an even faster pace.

Cower had been right the night before. The clouds were indeed heavy with rain. Sometime after what he guessed was noon, they engulfed the sun and the first drops began to fall.

In no time, the rain was coming down in torrents. They pressed on in spite of it, slogging through the soggy muck, ignoring the wet gusts in their faces. Each hillock became a torturous climb and then a treacherous slide once they gained the crest and started down the other side.

"I can't go on like this," shouted Malady above the roaring downpour. Her hair clung in sodden clumps to her head and shoulders. Rain dripped from her nose and chin. "I'm already soaked to me skivvies."

"We should keep going," called the Prince from the front of the line. "While there is light by which to travel. A little rain will not hurt you."

"A little -- !" Noim protested. "I can hardly see me hand in front of me face. I'm drownin' standin' up."

The rain fell in silky sheets one moment, then, buffeted by the wind, like a thousand stinging needles the next. So blinding was it that they could no longer tell if they were still upon the trail.

Finally, even Bryand could stand no more. "We'd best find some shelter!"

Cower glanced about them. "Where? There are trees aplenty but the ground is soaking wet and this wind is a villain."

"A hollow then, a ledge, anything that will shield us."

They trudged forward, stumbling, falling, covered with dead leaves and peat. They found another trail that wound through two outcroppings of mossy rocks. Here the ground was somewhat firmer, and once they had crested the rise they discovered a deep, round gully on the other side.

To their right was more dense undergrowth. To their left was a wide break where the splintered remains of some dead trees stood. Across the gully, about forty yards away, was a rock wall that glistened in the rain, and at its base was a deep gouge.

"There," shouted Bryand, and they hastened for it.

The gully turned out to be a muddy field. Here and there, puddles had already collected and some were deceptively deep.

They slipped and slid and waded across the expanse, falling at times onto their hands and knees. When at last they reached the far side, caked with mud and soaking wet, they approached the rock wall and discovered the gouge was actually the entrance to a cave.

"Wait here," said the Prince, water falling in a steady stream from the end of his chin.

"But I'm soppin'!" Malady complained.

"Even so. We need to know if it's safe."

Bryand drew his sword on the off chance the cave was inhabited by something that would take offense to their intrusion. He tossed his companions a quick look, tightened the grip on his blade and crept inside. His eyes took barely a moment to adjust to the darkness.

The cave was shaped like a funnel, wide-mouthed and long-necked, and ran straight back into the hill on a gradual downward slope. He listened for any movement from within. But the rain outside was coming down so hard that it was all he could hear.

"My lord," called Cower, his voice sounding distant

and puny. "Is everything all right?"

Bryand waited a moment longer. Finally, when nothing had come charging out of the darkness, he sheathed his sword and returned to the entrance. "It's all right! Come inside!"

The others plodded in, their spirits very low. Not only were they drenched, but they were tired and hungry as well. The berries they had breakfasted upon had curbed their appetites for only a short while.

Malady sneezed, then shivered and wiped her face with her sopping sleeve. "I'm frozen t' the bone. If I don't get warm soon I'll die of exposure."

Bryand peered into the darkness ahead of them. "Perhaps there's some dry brush and leaves further in, something we can use to start a fire."

"How about usin' that?" said Noim in a sarcastic tone. The boy pointed to a shadow along the side of the cave wall. In the deepest part of the shadow a short torch, about twelve inches long, rested in a sconce.

"What do you make of that?" Bryand said, approaching it.

"It's called a torch," supplied Noim. "Ain't ya ever seen one before?"

Bryand ignored the boy's remark. "But what's it doing here of all places?"

"Search me. You're the one wiv all the answers."

The Prince removed the torch from the sconce. "Interesting," he said as he examined it. "It's still well oiled." He sniffed it. "No rancid smell so the oil must be new." He stared at the cave's interior. "Strange."

Noim scoffed. "What's so strange about a torch. It's s stick wiv a smelly rag on th' end." Donoim chuckled at his brother's remark, which made Noim even bolder. "Would you like me ta tell ya whatcha can do wiv that stick?"

"That's enough!" said Malady, her temper flaring.

She gazed at the Prince. "I'm sorry, m'lord."

Noim scowled and threw a small stone into the gully. "There ya go with that m'lord stuff again. What is he a King or somethin'?"

Bryand brought the torch to Cower, who reached into his purse and took out his flint. A moment later the torch was burning.

Bryand held it overhead. "Funny how these walls are so smooth."

He proceeded deeper inside the cave, running his hand along the stone, and soon he came upon timbers and crossbeams evenly spaced along the walls.

"I thought so. This isn't a cave at all," Bryand called. "It's some kind of mine shaft."

Noim perked up instantly. "Mine? As in gold mine? Ya mean there may be gold down there?"

"I doubt it," said Bryand with a smirk. "From the looks of it, I'd say this place was abandoned long ago."

Noim took a few steps further in and peered into the gloom. "I'm gonna find out. Gimme that torch."

"You ain't goin' nowhere," said Malady, wringing out the bottom of her dress.

"But mum, we could be rich!"

"Ya think I want some rotted timber fallin' on yer head and crushin' yer brains in? Now sit down and dry off."

"But, mum--"

"Ya ain't goin' an' that's final."

Noim joined his brother and sat by the entrance of the cave, brooding as he squashed some ants that had scurried in from the rain.

Bryand returned to the others, replaced the torch in its sconce and slid down the wall next to Cower. Weary, he listened to the sound of the rain, and soon his thoughts drifted back to his brother and the foolish, foolish alliance he had formed with the Duke of Cunninghim.

What was Daron thinking? How could he have been so blind as to trust a villain like that? Daron was smart, he was devious, but he was no match for the Duke. Cunninghim had raised duplicity to an art form. Associating himself with such a man, placed the kingdom, perhaps all the kingdoms, in danger. Not from war; hopefully not from war; but from corruption and tyranny; things that were just as formidable and destructive.

Bryand sighed. The struggle he faced looked more and more bleak; more and more complicated. He hardly knew where to start.

Frustrated; miserable; he stared at the open field just outside the shaft. It was now a small pond. He wanted to start off again, but he knew the others were exhausted.

The boys appeared already asleep. They had settled down, one on each side of their mother, using her lap as a pillow. Malady's eyes were also closed. Her hair still wet and sticking to her face, she looked so bedraggled that he was reminded of the drowned rats he had seen on his tour of the city's sewers.

Let them sleep, he thought. They'll need it.

He shifted his weight, relaxing into a more comfortable position. He stared at the torch, watching the flame as it rippled in the breeze and cast an undulating shadow on the wall. He closed his eyes and was a breath away from falling asleep when he heard the sound.

Chink...... Chink...... Chink......

Slow and rhythmic, it was so barely audible, he almost mistook it for the rain. He cocked his head and concentrated upon it, and when the rain stopped momentarily, he heard it again more distinctly.

Chink...... Chink...... Chink......

Suddenly he realized the sound was not coming from outside as he had first assumed, but from somewhere within the mine itself. He looked at Cower, and from the expression on his face, Bryand gathered that the man had heard it, too.

"What is that?" asked Cower.

Bryand shook his head. "I don't know."

The Prince rose, his knees cracking, and grabbed the torch. Then he and Cower started down the shaft.

"Sneakin' off b'hind our backs, eh?" said Noim angrily. Apparently, he was not asleep. "Watcha doin'? Tryin' ta steal our gold?"

Bryand put his finger to his lips. "Quiet."

"You was right," said Donoim, also awake and supporting his brother. "First chance they got!"

"Listen!'

The boys continued to protest.

"I said listen!"

Chink...... Chink...... Chink......

This time they all heard the sound.

"What is that?" asked Malady.

"I don't know," said the Prince. He looked at the boys. "Stay with your mother."

Noim eyed him suspiciously. "What about the gold?"

"We'll split it," said Bryand, indulging him. "Half for Cower and me, and half for you and your family. Is that fair enough?"

The boy folded his arms and shook his head adamantly. "Uh-uh. Five equal shares."

"Equal shares it is," said the Prince, exasperated.

"Now be quiet."

Bryand took the lead. But he had only taken a few steps before he heard Noim whisper, "If he thinks I won't search his pockets, he's got another think comin'."

The shaft continued downward on a gradual descent, winding to their left, then to their right, and then straight ahead. The deeper they went, the louder the sound grew.

They rounded a sharp curve, and the shaft became brighter. There was light up ahead.

The sound stopped suddenly, and they halted. Then, tossing each other a quick glance, they hugged the wall and padded softly toward the light.

"Just a few more an' I thinks that'll do it, Picks," came a harsh gravelly voice.

"It..., better...," came a second voice, sounding winded. "With the rains startin'..., there's not..., much time left."

The sound resumed and was accompanied by a few labored grunts. Bryand leaned out from the wall for a better look. Ahead of him, the shaft ended at a chamber that had been hollowed out of the hill.

The walls had been shored up by wood planks, and thick beams stretched across the ceiling supported by large timber posts. Upon these posts, lanterns and miner's tools had been hung. In the center of the chamber stood a roughly hewn table, and about the perimeter were sacks and sacks of various supplies.

He handed Cower the torch, then sidled to the end of the shaft whereupon he peered around the corner. So amazing was the sight he beheld that the Prince blinked, shook his head, and looked again.

By the rear wall of the chamber - which was the

only wall not braced by wood - two dwarves covered from head to toe with dirt and grime stood on either side of the largest rough gem stone Bryand had ever seen. It was at least a foot in diameter.

One dwarf worked with a pickaxe, striking the rock along the side. He was bare-chested, and, though he was little, thick muscles knotted his arms and neck.

"Try this side now," said the one with the gravelly voice. He was taller than the other by about half a foot, and he had bushy red hair that winged outward from beneath his minor's cap.

"Right here," said the dwarf, placing a stubby finger on the rock. When the muscular one hesitated, he snarled, "well? Whatcha waitin' for?"

"But Digs," said the dwarf.

"C'mon, c'mon."

"But Digs," again the dwarf protested.

"Look, I knows what I'm doin'. Hits it right where I gots me finger."

Reluctantly, the one called Picks raised his tool over his head, and did exactly as he had been instructed, bringing the pick-axe down exactly on Digs' finger.

The dwarf howled like a dog and rolled back and forth upon the ground, cradling his hand. Then, at length, when the pain had lessened, he examined his finger, and gingerly pulled off his crushed nail. He shot the other dwarf a menacing look. "Ya dids that on purpose!"

"I dids not. Ya told me ta hits it, so I hits it."

To Bryand's surprise, instead of pursuing the argument further, the one called Digs shook his head and began to chuckle. "You're absolutely right, Picks, old chum. I said hits it, didn't I?"

"Aye," answered the other, grinning. He was missing a front tooth.

"Now anyone else would've realized I meant right by me finger, but, stupid me, forgots who I was dealin' with."

Again, the other, still grinning, said, "Aye."

Digs rose, grabbed a shovel and approached Picks casually. "So tell me, Picks, where da ya thinks we should strike next?"

"Well, let's see," said Picks, facing the gem and studying it.

Instantly, Digs raised the shovel, drew it back and whacked Picks squarely on his head. The dwarf spilled forward and landed unconscious with his feet resting on the wall. Digs dropped the shovel, waddled to a table, grabbed hold of a bucket from which mirky water sloshed, then splashed the contents in Picks' face.

In a moment he had sputtered, regained consciousness and was staring at his partner angrily. "Whatcha do that for?"

Digs tossed the bucket aside. "To remind ya that I'm the brains o' this outfit. An' 'cause I don't wants ya thinkin' ya can fix me the way ya fixed Haulsey."

"Why you-- ." Picks rolled to his feet, brandishing his tool like a weapon.

Realizing a struggle was about to ensue, Bryand thought it best to make his presence known. Motioning to Cower to follow, he took a bold step into the chamber.

"Hello, there!" said the Prince, smiling graciously. "Sorry to interrupt your little spat."

When the dwarves saw the two men, their feet left the ground with surprise. Then, recovering quickly, they glowered at them and stood side by side, facing what they assumed was a common foe.

"Hold," said Bryand, raising his hands chest high. "We mean you no harm. You've nothing to fear from us."

"Who are you?" demanded Digs.

"We're simply a pair of travelers who took shelter in your mine during the storm."

"Well, yer on private property," spat Picks. "So beats it or we'll beats you."

"Please," said Cower, in his most congenial voice, "we're tired and hungry, all we ask is-- ."

"That ain't no concern o' mine," said Picks, unyielding.

"You see, we were attacked by wolves, and lost all our provisions. Perhaps you might be willing to part with some of yours. You certainly have plenty to spare."

Digs laughed arrogantly. "Not a chance."

He sobered and eyed them with blatant malice. "This mine's ours. We claimed it years ago before the first flood. We worked it day 'n night, year after year before the second flood."

Bryand gave him a level look. "You?"

Digs avoided his stare. "Well... thems that we took it from did most o' the work. But we've done our share, too, 'n spilled our blood in the doin'." He showed Bryand his oozing thumb. "it's ours now. Now beats it before we gets rough."

Bryand held his ground. "We're perfectly willing to recognize your claim but we insist on purchasing some supplies."

Picks brandished his axe. "Looks, didn't ya hear what my partner said? Beats it! Or I'll beats you!"

"Wait a minute," remarked Digs, nudging him. This surprised Picks, and he eyed him curiously. Digs played with a wing of his red hair. "Did you say purchase?"

"Aye," said Bryand with a nod.

"Ya means, ya got cash?"

This time Cower answered. "Aye."

His eyes ticked from Bryand to Cower and then to Bryand again. "Hmmmmmmm," said Digs, rubbing his stubbly chin. He retreated a few feet, pulling his partner along by the sleeve. They turned their backs on Bryand and Cower and spoke in hushed voices.

"But they seens the gem!" said Picks incautiously.

Digs cuffed him on the forehead and whispered something more. Picks rubbed his head, then poked Digs in the shoulder and whispered something back.

The palaver went on like this for a moment more, with Digs cuffing his partner and Picks poking him in return until, at last, Picks grinned and nodded in accord.

Digs faced Bryand and Cower once again, and in a not too unpleasant tone, said, "Well, it's okay with me 'n Picks here. But you'll have ta ask our other partner, Haulsey."

"And where would he be?" asked Bryand, keeping his patience.

Digs stepped jauntily to a large round hole in the ground at the center of the chamber, and with a jerk of his head, he said, "Down there on the lower level."

Bryand crossed to the lip, taking note of a rope that had been tied at one end to a stake in the ground and neatly coiled. "Haulsey's down there, you say?"

"Oh, yeah," said Digs, grinning. He looked at his partner. "Ain't that right, Picks."

"I'm sure of it."

Before the last word had even escaped his lips, the Dwarf charged Bryand. Instinctively, Bryand's hand went to his sword, but he knew there was no time to unsheath it.

Luckily, the dwarf, being dwarfed, was slow and lumbering. Bryand pivoted, and Picks, with nothing between him and empty air, went plummeting head first down the hole.

Seeing his partner fall, Digs howled with rage. He jumped the Prince, and they grappled. Though the dwarf was only half as tall, he was strong, and he shoved Bryand to the very edge. But the Prince had no intention of falling, at least not alone. He held onto the dwarf, who, concerned now for his own life, struggled to break free. For one breathless moment they tottered together, and then they fell.

Cower, in the meantime, was still trying to dislodge the scream that was stuck in his throat. The attack had occurred so suddenly that he had hardly gotten his feet moving before Bryand had dropped out of sight.

"My lord!" he cried at last, falling prostrate by the hole. "Can you hear me?" Silence was his only reply. "Speak to me, my lord. Please!"

"Well, I found Haulsey," came the Prince's voice from out of the darkness below. "He's dead."

"Praise the Gods!" Cower exclaimed. "Are you all right?"

"Aye. But these other two weren't as lucky. They went and joined their partner the moment I landed on them."

Shaking with relief, Cower threw down the rope, and when Bryand had climbed out of the hole and was safe, the retainer hugged him.

Huffing, the Prince stared into the hole and then at Cower. "I think it's time I learned to be a little less trusting, don't you?"

They rejoined Malady and the boys and told them what had happened as they headed back to the chamber. Once there, the boys ran from one thing to another, examining the mining tools, digging through the provisions sacks, until Bryand called them over to the wall and showed them the gemstone.

"Am I supposed ta be impressed or somethin'?" said Noim.

It was clear to Bryand the boy had no idea what he beheld. Using Picks' pick, the Prince cracked off a few shards from the mother stone and handed them to the boy.

"What are these?" asked Noim skeptically.

"Those, lad, are diamonds. Uncut and unpolished but worth enough to buy a house three times bigger than my castle."

"What?!" Malady screamed. "What did you say they was?!"

Bryand smiled. "Diamonds. You're rich. We all are."

The idea of it was obviously too much for the woman, for she fainted on the spot. And while the boys danced around their mother, Bryand severed more shards from the stone, gathered them up from the floor, and placed them firmly in the retainer's palms.

"These, my friend," he said, smiling, his eyes shining for the first time in days. "Will buy us the army we need."

CHAPTER FOURTEEN

King Jasper stood outside his campaign tent under a canvas awning, listening to the rain over his head. His wife and daughter were inside the tent, attendants preparing them for their second night's sleep on a journey that would not end until they had reached Jasperland, their home.

The trip, he calculated, would take three weeks. The rain had slowed his progress some, but he had compensated for inclement weather in his figuring. No matter how well prepared, there were still some things about first class travel one was forced to leave to chance.

The King surveyed his encampment – horses tethered, tents pitched, wagons clustered, sentries posted, fires hissing and smoking. All was well.

Well, he thought, admitting the truth. All was not well. Would that MeAnne were with him, the King reflected.

Images from the past flooded his brain. MeAnne still a toddler; MeAnne a young princess; MeAnne his confidante and chess-buddy.

Such a sharp mind, he thought. How could she suddenly have become so witless? Was her love so blinding that she could not see the king for what he was?

A madman, came his answer. Worse than that; a despot. For a madman alone could be pitied and then restrained. But a despot; a mad despot at that, was dangerous, unpredictable, and vindictive.

"Is everything well, m'lord?" asked Jona, curious.

Realizing he had been observed, the King scoffed and cleared his throat. "Ach, aye. Damn wood smoke burns my eyes."

He wiped the tear that had run down his cheek. A stout man, a powerful man, a warrior feared in battle by his troops and his enemies alike, but when it came to his daughters, King Jasper was as tenderhearted as a blubbering troubadour.

"Go back inside, lass," he told Jona.

"Would you like something, m'lord? Some tea perhaps? I made a pot earlier for m'lady. It might help you sleep."

"No thank you. I'll be in shortly."

"Very well, m'lord."

"And Jona?"

"Yes, m'lord?"

"I understand your anxiety, being separated from MeAnne like this, but you needn't sleep at my feet. It's bad enough having a wife that snores without someone else kicking me every time I'm about to drift off."

"Yes, m'lord."

When he was alone again, His thoughts turned once more to the past. He had ridden by Audanot's side for twenty years; watched him forge an empire; served as his most trusted advisor. How could such a decent, hard-working conqueror produce such a worthless wretch? Two worthless wretches in fact! Why had the Gods been so cruel?

The answer lay beyond his reason and would forever remain a mystery to him. He sighed and gazed at the heavens where he assumed Audanot's spirit resided.

"Perhaps its best ya n'er lived long enough ta see the fruits of yer loins turn over-ripe and stench-ridden." A man like King Jasper did not mince words, not when addressing his friends, not even when addressing his dead friends.

"As for me, I did what I could. I hope yer not cross wi' me for takin' leave o' yer daft son's court."

His thoughts turned to the empire – Bandidon, Jasperland, the other united kingdoms of the council. What would happen now that he was gone? How long would order last without true leadership? How long before the old days were no longer the old days but new days that seemed like the old days? Sooner or later there would be a dispute, a raid, a battle, a war.

King Jasper shook his head. All that work for nothin', he thought. Angry now, he gripped the hilt of his sword. It was like gripping the hand of an old friend.

Slaybest was its name. It had been in his family since the first sword-maker molded the blade, so it was told, from the armor of the war god, Gunnakillya. Forged in the flames of the underworld, cooled in the frosty heights of the Heavenly Halls, inlaid with the gems from a dragon's belly, and enchanted by a four star wizard named Carle. It was a proud sword, a noble weapon. It was also very sharp.

"Blasted fool!" Jasper said aloud.

"Who is that, dearest?"

The King pivoted his bulky frame and found the Lady Inoya by the tent opening, holding the flap across the bodice of her nightgown. He scowled, and looking her straight in the eye, the right eye, for it was the one fixed on him, he pursed his lips and made ready to speak Bryand's name.

But then Jasper paused, struck by a new thought. Had he made the right decision leaving the court? With him gone, who was left to oppose the tyrant? Certainly, none of the other kings was as strong.

In that moment he knew he had erred, had made the wrong choice, allowed his personal feelings to cloud his judgement.

"Who dear? Who is the blasted fool?"

"Why, me, o' course," he said. Though angry with himself, he stepped to her and brushed a down-like feather from her shoulder. "You're not moltin' already, are ya?"

She snorted in amusement. "No, dear, it's the quilt."

"Aye," he said, placing the back of his hand gently against her cheek. "Get dressed."

"What?"

"Get dressed woman. We make for the capital."

Inoya's eyes darted this way and that. "But we just came from there."

Hearing the distress in the queen's voice, Blindella, their eldest, stepped to her mother's side. "What's wrong?"

"We're going back," the queen fretted.

"What?"

Blindella turned her good eye upon her father. She had suffered much angst and embarrassment over the past few months. Her betrothal to Prince Daron had not gone smoothly even before he had turned assassin. And now that he was rotting in the King's dungeon for the rest of his life, the chances of her getting to know him better seemed even more remote. "But father, I don't see why."

"O' course ya don't. But that's not yer fault."

"Jasper," the lady Inoya pleaded. "It's the middle of the night."

"Night, day, it does na' matter. The sooner we get there, the better. Jona! Jona! Where'd ya run off to, lass?"

Jona poked her head in between the two royals. "Here, your grace."

"Get the queen and the princess dressed. We're breaking camp." He did not wait for her to reply, but turned and stepped out into the rain.

"Where's my captain of the guard? Angoose! Angoose! Roust yerself!"

"Here, my lord," said Angoose, bursting from the tent to the king's right. His hair was tousled and his tunic was crooked. He held his sword belt in his hands.

"Assemble the men. Break camp!"

"Now, my lord?"

"Am I speakin' jibberish? Aye, now! And be quick about it!"

But before Angoose could shout an order, a great commotion was heard on the far side of the camp. Out of the darkness came men on horseback, helmeted, dressed for battle, wearing the colors of the Bandidonian guard.

Harsh cries rose up, horses whinnied, and under all was the sound of steel clashing in the distance. King Jasper stood agape, not knowing what to make of the intrusion.

He recognized the man at the head of the column as the Duke of Cunninghim's henchman. "Mortamour, is that you?"

"Aye, your grace," he replied.

"Why have you come?" Jasper demanded. "What is happening here?"

Mortamour halted his detachment and dismounted. In his hand he held a scythe-shaped blade with a crudely fashioned wood handle and crosspiece. Jasper had seen its like before, during the wars with the mad highlanders. "What have you there? A cuttintoo?"

"Right again, your grace," said the henchman, approaching him quickly. "We've arrived just in time."

Jasper gave him a stony look. "In time fer what?"

Mortamour looked at the king, at Angoose beside him. "Woolly-Bullies, your grace. Raiding the countryside."

In spite of the women's gasps, Jasper held his ground. "Woolly-Bullies? This far south?"

"Aye, your grace." He thrust the cuttintoo deep into Angoose's chest just below the man's ribs. Angoose gasped, died, and slid off the henchman's blade.

"Oh, and by the way," said Mortamour, smiling. "I believe you are under attack."

The rain began to fall even harder. It rarely rained in Bandidon, but, come the season for it, and it poured and poured.

So Bryand and the others spent the night in the mine chamber, and while he and Cower made an inventory of the supplies, Malady and the boys argued about what they were going to buy with their fortune.

At length, they decided to build a castle in the gully just outside the mine. By doing so, they could watch over production and, thus, continue to profit from their discovery.

After they had filled their haversacks with food and candles and lamp oil and flints, they filled their stomachs for the first time in days, and drifted off to sleep, contented.

The hours passed. Bryand slept heavily, at times lost in dreams that took him to castle hallways and green fields and misty forests. Every now and then, thinking it part of his dreams, he heard a rumbling sound, and once even a distant roar.

In this way, he passed the night until shortly before dawn. Suspended between darkness and consciousness, a vivid image took shape behind his eyelids. He was floating in a large pool of water. It had no walls to contain it, no borders of any kind. It was so real; so vast. He could feel its chill, and its wetness.

He went from dream to semi-consciousness. He was wet now, and cold. It was then, he realized it was not a dream. His eyes popped open and he sat up quickly, fearing he had done a boyish thing and wet his bedroll.

Much to his chagrin, he discovered the floor of the entire chamber was under several inches of water. This he found almost as disconcerting as the thought of having wet his bedroll.

He became aware of a low, rumbling sound. It was then the Prince vaguely recalled what Picks had said the night before; something about the rains starting and time running out.

And then he recalled the partner, Digs, had said something about a flood and a second coming. No. Recalling it now, the man had said "the first flood and the second."

The rumbling sound grew louder, and suddenly Bryand understood.

"Get up, Cower!" he called, startling the man awake. "Malady! Boys!"

"What's the matter?" asked the retainer, and then he stared at the water about him, puzzled.

"No time. Gather up our things!"

Bryand shot to his feet, grabbed the torch, and rushed up the shaft, splashing through the shallow stream that ran along the floor. How could I have been so stupid! What was I thinking?!

The farther up the shaft he traveled, the louder the rumbling became. So much so that, by the time he had reached the entrance, the sound was almost deafening.

He peered outside and in the grey light of predawn saw the entire floor of the gully was submerged. What had started as a small pond was now a huge lake.

Dearest Gods, he thought. How are we going to get out of here? But he had no time to think of anything more, for just then the ground began to tremble, and then to shake, and to his horror, a wall of roiling water hit the gully with a powerful roar. It splintered trees and pushed aside large boulders in its path. And seeing that it was heading directly toward him, his eyes went agog and, whirling about, he dashed at full speed down the shaft.

He found the others approaching, and waving his arms wildly about, he shouted, "Turn around! Turn around! Go back the other way!"

But they did not yet understand the urgency of the situation. They waited for him to join them.

"Go," said the Prince, shoving Noim. "We've no time to lose!"

"Hey," said the boy angrily. "Keep yer hands to yerself!"

It was then the water smacked against the outside wall, rocking the shaft and sending them spilling to the ground. Bryand dropped the torch, and it was doused with a hiss in the stream, plunging them into darkness. The Prince collided with someone, but before he could determine who it was, he was swept up by a wall of water and carried down the shaft.

He heard the boys shouting and Malady screaming. Though he knew not how she got there, he found her in his arms.

"Hold on," he shouted.

"Ya couldn't pry me off wiv' a crowbar!"

They were carried along by the rushing water, around the curve in the shaft and into the chamber, where, for a moment, the water's force was dissipated, and they lay in a bedraggled heap.

"It's all right," he said, trying to calm her.

"No, it ain't," she stammered.

"No. It's all right."

"No. It ain't!"

Bryand struggled to stand, but Malady would not let go of him. Yet it did not matter much, for the flood surged again, sweeping them off the ground.

In a moment, the room was filled to the rafters, and they would have gone to a watery grave had it not been for the hole in the center of the room, which acted like a drain. They soon found themselves in a whirlpool going round and round and round again, getting closer and closer to the vortex with each turn.

"What're we gonna do?!" Malady screeched, tightening her grip around the Prince's neck.

Bryand lunged for a post but missed.

"Hold your breath!" he cried.

Down they went into the hole, spinning out of control like a child's top, gaining more and more speed until the water covered their heads and darkness enveloped them.

At that moment, the one they assumed was their last, they hugged each other, so tightly that their bodies entwined. Cheek to cheek, then lips to lips; not lovers, but a man and a woman, seeking comfort as they faced what they thought their final moments of life.

But the shaft leading to the lower level was wider than the hole. For a moment, they found themselves falling, and then they hit more water with a loud slap that stung their backs and shoulders.

They broke the surface, gasping for air, and were carried along with the current until the shaft ended at a natural cavern where the water dispersed into what appeared to be an underground lake.

Sputtering, gagging, they somehow found higher ground and crawled to safety onto a sandy beach. Then, when Bryand had coughed up the water he had swallowed and Malady had regained her wits, they waited anxiously, hoping to find Cower and the boys alive.

The only sound was that of the rushing water.

Malady began to whimper. "Where are they? They shoulda been down by now."

"I don't know," said Bryand irritably, peering into the gloom. "Cower! Boys!"

No response.

The woman was fast becoming hysterical. "I can't see a blinkin' thing. It's too dark."

"Calm yourself," Bryand snapped. "They're probably right behind us."

But even he was growing concerned.

She began to cry in long, pitiful wails. "Noim! Donoim! Me boys is drowned!"

Bryand did not know whether to comfort the woman or rebuke her. Perplexed, frustrated, he started toward the water's edge. "I'm going to look for them. You stay here."

"Alone?" she asked immediately. "In the dark? Suposin' you drown?"

"I won't drown."

A sound reached them at that moment, one distinctly human, rising above the din of the rushing water.

"Wheeeeeeeeeeee!" shouted Donoim gleefully on the crest of a wave.

"Donoim!!!" Malady shrieked, tears streaming down her cheeks.

"Hey mum! Lookit me!"

Having never fathered any children, I cannot say conclusively what it is about them that makes them fearless. Perhaps it is because they are too innocent to recognize mortal danger. Perhaps they merely rely on their elders to fear for them. And perhaps that is why - as incongruous as it may seem - most parents at one time or another want to strangle their own children.

"Get your arse over here!" the woman raged, shaking her fists at him.

Bryand waded out for the boy and brought him ashore.

Noim followed shortly afterwards. Being older and somewhat wiser for his years, he was frightened, and he quickly scrambled into his mother's outstretched arms.

The Prince stood and watched the draining water for what seemed an eternity. But still there was no sign of the retainer.

"Cower!" Bryand called. Echoes reverberated through the cavern. "Cower! Over here!"

The roaring water was his only reply.

Make it, Cower! Bryand prayed. Please, make it! Finally, he could bear waiting no longer, and he jumped into the water and slogged toward the shaft until his feet could no longer touch the bottom. He tried to swim, but each time he took a stroke, the force of the water carried him back again.

Still he persevered, and like a fish fighting its way upstream, he reached the side of the shaft and gripped the wall.

"Cower!" he shouted, though he could hardly hear his own voice above the roar of the water. "Where are you?!"

The Prince lost his grip, and he was dragged from the wall. He tried swimming again, but by now his strength was spent, and the swiftness of the current carried him toward the others.

He was close to hysteria. Without Cower he could not go on.

"Cower!" he bellowed with all his strength, tears rushing to his eyes. "Cower, where are you?"

Whereupon the retainer, holding two haversacks like a pair of water wings, rode into the cavern on the crest of a new wave and sailed directly into his arms.

"You called, my lord?" he sputtered.

Bryand cackled like a loon and kissed the man's forehead. Helping each other, they swam back to the island, dragged themselves out of the water, and collapsed upon the wet sand, where they lay panting for air.

Suddenly Malady screamed.

"What? What is it?" shouted Bryand, straining to sit up.

"Me diamonds! I've lost me diamonds!"

Bryand fell down again upon the ground, too exhausted to care.

But Malady cared. So much so that she began to have a fit. "A minute ago I was a blinkin' duchess," she raged, stamping her feet and striking the air with her fists. "An' now I'm a pauper again! It ain't fair, I say! It just ain't fair!"

She whirled on the Prince and, forgetting the differences in their stations, shouted, "This is all your fault!"

"Mine?!" said Bryand, trying to catch his breath.

"Aye! If it wasn't for you, we wouldn't be in this fix. If it wasn't for you, I'd be home wiv me husband. An' now I got neither!"

Bryand stared at her, wondering how he was going to keep himself from throttling her before they had reached a conclusion to their journey. "Calm down, Malady."

"I won't calm down!" she railed. "I'm wet an' I'm cold, an' I ain't had a decent night's sleep in days!" She began to convulse. "Now ya've done it. Now ya've done it. Here comes one o' my seizures!"

Bryand scrambled to his feet. "Calm down, Malady," said the Prince, watching her twitch. It was like nothing he had seen before.

Her face contorted into a shapeless mass; her head snapped back and forth. From her throat came a guttural moan as drool spilled down her chin.

Bryand turned to Cower and then to the boys, confused, dismayed. "What should I do?"

"Well," admitted Noim, studying his mother carefully. "Me dad usually gave her a crack on th' chin 'bout now."

"That doesn't sound right to me," said Bryand doubtfully.

"Go on," said the little one. "It's okay."

Bryand looked to Cower for reassurance.

"I'll do it if you don't want to," said the retainer with a strange gleam in his eye.

"No," answered the Prince quickly. "I want to. I mean, I'll do it."

Normally he would never think of hitting a woman. The laws of chivalry were adamant about that. Hitting a woman was a despicable act perpetrated only by cravens and drunkards.

But the circumstances were not normal. He had to do something. Her head kept snapping back and forth. Her chest heaved up and down. He did not know how much more punishment the woman's body could take.

So, with a grimace, he drew back his fist and punched her squarely on the jaw. Malady stopped abruptly, her eyes crossed and rolled up into her head, and she collapsed in a heap upon the ground.

"It worked!" said Bryand, surprised.

"Told ya," answered the little one.

The Prince stared at the woman, noting that her facial features were once again symmetrical. Feeling completely ashamed of himself, he gathered her into his arms and sprinkled some water on her face.

"Malady? Can you hear me?"

The woman groaned and her eyes fluttered open, and finding herself in Bryand's arms, first she smiled, then, a thoughtful look came over her face. "Thank you, m'lord," she said, freeing herself and standing. "I thought only Cleave knew how ta do that."

"Well," said Bryand with irony. "I promised him I'd take care of you."

They rummaged through the haversacks to see what was salvageable. The sacks, being made from oiled skins, had kept most of their supplies dry.

Cower produced a few candles and lit them. "By the heavens," said the retainer breathlessly, gazing at the ceiling.

The others looked up and marveled as well. Catching the glint of the candles' flames were what seemed to be a myriad of tiny stars.

"Looky at all them diamonds," said Noim, awed.

"It's like the night sky," added Bryand in wonderment.

Malady sighed deeply and shook her head. "Now that's torture for ya."

From the wreckage and debris that had floated down from the chamber, Bryand scavenged a working lantern. And holding it aloft once it was aglow, he left the others to explore the reaches of the cavern in search of a way to escape.

He went from one tiny island to the next, wading across water that was sometimes knee deep, sometimes chest deep, depending on the height of the land. He made his way to the perimeter, then proceeded to follow its broad curve hoping to find any passable openings in the rock.

The lantern light cast many shadows upon the broken walls and, at times, gave him the impression he had come upon a hole. But upon closer inspection he would discover it was only a gash in the rock or a ridge, and with each disappointment, he went away feeling a little more desperate.

He glided through the inky water from crag to crevice, swimming at times, at other times pulling himself along the face of the rock, leaving nothing unexplored. And still he found no way out of the cavern.

He was in shallow water once again when he came upon a small crevice. Thinking he had at last found the means of their escape, the Prince bent low and entered it, limping along on his knees, one hand supporting his weight while the other held the lantern out at arms length just inches above the water. He went on in this way for about ten minutes, the muscles in his arm beginning to ache, the back of his neck burning.

He came to a dead end. Worse, he realized the crevice was too small to turn around. He was forced to make his way out backwards, ignoring the sharp pain in his back and the sweat that dripped into his eyes.

At length, he reached the cavern and promptly stretched to his full height, loosening the kinks in his body. At that same moment, a large wave crashed against the stone wall, almost dousing the lantern.

Bryand turned and peered into the darkness. That was strange, he thought. Up until then, there had been very little motion to the water.

He came upon a small promontory that jutted out from the wall, and being tired and depressed, he pulled himself up and stopped to rest. He glanced back toward his companions and saw the tiny flickers of their candles.

It was then, as he was sitting there, almost mesmerized by their luster, the darkness came up as if it had a life of its own, and swallowed the points of light. It was so fast that Bryand did not realize they were gone until they had appeared again, and he stared into the gloom, even more puzzled.

He slipped into the water once more. Here it was only waist deep.

He had gone another fifty yards, and was approaching a small island, when he noticed something floating in the water to his right. He held the lantern out, and soon Digs' body drifted into the circle of light, his eyes glassy and fixed upon the glittering diamonds that would never be his.

Bryand grimaced, and pushed the body away. He started again for the island. There came a large wave and a loud splash, not unlike the one that had smashed against the cavern wall earlier, and turning in that direction, the Prince saw the dwarf's body was now gone.

He waded out a few more feet, and then he noticed the pinkish tint around him. Blood, he thought repugnantly. He peered into the gloom and a chill ran up his spine.

Suddenly, he was afraid and wanted nothing more than to be out of the water. Quickly, man, he told himself as he slogged toward the tiny island. He was greatly relieved when he felt the lay of the land rising beneath his feet. In a moment, he was standing on the shore.

He watched the surface for any unusual movement.

But there was nothing. At least nothing he could see.

He was done with this; ready to quit. The thought of going back in the water filled him with dread, and this made him feel like a helpless child.

But he knew he had to press on. The others were depending on him to find a way out. Back into the water he went, shivering, his eyes darting this way and that.

He had traveled another thirty yards or so along the perimeter, and was back again in waist deep water, when he came upon what was unmistakably a large hole in the wall. Encouraged, he thrust the lantern into it and saw it was a tunnel of sorts, then he climbed out of the water and onto the ledge that was the tunnel's floor.

"My lord," came Cower's voice, echoing, sounding very far away.

Bryand faced the cavern and waved the lantern from side to side. "Over here! What's wrong?"

When the last of the Prince's echoes had died away, Cower replied, "The water's rising fast. We're losing dry ground."

"Then we'd better join up. I've found something here."

He watched the tiny specks of their candles dance up and down and slowly head his way. There came a splash in the distance and suddenly the same anxious feeling came over him again. He tensed and peered into the darkness, knowing not what he was looking for.

"Will ya stop throwin' rocks an' keep up," came Noim's peevish voice.

"Awright, awright. Quit pullin' at me," replied Donoim.

Bryand shook his head and breathed somewhat easier. But then Malady screamed. He reacted instantly, jumping off the ledge and into the water.

"What is it?" he shouted, the echo of his voice mixing with those of Malady's scream.

"Somethin' brushed me leg!"

"Aw, mum, cut it out," said Noim.

"I tell ya somethin' brushed me leg!"

"Quickly!" Bryand called, wading further out.

He looked down, very much aware now that half his body was lost from sight beneath the murky water. "Hurry!" he shouted, his voice tight and shrill.

A cacophony of splashes erupted as the others hastened to him. It seemed like an eternity, and it took all of Bryand's will to stand his ground.

But soon, to his relief, Cower entered the lantern's light, carrying Donoim in his arms, followed by Malady, wearing an anguished look, and Noim bearing the haversacks. Bryand took the little one from Cower, sloshed to the wall, and placed him on the ledge, then he and Cower helped Malady up, Noim next, then hoisted themselves out of the water.

When the echoes died, all was silent save for the sound of the draining flood.

"I hate the water," said Malady with a shudder.

Bryand stared at the blackness before them. "I've discovered I'm not too fond of it myself."

"So whaduya think?" asked the little one, peering down the hole. "Is this the way out?"

"We'll soon see," replied the Prince. Then, with a labored grunt, he stood, mopped the sweat from his brow and, taking up the lantern once more, entered the tunnel with the others close behind.

The angle was on an obvious incline, and this he found encouraging. Yet they had not traveled more than a hundred yards or so when the tunnel dipped again. The air grew hot and moist, and they became aware of a foul odor.

"Phew!" said Donoim, crinkling his nose with distaste. "Smells like them eggs we had last week."

"Last week," sighed Malady, a far off look in her eyes. "Seems like a lifetime ago."

It wasn't until the tunnel ended at a round chamber that they realized how aptly the little one had described the smell.

They halted as if they were one, and stared in awe as if they were one. For directly in front of them, in the center of the chamber, wedged between some jagged rocks and dry timbers, were three brown spotted eggs, each about two feet tall.

"What kind o' bird laid those?" asked Noim, eyeing them with wonder.

"Not a bird, lad," said Cower ominously as he gazed at the Prince.

"Stay here," said Bryand, unsheathing his sword. He circled the nest with caution.

He had never seen eggs like these. Why, they were twice as large as the giant Plumy birds of the southern plains.

Though he could not say for certain, something told him that Cower was right. No bird had laid these eggs.

Given the subterranean cavern, the lake, the perpetual darkness, he deduced they were reptilian. But he knew of no reptile that grew this large, and this sent a chill running through him.

When he had come around to the far side of the nest, he noticed the rear of one egg was missing. Pieces of shell, some as big as six inches across, lay nearby, coated on the inside with a green tinted slime.

Suddenly he thought of Digs' body, disappearing in the water as it had, leaving only a stain of blood. His hackles rose. He started toward the others with a grim look upon his face.

"Let's get out of here; fast!"

The words had hardly escaped his lips when Malady screamed. There was a loud hissing sound, and before Bryand could rejoin his companions, the egg's inhabitant rounded the other side of the nest and cut off his retreat.

It was like nothing he had ever seen; indeed, reptilian in nature, though Nature had probably considered it an abomination.

It was easily six feet long, with the body and legs of a lizard, yet thicker, more squat. Its hide was armor plated down to the tip of its long tail, and it had two yellow eyes that sat atop its conical-shaped head.

It truly was alarming; most of all its jaws - long and powerful, and lined with sharp teeth designed for ripping.

He stared fixedly at the creature, fear rising inside him, more complete than he had ever felt before. He had faced men in battle, risked death by their blows. Yet in spite of their enmity, there had always been an unspoken code between them that dictated striking quickly, killing quickly, and moving on to the next foe.

This creature, however, was something else. He saw nothing but the desire to kill in the way it looked at him, nothing but insatiable hunger in the way it licked its jaws. Dying in its clutches meant slow, unbearable torment while being eaten alive.

The creature hissed and started forward with frightening agility. Bryand retreated, almost stumbling. The creature slowed, hissed again, stretched wide its jaws almost as if it were toying with him.

The Prince gripped the hilt of his sword, his heart racing at the gallop, his lungs in need of more air.

Get hold of yourself, he thought, struggling to control his fear. If it gets you, there'll be no one to protect the others.

He took a deep breath, another, felt his courage returning, his intellect sharpening, and when next the creature advanced, the Prince held his ground.

Being closer now to the lamplight, the creature halted. Bryand took note of this and held the lantern out at arm's length. A small membrane came down over the creature's eyes; and taking advantage of its momentary blindness, the Prince rushed forward, his sword raised in the air.

He cried out, more from terror than anything else, and bringing down his blade with all his strength, he sliced deeply into the creature's neck. The monster roared and snapped at the air. Bryand struck again, savagely, and with no remorse. The creature writhed upon the ground like a crimped worm, rolling on its back, on its stomach, over and over again.

The prince raised his sword one last time, and with one last sweep of the blade, the creature stopped its writhing and lay still, its head severed completely from its body and its blood emptying on the floor.

Breathless, shaking from the effort, he staggered to the others, who, frozen in sheer terror, had been looking on the creature's death throes with a morbid fascination.

No one spoke. No one moved. Though it was only yards away from their feet, before them lay something whose existence seemed almost impossible to believe. At length, Donoim stepped closer, avoiding his mother's unwieldy clutches.

"What're you doin'?" asked Noim, his eyes still agog.

"I want its head. No one's ever gonna b'lieve me 'bout this if I can't show 'em its head."

"You ain't gonna touch that thing," Malady growled, summoning the courage to run after him and drag him back to Cower's side.

"Come," said the Prince, still grimacing. "We don't want to be around when the others hatch."

And without another word, they hastened back the way they came. However, cresting the rise, they saw the water within the cavern had risen sharply and had already penetrated the tunnel. But far worse than this were the two huge yellow eyes that broke the surface and glinted at them.

Malady screamed. Again.

"Dearest Gods," Cower gasped, and he clutched the children to him.

"Back! Fall back!" shouted Bryand. "As fast as you can!"

The boys dashed ahead, Cower waving them on like a shepard, while Bryand, pushing the stricken woman along, held the lantern behind him, hoping the light might keep the creature at bay.

They entered the chamber, rounded the nest, and hastened for the far wall. Bryand shielded Malady. Cower stood in front of the children and went rigid as a stone wall.

"I wanna see," said Donoim, peeking out, whereupon the retainer took his face and shoved it behind him.

They heard a low, guttural growl. A moment later, the creature appeared at the chamber opening.

First came its snout, four feet long, then the rest of its bony head, and then, having no real neck, came the front part of its body.

From what he had seen thus far, the Prince guessed it was somewhere between twenty-five and thirty feet long. The thought of it being in the cavern pool, chiefly responsible for consuming Digs and the other dwarves, sent a shiver through him.

The creature stalked into the chamber, its scaly hide glistening and dripping wet, its claws scratching on the rock floor. Ivory colored teeth sharp as daggers lined its jaws, and it smelled of slime and brine and rotting flesh.

When it came upon the carcass of its offspring, the creature halted its advance. It prodded the body with its snout. Then, opening its mouth wide, revealing its pink glutinous maw and the remains of Digs and Picks as well, it gave out with a deafening roar that shook the entire chamber.

In that brief pause, while Malady screamed and pulled at her hair, the Prince looked about, and his eyes fell upon a small hole in the wall about ten feet above their heads. He dropped his sword, grabbed Donoim, and hoisted him onto his shoulders.

"Tell me what you see?" he shouted.

"It's a tunnel," called Donoim, scrambling inside.

It was what he had hoped to hear. "Up you go," said Bryand to Noim. And he and Cower boosted him together.

They lifted Malady, ignoring her as she screeched,

"I can't, I can't, I can't!"

"Now you, " said Cower.

"No, you," answered the Prince, spinning the retainer to the wall. Then meshing his fingers together for Cower's foot, he bent low and, with a grunt, boosted him up.

Cower wriggled inside and began to turn around. But the hole was a tight squeeze, and for one brief moment the retainer became stuck.

"Help me!" he shouted, panicking, his hands groping for a better hold. Suddenly he felt a blow to his shoulder, and he was free. He realized Malady had just kicked him, kicked him hard, but there was no time to confront her about it.

In the meantime, stealing quick looks at the creature, Bryand danced from foot to foot, waiting for Cower to appear and offer him a hand up. He jumped for it, but the hole was too high.

And then, there was no more time to wait. The creature had rounded the nest. It had seen him, and now, with a hiss, it was barreling toward him with its mouth agape.

Bryand screamed and grabbed his sword, rolling clear of its snapping jaws.

He came up by its shoulder and, with all his strength, brought the blade down across one eye. Instantly, he was splattered with hot blood.

The creature roared and thrashed its head, knocking the Prince off his feet. It came at him, but Bryand wriggled clear of its maw, scrambled to his feet, and ran, putting the nest between them.

What happened next was basically a game of "If you go this way, then I'll go that way". Each time the creature rounded the nest, Bryand raced to the opposite side.

It was during this standoff, the Prince saw the

lantern and haversacks. Bryand sprang for them. He grabbed one, rummaged through it, came up wanting, then – frantic now - tore through the second sack. The creature rounded, saw him, and charged.

Where is it? he thought. I know it's in here! And then his hand was upon it, the flask of lamp oil he had seen Cower pack.

But before he could remove it, the creature was upon him. He shot to his feet, bringing his sword down with all his strength, cutting deep into the creature's top jaw. It gave out with an earth-shaking roar, allowing Bryand the chance to retreat once more.

Round they went again, and this time, reaching the haversack, Bryand pulled free the flask of oil, tore off the leather stopper and doused the eggs in front of him. He hurled the lantern just as the creature came about, and the nest went up in flames.

The creature shrank back from the fire, confused, enraged. Bryand fell back and hugged the chamber wall opposite it.

What to do? What to do?

Through the billowing smoke, Bryand saw Cower appear at the mouth of the hole, his arms outstretched and waiting. He was just above the creature' shoulder.

It was then, the Prince did something he had never done before. Taking no time to weigh his chances, no time to sort his options, but summoning all of his boldness, he raced across the chamber, jumped onto the creature's hindquarter and, using it as a springboard, leaped for Cower's outstretched hand.

He caught it and landed against the wall with a thud. But though he smarted, the Prince hung on, and was just scrambling inside the hole when the creature's head blotted out the fire's light.

He felt hot breath upon his legs; felt something snare his left foot. Suddenly he was being dragged backwards. But Cower grabbed him and held on, and Malady grabbed Cower and held on, and the boys grabbed Malady and held on.

Bryand kicked and kicked at the creature's snout. And then, there was a thunderous burst of light and sound from inside the chamber. The creature let go and pulled its head out of the hole. And looking below, before scrambling to safety, Bryand saw the unhatched eggs, cooked now from the fire's heat, had exploded.

The creature's bellow shook the chamber, dislodging rocks from the ceiling above. It lumbered first one way and then the other, slapping its bottom jaw on the stone floor in what was obviously a fit of rage. And then it saw Bryand. And it charged the hole once more.

"Go! Go! Go!" shouted the Prince, whereupon Bryand scrambled backward into Cower, who scrambled backward into Malady, who scrambled backward into the boys.

The creature's head filled the opening. It thrust its snout inside as far as it would go. But this time, Bryand was facing the right direction, and he was ready to do some thrusting of his own. The first, buried his sword down a nostril almost the length of the blade. The second found the creature's good eye. One or two more, and it dropped to the ground, bellowing in frustration.

"Now I know how a mouse feels when a cat is after it," said the Prince with a shudder.

Once Cower had turned around, they crawled along the tunnel, and they did not slow down until long after the creature's roars had ceased.

Hours passed, and still the tunnel had not widened. The air was stifling, and they were soaked once more, only this time from their own perspiration.

Since escaping the creature there had been nothing but darkness, darkness, and more darkness, complete and inscrutable, and with the finality of a grave.

"I've had 'bout as much o' this as I can stand," said Malady at last. "It's drivin' me dotty."

"Well, don't faint now," replied Cower in an exasperated tone. "You'll plug up the hole."

But though he would never admit it to the woman, the retainer knew that, if the tunnel did not widen soon, he would join her in her dottiness.

Even Bryand felt unbearably confined. The limits of his prison cell had been luxurious compared to this. Worse still, he thought fearfully, what if the tunnel should dead-end and we're forced to go back the way we came?

They pressed on, grunting, groaning, their eyes stinging from the salt that ran down their brows. The air was so hot that it parched their throats and burned their lungs, and still the tunnel did not widen.

"Please," gasped Malady, as she crawled. "I gotta rest. Me back is killin' me."

"Don't stop," wheezed Bryand. "No one is to stop. We must keep going."

"I can't!"

"You must," he said, his voice hoarse and barely a whisper. "Or we'll surely die in here."

She began to cry, uttering a low, pitiful moan, but even so, she continued to crawl. And listening to her suffer, Bryand wondered how long it would be before he began to cry, too. For even in the deepest, ugliest reaches of his soul he had never imagined a torture such as this.

"Ouch!" came Donoim's voice from out of the darkness.

Whereupon each of them collided with the rear of the person in front.

"Watch it there!" shouted Malady sternly. "That's me private zone!"

"How was I to know you'd stopped," the retainer

replied, mortified that he had stuck his nose someplace he shouldn't.

"What's going on?" the Prince called, wincing from the pain in his throat. "Donoim, why'd you stop?"

"Because I hit me head, is why!"

"On what?" asked his brother, punching him on the buttock.

"On the bloody wall in front o' me!"

No one spoke; and the dread each of them felt was like a tangible element that engulfed them as consummately as had the flood.

Noim was first to break the silence. "What're we gonna do?"

"I ain't goin' back," said Malady, her voice thin and strained. "Leave me here if ya want, but I ain't goin' back."

"You will," said Cower firmly. "Even if I have to drag you by the feet!"

"Don't you talk that way to me mum!" cried Noim.

And they began to argue.

"Calm down," shouted the Prince, pounding his fist on the ground. "All of you!"

But no one obeyed. And, having pushed themselves to the limit of their endurance, their harsh words spilled out along with their tears.

"Wait a minute!" said the little one, the only one who had not lost his head. "Hey, everyone, it goes up! Do ya hear? It goes up!"

Bryand shook Cower's leg. "Quiet, I can't hear Donoim. Quiet!"

The others fell silent.

"I said it goes up."

"Test it, lad," said Bryand eagerly. "See where it leads!"

Donoim stood and felt along the wall in front of him. His fingers touched a ledge in the rock just above his head, and he pulled himself onto it.

"Looks ta me like another tunnel."

And indeed, it was; though it was not much wider than the crawl space they were in.

"An' the air's cooler up here, too!"

Encouraged by this news, they delved within themselves once more and found an extra ounce of strength. They scrambled up the hole one after the other, and their efforts were soon rewarded, for not more than fifty feet beyond the first turn, the darkness no longer seemed absolute.

At first the Prince thought it was his imagination until he heard Noim say, "Hey, I can see me hand."

This gave them even more inspiration and after another hundred feet, they came upon a cave that was big enough for them to stand again.

They rose stiffly, their muscles screaming from their ordeal, and they lumbered along the floor of the cave, the light growing stronger with each bend they rounded.

And then suddenly there it was ahead of them, at the top of a twenty foot climb: an opening, with daylight streaming through! So bright was it that they had to shield their eyes.

They were exhausted, yet they hastened towards it, climbing hand over hand up that final grade, until, at last, they emerged into the daylight and found themselves on the side of a wooded hill. It was still pouring, but no one cared; and they ran into the open, whooping, laughing, dancing about.

Everyone, that is, except Noim, who remained by the entrance with his arms folded and a scowl upon his face. "What's so bloody marvelous?"

"Life, boy!" cried Cower, grinning from ear to ear. "And the fact that we're still healthy enough to enjoy it!"

Noim waved him off. "We got no food an' we're lost

in th' wilderness. I don't see no reason ta celebrate."

But the others ignored his remark, and they hugged out of sheer joy. Then, breathless, they stood with their faces raised to the sky and let the rain wash away the last of their fears.

CHAPTER FIFTEEN

Exhausted from weeping, MeAnne sat upon the floor at the center of the North Tower chamber, her arms folded and resting on top of a long pine box, her head resting on her arms. A week had come and gone since Daron imprisoned her; a week without contact with another human being. At first she thought she would be missed; that someone would come looking for her.

But no one had.

She still wore the riding shirt and leggings she had donned the night of the feast, but they no longer smelled very fresh nor looked very crisp. Her hair hung in tangled mats to her shoulders and had that unwashed odor she despised. Her teeth felt ever so scummy.

Upon entering the tower, she beheld a stark room save for a few pieces of ornately carved furniture along the walls, a canopy bed, and the pine box. The Queen Mother, however, was nowhere to be found. Confused, MeAnne walked about the room, looking for her, though it could not have been more than twelve feet across. She even checked under the bed. (*The Queen had exhibited some odd behavior since her husband's death.*)

But indeed, the Queen Mother was not there. It then occurred to her that the guards had locked her in the wrong tower. Dearest Gods, she thought, panicky. Am I to be confined here by myself? Without even the Queen Mother to talk to?!

What will I do? MeAnne thought, struck with fear.

How will I pass the endless hours? Surely, the silence will drive me mad!

She was about to despair when suddenly she remembered something her tutor had said the day they departed for Bandidon.

"Dignity, your highness, is a Princesses taskmaster. Without it, she is no better than a common milkmaid. And composure! Composure is just as important. Perhaps even more so, depending on the circumstance. Keep them both ever in your mind. For at times they are a lady's only defense, nay, only weapon, against her enemies."

Here she had paused, a far-off look in her eyes, and when next she spoke, there was a different tone in her voice. "Aye, her only weapon. But not just against her enemies. Oh, no! She must also contend with her husband. And those filthy urges of his! Oh, he'll ply you with threats. He'll berate you with curses. And when those efforts fail, he'll even cry and plead upon his knees. But do not weaken. No matter how much he begs. Let him go back to that little kitchen slut he's been shagging. Let him slither between her legs. Because it will be a cold day in the nether-world before he gets beneath your skirts again!"

It was here, she had taken a deep breath to calm herself, and when next she had spoken, she was her old self again. "Remember that always, my dear. Dignity and composure, and you can weather any crisis."

The woman had proven a shining example of her own advice. For even on the day she was executed for murdering her husband, she had acted quite dignified and composed.

Keeping her tutor's advice in mind, MeAnne tried hard to control her fears. But all her training, all her strength, had not prepared her for this kind of isolation.

She wanted desperately to be reunited with her

family, despite the fact that she hated the outdoors and found camping terribly inconvenient. No matter how many furs that were placed upon the tent floor, she always awoke soaking wet from the morning dew. And who was it that decided woodsmoke was refreshing and added an authenticity to one's outdoor apparel?

She thought of her father. Though they had argued bitterly, he would be outraged at the treatment she was receiving. For as long as she could remember he had always tried to protect her, comfort her. She remembered how, long ago, he would sit beside her bed at night, sword in hand, ready to fight off any trolls that might steal into her room and spirit her away.

This was, I should mention, a real threat and not the wild imaginings of a frightened little girl. There had been much rain that year, and trolls, like mosquitoes, proliferated abundantly whenever there was stagnant water about.

But this was no consolation to her, for she knew her father was far away by now. Even if she could find a way to get word to him of her plight, it would take months before he could muster an army and rescue her.

MeAnne chewed on her lower lip, trying to think of someone who could help her, now, when she needed it most. But this proved to be fruitless. Apart from the royal family and a few of Bryand's friends, she had not had time to meet anyone else.

Realizing just how alone she was, MeAnne began to tremble. Stay strong, she told herself. Stay strong.

But even as she formed the words, tears sprang to her eyes. Everywhere she looked, she saw dark, cold stone, and knowing she was trapped inside the chamber and a prisoner of Daron's whims, her courage fled like a routed army. She fell upon the pine box and buried her face in the crook of her elbow, and there she stayed, weeping uncontrollably once more.

◆ ◆ ◆

She awoke with a start, and she gazed about her, trembling. For a moment she did not know where she was, until she looked down and saw she had fallen asleep on top of the pine box. Everything was the same, except the light. The room was dimmer now. There was something else as well, a steady swishing sound that came from outside.

She rose and approached the narrow embrasure. Peering outside, she saw the sky was choked with clouds. Rain was pouring down in torrents. A gloomy day, she thought. One befitting my mood.

She watched the rain as it struck the small section of the battlement that was visible to her. A large puddle had collected on the wallwalk, whose surface was kept in constant turmoil by the heavy downpour. She was watching this for a while, when a sentry - his head bowed and shoulders hunched against the rain - stepped into her line of sight.

She sucked in her breath, so excited was she to see another human being.

"Hello down there!" she called, squeezing into the stone casement and waving. The soldier stopped and glanced about, but did not think to look up in MeAnne's direction.

"Up here!" she called again.

But the sound of the rain as it pelted the battlements was far too loud for him to hear her. Frustrated, the Princess wriggled free of the casement and searched about for something to throw in the sentry's direction.

Her eyes fell upon a piece of juicy fruit that she had not eaten for breakfast that morning (*the fall kind with the pock-marked orange skin. Not to be confused with the summer kind that is yellow and fuzzy and is more to my liking.*)

Scooping it up, she rushed back to the embrasure. But by the time she had jammed herself far enough into the casement, the sentry was no longer in sight. Disgruntled, she let the fruit fly, only to be further piqued when it landed just short of the battlement, hitting a merlon and falling out of sight.

She pulled herself back inside and left the window, wiping her scowling face on her sleeve. Of all the cursed luck!

Her mood now sullen and peevish, she plopped down upon her bed and stared about the room, her jail, hating it more than ever.

She studied the furniture and the sparse appointments. Whoever decorated this place should have been drawn and quartered, she thought, placing her chin on her palm. About the only thing of real value was the candlestick by the side of her bed and the silver salver that sat atop the low drop-leaf table against the wall.

Apart from the two straight-backed chairs and the faded tapestry that hung over her bed, there was nothing else in the room. Except, of course, for the pine box.

Strange, she thought, that it should be there, sitting by itself in the middle of the floor, and the longer she stared at it, the more out of place it seemed.

Having nothing better to do, she decided to examine it. She walked around the box, placing heel to toe, determining the dimensions to be just about six feet long and three feet wide.

The box smelled like a fresh pine forest, which she did not mind at all. The wood was so new, it still dripped sap in places. These she avoided because sap was extremely sticky and most difficult to remove when having made contact with the skin.

She walked around it once more and tapped it with her foot. She reversed direction, then knelt and rapped on the top with her knuckles in several places. The sound came back differently each time, and from this she determined there was something inside.

She tried to lift the box. She failed. There was definitely something inside and it was heavy. She examined its construction, noting how the top, or lid, had been nailed into place all along the perimeter of the box.

"If only I had something to pry it open," she whispered aloud. She glanced about the room, but she found nothing that was strong enough to do the job.

Sighing deeply, she went to her bed, where she sat and rested her head against a bedpost, depressed once more.

At length, the light dwindled within the room, and she sat in the darkness, listening to the rain. Her dinner tray was slid beneath her door, yet she let it sit there untouched out of spite. For each time a meal was delivered in this manner it rankled her.

Once during the past few days she had resolved to starve herself to death and by doing so protest against her mistreatment. But she had relented, thinking it more important to maintain her strength for a possible escape.

Now she was not so sure.

For the present, her hunger won out. So, she retrieved the tray and placed it on the table. One thing about which she could not complain was the fare. There was a mutton joint as big as a mallet and some capon wings, a large bowl of bread pudding, half a wheel of cheese, fruit, and a short pitcher of wine. It was a meal large enough to sustain her for at least two days, yet in the morning another tray would be slid beneath her door, and it, too, would be overflowing with food.

She lit a candle. Then she served herself some bread pudding with the silver spoon that had accompanied the tray. She had eaten only a few mouthfuls when it dawned on her that she could use the spoon to pry open the lid of the pine box.

Licking it clean, she knelt by the box and applied it to the top seam. The spoon bent. But she did not give up.

She turned the utensil around and pressed the tip of the handle into the seam, working it back and forth until she had created a tiny gap. Encouraged, she repeated the process along the entire perimeter, until there was a quarter of an inch between the box and the lid.

She rested a moment, her back tight from bending over for so long, her hands aching. After all, she was a princess, and being such, she was not used to labor of any kind.

When she looked up at the candle, she was surprised to find it half as tall. She rose stiffly and poured herself some wine, her hands shaking as she brought the cup to her lips. Then, refreshed, she went back to work, but now she used the front end of the spoon for greater leverage.

By the time she had pried the lid up high enough to slip her fingers in between the nails, the skin on her hands was cracked and bleeding, her knees were raw, and the muscles in her shoulders and neck burned like a firestorm out of control.

Yet she was too close now to allow pain to stop her from seeing what was inside. She peered through the gap, but with the only light being her dying candle, it was too dark to see anything. She shoved her hand through the gap as far as it would go, felt something soft and pliable and pulled out some wood shavings.

Oh, no, she thought, dismayed. All that work for nothing!

But wait--!

This box is far too heavy to contain only wood shavings. There must be something else inside, something underneath. She dug her fingers into the shavings. But she found nothing.

She worked long into the night, until at last the lid was a good yank away from coming off. She struggled to her feet and stretched the kinks from her muscles. Then, with her remaining strength, she gripped the edge and pulled.

The lid groaned, she groaned, and before she could recover, MeAnne found herself sailing backwards through the air, landing on the floor with a loud thud.

"This better be worth all the trouble," said the Princess from where she lay. She raised herself onto her elbows, pushed back the hair that had fallen into her face, and looked. To her relief, she found the lid lying on the floor and the box waiting to be examined. She scrambled over to it on hands and knees, too excited now to care about her sore muscles.

She reached for the candle and held it aloft. Then she dug her free hand into the wood shavings and shoveled them to the side.

She had not been doing this long when she found the toes of two soft leather slippers that were embroidered with strands of gold thread.

"That's odd," she said aloud, her brow furrowing. "Why would someone want to pack up his shoes?" There was something vaguely familiar about them, too, and the more she studied them, the more she knew she had seen them just recently, though she could not remember on whose feet they had been.

She dug away more shavings, heedlessly spilling them onto the floor. She cared little about the mess she was making. For the first time in days she had something to do and something to think about other than her imprisonment.

There was no doubt now they were a woman's shoes. I wonder if the owner will mind my wearing them, she thought to herself. They're very stylish. Oh, I hope they fit. I'm dying to get out of these boots.

She dug past the tongues, feeling something cold and smooth to the touch, and when she brushed more shavings aside she discovered the shoes were far from empty. She gasped, almost dropping the candle, and scrambled away from the box.

Feet, she thought, cringing. Those slippers are filled with feet!

For a long time, she sat by the wall, staring at the box, fighting her growing fear.

Dearest Gods, that thing's a coffin! I'm sharing my cell with a dead person!

She scrambled for the lid, intending to seal the box up again. She inspected the nails to see if any had bent. When she was sure all were straight or nearly straight, she carefully put the lid back on the box, making sure each nail had found a hole. She removed her boot, intending to use its heel as a make-shift hammer, and was ready to begin when something stopped her.

She set the lid aside and stood looking down at the coffin. What's wrong with you? she chided herself. Seal it up and be done with it.

But she did not listen to her inner voice. For the morbidness of the situation was overshadowed by the Princess's curiosity, the same curiosity that had propelled her to watch her tutor's execution.

She stared at the pair of feet, then at the other end of the box where the wood shavings were still undisturbed. If she had to share her room with a corpse, she was going to find out whose corpse it was.

But was she strong enough to look? Just the thought of digging out the face sickened her and filled her with dread. Yet at the same time, her curiosity begged to be satisfied.

She took a deep breath. She went to the other end of the box, knelt, and gingerly picked off the wood shavings a piece at a time.

First the tip of the nose appeared; the bridge, the eyebrows, the eyelids, the forehead and the cheek bones. Who is this? she thought, perplexed.

She brought the candle closer for a better look, the dim, undulating light, casting shadows across the fixed countenance before her. She removed more of the shavings, revealing the face in full, and then, with a gasp, it dawned on her. She knew exactly who was occupying the box.

MeAnne felt the world shift, felt her reason leave her. The color drained from her face and her mouth fell agape.

It was the Queen. She was indeed in the north tower, and together, one dead and one alive, they would be roommates for as long as-- .

"Dearest Gods!" she cried aloud, dropping the candle and retreating to the corner of the room. She huddled herself into a tight ball and clutched her head lest it crack into a dozen pieces.

He's killed his mother. His own mother!

Such evil was unfathomable to her. She knew monsters existed. But not the human kind. And he truly was a monster if he could commit such a heinous crime.

The darkness seemed to come alive. It crept up the walls and along the floor. In her tortured mind she saw the Queen sit up and reach out to her just as she was enveloped by it.

The entire box fell out of sight. So, too, the candle's light. Stone after stone turned to nothingness and joined the growing void.

What lay beyond, she did not know, and it terrified her. Desperate now, she pressed herself against the wall, her tiny space, all that was left of the world as she knew it. And as the darkness fell upon her, she uttered a piercing scream that went on for as long as her breath could sustain it. Her own voice; the last thing she heard before she disappeared.

Dwayne Pepperill was asleep in his bed, a state that was about to change if he did not stir soon, for with his rear sticking out as far as it was, the whole bed was dangerously close to tipping over. Yet, even so, it was lucky he was sleeping in this position; lucky for the rest of the household, that is. When Dwayne was flat on his back, he snored.

Now this was not ordinary snoring, the kind that has disturbed most everyone's sleep at one time or another. This was snoring that could start rock slides.

So deep and resonant was it, that even a person who was hard of hearing would have trouble sleeping.

And there was no meter to it, either.

Sometimes it lasted for a minute, sometimes an hour, then suddenly, silence, delicious silence, that lulled your jagged nerves and deceived you into thinking the interruption was over. And just as you were a heartbeat away from falling asleep, off he'd go again, jolting you awake.

It was morning, but with the sky grey and overcast, only a slight glow filtered into the room through the oiled skin across the window. Last night's candle had burned down to its tray, the flame long since drowned by liquefied wax. Outside, the rain fell in heavy drops rap-tapping against the window skin, drumming a more deliberate beat whenever the wind gusted.

But it was not the pounding of the rain that woke him. It was the sound of something else. Something more insistent, more urgent, that rose above the din of the rain, and when he sat up, he realized the sound was coming from somewhere within the house.

He rose, noting how cold and clammy his bottom was as he pulled on his braces, and when he opened his bedroom door, the sound grew louder still. It was then he realized someone was pounding on the front door.

He lumbered down the hall, the cold floor nipping at the soles of his feet, and when he reached the top of the staircase, he found his manservant, Trip, waiting for him at the bottom, holding aloft a candle in one hand and a cudgel in the other. Dwayne descended shaking the sleep from his head, then taking the cudgel, which was like a child's toy in his massive hands, the young lord approached the door.

"Who knocks in such a manner?" he said, annoyed.

"Open up, you overgrown infant!"

Dwayne turned to Trip, surprised. "It's Niles."

Trip tripped the bolt and swung the door inward. Niles Willowbrook flew in at the head of a gust of wind that sprayed rain everywhere and snuffed out the servant's candle.

Even in the dimness, Dwayne could see his friend was in an agitated state. Apart from being drenched, his clothes were torn and singed, his arms were smeared with oily pitch, as was his face, and down his cheek, issuing from a cut at his temple, fresh blood trickled.

Out of breath, Niles collapsed upon the stairs and leaned his head against the newel post. "Drink-- . I need a drink."

Dwayne turned to Trip and bade him bring a cup of fresh water.

"Something more bracing than that," snapped Niles. "Bring me hot wine. And lots of it."

"Make that two," said Dwayne to Trip, who, after lighting the candle again, departed.

"What happened to you?" asked Pepperill, though he was not overly concerned. For he had known Niles since his childhood, and over the years Niles' mouth had gotten him into trouble on many occasions.

But when the young man beside him began to weep, Dwayne was shocked and suddenly alarmed, and sitting on the step beside his friend, he said, "What is it? Tell me?"

Niles took hold of himself almost at once. He wiped away his tears, and took a deep breath. Then he paused and stared at the floor. "I watched my father and mother die last night," he said at last. "Along with the rest of my household."

"How is this so?" asked Dwayne, rocked.

"The guards fell upon us. We had no warning. Before we knew what was happening, they'd scaled the courtyard walls and had broken down the door."

"Guards? What guards?"

"His guards!" Niles' lips curled into a contemptuous sneer. "Bryand's!"

"That cannot be," said Dwayne, shocked.

"I tell you it's true. He's betrayed us, Dwayne. Now that he's King, he wants nothing more to do with us."

"I don't believe it."

Niles stared at him with a hateful countenance. "They plundered my home and set it on fire. Then they took my parents and led them outside, and executed them without so much as a charge. I managed to break free and steal a horse. But before I was well enough away, I heard my parents' screams." He paused, turning inward once again. "I hear them still."

"But why would he do this?" asked Dwayne. "Your family has always been loyal to his. Our fathers helped Armadon found the Kingdom. They fought at Audanot's side. You are Bryand's friend, why would he want to hurt you in this way?"

Niles turned to him and scowled. "B'Gods, man! Haven't you been listening? Or is your head as dense as your ass?!"

Dwayne would usually take exception to a remark like this, but he let it pass.

"It makes no sense, Niles. True, we argued with him and quit the court, but we've argued in the past, haven't we? On numerous occasions. When have you ever known Bryand to hold a grudge or be unscrupulous or deceitful? It's just not like him to do this."

"Nevertheless, my parents are dead and my home has been destroyed. He's changed, Dwayne. Can't you see that? Being King has gone to his head. He's drunk with power. I might have thought differently myself two days ago. But not now. Not after all that I've witnessed."

Dwayne sat for a moment, dazed and bewildered. The news, it was so horrific! So outrageous! Had anyone other than Niles brought it, he would have thrown the person out on his ear.

Bryand a tyrant? It didn't seem possible. It didn't make sense! But before Dwayne could consider things further, a crossbow bolt punctured the skin covering an embrasure by the door and lodged in the bottom step between the two young men. They jumped to their feet, startled.

"Perhaps now you'll believe me," spat Niles. He slapped the candle out of Dwayne's hand. It landed on the wet floor and was snuffed out.

There came a pounding at the door. "Open in the name of the King!"

At that moment, Trip came rushing into the hallway.

"Master Dwayne!" he called urgently. "There are men at the kitchen door! I tried to stop them but-- ."

He said no more. For suddenly his chest rose up and

his head went back. He staggered, gazed at his master with a shocked look upon his face, and fell to the floor with a crossbow bolt protruding from his back.

Just then soldiers entered the hall from the rear of the house. Their swords were drawn and ready to strike.

"Come on," shouted Niles, grabbing Dwayne by the arm and starting up the stairs. Though Dwayne followed him, he was unable to tear his eyes from his servant.

"This can't be happening!" said the young man.

"Trust me," grunted Niles. "It's happening."

The soldiers opened the front door and were joined by more of their own ranks, and when they saw the two young men upon the upper landing, they pursued.

Dwayne, in a rage now, grabbed a heavy chair from the hallway, lifted it over his head and, despite the crossbow bolts that whizzed by him, threw it down the stairs. The chair smashed into the leader and sent him tumbling backwards onto the men behind him, and they fell backwards onto the men behind them, plugging the staircase with their broken bodies.

"This way," said Dwayne, already on the run.

The two friends raced down the hallway toward Dwayne's room, stopping only briefly to struggle with some swords that hung ceremoniously upon the wall.

"Never mind," said Dwayne, grabbing hold of NIles' arm and dragging him along. "My sword and belt are my room."

They burst inside and shut the door, then using his brawn, Dwayne shoved his heavy wardrobe across the floor until it was flush with the door. "That ought to keep them out for a while," said the young man, huffing.

Niles looked about the room. "All right, now what do we do? Wait until they burn the house down around our heads?"

There came a sudden pounding at the door, and the

shouts of men. The soldiers had reached them.

"Don't be so smug," chided Dwayne, retrieving his sword and belt. "I've a plan."

"Well then, I'd say now's a good time to implement it. Wouldn't you?"

Dwayne handed Niles a belt, tore the blankets from his bed and tossed them to his friend. He hastened to the embrasure, a matter of two steps for a man his size, and, with the point of his dagger, punctured the oiled skin. He ripped it back, exposing a stout tree limb just outside.

"This is your plan?" said Niles following Dwayne through the embrasure.

The tree was old and had grown quite tall over the years. Dwayne's father had planted it long before he was born. Shading a corner of the courtyard, its limbs stretched from the side of the manor house to the wall. Dwayne had often used it to access the wall, and he thought of this as he slid his rear over the smooth stone and dropped to the ground on the other side.

"Ouch!" cried Niles in a loud whisper, landing next to him. "These slippers of mine. I had no time to grab my boots last night."

It was then Dwayne realized his own feet were bare.

But there was no time to do anything about it, for they heard the tromping of horses' hooves rapidly approaching.

They ran toward a copse of trees and had just tumbled into a thicket when mounted soldiers rounded the corner and dispersed at regular intervals along the wall.

Soon, the gloomy break of day was made brighter by the glow of flames. For though the rain still fell, the inside of the manor had been set to the torch, and its dry timbers, wooden floors and furnishings had caught at once.

Dwayne lowered his head, no longer able to watch. It was the only home he had ever known. His happiest memories were of his life there.

His parents' ashes were interred in the family vault where he had always assumed his ashes would be placed as well. But now-- . Now he had nothing.

He felt bewildered and adrift, like a boat torn from its mooring and tossed upon a violent sea. Behind the glassy sheen of his tears, his eyes smoldered with hate. He dug his fingers into the moist ground, ripped out clods of dirt, and crumbled them in his fists.

At length the roof collapsed. After making a thorough search of the grounds, the soldiers formed ranks and departed.

When the last of them had rounded a bend and was no longer in view, Dwayne and Niles left the thicket and went back to the house. They stood upon the wall and stared in silence as the rain put out the fire.

Dwayne shook his head in disbelief. "How could Bryand do this. Our lifelong friend."

"I'm sorry," Niles said at last. "But I told you."

"If it takes my whole life, even if it means forfeiting my life, I will learn the reason why."

"Come," said Niles, lowering himself to the ground.

Dwayne remained upon the wall, surveying the ruins. "Where? Everything I had in the world was here."

"Dillin has to be warned."

Dwayne looked at him, his brow furrowing. "Dillin?"

"Certainly. Don't you see the pattern? First my household is destroyed, then yours. It's obvious Dillin's will be next."

He started off, then stopped to see if Dwayne was coming. He found him still upon the wall, staring at his home.

"Dwayne," Niles called, feeling sorry for his friend.

Dwayne looked at him.

"We must go."

They came upon a patch of rocky ground. After stepping on one or two sharp stones and wincing, or in Niles' case, swearing oaths, it became apparent they were both in need of a decent pair of boots.

Dwayne knew of a cobbler in a nearby village.

"Now let me speak to him," said Pepperill, once they had reached it. "The people around these parts can be rather stand-offish at times, and that mouth of yours could get us into trouble."

"Fine with me," replied Niles, rubbing his aching feet. "Just make sure you can get that bum of yours through the front door."

"Don't start with me. I'm in a terrible mood right now."

Dwayne entered the shop. But no matter how he emplored, the cobbler was not willing to part with two of his best pairs of boots just on credit alone. Especially when the man asking for credit wore naught but a ragged nightshirt and braces, and was barefoot, too.

At length, Dwayne nodded his defeat and left, then joined Niles, who had gone to the side of the shop to sit beneath a large tree.

"Wait. Don't tell me," said Niles in a mocking tone. "He gave you magic boots. Invisible to the naked eye."

"No," grumbled Dwayne as he stood in the rain.

Niles sighed deeply and rose to his feet. "Stay here."

"Where are you going?"

"To talk to the cobbler." Niles reached for the dagger at Dwayne's belt.

"What are you doing?" said Dwayne, slapping his hand away.

"Give me your dagger," Niles insisted.

"I won't have you threatening the man. He has a right to be paid for his labors."

"I won't threaten him," said Niles, taking the dagger anyway and slipping it under his belt. "I'll simply reason with him. After that, I'm sure he'll see things differently. I'll be back with the boots in hand."

Niles marched around the corner and into the shop. The cobbler looked up, saw him, and scowled at once.

"My good man," said Niles, smiling. "My friend was just in, seeking two pairs of boots. Yet he has neither of them still. Perhaps you could you tell me why that is so?"

The cobbler, who had steely eyes, a pronounced forehead, and deep lines around his mouth, stared at him in disbelief. Another lunatic, he thought. What's happening to this country?

"Your friend had no money to pay for the boots," said the man in a harsh tone. "And if you have none yourself, you'd best join him and leave me to get on with my work."

"But sir," replied Niles cordially. "We are off to Torkelstone on urgent business. Time is of the essence. We cannot travel at the pace we must without a good pair of boots. If you, out of the goodness of your heart could extend us credit, your kindness will be generously rewarded upon our return."

"As I've already explained to your friend," answered the cobbler, whose voice grew more strident as he spoke. "I'm not in the habit of giving away the efforts of my labors."

"But, sir-- ."

"I'll hear nothing more on the subject of credit! You either pay for the boots now, or be on your way!"

"Were I to tell you that our mission is one of mercy, would that change your mind?"

"Not even if you were a high priest for the Gods," said the cobbler emphatically. "Instead of some short, annoying lunatic walkin' around in his night shirt."

There were certain words that Niles could not abide. Perhaps because he had heard them far too often in his lifetime. One of them was 'short', the other 'annoying'.

Offended at once, Niles' temper flared, and with his blood rushing into his cheeks, he snatched the dagger from his belt.

"Look here, Cobbler, I am not annoying. Irritating, perhaps, even exasperating at times, but never annoying. And, mind you, you'll find my agility with this dagger more than makes up for my height. Now, I've grown tired of this conversation. Give me the boots I want or you'll wind up with my blade in your gullet."

The cobbler, truly vexed by this, replied, "Yes, you *are* annoying. If I had my axe in hand, you'd wind up split in two and, mind you, it would be *'short'* work indeed."

"But seeing that it is nowhere to be had," snapped Niles. "I'll take the largest boots you have, and a pair that will fit me. And be quick about it! I'm a desperate man and would not hesitate to use this!"

The cobbler did as he was bade, though not as quickly as Niles had expected. When the boots were in his possession at last, the young man backed his way to the door.

"Let this be a lesson to you in civility, if not charity. Perhaps next time, you'll be more willing to help someone who asks for it."

"Next time," answered the cobbler, unafraid. "I'll have my axe closer to hand."

Niles slammed the door behind him and rounded the corner of the shop. Then with a smug look upon his face, he tossed a pair of boots to Dwayne, who stared at him in disbelief.

"I told you I'd get them," said Niles as he sat upon the ground and pulled off his slippers.

"And so you did," replied Dwayne, amazed. The brawny young man sat beside his friend and chuckled. "I thought for sure you'd come back empty-handed."

"Well, in truth, I almost did. But then I let your dagger do the talking for me and the cobbler quickly came around."

Dwayne stopped and looked at him. "What do you mean? You said you wouldn't threaten the man."

"I know. But he made me mad."

"You stole these boots."

Niles grinned wickedly. "Aye, I suppose I did."

Dwayne removed the pair from his feet and stood before his friend. "Give me those."

"Sorry, big fellow, they fit perfectly. You'll have to make due with what you've got."

"We're not keeping them," insisted Dwayne, for he had never stolen anything in his life. Just the thought of it filled him with self-loathing.

Niles snorted. "What are you, barmy? Of course we're keeping them."

"I said, let me have those boots!"

From Dwayne's expression and the tone of his voice, Niles realized he was serious. "Why are you getting so miffed?" Then trying to make light of the situation, he added, "Didn't I steal a pair for you, too?"

But this only made the young man angrier. "No one makes a criminal of me. Not even my best friend."

Niles stared at him, incredulous. "Lest you've somehow forgotten, we've just had our houses burned and our lives threatened by the King's guards. What do you think that makes us? His ambassadors?"

"I may well be outside the law, but I can still be a man of principle."

"Oh, stop being ridiculous," said Niles, growing impatient.

"I said give me those boots!"

Nothing made Niles more obstinate or inflexible than being told what to do. Especially when he thought he was in the right. He stood and dug in his heels (*literally.*)

"They're on my feet and that's where...." He paused, staring past Dwayne, whereupon, his curiosity aroused, Dwayne turned in the same direction.

It was then he saw the cobbler, who had grown extremely irritated over the loss of his boots. He had come looking for the criminal, hefting his axe in his hands.

"Ahhh," called Dwayne cordially, holding his boots aloft. "I suppose you'd be wanting these back."

"I'll have those in a moment," cried the cobbler, a maniacal look on his face. "It's your heads I'm wanting first!"

"See here, cobbler," said Niles, stepping in front of Dwayne with dagger in hand. "You've still time to change your mind and save your life as well."

But the cobbler was done talking. Instead, he came toward them, growling deep in his throat.

Dwayne shoved Niles aside. He reached for his sword and unsheathed it. Seeing this, the cobbler snarled aloud and quickly brought his weapon to a striking position above his head.

But apparently he had not used the axe in a very long time, for raising it as quickly as he did caused the axe-head to fly off its handle and land somewhere in the nearby bushes with a thud.

Cursing his ill luck, the cobbler went to retrieve it, and while he did so, Niles and Dwayne ran for their lives, and did not stop again until they were absolutely certain the cobbler had given up the chase.

The sky ahead of them was darkening. Each gust of wind came with a cold spray in their faces. They decided to camp for the night and took shelter within a cluster of trees where the ground was mostly dry.

Drenched, feeling miserable, Dwayne sat apart from his friend and avoided his eyes as he rubbed his aching feet. He had refused to put on the second pair of boots, which Niles had remembered to grab, and he did not intend to change his mind.

Stealing was wrong. That was what his parents had taught him, and he would not dishonor his parents or himself.

Then there were the Gods to consider. Did they not see everything? What would he say to Puritanicus, the God of honesty and fair play, when it came time to stand before him? The Gods were not interested in excuses. Especially Puritanicus!

At length, Niles sat down beside him, and in a patient tone of voice, one quite rare for Niles, he said, "Look, Dwayne. I understand how you feel. It was wrong of me to steal the boots. Someday I will find a way to make amends for it. But keep in mind, we've a job to do. Dillin's life depends on our speed. We'll never reach Torkelstone in time if we can't travel quickly. And we can't travel quickly if you don't put on those boots."

"But the Gods," insisted Dwayne. "They judge us by our deeds. I had always hoped that when my time came, I could go before them unblemished. You know how uncompromising Puritanicus can be."

Niles considered for a moment. The Gods were as much a part of his life as Dwayne's. But Niles had never taken much time to consider what they thought of him, or if they thought of him at all.

"Perhaps Puritanicus will understand. Think you about this; what is more important in the greater scheme of things, Dillin's life or a pair of boots?"

Dwayne saw Niles point immediately. He knew exactly which of the two was more important.

Dillin was not just a friend. He was family, too, especially since Dwayne's parents had passed on. If truth be told, there was nothing he would not do for Dillin, or Niles, or Bryand.

It seemed there were many levels of integrity, some less spotless than others, and the Gods would simply have to accept that. Even Puritanicus.

"Very well," said Dwayne, and he put on the boots.

Niles had never been the type to let matters settle or to walk away from an argument he had won without gloating a bit. It simply was not in his nature. Still, when he did gloat, it never stemmed from arrogance or conceit, but rather, from his irrepressible wit, something that had always served him, even at the worst of times.

He grinned and clapped Dwayne on the back. "Excellent. Now I can truly say to all our friends that I gave you the boot."

Dwayne responded to the remark with a baleful look. "I have one. How about, shut your mouth or I'll plant my booted foot in it."

"That works, too," said Niles, lying down. He was silent after that.

That is, until he sat back up again and said, "I'm glad you accepted the boots. That way, tomorrow, we can make some real tracks."

CHAPTER SIXTEEN

The first thing MeAnne saw when her eyes fluttered open, was the faint shaft of light coming from the embrasure. She did not know exactly how much time had passed, only that it was dark when she had fainted.

Her internal clock told her it was not quite dawn. This she confirmed when she went to the embrasure and saw the slight glow just above the hills in the distance.

The incident of the night before came quickly to her mind. She stole a look at the center of the room, hoping it had been just a horrible dream.

But there it was, the pine box, where it had been since her stay in the north tower began. And there was its occupant, Queen Benethia, in all her majesty, laying ever so still.

A shiver ran up MeAnne's spine. She did not want to go anywhere near the body, but being in the dark with it frightened her even more.

She took a deep breath to steady herself and, summoning her will, crept to the box and retrieved the candle. MeAnne set it alight and felt somewhat comforted by the flame.

Yet the thought of confinement with the queen in such a state, (*that, being dead,*) was something she could barely tolerate. MeAnne knew that if the situation did not change soon, she would most certainly lose her mind.

"I've got to escape," said the Princess aloud, her

voice trembling. "I've got to."

She looked about the room. But she found nothing that she had not seen before.

Skirting the box, she made her way over to the bed, then to the embrasure, where she peered outside once more.

It was still raining. She waited for a long time, hoping to see the sentry again, not just because he might be willing to help her, but because he was her only link to the world of the living.

Where are you? she thought, miffed. Exactly how much of the wall are you supposed to watch? Minutes passed and then she saw him.

"Hello," she called at the top of her voice. "Hello! Up here! Please look up here!"

But the rain was coming down in torrents, shouting along with the wind. Once she thought he might look up, turning this way and that. But it was only to insure his privacy as he unlaced his braces and urinated off the castle wall.

She turned her head, wishing to be discreet. Although she was curious to know what his sex looked like, never actually having seen a man's sex before.

No, she thought, suppressing the urge. Remember you're a lady.

Her resolve took less than a minute to crumble. She turned, hoping for a quick peek, only to discover the sentry was gone.

No sentry. No peek.

Frustrated, she pulled herself clear of the embrasure and returned to the bed. She had not felt this forlorn in years.

Growing up, her father and mother were often preoccupied with the intrigues of the court and with the betterment of the kingdom. Days, sometimes even weeks, would pass without her seeing them; not even for a quick hug or pat on the head.

Her sister, Blindella, was older and understood better the demands of state. Even she was sometimes shortsighted when it came to her younger sister's needs. But that was not her fault.

Once, feeling very depressed, MeAnne had tried to coax a little bastard boy up to her room, hoping they might play dress up together. But he had refused.

She understood now, as an adult, that striking him with her riding crop had been wrong. But he had been so churlish. He had even spat at her before leaping from the battlements and plunging into the moat. And that gesture he had made with his finger after crawling onto the opposite bank!

She remembered being angry. But that had passed swiftly and was replaced by the deepest sense of lonliness.

It was the same for her now.

MeAnne stared at the Queen and shivered. She was loathe to go near the corpse, but neither could she look at it one more minute.

Screwing up her courage, she retrieved the coffin's lid. If she could not order the box removed, the least she could do was to close it shut.

But just as she was about to do so, something caught her eye. Protruding from the wood shavings above the queen's head was a large green jewel about the size of MeAnne's thumbnail.

Is that an emerald?

This intrigued her. For she had always loved jewels. But even more important than that, she understood the emerald's value. A gem that size was worth a great deal, perhaps even enough to buy her freedom.

MeAnne sat by the box. A shudder ran through her. Oh, how morbid; how ghastly, she thought.

Nevertheless, she brushed aside the wood shavings and discovered the emerald was one of a cluster mounted on a fan-shaped silver ornament. Though she did not relish robbing the dead, she had no other choice, not if she wanted some leverage if and when the opportunity arose to negotiate her freedom.

Her hand trembling, she took hold of the ornament, half expecting the queen to grab her wrist as she did so.

Don't be a fool, MeAnne told herself, trying to remain calm. To think the Queen capable of doing something like that; why, she's probably stiff as a board by now.

Even so, she grabbed the ornament and pulled back quickly. She stared at it in her hand. It was attached to a smooth wooden dowel about six inches long that tapered to a point.

"A hair pin!" MeAnne said aloud, her heart fluttering with excitement. Bargaining power at last and a weapon too if needed!

She was excited now. The Queen was not one to flaunt her wealth by wearing excessive amounts of jewelry. But she was not ashamed to wear it either. It was highly likely that she had more than just a hair pin on her person at the time she was placed in her coffin.

Dare I? thought MeAnne, her heart quickening in pace. She felt heat spread throughout her body and this somehow emboldened her.

The shavings went this way and that. Soon, the queen's front was completely uncovered.

Oh, I've always liked this dress, said MeAnne to herself. It has such intricate embroidery. I wonder if her seamstress in the palace did it for her. As soon as she thought this, she realized she was losing sight of her objective.

She returned to her task, removing a gold-backed broach in the shape of a hammer and anvil from above the Queen's left breast. Both the hammer and the anvil were covered in small red, blue and violet diamonds.

Around her neck, hanging on a thin silver chain, was a large moon-pearl pendant worth a fortune, especially to the pearl traders on the coast. This she pulled free, (*with her apologies, of course*), along with a small square-cut ruby ring from the Queen's pinky.

She was about to check if there were any pockets in the dress, when her conscience chided her. MeAnne nodded, reminded of her purpose. She had found a small fortune. It was enough.

"Thank you, my lady," she said to the queen. "I promise to put these jewels to good use. I will also light candles in your memory and place them beneath the Goddess Tiffany's statue for the rest of my life."

It seemed to MeAnne that a peaceful look came over the Queen's face just then, even a hint of a smile, or perhaps it was just the poor lighting.

She did not hesitate this time, when she covered the queen with the spilled wood shavings or when she hammered the lid down with the base of the candlestick. She had an objective now, and she was determined to see it through.

She sat on the bed, looking at her treasure, tallying in her head what she thought each piece was worth. Once; twice; thrice; pretending to bargain with the city's shrewdest jewelry brokers; she walked away from the exchange each time with a fortune large enough to buy her freedom plus a small army, and if not an army, at least a regiment or two.

She gathered up the jewels and placed them under her pillow. Just having them in her possession gave her confidence. Nothing would stop her from escaping now!

All she needed was someone whose loyalty she could buy.

She rushed to the embrasure and wriggled through, ignoring the rain that pelted her face. At length, the guard appeared. "Yoo-hoo! Guard!" she called, waving her arms over her head.

He stopped and looked about.

"Guard!" she shouted at the top of her voice. "Hey stupid! Up here!"

But still the storm was too loud in the man's ears.

Oh, how frustrating! she thought. There must be some way to get his attention!

She wriggled her way back into the room and grabbed some juicy fruits off one of the trays by the door. Back to the embrasure she went, leaning out as far as she dared before throwing a piece toward the battlement.

Once again the fruit fell short and hit the outside of the wall, and once again, the sentry marched out of view.

"Nooooo!" she cried. "Come back! I'll make you rich!"

She hung there for a moment, exasperated, then she returned inside. She wiped the rain from her face and flopped on the bed.

Curse Daron! she fumed, punching the air. That he could leave her stranded like this; without any contact with another human being!

She realized she was still holding a piece of fruit. So irked was she, that she threw it across the room.

It squashed against the door; sticking for a moment, then fell and hit a food tray.

MeAnne stared at it, wishing she had as strong an arm when it came to longer distances.

Irritable; peevish; she glanced at the two trays. What a waste of good food.

It was then a thought struck her, one that caused her to leap to her feet. For it occurred to her that she indeed had contact with someone two, three times a day whenever her meals were brought to her or her emptied chamber pot was returned.

"Oh, you ninny!" she said, furious with herself. "Wasting time like this, when the wherewithal was always within reach!"

Reach she did, for a spoon, which she used to pry one of the smaller gems from the hair pin. She placed the gem in her palm and stared at it.

"Such a small thing," she murmured, watching it glint. "But large enough to do the job, I'll warrant."

She held it tight as she hurried to the door. Down she went on hands and knees, then lower still until her cheek was flush with the cold floor. She peered through the slit. But all she could see was the dull grey maw of a narrow castle stairwell.

"Hello!" she called. "Is anyone out there?"

Yeoman Grumble, who was a tall, lanky fellow with a long face that tapered to a pointy chin, was standing at his post on the lower landing of the tower. He was aptly named, for just then he was grumbling as he leaned upon his pike.

The Sergeant of the Guard had fined him ten coppers for falling asleep on duty the previous night. Why the man had made such a fuss was beyond him.

This was the loneliest, most boring post in the whole city; with nary a thing to do but slide food trays under the tower door and empty out - here he made a face meant to reflect his repugnance - someone's chamber pot.

Slide and dump; slide and dump. Was it any wonder that he had closed his eyes for a few minutes?

He recalled how his friends had mocked him. They

wouldn't have thought it so funny if they were the ones who had gotten pinched. Ten coppers is practically my entire pay for the month!

He reached into his purse, and scooped up the few coins that remained. He counted them slowly, knowing full well he lacked the funds to cover both his gambling debts and a night at the town brothel.

He stared at the coins, torn between what he should do and what he wanted to do. He decided his debts could wait one more month.

I'll just avoid the Slaughter House crowd for a while, he told himself. But when he remembered with whom he was dealing, he decided to give it more thought.

The Slaughter House crowd took their money-lending seriously. For instance, when people fell behind on payments, they tended to break things, like arms and legs; even heads from time to time.

Forget the brothel, he told himself. A roll in the hay lasts just so long; when you're dead, you're dead forever.

"Yessir, yessir, yessir," he said aloud. "That is what I'll do. I'll keep me willy in me pants and cry the whole night through."

The only good thing about guarding the most isolated post in the castle, was that he could take certain liberties at times. He could sing out loud if he was in the mood and make up silly rhymes, which he particularly liked to do.

He was still chuckling over his own cleverness, muttering, "Do; through; do; through," when he heard a voice calling from inside the tower room.

He alerted instantly. For the voice seemed strangely out of place and did not fit the prisoner he had pictured in his mind.

He had never seen him. As a matter of fact he had been expressly forbidden to look upon him, though he failed to understand why.

He was far from dangerous. He had never banged on the door or shouted curses of any kind. And having such a dainty appetite, it was no wonder his bowel movements were so slight.

Yet that voice.

His curiosity provoked, he grabbed a torch from its sconce upon the wall, then climbed halfway up the stairwell, stopping at the point where his eyes were level with the slit at the bottom of the door. Much to his surprise, he saw the face of a woman staring back at him.

It was a beautiful face, though slightly flattened on one side by the floor, and this took him completely off guard (*no pun intended here.*)

Can it be? Reggie thought. Was this really a female prisoner?

For he had heard tell of some men who enjoyed dressing like women.

Thank the Gods, thought MeAnne, feeling ecstatic and relieved. Another human being! And this one's alive!

A radiant smile stretched across her face. "Hello there!" she called. "Good morrow to you."

The guard did not respond. In fact, he looked most confused.

"Aye, you!" said MeAnne, in a bright, encouraging tone of voice, though inwardly she was thinking, I hope he's not an idiot. "Good morrow!"

Grumble kneeled on the stairs and tilted his head in the same manner as the prisoner. Without a doubt, she was the prettiest girl he had ever seen. When she smiled he could see she had all her teeth.

"Good morrow to you," he replied tentatively.

"What's your name?" asked MeAnne, even more encouraged now that she knew he could hear and speak.

"Grumble, Miss. Reggie Grumble."

"And I am MeAnne. Perhaps you recognize the name?"

Reggie shook his head. "No. Can't say that I do." He smiled shyly and avoided her eyes. "Though it's a pretty one."

His ignorance concerned her. She thought it best to be direct and to the point.

"Reggie, you must listen carefully. I am Princess MeAnne. Of Jasperland. The King's betrothed."

"Beg pardon?" said Grumble, his brow knitted.

"The Princess MeAnne. The King's betrothed. A terrible thing has happened. The King's brother has usurped the throne and stolen his identity."

The yeoman's eyes went wide. "Really?!" He had heard nothing of this. "When did that happen?"

"Months ago. I only discovered the plot just recently. But before I could expose it, the King locked me up. I am being held here against my will by a madman and a thief who would rob us all of our freedom."

"Usurped, you say?" said Reggie, trying to keep things straight. "The throne?"

I'm going to have trouble with this one. "Aye."

"By the king's brother."

This is not good, she thought. "Aye."

"You mean Prince Daron?"

"Aye! But being on the inside rather than the outside, I cannot unlock the door myself. I need your help if I'm going to escape."

Well, that makes sense, thought Reggie. He had never heard of anyone unlocking a door from-- .

"Wait!" he said, alerting. "Did you just say escape?"

"Aye. And quickly."

Grumble knitted his brow. "Oh, I can't do that, my lady."

"Why not?" asked MeAnne, frowning.

"Because I don't have a key."

Though he tried her patience sorely, she took a deep breath and went on. "But it is possible for you to acquire one, is it not?"

"Come again?"

"Can you get a key?"

"I don't know, my lady. I've never tried."

"But if you did. And you could find one. Would you help me?"

He sat up and frowned.

Sensing his reluctance, she added, "I'm prepared to pay you handsomely if you do."

Get a key, he pondered. Now where would I go to--.

"Wait!" he said, alerting once again. "Did you just say pay?"

"I did, indeed," said MeAnne, thinking they had finally made some headway.

His interest had indeed been peaked. He also made a mental note to use 'pay' and 'say' in his next rhyme. "How much?"

She stretched her arm through the slit and opened up her palm. "This could be yours," said MeAnne in an enticing tone. "Consider it a down payment for your services."

When he saw the stone, his jaw fell slack, and he drew closer to the door. "Is that an emerald?"

"Help me escape and I'll give you the mate to it as well. Escort me to Jasperland and I'll give you much, much more when we reach my father's castle."

"Jasperland," repeated Grumble, looking up from the gem. "I've never been there." In truth, he had never been anywhere outside the capital not in all his thirty years.

"It's a lovely place. Lots of greenery. Tall mountains, too. You'd like it very much."

"But what would I do there?"

"Anything you'd like. You'd be rich enough to be a country squire if you so choose."

"Oh, I don't like the country. There's too much open space." Actually, he was thinking he'd be too far from any drinking or whoring establishments.

"Then live in the city. The Hilltop Towers is a very exclusive district with a lovely view of the castle."

"Towers, huh? I don't much care for heights."

"In that case you could take a place at the bottom of the hill."

"Oh, no, no, what about run-off during the rainy season? There's nothin' I hate more than damp floors."

"Look," said MeAnne, wanting to hit him. "Live wherever you choose. Just tell me, man, are you willing to help me or not!"

"Well," said Grumble with a pained expression. "That's something I need to think about."

He peered at the stone.

"I could certainly use the money. Who wouldn't? But if I let you out, I'd be disobeying my orders, and my sergeant's angry with me already. If we got caught, I'd surely get my head cut off, and where would I be then? Dead, of course. Even if we did manage to escape, there's the move to Jasperland to think about. That's quite a journey, and when I got there I'd be looked on as a stranger. I'd have no friends."

"But you'd be wealthy," said MeAnne, trying yet another tack. "You could buy some friends."

"Aye, that's true."

Reggie turned away and was silent for a moment. He liked the idea of being wealthy, but he liked not the idea of risking his life for it. So he set his mind to thinking of a way he could obtain one and avoid the other.

What was it the Princess had said? The King is an impostor?

Perhaps he could use this information to his advantage. Perhaps it might be valuable.

But to whom?

"I'll have to give this careful thought, my lady," said the guard. "After all, what you ask is very dangerous, and our lives will depend upon its success."

"Our lives," she said, picking up on what he said. "As in, yours and mine? Does that mean you will help me escape?"

He bit his lip, then nodded. "Aye, my lady. But for that to happen, I must get hold of the key to your door, and at present, I don't know who I can approach without putting us both in danger, or worse getting us both killed. Therefore, keep your gem for now. I will let you know when it is time for payment."

"Very well, " said MeAnne, encouraged. "And Reggie?"

"Aye, my lady?"

"Thank you."

"Oh, no, my lady, thank you," replied Grumble with a quick bow.

He departed; much already on his mind. There were lots of ways he could go; lots of variations.

But soon, he had worked things out to his satisfaction, and, with a broad smile, he said to himself, "You'll pay, you say; without delay; and when you do, I'll shout 'horray.'"

She maintained her composure just long enough to reach the bed, whereupon she jumped onto her mattress and bounced up and down like a giddy child over and over again.

Oh, the joy and the relief she felt. She was a bird, no - a spirit!

Any second now she was going to spring into the air, her arms spread wide, and soar first about the chamber, then out the embrasure and climb high into the limitless sky.

She rushed to the window and leaned far outside, welcoming the rain that hit her face, comforted by it. For each new drop helped to wash away a little more of the torment and apprehension she felt.

She balanced there, her face dripping wet, until her hair was soaked and plastered to her skin. Then, feeling clean, almost purified, she pulled herself back into the room and shook off the rain like a dog drying its coat.

This amused her, and she laughed; quietly, so that Reggie would not hear; but hard and long, until tears had filled her eyes, her stomach muscles ached, and she was out of breath.

She tiptoed to the pine box and sat down beside it, patting the lid affectionately.

"Good-bye, my lady," whispered MeAnne. "Though your presence here has nearly driven me mad, there is a part of me that will always miss you. Sleep well."

She would have packed had she had anything other than the clothes she was wearing. For the first time in weeks she became conscious of her appearance. She touched her cheek, still wet from the rain, then ran her hand over her hair. She looked down at her shirt and pants, noting the various stains, the rip at her knee, the scuff marks on her boots.

"Oh, dear," she thought, perturbed. "I must look like a frightful hag."

But any awkwardness she might have felt regarding her appearance was far outweighed by the excitement she felt for her anticipated release, and it was upon that she dwelled for the remainder of the day.

The light within the chamber dimmed steadily until it was extinguished. She heard Yeoman Grumble depart.

Weary now, MeAnne climbed into her bed, and began the ritual that she used each night to induce sleep.

She thought of her father, then of her mother and sister, and a cozy feeling came over her. She pictured Bryand in her mind, not as she had last seen him, bedraggled and filthy from his stay in the dungeon, but the way he had appeared on the day of their betrothal.

A tender smile curled her lips and lingered there as she closed her eyes. Soon she had shed the limits of her chamber and was standing beside him in the Great Hall.

His arms came round her, and the warmth from his embrace spread throughout her frame and filled her with a quiet joy.

And that was all she needed to fall asleep.

In another part of the castle, the King of Bandidon strode down the corridor at a heated pace, weaving in and out without so much as a grunt or a nod to the many castle workers who had stopped to bow to him.

He was in a foul mood, one that had been growing more and more erratic since he had learned of his brother's escape. At times he suffered from fits of rage so violent and destructive that all fled from his person, while at other times he turned into a whimpering, quivering wreck of a man, huddling behind the furniture or the tapestries, replying to anyone who sought him out, "King who? Uh-uh. No one here by that name!"

He could not sleep. Though his body and his mind were weak and weary. He could not eat. Though his stomach gurgled and grumbled in want of food. But worst of all, he could not perform in bed. Though he tried and tried and tried again, the royal sex would not respond, and this filled him with a fear that far eclipsed any he might have had of his brother's vengeance.

Everything seemed to be in working order, judging from the way he rose in the morning. But come the darkness and he was overwhelmed by a nervous feeling that started in his stomach and went south, and no matter the prompting, he stayed limp, even puny, looking much like a turtle tucked into its shell.

So preoccupied was he by his present condition, that he had begun to neglect the affairs of state. He had missed the last three sessions of the Council of Kings, and without his iron rule, fights had broken out among the other leaders.

Blunderon and Odius had actually come to blows, and King Mittashmeer, while trying to break them apart, had been pummeled by both. But that did not bother Daron one bit. For all he cared, they could kill each other, and thus save him the trouble. It was what he had planned, anyway.

But at that moment he was not concentrating on anything so pleasant. He was worried about his doodle, and when he wasn't worried about his doodle, he was worried about his brother, whom he blamed for the current ineffectiveness of his doodle.

"I'll make him pay," he grumbled. A muscle in his cheek began to tick involuntarily.

"Mess with my manhood, will he? I'll teach him. I'll turn him into a eunuch. Aye, I'll leave him the itch but nothing to scratch; just as soon as I've nabbed him."

Yet even as he said this, doubt crept into his mind. Two weeks had passed and still Bryand had not been captured, despite the fact that they now knew he was traveling with Cower and the executioner's wife and children, and despite the huge net of men he had spread throughout the United Kingdoms.

He came to a turn in the corridor, rounded it, and strode directly to a door. He threw it open without even knocking and stormed inside.

The Duke of Cunninghim, who was sitting at his desk, scowled at the intrusion; but when he saw the King, he blinked and sprang to his feet. "Your majesty!"

Nightshade was there as well, sitting with his back to the door and draining a large tankard of ale. So startled was he by the Duke's sudden exclamation, that the tankard went sailing across the room along with what he had intended as his last gulp.

"Sire!" he wheezed as he struggled to rise. But his recent prosperity was most evident in the weight he had gained, and now he was so corpulent that more of his buttocks hung over his seat than was actually upon it.

"Don't bother getting up," snapped Daron. "I haven't the time to wait."

He strode directly to Cunninghim. Down came his fist upon the desk.

"You said you'd capture him. Well? Where is the Prince? Tell me you have him."

"I wish I could, sire," said the advisor, flustered. "I'm doing everything humanly possible. Why, right now, Mortamour is scouring the countryside, and I assure you, sire, if anyone can find the Prince, Mortamour can."

"Well, it's not enough! I want him taken. Do you hear?! I cannot sleep! I cannot eat! I cannot even forn-- ."

He glowered at the man. "That is all I'll say on the matter, save this! If my brother is still at large by the end of the week, I'll send you and Nightshade packing, and it won't be to some cushy post but to the frontier."

Nightshade yelped and shot to his feet like he had been jabbed with a pin in his behind.

"But sire-- . Surely, you wouldn't send away the most loyal of your subjects; especially to that wasteland?"

"I'd do it with glee. With glee, do you hear?! I want men about me who will not make empty boasts but do as I command." He shot them both a venemous look. He pointed toward the door. "Go! I cannot abide to look upon you!"

Cunninghim and Nightshade glanced at one another, confused.

Daron bristled. "Do you no longer heed any of my commands? I said, go!"

"But sire," ventured the Duke humbly. "This is my chamber."

Daron eyed the surroundings. "Oh. Very well then, you may stay. I will go."

And without another word, Daron strode to the door and exited.

Shaken, Nightshade retrieved the flagon, then poured himself some more ale. "Of all the nerve. Ordering us about like that. Why, the man's nothing but an imposter!"

"Nevertheless," said Cunninghim, staring at the door. "He's still the King, which means he can do as he pleases."

Nightshade's face went pale. For the last thing he wanted was a career as an assistant administrator for some obscure garrison post along the frontier.

Poisons abundant! Not the frontier and those heathen Woolly-Bullies! And with that, he conjured up the image of wild clansmen pouring out of their huts, brandishing their fearsome cuttintoos and nogginknockers.

He shuddered and turned to Cunninghim. "Do you think he was serious?"

"Possibly," said Cunninghim. "But before we panic, let's wait to hear from Mortamour. I have great faith in his abilities."

Nightshade turned away, nettled. He used to say

the same thing about me. Maybe I've been thinking of poisoning the wrong person.

Daron wandered the corridors, for there was much still praying on his mind, and as he proceeded toward the royal wing, he could not keep his thoughts from returning to his brother.

Perhaps I've underestimated him, he reflected, coming to a halt. Perhaps he's not the weak-minded fool I've always taken him for.

Daron's stomach churned and he suddenly felt queasy. Things had gotten so complicated; so out of hand.

If only Bryand had stayed locked up; if only his mother had not died; if only MeAnne had not learned the truth!

"All I wanted was to rule," he said aloud, sounding most pathetic. "Was that too much to ask?"

"No, your majesty," came a timid voice.

He had not expected a reply. It startled him. He turned quickly, whereupon he discovered a young chambermaid by the wall, bowing.

He stared at her a moment, saying nothing. From the way she had bowed, he could see down the front of her kirtle and spied the fleshy mounds of her breasts.

His heart quickened as the familiar excitement he had known since the age of eleven, returned to him unencumbered by fears or doubts. He felt the royal sex stir for the first time in a fortnight.

"Rise," he said in an impassioned tone.

Though he was coaxing himself, she thought he was addressing her. So, she stood and lifted her head.

He shifted his gaze quickly to her face. He did not want her to think he was staring down her blouse and, thus, objectifying her. Many of the men at court had been accused of that as of late. Being king, it was important for him to set an example for others, but secretly, as far as he was concerned, he considered himself exempt from such dictates.

The moment he beheld her face, Daron's heart began to pound in his chest. She was the loveliest peasant girl he had ever seen.

So clean and wholesome-looking; there was even a scent of wild flowers about her instead of that rancid odor so common to her class. Her face was delicately molded and perfectly balanced. Not a single wart or pimple blemished her skin, nor had she any of those unsightly mustache hairs above her upper lip.

Her eyes were alive and full of mirth. And boldness, too. For she was smiling at him as if she knew not or cared not that he was her sovereign lord.

"What is your name?" he asked, genuinely intrigued.

"Gabble, sire," replied the girl in a sweet voice.

"Gabble," repeated the King, delighted. "That's an odd name."

"But one befittin' my nature, sire. For I do tend ta run on at the mouth."

"Really? Well, I'm in the mood to hear someone run on for a while. Walk with me."

And talk she did, stopping only long enough to take a breath every now and then. Yet, she never once completed a single thought or anecdote or statement. One thing was always leading her to another thing, and by the time she had returned to her original topic, she had forgotten what she was trying to say in the first place.

Daron knew this trait could be irritating in the long run. Still, at that moment, he found her company soothing to his jangled nerves. She was beautiful and alluring, and for the first time in a long while he felt confident about making love. So, he smiled and nodded every now and then, pretending to listen to her drivel as he led her to his apartment, and then to his bed.

CHAPTER SEVENTEEN

After their encounter with the subterranean creature and torturous escape through the tunnels, Bryand and his companions spent the rest of the day and the following night camped in the entrance of the cave huddled around a meager fire. The joy and euphoria they had felt upon escaping the tunnel had carried them into the evening. But soon, as their hunger began to gnaw at them, their spirits began to fall, and after a while, as each of them reflected upon the horrors they had experienced, one by one they fell into a stunned silence.

In the morning, the sky was overcast but the rain had stopped, leaving the air fresh and perfumed. Bryand was in a buoyant mood, and he hummed to himself softly as he mashed some nokilya beans that Cower had foraged.

Though he knew not where they were at present, nor how far off course they had drifted by taking their subterranean route, he felt revitalized, and he was ready to start out again for Willowbrook at top speed.

He paused at his chore, struck by an odd thought. Wouldn't it be funny if someday people traveled under the ground to get where they were going, thus avoiding inclement weather, not to mention wild beasts?

He pictured enormous tunnels, miles long, and wagon trains full of people rolling through them. He chuckled to himself. But, of course, no one would ever be so foolish as to travel that way.

Perhaps then, he thought, sitting back on his

haunches, there would be expansive road systems that were wide enough for two or three wagons to travel abreast, and these would have smaller roads leading on and off with nearby inns and shops of all sorts to service peoples' needs.

Silly notion, he mused, shaking his head, and he returned to his chore.

"Good morrow to ya, m'lord," said Malady, rubbing the sleep from her eyes.

"Good morrow to you. I trust you slept well?"

"Very well. 'Cept for when me nose clogged up. Night air always makes me nose clog up."

Bryand smiled politely. "I see. Well, I've heard it does that from time to time." He went back to work.

Malady ran her fingers through her tresses, then frowned at all the loose hairs she had collected. She glanced at the Prince to see if he had noticed, but he was busy mashing the last of the beans.

She leaned on her elbows and watched him for awhile, scratching herself occasionally. He certainly is handsome. I wonder what it would be like to be married to a prince.

Now there's a cushy life for ya, she thought, picturing herself bedecked in jewels and fine linen, gobbling sweetmeats. I could get used to that real easy.

It was then it came back to her, among a tumult of images, from the gully, the mine shaft, the diamond, the flood, the whirlpool, the cavern, the creature.

Wait a minute, wait a minute, she told herself. Go back a bit; back to the whirlpool. Specifically, the moment when they were clinging to each other; when they thought they were going to die.

Was she mad?Was it just in her head? Or did he really kiss her? And if he really kissed her, did she not really kiss him back?

For as long as she could remember, she had thought

of herself as a wife and a mother. Thinking of that kiss and that desperate moment they had shared, and she suddenly thought of herself as a woman. A desirable woman.

But then her conscience chided her, and she recalled that, in reality, only a few weeks had passed since Cleave's death. Is that all? she thought, amazed.

So much had happened in that time, she had risked death so often, that her life with Cleave now seemed to be nothing more than a distant part of her past.

She pictured him alive and in all his glory, swinging his axe upon the block, and instead of sadness, her heart filled with warmth in the same way that it did when she thought of her parents, whose spirits had ascended to the Gods long ago.

Since she had never known the Gods to send anyone back again, she assumed Cleave was gone for good unless she happened upon a sorcerer who could restore him to life. But by then he'd be plenty moldy, wouldn't he? Malady thought, grimacing. An' what if I hugged him too hard one day an' he fell apart?

That particular image seemed to make up her mind. Best leave things the way they are, she thought, sitting up and crossing her legs. Cleave's dead, right? Life's gotta go on, right? And-- . She looked at Bryand, who was walking toward her. And the Prince has promised ta take care o' me, right?

"Here," said Bryand cordially as he handed her a thin slab of bark with some brown paste on it.

"Why, thank you, m'lord," said the woman, smiling. "But ya shouldn't be waitin' on me. I should be waitin' on you. What wiv you bein' royalty 'n all 'n me a lowly commoner."

"Please don't think that way," said Bryand. "I certainly don't."

"Really?"

"Of course." He chuckled. "We've lived through far too many dangers to allow our stations to stand between us. I dare say, in spite of everything we've been through, this is turning out to be a fruitful experience for me. I'm glad we fell in together."

She looked at him, confused. "Fell in?"

"Aye. At any other time, our paths would not have crossed. We'd have lived our whole lives and never even met."

"How true," she replied, smiling. But to herself, she thought, "What's he talkin' about?"

"And I want to get to know you even better. And the boys, too."

"What was that?" she asked. "I didn't catch that first part."

"I want to get to know you even better."

"You do?" Her heart fluttered, and suddenly, to her surprise, for it was a long time since she had felt such things, she was moist under her arms and between her legs.

"Of course." He pointed to her repast. "I'm afraid that hasn't the best of taste, but eat what you can of it. Who knows when we'll come by our next meal."

"I'm sure m'lord is an excellent provider." She wiped her hand on her chest and stuck her finger into the paste. Then, without taking her eyes off him, she slid her finger into her mouth and slowly sucked it clean. "Mmmmmmm! Very tasty."

"Glad you like it," replied the Prince, suddenly uncomfortable.

It was then it came back to him, among a tumult of images, from the gully, the mine shaft, the diamond, the flood, the whirlpool, the cavern, the creature.

Wait a minute, wait a minute, he told himself. Go back a bit; back to the whirlpool. Specifically, the moment when they were clinging to each other; when they thought they were going to die.

Was he mad?Was it just in his head? Or did he really kiss her? And if he really kissed her, why in the Heavens name did he do that?!"

"Are you all right, m'lord?"

"Huh?"

"Are you all right, m'lord?"

He broke from his thoughts. "Did you say something?"

"Yes," she said, swatting away a fly that was circling her head. "You've gone as white as a sheet."

Bryand busied himself with the paste. "I have? Uh, it must be because I have an empty stomach. Perhaps you'd better rouse the boys."

"Rouse the boys?"

"Aye. Get them up."

Her smile collapsed; and she turned to her children, feeling vaguely resentful of them. "Awright you kids; get up!" They awoke with a start. "C'mon, c'mon. We ain't got all day."

"Here," said the Prince, offering them each a trencher with bean paste.

Donoim grimaced. "That stuff looks like donkey puke."

"Eat it," ordered Malady.

Donoim shook his head firmly. "I ain't eatin' donkey puke."

"You will!" snapped Malady. "An' no more o' them comments, neither. His lordship went ta a lot o' trouble makin' that fer ya."

Noim frowned. "There ya go again. Why do ya keep callin' him that?"

But she refused to answer him. And while the boys struggled with their portions and Bryand's back was turned, she scraped off the remainder of her paste with her finger and flicked it out the entrance of the cave.

When they finished their repast, Cower doused the fire with dirt. Blankets rolled, they proceeded down the hill, winding their way through the trees at a brisk pace.

The air was full of moisture and pungent with the smell of pine needles and whispering ferns and climbing ivy. Though the sky above was a solid shade of gray, the forest floor was awash with color. Purple jump-ups dotted the ground between patches of viridian clover. Here and there, they passed a fallen tree covered with the scarlet and yellow moss that grew in abundance in the eastern shires. Even the ground sparkled with flecks of quartz and feldspar.

Soon they came upon a beaten path and halted.

"Which way?" asked Malady, staring first in one direction and then the next.

Bryand studied the path for any signs of recent use.

"No scat," he said. "And no prints."

All right, he thought. Which way. You must have learned something in the past few days. He studied the ground, the moss on the tree trunks, the crisscrossing branches overhead.

"Well?" asked Noim.

"It's coming to me." He stepped away from the others so they could not hear him.

"Eeny, meeny, miney, mo. Catch a dragon by the toe," he muttered under his breath, pointing his finger at the path in opposite directions in rhythm with the rhyme. "If he bellows let him go. Or a hot foot you will know."

"Right. This way," he said confidently, calling to the others; and he took the lead.

Though the path itself was free of stones and exposed roots, they often found themselves climbing up steep rocky slopes that were dangerously slick from the rain the day before, only to discover - once they had gained the crest - the climb down the other side was even more treacherous.

However, by late afternoon, they had left the hilly terrain behind. The forest was not as tangled or overgrown, and they could see the sky through the trees.

A breeze picked up, and for the first time in three days, the sun broke through the clouds. The forest came alive with light, and the leaves fanned out and lifted themselves to the sky like the brilliant feathers of the male primp.

By now they were very hungry. Luckily, the rain had created a dearth of phallic-looking growths, fungus really but, according to Cower, safe to eat and even quite tasty. The retainer gathered them up as they walked along, and when the small band came to a tiny brook, they boiled the growths and ate them with relish.

They started out again, braced for the next leg of their journey. Bryand was in the lead, not concentrating on anything in particular, keeping pace with the beat of his heart, when he saw a break in the trees ahead of them.

He halted. Not because he had sensed any danger, but because of the foul smelling breeze that wafted in his face. Unlike the tainted air of the egg chamber, this time he recognized the odor, for he had often smelled it after a battle had been waged.

It was the stench of carrion flesh.

"Pee-yew!" said Donoim.

Bryand spun about, a stern expression on his face. "Shhhh!"

The boy struck an arrogant pose and made to reply, but before he could, Malady slapped both hands over his mouth. "You heard his lordship," she whispered fiercely. "Shhhh!"

Bryand drew his sword. "There appears to be a clearing ahead. And from the smell of things, something is amiss. Stay here, while I have a look."

"Shall I come, too?" Cower asked in a voice just above a whisper. "You may need my help."

"No. If it is safe I will return shortly. If it is not and I am taken or slain, you must get yourself and the others to Willowbrook. You alone stand between this family and disaster."

Malady let go of Donoim and clutched her midsection. "All of a sudden I don't feel so good."

"Mushrooms," Bryand heard the retainer say as he went ahead. "Perhaps a bad one slipped in with the rest."

Bryand padded softly for the break in the trees. It was indeed a clearing, and in the center was a plundered encampment.

The tents that had been pitched were mere remnants, torn or burned to the ground, and there were wagons that were also badly charred.

He studied the tree line on the opposite side of the clearing, looking for any movement within. But he saw nothing.

Leaving the cover of the trees, Bryand took a cautious step into the high grass. The smell was almost overpowering now. He had not gone very far before he almost tripped over a body.

It was a man, or what was left of him, for much of him had been ripped or chewed by the carrion eaters of the forest. He wore mail and tunic. His face, the half that remained, was frozen in a look of surprise.

A deep gash ran from his left shoulder into his chest, and he was covered with dried blood. Bryand recognized the soldier's coat of arms immediately. This was one of King Jasper's men!

He moved on, discovering more bodies until he had reached the wagons. But bodies were not all that he found. Scattered here and there were noggin-knockers and cuttintoos, the characteristic weapons of the Woolly-Bullies. From time to time, a band of their misguided youth would break the truce between them and raid the frontier provinces, but he had never heard of a band attacking so far west before.

He picked up a nogginknocker and examined it. Most peculiar, Bryand thought. From the explicit carving on the shaft, he knew it belonged to a Woolly-Bully of the Shaggingoats clan that populated the uppermost hillsides of the Northside Mountains. The Shaggingoats, so named for their propensity to fornicate with livestock, were possibly the most barbaric of all the clans and certainly the most deviant.

He studied the field for any other signs and shortly his eyes fell upon a small leather pouch. He picked it up and examined its contents, finding three small bones, a handful of feathers, and some dried gizzards. It was a Wooly-Bully billybag, and its contents were often the representation of a clansman's spiritual beliefs. That or the remains of his lunch.

Strange, thought the Prince, studying the markings on the billybag. This belonged to a clansman of the Zigginzaggers. But they lived nowhere near the Shaggingoats.

He had never heard of two clans raiding together. Woolly-Bullies were notoriously territorial. They disliked each other almost as much as they disliked lowlanders. Not since the MacBrutish Uprising had the clans united, and that was seventeen years ago for the purpose of defending their own lands.

Still, he thought, scanning the clearing's perimeter, watching for any movement, who can truly say what Woolly-Bullies are apt to do. A man's as good as dead who underestimates them.

Yet he saw nothing among the trees except for the blackbirds and other carrion-eaters that were gathering to sup. Bryand ventured forward, his hand tightly gripping the hilt of his sword. He rounded the near wagon and halted abruptly, struck dumb with horror. This cannot be! Dearest Gods this cannot be!

Upon the ground, an arrow protruding from her breast, lay MeAnne's sister, Blindella. He could tell this from her wall-eyed stare. A short distance away, Jona, MeAnne's hand-maiden, was sprawled upon the ground, a deep gash in her neck, her face frozen in terror.

The clearing began to spin. He dropped to his hands and knees and vomited. He had seen death in battle before. He was a soldier; and a soldier understood that ripped flesh, and gore, and stench were part of war. But what had war to do with two defenseless women?

He took a deep breath to steady himself, swallowed hard, and struggled to his feet.

This was King Jasper's train.

He rushed first one way and then another, all the while glancing at the dead bodies strewn about. Until at last he found the King lying on his back across the roots of a tree at the far side of the clearing, two deep gashes across his blood soaked chest.

Dearest Gods, he thought, staring up at the sky. First you took my father, then my mother, then my kingdom and my crown, and now you've taken all those dear to my beloved!

"Why?!" he cried to the heavens, agonized. "If this is a test of my mettle, the burden is too great! I want no one else destroyed because of me!" He waited for an answer to his plea, but all was silent save for the sighing of the leaves in the wind.

He looked down at King Jasper. He had fallen with his right hand behind his back still clutching his sword, and in the other-- .

Bryand picked up Jasper's left hand. It was clutched into a fist, and protruding from it was a piece of cloth. He pried the stiff fingers apart, and the cloth dropped to the ground. Bryand's face went ashen.

Before him was something he had seen practically every day of his life. It was a piece of purple and green wool, the uniform of the Bandidonian Guard.

Suddenly he remembered the detachment along the road. He studied the ground. There were fresh hoof prints all around, and in some tall grass he found a broken spur. This was not the work of marauding Woolly-Bullies! This was Daron's doing!

He gazed at the carnage around him, his anger boiling into a scalding rage, and shaking his fists in the air, he cried aloud in the hope that his brother might somehow hear, "I will see you pay for this! No matter how long it takes, no matter what lengths I must go to, I will not rest until I have avenged these deaths! This I swear to you, brother, and to all the Gods of Bandidon!"

He was about to leave, when a single feather, soft and downy white, gently floated toward the ground in front of him. It landed at King Jasper's feet. Another feather came from above and landed in the king's hair.

Bryand looked up at the tree, and there among the higher branches and the last thing he expected to see, was Queen Inoya, pinioned by a score of arrows.

Bryand stared, incredulous. But how-- ? It was then he noticed something odd about the queen. Behind her drooped a small pair of diaphanous wings fringed by white down.

But that was impossible? How could it be? Perhaps she had trapped a bird behind her; a forest sprite or an unusually large fairy. Yet somehow he knew the wings were hers and that she had flown up into the tree.

He looked again at King Jasper as he lay across the tree's roots. And though he could not confirm it as so, Bryand knew in his heart the man had died trying to protect his wife.

He returned to the others and prepared them for

what they would see. But if the Prince had possessed any misgivings about exposing the boys to such carnage, he soon felt no qualms about it at all, for, as Malady explained, they had seen beheadings since they were mere babes.

Trust a mother to know her sons, he thought, watching with true amazement as the boys, acting very calm and detached, went from one body to the next, discussing the type of wound or the angle of blade penetration.

Bryand returned to King Jasper. There, he stood for a long time, staring at the body, saying not a word.

Cower joined him. As a castle servant, he had never spoken to the man. Still, knowing his long history as a friend of the royal family, Cower thought of him with great respect.

"Tis tragic," uttered the retainer. "So much pain and death."

Bryand made no reply. Instead, the Prince unbuckled his swordbelt and handed it to Cower, who looked at him, perplexed.

The Prince bent low and unfastened King Jasper's belt. Then he took the sword from the King's cold and rigid hand.

Slaybest.

He had heard the tales about it. They mattered not to him.

Bryand wiped it clean on the grass and held it so the blade caught the light. In a cold, remorseless tone, he said, "This will be the sword that slays my brother. And may I be worthy of the deed."

He sheathed the blade in its scabbard, then, wrapping the belt around his waist, he buckled it securely. He gazed at King Jasper.

"I will see your death avenged. And your wife's and daughter's, too." Bryand knelt and clasped his hands in front of him. "This I swear to you. One King to another. In fealty and at your feet."

"I do not care to hear you talk this way, my lord," said Cower, troubled.

"And what way is that?"

"With such hatred."

Bryand gave him a stern, dismissive look. Nevertheless, the retainer went on.

"The struggle ahead may be long and arduous, and perhaps filled with even more heartache before drawing to an end. I fear you may turn bitter and forget that mercy is perhaps the greatest quality a king can possess."

Bryand's temper flared. "You speak to me of mercy? For whom? He that stole my life and murdered all whom I hold dear? How can you ask me to be merciful after what I have witnessed and endured?"

"Aye, you have endured much," replied Cower, standing his ground. "But do not forget it is your compassion that sets you apart from your brother. Give in to vengeance and you become like him."

"But he must pay for these crimes."

"And he will. The Gods will see to that. He has sentenced himself to an eternity of suffering for what he has done."

Bryand turned from Cower and stared at King Jasper's waxen features. "It is not enough. I have made my vow, and I will not break it."

"My lord-- ."

"No," said Bryand, looking directly at the retainer. "I will hear no more."

It was then the Prince looked up into the tree, expecting to find Queen Inoya hanging there. But much to his surprise, her body was gone.

"What is it, my lord?" asked Cower, seeing the confusion upon the prince's face.

"The Queen-- . She's gone."

"What do you mean?"

"She was up there among the branches."

"Up there?"

"Aye. I saw her. She had wings." When Cower did not respond, the Prince looked at him. "I know it sounds insane. But it's the truth."

"Wings, my lord?"

"Have you ever known me to make things up or even embellish upon the truth?"

"No, my lord. You have never had the imagination for that."

Bryand, though piqued, found it hard to disagree with the man. "Ask me not where she is now, but the queen was up there. I swear it."

They spent the rest of the afternoon and early evening digging shallow graves for King Jasper and his train. They placed the bodies in the ground and covered them with earth and stones to protect them from the beasts of the forest.

"We'll come back when we can give them all a proper funeral," said Bryand, a sullen look upon his face. "For now, though, this will have to do."

They climbed aboard the wagons and rummaged through the packs that the fire had not consumed. They found some blankets in one and some biscuits and salted meat in another, which they quickly, almost shamelessly devoured.

The light was waning fast, and the wind, laden with moisture, now blew in sudden angry gusts. Though the Prince would have preferred to move on, he decided it was best to stay where they were for the night.

"Do you think that's wise?" asked the retainer, gazing fearfully at the graves about the clearing.

Despite his intelligence, Cower was a superstitious man. His quarters at the castle were filled with charms to ward off evil, and he could not pass the statue of any deity without leaving a copper or two at its feet.

"I mean, with so many murdered men, might there not be some angry spirits lurking about?"

The answer to his question came in the form of a rainstorm that quickly trounced the forest, and the raw, unrelenting wind that accompanied it.

Malady and the boys took cover beneath a wagon, while Bryand and Cower built a shelter from what remained of the wagon's canvas. Fighting the gusts and the constant downpour, they stretched it across the sidewall and anchored it to the ground with tent stakes. At length they crawled inside, drenched and exhausted.

The canvas had been well oiled, and it kept them dry. They slept undisturbed, which is not to say they had a good night's sleep. For Donoim chose that night to wander about, and the Prince, not wanting the boy to get hurt or lost, followed him around until he had settled down again.

The rain stopped sometime before dawn, but the sky remained cluttered with brooding clouds. They ate the last of the biscuits and salted meat in silence, cold and miserable from a dampness that had saturated their clothes, their skin, and their bones.

The Prince and Cower folded up the blankets and canvas and were tying them into packs when they heard Malady clear her throat.

"Just what do you two think yer doin'?" she said.

They turned and found the boys had armed themselves with three or four swords apiece, a cuttintoo and a nogginknocker, and a dearth of dirks. Along with these, they each had donned a yeoman's helm.

Cower had always tried to maintain a serious air around the boys, but even he found it hard not to smirk.

"Scoff if ya wants," said Noim, placing his hands upon his hips. "But I seen how you two have handled things so far, and I say, we're gonna need as many weapons as we can carry in order to get where we're goin'!"

Halfway through this bold statement, his voice cracked, embarrassing him, and he stared at the ground. "I mean, I thought I could help."

"Me too," said Donoim. He lifted the noggin-knocker over his head, but the weapon was so heavy that it sent him tottering backwards until he had fallen on the ground.

"That's enough o' that nonsense," groaned Malady.

"But mum!" Noim protested. "I'm old enough now ta carry a sword."

"An' just as likely ta stab yerself as one o' us, no thankee."

"Aw, mum! We buried some yesterday what was only a bit older 'n me."

"An' look what it got 'em," Malady stated flatly. "I said no, and I means it."

Noim pulled off his helm and dashed it to the ground. "If Dad were here he'd let me! He'd unnerstand."

Malady glowered at him. "But yer dad ain't here, I am. An' I don't want ya carryin' no swords! Now take them things off now."

Bryand saw the frustration on the boy's face, and remembering his own youth, said, "Perhaps you should let them."

Noim turned to the Prince, surprised, then shot his mother a hopeful glance.

Malady chewed on her lower lip, deliberating. She had not made many decisions on her own and none in a very long time.

She looked from Noim to the Prince, then back

again at Noim. Her head began to hurt, causing her right eye to twitch.

"Very well then," she said at last. "But just one. A dull one."

Bryand went to Noim. "Let's be smart about this." He leaned down and picked up a short sword that was well balanced. "Here. This should work for someone of your size and stature."

"Thanks," said Noim genuinely, his lips curling into a smile, revealing his yellowish brown teeth.

"What about me?!" protested Donoim, struggling to get up.

"Aye, what about you?" said Bryand, lifting him onto his feet and removing the boy's weapons.

"These things are far too heavy for someone your size." He came upon a small dagger. "Now this is more like it. Do you think you're big enough to handle this?"

"O' course I'm big enough," retorted the boy, taking it from him; and as Bryand walked away, pleased with himself, Donoim added, "What a stupid question."

CHAPTER EIGHTEEN

The path they had used to first enter the clearing continued on the far side. Having no other option, they followed it until they came to a trail that was wider than most they had taken thus far, with wagon wheel ruts here and there. After peering in one direction and then the next, Bryand shook his head in bewilderment. Feeling quite vexed, he turned to Cower and said, "I have no idea which way to go."

"Whadduya mean?" asked Donoim.

"Whadduya mean, whadduya mean?" said Noim churlishly. "He don't know which way ta go."

"Let's go that way," said Donoim, pointing to the left.

"Why that way?" asked the prince, frowning.

The little one shrugged. "I dunno."

Bryand peered down the road in the direction the boy had chosen, then sighed. "Well, that's as good a reason as any I know."

So they started off to their left, following the road as it wormed its way through a deep gully lined with leafy sapling trees named thusly for the sap dripping freely down their trunks.

"Stay in the center of the road," said Bryand. "And don't touch the trees."

"Why?" asked Malady. "What's with the trees?"

"The sap," said Bryand. "If you touch it, you'll be stuck for good."

Indeed, leafy sapling tree sap, when mixed with water,

was a most effective glue. Because of this, it was very valuable and much sought after at local markets and wherever hard wares were sold.

The sun broke through the clouds for a short visit. Shafts of light, silvery and translucent, pierced the overhanging boughs and touched the ground. After many hours, the forest dwindled and they found themselves flanked by meadows of wild grass and wheat that bowed before the wind.

The forest sounds were replaced by those of the field, and all about them zoomer bugs zoomed and ratchets ratcheted. The light turned from gold to grey with each cloud that drifted past the sun, and by late afternoon the rain was pouring down once more.

"Rain, rain, rain," said Malady, grousing. "I'm sick o' rain. Ain't Blubberus got nothin' better ta do up there in the heavens than cry all day? I been wet so long, I got mold growing-- . "

She paused, and when she saw she had gained everyone's attention, she added, "that's all I'm sayin', thankee."

They came to the edge of a dense copse of trees and ventured under the canopy of leaves. By now the light was fading and dark shadows quickly enveloped them.

"Do you think we should make camp?" asked Cower above the swish of the rain.

Bryand shook his head. "A little further and then we'll stop."

They rounded a bend in the road and halted as one. Ahead, in the dimness was a light, swaying back and forth, back and forth, growing larger by the minute.

"What's that?" asked Donoim, squinting.

Noim rested his hand on the pummel of his sword. "Well, it ain't no glow bug, that's fer sure."

Now the light was close enough for them to see that it was not just one, but many, all headed their way.

Bryand took a step forward, shielding his eyes from the rain. "Lanterns."

"Soldiers?" asked Cower, immediately on the alert.

"From this distance, it's hard to say. We'd best take cover, though, just in case."

They left the road and scrambled into the thick undergrowth, huddling behind a gnarled tree. It was not long though before they realized they had nothing to fear.

For instead of soldiers approaching, they spied a band of travelers driving brightly painted wagons that looked much like ramshackle cottages on wheels. Bryand recognized them at once.

"It's all right," he said, stepping out from their hiding place. He motioned for the others to join him. "We're not in any danger. They're Jangaloni."

Centuries ago, at the beginning of what has since come to be known as the Age of Reprisals, the Jangaloni were welcomed everywhere. And rightly so as they were a generous people who roamed the continent, selling trinkets and elixirs, telling fortunes and, in general, spreading their good cheer.

However, it was soon discovered that, along with their good cheer, they had also been spreading the plague. No matter what town or village they visited, by the time they had moved on, anywhere from one fourth to one half of the population had died. Yet, for some strange reason not a single Jangaloni ever succumbed, and because of this peculiarity, they came to be feared, and out of fear grew hatred.

Soon, they were hounded from one shire to the next until all but a handful had perished.

Many decades passed. Yet, though the plague had long since run its course, with the outbreak of any blight or disease, the local people would seek out the nearest band of Jangaloni and promptly burn them at the stake. Consequently, life was a fleeting quality for these wanderers. A summer of manhood, an autumn of womanhood, and they were gone - snuffed out by some irate farmer whose crops had failed.

The moment Malady heard the name Jangaloni, she cursed, picked up a rock in the road and made to hurl it at them.

"What are you doing?!" said Bryand sternly, grabbing her wrist.

"You said it yerself," replied the woman, her eyes alive with fear. "Them's Jangaloni! Don'tcha know they carry the plague?! Quick, kids, hold yer breath!"

But they paid her no heed, for they had never seen a house on wheels before, nor people dressed in such flamboyant garb. Add to these the clomping of horses' hooves, the jingle of rigging, the clunk of hanging pots and pans, the complaint of squeeze boxes, surrounded by the most brilliant of colors, and it could easily have been Knock-Knock, the annual holiday of feasts and games commemorating the day Bryand's grandfather, Armadon, had broken the prophecy stone with his head.

Sitting atop the lead wagon was a wiry little man of about seventy (*ancient for a Jangaloni,*) who wore a trim mustache that curled up at the ends and a gold ring through his left ear. A stocking cap with a long tassel (*known as a datswarmer*) covered the top of his head and was fringed by his bushy white hair.

"Hello dere!" he called jovially, smiling a toothless smile.

"Hello to you," replied Bryand in a friendly tone.

The old man looked at Malady and narrowed his eyes. "Why for dat lady turning blue? Can't she breathe?"

Malady expelled the air from her lungs and scowled. "O' course I can breathe."

The old man nodded. After a lifetime of being shunned he had come to recognize the disdain of others, and Malady, by holding her nose, was acting no differently. "Ain't you got no wagon?"

"We lost it," said Bryand.

"We was attacked by wolves," added Donoim, swaggering to Bryand's side.

The old man gasped and addressed the boy. "Wolves, you say? Oucha, dat's bad."

"That ain't all. We was almost drowned in a mine shaft an' eaten by a dragon."

"He wasn't no dragon," said Noim, cuffing his brother from behind.

"Sure he was! He was about a hunnert feet long, an' had teeth the size o' me!" Donoim turned to his mother. "I told ya I shoulda kept that head."

The old man looked at him and cocked an eyebrow. "You know sometin', kid? You could be a Jangaloni wid a tale like dat."

"Heavens forbid," grumbled Malady, and she grabbed Donoim to her.

"So where you folks headed?"

"To Willowbrook," replied the Prince.

"Oooo, dat's a nice place. Fulla nice people, too. Only one ting."

"What's that?"

"You never get dere da way you headed."

Bryand pursed his lips and shot Donoim a sidelong glance.

Seeing this, the little one replied, "Don't blame me; you're th' one what's in charge around here."

Bryand cleared his throat and addressed the old man. "Perhaps you could point us in the right direction?"

"Oooya, I do better 'n dat. I take you dere myself."

Bryand blinked at the man's generosity. "That's very kind of you, but we wouldn't want to cause you any trouble."

The old man chuckled. "Dat ain't no trouble to a

Jangaloni. Now, a spear in da chest, dat's trouble."

"Are you sure?" asked Bryand, delighted.

The old man shrugged. "Hey, we go dis way, we go dat way. It don't much matter. Besides, we headin' towards Willowbrook anyhows." He leaned over and waved to the wagons behind. "Listen up dere! We makin' a stop at Willowbrook!"

And instead of protests as the Prince expected, the others, who had been observing him cautiously, gave out with cheers.

Much to his chagrin, Bryand learned that he and his companions had drifted well off course. Willowbrook was almost as far as it had been the night they started out from Castle Bandidon.

But at least they no longer had to walk; so they climbed aboard the wagon, which they later learned was called a jalopy, Bryand and the boys up front with the old man, and Malady and Cower in the rear.

The old man introduced himself as Poppa Pokissamo, whereupon hearing his name, the boys began to laugh. He looked at them in mock surprise, which set them convulsing even harder. Then he smiled a toothless smile and winked at the Prince.

He explained that, in strict Jangaloni, his name meant, "He who puckers." But he liked to think it meant, "He who loves."

Either translation was appropriate, for, as the old man continued to explain, of the forty-two members of the band, he had sired seventeen. Those who were not his children were either his wives *(he had three,)* his in-laws, or his grandchildren.

"My life been pretty bountiful, yes?"

"That it has," agreed the Prince, astounded.

"So tell me, you got a name?"

"Aye," said Bryand tersely and nothing more.

Poppa Pokissamo nodded. Being a Jangaloni, he

knew how to mind his own business. He turned to the boys, inquiring, "an' what about you two?"

"My name's Noim," said the older one. "After me dad's brother Noim who was crushed beneath a boulder before I was born."

"Uh-hummmm," answered the old man.

"An' my name's Donoim, after me Dad's other brother who died from this bad cut what turned black an' smelly."

"How you know dat?" asked Poppa Pokissamo, intrigued.

"I gave it to 'im." And in response to the old man's shocked look, the boy responded. "It was a accident, I swear."

While on the road, Poppa Pokissamo helped pass the long hours by telling the boys outlandish stories. These, they challenged fiercely, all the while giggling and enjoying themselves completely.

"So den da bear cornered me and kilt me dead."

"How could th' bear kill ya, when you're here tellin' us about it?" asked Donoim with a skeptical sneer.

"What you tink, I'm lyin' or sometin'? Oucha! You got some nerve, kid!"

"I still don't believe ya."

"Okay, okay, you right. Da bear didn't kill me, but he woulda if I didn't give him da Jangaloni stare."

"The what?!" Noim guffawed.

Poppa Pokissamo snuck a playful glance to the Prince. "Da Jangaloni stare! Don't say you never heard of dat."

"'Course not. There's no such thing."

"Well, da bear didn't tink so eeder. But I gave it to him just da same. An' to dis day, whenever he sees me comin', dat bear lies down and lets me use him as a rug!"

Though the old man and his family had thoroughly captivated the boys, Malady was unable to forget the fears instilled in her growing up; and she spent her days with the Jangaloni in torment, convinced she had caught the plague.

Poppa Pokissamo, having a truly impish nature, did all he could to foster this belief and drove her to near hysteria. One night, after they had just made camp, the old man studied her as she was passing by and said, "Uh-oh, you don't look so good."

Hearing this, Malady halted abruptly. "Whaduya mean?"

"Is dat da color of you skin normally?"

"I dunno. What color is it?" asked the woman nervously.

"Green. Oooya, dat's green all right."

This brought on one of her seizures, which astounded the old man. Then, once Bryand had punched her lightly on the chin, which astounded the old man even more, Malady rushed to the nearest bucket and scrubbed her face raw.

The oldest of Poppa Pokissamo's wives was a corpulent woman with multiple chins. Her name was Aldina, and, though she bore a stern countenance most of the time, she was a kind person, who saw to the comforts of her guests unfailingly. Of the old man's three wives, she was probably the least attractive, but she was the one person to whom he would always turn whenever he was feeling troubled.

She wore her raven hair in a tight bun and pulled back from her fleshy face. Her black eyebrows converged in a small tangle above the bridge of her flat nose, and from her wattle-like earlobes dangled brightly painted beads that she and the other women had made from flour paste.

She was the family Boogiemuster, which in Jangaloni meant: Conjurer of the dead. Along with this talent she specialized in the making of charms and spells to ward off evil spirits and a pungent smelling ointment that, when applied just below the nostrils, immediately opened one's clogged nose.

The boys were wary of her. For she would act most stern in their presence and never allowed more than a hint of a smile to escape.

Malady was terrified of her. She did everything the woman told her to do. And if perchance she did show some defiance, Aldina would simply pretend to go into one of her trances, and Malady, fearful of having a ghost haunt her or a curse placed upon her, would immediately obey.

"Here, you wear dese around you necks," she said to Bryand and the others, handing out tiny medallions she had sculpted from clay. "Dey keep you safe from evil."

I have endeavored to draw its likeness.

Admittedly, it's crude and simplistic; I'm a mapmaker not an artist.

She waited until all of them had placed the charms around their necks, then, turning first to the boys, she scribbled an enchantment in the air over their heads. She did the same for Cower, and then for Bryand, and when she came to Malady, she smirked and said, "I give you special one to help wid you aches and pains. Maybe it also make you not so crabby."

Each night, after making camp, the entire band would gather together to partake of the evening feast, and while they ate and drank, they sang their favorite songs, one lively ditty being:

You go about from place to place,
When all dey do is kick you face,
Den bury you widout a trace.
Gee, ain't life a treat.
(Chorus)
Jangaloni, love bologna!
And though we spell them differently,
We rhyme them just the same!
(Second verse)
Dey seek you here, dey seek you dere,
Dey shave you head of all you hair,
Den steal you clothes, and leave you bare.
Gee, ain't life a scream.
Ohhhhhhhhhh!
Jangaloni, love bologna!
And though we spell them differently,
We rhyme them just the same!

Bryand would listen to their songs and come away amazed. How these people, who had been hounded and shunned for so long, could find humor in their suffering was beyond him. Along their journey, he had seen how people cursed them, threw rocks at them, even threatened them with death. Yet in the face of so much hatred, they had not once raised their hand in anger, nor spoken a word in their own defense.

A week passed; and Bryand grew genuinely fond of Poppa Pokissamo and his family. Yet, he could not help but feel troubled.

Every day lost made the possibility of taking the throne from his brother that much more remote. He had already seen the treachery Daron was capable of, not only to his person but to others as well, and, though he tried desperately to drive the thought from his mind, he feared that Niles, Dwayne, and Dillin had suffered the same fate as King Jasper. And then there was MeAnne, pledged to the wrong man; perhaps even married to him by now, and this filled him with despair.

"Beautiful night, yes?" said Poppa Pokissamo, stepping beside him.

Bryand surfaced from his thoughts and smiled weakly. "Aye."

"No rain for da last two days. Lotsa sun, lotsa moon. So what you bothered about?"

"How did you know I was bothered?" asked Bryand, his smile lengthening.

The old man's eyes danced in the firelight. "Ahhhh, you see, da wanderer's nose is very keen. He can sniff out trouble." Poppa Pokissamo shrugged and brought his palms up. "I just followed my nose."

Bryand chuckled but was silent.

After a pause, the old man said, "Look up dere. See dem stars? How many you tink are up dere? Couple of dozen? Uh-uh. Maybe couple of million. An' dey all a lot bigger dan a meatball, dat's for sure."

Bryand looked up at the sky.

"Sort of make you feel pretty small, eh?"

"Aye."

"Make you problems pretty small, too."

Bryand looked at him askance and smirked. "I suppose that's true."

Poppa Pokissamo continued looking up at the sky. "You know, dere's a star for each and every one of us. It's where we go when we-- . You know, croak. See dat one? Two above dat tree? Dat one's mine. Which one is yours?"

"I don't know. Whichever one shines over Bandidon."

"Oh, den you want dat one," said the old man, pointing to their left at a star that was low in the sky. "Oh, dat one must be yours. Look how it winks at you."

Bryand watched it twinkle, then sighed.

"So you from Bandidon?"

"Aye."

The warmth in Poppa Pokissamo's voice faded somewhat. "Dat's a nice place. We been run outa Bandidon lots of times."

Bryand looked at him and saw the pain in the old man's eyes; and, perhaps because he was an outcast of a different sort, he understood the plight of the Jangaloni for the very first time.

Bryand weighed telling him the truth about himself. But before he could decide, Jocco, Poppa Pokissamo's eldest son, rushed into camp, waving his arms over his head.

He was a big man, with curly black hair and a kind face. When he caught sight of his father, he doubled his pace.

"Poppa!" he cried, breathless. "Poppa, we in a fix again, oooya!"

"Quiet down you emotional boy," admonished

the old man, peering up at his son, who was at least two feet taller than him. "How you gonna be leader someday if you keep losin' you head?"

"But, Poppa, da soldiers, dey comin' dis way. An' dey carryin' torches!"

A frightened murmur erupted among those who had gathered.

"Of course dey carryin' torches," said Poppa Pokissamo, raising his voice so all could hear. "Ain't it dark outside?"

"We should run!" cried Roboosto, Poppa Pokissamo's brother-in-law. He was also tall, but lanky, with a long face, a disproportionately large nose, and pocked skin. "Quick, everyone, pack you bags!"

Some ran, while others debated, or stood by in fear.

"Hold it! Hold it!" shouted the old man, glaring at Roboosto. Poppa Pokissamo had never liked him. He was always putting on airs and pretending he knew everything.

"You not da leader here!" said the old man sternly. "You da leader's broder-in-law. Dat makes you just a little more important dan da compost heap!"

"Look!" shouted Jocco, alarmed.

The flames from the soldiers' torches were clearly visible, and the sound of galloping hooves was everywhere now.

It was then Malady muscled her way through the gathering with Cower and the boys close behind. "What're we gonna do?" asked the woman, her eyes locked upon the Prince. "Th' soldiers!"

Poppa Pokissamo regarded them. "What for you worried? Dey want only da Jangaloni."

But the grim expression upon Bryand's face told him otherwise.

"Da soldiers, dey lookin' for you?"

"It's very possible," replied the Prince, drawing his sword.

The old man stared at the weapon. "Dat ain't no peasant's knife."

Aldina had seen it too, and suddenly, for no apparent reason, she flinched as though she had been struck by a physical blow.

"Dat sword-- ." she said breathily. Curious, Bryand held it out with the blade flat across his palm. Aldina approached, bent low, and ran her fingers gingerly along it. "Oooya, you got sometin' powerful dere. I feel it."

Bryand had heard the name of Slaybest, for it was what King Jasper called his sword. As a child, he had also heard the stories about the sword's powers. Apparently, Aldina had heard them, too.

"Poppa," said Jocco, wringing his hands. The clattering of horses' hooves was even louder now. "Dey comin' fast."

The old man turned to Aldina, and, though she said nothing, he saw all that he needed in her face. With a nod, he turned back to the Prince.

"You never fight dem all. It be smarter to hide in da wagon."

"What?!" cried Roboosto. "Am I hearin' right? We gonna protect strangers?"

"Shut up, compost heap," replied the old man sternly, then he looked at Malady and the children. "Don't worry, we keep you safe."

Bryand hesitated. But a wink from the old man assured him they were in good hands, and he sheathed his sword.

Poppa Pokissamo had just shut the door behind them when the soldiers entered the camp.

They reined their mounts to a halt and

jumped from their saddles. They dispersed, entering wagons, evicting occupants, plundering anything of value. And while they jeered and performed their dirty work, the men and women of the Jangaloni stood by, their eyes filled with a sorrow their people had known for centuries.

A yeoman pushed his way between Poppa Pokissamo and Aldina, and started up the steps of the leader's jalopy.

"I wouldn't go in dere if I was you," sang the old man discordantly. "Not if I didn't wanna die a horrible det."

The yeoman halted, his hand resting on the door latch, and tossed him a dubious look. "What're you talkin' about?"

"Nuttin'. Go ahead den. Just don't blame me when you tongue turns black an' you groin swells up."

The yeoman's eyes filled with misgiving, and Poppa Pokissamo smiled to himself. But he had not yet succeeded in his charade.

"What's the delay there?!" barked the officer in charge from atop his horse.

It was Mortamour.

"I told you to search these wagons."

"Dere's sick people in dere," offered Poppa Pokissamo, gesturing behind him with his thumb.

Mortamour jumped from his saddle (*more gracefully than one would expect for a man of his size. Indeed, it was known in small, very private circles, that he practiced dancing in toe shoes not just because he had a particular penchant for it but because it also improved his balance.*)

He approached the old man, who looked quite puny next to the henchman. "Sick in what way?"

"I don't know for sure," replied Poppa Pokissamo, and then a worried look fell across his face. "I tink it's da plague."

The yeoman, who had been standing at attention all this time, gasped and leaped from the steps. But Mortamour was not so easily duped.

"You might be telling the truth. And then again, you might not. There's a traitor loose, and it would be just like him to hide among scum like you."

Poppa Pokissamo maintained his poise and his dignity. "I'm tellin' you, dere's only sick people in dat wagon."

Suddenly, the old man found the point of a dagger under his chin.

"You're a bold one for a Jangaloni," said the henchman.

Poppa Pokissamo made no reply, but neither did he look away.

Mortamour grinned. He welcomed defiance in men. Without it, killing them could be so boring.

Leaving his dagger beneath the old man's chin, Mortamour shouted to the yeoman, "Search the wagon!" and to Poppa Pokissamo, he said, "Know this, old man. If you're lying to me, I will nail your hands and feet, and then your tongue to the nearest tree." Looking askance, he saw the yeoman had not moved yet. "What are you waiting for?!"

Whimpering like a frightened dog, the yeoman climbed up the jalopy's stairs, and reached once more for the handle on the door.

Bryand, who was just on the other side of the door, drew his sword stealthily and made ready to attack. But suddenly, though he knew not why, Malady was in front of him, pushing him toward the others at the rear of the jalopy.

"Trust me," she whispered as she drew a motley curtain between them.

Outside, the yeoman lingered. His hands shook. Sweat poured down his face.

"Open it!" shouted Mortamour. "Or I'll nail you to the same tree as the Jangaloni."

Cursing his luck, the yeoman obeyed. He opened the door, and it was as if his greatest fear had been realized. His face went pale and he gasped in terror.

Standing before him, twitching and moaning, stood Malady, spittle dripping from the corner of her mouth. And with her sunken eyes and gray pallor, she looked every bit the victim of the plague.

"Water," she pleaded, grabbing hold of him. "I need water. PLEASE, I MUST HAVE WATER!!"

Terrified, the yeoman lost his footing and tumbled down the steps, nearly colliding with Mortamour who, upon seeing the woman for himself, recoiled from the old man.

"Unclean!" the henchman cried, his eyes wide with fear. "Into your saddles! Quickly! This place is unclean!"

Whereupon he leaped atop his horse and galloped out of camp.

Panic swept among the soldiers; they dropped everything, and while some rolled in the dirt, hysterical, others doffed their tunics and gloves, trampled them, and bolted into the night, running as fast as their mounts if not faster.

In less than a minute, they were gone. A minute longer and the last of their cries had faded completely, replaced first by silence and then by the familiar sounds of night-callers and hoop-hooper birds.

It did not seem possible. It had happened so quickly. For a brief moment, no one said a word. But then, as the realization took hold of them, laughed erupted, then shouts and cheers from all around the campsite.

They had won their first victory over oppression in a thousand years. True, it was a tiny victory, but nevertheless it was one that would live in their hearts and be told in their stories for ages to come.

Soon, every man, woman and child danced about, laughing or weeping for joy. They cheered Poppa Pokissamo for his courage, and they tossed him into the air. They cheered Aldina, and they kissed her plump cheeks repeatedly. And they tried to do the same to Malady, but she fended them off, deferring, "Awright, awright. Just don't get personal."

Bryand emerged from the wagon, observing the elation all around him. Swept up by it, he went to Poppa Pokissamo, ready to congratulate him and his family.

But when the old man saw him, he sobered. Others did the same. In no time, the dancing and singing had ceased, and dozens of eyes were staring at the Prince.

"Why for dat soldier call you a traitor?" asked Poppa Pokissamo, disapproval in his voice. "Who are you, an' what have you done?"

Bryand's smile collapsed, and he knew it was time for the truth. "They hunt me because they think I am Prince Daron."

A murmur ran through those nearby. They gathered around their leader. Those on the outskirts stepped closer, too.

Poppa Pokissamo blinked. "Dey tink you Daron--? Da much-a-crazy Prince?"

"Aye. But they are mistaken. I am not him."

"Well, I'm glad to hear dat."

"I am actually his brother, Bryand, son of Audanot, son of Armadon. The rightful King of Bandidon."

An audible gasp arose from the crowd. The Jangaloni were renowned liars and storytellers, but none had ever been so bold as to call himself a king.

Noim was the first to speak his mind. "Snipes 'n such! We've been travelin' with a blinkin' loon!"

"I speak the truth," said Bryand, ignoring the youngster. "If you would but hear me out-- ."

Poppa Pokissamo stared at him, full of doubt. Yet there was something about the young man's directness that impressed them.

From the moment they met, he had suspected there was something different about him. He was too well mannered to be a commoner; and the words he used - he had never heard anyone speak so well.

"Hey," said the old man with a shrug. "It ain't like I got an appointment somewhere. Go ahead. Take all da time you need."

Bryand smiled, encouraged. Then he related his tale.

One by one, the Jangaloni sat before him, the youngsters with their eyes transfixed, the elders with their upraised eyebrows, and the old ones, nodding slowly as they processed what they heard.

At length, he concluded by saying, "If you could just take me to Willowbrook. From there my friends and I will raise an army to stop my brother from destroying what good remains of the kingdom and the commonwealth."

He had spoken winningly; he was sure of it. Yet, much to his surprise, Poppa Pokissamo was silent.

It was Roboosto who spoke first, stepping forward and striking an arrogant pose. "Why for we help a land what's hounded da Jangaloni since dey first born?"

There were many in the crowd who agreed with him and said so openly.

"What's da diff'rence who's da rightful king," Roboosto continued with even more assurance, "when dey all treat us da same. Like dirt. Like wood for dey fires!"

Poppa Pokissamo raised his hands, and when his family had fallen silent, he smiled apologetically at the Prince.

"I'm sorry for da bad tings my people say. Dey make me sick inside sometimes." He sighed deeply. "But what makes me even sicker is dat I agree wid my broder-in-law."

"You do?" said Roboosto, astounded.

Poppa Pokissamo scowled. "Oooya, dat's sometin' I never thought I'd say."

He gave the Prince a kindly smile and shrugged. "I'm da oldest Jangaloni I know. I feel helty enough, but sooner or later somebody's gonna come along and clobber me dead. Do I mind? You bet I mind. What, you tink I'm crazy? But what can I do?" His eyes became moist with tears. "I'm a Jangaloni."

Bryand's heart went out to the man, and he spoke so the entire assemblage could hear. "When I am proclaimed king, you will never again have to live in fear. As in the olden days, the Jangaloni will be free from persecution and welcome everywhere; for as long as my house reigns. This I swear to you."

Poppa Pokissamo shook his head sadly. "Dat

sounds very nice. But how you gonna change people what tink one way for so long? Just by you say so?"

"Granted, it won't happen overnight. It will take time; years perhaps. Some may never change in their hearts. But this I promise you, deliver me to Willowbrook and you can consider Bandidon your home forever and its King your staunchest protector."

The old man's chin quivered. "You do dat for us?"

"Aye," said Bryand genuinely, and he offered him his hand.

Poppa Pokissamo looked at it, awed, then turned to his family. "I tink he really means it!"

His family cheered, everyone except Roboosto, that is, and the old man shook the Prince's hand.

"Dere's just one ting."

"What's that?" asked Bryand, feeling more encouraged than he had in a long time.

"What happens if you lose dis fight against you broder?"

"Then you'll have made the trip for nothing."

"For nutting, you say?" the old man chuckled. "Who cares about dat. We Jangaloni, remember? We got no place better to go."

Two days later the wagon train emerged from the forest on the outskirts of Willowbrook, and when it crested the rim of a wide valley, Bryand saw Niles' home in the far distance.

Thrilled, the Prince unhitched Poppa Pokissamo's lead horse.

"My lord," said Cower, concerned at once. "Would it not be wiser to travel with the band?"

But Bryand did not heed the retainer's advice. He prodded the horse's flanks with his heels and galloped down the grassy slope.

He had told himself over and over not to get his hopes up. Yet, with the manor house in sight, he could not help but feel that the hardships he had endured were finally coming to an end.

He spurred the horse onward. Each mile he traversed, his excitement grew until he could hardly contain it.

But when he came to the top of a rise just above the manor, the smile on his face collapsed; and he tugged on the horse's reins so hard that the animal skidded to a halt along the grass.

"Oh, no," he muttered aloud as he eyed the scene before him.

The walls of the manor house were scorched. The roof had collapsed in places, leaving charred timbers exposed, and the manor door, which had always impressed Bryand with its girth and ornate ironwork, lay upon the ground, ripped from its hinges.

"This cannot be," he said, his heart wrenching in his chest, and the wind moaned in accord.

Bryand spurred the horse forward; and minutes later he galloped into the deserted courtyard, leaping to the ground before the animal had even slowed. He eyed the ruins, the burned out cottages, the broken furniture and casks.

"Hello!" he called. "Is anyone here?!"

He raced inside the manor, stopping short just beyond the doorway. He had spent so many years here. He had always thought of it as his second home. Now it was an empty shell.

"Hello?" he called again, anguished. "Is anyone here?" But the silence was his only reply.

He returned to the courtyard, dazed and confused. His eyes fell upon the remains of a pyre, and he immediately felt his stomach turn.

He approached the pyre, crouched, and fingered the coals. Cold, he thought.

Was this fire for you, Niles? Have you joined all the others roaming the heavens? He ran his fingers through his hair, feeling lost and bewildered.

It began to rain, but he took no notice, and he remained by the pyre while the rain dripped down his face and mingled with his tears. At length, he heard the wagon train approaching; and he thought immediately of the promises he had made - to Cleave the executioner, to Malady and the boys, to Cower, and to the Jangaloni. He knew he could do nothing for them still.

He found himself back on his feet and on the move, without questioning what he was doing or where he was going. First a trot, and then he broke into a run, head low and at breakneck speed, rounding the house, passing the guard quarters and the empty stable. All he could think of at that moment was to hide. Hide from everyone and everything, abandoning reason and logic, all the things that had grounded him thus far, in favor of despair.

Ever since the night the Jangaloni had agreed to help the Prince reach Willowbrook, a hope had been growing inside Cower. One that was similar in feeling to the anticipation of a long-awaited spring.

Yet the moment he caught sight of the destruction, that hope was dashed. "Oh, cruel, cruel fate," the retainer muttered, concerned at once for Bryand.

He turned to Poppa Pokissamo and, in a tone that suggested he would not take no for an answer, the retainer requested the use of a wagon. Poppa Pokissamo quietly agreed, for he too was worried about the Prince.

The moment Cower rolled through the manor's shattered gate, he reined the horses to a halt, overwhelmed by the extent of the damage before him.

"My lord?" he called.

Bryand's mount stood grazing, but the Prince was nowhere in sight.

"My lord?" he called again. The hairs on the back of his neck stood on end. "Can you hear me?"

The swish of the rain was his only reply.

Cower descended, his eyes taking in the charred remains of the pyre. There was no mistaking this was a place where death had visited, and it was more than likely some angry spirits were lurking about.

Wearing a grim expression, he took hold of Bryand's sword, which he now carried at his hip. He did this for effect only, for he knew it would be useless should a spirit decide to confront him. Spirits were incorporeal by nature. Things tended to pass right through them, including swords.

He began to search the courtyard. He passed the pyre, keeping his distance, then worked his way along the wall.

"My lord," he called anxiously. "My lord, where are you?" He halted in his tracks and listened, but still there came no reply.

Very worried now, he drew his sword from its scabbard. He gripped it tightly. So tightly he could feel the hilt's braiding pinch his flesh.

"Answer me, please, if you are still among the living."

Holding the weapon in front of him, Cower started forward again. He checked each cranny in the wall, each billet, until he had reached the rear of the main house.

It was there, in the corner where the courtyard wall joined the side of the house, he found the Prince. He was sitting with his legs folded in front of him and his knees against his chest.

"My lord!" called the retainer, deeply relieved. Cower rushed to him and knelt by his side.

Even in the dimness he could tell the Prince was crying, and though he wanted naught else but to put his arms around him in the same manner as he had when Bryand was a lad, Cower said nothing more and waited for the Prince to speak.

At length, the Prince wiped his eyes with the back of his hand. "It was foolish to think Niles was still alive. It's foolish to think the others are alive as well."

"You don't know that for sure, my lord," said Cower respectfully.

"What difference does it make? Even if they are alive, they cannot give me back my good name. And without that, I am nothing."

"You are Bryand," answered Cower in a firm tone of voice. "Prince of the realm, the rightful King of Bandidon."

"Look you, Gods," the young man scoffed, addressing the heavens. "It is I, Bryand, the rightful King."

He chuckled sardonically. "A Prince of a King."

His smile vanished. Suddenly he was angry and shot to his feet. "Prince of fools is more like it."

He turned to Cower. "I know what you expect of me but I can't do this any more. I can't go on pretending to be something I am not."

"Is that what you want?" asked Cower pointedly. "To give up your cause?"

"Cause? What cause? Tis a delusion at best."

"Not so, my lord. For a delusion is a false belief. You are the rightful king. That is a truth. Just as regaining your throne is another."

Bryand began to pace. "So much has changed. So many lives have already been lost."

Cower rose to his feet. "Very well then. Give it up. And right away, please; so we can stop all this trudging about in the rain. And then what?"

Bryand halted and turned to him. But before he could utter a word, Cower was answering his own question.

"I know, we can set up housekeeping in a little village on the coast of Fluug. The most isolated part of the United Kingdoms, where your brother would never think to look for you."

His voice grew more intense. "I can see us now. You, me, and Malady and the boys. You can fish for our supper. The boys will want to help you. I can see them now, standing eagerly on the jetty with their clubs in hand, waiting for you to catch something they can bludgeon to death. I won't be there, of course. I will be tending to my garden trying to grow something, anything, in such a harsh climate. Malady can cook. If she's well enough, that is. I'm sure she could turn out a delicious mollusk stew. At night, if the wind isn't at gale force and the air too frigid, we can sit outside our front door and watch the tide come in. Then we'll all retire. Me to my room, the boys to theirs, and you and Malady to yours."

Bryand paled. Seeing this, Cower presented him with a look of mock surprise, "Isn't that what you want?"

Bryand shuddered at the thought. He looked at Cower, crafty Cower, and in a voice filled with sarcasm, he said, "You have a way with words, my friend. You paint such lovely pictures with them."

Cower grinned. "I only speak the truth, my lord. You should know that by now."

Bryand nodded his head, conscious of the love and respect he felt for the man at his side; always ready with some insight; always standing by lest he fall. "Thank you for the reminder," said the Prince in a grateful tone.

"Any time, my lord," replied the retainer. "Now I believe you could do me a favor."

"Of course, what is it?"

"Help me pry my hand from this sword."

Indeed, the retainer had gripped it so tightly his knuckles were white.

Moments later, they met the wagon train at the entrance of the courtyard.

"Oooya," said Poppa Pokissamo, scratching his head as he eyed the ruins. "Looks like tings have pretty much fizzled for you."

Bryand snorted grudgingly. "For the time being, perhaps."

"What you gonna do now?"

"Now?" echoed Bryand. He scanned the destruction about him. This was all his brother was capable of – ruination and despair. Well, he would have no more of it.

"Now," said Bryand boldly. "I'll seek my friends at Pepperill. And if they are not there, I'll go on to Torkelstone, and if they are not there either, I'll follow any lead I can until I've found them or seen their funeral pyres with my own eyes."

Poppa Pokissamo nodded. "Well, da least I can do is give you a wagon. You take dat from me, yes? I be cross wid you if you don't."

"A wagon would be most helpful," said Bryand with a grateful smile.

"Den it's settled. Hey, Jocco! You movin' in wid you mudder and me!"

When the jalopy had been fully provisioned, they said their goodbyes all around. The boys hugged Aldina and shook Poppa Pokissamo's hand.

"Take care of you mudder," the old man said; and, with an impish grin, he added, "she don't look so good to me."

"Go on!" said Malady lightly, and, much to everyone's surprise, she hugged him.

It was then Aldina approached the Prince, her eyes locked upon the sword at his side.

Suddenly, Bryand remembered her reaction to Slaybest on the night the soldiers had invaded their camp.

"You take care of dat," said the woman in a reverent tone, pointing to the sword. "And it take care of you."

"I don't understand---"

"You will; if an' when da time comes."

And that was all she said.

Malady climbed into the back of the wagon, followed by the boys. Bryand and Cower settled themselves on the front seat.

"Ready back there?" The Prince called through the window behind him.

"Yeah, yeah," came Donoim's voice from inside "Try not ta get us lost again."

Bryand started the horses forward, then halted them again by the old man's wagon.

"Poppa Pokissamo-- ," said the Prince. He paused, searching for the words that would best express his gratitude.

But before he could speak, the old man said, "You keep you promise some day, yes? I mean, some day when you King."

"Aye," said Bryand, feeling a tug at his heart. He would miss him. He would miss all of them. "No matter how long it takes."

"Well," the old man sighed. "Dat gonna be a great day for da Jangaloni. In da meantime, though, I gotta get my family outta da rain." And with that said, he set his wagon rolling.

"I won't forget you," called the Prince. "Or your kindness."

The old man looked back at him, smiling. "Wid luck, I see you soon, okay?" He purposely crossed his fingers and held them up for the Prince to see. "You bet Okay!"

The wagon train headed back toward the forest, pots and pans clanging, wheels creaking. Someone played a push-pull, and a song came back to them upon the the breeze.

"***Good bye, so long,***
da merry rovers said.
Come look for us,
where da wind blows strong,
An' bury us if we dead."

When at last the song had faded, Bryand started off as well.

"Now," said the Prince over the sound of the horses' hooves. "Which way did Poppa say we'd find Pepperill?"

Cower pointed behind them. "That way, my lord."

Surprised, Bryand cast a look over his shoulder.

"Are you sure?"

"Aye, my lord."

Bryand knitted his brow. "Then I think it would be a good idea if we turned around."

Which he did, and they started off again, only this time in the right direction.

CHAPTER NINETEEN

As any map maker or ship's pilot knows, starting off in the right direction is only that - a start. Varying from one's course by even a single degree can, depending on the length of distance traveled, take one a mile out of the way or tens of miles out of the way. So it was without any wonder that the Prince wandered into...

I was about to call it unfamiliar territory, but with someone like Bryand, whose own courtyard was often unfamiliar territory, there really isn't much point.

In addition to the Prince's sense of direction, or lack thereof, the weather continued to work against them. The rain was unremitting, pouring down in glistening ribbons, making the road a sloppy, almost impassable mess.

So, in order to avoid detection and make better time, they left the road and rolled onto a wide plain of tall grass. This was, perhaps, their very first stroke of good luck, for, unbeknownst to them, they were heading straight for the Ankledeep River, which was the western boundary of the shire of Pepperill.

However, at this time of year, the Ankledeep was far from ankle deep.

The river's source was somewhere in the highlands and was said to be a mere trickle that could be crossed by a single stride. Many explorers had attempted to trace it, but most had fallen victim to the mad clansmen of that region and were never heard from again.

Only one man had ever returned and he by way

of the river itself. Unfortunately he had drowned and, therefore, was unable to impart anything about the Ankledeep other than the obvious conclusion that it was dangerous.

After two days upon the grassy plain, traveling in light drizzle, they came in sight of a tree line, and, from somewhere behind it, they could hear the sound of rushing water. By the time they had rolled beyond the trees and had reached the river, the rain had stopped - this being the first break in the weather in a week. However, because of the heavy downpours, the river was dangerously swollen and filled with forest flotsam and debris.

"We can't cross here," said the Prince as he and Cower watched a large uprooted tree sail by.

"Not unless we feel like drownin'," Noim's voice came from behind them.

Bryand turned and found him leaning on the casement. His hair hung down upon his forehead like greasy twine and pimples dotted his face and nose.

"I think you'd better shut the window and find a seat."

"Do ya now," croaked the boy, and in a brazen tone he added, "Tell me, m'lord, what loony bin was it you escape from?"

A hand appeared from inside and jerked Noim backward by the scruff of his neck, leaving Bryand staring at the empty casement.

"You keep a civil tongue in yer head, ya hear?" came Malady's voice.

"Why should I? 'Cause he says he's a king?"

"I know fer a fact he's a king."

"You can b'lieve him if ya want, but not me. I think he's crazy as a bed bug."

"Quiet, you! That's no way ta talk about our provider!"

"Some provider! So far I been wolf bait, monster bait, an' soldier bait! He's been doin' a great job, ain't he?!"

"I'm warnin' ya. Keep it up an' I'll whollop ya good."

"Why're ya defendin' him? Huh?"

"I ain't."

"Ya are. As a matter o' fact, you've been actin' all gushy around him ever since we left them caves! I seen ya!"

There came a crack, a loud thump. A tangle of conversation threads over grunts and groans.

"Don't you raise your-- ."

"You can't make me-- ."

"I can an' I will-- ."

A moment later, somewhat out of breath, Malady stuck her head out and smiled at the Prince. "Sorry fer the disturbance, m'lord." She noticed he was wet, and she frowned. "Deary me, you're soakin'."

She disappeared and quickly returned with a blanket.

"Here ya are," she said, placing it across his shoulders. "Just the thing on a miserable day like this." She smiled. "We don't want ya catchin' yer death now, do we?"

"Thank you," replied the Prince politely.

"Have you an extra blanket in there for me?" asked Cower, shivering.

Malady glanced his way. "No."

And she shut the window.

"You've a sticky situation on your hands, m'lord," said Cower, rubbing his arms.

"Aye, it seems that way," Bryand muttered, sharing half the blanket with him.

He tossed a quick look over his shoulder and added in a voice the sounded very tired. "One, I think, that will only get stickier the longer I wait to address it."

He did not know what dangers they still faced or what obstacles lay in their path. Someday soon, though, he would sit her down and explain that providing for her and the boys meant seeing them situated close to the castle in a comfortable, well-kept home with a generously stocked pantry.

He would see her cured of all her illnesses. At least those that were treatable. And if the boys wanted to better themselves that was acceptable, too.

He would see they received the finest education and training. Perhaps one day they could be squires or even knights.

But that was as far as he would go. There would be no romance, and certainly no cohabitation. Definitely no cohabitation!

He knew, for everyone's benefit, he would have to speak to her soon. Still, just thinking about the confrontation made his stomach churn.

They followed the river for nearly five miles until they came to what was an obvious crossing. On their right, a muddy road ended at the bank. Peering across the river, they could see the road starting up again on the opposite shore.

Here the river was much wider, about fifty yards across. The murky brown water had dispersed, lessening the swiftness of the current.

"What do you think?" asked the Prince.

Cower watched a spiraling log sail by, scores of tumblebrush, the roof to some poor homesteader's chicken coop. He frowned.

"There's much debris."

"Aye, but that's something we'll have to deal with no matter where we cross. And we may not find a place as good as this."

His mind made up, the Prince knocked on the window frame and called over his shoulder. "Hang on back there; we're about to ford."

He set the team moving down the bank, its tack creaking and chains jingling as the wagon lumbered into the river. It was slow going, but the horses were strong, stocky animals that had been bred for endurance rather than speed. They soon gained their stride and pressed on against the current at a steady pace.

"Hey! Hey! We're leakin' in here!" shouted Malady from inside.

The Prince called back in a calm and steady voice. "Don't worry. This jalopy may be old, but it's sturdy. With thick wooden beams along its sides. If it comes to it we'll float." And then, in a voice only Cower could hear, he added, "At least, I think we'll float."

All appeared to be going well, until they reached the middle of the river. It was then Cower raised up on his haunches and said, "Gods spit! Look, my lord!"

The Prince did so, and suddenly all the color drained from his face. Ahead of them, emerging from the woods on the far shore, was a company of mounted guards. They rode in a column of twos, and more and more appeared until their number was at least thirty.

"What do we do?" asked the retainer, his voice filled with fear.

Bryand felt his own fear taking hold of him. Dearest Gods, what do we do?

There was no way they could turn the wagon around in the middle of a rushing river. And even if they could, the guards would be upon them in no time.

"We'll have to keep going," said the Prince with little confidence. "Just act humble and hope they're not looking to give us any trouble."

The soldiers entered the river in two ranks that

parted and filed past both sides of the wagon. Bryand kept his head bowed and his eyes lowered. Thus, he looked very much like a cringing peasant.

Cower, on the other hand, was praying. For there had been no time to warn the others of the guards' approach.

Please, thought the retainer, casting a quick glance toward the Heavens. If any of you Gods is listening, keep Donoim quiet!

His prayer came too late. The boy had chosen the exact moment to look outside.

"Hey, mum!" his voice rang out from inside the wagon. "Lookee here. Them crummy guards is all around us!"

The retainer cringed and prayed harder, only now it was for a quick death. He hoped he would not face a long delay at the Heavens' weigh-station where his actions in life would be reviewed for improprieties.

There had been a few along the way. He was not proud of them. But, in his opinion, they were only minor offenses.

His one real concern was that his thoughts, especially those of late, might be weighed as heavily as his actions. If that were the case, he was in big trouble. He had considered strangling Malady at least half a dozen times just in the last three days, not to mention losing her children in the woods.

Bryand, in the meantime, reached under the blanket for Slaybest, expecting to be challenged then and there. Totally out-numbered, stuck in an indefensible position, he figured he could surprise two, maybe three, before he was floating lifeless down the river. Goodbye throne. Goodbye MeAnne. I declare you, Daron, the winner!

Luckily, the soldiers were more concerned with crossing the river and avoiding the floating debris than causing trouble for a single wagon; even if it did contain a loud-mouthed little wart like Donoim.

They filed past, hunkered down against the rain, shivering from the cold. Not a single one gave them so much as a glance.

But all too quickly, that luck seemed likely to change when the company commander, who was the last to ford, rode toward them.

Bryand recognized him at once.

"Mortamour," he said under his breath and through clenched teeth.

In his mind's eye, he pictured the clearing where King Jasper and his slaughtered family lay. Mortimour had been the instrument of their death. He was sure of it.

A raging voice clamored inside his head. Kill him! Strike him down as he passes! He wanted to see the look of shock and pain upon his face as Slaybest cut through his shoulder and into his chest.

Yet as much as he wanted his revenge, he kept his fury bridled. The time was not right.

You must think of the others. he told himself. Get them to safety first. Then... Then!

Their eyes met for an instant before the commander rode past. Bryand stole a glance behind him, then turned to Cower and whispered in an urgent tone, "Keep the horses moving. Don't stop for anything!"

The retainer responded by slapping the reins repeatedly on the horses' rumps. But the current was swifter in the deeper water and while the first team lurched forward, the two behind stumbled for a foothold. Despite the retainer's efforts, the crossing was slow and laborious.

Mortamour headed toward the opposite bank, his brow knitting. He had gained his renown as a top-notch assassin not only for his skill (*he had many methods, all of which were grouped into two categories - slow or fast kill,*) but for his instincts as well. They had never failed him; a failsafe, he liked to think; and now they were telling him something was amiss.

He rode up the bank, halted, and wheeled his horse about. More Jangaloni, he thought, and in so short a time.

He had never known them to travel alone like this; they always moved in bands. It was paramount to their survival.

He had even seen it carved on the sides of their jalopies:

Stay togedder!
Dey can't kill us all!

And then there was the driver.

You've seen him before, he brooded, staring hard at the wagon. But where? He had not gotten a very good look at him; only his eyes.

It was then the realization hit him like a thunderbolt. "Blistering irons!" exclaimed the henchman. "That was the Prince!"

He roared for his men to halt and commanded them to come about.

"Seize that wagon!" he shouted. "At any cost! I want them taken. All of them!"

And as the soldiers plunged back into the river, he called with pleasure to the Prince. "Well, well, my lord. Nice of you to drop right into my lap like this."

"They're on to us!" said Bryand, who had been observing the henchman's movements. The Prince threw off the blanket and unsheathed his sword. "Get us moving. Quickly!"

Feeling suddenly like a trapped animal, Cower's heart began to pound. He slapped the reins repeatedly across the horses' rumps, his teeth gnashed and his brow deeply furrowed.

But just then the horses reached deeper water, and, having to swim now, they lost all momentum and slowed even more. The wagon rose abruptly, buoyantly, and they began to drift along with the current as they continued to cut across the river.

It took a moment for the guards to bring their mounts about and reenter the water. That moment turned out to be the Prince's reprieve.

From upstream, a large tree that had been uprooted by the rain, came sailing toward the wagon with its dark, sodden roots looking like hundreds of outstretched arms.

Bryand saw it a moment before it struck, and his eyes went agog. "Brace yourself!" he cried, grabbing hold of the seat.

The tree hit the wagon broadside with the force of a battering ram, snapping the tongue and separating the horses from the jalopy. Before he knew what was happening, Cower found himself jerked to his feet and hanging overboard.

"Let go of the reins!" shouted Bryand, grabbing the retainer about his knees.

"But the horses!"

"Let them go! I can't hold you!"

Cower released the leather straps, and when he was safely aboard again, he watched with chagrin as the horses swam toward shore. The jalopy, in the meantime, had separated from the tree and was now a makeshift boat that coursed along the river turning round and round out of control.

Suddenly an arrow whizzed by Bryand's face. So close had it come, that the Prince fell backwards, landing hard against the wall.

He shook his head, dazed, then, as the wagon came about again, he saw the guards strung out along the bank, keeping pace with them and aiming from atop their horses.

Bryand pounded on the window frame and shouted, "Quickly! Let us in!"

Malady opened it. "What's goin' on? What was that big bump?"

"Not now!" said the Prince, pushing her aside and clambering through the opening onto the wagon's floor.

Cower followed close on his heels, falling on top of the Prince, and while they were untangling themselves, Donoim poked his head out the window and said, "Hey! Where'd the horses go?"

"Get down!" shouted Bryand, pulling him to the floor by the seat of his pants an instant before an arrow streaked through the opening and lodged in the wall with a loud twang.

"Hey, ya dinghy kingy!" protested Donoim, who was not the least bit concerned about the arrow, "keep yer hands ta yerself."

His patience sorely tested, Bryand thrust the boy into Malady's arms and said, "Could you please do us all a favor AND TIE HIM UP?!"

But before anyone could do anything, the wagon pitched drastically to the left and then to the right. Supplies fell all around them. Pots clanged and timbers groaned.

"What's goin' on?!" Malady bleated. "Why're we doin' that?"

Back to the left they went, then to the right. Each time the wagon lurched it seemed like they would capsize, but somehow they stayed upright.

They hit a rock with a jolt and stopped abruptly. Malady and Noim found themselves deposited on the floor. And while the wagon lingered there, slowly pivoting with the force of the current, Bryand crawled to the window and ventured a peek.

"Rapids," he shouted above the din.

"What?" Malady blurted.

"White water. And fast, too."

"Ya had ta tell me that?!" the woman shrieked.

The current dragged them from the rock and they were off again. Round and round they went, out of control, slamming against more rocks, sliding down cascades, bobbing this way and that until, after countless minutes of this abuse, they all became aware of a thunderous roar.

"What's that? What's that?" asked Malady, her eyes agog.

It occurred to Cower first. "I do believe we're on the Ankledeep and if that is so then we've reached Themstall Falls."

True enough, the Ankledeep flowed over Themstall Falls, which were known for being very... Need I say it?

"Falls?! Themstall Falls?!" cried Malady. "Oh, no! Oh, no! I'm not doin' falls!"

Bryand stole another glance. They were about three hundred yards from the brink. But he had seen something else as well.

"There's an island up ahead!" exclaimed the Prince. He pulled open the rear window and saw the guards far upstream, looking the size of ants. "Just pray the river takes us along the blind side."

It did, and in a moment, they had disappeared from the guards' sight. The island was now between them, and even more to their luck, the wagon entered a shoal.

"Everyone out!" shouted Bryand, pulling open the

window. "Let's go! Let's go!"

"I thought we was done bein' dunked!" protested Malady.

"Would you prefer going over the falls?!" offered Cower, fed up with her ranting.

That seemed to make up her mind, and she quickly climbed through the casement.

Bryand grabbed a hank of rope from the wall and tossed it to Cower. "Angle yourselves upstream so the current doesn't carry you past the island." Bryand peered at the little one. "Do you understand?"

"I told ya b'fore," responded Donoim. "I ain't no dummy."

"I am not a dummy; I am not a dummy," said Cower emphatically, pulling him through the window. He had taken it upon himself to teach the boys proper grammar.

Placing himself between them, he took their hands and jumped. The water was icy cold and stabbed him like a thousand knives. He broke the surface panting.

"I ain't been so wet so often in me life," said Noim by his side.

"You've never been cleaner, either," commented the retainer. "Now shut up and swim."

Bryand looked around for anything else worth salvaging. But the interior was mostly a shambles, and a sudden lurch told him that the wagon had left the shoal and was picking up speed. He saw a leather pouch and grabbed it, hoping there was food inside, then he pulled himself through the casement and onto the front seat where he found Malady waiting for him.

"I thought we could go t'gether," said the woman, trembling. "That way, if anythin' goes wrong, we can at least drown t'gether."

"We're not going to drown," said the Prince. He grabbed her tightly around the waist and they plunged into the water. It was numbing cold. He could hardly breathe, but that was probably more because Malady had wrapped her arms around his throat.

"Someday, I must teach you how to swim," Bryand said between grunts as he strained to keep them afloat.

It was a struggle, but they reached the island. Dragging themselves onto the narrow shore, they joined the others and, together, out of breath and drenched once more, they watched in silence as the wagon, even lighter now without their weight, sped down the river and approached the brink of the falls.

When at last it went over, it appeared to hang suspended in mid-air, then, with a finality that made its former occupants shudder, it dropped out of sight. They looked on at the raging water, silent, frozen in place, knowing exactly what their fate would have been had they not found the opportunity to escape.

"We got a knack fer losin' wagons," stated Donoim at last.

As much as he would have liked to disagree with the boy, even throttle him, he could not. After all, there they were, on foot once more, without food or shelter.

Suddenly he remembered the leather pouch he had thrown over his head. He peered inside. But all he found was a collection of Aldina's skin balms.

"Quickly now," he said, masking his disappointment. "Into the bushes, we want the guards to think we've gone over the falls."

Cower led the way while Bryand followed at the rear, erasing their footprints with the help of a fallen branch. They found a small clearing that was well hidden, and here Cower and the Prince left Malady and the boys and climbed to the top of a wooded hillock from which they could observe the soldiers upon the opposite shore making their way closer to the falls.

"Do you think we've fooled them?" asked Cower.

"We'll soon find out," said the Prince grimly and nothing more.

Mortamour signaled his company to halt just opposite the island. He dismounted and stood at the edge of the bank, absently rubbing his chin.

He had seen the wagon go over the falls, but he was not yet convinced the Prince had been in it. The instinct that had alerted him earlier was back again with the same nagging intensity, and he scrutinized the island with the keen eyes of a hunter, searching for any unusual movement among the trees.

So, my lord, thought Mortamour, were you clever enough to avoid the falls? And if so are you hiding right under my nose?

"We'll soon see," muttered the henchman aloud, his lips tightening into a grin. The one and only thing he loved more than the chase was the kill itself.

He ordered a detachment of four men to cross to the island. But before the soldiers were halfway, their mounts had faltered in the driving current and men and horses were dragged screaming toward the falls.

The henchman scowled and shook his head. That was a bad call, he thought. Those were good horses.

He puffed air into his cheeks and placed his hands on his hips. What now? he pondered. He did not want to deplete his ranks any more than he had to, but all his instincts told him the Prince was on that island.

Still, approaching it from this bank seemed impossible. Was it worth retracing his steps and fording the river at the crossing upstream? He would have to work his way down and cross to the island from the far bank. He had no idea if the terrain would allow him to do that or if it would take more of his men's lives during the attempt.

But he was willing to take the risk. The prince was a great prize. And killing him would be such a pleasure.

"Form ranks!" he cried. He climbed into his saddle and wheeled his horse about. "By twos!"

He started them off again upstream, but did not take the lead. Instead, he waited until the column had passed by, all the while keeping his eyes locked upon the island.

"I'll be right back, your lordship," he shouted. "So don't go away." He chuckled at his own levity. Being smug and cruel always tickled him.

Bryand and Cower scrambled down the hill and rejoined the others. "They know we're here. We've got to move fast."

"But how're we gonna get off th' island?" asked Noim. Then, with a haughty look, he added, "We ain't birds, ya know."

"Aren't birds," corrected Cower.

"Quickly," Bryand snapped. "To the shore. We haven't much time."

When they had done so, the Prince studied the river and the opposite bank. "There," he said, pointing. "Where the shoal is widest. We'll cross one at a time, using the rope."

"Wait a minute; wait a minute," blurted Malady nervously. "One at a time? I can't go by myself, I'll never make it."

True enough, once in the water she would sink like a stone and, though it seemed an answer to the Prince's romantic problem, he would never actually let that happen.

Yet, he knew he was not strong enough to carry

her beyond the shoal. Once in the stronger current, she would surely panic and cause them both to drown.

He thought for a moment, chewing on the inside of his cheek, and then an idea occurred to him. "I know, we'll float you."

"Float me?" said Malady, irked. "Whaddu I look like, a pig's bladder?"

"I mean, we'll pull you across. You'll have to stay behind, though. Everyone else must cross first."

Bryand tied one end of the rope around his waist. "Hopefully, it's long enough to reach across," said the Prince, handing the other end to Cower. "Once I'm on the other side I'll tie my end off, and then you can do the same."

He dropped into the water and, ignoring their anguished looks, tossed them a confident smile. He proceeded through the shoal, angling upstream as he went so the current would not carry him too far off the mark he had set for himself on the opposite bank.

Cower kept the line slack, feeding more and more of it through his hands as the Prince worked his way farther out. But when Bryand entered the rapids, he was carried along by the current faster than Cower anticipated.

The sudden force of the water jerked the line through his hands in the same manner as a fleeing fish after swallowing a baited hook.

The retainer tightened his grip, but the current remained overpowering, and he found himself being towed along the bank, unable to get a decent foothold.

"Where're ya goin'?" called Donoim, puzzled.

"To market!" Cower retorted angrily as he struggled with the rope. "Would someone care to help me?!"

Malady and the boys took up the line and, with their combined weight, they served as a mooring for the Prince.

Fortunately, the rope was long enough to reach the other bank. Bryand climbed out of the water, panting, his arms and legs quivering from the effort.

He rested for a moment, hearing only the air as it whistled through his nostrils. Then, gathering the remainder of his strength, he rose to his feet with a grunt and removed the rope from his waist.

He worked his way along the bank, until he had come abreast of his companions. There he found a stout tree and tied his end of the rope around it. Once that was accomplished, Cower did the same with his end.

"I wanna go first!" volunteered Donoim with glee. "Can I? Huh? Can I?"

Cower motioned him forward. "No showing off now," cautioned the retainer. "And don't let go of the rope."

The little one sneered and tossed him a dismissing wave. Then, gripping the line, he worked his way across the river, hand over hand.

Bryand waded out and met him, and together they climbed onto the bank.

"Well done, lad," said the Prince, clapping him on the shoulder.

Donoim shrugged and accepted the man's compliment humbly. "Piece o' cake, really."

Noim went next, then Cower, leaving Malady wringing her hands and fretting. She felt woozy, and her throat was parched; yet the thought of putting water inside her at that moment filled her with repugnance.

Come on, come on, she thought impatiently. Though she dreaded the river, she was, at the same time, eager to get the whole thing over with.

Bryand helped Cower out of the water, deposited him on the bank, then called to the woman. "Here we go now, Malady. Untie your end."

But Malady, realizing the time had come to cross

the river by herself, suddenly found her feet rooted to the ground. "I-- . I can't!"

"You can, Malady!" coaxed the Prince. "You've come through far worse than this!"

But from the panicky look on her face, he knew his words had had no affect on her. "Listen to me, Malady; Malady; you're not listening to me! You can do this!"

She began to cry.

"Stop that!" shouted the Prince. "I mean it! You'll bring on one of your seizures!" But all that did was make her cry harder.

Scowling, Bryand grabbed onto the line and waded out. Time was of the essence; any minute now the guards would return. He had to get Malady moving.

"Hear me, woman!" shouted the Prince sternly. "I'm the provider for this family, and as such, you must listen to what I say!" He suddenly felt contrite. "Please!"

That seemed to work. For, with trembling hands, Malady removed the rope from the tree and tied it around her waist.

"Now edge into the water," called Bryand. "And hang on!"

"O' course I'm gonna hang on," she whimpered, tears streaming down her cheeks as she waded out. "What else am I gonna do."

"That's good. That's good," Bryand called.

"One foot, then the other foot, mum," shouted Noim.

The water rose higher and higher up her torso. "I don't like this," she muttered. "Don't like it; don't like it; don't like it."

Finally, when the water was just under her chin, she tightened her grip on the rope, pushed off with her toes and set herself adrift.

"Yer doin' it, mum!" said Donoim, hopping up and down with glee.

"Good girl!" shouted Bryand as he gathered in the rope.

Malady found herself somewhat relieved and laughing nervously even as the current took her downstream from the others. This ain't too bad after all, she thought.

But when she entered the faster water and found herself being buffeted about, she became terrified and began to screech, "Pull me in! Pull me in, pull me in, pull me in!!"

"You're all right," said the Prince, dragging her onto the shore, and when she saw she was on dry land, she kissed his hands, and said, "Thankee, m'lord. Thankee; thankee; thankee."

Bryand coiled the rope, then placed it over his shoulder. He peered upstream, looking for any sign of the guards. But the trees on this side of the river came all the way down to the water's edge.

He did not want to linger long. An hour or more had passed since the guards had ridden off; it was a certainty they had already forded the river and were on their way downstream once again.

He looked at his bedraggled companions. They were exhausted, and Malady, with her eyes wide and glassy and muttering incoherently, appeared just short of losing her sanity.

Nevertheless they had to press on. "Come," said the Prince gently but firmly. "We must keep going."

"Which way, my lord?" asked Cower, regretting his words almost immediately.

The Prince pondered the question, (*which was always a bad sign.*) However, this time the odds were greatly in his favor. It did not take much foresight to know that heading upstream would land them in the guards' clutches. Only a fool would go that way, as only a fool would recross a river he had labored so hard to cross in the first place.

As Bryand saw it, there were only two directions from which to choose. They could head for the falls and, hopefully, find a way to climb down, or proceed away from the river directly from where they stood.

The Prince chose the latter and began to wend his way through the trees, and in no time at all, he had led them into a swamp, where clouds of insects descended upon them as if a dinner bell had just been rung.

The air here was still and pungent with the odor of decay. A soupy, torpid mist blanketed the ground and the further they traveled, the thicker the mist became and the deeper they sank into the muck beneath it.

"Uh, my lord," said Cower, shuddering, for he was reminded of the time, as a boy, he had been forced by the village bully to walk barefoot through a pig pen. "Don't you think we should try going another way?"

"Well, I thought of doing that," called Bryand over his shoulder. "But we seem to find trouble no matter which way we choose. So, with that being true, we might just as well continue in the direction we're headed."

Cower saw the logic of it and had to agree.

Naturally, they stumbled onto more trouble, this time in the form of a swallow-up, which was far worse than the worst kind of bog. For in a bog one tended to sink slowly and usually only to the knees. A swallow-up tended to swallow up all things quickly and whole. One step was all it took.

And with things going the way they were, one step was all it took, and Bryand, being in the lead, found himself up to his neck in muck and sinking fast before he or anyone else had time to react.

"No need to panic," said the Prince calmly, trying to assuage their fears. "Now then, who's got the rope?"

"You do!" the others shouted.

"Oh."

And he went under.

With a strangled cry, Cower threw himself down and clawed at the muck while Malady fanned away the mist with the remains of her skirt. But, though the retainer worked feverishly, he made no headway. The muck simply filled itself in again with every channel he dug.

"My lord!!" bellowed Cower, crawling out. The top part of his body sank instantly, and he too would have gone under had not Malady and the boys grabbed hold of his ankles and pulled him back to safe ground.

The retainer wiped the mud from his eyes and stared with disbelief at the spot where Bryand had gone under. There was no disturbance in the mist. Nothing that indicated the Bryand was alive and attempting to break the surface.

Cower pounded the ground with his fists and raged, "Dearest Gods, I swear this now; I will quit you! If you do not save my Prince, I will quit you this minute!"

"Please, oh, please, oh, please," whimpered the woman as she squeezed her hands together and pressed her eyelids shut. "I lost one man already. Don't take this one away from me, too!"

For one long, horrible moment, they waited, hoping for a response from the Gods.

But none came.

"Hey, Noim," said Donoim, breaking the silence. "How long ya think he can hold his breath?"

"'Bout two minutes, or so."

"Ain't it been that long already?"

"Oh, yeah."

Donoim stared at the misty blanket. "Guess he's dead, then."

Malady began to wail, and Cower, distraught and almost at his wits' end, chewed on his hand. Yet, just when he too was about to completely despair, a mud-caked head appeared, sputtering and gasping, then a neck and a pair of shoulders, and slowly the Prince rose out of the swallow-up.

The others stared in shock and disbelief, convinced they were witnessing a miracle, until it became apparent that the Prince was standing on the back of an animal. A goo-sifter to be precise, which was a large but passive creature, indigenous of bogs, that sucked mud through the gaps between its teeth in search of insects and small reptiles.

This was a baby, so it was a goo-goo sifter; yet it was still big enough to support the Prince and serve as a bridge for him to rejoin his companions. As soon as Bryand stepped off its back, the animal snorted, then submerged again to indulge itself in its favorite pastime of wallowing in the mud.

"I suppose we should choose another way," said the Prince, unscathed by the experience though somewhat wiser for it.

Cower nodded, trembling with relief, his heart filled with joy. Then, to keep from breaking down in tears, he relied on what he knew best and began to wipe the Prince's face and scrape the mud from his shoulders.

"Oh, my lord," cried Malady, still shaken. "I thought ya was dead fer sure!"

Her first impulse was to embrace him but, after one look at the slime that covered him, she decided against it. Instead, she turned to the boys and said, "Well? Ain't ya got nothin' ta say?"

Noim shrugged. "Nice ta have ya back."

"Yeah," added Donoim, mimicking his brother. "We thought you was dead for sure."

"Now what?" asked Noim, flicking some slime from his fingers.

"Back to the river, as fast as we can travel," said Bryand, turning in what he imagined was the proper direction.

"No, my lord," blurted Cower. "That's the swallow-up."

With a smug smirk, Noim jerked his thumb, indicating the correct direction lay behind him. "The river's this way."

"No it ain't," said Donoim impatiently. "It's that way." And he pointed off to his right.

"No it is not," said Cower, correcting him.

"Awright, if you know so much, you pick a way."

Cower scanned the area, then shrugged. "I can't say."

Malady frowned. "Well, someone better choose."

Bryand cleared his throat and opened his mouth to speak, but the bald look he received from everyone else, convinced him he was not the best person at the moment to decide the issue.

"Any ideas?" asked the Prince, keeping in mind that a good leader was always willing to listen to the suggestions of those he led.

But before anyone could reply, they heard the distant shouts of men, and turning in that direction, they immediately saw a string of tiny flames in the dimness. The guards were trailing them through the swamp.

"I told ya the river was that way," said Donoim pointedly.

"Quiet!" Bryand snapped in a hushed voice. He watched the tiny lights bobbing up and down, trying to judge the distance between them. This man Mortamour, he acknowledged, was indeed a formidable adversary to track them in a swamp of all things. Wasting no more time, the Prince grabbed a tall stick and tested the ground ahead of him and, in this way, blazed a trail around the swallow-up.

They slogged through the mire in single file, stepping into the rapidly filling hole made by the person in front of them. They had gone about three hundred yards or so when they heard the first screams.

They halted and peered at one another, then back the way they had come. The soldiers' torches were barely pin pricks now, and they danced this way and that in a confused pattern.

Mortamour had reached the swallow-up.

Hours passed. They traveled deeper into the swamp, peering over their shoulders again and again for any sign of their pursuers. But the lights had long since disappeared.

The air became hot and moist and hung about them like a shroud. So tangled and vine-covered were the trees that soon they could not see the sky. The little light that did filter to the ground was of a grayish hue, giving everything around them a lusterless, moribund appearance.

Not a bird chirped. Not a frog croaked. The silence was so complete and overpowering that it was truly a sound unto itself, droning everywhere and nowhere all at the same time.

Bryand cast edgy glances about him, first left, then right, then front and back. He did not know what he expected to see. But there was something about this swamp that made him uneasy.

He gripped Slaybest's hilt. Almost immediately, he became aware of a light tingling sensation in his hand.

However, he did not have time to dwell upon it, for presently the mist rose up in a most unusual way, surrounding him so completely that he could no longer see anything but the mist itself.

"Cower!" he called, alarmed.

"Aye, my lord," came the retainer's voice.

He turned in the direction he thought it had come. "The mist, is it-- ?"

"Aye."

"What's goin' on here?" called Malady in a fearful voice.

"Who's this?" said Donoim, probing the mist in front of him.

"Yer mum, and get yer hands off me bum." She grabbed him and pulled him to her. "Where's your brother?"

"Hey Noim!"

"What?"

"Where are ya?"

"Over here."

"Over where?"

"Over here! Where're you?"

"Over here, o' course."

"Who's this?" asked Cower, touching someone ahead of him.

"I'm tired o' bein' pawed," groused Malady.

"I beg your pardon."

Bryand peered about him, feeling most disoriented. "Cower?"

"Aye, my lord."

"I don't know which way to go. The mist is baffling my senses."

"Then, stay where you are, and we'll find you." The retainer linked arms with Malady, who linked arms with Donoim, and together they inched along until they came upon the Prince.

"Now whaddu we do?" asked the little one.

It was then Bryand remembered the rope. "We can use this to stay together." He tied one end about his waist, then, leaving two or three feet of slack, tied a loop around each of them.

He stopped, and gazed about, confused. The mist was so thick that he had not realized Noim was missing. "Where's your brother?"

"Hey, Noim! Where are ya?!" called the little one.

"Over here!"

"Over where?"

"Over here! Over here!"

Noim peered into the mist. He was lost.

Awright, now, don't go losin' yer head. You'll find 'em.

The boy inched forward, his arms outstretched before him.

This bloody mist, he scowled; it's confoundin' me senses. He moved on in this way for a minute or two.

Some trip ta th' country this is turnin' out ta be. Runnin' around, followin' a lunatic, who couldn't find his way outta a room with one door.

"Hey!" he called. "Ya still there?!"

"Yeah," came his brother's voice, but now it was punier, as if he were farther away.

"Donoim?" he shouted nervously.

"Noim," came his mother's distant voice. "Where are ya?"

"Over here!"

"Over where?"

"Are you gonna start that again?!"

He walked on, his teeth starting to chatter, not because he was cold but because he was now quite afraid. And then a thought struck him. What if I can't find 'em? What if they leave me here ta rot?

"Hey you guys!" called the boy, tears springing to his eyes. "Where are ya?!"

He waited.

"Mum?!!"

But no answer came.

Panic gripped him, and he started to run. "Don't leave me here, mum! Please!"

Suddenly the ground was not where he expected it to be and, with a startled cry, he tumbled head over heels down a sharp incline. At length, he rolled to a halt with a grunt, and when he had shaken off his dizziness and had gathered his wits, he raised himself up on his elbows and discovered he was in a small gully.

He rubbed his aching head and winced. He had struck it on something on his way down.

He pulled himself to his feet; rocky; somewhat woozy. He looked up the hill in the direction from which he had come, and he saw the mist upon the crest, looking much like an impenetrable curtain.

Funny, how it just stays there, he thought. Ya'd think it'd creep down th' hill.

It was then he heard his name. It was barely audible; so far away that he could not tell if it had been his mother or not.

"Here!" shouted Noim, his voice cracking discordantly. "An' watch yer step!"

Noim, came a voice from directly behind him.

Startled, the boy whirled about. But there was no one there.

"Who's callin'" he shouted.

Silence was his only reply. He scowled and peered about the gully, then he rubbed his head. Must've hit it harder 'n I thought.

Noim, came the voice again, and again it was from behind him.

He spun on his heels, afraid now, his eyes darting back and forth searching for his tormentor.

It was then he saw the girl.

She was on the other side of the gully about thirty feet away, standing atop a grassy knoll among a tangle of branches.

Noim had never seen branches like these. They appeared to have no bark of any kind and looked completely devoid of leaves. They moved as if they had a life of their own, entwining above the girl, around her, forming an elaborate, lacy cocoon. As he approached, the cocoon suddenly opened up and drew back, framing her in an almost perfect arbor.

She was beautiful, the most beautiful girl he had ever seen. She had long auburn tresses that billowed about her though he was not conscious of any breeze.

She wore a plain white bodice that was cut low and laced up the front. He could not help but notice how her full breasts seemed barely contained.

The soft white skirt she wore was made of homespun. It clung to her in the breeze, revealing the line of her supple thighs and the conical shape of her sex.

Noim's heart quickened to a frantic beat and his manhood rose in tribute to her loveliness. When she beckoned him with a delicate wave of her hand, he stumbled forward in eager obeyance.

This can't be happenin', he decided. I gotta be dreamin'. The thought triggered something in his mind, and it was then he recognized her. For she was none other than the girl he would conjure whenever he was sure Donoim was asleep and he felt the urge to express himself.

Aye, it was her, in all her beauty and lusty appeal. But how could that be? And what was she doing here of all places?

She grinned at him coyly, her full lips pressed together. Somehow, though the boy could not explain it, her bodice laces came untied, the front of the garment, with nothing to hold it together, pulled apart and the girl's breasts, no longer restrained, were now partially exposed.

That all these things were exactly as he had fantasized mattered not to him. He was swept up by his desire and trapped in the throes of something beyond his control. Weaving across the gully, he came to the bottom of the grassy knoll and began to climb, only slightly aware of the crunching sound beneath his boots.

Bryand and the others plodded through the muck, enveloped by the mist, which by now was so dense and mordant that it was more like sulphurous fumes than anything else.

"Noim!" called the Prince, wincing. His throat stung more sharply with each breath. "Noim, lad! Where are you?!"

But the boy had not responded for many minutes.

"This ain't like him," wheezed Malady, wringing her hands as she peered every which way. So concerned was she that the woman no longer gave any thought to the mist or the way it burned her insides.

"Ya don't think he got swallowed up by a swallow-up, do ya?"

"We'll find him," said the Prince, indulging her the best he could, for his patience was strained to the limit.

"My lord," said Cower, clutching at his throat. "I can't breathe."

"Me needer," croaked Donoim.

Indeed, it seemed as though the fog were robbing them of their air.

Each of them began to cough, once or twice at first, and then uncontrollably. Malady fell to her hands and knees, gasping and straining. Cower felt his consciousness slipping away, while Donoim gave out with a fearful whooping sound as tears ran down his cheeks.

This fog, thought Bryand, struggling to stay lucid. This blasted fog! I've never seen anything like it! It's almost alive.

His hand involuntarily reached for Slaybest. Once again he felt the tingling sensation. This time, however, when the mist closed in, he drew Slaybest from its scabbard. To his astonishment, and to the astonishment of everyone else, an orange glow emanated from the blade. (*Aye, orange, I say, as opposed to blue, for it was well known that some blades emitted a blue glow when orcs and trolls were about. Orange, however, indicated a much more complicated smelting process, which meant the blade was capable of detecting far more monstrous species than just orcs and trolls. Also bad fungus, which was a good thing in a way.*)

Such was the glow, brilliant, pulsating. And at its appearance, the mist drew back abruptly as if it had a life of its own and found the light a threat.

Suddenly the air was not so tainted. In just a moment, they were all coherent once again.

"Clip my toenails, would ya look at it," rasped Malady, staring in awe at the blade.

"I ain't seen it do that b'fore," commented Donoim, rubbing his stinging eyes.

Cower marveled at the light. "How did you---?"

"I've no idea," said the Prince, feeling cheered by the glow. He cleared his parched throat. "But now I know what Aldina meant when she said there was something powerful about it."

The Prince extended Slaybest, took two quick steps forward, and, as he expected, the mist just as quickly shrank from the blade.

They moved on in this way, and though the glow never lapsed, there were moments when it brightened. Though he had no explanation for it, he believed the sword was acting like a divining rod. What it measured, he was not sure. Where it was leading them, he did not know. But he was no longer cheered by the light, and the brighter it grew, the more he was convinced that Noim was in terrible danger.

"I want you, Noim," said the girl, though she had not moved her lips. "Come to me. Come to me, my love."

Noim proceeded to climb, losing footing here and there. He did not even bother to look down, for the girl's breasts were exposed now in all their supple beauty.

Her skirt fell away, revealing the shock of auburn hair between her thighs. When he saw her naked sex, he longed for her, he hungered for her, and his manhood, throbbing now, strained against his braces.

He scrambled up the mound hand over hand, sliding backwards at times, regaining his ground. At last he had reached the top, and he stood for a moment; awed by her beauty; driven by her nakedness.

His heart pounded in his chest, sending his hot blood streaking through his veins like the fiery stone he had once seen crash to the ground from the Heavens.

Suddenly she was no longer standing before him, but resting on a pedestal of limbs, and when she spread her legs, two branches came up like stirrups to support her feet.

"Come to me, Noim," beckoned the girl. "I want you. I hunger for you."

He saw her sex, as he had seen it time and again in his dreams. He stepped into the arbor and let fall his braces in preparation of their union.

So consumed was he, so enraptured, he had no idea that behind his back, dozens of limbs were entwining, becoming a cocoon once more.

Bryand broke into a trot. In addition to the glow,

Slaybest now hummed.

"Hey! Hey!" cried Malady, "I can't keep up."

"You must!" called the Prince over his shoulder. "Noim's life depends on it!"

The mist parted like a curtain before them revealing the crest of the hill and the depression below. They scrambled down the slope, the rope tugging at their waists, going slack, then taught once more.

Slaybest glowed now with the intensity of a coal and the hum was now a full harmonic chorus. As they descended, the light from the blade illuminated the ground before them spilling across the gully when they reached the bottom of the slope. It was then, they came to an abrupt halt, so stunned and horrified were they.

For there, atop a pile of bleached bones of every size and shape, locked in a strange-looking cocoon, was Noim with his pants collected about his ankles.

"Strange place ta take a pee," observed Donoim.

Bryand spun around and severed the line between them with one quick slice from Slaybest. He said not a word. Instead, he broke into a run; fast as his legs would carry him. For the Prince knew Noim had only minutes to live, perhaps less.

He had heard tell of creatures such as this, though he never in all his days had expected to come across one. For they were of a time that had long since passed, a time when men huddled in caves and monsters ruled the world.

Nevertheless, there it was; a Gormandizer! And the hairs on the back of his neck stood on end.

According to the ancient texts, they had strange powers over the mind, which they used to lure their unsuspecting prey to them. Once within their clutches, the victim's flesh was stripped away and devoured. Bryand knew if he did not reach the boy in time, Noim's fate would be the same.

"Noooooim!" he bellowed as he reached the bottom of the mound.

The boy stepped back. Through the coiled mass of tendrils, he saw Bryand climbing toward him, sword glowing in his hand, a menacing look on his face.

"Hey!" Noim snarled. "Get yer own girl!"

It was then the limbs grew closer together, pressing him toward the woman. Embarrassed now, Noim turned to the girl, wanting to apologize. But what he saw instead made his eyes go wide and his mouth fall agape in horror. For where the nude girl had been, so lovely, so inviting, was now the sickly grey trunk of a bare tree, and there in the center of the trunk, were two small hollows above a mouth filled with jagged teeth. Noim screamed. He clawed at the limbs, but they merely flexed and drew him closer to the creature's jaws.

It was then Bryand reached the top of the bone pile and, without a pause, sliced into the mass of tentacles surrounding the boy. Instantly, the gully was filled with a blood-curdling scream that rose up from the creature's maw. The tentacles flew apart and spread to their fullest height, and as they did, Bryand grabbed Noim by the back of his neck and pushed him off the bone pile.

The boy was safe. The Prince, however, having traded places with him, was now the one in danger.

He was turning toward the creature, intending to attack, when the creature's stalk, though thick and rooted to the ground, stretched forward at a speed the Prince did not expect. Having no time to raise his sword, Bryand lurched to his right, narrowly escaping its jaws, which clamped shut, cutting off one of the Prince's shirt laces.

Overhead, tentacles snapped at him like whips; some with long, curved talons at the end. Bryand dodged these, dropping to the ground, rolling to his right, then to his left as talons dug deeply into the ground.

He swung Slaybest across his body, slicing off the talon on one whip and then severing another. The Gormandizer convulsed, and during that reprieve, Bryand scrambled to his feet.

When next the trunk attacked, the Prince was ready for it. Just as the Gormandizer spread its jaws, he drove Slaybest down its throat, the glow from the blade lighting its hollow orbits from within. Using all his strength, Bryand pulled out the blade, angling it upward as he did, cutting through the top of the creature's mouth all the way to its eyes.

The gormandizer shook violently, black gore oozing from its wound. Bryand clutched Slaybest with both hands, brought the blade up and closed for another attack.

It was then, the Gormandizer vanished.

Bryand halted in his tracks. His mouth fell open. For there, where the Gormandizer stood just a moment before, was now MeAnne, dressed in the gown she wore the night he had escaped, surrounded by an ethereal glow.

"I want you, Bryand," she said longingly. "I hunger for you."

Bryand stood, completely arrested; captivated by her beauty. In an instant, the had world vanished. Nothing mattered but the two of them.

He was a breath away from surrendering completely to the Gormandizer's vision, when Slaybest shot forth a blast of light so intense that it blotted out the image in his mind.

Bryand blinked, saw the Gormandizer awash in Slaybest's glow, saw the tentacles closing around him, and he was once again in control of his mind. "I know what you are," he said, snarling.

"My dearest love," she replied, arms outstretched and waiting to close around him.

"You are not MeAnne!" he exclaimed. He raised Slaybest over his head and calling on all his willpower, he slashed her twice across the chest.

MeAnne disappeared instantly and was replaced by the slick gray visage of the Gormandizer. Tentacles lashed out at him from all sides, brandishing their sharp claws. But the Prince, consumed by bloodlust now, engaged each one and left them wriggling on the ground like crimped worms.

The Gormandizer, desperate now, reached deeper into his mind, changing into all those he loved; from MeAnne to his mother, to his father, to Dwayne, to Niles, to Dillin, to Cower, and finally to Daron.

The moment he saw his brother, Bryand broke off the attack. "You," he said in barely a whisper.

"Brother," said Daron, sounding most concerned. "Brother, I feel your pain."

"Do you now," said Bryand, his mouth twisting into a hateful sneer. "In that case, here's some more."

He pounced, hacking away at his brother's image again and again, gore splattering everywhere, the gully echoing with his screams.

"My lord!" shouted Cower from the base of the bone pile. "It is enough! It is enough!"

But the Prince did not stop until the vision faded and all that remained was the Gormandizer's mangled trunk.

It twitched and quivered, its remaining tentacles straining toward the sky. There they lingered for just a moment, went rigid, then limp, and fell upon the pile of bones.

Bryand knew it was dead, for Slaybest's blade had stopped glowing and was once again only burnished steel.

Sheathing his sword, the Prince turned and climbed down the mound, sick to his stomach and trembling from fatigue. He rejoined the others and watched Malady smacking Noim upon his bare buttocks, too tired to interfere.

"If I ever; catch ya; doin' that again; Ya won't; be able; ta sit fer a year!"

Winded, her hand smarting, she let him go. "Now put yer pecker in yer pants an' keep it there."

The boy obeyed his mother, trying hard to maintain his dignity as he laced his braces. But even when he was done, he could not bring himself to look at the Prince.

"Let's away from here," said Bryand in a tired voice. He started toward the hill. At that moment, he did not even care if the others followed him.

Ingrate, he thought, stewing. The boy's an ingrate. I suppose I should have left him to be eaten!

But moments later, when they had emerged from the gully, the Prince found Noim walking beside him. He tossed him a curious look, but Noim kept his eyes straight ahead. So, the Prince said nothing, and concentrated on blazing the trail.

At length, Noim cleared his throat and said, "Thanks fer savin' my life."

Bryand waited for the boy to improve upon the remark with one of his sardonic comments. But to his surprise, none came.

"You're welcome," rejoined the Prince, making sure not to look at the boy and thus embarrass him even more.

He came to a gooey patch of ground and tested it with his stick before continuing across it.

"Look," Bryand said somewhat stiffly, eyes straight ahead, on the lookout for any other Gormandizers or swallowups. "I know it's difficult for you to think of me as a friend just now, what with your father's death still so recent; and with everything else that has happened on this misbegotten journey. But, I want you, and your brother, and, of course, your mother, too, to know that you can depend on me; not just now; but in the future as well. Perhaps, you and I, eventually, might even be friends."

He waited for the boy to reply. "If you'd like; I mean, if and when you're ready."

Again he waited for the boy to speak, and again, the boy did not. Bryand decided the time had come for them to clear the air.

But when the Prince turned to look at him, he realized the boy was not there. Noim had dropped back to the end of the line.

Realizing he had been talking to himself all that time, Bryand shook his head, nonplussed. "But, of course," he muttered under his breath. "I should have known--."

"Did you say something, my lord?" asked Cower in a weary voice. "I thought I heard you speak."

Bryand snorted, feeling somewhat peevish and annoyed. "Nothing important," he replied, after which he proceeded in silence, poking the tar-like ground ahead of him, wondering somewhat dubiously if there ever was any real joy in parenting.

CHAPTER TWENTY

Niles awoke to the lyric sound of chirping. Dawn already he thought as he gazed with bleary eyes at the branches overhead. There he saw a flock of birds, displaying their brightly painted plumage, flitting this way and that, greeting their neighbors and bobbing their heads while singing their praises to the new day.

"Cut out that racket!" snapped the young man.

The birds obeyed immediately by scattering every which way.

"What's wrong?" asked Dwayne sleepily.

"Too much noise," grumbled Niles, and he curled up beneath his half of the blanket. But though he tried, he could not go back to sleep.

He had been having such a wondrous dream. He was in a room the size of the Great Hall of Castle Bandidon, and it had been stacked to the rafters with plates of food. It was a feast for a King, for a God even, and he with an appetite to match any deity!

Disgruntled, Niles sat up and rubbed the sleep from his eyes. He looked about, observing the way the sunlight sparkled on the dew-covered grass.

This was the first time in days he had awakened to sunshine instead of hammering rain. But though he was no longer cold and drenched, he was far too hungry to be cheered by the change of weather. He rose stiffly, grunting. Some bed, he brooded, massaging his back, Is there no justice in the world?

He stood and stretched his achy muscles. Fully

awake now, he glanced about the small clearing they had chosen for their camp.

He became aware of two things. The first, that he was still hungry, ravenously hungry, and the second, that there was a medium-sized brown rabbit observing him from the clearing's edge.

Niles shut his eyes, afraid his hunger was causing visions. But when he opened them again, the rabbit was still there. My stars, he thought, what a stroke of luck!

Niles was a skillful hunter, the best of all his friends. Had he a bow in his hand just then, the rabbit would most definitely have been breakfast. But the only weapon he possessed was his dagger, and to use it effectively, he needed to be much closer.

He reached for the weapon, keeping his movements as slow and fluid as possible, all the while presenting the rabbit with an ingratiating smile.

"Hello, little bunny," he cooed, taking a careful step forward. "How are you this morning? I hope you don't object if I turn you into stew."

The rabbit's ears perked up at this, and it raised itself onto its hindquarters. Still, it made no attempt to escape, and sat there inviting him to snare it.

He was now about six feet away. One hot breakfast coming up, he chortled to himself as he made ready to pounce.

But what Niles did not realize, was that Dwayne, having fallen asleep once more, had rolled onto his back. At that very moment, the brawny young man gave out with a snore that sounded like an enraged moose during mating season.

Startled, the rabbit, spun about and darted into the woods.

Desperate now, Niles lunged, trying with his short dagger to skewer the animal. But it was already out of range, and he landed with a thud upon the soaked ground.

Furious, he shot to his feet, marched over to Dwayne, and unceremoniously kicked him in the leg.

"What-- ?" responded Dwayne, sitting up abruptly. "What's wrong?"

"You dim-witted oaf! Because of your confounded snoring we just lost our first hot meal in days!"

And without waiting for Dwayne to reply, he bolted after the rabbit, calling, "Here bunny! Here bunny-bunny-bunny!"

Unperturbed, Dwayne yawned and scratched his head. He contemplated going back to sleep. But the sun was up, the birds were up, and unless the clouds returned later on, it looked like it was going to be a beautiful day.

He stood and took the crisp morning air deep into his lungs. The land was such a marvel, he thought, taking in the trees and bushes around him. No matter how many wounds it received, it always found ways to heal itself.

He felt akin to it. The life he had known, everything that was familiar to him, had been snatched away. He still could not understand the reason for it. Yet, for the first time in days, the sadness inside him seemed less burdensome. Like the land, he was healing.

He heard Niles approaching fast. Dwayne expected him to be quite churlish. But much to his surprise, when Niles entered the clearing, there was an eager look upon his face and a bounce to his step.

"There's a road up ahead," said the knight. "And just beyond it, I saw some laborers working in a field. We must be near a farm or perhaps even a village where we can steal something to eat."

Dwayne scowled disapprovingly. "Steal?"

"Did I say steal?" replied Niles, an innocent look upon his face. "I meant to say borrow."

While Niles gathered up the blanket, Dwayne stood and stretched, then placed his hands on his hips, took three deep breaths, and began his daily exercises.

"Must you do that now?" asked Niles a bit impatiently. "I'm starving."

"This won't take long," answered Dwayne, concentrating. "I've got to keep in shape."

"You're not going to fall apart if you skip a day every once in a while."

"Of course not; I know that. But I do this for another reason. Keeping my body physically fit gives my mind a sense of calm. You should try it sometime. Perhaps you wouldn't be so jumpy."

"Jumpy? I'm not jumpy. I'm never jumpy. I'm hungry, is all."

"Just one more minute." He stretched out upon the ground face down, then pushed himself up with his arms and dropped again slowly, repeating this fifty times before hopping to a standing position.

"Ready," said the young man, smiling, his cheeks flushed and his eyes shining.

"Are you sure? Maybe you'd like to stand on your head or hang upside down from a tree for a while?"

"No," replied Dwayne, unperturbed. "We can go now."

And so they did, with Niles in the lead, retracing his steps to the road.

They passed fields of sand colored wheat and rows of corn with ears so large they had burst from their husks.

Niles looked at it longingly, his mouth watering. Cooked or not, at that moment he did not care.

"I know what you're thinking," said Dwayne just then.

"What? What am I thinking?"

"You going to take some of that corn."

"I am not. I'm going to eat it without removing a single ear from its stalk."

"That's the same as stealing."

"Just the kernals. I'd be leaving the cob."

"See that scarecrow yonder? It's there because the farmer doesn't want anything or anyone pilfering his crop."

"But I'm starving!"

"So am I."

Grumbling, Niles trained his eyes upon the road ahead. "Very well. I just want you to know that, if I had not grown up with you and invested all those years in our friendship, I'd seriously consider quiting your company right now and striking out on my own."

"Really?"

"No. Now leave me alone."

About an hour later they noticed a distinct odor in the air that grew more acrid with every step they took. From this, they knew exactly where they were. In all the United Kingdoms, there was no place that smelled like the town of Anapest.

I visited Anapest once, very early on in my travels as a Gudi-Gudi. As I recall, it was a quiet community but one that was rather uninformed and narrow-minded in its thinking.

What news they did acquire was obtained from those travelers like myself who would linger long enough for a pint or two in the town pub. But these were few and far between.

Most people avoided Anapest not just because of its lack of basic comforts, but because of the noxious odor hanging over the town, caused by its one and only industry - the preparation of cow manure for use as a soil restorative.

In all, the town consisted of six rows of houses; three rows on one side of the road; three rows on the other. Though it was only a small town, its residents lived each day by a strict moral code that originated from a rigid social order.

That such an order existed in a town like Anapest was completely nonsensical. For it had been founded in ancient times by a pair of common thieves who had fled beyond the reaches of civilization to avoid execution.

During the years that followed, their two families intermarried. The ancestors of those families intermarried. Eventually, everyone from the manure monger to the Manure Queen (who was chosen once a year) was related in one way or another.

But as far back as anyone could remember, the people living on the north side of the town had considered themselves better than the people living on the south side. This was because the north side was not just on the opposite side of the street from the manure depository but up wind of it as well.

A person from the north side would never think of marrying someone from the south side. It simply was unheard of. Though, long ago there was a north side girl named Julianna who fell in love with a south side boy named Roomero

The story goes: their families feuded, they married secretly, he killed her cousin Tipler in a duel and was banished for the deed, she pretended to kill herself so she could join him, he thought she was really dead and poisoned himself in despair, then she woke up and found his warm but lifeless body at her feet, so she took his dagger and killed herself because she couldn't live without him.

If it sounds familiar, it is because the story has inspired many theatrical productions over the ages even some with elaborate songs and dances.

But that is of no consequence to this story.

By the time Niles and Dwayne reached the southern entrance to the town, the smell of manure was almost overpowering, clinging to their clothing, their skin, their nose hairs. In spite of this fact, they were ravenous with hunger.

Luckily, the one and only tavern was past the manure factory on the north end of town. It was called A Breath Of Fresh Air, and true to its name, it was.

Just outside, they discovered a horse-drawn cart laden with stores. Loading it was an old man, who, at that particular moment, struggled with two large baskets of food. Six guards dressed in grimy green and purple tunics stood idly by, picking their noses or their teeth.

As with most towns in the Kingdom, there was a small garrison posted in Anapest.

Actually, it was not in Anapest, but just north of it. Actually, it had not always been north of it, but when Daron's replacements arrived - a dozen rough, hardbitten men fresh from the Slaughter House - they evicted the mayor and his family from their home and proclaimed it their new headquarters.

"Here," said Dwayne, approaching the old man. "Let me help you." He took both baskets from him and placed them easily onto the pile of stores. "There now. That does it."

"Thank you," said the old man, huffing.

"You does that quite well," remarked one of the guards. He wore a patch over one eye and his upper lip was missing, giving him the appearance of a snarling dog.

"Nothing talented about it, I assure you," replied Dwayne humbly.

The guard was being anything but congenial. "There's more inside. Get it. An' you," said the man with a nod towards Niles. "'Help 'im."

Niles' right eyebrow arched indignantly, but before he could open his mouth and get them into trouble, Dwayne grabbed his arm and said, "He'd be happy to."

They entered the tavern and found it in a shambles. The chairs and tables had been overturned and shoved back against the walls. In the middle of the floor, baskets overflowing with cheese wheels, fruit, vegetables, roasts of mutton and beef, rashers of bacon, whole chickens, and various other culinary delights had been gathered along with six or seven kegs of ale.

When Niles saw the mound of food, his eyes went wide and he immediately thought of his dream that morning. "Thank you," he said, staring at the heavens.

He fell to his knees before the mound of food. He took hold of a mutton joint and almost had it in his mouth when a sharp pain erupted in his side and he found himself lying upon the floor.

"Keep yer grimy mits off the fare," said the guard with no upper lip. "That's for the garrison."

Niles sneered and sprang to his feet, but before he could respond in any way, Dwayne had him locked in a bear-like grip. "We understand."

Barrel upon barrel, basket after basket, the delicious smells – sweet, tart, smoky, briny - wafted under their noses like a wicked prank.

"Oh what torture," Niles whimpered, eyeing the food he carried. "What cruel and merciless torture."

At length, Niles and Dwayne finished loading the cart and tied a patchwork canvas over the top. The guard tossed them each an apple for their trouble, which they devoured.

"And you'll earn another one of those when you unload everything at the garrison."

Niles made to speak, but once again Dwayne answered for him. "We thank you for your generosity. But we hadn't planned on traveling any farther this day."

One-eye trained his eye on him, not quite sure how to take the young man. "Well, ya just changed yer plans. Get on board. An' if I catch ya filchin' a single fig, I'll cut yer hands off.'"

As Niles and Dwayne climbed atop the wagon, One-eye turned to the old man and handed him two silver pieces. "'Ere ya go."

Aghast, the old man stared at the two coins in his palm. "But this is hardly payment enough. You've emptied my entire larder."

The guard nodded indulgently. "At any other time you'd be correct. But I've taken the liberty of holdin' back yer next installment of the cost of livin' tax."

"I just paid that three months ago," protested the old man.

One-eye shrugged. "Yer still livin', ain't ya?"

The other guards laughed. Realizing he had been funny, one-eye smirked at his cronies and went on.

"I mean, I can change that with a quick thrust of me sword if ya like. You could keep yer money then. 'Cept you'd have no use fer it, bein' dead." The other guards laughed harder still, and feeling especially pleased with himself, one-eye joined them.

Powerless, frustrated, the old man frowned and bowed his head. "Very well, take it."

The guard wiped away some spittle that had dribbled down his chin. Having only one lip, it was hard to contain the juices that flowed from his mouth.

"I thought you'd see it my way." The guard looked at Niles and Dwayne and found them scowling at him. "Either o' you got a problem with that?" The other guards stood firmer on their feet, readying themselves in case Niles or Dwayne objected.

This time it was Dwayne who was about to protest when Niles quickly spoke up. "No, sir; no problem."

One-eye pointed over his shoulder. "Get movin' then. The big house up the road. And we'll be right b'hind ya."

Niles grabbed the reins and did as he was told. The guards, having mounted their horses, caught up to the cart almost at once, and soon they had come to a halt in front of a large house north of the town.

It was a stone structure covered by a slate roof, with oiled-skin embrasures and a heavy wooden door fashioned with ornamental iron dragons. Two guards sat upon a bench by the door. One sucked on a blade of foxtail grass as he whittled, while the other strung a bow and swatted flies.

"Where ya been?" the whittler called. He was a greasy sort, with dark smudges on his cheeks and forehead. "I'm up fer an hour already an' there's nothin' ta eat."

"Aye," said the bow-stringer, a willowy fellow with a birthmark the size of a fist on his left cheek. "I'm hungry!"

"Hold yer tongues," One-eye called. "You'll be stuffin' yer faces soon enough."

The guard ordered his troop to dismount and stable their horses. He climbed down from his own horse and tied it to a hitching post at the front of the house.

"Well?" he called to Niles and Dwayne atop the cart. "Don't take all day about it. I got hungry men ta feed."

He strolled to the cart, a smug look on his face. He watched them carefully as they climbed down and untied the canvas tarp.

"So," he said, grabbing an apple from a basket and leaning against the wagon. "'How come I never seen you two around here b'fore?"

"We're not from here," Dwayne responded, unloading a sack of beans.

"Where ya from then?"

"West of here."

"West, eh?" the guard said through a mouth full of spittle and pulp. His one eye went from Dwayne to

Niles and back to Dwayne. "What's yer business in these parts?"

"We're mercenaries," Dwayne said, patting his sword. "Soldiers of fortune. Selling our arms and loyalty to whomsoever has the money to buy them."

"Whomsoever?" One-eye repeated with disdain. "Didja hear that?" he called to the whittler and bow-slinger. "Whomsoever. You don't sound like no mercenary ta me. All the ones I ever known, couldn't put two words t'gether."

Niles was never one to allow the slightest opportunity to escape him. "I know two words," he said with a smug grin of his own. "And I'm sure you've heard them often."

The whittler and the bow-stringer immediately found this funny. One-eye, however, did not. He dashed the apple to the ground and took a quick step forward, his teeth bared even more so than normal. "An' what two words would they be?"

Niles feigned innocence. "Why, "nice day," of course." Again, the two on the bench laughed.

"Shut yer faces," said one-eye, whirling on them. They stopped at once.

One-eye turned back to Niles. His hand going for the hilt of his sword. "What do you take me for, a fool?"

"Well, actually," confided Niles, picking up a small keg of ale. "That's exactly what I take you for."

He threw the keg into One-eye's stomach, knocking the wind out of him, then planted his fist on the guard's jaw. Feeling most satisfied with himself, Niles tossed the guards on the bench a flippant wave.

"Nice to meet you," said the knight before jumping onto the front seat of the wagon and grabbing the reins. "Well?" he called to Dwayne, who was looking as astounded as the guards on the bench. "Are you coming or not?"

Niles flicked the horse's reins and set the cart in motion. Dwayne, not wishing to be left behind, tossed the basket he was holding at the two guards and leaped onto the rear of the cart.

One-eye staggered to his feet, unsheathed his sword and swung viciously at Dwayne. But having only one eye, he lacked the necessary depth perception, and with three feet of empty air between them, the young man escaped unharmed.

One-eye spun and faced the two guards on the bench. "Get yer horses, ya blasted pea-heads! An' ride down them fiends!

By now, the other guards were returning from the stables. Seeing them, One-eye shrieked. "Mount yer horses! Mount!"

"But we just put 'em down," one guard complained.

"I'll put you down," One-eye shrieked. "Six feet down. Now get them horses saddled again!"

One-eye peered at the escaping cart. "Two words, eh?! I got two words fer you! Worm's meat! Wadduya think o' them?!"

He sprang for his own mount. But again he misjudged the distance. Instead of his stirrup, his foot found empty air, and he landed flat against his horse's flank with a loud oof.

He sank to his knees, the wind knocked out of him once more. The other guards looked on, confused, wondering whether or not to proceed without him.

When One-eye saw they had not yet obeyed him, he went berserk. "Move, you useless baggages! Earn your keep or I'll send ya back to the Slaughter House one piece at a time!"

In the meantime, Niles and Dwayne had increased

their lead.

"Nice work," said Dwayne, climbing onto the front seat.

"Sometimes, I manage to surprise myself," replied Niles with a broad grin, slapping the horse's rump with the reins.

Secretly, he was enjoying himself. He loved danger. It set the blood coursing through his veins at a pace that nothing could match. In fact, it was the only time he truly felt alive.

"Did you see the look on those guards' faces when you threw your basket at them?"

Dwayne could not help but laugh. "How about when one-eye swung and missed?"

Niles chuckled. "Wonder what he'll eat tonight. Besides crow."

At that, they both laughed. For a moment, it was as if the hands of time had reversed themselves and neither of them had suffered tragedy. They were young again, or younger still, adventuring in the countryside like they had as boys.

But when the guards closed the distance between them and started loosing arrows, the conversation between the two friends took on a different tone.

"Can't we go a little faster?!"

"I'm doing the best I can."

"They're gaining on us, Niles. They're going to catch us, Niles!"

"Look, if you think you can do any better, you drive!"

The horse was lathered white with sweat and beginning to tire. An arrow whizzed by Niles' ear, and he knew that if he did not think of something quickly, they would be overtaken and hacked to pieces.

Think, he told himself. Use your head. But not a single thought came to mind.

Yet just when he was about to panic, he saw a sign by the side of the road that read:

SHERMAN OAKS
FOR THE EXPERIENCED ONLY!
THEM WHAT TENDS TA GET LOST, STAY OUT!

Niles laughed aloud, a laugh that came straight from his gut, and he kept on laughing even after he had veered off the road and had plunged into the forest.

"What are you doing?" cried Dwayne, aghast. "Are you mad? This is Sherman Oaks!"

"Aye," shouted Niles with wild abandon. "Our only chance."

In the early days of beasts and magic, when the land was as yet untamed and men huddled around their fires at night to stave off things that would eat them, there had lived a halfcaste by the name of Sherman. Part mortal, party mystery, (it's not quite clear if the mystery part was goblin or worm or rock beast.) One thing is certain, his mother had always claimed that the "no account" who'd sired Sherman was far more a monster than a man.

He was held in abhorrence by human and animal kind alike and thus was welcome in neither kingdom. Yet the Gods, for reasons of their own, decided not to tear the wretch asunder with a blast from the Heavens. Instead, they guided him to a place he might call home, one befitting his nature, with rotted trees and brambly thickets, scum-coated ponds, and swarms of belligerent hornets.

To avoid evoking any sympathy for Sherman, it must be noted that he was a thoroughly detestable little bugger with a foul mouth and a nasty temper who was completely deserving of the abuse he received.

Since that time it had been called Sherman Oaks and, though Sherman was now long gone (no matter what the Gods thought of him, he was not stupid enough to stay in a place that made the worst low-rent district in Bandidon look like a vacation resort,) it had been the haven for every outcast and thief that even Daron was loathe to employ.

I myself have managed to avoid Sherman Oaks all these years. Perhaps I've been remiss in my duty as a Gudi-Gudi, allowing miscreants and cutpurses to prey upon the unsuspecting travelers that fall into their clutches within the woods.

If that is the case I will be held accountable for this failure when my time comes to join my fellow Gudi-Gudis in the Heavens. Yet I am only human, with faults like everyone else. And fears, too.

For one thing, I have always been deathly afraid of angry hornets. Pardon me while I wipe the sweat from my brow.

Just the thought of them makes me nervous. Over the decades I have fought in many battles and come face to face with many enemies. I have been speared, slashed, punctured by crossbow bolts, even chewed upon by beasts. Yet, even after facing all those foes and enduring all that pain, encountering a hornet no bigger than my thumbnail will send me fleeing in a panic.

But again, that is of no consequence to this story.

"Duck!" shouted Niles gleefully.

They raced beneath a series of low hanging boughs, knobby and twisted and covered with withered moss. A moment later, they were galloping through a break in the tangled brush only to find a patch of wraith-like trees, wizened and stunted, blocking their way.

Niles pulled hard on the reins. The horse veered sharply to its left and then to its right, the cart careening each time and riding on one wheel.

"Slow down, you lunatic!" shouted Dwayne, clinging to the cart. "You're going to kill us!"

A crazed look came into Niles' eyes and he cackled stridently for his friend's benefit, and instead of pulling back on the reins, he slapped them harder across the horse's rump.

"Give me those reins!" said Dwayne fiercely, groping for them.

"Never!!"

They wove between a dense copse of trees, the horse's hooves digging up the forest peet and kicking it into their faces. Before they left the copse, they were covered in it, and seeing Dwayne with turf hanging from his chin, set Niles to laughing uncontrollably.

But just then, they came to a sudden dip in the ground. Seeing it, Niles' laughter strangled in his throat.

He pulled back on the reins with all his strength. The horse, responding to the command, dug in its hooves at once, whereupon, horse, cart, and riders were carried along, skidding down the slope out of control.

Had not the slope been barren save for some dead scrub, they would have crashed and more than likely killed themselves. It was a miracle they did not overturn.

But their luck was with them, including the horse's. They slid to the bottom of the slope and came to a gentle halt.

The two men sat for a moment, their faces reflecting their shock and fear. Then, slowly they began to breathe.

Dwayne turned to Niles, greatly concerned. "Are you all right?"

Niles, who had been cured of his waggery, *(at least for the time being,)* blinked once or twice and nodded. "Aye, I think so."

Whereupon Dwayne grabbed him by the shirt and began to shake him violently. "Don't ever do that again," he growled. "Is that clear?!"

"Fine," said Niles, his head bobbing this way and that. Sometimes, it was better to let Dwayne blow off steam than to resist. "Whatever you say."

After one or two more bobs, Dwayne released him. He even smoothed the wrinkles he had made in Niles' shirt.

"Feeling better now?" asked Niles, flicking the reins across the horse's back and setting the cart in motion.

Dwayne nodded. He looked at Niles askance and smirked. "Aye. Most definitely."

"You're sure? Because I could let you shake the stuffings out of me some more if you like."

"No, no," replied Dwayne. "That will do." And then he added, "For now."

They had not gone very far before the brush became too impassable to continue by cart. They did not want to leave it, or the food, or the horse, in the open, especially if the guards were still in pursuit.

The went searching for a place to hide them all. At length, they came to the base of a wide round hillock. One side was covered by a dense thicket of thorn bushes.

When they rounded the other side, they noticed a narrow path that led to a large outcropping of rocks at the crest. It was just wide enough for the cart.

They led the horse up the path , covered the entrance with some fallen branches, then proceeded deeper into the woods on foot.

When they came upon an enormous vine-covered tree, they climbed its misshapen trunk and hid among its branches. There, they kept watch for any sign of their pursuers, wondering if they would come at them in force while the light was still good or by stealth under an impenetrable cloak of darkness.

The sun had reached the peak of its arc and had

started its descent and still the guards had not appeared.

Waiting had never been an easy thing for Niles under the best of conditions. He found himself getting restless, and soon he began to brood. "I'm hungry."

"You're always hungry," sighed Dwayne.

Niles shot him an indignant look. "Pardon me. I've had nothing in my stomach all day save for a wormy apple."

"Mine wasn't wormy," said Dwayne. "Mine was sweet."

There were times when Niles had trouble letting go of small, inconsequential things. This was one of them. "Sweet, you say. I suppose you had to tell me that."

"It seemed a good idea."

"Fine. I hope you found it satisfying."

"Both the apple and the remark."

Niles was about to continue the exchange when a thought struck him and he sat upright. "Wait a minute! What am I complaining about?! There's a whole banquet of food in the cart!"

"True," said Dwayne, frowning. "But it doesn't belong to you."

Niles stared at him in disbelief. "You're not going to start that again, are you?"

"I most assuredly am. That food was taken from the tavern keeper. It belongs to him, and I intend to return it just as soon as I can."

"But -- ."

"I'll not hear another word about it," said Dwayne. "I've compromised my principles once already on this trip; I won't do it again."

"But we've got to get to Torkelstone, right? To save Dillin, right? Well, we certainly won't be able to, if we die of hunger along the way."

"I'll be fine."

"Of course you will. You've enough fat in that ass of yours alone to burn for an entire week. But what about me? I'm nothing but muscle, and stringy muscle at that. I'm going to faint and fall out of this tree if I don't eat something soon."

"I don't care," said Dwayne adamantly. "I want to be clear about this, Niles. I will not pilfer food or anything else for that matter, from here on out, regardless of how desperate things get."

They sat for a moment, the sound of Niles' growling stomach filling the silence.

"Must you do that?" said Dwayne, annoyed.

"I can't control the noises I make," Niles retorted defensively. "Any more than you can." And then, a thought occurred to him.

"Look you, Dwayne, I understand your principles; I really do. But if we hadn't galloped off with the cart, it would be in the guards hands right now. True?"

"I suppose."

"And if it were in the guards hands right now, the tavern keeper would be out of business."

"So?"

"So, what is one missing mutton joint or a roast chicken when compared to an entire larder of food? Don't we deserve something for saving the tavern keeper's livelihood?"

Dwayne considered the question; and when Dwayne considered a question, he weighed all sides, all aspects, all consequences, before making a decision. Indeed, it seemed like the world itself could grow old and cold before Dwayne would make up his mind about something.

"Well -- . When you put it like that -- ."

Niles waited for him to continue, prompting him with only a, "Yes?"

"It wouldn't really be stealing."

"Not at all!" said Niles eagerly. "So, you agree?"

"The tavern keeper would have nothing if not for us."

"I remember saying that myself just a moment ago. So, you agree?"

"And we did risk our lives to help him."

By now, Niles' patience was wearing thin. "So, you agree?!"

"I suppose I do. Even though we don't have the tavern keeper's permission. It seems only fair. And it would provide us with the nourishment we need."

"Well then," said Niles gleefully, making ready to climb down the tree. "What's your pleasure? A mutton joint? A small capon? Stay right where you are, I'll get it."

"Perhaps a loaf of bread."

Niles looked at him, confused. "That's all you want?"

"That's all you'll take."

"A loaf of bread for each of us?"

"A loaf of bread we'll share between us."

Niles sighed, exasperated. "A single loaf of bread for risking our lives like we did? For performing such a valiant deed?"

"All right. A loaf of bread and a wheel of cheese. A small wheel of cheese."

"And two more apples," added Niles quickly.

"And two more apples. But that's all!"

Niles beamed. "Coming right up, your lordship."

He jumped to the ground, got his bearings, and started off for the cart. He proceeded cautiously in spite of his hunger. He had no desire to stumble onto any guards who might still be lurking about.

As a skillful hunter, he was quite adept at creeping silently through the woods. Though, it was fortunate he was not stalking anything today, for his stomach was growling so loudly that he was certain it would announce his presence to even a codger, which was, (*as everyone knows,*) the deafest animal in the forest.

He found no ground disturbed, no broken twigs, no scratches in the bark of any trees, no signs at all that indicated anyone or anything had gone as far into the woods as he and Dwayne. Based on that assumption, he was now quite certain the guards had long since given up the chase. In fact, if he bothered to retrace his steps to the road, he was certain he would find no evidence of the guards having entered the woods at all.

He breathed easier, feeling fully confident now. His mouth began to water as he pictured the cart with its baskets full of provisions, and his head began to spin when he looked upon it for real.

Before he could stop himself, he had gobbled down a personal-sized berry tart (*aye, they made them that way even back then.*) The last morsel was still in his mouth when his eyes fell upon a roasted capon, and without a second thought, he tore off a leg and sank his teeth into it.

Oh, my, he thought, savoring its flavor. I'll just pretend the bird had only one leg if Dwayne says anything about it.

He attacked the leg and bared it to the bone in just three bites. Then he tossed it away and ripped off the other leg, stuffing it into his shirt for a snack later that night after Dwayne had fallen asleep. After all, one of them had to keep his strength up, especially if Dwayne intended to act so self-righteous all the time.

He took a loaf of bread and placed it in the crook of his arm. He chose a small wheel of cheese and drank deep of its aroma. He started off for the tree, and then remembered the apples.

"Can't forget dessert," he said to himself with a

grin.

He returned to the cart, whereupon he devoured one more berry tart and a minted lamb pie before he left for good. Such a naughty fellow, you are, he thought, a smile curling his lips, and the smile remained upon his face as he made his way down the slope and into the thicker part of the woods.

But when he returned to the tree his smile faded. For he found his friend hanging upside down at the end of a vine, his face red from the blood collecting in his head.

"What, may I ask, are you doing? Wait; don't tell me. You've discovered a new exercise."

"Perhaps he can tell you," said Dwayne with a nod of his head, staring past his friend.

Niles dropped the food and spun about at once, reaching for the dagger in his belt, thinking he had been careless in reading the signs, and that somehow One-eye and the guards had followed after all.

But much to his surprise, it was not the guard that he beheld, but instead, a very large man even taller and stouter than Dwayne.

His head was shaved, and the beard on his chin was black and flecked with gray. Beneath a massive brow were two dark, piercing eyes.

His nose, having no distinct shape, looked like it had been broken at least a half a dozen times and each in a different place, and a long thin scar that was bluish in tint ran from the corner of his mouth to his right earlobe, which was pinched and shriveled like it had been reattached too hastily after being separated in the first place from the rest of his ear.

"Who are you?" demanded Niles boldly. "And state your business."

"Thot be'd me queshion, strengor," said the burly man, placing his massive hands on his hips.

Niles peered at him, perplexed, wary. "I say, could you repeat that? I didn't quite understand you."

At that moment, half a dozen rough-looking men with various and sundry disfigurements emerged from the brush. From among their ranks, a short, wiry man stepped forward.

By his bearing, he appeared more elevated than the rest inasmuch as he was cleaner and better dressed. Though his hair was grimy and plastered to his head, he had tied it back as was the fashion at court, and instead of a weapon, he carried a staff. "He said, that was his question, stranger."

"Ayeeee," growled the leader. "On whoot ere ya doin' en dis paht o'th' wooooze?"

Again, Niles stared at him, a blank expression on his face. "I beg your pardon?"

"He wants to know what you're doing in this part of the woods?" said the interpreter. "And you'd best speak the truth, if you know what's good for you. Your life depends upon it. Oh, and one more thing," added the man, stepping a bit closer. "Use small words. He responds better when you use small words."

"Ayeeee," again growled the leader.

"I don't think I care to tell you," answered Niles arrogantly. He looked at the interpreter. "Were those small enough?"

In response to the remark, the men flanking the giant drew their swords and dirks.

"On the other hand," said Niles, acquiescing, "It's not so personal that you can't be told. We're outlaws."

"Ahh thunk so," growled the giant, nodding to his companions, and they quickly overwhelmed Niles and dragged him to the tree, whereupon they placed a noose around his feet and tightened it.

"Wait a minute, wait a minute!" Niles protested. "What are you doing?"

"Wer mekin' a eckzampoo o'yooo."

"A what?"

"An example," supplied the interpreter. "You're to be left for spider food." He smiled and balanced on his staff. "Have you seen the spiders here in Sherman Oaks? They're quite big, you know. They wrestle the rats for their food."

"But why? What have we done?"

"Yer blooodi scebs," supplied the giant.

"What's a sceb?"

"Not sceb," said Dwayne from above, for he had heard all this before Niles had arrived. "Scab."

"Ayeee, a poorson whoot warks fer liss thin guiwd rites."

"I'm sorry," said Niles with a wan smile. "I'm not trying to be cheeky, I just don't understand a word you say."

"Scab," repeated the interpreter. "A person that works for less than guild rates. It gets his goat seeing amateurs like you and your friend, coming into the forest and stealing from passers-by without any regard for rules and regulations. It gives us professionals a bad name!"

"Ayeeee," growled the giant.

"But we haven't stolen anything from anybody. We're fugitives. We just got here a few hours ago."

"Yooo're oowtloowz, ain'tcha. Ya says so yooosewf."

"You're outlaws, are you not? You said so yourself. And you're not wearing guild colors, so you must not be members. And not being members makes you scabs."

"Ahhh hates scebs!"

"Colors. Members. I don't understand," said Niles, looking at Dwayne.

"You will," said the young man. His face was now a deep crimson.

"We're from the TCG of B," said the interpreter. "The Thieves and Cutthroats Guild of Bandidon. The official colors are brown and Lincoln Green. For forest work, that is. This gentleman here," said the interpreter, indicating the giant. "Is Kussensuch, the field representative for this district. You're in violation, mate."

"We're sorry," proffered Niles. "We didn't know."

"Ignorance is no excuse," offered Dwayne from above in a casual tone.

"That is correct. You cannot rob, waylay, kidnap, or detain any unsuspecting individual without first joining the Guild."

"Strings im uuup, lahds!"

The thieves hoisted Niles into the air until he was almost at the same height as Dwayne.

"You can't do this!" said Niles.

"I think they already have," remarked Dwayne.

Kussensuch picked up the apples from off the ground. They appeared to be miniature in his hands. Then he directed his men to grab the cheese wheel and bread and led the band away.

"Wait!" cried Niles. "Please!" But his plea went unheeded. And then an idea struck him. "What if we wanted to join?!"

Kussensuch turned and eyed him askance. "Yooo'd efta cough uuup th' fee."

"I beg your pardon?"

"Th' fee! Th' fee!"

"Oh," said Niles, pleased that he had at last understood something the giant had said. "How much?"

"That depends," answered the interpreter. "What do you want to be? A cutpurse? A highwayman? A beggar? You must choose."

"Ayeee, chooze."

"I must?"

"We're in the age of specialization," expounded the

interpreter, responding to Niles query. "You can't be a general practitioner any more. At least not if you want to earn a decent living."

Niles looked up at Dwayne.

"Do as you please," said Dwayne. "I've already told them I refuse to join."

Their earlier argument still fresh in mind, Niles knew it was useless debating Dwayne on the morality of joining a guild devoted to thievery.

"C'moan, c'moan," said Kussensuch impatiently.

"Was that, 'come on, come on?'" asked Niles.

"Ayeeeeeee!"

"Wasn't sure but I thought so."

In response, Kussensuch snarled and smashed his fist into a tree.

"You're testing his patience," said the interpreter. "I'd hurry up if I were you."

Niles pondered for a brief moment. "Well, if I have to choose, I think Highwayman. There's something about waylaying coaches and stealing kisses from beautiful maidens that appeals to me."

"A romantic, eh?" said the interpreter with a sly grin.

Niles was aware of the disapproving look on Dwayne's face but he ignored it all the same. "Aye. And as far as my friend here is concerned. Give him a moment and I'm sure he'll come around."

"No, I won't," grumbled Dwayne.

"Yes, he will," answered Niles.

The interpreter turned to Kussensuch, who, as a response, held up two crooked fingers. "Well, for a gold coin you can both have all the romance you want."

"That's very reasonable but we haven't any money. Perhaps you'd be willing to accept that wheel of cheese and loaf of bread as payment?"

"Nooo why!" The guild representative sneered and

shook his head. "Them's izz penuty fer scebbin'."

"Come again?"

"Penalty," said the interpreter. "He's confiscated your food as a penalty for scabbing in a guild district. You'll have to come up with something else if you want to join."

"Well then, can I do this on account?"

Kussensuch scowled. "Noooo!"

"That's against Guild regulations," said the interpreter. "I'm afraid you'll have to stay where you are."

Once again they turned to leave.

"Wait!" shouted Niles. He paused just long enough to glance at Dwayne. "Though we haven't any cash, we've still a cache from which to pay you."

Kussensuch eyed him skeptically and scratched his beard. "Izzat, a riddue? I don't lawk riddues."

"Be careful stranger," advised the interpreter. "He doesn't like riddles. They give him head pain."

"Ayeee!" growled Kussensuch.

"Then I'll speak plainly. Not far from here is a cart full of food worth much more than our initiation fee."

Dwayne stared at him in disbelief. "You can't! I won't let you!"

But Niles ignored him. "That bread and cheese is just a tiny measure of our stores. Lower me and I'll prove it to you."

"Why should we believe you?" asked the interpreter, eyeing him warily.

"I've a sample of it beneath my shirt. Right here beneath this grease spot."

"You've what?!" said Dwayne, outraged.

"I'm sorry, Dwayne," said Niles. "Go on. Reach inside."

The interpreter turned to Kussensuch for approval. The giant's eyes ticked from Niles to Dwayne, then to his crony, and he nodded.

The interpreter reached inside the young man's shirt and produced the capon leg, whereupon he and the others gawked at it as if they had never before seen its like.

"Izzat meat Ahhh sees?" asked Kussensuch as he gestured for the interpreter to bring it to him.

"Aye," said Niles, smiling craftily. "And after you've whet your appetite on that, I'll lead you to the rest."

"You're insufferable sometimes!" raged Dwayne. "If I was on my feet right now, I'd thrash you! I'd pound you into the ground!"

"It's the only way!" said Niles in his own defense. "Would you prefer to be spider food?!"

"I would! And I consider hanging near you even more unpleasant than being slowly digested. As far as I'm concerned we've quit each other's company. Henceforth, you and I shall be former friends and nothing more." And having said that, Dwayne turned his head and would no longer look upon him.

Niles sighed, feeling more impatient than anything else. For he had heard Dwayne say the same thing, (*minus, of course, the slowly digested part,*) many times before. "You know you don't mean that."

"I most certainly do."

"No, you don't. You know I'll do something clever to weaken your resolve, then I'll say something witty to win you over. I always do. So can't we just assume we're friends and move on?"

"No," replied Dwayne coolly.

"I wish you'd reconsider. My head is about to burst and I wouldn't want my brains splattering someone who doesn't fully appreciate them."

"I'll not be persuaded this time."

"Very well then," said Niles, though he was still not overly concerned.

"If that's the cost of saving your life, I'll pay it. I'd

rather see you alive and in good health and be deprived of your company for the rest of my life, than to watch you die knowing it was within my power to save you."

He turned to the interpreter. "Set us free and I'll lead you to the food."

The interpreter, acting on his own initiative, nodded to the men controlling the vines who, upon his signal, started lowering both men to the ground.

"Whyt!" call Kussensuch, halting them, and he pointed at Niles. "Jist im."

When Niles saw he alone was being freed, he said, "Wait a minute, wait a minute. My friend gets untied as well, or the deal is off."

"Noooo," growled the guild representative, nudging the interpreter roughly. "Eee stys ear oor th' deew es oofff!"

"No! He stays here or the deal is off," said the interpreter in a harsh tone of voice. He was most adept at mimicking Kussensuch's demeanor.

Suddenly Niles found a dagger at his throat, then two, then three as Kussensuch's men closed in to help make their leader's point.

"All right. Let me up," he said, knowing it was useless to try to negotiate. And as they pulled him onto his feet and shoved him along, he shot a look at Dwayne and said, "Hang around. I'll be right back."

"Do whatever you like," replied the young man, looking away. "I care not."

It took a moment for Niles to regain his balance after so long a time hanging upside down. But once he had, he was off into the brush with Kussensuch and his men following close behind.

Yet as he traveled closer to the wagon and supplies, he could not help but feel more and more uncertain about the decision he had made. He did not trust the guild representative, or his interpreter. And the other guild members, despite being coordinated in their brown and green garb, looked most deceitful and untrustworthy.

It was not long before he came to the outcropping, and clearing away the small path, he smiled graciously and gestured for Kussensuch and the others to proceed ahead of him. "After you."

"Naw, naw," answered Kussensuch, with a scowl, giving Niles a small shove. "Issus yer shaww, so eeyew gaws fust."

"Beg pardon?"

The interpreter scowled. "This is your show, so you go first."

"Very well," said Niles cheerfully. "If you insist."

His smile had remained unchanged, but inwardly he was growing most concerned. The path, lined on both sides by tall boulders, was very narrow and ended at a thick wall of brush just beyond the cart. There was no escaping from it, not unless he managed somehow to carve his way through Kussensuch and his cronies.

But having been relieved of his dagger, there was not much chance of that.

"You see?" said Niles pulling the canvas off the cart. "I am true to my word."

The guild members replied with an assortment of ooohs and ahhhs as they crowded in behind the cart.

"True to your word, indeed," said the interpreter, his eyes scanning the mounds and mounds of food.

"Ayeee," said Kussensuch. The giant picked up a mutton joint and tore half of it off with his teeth.

Niles sidled past the cart to where the horse stood grazing. He stroked its withers, trying to appear casual both for the horse's sake as well as his own.

"I believe this should cover the initiation fee for myself and my friend."

"Ayeee. Yoo be membirs."

"Welcome to the Guild," said the interpreter with a flourish.

"Thank you. Now if you'll be so kind as to return my weapon, I can be on my way."

Kussensuch kept shoveling food into his mouth and had yet to swallow. "Nasafaft, nasafaft. Yerfon violumpfun o' mee dift-twict."

Niles found it difficult to understand the man normally, but with food in his mouth, it was next to impossible. "Come again?"

"He's citing you for violating his district," supplied the interpreter, nibbling on a capon wing. "Article three, section two, paragraph two, of the Guild bylaws. No member shall act in any way that might undermine the integrity of the Guild or of its members, specifically the engagement of non-guild employment or the concealment of earnings from the local representative."

"Datz meee," said Kussensuch through a mouthful of food as he poked his chest with a greasy thumb.

"Nor shall he plunder within the territory or district of another guild member. Behavior such as this shall be considered duplicitous and contrary to the spirit of these bylaws and punishable by fine, expulsion, and/or death."

"I see," said Niles with a knowing grin. "So it seems I'm out as fast as I'm in."

The interpreter smiled slyly. "That's very astute of you."

"And I'm to suffer 'and/or death'."

"Right again."

The other thieves began to laugh and snicker.

"Well, gentlemen," said Niles pleasantly. Though his demeanor appeared most calm and affable, inwardly his mind was racing frantically to find some means of escape. "It seems our newfound friendship is about to end much sooner than I anticipated."

To this, the thieves responded with more laughter. Even Kussensuch and the interpreter joined in.

"And it pleases me to know I depart this world leaving you in such fine spirits."

He feared he might actually be speaking the truth; that these were indeed his parting words. For there seemed to be no way to escape; at least, none that he could see.

But just then, the horse snorted and bobbed its head, reminding him of its presence.

An idea began to form. The narrowness of the path itself, Kussensuch's massiveness and the men crowding behind him, just might work to his advantage.

He knew there was no time to think things through completely, which did not really bother him. (*In all honesty, Niles was never one to think anything through completely.*)

Springing backwards, and at the same time flailing his arms wildly over his head, He shouted at the top of his voice:

Haaawww!
Haaawww!

Startled, the horse whickered loudly and raised itself up on its hind legs. The cart rolled backwards, colliding with Kussensuch. The guild representative, taken off-guard, stumbled into the interpreter, who, being the lighter of the two, fell into the thieves behind him.

Haaawww!
Haaawww!

Niles watched with unabashed delight as the horse backed up even more and forced the thieves to scramble down the path in disorder.

This gave him the time he needed, and he began to climb from boulder to boulder. It was steep and slick in places, with nary a ledge or a crevice to grip.

Any normal person, and by that I mean someone with a healthy respect for death, would have looked at the climb and deemed it impossible to achieve. Not Niles. He saw it as a challenge. To be completely honest, he saw it as great fun.

Perhaps it was his outlook that allowed him to succeed at things, or perhaps it was his lack of judgement instead. Whichever was the case, at that particular moment, he managed to climb a sheer rock wall some twenty feet in height without slipping even once.

By this time, the horse had calmed and the thieves were at last able to sidle past it. Kussensuch, however, being too large to get by, was forced to remain behind. From where he stood, he spied the young man escaping, and with a snarl, he reached for the dirk at his belt, shouting, "Kiwwim! Kiwwim!"

"Kill him! Kill him!" yelled the interpreter, taking up the cry. Instantly a dozen daggers went hurtling through the air at Niles, who stood boldly above the guild cronies with arms folded and a goading smile on his face.

The weapons, badly misaimed, struck the rock below Niles' feet and caromed into the brush.

"You'll have to do better than that," said Niles.

Though the thieves tried again, not a single throw came near him.

"You men are in need of some serious practice. Try aiming at one another for a while."

Now, had Niles simply scrambled to safety without bothering to taunt his pursuers, he might have saved himself some trouble and even some pain. But once again his mouth, (*or the bigness of it to be more precise,*) was his undoing.

For Kussensuch, fully provoked now, took that opportunity to let fly his dirk at the young man, and the blade sliced across Niles' forehead, stunning him, causing him to stagger backwards.

One step - rock soundly beneath his feet - another step - rock still beneath his feet - a third step - air.

Before he could regain his balance, Niles toppled off the far side of the rock. Though no longer in sight, the thieves heard his body crashing through the shrubbery. They raced down the path and rounded the low hill. But so dense and deep was the brush they found on the other side, not one of them penetrated it more than a foot or two, even after hacking away at it with axe and sword.

"Qua-et!" shouted Kussensuch. Though none really understood what he meant, just his shouting was enough to silence them.

They listened for any sign of life, and watched for any movement. Minutes went by; a quarter of an hour; three quarters.

But no sound came.

At length, after the breeze had carried the sweet scent of a spiced cake under Kussensuch's nose, he called off the search and they retreated.

The members of the TCG of B, Sherman Oaks branch, returned to the cart, backed it out, and led the horse and cart away with what remained of its contents, pausing only briefly to scan the brush once more for the benefactor of their new found feast.

"Lessgo" said Kussensuch impatiently. "Eee pwubly brookisnickk frimmdafoe."

As was their habit, the other thieves turned to the interpreter for a translation. He, being weary from the day's events and, at that moment, frustrated by the dumbness of their expressions, snapped, "He probably broke his neck from the fall! He probably broke his neck from the fall! Doesn't anyone around here speak Bandidonian?!"

Niles opened his eyes and looked about, confused, disoriented. What am I doing here? A moment ago, I was -- .

He furrowed his brow. I was, what?

He contemplated this briefly, and then it came to him. I was floating! Actually, floating! In the air! The thought of it was almost too much to fathom. How amazing!

But that was not all. I was right above some man! He was lying among the thorn bushes. Imagine that; why would anyone do such a stupid thing?

And then he remembered something else, something he had found extraordinary and even somewhat frightening. The light! That strange white light. So bright; so all-consuming. And the voices beckoning me from within it! They were so beautiful, so compelling.

Yet he had refused to listen to them and had turned away from the light.

But why?

He thought about this for a moment, and then it occurred to him. The man; the one in the bushes lying face to the ground. He had seemed so familiar. And as he descended to take a better look at him, he saw the man's chest heave and he heard air rush into his lungs. It was then some strange and powerful force took hold of him like a pair of invisible hands and pulled him down toward the ground, toward the man, until he thought they would collide.

His head started to hurt, badly, and rubbing his brow, he discovered it was cut and bleeding. He found other cuts along his arms and legs, and there was a long slash across his chest.

He cast a look at the rock wall, at the thorn bushes, at the broken branches above him, and suddenly everything fell into place. "It was me!" he blurted. "I was floating above myself!" And that brought him to yet another thunderous conclusion.

"I was dead!"

He sat there awhile, dumbfounded. I was actually dead, he thought, his mouth agape. And that light was the light of the Gods. The Gods!

And those voices -- . Those voices were the voices of the Gods!

"I would have come to you just now," he said, concerned that, by turning away from the light, he had offended them. "But, you see, I've this friend who's hanging from a tree. He needs my help."

He waited for a response. He did not expect anything as majestic as a Heavenly vision, but he thought perhaps a song would be nice.

No song.

He stared about him at the gnarled vines and branches, thick as his forearm, with thorns as sharp as dagger blades.

"I don't suppose you'd help me find my way out of here?"

Still no song.

Groaning, he struggled to his knees and scanned the tangle in front of him for a break in the bushes, (*a break other than the one he had created overhead, that is.*) He found a small space, almost a channel, at the very bottom of a bush to his right. He crawled into it, trying to make himself one with the ground, moving slowly, cautiously, a few inches at a time.

It was like the maze in his mother's garden, full of false turns and dead ends. As a boy, he had spent countless hours exploring until he had found the correct path.

He pressed on, following each twist or turn he thought would take him closer to an exit, peering into the dimness ahead of him, ignoring the thorn pricks he received from the branches he shoved aside.

He was moving along at a decent pace, (*though keep in mind it was still a crawl,*) convinced he would soon be free, when he rounded a bend and stumbled upon a gagger.

Believing Niles to be a predator, the animal bared its teeth and ruffled its fur. Niles froze. He had heard that some gaggers carried the foaming sickness. But this did not worry him half as much as something else. For a gagger's primary defense was the foul-smelling, even nauseating, musk it sprayed upon would-be attackers.

Please don't, thought Niles, slowly lowering his head until his cheek was flat upon the ground. He whimpered softly, hoping the animal would take this as a sign of submission.

But much to his dismay, it did not. The gagger pivoted about and raised its tail.

Niles scrambled backwards, wincing from the cuts and tears he received from the punishing thorns around him. But he had not gone more than a few feet before the gagger disgorged its musk.

The rankness of it fell upon him and clung to his skin and clothing like salty ocean air. This, in itself, was bad enough, but apparently not as far as the gagger was concerned. For the animal chose to squeeze again, and sprayed him with a second dose.

That Niles managed to crawl away, round a bend and work his way down a new channel before giving up the contents of his stomach was a testament to his endurance. He said goodbye to the roasted capon, the berry tarts, and the minted lamb pie. After that, it was one dry heave and then another.

◆ ◆ ◆

Retch and crawl; retch and crawl; his body alternately quaking and cramping, until finally, he located a way out of the thicket.

His head felt like it had been cleaved by an axe. His eyes burned like they had been branded with hot irons.

The stench was so pervasive, he could taste it at the back of his throat. It was in the water he passed, under his fingernails, the snot that ran from his nose. And he would have succumbed to it, let his reason bow to it, had there not been one thing fixed upon his mind more important than his own needs or his own life.

Dwayne still needed his help, and he would surely die if he was not lowered from the tree soon.

Niles pulled himself upright, which was a chore in itself after crawling for so long, and he started back toward the tree, weaving from side to side on legs that seemed barely able to support him.

He prayed for a brisk wind, for a downpour, anything that would rid him of the stink.

"It's me. Niles," he said, addressing the Gods. "I know you can hear me. And if you can't hear me, I have no doubt that you can smell me."

He fought the urge to vomit. "You're angry with me; I can tell. Forgive me for being so bold but I've already apologized for my earlier indiscretion. Don't you think it's time to put an end to this scourge?"

It was then his knees buckled, and he collapsed upon the ground.

"I guess not."

Niles retched once more, and this made his head pound even harder. He closed his eyes and covered his face with his hands.

"I swear," he muttered, attempting to ignore the

pain. "Once this is over, I'll never set foot in the woods again. Perhaps I'll live by the shore. I hear sea air is good for the lungs."

However, he did not dwell on this long. Even thinking made his head hurt.

When the pain subsided, he dragged himself to his feet. He studied the surroundings, no longer certain if he was heading in the right direction.

He tried to concentrate, but the stench was like a wall that had risen up to encase him. It confounded his senses and clouded his mind, and made even the simplest thing like taking a step a difficult task.

So, he trusted his instincts, confused as they were, and concentrated solely on reaching the next tree; the next; and then the next after that.

He had no concept of time, no perception of distance. Every minute that passed, his body responded less to his will.

Yet somehow he managed to reach the right clearing and the right tree, and before he was fully aware of what he was doing, the vine was in his hands and he was lowering Dwayne - who was unconscious - to the ground.

Niles stood over his friend, listing from side to side, barely clinging to consciousness himself. His muscles screamed for rest, his head felt ready to burst, and the smell -- . The smell!

He dropped to his knees with a loud grunt, and fumbled with the knot at Dwayne's feet. But his eyes no longer focused and his hands were useless weights. Tears, stinking tears, ran down his face, and making one last conscious effort, he loosened the knot with his teeth.

Niles collapsed and found himself gazing at the sky. It was swollen with dark clouds, and much to his amazement, the darkness suddenly had a life of its own, for it reached right from the sky and closed about him like a giant hand.

Yet he was not afraid of it. In fact, thinking the Gods had finally come to his aid, he welcomed them with a weak smile, and said aloud, "Thank you for coming. I appreciate the effort. You may need to bathe after this."

It was then the rain began to fall.

CHAPTER TWENTY ONE

A day's march from the Gormandizer's lair brought Bryand and the others to the edge of the swamp. Here the terrain was less marshy. By the time night had fallen on the second day, they had solid ground beneath their feet and were weaving their way between hardwood trees and leafy thickets.

The forest sounds returned. A fresh breeze wafted in their faces. Soon the moon rose, minus two quadrants; but a welcome visitor all the same.

They reached a wide break in the trees, and were halfway across before they realized they had stumbled upon a road. So great was their joy and relief that they hugged one another and danced about. They had left the realm of swallowups and monsters behind them and had found their way back to the world of men.

Still, they knew it was unwise to remain in the open for too long. The world of men was proving just as dangerous. Mortamour was out there somewhere, searching for them, and they knew he would not rest until he had located their trail once more.

"Come," said Bryand. "As much as I would like to camp right in the middle of the road, we need to find someplace a little more secluded to hole up for the night."

The Prince headed into the woods on the far side.

His feet were like stone weights, and his eyelids felt nearly as heavy.

Adventuring had always had its lure. (*This he had inherited from his father.*) It was as much a part of his nature as was governing and being king. (*His mother's side.*)

Even so, he was done with taking risks for awhile. He wanted nothing more than to find a small clearing among the trees, spread his blanket out, and sleep for a dozen years.

But he had not traipsed more than thirty yards, before catching sight of a small flicker from deeper within the woods.

He halted at once. What now? he thought, annoyed. Are we never to get any rest? He put his finger to his lips to silence the others, then he motioned for them to gather round.

"There's a campfire up ahead," said the Prince in a hushed voice.

Malady's shoulders slumped. "Here we go again. Why can't we just avoid this one? Why do we have ta stick our necks out all th' time?"

"Look," said the Prince dourly. "I don't want to do this any more than you."

"It might be someone friendly," offered Cower.

"Aye, that's a possibility. But it could also be Mortamour and his men."

"I can go and see," said the little one, removing his dagger. "I ain't stuck nothin' with this thing yet."

"I have not stuck a thing," corrected Cower.

"That ain't my fault."

"No one's doing any sticking, is that clear?" said the Prince, trying not to lose his patience.

Moving slowly through the darkness, trying to be as quiet as they could, they worked their way to a dense thicket of always-green shrubs.

"You'll be safe here," whispered the Prince, after

Malady and the boys had crawled inside. "Just be quiet and don't fidget."

"Where are you goin'?" asked Malady, fretting.

"Cower and I are going to have a look." He glared at Donoim. "And you're staying here."

The boy scowled and opened his mouth. But before he could retort, his brother cuffed him on the arm and said, "You're stayin' here."

Bryand tossed Noim a nod of thanks. Noim responded in kind. Well, thought the Prince, it seems we 've made some progress after all.

"How long're ya gonna be?" asked Malady, still fretting.

"We'll be back shortly."

"What if yer not?"

"We will."

"But what if yer not?"

"Malady-- ," said the Prince as patiently as he could. "You're going to work yourself into a fit. I promise we'll be right back."

Bryand and the retainer crept toward the light, weaving between bushes, the ground cool and damp beneath their hands and knees.

It was a campfire indeed, and seated about it were many strange-looking men with wild, bushy hair and braided beards that hung down to their waists. Their faces were blackened by pitch and smeared with paint in a variety of ways and colors. Some had tattooed their chests with crude images and some had pierced their nipples with small bones.

Bryand recognized them immediately, and, keeping his eyes locked upon them, the Prince leaned close to his retainer and whispered, "Woolly-Bullies."

Hearing this, Cower stiffened with fear.

Woolly-Bullies! The dreaded clansmen of the north so named for their shaggy appearance and belligerent natures.

The retainer had heard of their ruthless raids upon the northern shires, brandishing their deadly noggin-knockers and cuttintoos, butchering settlers and carting off their furniture, (*for it was well known they had never developed the skill to make their own.)*

Dearest Heavenly Beings whom I am so often beseeching, he said to himself, trembling. What more will you throw at us?

Bryand watched the clansmen with a growing sense of danger. This does not bode well, he thought. That they should be so far south. How had they gotten past the frontier outpost? The shire posts? Were there no more military patrols?

From the looks of them, the grey paste in their hair and lint woven through their beards, the Prince determined they were all from the NavelDiggin clan. Furthermore, he decided they were young Smellys, with no extra ears, or they would be wearing them about their necks.

It was well known that ears were a prized trophy among Woolly-Bullies, who pierced them and strung them around their necks. In this way, they could keep count of the enemies they had slain and, at the same time, maintain the foolish notion that the more ears they possessed, the better would be their hearing.

The younger men of the tribe were called Smellys for the baggy swaddling about their loins. This swaddling was worn until they had proven themselves in battle and were no longer wetting themselves in a fight or losing control of their bowels.

Seeing a Woolly-Bully in a swaddling cloth might lull a stranger into thinking he was not in any danger. But Smellys, wanting desperately to prove their bravery to the rest of the tribe, were actually the most fearsome of Woolly-Bullies.

One thing, of course, they seemed never to achieve, and that was the element of surprise. The rancid odor of their swaddling cloths always traveled in advance of their approach, no matter whether they attacked up wind or not.

He counted their number as they gesticulated and grunted amongst themselves. There were at least ten that he could see.

The Prince frowned and shook his head, dismayed. Far too many for him to handle. They needed to be gone from there; and quickly; even if it meant marching the whole night.

Malady won't like that, he thought ruefully. But better to walk ten miles than wind up without our ears.

The Prince tapped Cower lightly on his shoulder and jerked his head in the direction from which they came. However, as he started off, he heard a loud snort. He paused and scanned the encampment. Tethered at the far side, just beyond the fire's light, were the horses they had lost at the Ankledeep.

Just then, the Woolly-Bullies' gesticulating became quite animated, and one, who was obviously angry, shot to his feet and stepped closer to the fire. His face was terribly scarred. Woolly-Bullies considered this a mark of courage. The more scars the greater the courage. Thus, some of them went so far as to wound themselves in battle.

The warrior cast a dower glance back and forth between two particular clansmen who sat upon opposite sides of the fire, staring at the ground.

"Oofla, chicken-hearted," said the warrior, addressing one in a contemptuous tone. "No like mekka war."

The band booed the man, ripping up clumps of turf and throwing them at him.

The orator faced the other and sneered. "Moosta, got kablooey brains and no bring clan num-nums forda tum-tums." He too was pelted with divots.

A troubled look came over the orator's face. "Must choose one to chomp and gulp. But who?"

Oofla, the chicken-hearted one, rose and struck a proud pose. "Me say, biggy clan more important than bitty band, bitty band more important than singy man. So, if must choose one to chomp and gulp, me say... Choose Moosta!"

However, the one called Moosta was of a different mind. He bellowed in protest and sprang to his feet, snatching up his cuttintoo at the same time.

Seeing he had no choice but to fight, Oofla produced his own weapon, and the two men engaged each other at the center of the campsite.

During the struggle that ensued, Donoim crawled to Bryand's side, his eyes riveted on the strange-looking combatants.

"I told you to stay behind," whispered the Prince angrily.

"Take it easy, will ya," rasped the boy, scowling. "Mum sent me ta get ya. We got unwanted comp'ny."

Bryand frowned, shot Cower a concerned look, then followed the boy away from the encampment. A moment later and they had located Malady and Noim.

But there was no need to speak, for it was plain to see what Donoim had meant. About thirty yards away, where the trees ended, another fire now glowed; and creeping to the edge of the woods, Bryand saw the guards making camp across the road. He closed his eyes and rested his head against a tree.

This is getting ridiculous, he thought wearily. Fatigued as he was, he could have fallen asleep where he stood, but he forced his eyes open again, and with a deep sigh, started back to their hiding place.

When the Prince rejoined the others, he knelt beside Malady and said, "We're in a fix."

"When ain't we." said Donoim.

Bryand ignored the remark and went on. "We can't go that way or we'll run into the guards. We can't go the other way or we'll run into-- ." He paused and stared at Malady. "Promise you won't scream."

She hesitated, and looked about at the others. "I promise."

"Into Woolly-Bullies."

Malady's eyes went agog and she sucked in a deep breath. But before she could let loose with anything, the others jumped her, and smothered her beneath them.

"You promised you wouldn't scream," whispered Bryand crossly.

"I wasn't gonna scream," said the woman, once they had let her up. "Ya never said nothin' 'bout gaspin'."

Bryand could tell he had bruised her feelings. "You're right. I'm sorry."

"'Pology accepted," brooded Malady, straightening her bodice. "Now what're we gonna do? If they catch us they'll eat us alive."

Recalling the confrontation he had just witnessed, Bryand said, "I don't think there's much chance of that. They've got our horses, and I've an idea that will get them back as well as shake those guards off our tails. But we must separate for a while."

"How long?" asked Malady, instantly fretting.

"We'll be back shortly."

"What if yer not."

"We will."

"But what if yer not."

Bryand sighed. "Look, Malady, we're in another tight spot. You've got to stay strong."

"It's so hard," she sniveled. "I'm so tired. Me aches

and pains have aches and pains of their own. I ain't got nothin' left..." And she covered her face with her hands and began to weep.

"Of course you do," comforted the Prince, patting her shoulder. "In fact, you're one of the strongest people I know. Why, look at all the dangers we've overcome in the past few weeks. No ordinary person could have done it."

"But I'm so scared."

"So am I. I just pretend to be fearless. Can you do that? Pretend to be fearless?" Even in the darkness he could tell her nose was running. "Can you try?" And with a pained expression, he added, "For me?"

She thought a moment, blinking back her tears. Then she nodded her head affirmatively.

"Good," said Bryand, back on task. "Now stay here and keep yourselves well hidden. Don't move; don't even breathe. There's going to be a lot of noise and commotion. Just trust that I know what I'm doing, and Cower and I will be back when things have quieted down."

"But what if yer not?"

Bryand thought it best to leave the question unanswered.

When they were a fair distance away, Cower whispered, "Take comfort, my lord. This situation will not last forever."

The Prince stopped and looked at him, somewhat rankled. "I haven't said a word."

"I know. You don't have to. The frustration is distorting your face."

Bryand took a deep breath and nodded. "I'm a family man and I'm not yet even married. I wonder what MeAnne would think of that?"

Cower shrugged, not knowing how else to reply.

They tiptoed to the Woolly-Bully encampment

where they found the conflict resolved and Oofla being tenderized for consumption.

Bryand had never witnessed such barbarity. He had heard the stories of Wooly-Bullies carrying off their dead after a battle. He thought it was out of loyalty; or respect. He never realized it was so they could serve them up for lunch.

The Prince cringed and looked away. Don't think of it, he told himself. Keep the objective foremost in your mind.

They bent low, padding from one tree to the next, skirting the campsite until they had reached the tether line. Bryand and Cower stepped between the horses, carefully untying the reins.

Cower suddenly felt quite afraid. Two things plagued his mind, one contingent upon the other.

Firstly, he had never ridden bareback before. If by chance he fell off, he would surely be captured by the Woolly-Bullies.

Secondly, if he was captured by the Woolly-Bullies he would surely go the way of Oofla and wind up roasting on a spit.

Hopefully, he thought, wiping sweat from his brow, neither will take place and all will go as planned.

The retainer clutched his horse's mane and swung himself onto the animal's back, then, gripping its flanks with his knees, he looked at the Prince and signaled his readiness.

They were off, whooping, shouting, flailing their arms excitedly, which caused the remaining horses to scream and bolt through the center of the encampment. Taken unawares, the Woolly-Bullies scrambled out of the way, confused, rattled; and Bryand and Cower rode past them unharmed.

However, a Smelly provoked was a Smelly enraged. Once they had regrouped, they took up the chase like a swarm of angry bees.

But that was exactly what the Prince had hoped they would do; and he led them closer and closer to the road.

,At the same time as Cower and the Prince were disrupting the Woolly-Bully camp, Mortamour was sitting down upon a large boulder by the side of the road. He remained apart from his troops. He knew they did not like him. But that mattered naught to the assassin just as long as they feared him.

He was in a truly ugly mood. The excursion to the island had yielded nothing and had cost him four more men, and then the swamp and that befouling swallow-up had cost him three more before he had given up and turned back toward the river.

Blast him, he brooded, thinking of the Prince. Even though Mortamour very easily could have strangled the man, at that moment, he was angrier with himself for allowing the Prince to slip through his fingers. It was the kind of error a journeyman thug would make, not a master henchman and assassin. Once word got around, he'd be the laughing stock at the Slaughter House.

Mortamour drew his dagger and toyed with it. "I'll get him, though," he muttered. "Next time."

A bad taste rose in his mouth. For not once in his entire career had he used those words - next time. As reluctant as he was to say them, he hated their implication even more. "Aye, next time, my lord. And when I do, such pain will I inflict upon your person that you'll think of death as liberation."

He had just stuffed a piece of jerky into his mouth when the quiet of the evening was interrupted by loud crashes coming from the woods. Before he could make sense of it, two horses galloped into view and then two more with riders upon them.

Mortamour shot to his feet, his mouth falling open as he recognized the Prince. He spit out the jerky, and was about to shout the alarm, when a score of mad highlanders - and they were truly mad at this point - burst into the open and fell upon his command.

Mortamour turned and saw a nogginocker heading straight for his head. Being an assassin as well as a henchman, he had developed lightning fast reflexes. He ducked, just as the weapon whizzed by his ear. He may have been stout, but he was also very flexible.

The clansman rushed him, groping for his cuttintoo. But he had no time to unsheathe it, for Mortamour tackled him and plunged his dagger into the Smelly's heart.

The henchman looked up, and for a moment, he stared in horror as his men were hacked to pieces. You should help them, a voice said in his head, watching a Smelly bite off his bugler's nose. The man's screams turned to a pathetic gurgle as he choked on his own blood.

The look of horror slowly changed to one of detachment as the henchman calculated the chances of his surviving the attack. He decided they were next to nil.

"Right, then," said Mortamour, and he bounded into the woods and did not stop until he was well hidden among the trees.

Minutes later, the Woolly-Bullies stood over the dead, braying in triumph. They stripped the bodies of their clothes and weapons, gathered up the supplies, and took the soldiers' horses as payment for the ones they had lost. They gestured of their deeds and grunted their accord. When at last they could carry no more, they started back to their campsite, chanting:

"Hey, lowlanda whut yoo say,
Da Woolly-Bully cum yoo way,
But yoo dunt see or heer no mohr.
Cuz yoo be det upun da flohr."

Soon the only sound was that of the wind moaning as it caressed the dead. Then it, too, fell silent as Mortamour, moving stealthily, emerged from his hiding place among the shadows and crept into the road.

He glanced at the carnage, at the treeline, and made his way through the encampment, stepping over bodies here and there, drawing closer to the tether line where he hoped his horse would be waiting.

He never secured the mount. Instead, he allowed it to graze freely as a precaution against a situation arising just like this one.

He had chosen the animal himself and had trained it most diligently to sense the approach of danger, to flee from it without hesitation and to return with the sounds of the night or when the air was no longer tainted.

However, when he reached the tether line, he knew his training of the animal had fallen short, for it was not there. Nor was it in a nearby clearing, nor among some gooseberry bushes on the other side of the road.

Of all the ill luck! he thought, his hands curling into fists and shaking. Now I'll have to walk back to the capital!

He started off on foot, cursing the Prince's name, his determination to hunt Bryand down increasing with every step.

Ruin my record, will you, my lord? He sneered to

himself. Well, enjoy your freedom. But know you this. One day I will find you. No matter how long it takes, and on that day -- . On that day -- ." So angry was he that he could hardly find the words.

"On that day, believe me, it will hurt!"

Now if Mortamour had been just a little more patient, he would not have had to wait to face the Prince again. For shortly after he disappeared around the bend in the road, Bryand and Cower appeared from another in the opposite direction, leading their stolen horses on foot.

Soon they had reached the grisly scene. "Poor wretches," said Cower, overcome by the savagery and slaughter.

"Aye," the Prince agreed.

They went from man to man, checking to see if any was still alive. But the Woolly-Bullies had been most thorough, inasmuch as all were dead and none had been spared the loss of his ears.

They searched for any supplies the Woolly-Bullies might have overlooked. They were lucky, for they found a small pouch with salted beef and dried biscuits and some water skins that had been hung on a low hanging branch by the side of the road.

"Stay here," said Bryand. "While I get Malady and the boys."

"Aye, my lord," replied the retainer none too eagerly. More dead men, he thought. More angry spirits. But he said nothing; and he led the horses to the side of the road where he waited patiently, if not painfully, while Bryand slipped into the darkness.

Raucous laughter came from the Woolly-Bully encampment, and then the gutteral strains of a song.

"Chomp and gulp, chomp and gulp,
Oofla mek good chomp and gulp."

A single clansman took up the next stanza. Off-key and ragged in voice, he sang:

Moosta, Moosta he soh mahd,
Wen Oofla nogginkock his hahd.

Another clansman completed the line, sputtering with laughter as he sang:

But Moosta grab his cuttintoo,
Now Oofla mekkin' up th' stew.

The entire band took up the chorus once more.

"Chomp and gulp, chomp and gulp,
Oofla mek good chomp and gulp!"

After searching two or three thickets (*at night they all looked alike,*) Bryand located Malady and the boys.

"Everything all right?"

"Aye," answered Noim, tossing away a stone he had intended to hurl had Bryand proven to be someone else.

"Mum messed her pants again," said Donoim matter-of-factly.

Embarrassed, Malady punched the boy on the arm. "I told ya not ta say nothin'."

They padded softly out of the thicket and rejoined Cower by the side of the road.

"Oh, crimey, would ya look at that," said Malady, grimacing when she beheld the massacre. Her foot inadvertently touched the hand of a dead man and she yelped.

For an instance they all froze, thinking she had betrayed their presence. But to their luck, the singing and laughing continued uninterrupted.

"Look at that gash!" said Donoim, pointing to one of the bodies with its organs leaking onto the road. "Wadduya think, Noim. Was it made goin' in or comin' out?"

"Boys," said Bryand flatly, before Noim could answer. "We can discuss the impact of carnage upon viscera some other time."

"What's viscera," asked the little one as Bryand lifted him onto a mount. When Bryand did not answer him, he turned to his brother. "Hey, Noim. What's viscera?"

Noim was already sitting atop his horse and waiting to get under way. "I'll tell ya soon as I figger out who carnage is."

"Not who carnage is," said Cower, mounting his horse. "What carnage is."

Bryand lifted Malady, grateful for the darkness as she spread her legs wide and straddled his horse. He swung himself up behind her and felt her settle against him.

"Ready?" he said to her.

"Ready, m'lord," she replied, sounding very content.

"Right," said the Prince, resignedly.

He looked at Cower and then at the boys. "Now, let's keep our voices and our heads down and be well away from here."

They followed the forest road for two whole days,

until the trees thinned and were replaced by rolling hills broken here and there by striated rock formations. After another two days, the hills ended at the edge of a lush valley of grassy fields and clobbernut groves.

"We should have reached Pepperill by now," said the Prince, vexed. "It's an entire county, with a village, and a large manor. How difficult could it be to find the blasted place?"

"Do you think we should turn around?" asked Cower half-heartedly, for he knew that doing so would not rectify things; they would still be lost. He loved the Prince like a son but recognized his shortcomings.

"Maybe it's just up ahead."

"You said that yesterday."

Bryand shot him an irritable glance. "I know I said that yesterday."

Cower made no further reply. Having raised the Prince, he could go quite far before being considered forgetful of his place, but telling the Prince where to go was not permissible.

"I swear, if ever I'm king, the first thing I intend to do is erect signs along every major road and byway on the continent. And I'll hire a mapmaker to chart each and every hillock and valley between Bandidon and the Tanta Mounts!"

Thus the idea was born; and, though I was unaware of it, my destiny was soon to be forged with the Prince's. I say unaware, yet I must admit that for quite some time I had the strangest feeling that my life was going to change somehow.

Perhaps the Gods knew better than to grant me anything more prescient than a feeling, for if I had known exactly what they had in store for me, I probably would have changed my profession as well as my name and quietly slipped out of town.

"When're we gonna get there?!" asked Donoim impatiently nudging his mount alongside the Prince's.

"Soon," said Bryand flatly.

"Ya said that yesterday."

"I know! I know!"

"I gotta go."

"Me, too," said Noim.

"We'll stop soon."

"Now!" said Donoim urgently. "Or there's gonna be a accident."

"Why must you always wait until the very last minute?" groused the Prince as he steered his horse off the road.

The boys jumped down and ran deeper into the woods.

Bryand watched them disappear, a petulant look on his face. What was it about a child's bladder that needed emptying so often? But then he sighed, and after a moment more, he said, "Well, I suppose we could all do with a stretch." He hopped to the ground. "But I don't want to make any more stops after this," he announced as surely as if he had uttered a royal decree. "We go straight to Pepperill from here."

"If we can find it," muttered Cower under his breath as he climbed down from his horse. His joints were stiff; and his seat was sore; and if he had been able to see himself at that moment, he would have been as sorely depressed as was his seat.

Being a royal retainer, he had always prided himself on his grooming. Yet now he sported the makings of a silver and white flecked beard. His hair, or rather what was left of it, was matted and his clothes were so grimy and sweat-soaked that he intended to burn them the very first time the opportunity presented itself. Just the thought of them made him shudder.

Cower glanced at the Prince and shook his head sadly. For Bryand was just as unkempt. His hair had grown shoulder length; his cheeks and chin were covered with stubble; and, though Cower would never dare to mention it, each time the wind was right he could tell the Prince had gone unwashed for a very long time.

How many more hardships would they have to endure, he wondered. Noble as their struggle was, living it day after day was quite another thing. Would they ever again know the comfort of a bed; or the satisfaction that went hand in hand with a full stomach; or the pride of wearing a suit of clothes that was not mildewed?

Hang everything else! If he could be assured just those few things he could die a contented man.

"I found it!" called Noim excitedly as he broke from the woods.

Donoim followed, lacing his braces. "Ya did not! I found it!"

"Bite me if ya wasn't still peein' when I laced up an' peeked me head outta them trees!"

"I'll bite ya all right!" growled Donoim, and he pounced on his brother.

"Quit that," scolded Malady, sliding off the mount. But they did not heed her.

"Boys! Boys!" shouted the Prince.

"Allow me," said Cower, unperturbed.

He sauntered over to the nearest tree, reached up and pulled off a handful of clobbernuts, then pelted the boys until they had stopped.

"Now," said the retainer, having gotten their attention. "What exactly did you find?"

"Pepperill!" they replied in unison.

The boys grabbed Cower by the hands and led him into the grove. Bryand and Malady followed close behind, eager to have a look.

"See, that's where I went," said Donoim, pointing with pride at a wet spot on the ground.

Cower wrinkled his nose. "Well, I suppose it's better than doing it on your shoes. May we proceed?"

When they emerged on the far side of the grove, they were greeted by a wonderous sight. Below them was a large grouping of wattle and daub cottages nestled in a glen. The sun shone down on their thatched roofs, turning them a brilliant gold, and the hills surrounding the village were splashed with fields of colorful wild flowers. A herd of woolly sheep grazed on a lower plain, watched over by an energetic dog, and here and there field birds did madcap loops in the air.

"It's beautiful," Malady whispered. "Almost like a tapestry I once seen."

"This must be the village just before you come to the manor," said Bryand elatedly. "I think I remember it."

About an hour later they halted at the edge of the village. So excited were they to have reached their destination that they took no exception to the wary looks cast them by the locals they had passed. They simply attributed these to their ragtag appearance and the workhorses they rode.

Upon Cower's suggestion, Bryand sought out the local tavern, which was at the far side of the village, for, according to the retainer, it would be the best place to learn the latest gossip or news. If Daron's guards had been to Pepperill, the keeper there would know.

"Can I come?" asked the little one, jumping to the ground.

"No," replied the Prince adamantly.

"Why not?"

Bryand wanted to say, "Because I'm fed up with you and need a moment to myself!"

But instead he knelt before Donoim and, in a calm, tolerant voice, said, "Because I need you to look after the horses and keep your mother company. What say you to that?"

"You're breath is really bad."

After he had deposited the boy with his mother, Bryand returned to Cower and headed for the tavern entrance. "Was I ever like that?" asked the Prince, rankled.

"Oh, no, my lord," answered Cower. "You're brother on the other hand -- ."

Out of respect, the retainer said no more. He did, however, roll his eyes and shudder, which made the Prince laugh out loud and clap him on the back.

The tavern was one large room furnished with roughly hewn wooden tables and straight-backed chairs. Timbers ran along the ceiling, and from these, many colorful banners had been draped.

On one side of the room stood a long bar that rested on four beer barrels. On the other side was a wide stone chimney with a polished mantle, upon which some pewter dishes stood upright.

Sconces encrusted with mounds of candle drippings had been hung from the walls, and directly opposite the front door stood an open archway and a corridor that turned out of sight. When Bryand and Cower entered the establishment, all eyes turned to them and the room fell silent.

Feeling somewhat conspicuous, the Prince cleared his throat and said, "Hello. Good day. Good day to all of you."

But no one answered him. Instead, three men, who had been conversing at a table close by, stood and left the tavern, slamming the heavy door shut with a thud.

Bryand faced the others still about. "Could one of you tell us if this is Pepperill?"

Still no one spoke up.

Bryand and Cower exchanged a confused look. Then, finding the silence most irritating, the Prince took a step forward and said, "I beg your pardon, but would someone give reply?"

"Here now," someone said sternly from behind.

The Prince turned. In the archway stood a tall, well-built man with silver hair and a strikingly handsome face. At first Bryand expected a rebuff.

But it soon became clear the man was not addressing him. For he strode about the room, glaring at all the occupants, and in a remonstrative tone, he said, "Is that any way to make a stranger welcome? I'm ashamed of you! Why, you'll give us a bad name, you will. No one will want to stop here any more. And then where will we be. Alone. With no one but ourselves to blame."

He held a small keg in the crook of each arm, which he carried to the bar top and set down with ease. He looked at Bryand, and then at Cower, and his stern expression softened, "Good day to you, sirs. You must forgive my mates here. They're not used to seeing outsiders."

"Are you the proprietor?" asked the Prince.

With a smile that revealed clean, straight teeth, the man replied, "Proprietor. Mayor. Spiritual leader. Now how can I be of service to you?"

"You can tell me if we've reached the village of Pepperill."

"Is that the place you seek?"

"Aye," said Bryand, weary of pleasantries.

"Then seek no more. This is Pepperill."

"It is?" said Cower, surprised.

The man chuckled disarmingly. His cheeks were flushed; and he looked like he enjoyed sampling his ale as much as he enjoyed selling it. "As sure as you're born."

Bryand smiled, and his good humor returned. "That's grand! Grand indeed! I knew I could find it."

"The name's Daemon," said the tavern keeper, extending his hand, which Bryand shook willingly. "And yours?"

"Bryand."

"Like the King's!"

"Aye, I was born the same year," said the Prince humbly.

"Only not quite so nobly," said Cower, chiming in.

Bryand smiled and placed his hand on the retainer's shoulder. "This is my good friend, Cower, who likes to remind me of the fact every now and then."

They shook hands. Then the keeper slapped the kegs on the bar with his palms; and leaning toward them with eyes twinkling and an ingratiating smile.

"I'd be pleased to share a tankard or two with you!"

"Thank you, but no," said Bryand politely.

"'Tis my treat, sir."

"You see, we've come a long way and we're -- ."

"Then you must be parched!" said Daemon gleefully. "And there's nothing better to quench a man's thirst than a dram or two of ale."

He circled the bar, grabbed two tankards and plunked them down, then poured some frothy ale into them from a copper pitcher.

Bryand was about to beg off again when he noticed the longing look on Cower's face. Bryand sighed resignedly and stepped up to the bar.

"You men traveling alone?" asked Daemon, folding his arms and watching them with pleasure as they drank.

"No," gasped the Prince, for the ale was icy cold and bitter and burned as it ran down his gullet. "The rest of the family's outside."

"Family, you say?" said the keeper, intrigued.

"Aye. My wife and two children."

Bryand had said this for the keeper's benefit. But hearing the words escape his lips caused him to stop and reflect upon how much he had grown accustomed to his companions.

The boys weren't half as bothersome as they had

been at the start of their journey; a little polishing and they'd be proper gentlemen someday.

He paused. Perhaps that was expecting too much. He'd be happy if they learned to keep their fingers out of their noses and their mouths closed when they belched.

As for Malady... Well, he preferred to think of her as being healthy someday and nothing more.

"I thank you for your kindness," said the Prince when he had quaffed the ale. "Now could you tell us how far the manor house is?"

"Just up the road a ways," said Daemon, pointing off with a stunted forefinger. He was missing the first two joints.

Bryand couldn't help noticing it, and the keeper, seeing the Prince's reaction, added casually, "Hunting accident. Now as I was saying, it's just outside the village about a mile or so. Bear right at the fork. You can't miss it."

"Right," said the Prince. Then, remembering his original purpose, he asked, "There hasn't been any trouble here of late, has there?"

"Trouble? In what way?"

"The lord of the manor; I take it he's still in good health?"

"As far as I know."

This was excellent news. Bryand was excited now and eager to be on his way. So, with a tug at Cower's sleeve, he thanked the keeper for the drinks and headed for the door. The retainer gulped down the remainder of his ale, nodded, and hastened after the Prince.

But when they returned to the horses, they found Malady and the boys were gone.

They looked down the road in the direction they had come, then turned and peered in the direction they were headed, shielding their eyes against the sinking sun.

"Now where could they be?" grumbled Bryand. "Of all times to wander off, when we're so close to joining up with Dwayne."

"Perhaps we should look for them," Cower suggested. "They may have wandered into a shop."

But in their search they discovered there were only two shops, and no one who they stopped or on whose door they knocked could tell them anything of their companions' whereabouts.

"This is ridiculous," said Bryand, annoyed. But he was also growing concerned. "Where could they be?"

At that moment a shadow drifted slowly across the oiled skin that covered one of the tavern's embrasures.

Seeing it, Bryand started for the door, hoping Malady and the boys had gone inside while he and Cower had been searching for them.

He opened it halfway and glanced about the room. Daemon was behind the bar, leaning upon it as he conversed with two men. When he noticed the Prince, he raised his eyebrows and smiled. "Did you forget something, sir? More ale to take with you?"

"No, no thank you. I'm looking for my wife and children. They seemed to have disappeared."

"Disappeared?" said Daemon, not sure if the Prince was joking.

"Aye. Gone. Vanished."

Looking quite perplexed, the keeper rounded the bar and joined the Prince by the door. "That doesn't make sense," said the man, his brow knitting. "Are you sure they're not just off somewhere in the village? There's a woman what makes sweets at the other end. Perhaps they caught wind of it and went."

"No," said Bryand, shaking his head. "We were there."

Daemon placed his arms akimbo. "Well, this is odd

indeed," he said. "But I'm sure they'll turn up soon. With some fantastic story, too. Believe me, sir; no one's ever disappeared from here. It just doesn't happen. You're welcome to wait for them if you'd like."

"Thank you," replied Bryand, distracted. "But I think I'll remain outside."

He shut the door and joined Cower. They leaned upon the hitching post and waited while the sun sank closer to the tops of the trees. Finally, Bryand had had enough of waiting. "Stay here," he said, untying his horse's reins.

"Where are you going?" asked Cower.

"To Pepperill, to find Dwayne. They'll probably show up before we're back. But if they don't, we'll need his help to find them."

"Are you sure you want to do this?" asked Cower, fretting.

"Of course," replied the Prince as he swung himself onto the horse.

"Let me rephrase that. Are you sure you can do this?"

Bryand stopped and gazed at him, offended. "Of course I can do this. How hard could it be to follow the road for a mile or so?"

For anyone else it would be simple, but Cower knew with whom he was dealing. "Aye, but -- ."

"Not another word," said the Prince, annoyed, and he kicked the horse's flanks and started off.

"Remember!" shouted the retainer. "It's the right fork! The right fork!"

And Bryand raised his right hand to signify he had understood.

He followed the road beyond the village, past some rock outcroppings, and into heavily wooded terrain. These were gnarly trees, named thusly for their dense, twisting limbs. Gnarly trees were sometimes mistaken for knobby trees, which were much like them only... knobbier.

The Prince came upon the bifurcation and, without the slightest hesitation, guided the horse onto the road that veered to the right.

There, he thought, pleased with himself, I did it; and he spurred the mount harder, expecting to see Pepperill Manor at any moment.

The road took him deeper into the woods. Soon it narrowed, and a canopy of limbs stretched overhead, obliterating the sunlight. Bryand squinted in the dimness. But his mind was not on what he was doing. He was too excited about seeing Dwayne and enjoying the comforts of his home. Perhaps Dwayne knew what had happened to Niles. Perhaps Niles was there with him. And Dillin, too. Oh, it would be wonderful being together again! Almost like old times, before all their troubles had begun.

The road bent sharply behind some trees to his left. Bryand leaned over the horse's neck and into the turn, but when he rounded the curve, he sat erect and cried out with alarm, tugging hard on the horse's mane.

For only a few feet in front of him the road ended abruptly at a cliff and dropped off into empty air. The horse, seeing it, too, neighed with terror and turned drastically to one side, its hooves dislodging clumps of dirt and pebbles along the ridge. For a moment Bryand thought they would go over. But the animal was surefooted and headed into the trees.

However, it was far too frightened now to respond to Bryand's commands; and the Prince suddenly found himself parted from the animal by a stout limb that knocked the air from his lungs and sent him spilling backwards over the horses' rump.

Sparks of all different colors flashed behind his eyelids, then faded into blackness; and the thud-thumping that was the blood rushing through his head, gave way to the sounds of the woods.

He groaned and opened his eyes. When his vision cleared, he saw the sky above him through a patchwork of leaves.

He rolled onto his side, wincing from the pain in his chest. He rubbed it, finding his shirt torn and his skin raw where the limb had struck him.

When the pain subsided, Bryand pulled himself onto his feet. He was suddenly lightheaded, and he leaned against a tree trunk and waited for the spell to pass.

He was confused. Not so much by the blow - he recalled that all too well - as by the events leading up to it.

I'm sure I took the right fork, he thought, rubbing his chest. The keeper said right, right? I went right. I know it was right because I hold my sword in my right hand. He looked down at Slaybest and, with chagrin, found it hanging on his left side.

Wait a minute, maybe I did go wrong. He stood for a moment, frowning. But then he brightened.

No, no, that's right. My sword hangs by my left hand so I can unsheathe it with my right. There's something else, too. When I put my pants on I always start with my right leg!

So I'm right; I did go right. He frowned once more. Then what went wrong? (*As stated before, he was confused.*)

He looked about and saw the horse grazing a few yards away, no worse for the experience. He was about to approach it when he heard voices and rapid footfalls coming from the direction of the road. He turned, thinking someone had seen him in distress and was now rushing to his aid.

Three men came into view, the same three men who had left the tavern abruptly. They ran up to the cliff and peered over the edge. Two carried cudgels and ropes, and the third a drawn sword. From their manner, Bryand gathered their intentions were far from helpful.

"I don't see 'im," said one. He dropped his weapon, unshouldered his rope, and began to uncoil it.

"He's down there," said another, eyeing the trees and brush below him. "And remember, I get his sword."

It was then the horse snorted, and looking up, the villagers caught sight of Bryand immediately.

"You lads looking for me?" called the Prince with a broad grin. "As you can see, I managed to avoid that nasty fall. I'd be on my horse still if I hadn't caught a tree limb across the chest."

"Come on," said the one with the sword, nudging the man by his side. They started toward him, slowly fanning out as if stalking a prey.

"No need to worry yourselves," said Bryand, retreating a step or two. "It only knocked the wind out of me. I'm back on my feet. Perfectly fit. Healthy as yonder horse."

"Not when we're through with you," growled the one with the sword. He was an ugly brute with a birthmark the size of a man's fist upon his neck.

"Not when we're through with you!" The man at his side cackled idiotically, revealing a mouthful of crooked teeth. "That's a good one!"

"Remember," said the third, a dirtier version of the other two. "I get his sword."

If he had any doubt before, Bryand was sure now of their intentions.

"Before you start anything," said the Prince, raising his palms, "I feel it my duty to warn you, I'm a champion swordsman."

"Really now," scoffed the one with the birthmark.

"Really now," repeated the idiot, still cackling.

"This I've got to see."

"Aye, this I've got to see."

The man with the sword rushed forward. Bryand unsheathed his own blade and made ready for the attack.

Their weapons clashed and rang, but the villager was indeed no match for the Prince. In a moment he lay dead, his blood proliferating upon the hard ground.

"Ya killed him," said the idiot, gawking at his cohort. Then, looking up at Bryand, his eyes brimming with hate, he said, "Now who's gonna buy me dinner?!"

"Come on," said the dirty one, seething. "Let's bash his head in."

Together, they came at the Prince. However, the woods were too dense for them to wield their cudgels effectively, whereas Bryand's sword was sharp and to the point.

The Prince eluded the idiot and advanced upon the other, ducking a murderous swing that caromed off the trunk of a tree. With a quick feint Bryand lunged, the dirty one clutched his chest in agony, then fell to the ground dead.

The idiot, realizing he was on his own now, grunted and groaned as he swung his cudgel back and forth in short furious strokes that forced the Prince toward the cliff. Here the villager had more room to maneuver.

Uttering a maniacal laugh, he threw all his weight behind his weapon, slicing the air with a loud whoosh. But Bryand - not caring to have his head cracked open like a clobbernut - quickly ducked and slid out of the way.

They were reversed now, with the villager by the edge. Realizing the precariousness of his position, he swung his cudgel from side to side, attempting to force the Prince on the defensive. However, at that same moment, the ground along the edge of the cliff broke loose and the villager lost his footing. He tottered for an instant, his eyes wide with fear. Bryand reached for him; grabbing his cudgel. But it was too late, and the man fell with a strident cackle.

The clamor of snapping branches and swishing leaves drowned out his laugh. A moment later all was silent, and when Bryand peered over the edge, he saw the villager staring up at him with sightless eyes, impaled on a broken tree limb.

The Prince grimaced and looked away. It was then he saw a bridge that spanned the ravine about a mile in the distance.

Probably reached by the left fork, he surmised bitterly. But it did not matter.

He knew now that they were not in Pepperill; that they had been duped by the tavern keeper; and these men were Daemon's cronies come to finish him off had he by some chance survived the fall.

CHAPTER TWENTY TWO

He checked the men who lay among the trees; first one and then the other, and much to his surprise he discovered that each had the same stunted forefinger as the keeper.

"Lots of clumsy hunters around these parts," muttered the Prince, but he did not really believe it. Nor did he dwell upon it long because he was suddenly struck by a profound sense of fear.

Cower and the others were in danger. He knew it. All his instincts told him so.

He cursed himself for having left them unprotected, and, wasting not a single moment more, he retrieved the horse, leaped onto its back, and galloped toward the village with his heart in his throat.

But instead of riding directly up to the tavern and bursting inside as his wrath demanded, Bryand listened instead to the voice of reason in his head. He had no idea what to expect or how many adversaries he would be facing.

Stealth was his answer; at least until he had taken stock of the situation and had learned if there were any advantages in his favor.

Keeping this in mind, he slowed his mount to a walk about thirty yards from the village and guided it into the woods, where he left it tethered.

The sun had just dipped below the horizon when the Prince emerged from the trees and located the back wall of the tavern. The oiled skins covering the embrasures were dark. He could see nothing through them.

He rounded the corner of the building and came to a door. He tested the latch. It was unlocked.

Opening it gingerly, cringing with each creak, the Prince slipped inside and shut the door behind him. He stood motionless in the darkness, his hand upon the hilt of his sword.

This was a grueling moment, being blind, not knowing if anything would come at him. But soon his eyes adjusted to the darkness, and he found himself in what he thought to be the back room of the tavern and Daemon's living quarters.

He eyed the few sticks of furniture and the meager appointments. And this struck him as odd. For someone who made his living waylaying unsuspecting travelers as the Prince suspected, the man was obviously not of wealthy means.

Perhaps he's set up shop on the wrong road, thought Bryand. His eyes narrowed, and he clenched his teeth. Whatever the case, he's about to go out of business.

He headed for the interior door, opened it a crack, and peeked into the corridor. It was dark and empty.

He was about to exit when he noticed a strange looking dagger hanging on the wall adjacent to the door. He was drawn to it. The blade was curved and reminded him of a long thorn. A wooden crosspiece had been carved for it, upon which were engraved markings he had not seen before, even though he could read the four major languages of the continent and converse in them like they were his native tongue.

But the most curious thing about the dagger was its hilt. It, too, was wood and had been carved into a crude image. The head and upper torso were human, though barely; yet the lower half resembled the hind quarters of some type of beast.

There was something familiar about it. He knew he had seen its likeness somewhere before but where or when, at that moment, he was unable to recall.

The sound of approaching footsteps prevented him from deliberating any further on the subject. Springing like a cat-like, he leaped to the hinged side of the door just as it swung open.

The Prince held his breath and hugged the wall. Someone entered the room, though from his hiding place he could only guess it was Daemon. He was about to steal a look when the footsteps retreated hastily. A moment later he heard the tavern door shut.

Bryand expelled the air from his lungs. That was strange, he thought. The Prince stepped clear of the door and looked about the room. What could he have wanted?

It was then his eyes fell upon the empty pegs on the wall by the door. The dagger was missing.

A shiver ran through him. He still had no idea what he was up against, but he knew he had no time to waste; not if he wanted to see his friends again.

He hastened to the end of the corridor as quietly as he dared, and peering around the archway, he found the main room empty. The fire on the hearth still blazed, but the candles in the wall sconces had been extinguished. From these, oily black smoke still billowed, which meant the room had not been vacant very long.

A part of him clung to the hope that the attack in the woods had been masterminded by the three thieves alone and that he would find Cower and the others waiting for him by the side of the road.

But when he opened the main door and peered outside, he found no one there. Even the horses were gone.

Bryand stepped into the shadowy recess outside the door and hugged the wall. He glanced first one direction up the road and then the other. The cottages within sight were dark and the road was empty.

In fact, the entire village seemed deserted. His foot touched something, and when he looked down, his stomach dropped. Cower's purse lay in the dirt.

He scooped it up and examined it in the waning light. It was empty, and there was blood on the flap.

So filled with rage was he that he convulsed. He clutched the purse to his chest, wanting to scream. He stood for a moment, his chest heaving, and when he had regained a measure of control, he stuffed the purse under his belt and started off at a deliberate pace.

He proceeded door to door, throwing them open, kicking in those that were locked, only to discover not a man, woman or child remained in the village.

"Show yourselves!" he shouted, frustrated, angry, and he ripped Slaybest from its scabbard. "It's just me now. You've taken everyone else!"

Silence was his only answer. He slashed the air with his blade. "Come on! I'm waiting! Is there none among you with the courage to face me?! Or are children and women and old men all that you can handle?!" But no challenger stepped forward, and the silence was complete.

"Well," said the Prince under his breath as he adjusted his grip on Slaybest. "This is not over. By any means."

The darkness was complete now and would have halted someone less determined in his search. But the Prince was a driven man, fueled by a burning rage. And it was the darkness of all things that yielded up to him the whereabouts of the villagers. For as he passed the last of the cottages, his eyes fell upon the black silhouette of the hill above the glen, and there he saw a file of torches coiling toward the summit.

His lips curled into a vengeful sneer, and he bolted toward the lights like an animal on a savage rampage. He barreled headlong through a dense thicket, heeding not the cuts and welts he received from the tangled branches. At that moment, nothing short of a twenty foot wall would have halted him, and even that he would have somehow found a way to scale.

Up he went, leaping over rocks, dodging trees, scrambling onto ledges. His strength seemed boundless. He saw a dark, wide gap ahead of him and, running at full tilt, he sprang across it effortlessly, landing on the far side without breaking stride.

He raced onward, upward. Until at last he came upon a path and halted for the first time. He crouched and surveyed the hill with calculating eyes. He saw the last of the torches disappear over the summit, and he was off again like an arrow streaking toward its mark.

A single torch might have been difficult to follow as it was carried behind trees or below a fold in the earth. But collectively the lights the villagers carried formed a glow that radiated into the sky. He was a moth drawn to that glow. Only this moth was bigger than the villagers had ever encountered. And it had a stinger!

He reached the summit. He was sweating. Yet his heart seemed to be pumping molten steel through his body instead of blood, for he was not the least bit winded. He worked his way through some brush, drawing closer to the light, and as he did so, the strains of a chant reached his ears. He cocked his head and listened intently. The cadence of the chant remained the same and was repeated over and over again. Though he could not say for sure, he thought it went something like:

Boom-Shacka.
Boom-Shacka.

Boom-Shacka-Lacka-Lacka!

"What sort of nonsense is that?" he muttered to himself, and he slunk through a cluster of trees, coming out at the crest of a deep, round hollow. The chorus was louder now; and, peering over the rim, he saw the villagers about one hundred yards below him. They were gathered in a large semi-circle, facing a clearing. At the far side was a massive throne that had been hewn from stone, and between it and the villagers, four tall stakes had been driven into the ground.

It was then he became aware of the tingling sensation in his hand, and when he looked down, he saw Slaybest was glowing faintly; (*orange, as I said earlier; not blue.*)

His heart sank. For he knew the meaning of the glow. Something malevolent was in the hollow, but whatever it was and whatever it needed still remained to be seen.

He started off again, slipping the weapon back into its scabbard. For he did not want its glow (*orange*) to betray his presence.

He crept from one tree to the next, slowly working his way down to the base of the hollow. The ground leveled off and he crouched behind a copse of thorn bushes. He peered above it, and discovered he was just outside the clearing, the villagers to his left, the throne to his right, and the stakes directly in front of him.

The flames from the torches bathed everything in an eerie light that alternately dimmed and brightened each time the wind picked up. Shadows danced about and, in the inconsistency of the light, they seemed to have a life of their own, one that was nurtured by the villagers' chanting.

Boom-Shacka.

Boom-Shacka.
Boom-Shacka-Lacka-Lacka!

Just then, Cower and Malady were brought from the darkness and taken to the stakes where they were quickly bound. The boys followed shortly after this, struggling to break free from their captors. Their efforts proved fruitless, and they were tied to the two remaining posts between their mother and the retainer.

When first he saw his companions, Bryand's heart leaped for joy. They were alive, and he thanked the Gods for their mercy. But from everything he had seen so far, he knew they would not be alive for long.

He eyed the villagers as they chanted. All told there were about twenty, and of these, about half were men. At any other time he might question whether he could defeat that many foes, but at that moment he was a man possessed, and he welcomed the odds.

He reached for Slaybest's hilt, and was about to unsheath it, when he became aware of a someone's presence. His hand arrested and his whole body tensed. He held his breath, then slowly, painstakingly, he turned his head and found none other than Daemon himself standing ten feet away.

The keeper was dressed in a grotesque costume. His face and bare chest were smeared with red clay, and he wore wooly skins about his lower abdomen and thighs. Upon his hands were fur gloves with sharp talons protruding from the fingertips, and atop his head was a woolly cap from which two lyre-shaped horns rose into the air. He was, as Bryand quickly surmised, the incarnation of the figure upon the dagger he had seen.

And suddenly the Prince was a child again, sitting on a work bench in the kitchen of his father's castle, while Mouck, the royal chef, whose cooking he had never liked, tried to frighten him with tales of demon-worshippers.

According to Mouch, they practiced human sacrifice in the dead of night. And the most powerful and cherished sacrifice of all, he had emphasized with ghoulish delight, was an innocent child.

Suddenly Daemon leaped into the clearing and danced toward the stakes, whirling, undulating, flailing his arms and growling like a beast. And as he performed, the villagers' chant built in volume and tempo.

Boom-Shacka.
Boom-Shacka.
Boom-Shacka-Lacka-Lacka!!

Demon-worshippers! thought the Prince, and a chill ran up his spine. But that's impossible! These are modern times!

Yet he was undoubtedly witnessing some sort of demonic rite.

The keeper circled each of the captives, bearing his teeth and flexing his claws. Malady screamed and fainted, Noim shut his eyes and turned away, and Cower, whose head had been bloodied, tore at his bonds. Only little Donoim seemed unshaken, and he stood erect, his shoulders back and a brazen sneer upon his face.

The chant reached a feverish pitch. Daemon pranced to the throne. Then, with a sweep of his hand, he took from a smoldering brazier, the dagger that had hung upon his wall.

"Boom-Shacka!" he bellowed gutturally, raising the dagger overhead. The chanting ceased, and for a brief moment the only sound was the wind sighing.

"Boom-Shacka! He who is guardian of the night! Yours is the way of darkness. And in that darkness is found new light!"

The shadows coiled around him, caressing his torso and limbs, and his eyes reflected the fire of his passion.

"Hear me, Boom-Shacka! It is I, Daemon, High Priest of your temple and teacher of your ways. Accept these sacrifices as a token of our devotion and grant us, Your loving servants, extended life."

To this, the villagers responded with:

Boom-Shacka! Boom-Shacka!
You've got the knacka-knacka!

"Thus we have lived through the ages. Life by life. Life for life. A year for the woman's. A year for the man's. And ten times that for each child's!"

Boom-Shacka! Boom-Shacka!
No turning backa-backa!

He held the dagger before him, eyeing it with adoration. "Black as is his realm. Burning as is his touch. This he sundered from his own hand and delivered unto us."

Boom-Shacka! Boom-Shacka!
Time to go whacka-whacka!!

His eyes ablaze, Daemon started toward Malady and raised the dagger to strike. Bryand knew there was no time to waste. Plan or no plan, he had to act. So he drew Slaybest, which glowed like a fiery brand, and he rushed into the clearing, uttering a savage cry.

Startled, Daemon faltered in his step, and before he could recover, the Prince swung his sword and struck the dagger from the keeper's hand.

Sparks erupted when the two blades met, smoke

rose up, and the air was filled with the smell of burned flesh. Yet Bryand took no notice of it as he bore down upon the priest.

Daemon started for the dagger, but the Prince quickly blocked his path. Outraged by this, the priest snarled and slashed at Bryand with the claws on his gloves; whereupon, the Prince dodged the attack and smashed the pummel of his weapon into the priest's face.

Daemon fell to the ground, stunned, and before he could recover, Bryand was upon him, pressing the point of his blade into the priest's throat. For a moment he stood over the man, his chest heaving, his blood hot with rage, and he would have killed him willingly had not his reason prevailed.

"Make not a move," spat Bryand, his voice quivering. "Or your life ends here and now!"

He looked up and saw the villagers closing fast. "Stay where you are! All of you! Do as I say or I'll send him to your precious Boom-Shacka!"

They halted, and eyed him like savage beasts.

"That's tellin' 'em!" shouted Donoim gleefully.

"On your feet," growled the Prince. But the man made no attempt to do so. "Did you not hear me!? I said, on your feet!"

Daemon rose, wearing a smug grin. "You have entered the realm of darkness," said the priest calmly, confidently. "Try as you may, there is no escape for you or your family."

"Silence!" Bryand commanded, pressing the blade into Daemon's flesh. "Sacrifice yourselves for all I care, but you will not harm any loved one of mine."

From the corner of his eye, the Prince saw two villagers stealing toward him.

"Come any closer," called Bryand, addressing them, "and your High Priest is worms' meat!"

They froze in their tracks.

"Now set my family free!"

"No!" shouted Daemon to his followers. "They belong to our lord. The lord of our lives! The lord of our souls!"

Bryand took the hilt of his sword and smashed it against Daemon's skull, sending him to the ground again.

"Do it!" cried the Prince murderously, "Or he's dead!"

"No!" called Daemon from where he lay. "Do not fear for me! Ours is the way to eternal life. If I am struck down, I will rise again within the kingdom of our lord!"

"Not another word!" snarled the Prince, pressing the point of his blade into the keeper's chest until it had pierced his skin.

But Daemon seemed impervious to the wound. "Do not let them go," he shouted to his followers. "My life is insignificant compared to the years you will glean from their sacrifice!"

There was much confusion among the villagers.

Someone shouted, "No! You are our leader."

Another said, "We will not give you up!"

"You must!" replied Daemon. Then a wild look fell across his face.

"For I go to the land of darkness to pay tribute to our Lord. Hear me, Boom-Shacka. I come to you now. Take me to your bosom as I journey into the darkness that is your glorious keep."

Whereupon, he smiled triumphantly at the Prince, then slowly pulled himself onto Slaybest until it was buried in his chest up to the hilt. Bryand looked on, horrified, and the villagers wailed with grief.

"You will know the wrath of Boom-Shacka," croaked Daemon through a gush of blood. "Before this night is over, you will know."

The fanatical leer lingered on as the keeper's eyes drifted to Bryand's chest. But then the look changed to one of total shock.

He gazed at the Prince again, thwarted, betrayed, whereupon his knees buckled, and he slid off the sword in a heap at Bryand's feet.

The Prince stared at him, visibly shaken. Involuntarily, his hand came up, and he fingered the tiny charm that Aldina had placed around his neck.

But at that same moment, a villager rushed him, knife in hand, uttering a vengeful cry. The sound jolted Bryand back to his senses, and unleashing all of his fury, the Prince cut him down with a swipe of his blade, then met another, and another, and another still, until four men lay dead about their leader.

"Who's next?!" shouted Bryand, brandishing his weapon.

Two men accepted the challenge and came at him from opposite sides. Bryand locked hilts with one, and for a brief moment they balanced there, two equal and unyielding forces.

Then, using the man's strength against him, the Prince grabbed hold of his jerkin and together they spun about just as the other villager thrust his blade at what had been the Prince's back. Thus, one man was slain by his own comrade and the other fell victim to Bryand's fury.

During this, another villager had worked his way behind the Prince and now ran toward him holding aloft an axe. "Behind you!" cried Cower with alarm.

The Prince turned just in time and parried the intended death blow. Filled with renewed wrath, Bryand struck out savagely, wielding his blade back and forth, pressing the man against the base of the throne until at last he saw his opening and plunged Slaybest into the villager's chest.

The man's eyes rolled up in his head, his mouth fell open, and he slid to the ground, leaving a smear of blood upon the stone. Bryand removed his sword and whirled about toward the clearing, ready for the next assault. But none came. The remaining villagers, fearing for their lives, had scattered into the surrounding darkness.

Wasting not a moment more, the Prince rushed to the stakes and hacked at his companions' bonds until all had been set free.

"My lord," said Cower, anguished. "My purse... The diamonds..."

Remembering the purse, Bryand pulled it from his belt and handed it to the retainer. Cower tore it open, hoping beyond hope their fortune had been somehow saved. But when he saw the purse was empty, his shoulders slumped and a look of disappointment fell across his face.

"Never mind the diamonds. We've got to -- ."

"But, my lord. Our fortune. Our army!"

"What a fight!" said Donoim gleefully, slicing the air with an imaginary sword.

"No time to waste," said Bryand in a husky voice. His throat was tight; only now did he become aware of a terrible thirst. "We've got to get out of here!"

He propped Malady up against the stake to which she had been tied, then slapped her repeatedly on her cheeks, coaxing her back to consciousness.

Upon seeing the Prince, she wrapped her arms around his neck.

"I thought I was dead for sure." But when she spied the carnage about them, she paused abruptly and said no more.

It was then the look on her face went from joy to horror and then to revulsion.

So quick was the change that Bryand turned to

see what had caused it, and together they watched in stunned silence as the bodies on the ground aged at an accelerated rate. First their skin and muscles withered. Then their organs shriveled, popping from the air left inside them, juices escaping everywhere. Until at length, *(which was only about a minute or so,)* they were dry and brittle, and crumbled into dust.

"Didja see that?" asked Donoim, amazed. "That weren't natural."

Though Cower remained transfixed, he still managed to correct the boy. "Wasn't natural."

"Wait a minute," said Malady, aghast. "Maybe we're all dead, an' this is the netherworld."

"You're alive," choked Bryand, prying himself free of her strangle hold. "But we've got to hurry. The others may return." He placed her arm behind his head and lifted her onto her feet. "Anyone know what happened to the horses?"

"Aye," said Cower, supporting Malady under her other arm. "When they jumped me, I saw them being led away behind the far side of the village."

"Then we've got to go back there. Quickly now, lads... Lads?!"

Noim and Donoim were fighting over the ceremonial dagger, tugging it back and forth between them.

"I saw it first!" whined the little one.

"But I grabbed it first. Let go!"

However, they did not have time to decide the issue. All at once, the earth began to tremble, and then to quake. Behind the throne, a massive boulder cracked as if it was as thin as an eggshell. Trees, one after another, on all sides of the hollow, rose as if the earth beneath them had spit them out, then, limbs cracking, branches snapping, they toppled in heaps onto the floor.

"What's this, what's this?!" Malady screeched in terror.

"Boys!" shouted Bryand above the growing roar. But they did not hear him, or would not hear him, for they stood arrested as the ground began to crack around their feet.

"What's happenin'" said Noim as Bryand grabbed them both and rushed them away.

Suddenly the ground between the stakes and the throne split open and a violent upsurge of flames and molten rock spewed into the sky in a fiery effulgence. A deep, guttural growl erupted from the fissure; another; and another still, resounding like a deafening roar, and from out of the blazing release, in all his demonic hideousness, Boom-Shacka emerged.

He was as tall as the trees, the color of rancid blood, with dagger-like teeth and ripping claws. Everything about him was evil and malignant and reached from a time before time itself, when chaos reigned and all was darkness.

Bryand clutched Cower's sleeve. "Get the others away," he whispered, his eyes glued upon the demon. "And don't come back."

However, doing such a thing was contrary to Cower's personal code of honor, needless to say his unwavering devotion to the Prince. "No, my lord, I won't -- ."

"You will!" said Bryand with a hard look. "I command you!"

The Prince did not wait for a reply. He rose to his feet and circled cautiously around Boom-Shacka, who followed him with his eyes.

Bryand hefted Slaybest, which was as brilliant as the sun, and, with a boldness that surprised even himself, the Prince bowed most graciously

"Boom-Shacka, I presume. What brings you up from the depths?"

Boom-Shacka's eyes blazed. "Mortal!" he boomed in a sonorous voice that shook the ground and sent tremors through the Prince. "You have slain my priest and defiled my temple!"

Bryand's jaw slackened with surprise. He had never expected the demon to speak. And so intelligently, too.

This gave the Prince an idea. He would engage the demon in a conversation, and hopefully, by doing that, give the others the time they needed to escape. He knew it was ludicrous, even outrageous. But then again, this was a demon he intended to address. What could be more ludicrous or outrageous than that?

"Well, there I must differ with you," said the Prince judiciously. "True your priest is slain. But technically Daemon took his own life. Let's be clear about that. And I'm not the one who tore up the ground and spit hot rocks everywhere. We mustn't blame others for our own sloppiness, must we?"

The demon bellowed with contempt and rage, a sound so fierce that even the trees seemed to shrink from it.

"I take it you disagree."

"Impudent fool!" thundered the demon. "You know not with whom you trifle. I am Boom-Shacka! All that I touch turns to fire and ash!"

To emphasize this, the demon reached out his hand and placed it lightly on the top of a tree. It exploded instantaneously in a mass of flames and billowing smoke.

Bryand nodded with respect. "You must be very popular during the colder months. Have you ever thought of hiring out?"

The demon's eyes narrowed menacingly. "You will not be so arrogant when you smell the stench of your own flesh burning."

"Oh, I've no intention of doing that," said the

Prince, his eyes darting about the clearing.

And when he was certain Cower and the others had slipped away, he presented the demon with a defiant look.

"As you can plainly see from the number of dead, I'm a very handy swordsman. And I've a blade here," said Bryand, bringing Slaybest up for the demon to see, "that was made for folks like you."

Boom-Shacka laughed aloud, a sound so deafening the Prince could do naught but cover his ears. "Do you really expect me to shrink in fear from that? A branding iron?"

"This is no branding iron," rejoined the Prince. "This is Slaybest, sword of the Jaspers, destroyer of evil and defender of righteousness."

The demon nodded. "I've heard tell of it."

"Then you should be impressed."

The demon crouched and bared his teeth. Spittle fell from his mouth in smoky streams that hissed when they hit the ground.

"Tell me," the demon chortled. "Is that all you rely on to save yourself?"

Bryand readied himself. Yet even as he did so, the Prince knew he could never withstand such an onslaught as the demon was capable of rendering. "'Tis enough, I'll warrant it."

"Then say farewell to your world, mortal," said Boom-Shacka, his eyes narrowing. "And prepare yourself for the agony of mine."

Boom-Shacka pounced, raking the air with his claws. Bryand dodged one hand and met the other with a powerful swipe of his weapon. Slaybest glowed like a red hot poker, and cut into the demon's flesh with a hiss. Boom-Shacka drew back, startled, and examined the wound. "No one has ever done that to me."

"Well, Boomie, there's a first time for everything."

The demon roared in angry frustration, then stared at Bryand with smoldering eyes *(literally.)*

"I will cook you slowly, mortal, till you are crisp on the outside, but tender and juicy on the inside."

"Don't plan your dinner menu around me, demon. You'll find yourself lacking a main course."

Boom-Shacka pounced, attempting to grab the Prince. But with a quick leap, Bryand avoided his clutches, and brought his weapon down, severing a finger from the demon's hand.

Boom-Shacka howled in pain. But this time, instead of breaking off the attack, the demon intensified it.

Though Bryand used all his skill, he found himself being pushed back toward the base of the alter. (*After all, the demon was tree-sized, which made the Prince - when compared to Boom-Shacka - not much bigger than a woodchuck.*)

Bryand began to tire, and the demon, seeing this, gave out with a demoniacal laugh (*as demons are apt to do.*)

"Puny, mortal," sneered Boom-Shacka. "Did you think you could outlast me? My strength comes from evil itself. It is as boundless as the sea. As endless as the sky."

"Let me guess. You enjoy using cliches whenever possible."

The demon had had all he intended to endure of Bryand's insults and came at the Prince, his claws raking the air. Bryand repelled the attack for what seemed an eternity, using all of his prowess and wits.

Finally, however, the demon proved to be too great a threat, and the Prince found himself back-handed with such force that he went sailing through the air and landed on the seat of Boom-Shacka's throne.

It's over, thought Bryand, hanging onto consciousness by a thread. I'll never be king. King?! I'll never be found!

Boom-Shacka's face blotted out the sky. The Prince stiffened even in his dazed state, and he felt the heat, the blistering heat, though for some reason in his confusion, it felt as if it rose from him and not the demon.

Bryand saw the demon's hand come up, rippling in the heat. His claws closed around the Prince, but suddenly the demon lurched backwards as if in pain, and let go of him. Yet the heat still remained, so intense now he thought his brains would fry.

Boom-Shacka stared at the burned flesh on his palm, incredulous, then bent low and scrutinized the Prince.

Just as the innkeeper's eyes had drifted to the Prince's chest, so too did Boom-Shacka's. It was then a combination of horror and shock swept across the demon's face. He stared at Bryand, at his chest again. Then he bounded backwards, repelled in some way.

"No! No! No!" he ranted, stomping the ground like a child in the throes of a tantrum. "It can't be! It can't be! I'm too evil to be cheated by such villainy!"

He swung at the trees about the clearing, shredding limbs and splintering trunks in a blind fury. Fiery leaves drifted everywhere. Brilliant embers rose up into the night.

And when everything about him was ravaged and in flames, he spun about and loomed over the Prince. "You are lucky today, mortal!"

Bryand's hand came up to his chest and touched the tiny medallion that lay there. Somehow it was protecting him.

"I guess -- ; I lead -- ; a charmed life," muttered the Prince, which sent the demon raging once more.

Finally, the demon took one last swipe at the

empty air. Then, grumbling, cursing, he strode to the fissure and began to descend.

But before he was completely out of sight, he cast the Prince a menacing look and said, "Listen carefully, mortal. Never take it off; that charm of yours. Not if you care to live. For the day you do, will be the day I claim you."

And with that, he dropped out of sight.

At length, Bryand dragged himself to where Slaybest had landed and took hold of the sword. Once again the blade was its normal self, but it was now scorched and covered by a thin layer of black ash.

He stood, tottering actually, barely conscious, and wiped his sweat-covered face with the back of his hand.

It's so hot, he thought. Why is it so hot?

His clothes were drenched. His throat was on fire. Water, he thought, I need some water.

He tried to walk, but the heat had sapped his strength. His knees buckled under him and he collapsed upon the ground.

He gazed from where he lay at the sulfurous smoke rising out of the fissure. It swirled and coiled into the air, lulling him into a dream-like state.

And then, from the recesses of his mind, emerging from a time long forgotten, he heard a voice calling. A child's voice, filled with innocence and glee.

It might have been his own voice when he was younger. Or Daron's, perhaps; he did not really know. Nevertheless, it filled him with peace as it chimed ever so sweetly, "Night, night, dear Cower. Until the morrow and the sun is up. In the meantime, I'm off to beddy-by land."

CHAPTER TWENTY THREE

The Duke of Cunninghim stood at his window. Draped across his shoulders was a soft woolen shawl, the greenish-blue color of clingtuya ivy. A steaming cup of spiced redfruit cider warmed his hands.

From his window, he could see the distant hills to the east. He watched the darkness slowly recede and the morning light broach the hilltops.

He did this often, but he enjoyed it most on sunny days. There he would wait in eager anticipation for the moment when the light first struck the battlements of the city. At that hour, they were always moist with dew.

He held his breath. And then, in an instant, the sunlight touched the wall, transforming it into a monument of dazzling colors. It was a thrilling sight, and perhaps the very reason why he wanted to own the city.

Bandidon; it had always held a strange fascination for him. Even when he was just a lad. The sights, the sounds, the smells - at times they had almost overwhelmed his senses.

And the people! They had taught him so much! Up to their knees in offal, struggling day after day to make a living - it was from these simple men and women he had learned the futility of work.

He knew at quite a young age he was different from them. The way they embraced each other in harmony and good fellowship; such mawkishness had always seemed useless to him, even somewhat sickening.

Perhaps if he had known his mother and father better, his life might have turned out differently. He might have developed feelings like kindness and empathy, generosity and humility.

But the fire he had started at the foot of their bed, had ruined any chances of that long ago or of his further understanding the mysteries of the heart.

The heart. What was so important about it, anyway? All it did was confuse things with sentimentality. What did a good ruler need with that? A good ruler, kept himself aloof; detached; removed from the people. In this way he could best see what were their overall needs.

Take this new tax, he thought. What kind of way was that to support the royal treasury? Being chiefly responsible for its collection, he had seen the trouble it had caused, the anger, the suffering. None of it was necessary.

Under his rule, people would be forbidden to earn any income at all, thus there would be no need to tax a portion of it. All commerce and trade would be done in his, the King's name, and he, as the patriarch of the nation, would provide for his subjects according to their individual needs.

Therefore, the poor man who managed to get by on little, would get little, and the rich man who required more to suit his lifestyle, would get more. So simple, he thought, pulling the shawl tighter around him.

From below him came the sounds of the city waking up. The clang of a blacksmith's hammer. The town cryer calling out his morning salutations. The street urchins begging for coins.

Ah, the city! So alive; so vital. He cherished every aspect of it; save one - its name.

He scowled and shook his head. Bandidon was too reminiscent of bygone days, and of Bryand's, or rather, Daron's rule.

He wanted to be free of any attachments to the past (*actually, he wanted to erase the past completely and start History over beginning with his reign,*) and one way of doing so was to rename the capital the moment he took control.

He had chosen the name long ago, upon the very day he decided to murder and conspire his way to the throne.

"Cunhimia," said the Duke, grinning. "Cunninghim of Cunhimia." He would often say it aloud, though only when he was alone, repeating it again and again, emphasizing each syllable for dramatic effect.

Am I deluding myself, he thought, glowing with pride. Does it not have a distinctive sound to it? He already knew the answer to his query. But sometimes, he wanted the pleasure of hearing someone else say it, too.

He turned to Nightshade, who, having fallen asleep the previous night in a drunken stupor, was slumped in a chair and snoring softly.

"Nightshade!" called the Duke eagerly. "Wake up man, I want your opinion about something."

Nightshade twitched and raised his head, but his eyes stayed closed. "What's that?"

"What do you think of Cunhimia?"

Nightshade opened his eyes, smacked his lips, and let some gas escape first from one end and then the other.

He looked about, confused. "What am I doing here? This is not my room. Mine's the one with the beige settee."

Cunninghim stared at him, filled with sudden repugnance. "Never mind. Go back to sleep. You make things less difficult that way."

There was a knock upon the door. Cunninghim heard it and turned to his servant, Gofor, who was lying on a bench at the front of the room.

"Well?" said the Duke. "Are you going to answer that?"

Gofor, a small man whose features resembled a field mouse's, stared absently at his master and made no attempt to get up. Cunninghim frowned and was about to rebuke the man, when he remembered Nightshade had tested a new concoction on him the night before, one that had left him seriously paralyzed.

"Don't you dare take anything else the Earl offers you," groused Cunninghim as he crossed the room. He took a moment to adjust his shawl and opened the door. Outside stood a tall, lanky fellow wearing a soldier's tunic and helm. "What do you want?"

"I must speak to the Duke of Cunninghim," said Reggie Grumble.

"Do you know what time it is?"

"Aye. Tis early, I know. I should be heading for my post right now, but I have information the Duke will find most interesting."

Cunninghim scowled. Another weasel attempting to profit from some useless gossip. Was there no end to them?

"Get to your post, yeoman, before you're listed as absent."

"This concerns my post. You see, I guard the north tower and the person who presently occupies it."

Cunninghim, who had been poised to slam the door in the man's face, suddenly found himself intrigued. He had sent no one to the tower, nor had Nightshade. If indeed anyone was captive there, it could only have been the King's doing. Yet why had he kept it a secret from him?

"I see," said the Duke. He scrutinized the man for

any weapons, and finding none, Cunninghim bade him to enter.

"Very well then," said the Duke. "Tell me what you know."

"I'm sorry," replied Grumble, glancing at Nightshade. "But it is for the Duke's ears alone."

"I am the Duke."

Reggie was surprised. "You? But you answered the door like a common servant."

Cunninghim shot Gofor a withering glance. "Aye. I do that from time to time. It keeps me humble. Now what is it you wish to tell me?"

Reggie hesitated. Planning this confrontation had been far easier than carrying it out. He was nervous in the Duke's presence and uncomfortable.

"Well, m'lord, you see -- . I'm a poor man. I've many debts. A yeoman's pay doesn't go very far these days, and, well -- . I've been told you're a generous man."

"Whoever told you that should have also mentioned I never pay for anything in advance of delivery. If I consider this information of yours worthwhile to me, then and only then, will I reward you. But know you this as well. I enjoy not being disturbed by someone who brings me useless information. Especially at this time of day."

Fearful now, Reggie told him everything about the woman prisoner who claimed the King was really an imposter.

"Most interesting," said Cunninghim cagily. "Did she happen to mention her name?"

"Aye, m'lord. She called herself the Lady MeAnne."

He was excited now. But years of duplicity had taught him to keep a placid expression upon his face.

"You were right to come to me." Cunninghim crossed to his table and picked up his purse. He paused.

"How many others have you spoken to of this?"

"No one, m'lord. You were the first person that came to mind."

Cunninghim nodded his approval. "What is your name, man?"

"Grumble, sire. Reggie Grumble."

"Good work, Yeoman Grumble," said Cunninghim as he tossed him the purse. "You deserve that and more. And you shall have it."

"Thank you, m'lord," replied Reggie, ecstatic.

"Now wait outside while I decide how best to employ your services."

"But my post, m'lord."

"Yeoman, do I not command the Royal Guard?"

"Aye, m'lord."

"Then stop worrying about your post and do as you're told."

Reggie bowed, a bit too dramatically. But his mind was already on his newly found wealth.

He went to the door and opened it, whereupon a look of fear fell across his face.

"Godzilla!" he shouted as he jumped backwards into the room.

Godzilla - a contraction of the older idiomatic phrase 'The Gods' will upon us.'

For standing in the doorway was Mortamour, the Captain of the Guards, so disheveled and covered with dust that he looked much like the ghost of his former self.

"What happened to you?" said Cunninghim, aghast.

Mortamour staggered into the room, ignoring Grumble completely. He went directly to the pitcher of wine upon Cunninghim's table, scooped it up and drained it without pausing to take a breath. "I had to walk nearly thirty miles, is what happened. Not a horse in sight in all that time. Not even a blasted cart."

The sudden outburst had awakened Nightshade,

and he sat up and looked about, confused. He noticed Mortamour immediately and frowned - not because of his appearance, but because he was drinking up all the wine.

"Easy there, my friend," said Nightshade, watching Mortamour drain a second cup. "Wouldn't want you to choke."

Mortamour ignored him, and drank until the pitcher was upside down and altogether empty.

"You might have saved me a drop," said the Earl peevishly in a dry, hoarse voice. "How's a man to get started in the morning?"

Mortamour collapsed into a chair by the table and sighed deeply. Yet before he settled himself and yielded to his fatigue, he leaned over and removed his boots, grunting with the effort.

He let each boot fall to the floor with a thunk and worked his toes back and forth until all ten had cracked.

"Ahhhhh!" he sighed "I've been wanting to do that for nearly fifteen miles."

"Perhaps the Captain would like some water?" asked Grumble timidly.

Scowling, Mortamour looked at him for the first time, but said nothing. Reggie felt his stomach drop. He had never met the man, but knew enough from the stories he had heard to avoid him whenever possible. "Perhaps some more wine instead?"

"That's a good idea, Reggie," said Cunninghim. "Find the Castle Steward and beg some in my name."

"Aye, m'lord," said Grumble moving instantly. In a moment he was out of the room.

"Who's he?" growled Mortamour.

"That's what I'd like to know," muttered Nightshade. But then he remembered the man was going for more wine. "Though he seems like a nice sort of chap."

"I'll explain his presence in a minute," said Cunninghim, leaning on the table. "First you must tell me how you came to be in such a frightful state."

Mortamour snorted and shook his head, and after a moment's pause, he said reluctantly, "We were attacked by Woolly-Bullies." The doubt on Cunninghim's face was unmistakable. "I knew you wouldn't believe me."

"Oh, please!" rejoined the Duke sternly. "You forget it was I who first concocted that tale."

"I tell you it's true. We'd just made camp for the night on the Eastern road, when all of a sudden the Prince came bounding out of the woods several strides ahead of a dozen Woolly-Bullies. They were Smellys. I'm sure of it."

"How do you know that?" asked Cunninghim coolly.

Mortamour furrowed his brow and shot him an incredulous look. "They smelled, of course!"

At the mention of the Prince, Nightshade alerted. "Bryand, you say?" He rolled forward, and with a hopeful look in his eyes, he said, "Did you snare him?"

Mortamour sneered and lowered his gaze. "No."

"Why not?" asked Cunninghim, who was most displeased with the news.

"Because there was no time! Before we knew what was happening we were set upon. Blistering irons! They're a fearsome bunch. I was lucky to escape with both my ears."

"And how many men escaped with you?" asked Cunninghim in an icy tone.

Mortamour's cheeks flushed. "None."

"You mean to say a whole company of guards couldn't defeat twelve Woolly-Bullies?!"

"We weren't a whole company by then," answered Mortamour defensively. "I'd lost some men in the Ankledeep and some in the swamps while chasing the

Prince."

Reminded now of the humiliation he had suffered, the henchman gnashed his teeth and pounded his thighs with his fists. "Blast the man! I'll roast his liver when I see him next."

"Really," said Cunninghim dubiously. "You might try catching him first."

Mortamour scowled at the rebuke but made no attempt to reply, and he sat there with his arms folded, devising hideous tortures to perform upon the Prince once the royal had fallen into his clutches.

Nightshade, however, was not as calm or deliberate as either of his companions. He was perspiring and his head ached. Oh, for a cup of wine, he thought, wiping his brow.

He stood and shot Mortamour a contemptuous look. "Bungler!" he snapped, surprising the henchman. "Do you know what you've done? You've sunk us! Because of you, we'll be sent to the frontier, or worse: to the block!"

Mortamour jumped to his feet and snarled, "Don't you dare try to blame this on me. If you hadn't provided Daron with an antidote to your poisons, things would be all together different right now!"

"I will not be spoken to like that!"

"I'll speak to you any way I like, and if I see you anywhere near my drink, I'll slit your gullet and strangle you with your own innards!"

"Stop it. The both of you," Cunninghim commanded. He crossed to the large map on his wall, depicting Bandidon and the adjoining kingdoms. "You say this happened on the Eastern road."

"Aye," grumbled the henchman.

"He's obviously heading for his friends."

"Willowbrook and Pepperill can no longer help him. I've seen to that. And I was just starting off for Torkelstone when I stumbled upon the Prince."

"And King Jasper, what of him?"

"He's dead."

"Well, that's something at any rate," conceded Cunninghim.

"I'd say that's a bit more than just something," argued Mortamour.

He understood he was not of their station, that as a commoner he was obliged to bow to them and do their bidding. But that did not stop him from speaking his mind when he felt justified. He was not afraid of either of them. He knew every heinous act they had perpetrated over the past fifteen years, had been the instrument of their deviousness for most of them, and they knew he knew.

"Stop brooding," said the Duke. "Look, you, I appreciate your efforts, I really do, and I recognize how frustrating it must have been when the Prince eluded you."

"Thank you," said Mortamour reluctantly. "You've no idea how difficult it can be in the field sometimes. The obstacles that get in your way-- . A man needs a little encouragement every now and then. A pat on the back. That's not asking much. Not for all I do."

"You are absolutely right," Cunninghim agreed. "Isn't he Nightshade?"

"Yes, yes," the Earl replied without any real enthusiasm. For inwardly he was thinking, "What a baby."

Presuming all grievances had been aired and settled, Cunninghim went to the window and considered the information Reggie had brought him. Obviously, MeAnne had learned the truth about the King, or why would Daron have locked her up? He wondered how he might use this knowledge to his best advantage, and how, with Bryand still at large, he was going to avoid losing his head?

But nothing came to him, and turning to his associates, Cunninghim found them arguing again.

"He's just one man," bleated Nightshade. "With those tracking skills of yours, one would think you could actually catch someone."

Mortamour smashed his fist upon the table. "I tell you, I'd've nabbed him if it hadn't been for them blasted Woolly-Bullies!"

"Well, you'd better get used to them, my friend, for we're off to the frontier for sure now!"

Woolly-Bullies, Cunninghim reflected. Nightshade was right to fear them. Whole armies had broken the moment their savage war cries rose up. Even the bravest of men had been known to faint in their presence. If only they were his to command. He would be invincible, unstoppable. He would explode like a firestorm across the land.

Cunninghim's eyes glowed with a fierce intensity as he pictured himself at the head of the screaming highlanders. And then it struck him, a plan so complete in every detail that he was convinced Rapscallion, (*the God of mischief and intrigues,*) had reached down from his dungeon cell beneath the Heavenly Halls and touched him upon the head.

The Heavenly Halls being the palace where the one hundred and eighty three Bandidonian Gods reside. It was quite crowded for the first millennium or so, until several wings were added on by Condominius, the God of multiple dwellings. Although some like Humble-Pious thought it much too lavish and overbearing, most of the other deities were pleased - especially those on the upper floors who had better views.

It was daring. No, it was downright dangerous. But it intrigued him nevertheless. Ally myself with the Woolly-Bullies, he thought. Now there's a madcap scheme. But at the same time he knew it was brilliant. All it would take for the plot to succeed was a clever man to execute it, one with high aspirations and an overwhelming desire to subjugate the world.

Ignoring his associates, Cunninghim turned back to the map, and he saw the whole plan unfold before him. I could sweep down from the north and cut off the frontier outpost before anyone there had time to alert the kingdoms. Once it was leveled, I'd drive through Cumberland, then straight into the heart of Bandidon before the King could muster a command.

From each town along the way, I'd recruit the very same cutthroats and thieves I'd sent there to defend the crown. We'd be at the capital gates in four month's time. Perhaps even less. And faced with such overwhelming odds, Daron would have to surrender the throne.

Cunninghim faced his associates once more and strode to the table, barely able to contain his excitement. But though he tried to get their attention, Nightshade and Mortamour paid him no heed.

"A stuffed pig's bladder!" growled the henchman. "That's what you are!"

"Go on," snapped Nightshade, his face beet red. "Strike me if you dare. I've enough poison in me that I need only to spit on you and your face would rot!"

"Enough of this!" shouted Cunninghim harshly, getting their attention at last. "I've no time for this foolish bickering. There's much to do!"

It was then they heard a discrete knock on the door, and Grumble poked his head inside.

"Come in! Come in!" said Cunninghim, crossing to the door. The Duke guided him to the table and took the wine from him.

"I'll take that," said Nightshade, reaching for the pitcher.

Cunninghim shot him a baleful look and placed the wine deliberately on the table. "Let me introduce you to my friends." And he did so most graciously.

"Reggie came to me this morning with some rather distressing news," continued Cunninghim, and it was here he lowered his voice and sounded most conspiratorial.

"I commend his bravery, for such knowledge could have sent him to the block were I a different person. I entrust it now to you, my friends, should something sinister happen to me, so that you might prevail against the evil that has been perpetrated against our beloved country."

Nightshade and Mortamour glanced at each other, then back at Cunninghim.

"The King is an imposter. He calls himself Bryand, but he is really his twin. Daron has stolen his brother's identity, and his throne, and now rules in his stead."

Once again Nightshade and Mortamour looked at each other. This was no news to them, they had known the truth for weeks already. But being well practiced in the art of deception, they pretended to be shocked for Yeoman Grumble's benefit.

"You can imagine the implications," said Cunninghim gravely. "I've also learned, thanks to Reggie here, that the Princess MeAnne is being held in the north tower."

This news genuinely grabbed their attention.

"We must see she is taken to safety before that madman causes her more pain. It is our duty."

Cunninghim turned to Grumble, smiling. "As for you, Lieutenant," said the Duke, clapping the man on his shoulder. "I've an important job for you."

"Lieutenant?" echoed Grumble, his eyes agog.

"Aye. We know not one another very well yet, but something tells me you are a stalwart fellow. One worthy of my faith and trust. Therefore, I am awarding you with a field commission in advance of your mission."

Things were happening so fast, his head was spinning. He had never expected to be taken into the Duke's confidence like this, and as a lieutenant, he had just been elevated to a position far above one he could ever have obtained by his own means, even if he had remained in the guard his whole life.

"My sword is yours!" proclaimed the new officer, and he slapped his hip. However, in his exuberance he had forgotten he had no sword.

"That's quite all right," said Cunninghim, seeing his embarrassment. "The sentiment is what counts. Though it would be wise if you found a weapon soon. Now! About your mission."

Cunninghim leaned in closer. This he did for effect.

"You must set the Princess free and bring her safely to the main ward. The Earl and I will be mounted and waiting there for you and, together, we will spirit the lady away to Castle Nightshade."

Cunninghim unsheathed his dagger and cut the money purse from Nightshade's belt.

"What-- ? See here!" protested the Earl.

But Cunninghim ignored him. "Find the Dungeon Warden and show him this." He tossed Grumble the purse. "He'll recognize the Earl's sigil. Buy yourself a key to the north tower door. Be careful. He is not a very trustworthy person."

This he knew for certain, having chosen the man himself.

"Say nothing to him about the lady MeAnne or about anything else you've learned. Do it quickly, for we should be well away before the King awakens."

"Aye, m'lord," said Grumble, hefting the purse, and he started for the door.

"Hear you this, Reggie," added Cunninghim. The lieutenant halted and turned to him. "You must not fail.

Were it just our lives, I would not be half so concerned, but the fate of the country, the land we love, depends upon it as well."

"Aye, m'lord," answered Grumble exuberantly, and with shoulders back and head held high, he pulled open the door and slammed it shut behind him.

"Weren't you laying it on rather thick?" asked Mortamour.

The Duke grinned. "Perhaps."

"I wish you'd let me in on what you have in mind," said Nightshade petulantly. "I don't like being left in the dark."

"I'll explain everything to you on the road. Once we're a safe distance from the capital." Cunninghim turned to Mortamour. "Now for you."

"But I've just returned," growled the henchman.

"That can't be helped. Gather another command. Take a whole regiment. Two if you must. But I want Torkelstone Castle destroyed and the Prince dispatched for good."

A steely look came into Cunninghim's eyes and his voice became deliberate. "Understand me, Mortamour. You must succeed at this."

"Aye," said the henchman obediently, yet with little warmth.

His hand went to the gold ring on his finger; the only piece of jewelry that he wore or owned. It was awarded to him the day he attained the rank of Master from the Assassin's Guild. Since that day, he had not taken it off.

"Oh this ring, I swear it." And gathering what dignity he could along with his boots, Mortamour departed.

"Answer me this," asked Nightshade, fingering his goblet, for he had managed to sneak himself a sip when the Duke was not looking. "If we have to leave so quickly, why are we bothering with the girl?"

"For insurance. In case Mortamour fails to eliminate the Prince and he turns up down the road."

Cunninghim strolled to the bench where Gofor still lay. "And how are you? Any movement yet?"

The man could do nothing more than look at him and drool. Cunninghim shook his head regretfully and sighed.

"Then I'm afraid, my friend, you'll have to stay behind and shoulder the king's wrath."

Gofor's eyes opened wider.

"One consolation, though," said the Duke, patting his servant's hand. "You won't feel a thing."

MeAnne went to the door and dropped to her knees. Dearest Gods, she thought. Please let it be today. I don't think I can stand much more of this confinement. It's already changed the texture of my hair.

She leaned over, pressed her cheek against the cold stone, and peeked out through the narrow gap below the bottom of the door. To her dismay, she found the hallway empty and Grumble nowhere in sight.

"Reggie?" she called, thinking him temporarily away from his post; for there were times when he would visit the nearest garderobe to answer Nature's call.

But after many minutes, he still had not appeared. Perhaps it's earlier than I thought, she told herself, and he has yet to report for duty. So she waited there until her back ached and she was thoroughly chilled from crouching upon the floor.

At length, MeAnne sat up and peered about the room, knowing that, if she did not set her mind on something else, she would succumb to the fear that had taken root inside her lately.

Each day it had grown a little stronger and a little harder to control. Though she tried to deny it, in her heart she knew the isolation had already done something to her thinking. Not that she was coming unhinged. Certainly not that.

She was royalty; and royals never came unhinged. Royals acted peculiar, and that was all.

Oh, this is silly, she thought. It is nothing. A trifle! Merely some unwanted behavior of which I can rid myself whenever I so choose.

The behavior she was referring to had started as a simple game, a fanciful diversion, with her imitating the birds as they flew by. Each time she heard them chirping she would hasten to her window and watch them soaring through the sky.

It was so liberating to her bruised and ailing spirits that soon she was racing around the room in large overlapping circles, her arms outstretched like wings, fully cheered, pretending to be just like them as they glided on the wind.

But just the other day, and this she hated to admit, with no recollection of how or when it had started, MeAnne had found herself, as if coming out of a dream, standing on the bed, flapping her arms and squawking.

As much as this disturbed her, she found the empty void from which she had emerged, even more distressing. Where had she gone? Certainly no where in a physical sense. It was obviously somewhere within her mind. And this undermined her courage.

She rose to her feet and plodded toward her bed, but with every step it seemed more and more like a futile journey. She came abreast of the pine box and halted. She gazed at it, at the simplicity of its design. Nothing to fear, she told herself. Just a box with a dead body in it. That is all.

It was then a far-off look came into her eyes. In

the time between two heartbeats, she had crossed once again into the realm she feared. And there she lingered, completely unaware.

When Reggie opened the door and saw her, he could not help but falter in his step. "My lady?" he called, shocked, for the last thing he had expected to find, was the Princess MeAnne perched atop a coffin. "Do you always relax like that?"

MeAnne blinked. Are those words I hear? Presently, she had no idea where she was. Just a moment ago, she had been high up in the air, above the battlements of her father's castle, making broad lazy circles like a sparrow hawk.

"My lady?" asked Grumble tentatively.

"Reggie?" She hardly noticed his new uniform and cape. "Is that you?"

"Aye, m'lady." The soldier took a small step closer. "Are you feeling well?"

"What do you mean?"

"It's just that -- . You're, uh, standin' on a coffin."

MeAnne did not believe him at first, but looking down she noticed that, not only was she standing on the box, but she was standing on it using only one foot. In addition to this superior feat of balance, she also noticed that her hands were tucked under her armpits giving her arms the appearance of wings.

"Oh, no," she muttered, her stomach dropping. The strange behavior had emerged once again.

"My lady, are you all right?"

Out of sheer panic, she leaped from the box and hugged herself. "No! Can't you see what this place is doing to me? Take me away from here. Please, Reggie; I implore you!"

"But that is exactly why I've come. Haven't you noticed the door? It's open. I found a key!"

She looked at him, trembling. "What did you say? My mind is not working very well these days."

"You're free, my lady! Your escape is at hand!"

"Free?" she repeated, barely daring to believe it.

"Aye, but we must hurry! I've brought you a cloak," said Grumble as he threw it around her shoulders.

"It's nothing fancy, but it will keep you warm against the morning chill. Oh, before I forget. Those gems of yours? I'll need that stone you promised me; it took all my cash to secure the key."

"There," she said, nodding toward the table, upon which sat the ornamental comb. "It's yours. The whole piece. Just tell me this is really happening."

How odd royalty is at times, he said to himself. "Aye, my lady. This is really happening."

She thought she had spilled the last of her tears, but her eyes filled with more, and, overflowing, they ran down her cheeks in two streams. This time, however, they were tears of joy, and she put her arms around him and hugged him out of gratitude.

He did not know how to react. So, he stood with his hands at his sides and waited until she was done. "Ready, m'lady?"

"Aye."

She started forward but then remembered the other jewels. "Uh, Reggie, perhaps you would give me a little privacy before we set out."

He gave her a quizzical look. "Privacy, my lady?"

"Aye," she replied looking purposely at her chamber pot and then back at him.

It took him a moment, but then he understood. "Oh!! Of course, my lady. I'll be right outside."

He hastened out of the room and shut the door behind him.

MeAnne hurried to her bed. She removed the jeweled pin, the pearl, and ring from beneath her pillow and placed them in the inside pocket of her riding cape.

After that she took care of her other business, knowing it was always better to start a journey with an empty bladder no matter what the situation.

"Ready," she called, standing by her bed.

When Reggie opened the door, a rush of cool air came through the embrasure. She drew some deep into her lungs, nodded to herself and started across the room.

She said goodbye to the queen beneath her breath, then skirted the box and joined the guard at the threshold.

She took his arm and held it tightly, afraid something unseen might draw her back into the room. She shut her eyes, allowing him to guide her, and when she opened them again, she was outside the chamber and they were starting down the tower steps.

She gasped with relief and began to tremble.

"Stay here," said Grumble leaning her against the wall.

"Where are you going?" she said at once.

He looked at her; saw the fear on her face. "Only to lock the door behind us," he said. "We don't want people to know you've escaped."

"Escaped," she said, a nervous smile slowly curling her lips. "We have, haven't we?"

"Aye, my lady," said Reggie, patting her hand. "But let's not get too sure of ourselves. We've only just begun."

By a dark and forgotten stairwell, they reached the ward and headed for the stable. It was on the wall opposite the keep, separated by an open stretch of ground some twenty yards wide.

At any other time they would have been seen by the guards upon the battlements. But there was much smoke from the kitchen fires at that time of the morning and very little breeze. They crossed the ward and entered the stables without being discovered.

Reggie led her down the row of stalls, stopping at the far end where two well-groomed horses stood saddled and waiting. He handed MeAnne one set of reins, boosted her up, and mounted the other horse.

"Ready?" he asked.

"Yes," said MeAnne. But then, her voice quivering, she added, "Thank you, Reggie. I won't forget you for this."

"M'lady has already paid me more than I deserve," said Grumble. To himself, he also noted, between the gems and what the Duke gave me, I'm as rich as the best of 'em.

They prodded their horses into motion and were about to exit the stable when Cunninghim and the Earl of Nightshade, astride their own horses, greeted them at the opening.

"What goes here?" asked MeAnne, reining her mount to a halt. She turned to Reggie for an answer, defiance in her eyes. He was about to respond but the Duke spoke first.

"My lady, if we are to escape we must move quickly."

"Escape? You?" she said suspiciously. "I don't understand."

"When there's time I'll explain more. For now, please pull up your hood and play your part at the gate."

"My part?" asked MeAnne.

"Aye, as Gofor, my servant. Speak not a word no matter what you hear me say. And do nothing that would attract attention to yourself in any way. Your hood, please, my lady?"

They worked their way through the city, whose streets were filled now with people about their chores or selling their wares. The activity served as a miracle tonic for MeAnne's ailing spirits.

She had hungered so long for the company of others that everyone she beheld seemed wonderfully alive; everything they touched appeared vivid in texture or color. There, a row of brilliant ribbons and garlands. There, baskets of red and green melons. There a rack of polished daggers and swords. Oooo, swords!

She was like a child again at her first bazaar, and it took all her willpower to keep from jumping off her horse and shopping for an hour or two.

When they approached the checkpoint before the city gate they were halted only briefly. Being the Commander of the Guards, Cunninghim could come and go as he pleased. Still, he did not want anyone discovering MeAnne.

But when he turned in his saddle, he saw there was nothing to fear. The Princess, acting like a good manservant ever mindful of his place, had drawn her cloak about her and very humbly bowed her head.

"Inform the king once he has awakened," said the Duke to the officer in charge, "that the Prince was last seen headed for Torkelstone."

"Is this good news or bad, my lord?" asked the officer, who was not eager to approach the King about anything.

"And what difference does that make?"

"Just tryin' to figure out what I'm facin' is all, my lord."

Cunninghim pursed his lips. My these new guards were cheeky.

"Good news for sure," said the Duke. "Tell him two regiments have already been dispatched and that I, ever diligent in my duty, am on my way there to witness the Prince's capture. Inform his Majesty, every effort will be made to take the Prince alive and to keep him in good health until I have returned with him. He should be most pleased to hear that, too."

"Very good, your lordship," said the guard, waving the party on, and turning toward the gate, he called to the men posted there. "Make way for the Lord High Protector and the Commander of the Guard, his servant, a lieutenant and one corpulent gentleman who looks very hung over!"

The men at the gate stood at attention, looking straight ahead, without even so much as a glance at the Commander who saluted them with his riding crop as he passed.

"Well, that was easy," said Cunninghim, pleased with the way things had gone.

"That was insulting," said Nightshade, his cheeks flushing (*more from drink than indignation.*) "Why didn't you tell that man who I was?"

Cunninghim glanced at him, unperturbed. "Because I didn't want the King thinking we had deserted him entirely."

"But what if he comes looking for me?"

"What for?"

"I don't know. Perhaps to ask my opinion on some important matter of state?"

Cunninghim's lips curled into a grin. "Don't worry. He won't."

They crossed the outlying fields and entered a dense cluster of trees. When the city was no longer in sight, they spurred their horses and road at the gallop.

They proceeded this way for close to an hour before they slowed and walked their mounts down a gentle slope covered with flowering clover. It was here Cunninghim dropped back to the Princess and revealed the events that had led to their flight.

"So you see, my lady, we are all fugitives now. My deepest regret is that I only discovered your plight just a few short hours ago. Thank the Gods Reggie here had the good sense to inform me."

"Aye," said MeAnne, glancing at the guard fondly. "And for that I will be eternally grateful. But tell me something, my lord. Why is it we travel West when Jasperland lies to the Southeast?"

Cunninghim was not often taken by surprise, but the girl had found a way. He had never expected her to be so astute, and he found himself at a loss for words.

Nightshade, however, attempting to remedy the situation, chuckled and said, "But we are traveling East."

"Really? Am I now to assume the sun rises in the western sky, my lord?"

"No, no," fumbled Nightshade, digging himself an even deeper hole. "The sun rises in the East, but -- ."

"Then it should be in our faces and not at our backs as it has been since we left the capital."

"You are correct, my lady," said Cunninghim plainly. "We make our way west, to Castle Nightshade."

"You are to be my guest," added the Earl.

MeAnne frowned. "But what can be accomplished by that? Surely, Jasperland should be our destination. My father must learn of Daron's treachery. Not only does he have an army to oppose the usurper, but being the Council Majority Leader, he has the means to organize the other kings as well."

Which is exactly why I had him eliminated, thought Cunninghim shrewdly. But to the Princess he presented a sorrowful look and reined his mounted to a halt. When MeAnne and the others had done so as well, he said, "My lady, I had hoped to see you stronger before I informed you of this."

"Informed me of what?" asked MeAnne.

"Your father, my lady." He paused, trying to appear concerned but in reality, it was more for dramatic effect.

"Tell me," said MeAnne, gripping the pummel of her saddle.

"He was one of the first to suffer Daron's cruelty."

Just from the tone of his voice, she knew tragic news was in store. "He's dead, isn't he?"

Cunninghim reached for her hand. "I'm very sorry, my dear."

MeAnne swallowed hard. No more tears, she told herself. No more tears. "And the rest of my family?" She had barely gotten the words out.

"They are also with the Gods."

She had never known such pain. It stole her breath away. She wanted to scream but her jaw was clenched so tightly, she could not utter a sound.

Everything, time, the seasons, the wind, her heart, with the utterance of just a few words, had come to a sudden halt, and for an instant, she expected darkness, like the darkness of her nightmares, to descend with the same finality upon her and the rest of the world.

But the darkness did not come, and air somehow found its way into her lungs. Her heart, though still aching, began to beat again, furiously at first, and then its normal rhythm.

The sounds and smells of the world returned, led by a vanguard breeze that brought with it the fragrance of honey, and lastly, with the same inevitability that made it lord of everything, Time started up as if it had never stopped.

"Thank you, my lord, for telling me," she said at last, staring hard at the road ahead.

He had expected her to burst into tears or to faint. But to his surprise she shouldered the blow with the endurance of a veteran soldier - in silence.

"Forgive me, my lady," he pressed. "That I should be the one to hurt you, is something I must bear. But know you this: I would as lief besmirch my own good name than ever hurt you again."

He paused, waiting for some kind of response from her. When none came, he said, "I believe we are a safe enough distance from the city now. Would you like to rest?"

"No," replied MeAnne in a flat tone of voice.

"Perhaps a sip of wine, then," offered Nightshade, concerned. "I've a skin right here on my saddle."

"No!" she said adamantly. It was then her lips curled down into a hard frown, and with a swift kick and a slap of her reins, she set her horse running at the gallop.

The three men watched her for a moment, then Cunninghim said, "Reggie, stay with her."

"Aye, m'lord," responded the officer, and he galloped off in pursuit of the girl.

Cunninghim watched her ride. As good as any man, he thought. And with a disciplined mind, too. She would make an excellent queen some day. "Excellent indeed," said the Duke aloud.

Nightshade, who had tempted only himself when offering MeAnne some wine, was just wiping his chin. "I'm sorry. Did you say something? I was swallowing."

"Merely thinking aloud."

"I see. Every time I chew or swallow, something happens to my hearing."

"Is that a fact," said Cunninghim dryly. And staring at the man's rotundity, he added, "It's a wonder you ever learned a thing."

CHAPTER TWENTY FOUR

Dwayne Pepperill sat with his hands folded in his lap as the orange glow from the campfire cast undulant shadows across his face. He bore a sober look, and every now and then he pursed his lips and ground his molars together. It had been three days since they had fallen prey to Kussensuch and his band of thieves, and for three days they had followed a trail of mutton shanks and capon carcasses and other assorted litter.

However, due to the inhospitable nature of the terrain and the inclement weather, they had been unable to narrow the distance between them, and he feared by the time they finally caught up to Kussensuch, the entire cartage of food would be gone.

"How much longer are you going to act like this?" asked Niles from the other side of the campfire. Dwayne ignored him. Niles picked up a makeshift skewer that had been resting over the flames.

"Look. I made you a local delicacy: roast lizard. Don't worry about picking the meat off the bones, the full enjoyment is in eating it whole."

"I don't want any, thank you," replied Dwayne courteously but with no real hint of warmth, and he tossed a twig into the fire.

Niles shrugged, then pulled a lizard from the skewer and bit off a piece. Save for the muffled crunch of bones, all was silent for a beat.

After he had sufficiently chewed the morsel into pulp, Niles swallowed it with a grimace. But for Dwayne's sake he grinned and said in an exaggerated tone of voice, "Mmmmm! Very tasty. And so tender, too. You have no idea what you're missing."

"I said I didn't want any," retorted Dwayne.

Niles placed the skewer back into the fire. "You know, you could try being a bit more gracious. After all, I did go out and find us the only decent meal in this entire wasteland."

"Well, you needn't have done it. Not for my sake at any rate," said Dwayne, staring into the darkness. "So let's drop the subject."

"All right," replied Niles, adjusting the bandage across his forehead. "If that's what you want."

"That's what I want."

They sat in silence once more. But if there was one thing Niles truly hated, it was silence. "I think we've seen the last of the rain for awhile," he said, looking up at the heavens through a break in the trees. It was a clear night save for a cloud or two, and the sky was rich with a treasury of stars.

"The air no longer smells like it. And speaking of smells, I think I've lost the last trace of gagger stench."

He glanced at Dwayne and waited for a response. But when none came, he said, "Unless, of course, I've just gotten used to it."

He chuckled, a bit too loudly. Still Dwayne made no effort to reply.

More silence.

Niles felt his stomach muscles tighten and the blood rush to his face, and with a scowl, he said pointedly, "It's your turn."

Dwayne looked at him, slightly puzzled. "My turn?"

"To say something! You might try: "Is that so?" or "Isn't that interesting," or "I couldn't care less what you smell like!" Anything. Just say something, will you?!"

"I don't wish to discuss it, thank you."

"Very well then," insisted Niles, springing to his feet. "Let's discuss something else. Like, what an ungrateful ass you are at times!"

"Don't you start on my bum," growled Dwayne, pointing his finger at him. "With the mood I'm in, I'm likely to twist you around a tree."

Niles snorted. "You've a far bigger problem than your buttocks, my friend. This self-righteousness of yours is positively insufferable."

Dwayne rose slowly to his feet, his eyes smoldering. But Niles stood his ground.

"That's right - insufferable! From the way you act, one would think you were the only person around here with any character."

Though they differed in height by at least ten inches and in weight by more than forty pounds, Niles was too angry now to concern himself with the thrashing he was risking.

"Let me remind you that if it weren't for me you'd still be hanging by your heels from a tree like a freshly slaughtered pig. Though right now, I can't imagine why I made the effort. I should have listened to you and let you martyr yourself over that stupid cart of food."

Niles felt something tickle his nose, and he scratched it. His fingers came away wet with blood.

"That's what you wanted, wasn't it, to sacrifice yourself for a pair of hams?" And in a tone dripping with sarcasm, he added, "Aye sir, the world would have long remembered you for that gallant gesture; you'd have been immortalized for sure!"

"Now you've done it," said Dwayne churlishly. He was looking at Niles' forehead. "You've opened up your wound again."

Niles hand went immediately to the cut on his forehead.

"Who cares about that?" retorted Niles, brushing away the blood that had trickled down his cheek. "It's nothing."

Dwayne shook his head and snorted. "Now who's being the martyr? Sit down by the fire and let me have a look at it."

"I don't need your help," said Niles irritably as he adjusted the bandage, the front of which had turned dark brown with his blood.

"Niles, it needs tending."

"Absolutely not. If I allowed you to help, you'd no longer be beholden to me. Then I'd have to suffer your pomposity forever."

"Sit down, Niles."

The young man grudgingly obeyed.

Dwayne removed the bandage and examined the wound. It had bled many times. Having no water in the area that was not tainted or crawling with one thing or another, the wound had been difficult to clean and soon began to fester. And now Niles' whole forehead was red and puffy.

"Ouch!"

"Sorry," said Dwayne.

"I forgive you," replied Niles. Then, with a haughty grin, he added, "For everything."

Dwayne stared at him and chuckled in spite of himself. But he quickly sobered and said, "It's bad, Niles."

Niles' grin waned. "How bad is 'bad'?"

"It will kill you unless we do something about it."

"Like what?" asked the young man warily, feeling his heart quicken in pace.

Dwayne glanced at the fire, then back at Niles. "I'll

have to cauterize it."

"You mean, burn my face?" said Niles incredulously. He felt a bead of sweat trickle down the gully between his shoulder blades. "Oh no you won't. No one burns my face. Burning my face is definitely out of the question."

"It's the only way."

"Not as far as I'm concerned," said Niles, scrambling to his feet.

Dwayne followed him. "Listen to me-- ."

"No!"

"Do you want to die?" asked Dwayne. Niles purposely looked away. "Do you? Because that is exactly what will happen if you don't let me cauterize that wound."

The blood was flowing freely down Niles' face now, and he dabbed at it with the sodden bandage. "There's no chance it will heal by itself?"

"I've seen its like many times, Niles. Believe me. If you let it fester much longer, the poison from it will get into your blood, and when it does, there will be no saving you. We can wait if you like, but the odds will be even greater that you'll die."

Dwayne's voice was filled with such sincerity that Niles could do naught but agree.

Dwayne pulled a vine free from over their heads. "This should do well enough," he said, tying one end around Niles.

He guided him to the trunk, stood him with his back to it, then began to wind the rest of the vine around Niles and the tree. "Normally, there would be two or three surgeons to hold you down lest you squirm too much."

"Well, you know me," said Niles nervously. "I can squirm out of anything. What's the difference between a wiggle and a squirm?"

"What?" said Dwayne, looking at him.

"I don't know. But I think one involves pain and the other doesn't."

Dwayne continued with his winding.

"Tell me something," said Niles with a nervous snort. He was sweating profusely. "You're not just doing this to get back at me for jesting about your bum all these years? You wouldn't be that cruel, would you?"

"Certainly not," said Dwayne, pretending to be insulted. Then a smile played at the corners of his mouth. "Although, I must admit, it is a just reward."

He placed his foot upon the tree, and using it for leverage, pulled the vine tighter. "Too tight?"

"No," replied Niles tersely.

"That's no good," he grunted, pulling harder. "I can't have you moving about on me. How's that?"

"Much better. Who needs to breathe."

"I'm glad to see this hasn't effected your sense of humor. You're as obnoxious as ever."

Dwayne tied off the vine, then strode to the fire and knelt before it. "I have to say, this is the hardest thing I've ever had to do."

"I believe it. But don't let that slow you any. I'm already having trouble breathing and my courage is dwindling as I speak."

"Then here we go," said Dwayne, selecting a flame-stick the size of a dagger and, shielding it from the breeze, he returned to his friend. "Ready?"

Niles' chest was heaving. He could not answer, but he nodded his head affirmatively, then shut his eyes and gnashed his teeth.

Dwayne placed his hand over Niles' mouth. He pressed Niles' head firmly against the tree. "Shut your eyes," he said, and brought the flame stick closer.

Niles felt the heat from the flame. He went rigid and sucked in a breath through his nose. And then there was such an intense pain that his whole body convulsed, and from deep within his throat a scream erupted. But it never had time to escape. Niles had fainted.

Thank the Gods he's out, thought Dwayne, proceeding with his task. The stench of burning flesh was all around him, in his face, in his eyes, up his nose, and it made him sick to his stomach.

At length he finished sealing the wound, and with a grimace, he dropped the smoking cautery by his foot and ground it into the dirt.

He untied the vine and carried Niles to the fire, sat, and held his friend in his arms, blowing on the wound and fanning it throughout the long night.

And when the campfire was only embers and the sky was growing light, Dwayne placed Niles gently upon the ground and covered him with their blanket. Then he, too, laid down and waited for sleep to overtake him.

Soon his eyelids were very heavy, and the darkness behind them was all he saw. His breathing slowed, became rhythmic and deep. He was just drifting off to the land of slumber, when a voice interrupted his departure and shook him abruptly awake.

"Hey there! I'm hungry. And with all this pain you've put me through, you could at least scare up some breakfast."

Two days later, after Niles had regained a measure of his strength, he and Dwayne set off to find Kussensuch and his band of thieves. They shared the same purpose (*with a few subtle differences, that is. For Dwayne, it meant recovering the food at all costs.*

For Niles, however, someone who had always believed

in the ancient saying "Lose and eye, take an eye; lose a tooth, punch them harder," it meant recovering the food, and then changing the current leadership of the TCG of B, Sherman Oaks chapter.)

"Look," said Niles, pointing to a pile of dark brown spoor upon the trail. He and Dwayne knelt beside it. "See how course and irregular it is. That's a strong indication of a varied diet."

I must say that Niles never felt more alive than when he was hunting or tracking. From what I learned of his past, he had spend most of his life among the trees, sleeping under the stars. He admitted to me once, over a large tankard of ale, that he did not completely understand himself; the way he would quit his friends for weeks at a time just to pit his skills against the rigors and challenges of the woods.

Yet as perplexing as it was to him, he felt no shame about it. In fact; it was a source of pride. So much so, that he hoped one day in the distant future to organize a competition where contestants from all walks of life could test themselves using only the crudest of weapons, to see just how long in the savage wild they could survive.

Being his loyal friend, and, I like to think, someone with a good measure of common sense, I never had the heart to tell him what a truly stupid idea I believed it was.

Niles grabbed a stick and cut off a piece of the spoor. "Notice its consistency. Do you see how the surface has hardened slightly but the inside is still soft?" Dwayne nodded. "I'd say this is only a day old. Perhaps even less."

Niles brought the stick to his nose. "And from the strong smell, it was definitely a man who made this shit."

"Aye, but is it the right man's shit?" asked Dwayne staring down the trail. "We haven't seen any wagon tracks for a long time now."

"Well," replied Niles, undaunted. "That could be

because the ground here is hard. Or because the cart is considerably lighter now."

Dwayne made a grumbling sound in the back of his throat much like a dog did right before it growled. "Come on."

And he was off and running.

The following day, they came to a hillock, and climbing to the top, they found, just behind a ring of tangled brush, a small clearing.

I say a clearing but it was anything but. For it was -- . It was -- .

A small pause here while I gag.

For it it was littered with mound upon mound of human excrement and various other offal and debris.

The pungent odors of decay, filth, and sweat hung over the place like a stubborn fog. Nowhere had they seen such a collection of garbage or smelled its like, except perhaps the yeomens' billet at the capital which was famous for its stench.

I do not pretend to understand what it is about men that, when collected in a confined space, causes them to abandon all the things about their natures that would be consider civilized. Bodily functions such as the passing of gas become the source of their humor; picking snot from their noses and rolling it into tiny balls with which they can flick at one another; and worst of all, snapping towels at unprotected rears.

They worked their way between mounds of waste, food scraps, hoary bones and feces, swatting flies away with one hand, covering their noses with the other. At the far side of the dump, (*which, by the way, would have made any farmer rich from the wealth of compost he could harvest,*) they came to a small path.

Being careful not to make a sound, they followed the path a short way, and rounding a bend, they discovered a second clearing, wherein stood almost a dozen ramshackle huts made from sod and stone and dead leaves and branches.

They had found Kussensuch's camp. But much to their consternation, nary a guild member was to be seen.

Scattered about the camp were more piles of rubbish that smelled almost as bad as the dump. But here were also collected the prizes Kussensuch and his men had stolen during their tenure as Sherman Oaks' only authorized group of thieves.

There were wardrobes and chairs and tables and carpetbags full of clothing and chests full of tools and armor and kitchen utensils. There were sacks of grain and bales of fodder, cut timbers, carpenters' saws, blacksmiths' anvils, and even several tanner's frames with hides still stretched upon them.

"Well, it appears they've kept themselves quite busy," said Niles, eyeing the various stores.

"Aye," agreed Dwayne, frowning. "Very busy indeed."

A large fire pit had been built at the camp's center, and to this Niles went directly. He crouched, and held his hand inches above the coals.

"Still warm," he said. He took a stick and stirred the ashes, and from under the top layer, he turned up some glowing coals.

"They were here this morning," announced the young man, eager now as he studied the ground. There were many overlapping footprints about, but the freshest of them converged at the far end of the clearing.

"And I think I just found the way they went."

When Dwayne did not respond, he looked up and discovered he had been talking to himself. Niles scanned the surroundings.

"Hello, hello; where did you go?"

"Here," replied Dwayne, stepping from the side of a hut. He bore a grim expression. Joining him, Niles saw the empty cart, and his heart sank.

"I'm sorry, Dwayne."

"It's not your fault," said the young man, scowling. "Some wrongs can be easily righted, while others-- ."

He did not complete the sentence, but, instead, picked up a lone grape from the bed of the cart and threw it into the bushes.

They continued their search, passing more piles of booty. On the perimeter of the camp in what was a small natural goiter surrounded by dense shrubs and pinenut trees, they discovered a shed built mostly of stones with a heavy wooden door that had been padlocked.

"This is interesting," said Niles, examining the door. He peered through a knothole. "I wonder what's in here?"

"Let's find out," said Dwayne, backing up.

Nile shook his head. "You're not really going to try and break it down, are you?"

"Aye," Dwayne said.

"That only works in stories."

Dwayne backed up a few more paces, his eyes locked upon the door.

"Stand aside, Niles," He said resolutely.

"If you'd just listen to me-- . "

"No games, Niles. Stand aside."

Niles purses his lips, shrugged, and did as Dwayne bade. "Do it if you must."

The path now clear, Dwayne charged the door like an angry bull, which, upon impact, remained firmly in place as Niles predicted.

"I told you," said the young man, helping Dwayne

to his feet. "You're a brawny fellow, but a human battering ram, you are not. Can we try my way now?"

Dwayne rubbed his shoulder. "By all means."

Niles went about the camp perusing the stolen goods, whereupon he located a hammer and a chisel. With a smug grin, he held them up for Dwayne.

"What good will those do? That padlock is far too heavy to cut through it with a hammer and chisel."

"If you were half as observant as I, you'd know that the man who hung this door had the intelligence of a pea. For no one, who wanted to protect what's inside, would hang a door with its hinges on the outside."

Indeed, there they were, three in all, made of ironwork.

"Step back, please. I need some room; thank you." After just a few whacks, he had removed all the hinge pins, tossed aside the tools, and was brushing off his hands. "Now you may hit it."

Dwayne obeyed and gave the door a swift kick, and this time it surrendered to his strength, smacking against the inside wall, splintering its frame and tearing free from the padlock.

Light spilled inside the shed, clouded by billowing dust, and when the dust had settled, they found a cache of arms piled haphazardly upon the floor.

"What have we here?" said Niles eagerly. A crossbow lay just beyond the door, and behind it sat a leather pouch full of quarrels. "This should even the sides somewhat, eh?"

"Aye," said Dwayne, admiring a long pole overlaid with iron filigree. One end tapered to a point as sharp as a spear. He hefted it, noting its weight. Though a bit too heavy for other men, it was perfect for someone his size and with his strength.

"I'll take it," he said to himself with no misgiving, no pang of conscience this time around.

Seeing the weapon, Niles nodded. "That stick of yours looks quite formidable."

"Hmmm," said Dwayne. "I think that's what I'll call it."

"What? Formidable?"

"No. Stick." And he thrust it at an imaginary foe.

They armed themselves each with a sword and dagger, Stick, and the crossbow and quarrels Niles had chosen. Then, one by one, they cast into the woods in all directions the remaining swords and axes and cudgels they had found.

Nothing had changed about them physically save for the addition of their weapons. Yet the grim look on their faces and the deliberateness of their strides, said otherwise.

Wasting not a single moment more, they crossed the clearing and entered the woods, picking up Kussen-such's trail almost at once.

"Our initiation fees were a bit too high." said Niles, reading the signs upon the ground. "Don't you think? Or do you still insist you never joined."

"It makes no difference," Dwayne replied, hefting Stick. "Either way, we've a refund due us."

And with that said, Niles broke into a fast trot with Dwayne following close behind. The time for vengeance had come at last.

CHAPTER TWENTY FIVE

And speaking of vengeance, please forgive me, for I must pause to chastise my servant, Rolfo, once again. Though he is well on in years, the man still finds some fiendish pleasure in vexing me whenever he can. For example: just this morning, which was exceptionally cold, I awoke shivering, only to find my blanket missing. When I discovered it on Rolfo's bed and confronted him about it, he pretended to be innocent of the deed. The fool! With but the two of us living in this cave, who else could have been responsible!?

He says he's going vague in the head. To that, I say ha! And ha again! True the man's a dimwit when it comes to scholarly things, but he remains every bit as keen as me. He even knows I'm scribbling something about him now; I can see it in his beady little eyes. Oh, he pretends to go about his business, but I know him better than he thinks. Later, when I'm asleep, he'll unroll this scroll to see if I have written anything disparaging about him. Therefore, to you dear Rolfo, I say: GO BACK TO SLEEP, YOU NINNY! I WANT MY BREAKFAST SHARP AT SIX!

Now then...

With all that has transpired thus far, you might be wondering what the King, or Daron, I should say, was doing. And the answer to that is: nothing. Nothing, that is, outside of what he normally did, which was chase women and lavish himself with new clothes and jeweled buckles for his shoes.

Though he worried constantly about his brother turning up with an army or two, causing him much physical discomfort in his lower regions, the feasts went on as usual, as did the jousting and the archery contests, the horse races, and the new game he called, "Groping In The Garden."

Life at court was never more lavish, and those who thought of naught else but the gratification of their own personal needs were never more pleased to be present.

There were foods and wines from all over the United Kingdoms (Daron had ordered his storehouses stocked to the rafters,) nightly entertainments that could be anything from fifty exotic dancers, a troop of dueling magicians, or something the King called his "private showings," which entailed taking the members of the court to his chambers and modeling his newest clothes.

To those who were as shallow as the King, Bandidon was at the height of its glory. But in reality the country was going to ruin, and this was nowhere more apparent than in the Council of Kings.

"Order! Order!" shouted Daron irritably. "I cannot hear myself think!"

The other Kings around the council table quieted at once.

"That's better. My lords, with all that we have to accomplish today, could we not at least try to get through this first piece of business!?"

The other Kings stubbornly agreed.

"Good." He rubbed his face out of frustration. "Now then, the question still remains upon the table: who ordered the sliced ham!?"

"Certainly not I," said Mittashmeer, shuddering. "I never touch the stuff."

"I might have," said Fallacius, cocking an eyebrow. "But then again-- ."

"Well, someone did!" barked Daron.

Blunderon raised his hand. "It was I. I remember now."

The servant placed the platter in front of him. Blunderon picked up his knife and was about to commence when he noticed King Odius staring at him and frowning. "Is there a problem?"

"Oh, no," said Odius. "It's just that my brother died while eating ham."

The council chamber was a large room, with a massive stone fireplace whose mantle had been meticulously carved into the head of a dragon. The fire on the hearth was set each day, mostly for the effect, for once ablaze, it gave the appearance of being the dragon's own issue, and when the wind blew across the chimney in just the right way, a growl seemed to rise from deep inside its throat.

In front of the hearth was a rectangular table whose top was inlaid with tiny squares of wood, all different in shade and polished to a shine.

Daron insisted upon sitting at the end facing the fireplace. The other end was reserved for whomever he was angry with at the time.

For from Daron's point of view, the occupant was framed by the jaws of the dragon and looked as if he were about to be consumed.

He called it his "hot seat;" though he told no one. There were times when, becoming suddenly angry with someone else at the table, he would command the hot seat's occupant to switch places with the new offender. But this did not happen very often.

"Are you not hungry, my lord?" asked King Gluttonus, speaking with his mouth full.

Daron folded his arms and sighed. "No."

"In that case-- ." Gluttonus took Daron's plate and scraped it onto his own. "My mother told me never to waste food."

Daron suddenly found the man overwhelmingly repugnant. Needing to escape, he pushed his chair away from the table and went to the fireplace. He stared into the flames, feeling angry, discontent, but mostly confused.

A week had passed since he was informed of Cunninghim's departure for Torkelstone. Not a word had arrived since. What Daron thought particularly odd, was the fact that Cunninghim had left what's his name behind; the servant; prostrate on a bench and unable or unwilling to move.

Three days ago, after sending Pomp to look for Nightshade, the chamberlain had returned with a hastily scribbled note in Nightshade's handwriting. According to the Earl, he was on a foraging expedition for poisonous spores and fungi, and as this year had produced a bumper crop, he did not know when he would return.

It was almost as if they had abandoned him; left him flat, like he was some country cousin.

Just then, his stomach grumbled loud enough for the others around the table to hear.

"Are you sure you're not hungry, your grace," said Gluttonus through a mouth full of food. "I can always spit some back onto my plate."

"No," said Daron with a rancorous sneer. "Once chewed, it's pretty much yours."

His thoughts returned to Nightshade and Cunninghim. I should never have treated them so shabbily. Or threatened them with the frontier. He would have to go a long way before finding men as capable; and with such specialized skills.

Though Daron had never liked admitting he was wrong, not even to himself, he decided to be especially attentive to their needs when next he saw them, which, with any luck, would only be a few more days.

How long could gathering fungi take? And Cunninghim had Mortamour with him; a very capable fellow. Surely they were already heading back to the capital with Bryand in chains.

He thought of Bryand trudging along behind Cunninghim's horse, beaten, weary, without a single hope; and this cheered him.

Aye, I'd like to see that, Daron mused with a private smile.

However, it was then a new thought struck him and the lift in his spirits deflated like a punctured pig's bladder. Bryand was a capable man; a fact that Daron could no longer deny. Suppose, during the march back to the capital, Bryand managed to convince Cunninghim of his true identity? Then all would be ruined.

He would return to the capital not in chains, but with Cunninghim's support. Unlike Willowbrook and Pepperill, or even Torkelstone for that matter, Cunninghim was a man with real power. Daron himself had proclaimed him Lord High Protector and Commander In Chief of the Royal Guard.

The Royal Guard! he thought, his stomach twisting into a knot. More than enough men to kick me off the throne and proclaim himself king.

This is bad, thought Daron, sweat beading on his forehead. This is very bad. Worse than that, it's catastrophic!

He stood for a moment, plagued with fear, wondering - of all things - if they would let him keep his wardrobe.

"My lord," someone spoke in a respectful tone.

"Aye," replied the King, distracted.

Blunderon joined him at the fireplace. "We've a dispute on the table."

"What is it this time? Did someone forget who ordered the roast beef?"

"Roast beef, your grace? I didn't see it on the menu. If I had, I surely would have-- ."

"The dispute, man!" Daron exploded. "Tell me about the dispute!"

Bluderon cringed. "The issue of the river Gentleflow, your grace. It remains unsettled between lords Ikenfloss and Gallstone. Since the river divides Gonad from Upper Thorax the entire council has taken up the issue. Fallacius now claims it has always belonged to Upper Thorax, but Mittashmeer insists he's lying."

Suddenly Daron had had enough of being King, of being Bryand. He wanted nothing more than to cast everything aside and run away.

He whirled on Blunderon, his face contorted in a hateful sneer, shouting, "Damn the Gentleflow! Damn it all!" And without another word, he smashed his fists upon the dragon's nose and stormed out of the room.

Blunderon stood for a moment, contemplating. Then he faced the others, and with a shrug, said, "You heard him. Dam the Gentleflow."

"Aye," said Mittashmeer, staring at Fallacius, who was nodding in accordance. "That's an excellent solution. Perhaps just above where the river has changed course?"

More "ayes" came from around the table. Also, King Gluttonous wanted the relish passed his way.

Indeed, it was the first time they had agreed upon anything since before the old King's death.

With the sound of his footsteps echoing all around him, Daron raced along the castle's corridors, heedless of the strange looks he received from the lords and ladies he passed. His face was very pale, and he was sweating profusely. He held his stomach tight as if by doing so he could prevent himself from being sick.

At last he reached the Royal Apartment, whereupon he threw open the door, dashed across the outer room, and into his private chamber.

"Mercy!" cried Gabble from atop his bed. "Whatever is the matter, my lord!?" Since the day he met her and brought her to his room, she had remained in it, and was by this time, too him, as much a part of its appointments as were the goose down pillows.

"Not now!" he barked, rushing toward his commode.

"Can I help in any way?"

"No!"

She knew he was serious when he pulled down his leggings and bared his bottom.

"Oh, dear," said the girl, flustered. "I'll--. I'll just give you some privacy."

She fled the room, shutting the door behind her. She stood there for a moment, trying to ignore the sounds coming from the other side.

"Strange, how you've been sick so much lately," said Gabble to the door. "You must have a touch of something. Or perhaps you ate a piece of tainted meat. Did you have any fruit today? Too much fruit can give you the runs, you know. That's why I'll only eat one piece a day. My Aunt Anadda gets the runs. Though why, I couldn't say. She hates fruit. Never touches it. On the other hand, my Uncle Clobber, her husband, eats fruit all the time and never ever has loose bowels."

A thought struck her as funny, and she giggled. "Perhaps it is he who gives Aunt Anadda the runs. A distinct possibility, knowing Uncle Clobber as I do. The man is such a grouse! Grouse, grouse, grouse! That's all he ever does. If I had to live with someone like that, I'd be going to the pot all day, too."

"Gabble! Please!" called Daron.

"I'm sorry. I must be distracting you. I know how important it is to concentrate when you're answering Nature's call. As you've said in the past, it's when you do your best thinking. I for one find standing in a pitch-black room the quickest way to obtain some wanted insight. Of course it only works at night. However, if I find I must think decisively during the day, I try standing close to a wall. So close that my nose touches the stone, and in this way I can see only a dark gray blur."

She waited for a response but none came. She waited a moment more, then she pushed open the door and peeked inside, finding the King on the edge of his bed, his face buried in his hands.

"Would you like me to bring you something for your stomach? Perhaps a sprig of mint? You know, my mother used to chew on the leaves whenever her stomach was feeling poorly, that or-- ."

"No," said the King abruptly, before she went off again on another extemporization. "Just come and sit beside me."

"Aye, my lord," said the girl dutifully.

Daron watched her approach. How strange it was that, out of all the women in the entire Kingdom, he had chosen a servant girl to befriend. Though she would talk and talk - sometimes for hours on end - there were also times she would listen attentively, and without being judgmental.

"Gabble," said Daron, his eyes awash with tears. "I don't know what to do."

Her face, always well scrubbed and full of color, became the reflection of her concern. "What troubles you, my lord?" said the girl, slipping her hand into his.

Daron stared at the floor. "I've done so many hateful things, and soon I'll be held accountable for them."

"You, my lord?" said Gabble, surprised. "I find that hard to believe. You have never been anything but kind to me."

"All the same, it is true. I've hurt people. I've caused them much pain."

"In what way?"

"I've stolen something that doesn't belong to me. I lied and cheated to obtain it. And now that it's mine, I can hardly sleep or eat or-- ." He glanced at her, embarrassed. "You know."

She squeezed his hand and said, "Then you should make amends."

He turned to her. She smiled compassionately. "You really think so?"

"Aye, my lord. When he was younger, my grandfather stole a sack of grain. But when he was questioned by the local magistrate, he blamed it on another man, a neighbor, who then suffered great pains because of my grandfather's lie. My grandfather, however, the one who caused all the trouble, bought the neighbor's property for a song, married the man's widow, and prospered for the rest of his life."

"Forgive me, my dear," said Daron, frowning. "But I fail to see the point you are trying to make."

"Simply this, my lord. Though he lived well into his sixties, had nine surviving children and a dozen healthy grandchildren, he was bereft of the one thing he wanted most."

"And what was that?" asked the King anxiously.

"A hammock. There was nary a tree to hang one from."

Daron stared at her in disbelief. "A hammock!? That's it!?"

"Don't you see? It wasn't the hammock itself that was so important. But what it represented."

"And what was that?" rejoined the King, dubious.

Gabble patted his hand and looked into his eyes. "Peace of mind, of course. That's what he really wanted."

In silence, Daron rose and walked to the window. He leaned against the frame and looked outside, finding a solitary mason atop the inner curtain, humming to himself as he repaired the wall. And for the first time in his life he found himself envying someone of the lower class. "It would be so nice to sleep again."

"Then you must do what you need to. In order to accomplish what you desire."

He thought of MeAnne at once, shut up in the north tower all this time with only a corpse for company. "Aye. I've got to make amends."

He turned to Gabble. "Thank you, my dear."

She smiled at him. "My lord is too kind."

He felt a sudden urge to make love to her, to stroke her hair and kiss her face. But he knew he should settle things with MeAnne first. So he ignored the stirring in his loins, (*which in itself was an accomplishment for Daron,*) and bid her to wait for him in bed.

He went directly to the Castle Warden whereupon he secured the key to the north tower.

He took note of the filings along the shaft and bow. "Is this new?" he asked, turning the key in his hands.

The Warden cleared his throat and said, "Aye, your grace. The old one needed replacing."

"I see," replied Daron. But he was not really listening. "Glad you're keeping the place up."

There was a jauntiness to his step now as he made his way along the corridors. He was filled with a calm he had not felt for a very long time.

Perhaps Gabble is right, he thought. Being honest and reputable must have some reward. I'm feeling much better.

So much so, that when he rounded the corner and saw the tower door upon the landing just ahead, he became giddy and even light-headed. He knew not what he would say to MeAnne once they were face to face, nor did he care what the consequences would be once he had released her. All he wanted was his peace of mind restored.

He bounded up the short flight of steps two at a time, a smile stretching across his face. He unlocked the door, opened it, and took a bold step inside.

He was surprised to find her not yet up and about, but then it occurred to him, being confined as she was, there was no reason for her to rise at a specific time of day.

He padded to the bed, thinking to awaken her with a gentle tap. But when he drew near and saw the bed was full of covers and pillows only, he faltered in his step. He looked about the room, at the key in his hand, and then it dawned on him.

MeAnne had escaped.

"Oh, no," said Daron aloud. "This cannot be."

Suddenly, the weight that had been lifted from his shoulders just a short time ago, came crashing down upon him with such finality that he literally crumpled to the floor.

On hands and knees, he crawled to the pine box and huddled against it for support. There, he sat, chewing on his fingernails and looking about the room.

"I think I could live here," he thought, distracted. "But I'm not sure Bryand would allow me to; Live, that is."

At length he realized he was leaning on his mother's coffin. He was not repulsed. Instead, he ran his hand adoringly along the lid.

"Mummy?" he said softly. "It is I, Daron."

He waited, though he did not really expect a scream to erupt from inside.

"You're probably mad at me, I know. Shutting you up the way I did. I'm sorry for it now. I really am. Do you hear me, mummy? I'm sorry for it now. You see, I've really made a mess of things. I've gotten myself into quite a stew."

He looked about the empty room, reminded of MeAnne's escape, and then he thought of what would happen when the court had discovered the truth.

"You don't suppose they'd look at it as just one of my little pranks? An elaborate jest?"

The silence that came next confirmed for him the truth.

"I don't think so, either." He stroked the box once more.

"Was I such a horrid child? Growing up, I mean? You must admit, I never once caused Bryand any lasting pain."

He thought of his brother; of the crime he had committed against him.

"That is, until now."

He thought of MeAnne. On the road to Jasperland, he surmised; proclaiming to all who'd listen that they had an imposter for a king. He thought of the council and the court, the priests, the people, crying out for justice, crying out for his execution, dragging him off to the block before he could say one word in his own defense.

I am innocent!

But actually...

That was not true.

They say its a tickling sensation, he told himself in desperation, as the blade slices through your neck. Perhaps, then, I won't feel anything.

This next he directed to the Gods above. "After all, I am a noble person, in spite of the things I've done. Might you not grant me some special dispensation?"

The sickness in his stomach chose that moment to return.

"I assume that's your answer," he said aloud, shooting to his feet and rushing to the embrasure. He leaned over the sill, and retched and retched until his muscles gave out.

He rested his head against the stone, gazing absently at the battlements below. It was then he realized he had been observed by the sentry there, who, upon recognizing the king, smiled and snapped to attention.

This brought tears to Daron's eyes, his lower lip began to quiver and, addressing the man as if he were the only friend left him in the world, Daron said, "Don't you see? All I wanted was to be liked!"

CHAPTER TWENTY SIX

Castle Nightshade was not really a castle but, instead, a large, cylindrical, stone keep three stories tall. It had no ramparts, no parapets or crenellated walls, or even breastworks to protect it from attack. Nevertheless, it was considered by many to be a castle, and particularly, one that was impregnable.

It had been built upon a small island in the middle of Lake Dongo-Neardat, which was the most foul and cursed place in all of Bandidon save for Sherman Oaks. Technically, with its salt water, it was a lagoon, though it was more than twenty leagues inland from the actual sea.

According to legend, ItzMynus and DatzYorus, the Gods of sibling rivalry, had an argument that came to blows. ItzMynus, who was quite a selfish fellow and completely deserving of a good thrashing, was knocked clear out of the Heavens. It is said he landed in the Sea of Ill Luck, causing such a splash that the water all but swallowed up the land. I, for one, being more scientifically minded than most, am convinced the ground quaked, nothing more, but so violently that the Sea of Ill Luck was frightened and leaped upon the shore.

Eventually the waters receded, leaving behind giant pools in the areas that were lower than the sea itself. The largest of these came to be known as Lake Dongo Neardat, for within its black and slimy depths swam a hideous crea-

ture five horses in length, whose jaws were lined with deadly teeth.

How long it has dwelled there no one knows, but once, while reading the Great Book, I discovered an obscure passage that may indeed refer to it, thus making the creature at least a thousand years old. It is written:

"And Yugo, being the chosen one, took up his father's sword and drove the beast back into the water, whereupon, with his dying breath, Yugo rescinded all fishing rights for the safety of his people."

I myself have seen the creature. Once. But once was all it took to see it time and again in my dreams.

Below is a drawing I copied from an etching made of wood.

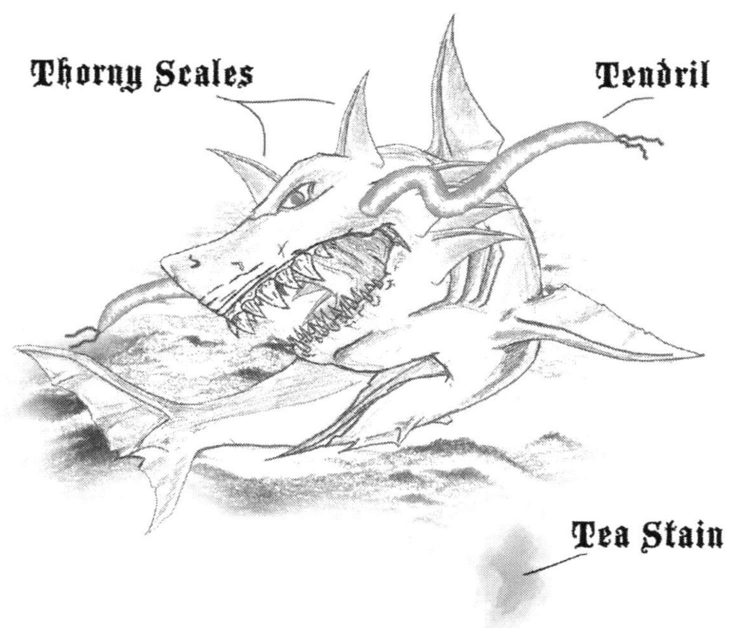

Far worse was it than any dragon I have encountered. For dragons, though malevolent and cunning, are discriminating about what they eat.

This thing consumed my boat!

The lake was surrounded by a forest of trees so overgrown with clinging moss that only a soft half-light touched the ground. Though from far away it made a lovely, tranquil sight, upon closer inspection one found the trees themselves were dead and brittle. For this was no ordinary clinging moss.

A pale, sickly yellow, with translucent tendrils shaped like withered hands, if this moss liked you, it never let go. Thus, among its leafy strands hung the skeletal remains of many forest creatures and a few amateur botanists as well.

The one and only way to stave off the moss's advances was to carry a lighted torch. Somehow it knew that fire was not healthy for it.

Perhaps it was the heat, but come within two feet of a lighted torch and the moss curled up like a moat frog's tongue. Therefore, to keep the one and only access to the castle clear and free of danger, wooden canopies had been erected on both sides of the road leading up to the lake's shore, and beneath these were two rows of firepots, which were kept burning day and night no matter what the weather.

But not even the sight of dangling skeletons along the sides of the road could evoke a response from MeAnne. The dense fog that had appeared so often during her captivity had returned once more. No matter how far she traveled, and the trip had lasted three days, the fog enveloped her like the folds of a heavy woolen cloak.

Along the way, there were some moments when she was conscious of the sunlight. She could feel its warmth upon her face and see her shadow traveling on the ground. But with this consciousness came thoughts of her family, which only led to heartache, which only prompted a desperate longing to escape again within the fog.

For deep within it came the feeling she was floating, that somehow she had been set free from a world of physical restraints where nothing existed save for the occasional squawk of a dither bird or the call of a lonesome dove.

"She makes me very nervous when she does that," said Nightshade, eyeing her askance.

"She's had a terrible blow," replied Cunninghim. "She's hurt and in pain. Some people crawl inside themselves when that occurs."

"Agreed," said Nightshade, frowning. "But they don't start acting like a chicken."

Cunninghim watched her as she rocked in her saddle, cocking her head first one way and then the other. So beautiful, he thought. The man who weds her will truly be a lucky fellow; unless, of course, she's gone completely off her nut.

"She'll come out of it," said the Duke, though he sounded not at all convinced. "She just needs some rest."

Two days later, they reached the border of Nightshade's lands. By late that afternoon, they stood on the edge of the forest and found the moss had grown dangerously close to the sides of the road.

"I hate it when they let the grounds go," said Nightshade, frowning. "I must talk to the gardener if he's still around. Trouble is, I go through so many trying to keep the moss under control."

He sighed and rolled forward in his saddle. "Well, at least the firepots are still lit. But we mustn't dawdle. The moss gets bolder by the year. Why, I've seen vines creep right between the pots for the chance at a horse and rider."

They spurred their mounts to a trot until they came to the lake. There the canopies and firepots ended at an adjoining cover where, instead of more firepots, long cast-iron troughs had been placed filled with blazing coal oil, creating a wall of flames and a "safety zone" as the Earl explained.

They dismounted at the foot of a short pier to which was tied a large, rectangular ferry. Nightshade waddled onto the pier and rang a bell that had been hung upon a tall mooring post. "You'll want to stay back now," said the Earl, calling over his shoulder. "He comes up whenever the bell's rung."

"He?" said Reggie, forgetting himself. (*One did not speak to royalty unless spoken to first. In those days, especially, it led to a great deal of pain.*)

"The monster, of course!" replied the Earl with a sneer. Now that Reggie was there, Nightshade had someone he could bully in the same way Cunninghim bullied him.

Fool, he thought. Hanger on. Always in your face whether you needed him or not.

Reggie helped MeAnne out of her saddle. But he was hardly conscious of her as he scanned the surface of the lake.

Like everyone else, he had heard the tales of the creature. However, being a city-dweller, immersed in the comings and goings of city-life, he had never really given them much thought or credence.

If he had known the monster was real; *really* real; he never would have agreed to join the Duke's service. In fact, he never would have listened to the girl.

A loud splash somewhere in the lake pulled him abruptly from his thoughts. He scanned the lake but saw nothing outside of the choppy water. What have I done? he fretted. I should be home right now (*meaning the Slaughter House.*)

"Reggie?" said MeAnne, her voice barely above a whisper.

Grumble was momentarily distracted. "Aye, my lady?"

"Where are we?"

"At our destination. Look you there," he said, pointing with a trembling hand.

MeAnne stared at the fortress on the island across the lake. "What is that?"

"That, my lady," interjected the Duke of Cunninghim with a congenial grin, "is Castle Nightshade."

He approached and took her hand. "I'm glad to see you more responsive today. We've been worried."

"And why is that?" asked MeAnne, frowning. She truly did not know.

"Well," replied the Duke somewhat awkwardly. "You've been a bit; shall we say; distracted these past few days. Which is perfectly understandable," added Cunninghim quickly. "What with the hardships you've endured."

"You needn't worry about me, my lord, I've simply been tired of late, that is all. Probably caused by the moon.

"The moon?"

"Aye. Tis not well known, but its beams have strange properties that can, among other things, sap a person of his strength, or reverse the aging process in the skin."

"Imagine that," said the Duke, his voice betraying his doubts.

"Achh, aye. But you mustn't stare at it too long," said MeAnne, sounding much like a lunar expert. "It can steal your sanity from you without your even knowing it. To be completely safe, you should really look out your window only on moonless nights. Of course on moonless nights there isn't very much to see."

"Of course," said the Duke.

"And moonlight is so pretty. Therefore, to stay safe, when looking out on nights the moon is visible, you should shut your eyes before looking out."

"Excellent advice, my lady," said Cunninghim, indulging her, while inwardly he was thinking: Daft; the girl's gone daft. Yet he did so want to be wrong.

"Well; now that you're here," added the Duke, squeezing her hand gently, "you'll have plenty of time to regain your strength. I've been to Castle Nightshade before, and though it appears stark and uninviting on the outside, it is warm and comfortable within."

It was then, as he was gesturing toward the castle, the creature surfaced just a few feet from the pier. Seeing it, MeAnne shrieked in terror, and Cunninghim, startled by its presence, retreated, pulling her with him.

"Godzilla!" blurted Reggie, taken by surprise, and he fumbled for the sword he had removed from the castle armory.

"Don't draw that!" cried Nightshade, alarmed.

Reggie froze in place and stared wide-eyed at the Earl.

"Leave it right where it is. I promise, he'd do far more damage to you than you to him."

It was indeed a ferocious-looking creature. Its skin was greenish black where it wasn't covered by barnacles and sea spores. It had a conical-shaped snout and teeth the size of daggers. Between its pupiless eyes and the corners of its mouth, grew two eel-skinned tendrils that whipped about in the air. At the end of each of these tendrils, were two long, curly filaments. Bridging the gap between these filaments, was something Nightshade called a "current" that glowed and sizzled and threw off the same type of sparks produced when a flint hit a strikeplate.

Yet, as fearsome and predatory as the creature appeared, it made no attempt to attack, but remained where it was, with its head above the water and its mouth sitting open.

"Your sword is metal," Nightshade explained. If

one of his feelers had touched it, you'd've been shocked to death."

"Shocked?" said Reggie, who was unfamiliar with the term.

Nightshade gave him a condescending look "As in lifted off the ground convulsing and sent flying backward some fifteen feet through the air."

Reggie quickly removed his hand from the hilt of his sword and made no other move.

Pleased with himself for having put the lieutenant sufficiently in his place, Nightshade went straight to work. He flipped open a small wooden box that sat on a shelf just below the ferry bell. Inside was a white crystalized powder from which protruded the handle of a small spoon.

Using the toe of his boot, he flipped up the lid of a larger wooden bin that sat upon the pier. Inside, resting on shaved ice, were half a dozen good-sized fish.

"I hope these are fresh," Nightshade muttered, grabbing one. "He likes his food fresh."

He tapped a heaping spoonful of the powder into the fish's mouth, then another into each of its gills. He waited a moment, whistling to himself. He looked into the fishes' mouth, and when he was satisfied enough of the powder had dissolved, he grabbed several more fish from the bin.

Arms full, the Earl stepped to the edge of the pier and addressed the creature. It had been bobbing quietly, all this time, it's mouth open and ready for feeding.

"He's trained the thing!" blurted Reggie, awestruck. "He's gone and trained it!"

"Aye," said Cunninghim, watching Nightshade feed the creature. "I must admit the Earl has some surprising talents."

Nightshade tossed the last fish into the creature's

mouth, then wiped his hands on the end of his tunic.

"That's it for now," he said, and the creature blew some spray at him just before shutting its mouth. "Cheeky! Very cheeky! Try that again and there'll be no supper for you."

It was almost as if the creature understood him. The feelers on its snout went limp and it submerged.

Nightshade shaded his eyes as he tracked the creature's movements. This he did from the trail of sparks that broke the surface of the lake. Soon, the sparks became more intermittent, until at last, they stopped completely.

"Well, that should do it," said Nightshade joining the others. "In about a minute or so, he'll float to the surface."

He noticed the puzzled look on Reggie's face. This gave the Earl the opportunity to be condescending once again.

"You see, he allows me to feed him, but that doesn't mean he wouldn't devour us all if he got the chance. So the only safe way on or off the island is to render him unconscious."

Nightshade paused a moment and stared at the lake. "The trouble is," said the Earl, reflecting aloud, "though the dose is always exact, he never regains consciousness at the same time."

He shook his head, returning to the business at hand. "Therefore, we'd better hurry along if we don't want him snapping at our heels. He's most unfriendly after he's been drugged."

Nightshade started toward the mooring rope, but when he glanced back at Reggie and saw the lieutenant had not yet moved, he barked, "What are you waiting for?! We haven't a moment to lose."

Somehow Reggie found the will. He untied the horses and led them onto the ferry. Cunninghim followed behind with the Princess. Nightshade made ready to cast off.

When the Earl had first rung the bell, in addition to summoning the beast, some castle workers had also responded, hastening to the island's shore where they stood ready to haul the ferry to their side the lake.

As Nightshade had predicted, the beast rose to the surface, twitching at first, snapping its jaws. But soon it quieted and lay on its back, bobbing up and down in the gentle waves with its tongue lolling out.

They pulled away from the pier, and with the sudden jerkiness, Reggie gasped and lunged for the railing. This being his first time upon water would have been terrifying enough without an unpredictable monster floating directly in his path. His heart raced, sweat poured down his brow, and he felt the bile from his stomach rise to the back of his throat.

"You don't look very well," said Nightshade, eyeing him appraisingly.

"No, my lord," replied the lieutenant after a difficult swallow. They had come within ten feet of the monster.

Nightshade bent down with a grunt and picked up a long wooden pole. He swung it out over the railing, placing the far end against the creature's belly.

"Lend us a hand, man," said the Earl to Reggie. He waited a beat, and when Grumble was slow to react, he shouted, "Come on, come on! Do you want to be eaten?"

"No, my lord," answered the lieutenant, trembling miserably.

"Then get over here!!"

With a whimper, Reggie tore his hands from the railing and gripped the pole, and together they shoved the creature clear of the ferry's path.

Grumble stared at it as they went by, his eyes agog and his mouth agape. To be so close that he could actually smell its breath and see the definition of its skin!

Godzilla, he thought, surely this can't be happening! And he covered his eyes with his hands, knowing he had reached the limit of what his senses could endure lest he go as mad as the Princess.

For a moment he was conscious of only his chattering teeth. But then he heard, "The horses, Reggie!" It was Cunninghim's voice. "Quickly, man!"

Reggie looked up, and through the blur of his tears he saw they had reached the island landing. A chuckle escaped his lips, and with trembling hands, he untied the horses' reins and led them onto the shore, whereupon, feeling suddenly sick to his stomach, he collapsed upon the ground and retched until his insides hurt.

"No need to feel ashamed, man," said Nightshade, offering him a hand up. Secretly he was very pleased to see him in such a state. "I do that myself quite often. Remind me to give you something for the queasiness when we get inside."

"Aye, my lord," said Reggie, his face flushed and his head pounding.

Nightshade proceeded up the path, his attention turned now to the awaiting servants.

Cunninghim, however, having overheard his associate, gripped Reggie's arm, and, pulling him aside, said, "Accept nothing from his hand. You'll live longer."

"Live longer, my lord?" said the lieutenant. But the Duke did not reply. Instead, he escorted the Princess through an open guard door in the gate, leaving Reggie with his mouth hanging open and feeling even more uneasy than before.

This won't due, thought the Lieutenant. He was sure now he had made a terrible mistake swearing allegiance to the Duke. In his purse was at least twenty gold coins and a hairpin broach topped with emeralds and rubies; a treasure large enough to buy him his own title and a manor filled with servants. But what good was having any wealth at all, if he was to be stuck on an island, practically a prisoner, and with only one extremely dangerous way on or off.

Suddenly he wanted nothing more than to run away; to escape before he was hopelessly embroiled in the events he himself had instigated. He turned to the lake and saw the monster floating on its back.

You still have a chance. It may be your last one. Do it, man, he thought, licking his dry lips. Do it while there's still time!

But he had not taken two strides toward the ferry before he saw the monster flip onto its stomach and swim closer to the shore. Grumble stiffened, daring not to move a muscle, and it was as if the monster knew someone was watching because it turned and looked directly at him with its dark and fearsome eyes.

It spread wide its jaws, revealing its razor-sharp teeth, then slowly, deliberately, it sank below the surface of the water and disappeared from sight.

It's seen me, thought Reggie, frightened beyond reason. Now it knows who I am!

On wobbly legs that seemed ready at any moment to buckle, Reggie pulled the horses up the path. "Open up," he called, somewhat frantically. "Open up this bloody gate!"

A moment before he would have done anything, given anything, to be anywhere but Castle Nightshade. Now, after what he had just witnessed, all he wanted was to be safely inside.

When the gates at last swung apart, he led the horses through. "Quickly, man!" he shouted to the approaching groom, who, though already on the run, was not moving fast enough for Reggie.

He tossed the reins at him, and being in no mood

for idle conversation, he ignored the groom's salutations. He marched quickly for the inner curtain door, wanting only to find his billet where he might drink a few pints and forget what he had seen.

But something told him, no matter how many pints he drank, he would never forget what he had seen. From this day forward, he would know that monsters truly existed.

And with that thought in mind, he pulled open the keep door and disappeared inside.

Alone, Cunninghim sat at a large desk in the Earl of Nightshade's private chamber, his back to a pair of lofty stained glass windows in which were pictured many colorful herbs and fruits and ground covers that were poisonous. A massive fireplace made up most of the wall in front of him. On its hearth, a fire blazed, warm and comfortable, and fragrant, too, the wood having been treated by special incense developed by the Earl. Air freshener, he had called it, after Cunninghim had commented on its pleasantness.

This had pleased Nightshade. "I've often entertained the idea of selling it," said the Earl.

"To whom," Cunninghim had asked, only partially curious.

"To the public should my other talents begin to fail me. A good air freshener would do much to improve their lives. Just think how it could improve commerce. I for one am loathe to enter some of those markets. It matters not that they are outdoors. You can smell them from a mile off, and it's not the produce that is smelling."

"I suppose," said Cunninghim. He meant what he said, too, for he had never actually been to any outdoor markets.

"And not only that, with water being so difficult to access in the cities, if people applied my air freshener to their persons, they would perhaps need only bathe once or twice a year. Why, I'd wager it would start a whole new industry of beauty products."

Cunninghim had smiled wanly, thinking it best not to respond and thus encourage such a ridiculous notion.

Above the hearth was a stone mantle with a delicate relief carved at the center. Most everyone who looked upon it, saw only a sprig of flowers and berries, but those well-versed in the arts of poison and apothecary recognized it as belladonna and Nightshade's family crest.

Etched into the stone above the mantle, reaching almost to the ceiling was the likeness of the Lady Belladonna, the Earl's mother and tutor. Before the Earl had taken his leave, he had stood for a moment to appreciate it.

"What do you think," said Nightshade, having puffed out his chest. "I commissioned it ten years ago. An artist from Lower Thorax. Up and coming then but quite famous now. Took the fellow almost three years."

"Lovely," Cunninghim had been compelled to say. "From what did he take your mother's likeness?"

"From her, of course."

"But your mother's been dead fifteen years."

"I preserved her body just for this purpose." Reacting to the odd look he received, the Earl had quickly added, "Fear not. She's below ground now. And will stay there." With that, he had gazed at the etching again. "She was a master of poisons and a vile creature in all respects. Did I ever tell you one drop of her blood could fell a full grown horse in less than a minute after its ingestion?"

"No," said Cunninghim awkwardly.

"Truly. The things she could do with her bodily fluids was simply amazing."

It was then the Duke had requested some time alone to, as he put it, "explore certain possibilities."

Nightshade, his feelings a little bruised, reluctantly agreed and had left the room. But not before sneaking a peek or two before shutting the door completely.

Two hours later, he was satisfied with the plot he had devised and was laboring over a scroll of parchment at Nightshade's desk.

He fancied himself an eloquent writer, one whose words could persuade, entice, or enrage. No matter the content, every document he had ever written was carefully drafted with the belief that it was a relevant part of Bandidonian History and worthy of being preserved.

The next phrase came to him, and he attacked the parchment with his pen, scratching furiously, dipping the tip into the well for more ink, scratching again. After repeating this process half a dozen more times in exactly the same way, he put the pen down and leaned back in his chair. He stretched and reached for a goblet of water, took a large swallow from it, and sighed contentedly.

"Finished yet?" asked Nightshade, poking his onion-shaped head into the room.

Cunninghim toyed with the goblet and grinned. "Just now as a matter of fact."

"It's about time," said the Earl irritably, entering. He plunked himself down into a wide chair in front of the desk. "Perhaps now you'll tell me what you have in mind."

Cunninghim replaced the goblet, grabbed the shaker next to it and poured some sand over the document. "You'll know shortly." He blew away the sand and examined the parchment for any wet ink. "I want to see the look on your face when I set things in motion."

"Fine," said Nightshade, though under his breath he muttered something truer to his feelings. "Use my castle. Use my sand. But don't bother telling me what's going on."

"Have you a problem with this?" asked Cunninghim as he fixed his seal to the bottom of the scroll.

"No. I mean, yes!" Nightshade stood, his knees cracking loudly. "Why don't I ever get to tell you the plans?"

The Duke eyed him contemptuously. "Probably because I'm the one who thinks of them."

That, unfortunately, was the truth. "Oh," said the Earl, sinking into his chair once more.

"I don't like being left in the dark," he groused, resting his fat chin upon his oversized chest.

He paused for a moment, lost in thought. A wistful look came over his face.

After a beat, he sighed and said, "Funny, what comes to mind sometimes. When I mentioned being left in the dark, I suddenly remembered the servant my mother kept in here while I was growing up. His one and only job was to hold a lit candle. Day in, day out, he'd stand right there," said Nightshade, pointing to a mound of old wax by the side of his bed. "Lighting one after another. Tireless, he was. Never sat down once. By the time I was nine, the drippings were so high, he'd become permanently attached to the floor. They had to hang a tray over his shoulders so he could eat, and built him a special commode to move his bowels."

Before Cunninghim could respond, there came a knock on the door, and Reggie poked his head into the room. "You wanted to see me, m'lord?"

"Aye, Reggie. Come in," said Cunninghim, standing. "How is the Princess?"

"She is resting comfortably, m'lord."

"Any more episodes?"

"Episodes, m'lord?"

"How shall I say it? Has the Princess shown any peculiarities?" It was clear Reggie still did not understand.

"Oddities, man. Strange behavior."

"He means," interjected Nightshade. "Has she been flapping her arms and squawking again?"

"Oh, no, m'lord," said Reggie, understanding at last.

"Well, that's good," replied Nightshade. "All we need is a lunatic princess on our hands."

Cunninghim found the remark irritating but he made no reply. Instead, he strolled to a table and filled a goblet with wine from a silver pitcher.

"Thank you," said Nightshade, extending his hand.

"Get your own," replied the Duke, offering the goblet to Reggie.

"Thank you, m'lord," said the lieutenant, surprised.

"Tell me, Reggie. What do you know of the frontier?"

Though he had been elevated to an officer's rank, Grumble still acted like a common yeoman, which was akin to a brick wall. "It's very far from here?"

"How astute," said Cunninghim with an ingratiating smile. "Anything else?"

Reggie thought hard. "It's a dangerous place. Lots of woolly-bullies about."

"Aye, woolly-bullies," said the Duke eagerly, pleased that the conversation had, without much effort, steered in his intended direction. "The highland clansmen. Know you anything about them?"

Grumble shrugged. "They're madmen. Or so I'm told."

"Small wonder," said Nightshade disdainfully as he poured himself some wine. "From all that inbreeding. Good stock comes from mixing blood, any fool knows that. Now I've a bitch in my kennel-- ."

Cunninghim turned to him, glowering. "May I continue?"

"By all means," replied Nightshade obliviously.

The Duke paused to collect his thoughts, then took up his water goblet in a salute to the lieutenant. "You're a very brave man, Reggie. No, no, it's true. Do not look so surprised. Most men break and run the first time they encounter the Dongo-Neardat Monster. I myself blanched and fainted."

"You, m'lord?"

"Aye. Dead away."

"I don't remember that," said Nightshade, intrigued.

"You were busy at the time," replied Cunninghim, shooting him a baleful look. He turned back to Reggie and shrugged. "I can speak of it without embarrassment, knowing that so many have reacted far worse than I. But you, Reggie. You stood there. You held your ground. And never once did you attempt to run."

Reggie felt his stomach drop, and he could not look at the Duke. "Well, there was a moment-- ."

Cunninghim brought his arm across the officer's shoulders and embraced him. "We've all known that moment, Reggie. When the urge to run threatens to overwhelm our reason. But my point is, you refused to allow your fear to rule you. And that is a rare quality in a man these days."

He was blushing now. "Thank you, m'lord."

"You're very welcome." He clinked cups with the lieutenant, and after they had sipped, he returned to the desk.

"Which brings me back to the first part of our conversation. The frontier. A brave man like you could survive there, don't you think?"

"I suppose I could, m'lord. Though it would take

some doin'."

"Oh, don't be so modest, Reggie. I'm convinced of it. You're a resourceful fellow. If you weren't, you never would have come to me in the first place."

"Thank you," replied the Lieutenant, feeling welcome enough now to drink deeply from his cup.

"So that is why," said Cunninghim, placing his own goblet on the desk and looking squarely at Grumble, "After much consideration, I have decided to send you north."

Reggie lowered his drink, confused. "Beg pardon, m'lord. Did you say north?"

"Aye. To the highlands, to find MacBrutish, the leader of the woolly-bullies."

It took a moment for this to sink in, and when it did, Reggie's mouth fell open and the wine goblet slipped from his hand.

"Now that's a waste," Nightshade grumbled.

"Never mind," said Cunninghim, walking Reggie to the desk.

He looked squarely into the lieutenant's eyes. "It's dangerous. You'll need your wits about you every minute. But I know you will not fail."

Cunninghim produced the scroll.

"You must deliver this to MacBrutish, and only to him. You must not let it fall into anyone else's hands. Now take it back to your chamber and memorize it lest MacBrutish isn't fluent in Bandidonian."

"No, m'lord, I cannot," said Reggie, finding his voice.

Cunninghim frowned. "And why is that?"

"I don't know how to read."

Cunninghim stared at him, incredulous, then, deciding to forge ahead, he guided the lieutenant into a chair.

"In that case I will help you put it to memory. But

before I do, let me emphasize once again the importance of your succeeding. The future of the kingdom depends upon it. Our very lives as well. Do you understand, Reggie?"

"Aye, m'lord," replied the lieutenant. But he was far too stunned to understand a thing. Every time he thought nothing worse could happen, something else did.

Now it was woolly-bullies! Madmen! Flesh-eaters!

Dearest Gods, he thought, tightening his grip upon the arms of the chair until his knuckles had gone white. I am lost. I am a dead man.

MeAnne felt like she had awakened from a very long, very disturbing dream. She lounged in a large copper tub, immersed to her shoulders in steaming hot water scented with vanilla.

A large, broad-shouldered attendant, Yamooka was what she had called herself, sponged away weeks and weeks of dirt and grime while her other attendant, Yudini she believed was her name, straightened the sheets on her bed.

It was so luxurious to have people attending her once more. And the gowns they brought her! The shoes! So beautiful, so well made. It mattered not that they were perhaps ten years behind the fashion and the property of the Earl's dead mother.

When Yudini had asked MeAnne what she wanted done with the clothes she was wearing, MeAnne had ordered everything burned without a moment's hesitation.

The servants had been discrete, allowing her the privacy to remove her clothes behind a screen. This allowed MeAnne the opportunity to stash the queen's jewels in an ornamental vase before stepping into her bath.

"More hot water," she sighed, not wishing to stir; ever. "Please."

"Certainly, your grace," said Yamooka with a gleeful smile. She poured some into the tub.

MeAnne felt its heat mingle with the cooler water. "Thank you," she said, contented.

She closed her eyes and slid deeper until her chin was touching the water. It seemed wrong, almost shameful to be so shiftless, so self-indulgent, while the country was in such a horrendous state.

The Council of Kings needed to be informed about the usurper, knights sworn, soldiers conscripted, arms secured, siege towers built, trebuchets assembled, catapults, giant crossbows, battering rams.

Still -- . There was no need rushing off to war dirty. Wasn't good hygiene important, too?

"Sit forward, dear," said Yamooka. "So I can scrub your back." MeAnne obeyed willingly, her eyes still closed. "There you go. Wash away that grime. Scrub off the old skin, stimulate the new. That's good. That's very good. You certainly have a lovely back, my dear. Now rest your head on the tub again while I do your front."

It felt good to place herself in someone else's hands. And what hands! So large and so strong! MeAnne glanced at Yamooka. It seemed odd to her that a woman should don a manservant's garb. Instead of a dress, she wore nubby woolen hose and a homespun tunic. Beyond a doubt Yamooka was the most masculine looking woman MeAnne had ever seen.

Dark fuzz grew just above her upper lip and along her jawline by her ears. Her nose was big and bulbous and her eyebrows were really one.

But more masculine than any of her features, was the way she wore her pitch black hair. Short on top and sides, ears showing, and long in the back. She reminded the Princess of Sir Milfred of the Mullet, the most quarrelsome knight in her father's kingdom.

"Aye, aye, scrub off the old skin," said the attendant, soaping up her sponge. "Stimulate the new." She sponged MeAnne's breasts, round and round and round.

"Not too hard, not too soft. Being careful not to hurt my lady's nipples." MeAnne opened her eyes and stared at Yamooka.

"Sensitive they are," the servant was saying. "Little pink rosebuds, perky and pliable, standing up like they was proud of themselves." The sponge was making wider circles now.

"And let's not forget the tummy, that supple cushion covered with the finest down. Oh, your grace, you have such a cute bellybutton!"

MeAnne eyed her with growing concern. Were it not for the fact that Yamooka had breasts the size of honey melons, MeAnne would have thought she was a man.

"And what's below the bellybutton, eh? But that miracle of miracles, that mound of silkiness, that sweet nubbin of pleasure, that..."

"I think I'm clean enough," said MeAnne, grabbing the woman's hand with both her own.

"Think so, your grace?" said the attendant, surprised. "I haven't scrubbed between your hiney cheeks yet."

"Where I come from we do that ourselves."

"Really?" said Yamooka, surprised.

"Really."

"Very well, my lady," said Yamooka sounding somewhat disappointed. "If you so wish."

Blushing, MeAnne completed washing herself as quickly as she could, and when Yamooka brought her a silk robe, she all but sprang into it and wrapped it tightly about her body.

The attendant smiled and shook her head. "Such a slender thing you are, my lady. So lithe and nimble, too. I'd wager you're a sight upon the ballroom floor. Do they line dance in Jasperland? I could show you one or two."

"That is most kind of you," MeAnne replied feeling very awkward. "Perhaps sometime soon."

"A pleasure, my lady. It's not often castle Night-shade receives such a noble guest."

Yudini returned from her trip to the kitchen, bearing a platter upon which sat a cup of red wine, a trencher of creamy soup with potatoes, onions and clams, crusty brown bread, deep fried fish filets, more potatoes deep fried like the fish, and a side dish of diced cabbage and carrots in a pearly white sauce that the attendant called "slaw."

Yudini was the opposite of her companion, being slight of frame and more feminine in appearance. Her long blonde hair was pulled back from her face, except for short bangs that hung like a valance across her forehead. Her eyes were a soft green and her nose was straight and pointy like a beak.

Yet, even she had opted to dress like a man, dressing in much the same way as Yamooka.

MeAnne smiled at her as she placed the food upon a table by the tub. But the attendant did not return the smile. Instead, Yudini gave the princess a resentful look.

"Eat my lady," said Yamooka, pulling out a chair for her. "Fill that dainty stomach of yours with nourishment. Keep up your strength for the challenges ahead."

MeAnne sat, clutching the robe tightly, and glanced at Yudini once more. By now, the look had turned to scorn.

"I thank you for the fare," said MeAnne, attempting to make friends. "It was kind of you to bring it."

Yudini gave her a limp smile. "Tis me duty, yer highness." She shot Yamooka a hostile glance. "And nothing more."

Yamooka glowered at Yudini. Her mouth opened, but remembering MeAnne was present, she chose not to retort.

Instead, the attendant presented MeAnne with a forced smile and said, "Should you require anything, my lady, do not hesitate to call."

"Thank you again," said MeAnne.

Yamooka joined Yudini at the door. "Whatever you need. Whatever your pleasure. Isn't that right, Yudini?"

"Of course, we're just down the hall," said the woman grudgingly, casting MeAnne one last sullen glance before following Yamooka out and shutting the door behind her.

"So that's how it is," MeAnne heard her say on the other side. "Soon as my back is turned you're flirtin' with another woman?"

"What are you talking about?" Yamooka said, annoyed.

"I seen the way you was lookin' at her, moony-eyed an' all."

After that, their conversation came to her in bits and pieces, growing fainter as they headed down the hall.

"Oh, stop... so jealous..."

"Yer not foolin'...."

"... the only one..."

"I doubt..."

"... want to..?"

"If you do..."

"... get the oil."

Recalling she was famished, MeAnne turned her attention to the food in front of her. In all the time of her captivity, not once had she been deprived of food, but no matter what she ate, the taste was always bitter in her mouth. Now that she had been liberated, everything was delicious, and she stuffed herself with delight.

Cunninghim and Nightshade accompanied Reggie down the path leading to the lake. They stopped just short of the island pier. Behind them the castle groom towed a saddled horse and another laden with packs.

Reggie stared at the lake ahead, his legs stiff and unresponsive as he approached. He was sweating and at the same time he was chilled.

What more; what more, he thought ruefully. There was nothing hidden or cryptic about his answer.

In but a few short days he had stolen a princess, turned outlaw and traitor and was now going in search of the craziest woolly-bully in the annals of History.

All he had wanted was to pay off some debts. Which was another thing that worried him. He owed money to many a brigand from the Slaughter House and it was well known that no one ever escaped their reach.

He thought of the ornament he carried in his purse. It was worth a fortune, even after a moneylender changed it to coin.

He could pay his debts and be free of the Slaughter House threat. After that, he could head for another country.

Bag it all, he thought, his mood quarrelsome and edgy. Why should I care what happens to the princess or Cunninghim or Nightshade. Why should I care what happens to anyone other than myself?

He watched Nightshade follow the same routine as the day before. Fill the fish with powder. Ring the dinner bell. Feed the monster. Hear it bellow. See it flip and flop. Wait a bit. Out cold.

Just as he expected, in no time at all, the thing floated to the surface and rolled onto its back.

"Well, then," said Cunninghim, extending his hand. "I'll expect to see you in two months."

Reggie shook it, nodding, for he was too terrified to speak.

MeAnne had finished all the food and was washing it down with wine, when from outside her window came what she thought was the blare of a thousand bass basoondas sounding all at once. So loud was the bellow, that it almost knocked the cup from her hand.

She knew at once it had come from the monster. Don't look; don't look, she told herself. It's evil. It's horrific. But her curiosity drew her to the window in spite of her better judgement.

The monster was nowhere to be seen. Instead, she found Nightshade, the Duke of Cunninghim and Reggie standing by the pier.

What are they doing? she thought fearfully. They're far too close to the water?

But before she could call out to them, the monster breached the surface and leaped into the air, its green scales gleaming in the light, its tendrils darting this way and that. It hit the water and gave out with another blood-curdling bellow. It dove below, but a moment later, it had surfaced again and was floating on its back.

Drugged again, thought MeAnne. But why?

She saw Reggie shake the Duke's hand and then Nightshade's. She watched in disbelief as he led the horses onto the ferry and clutched the railing for dear life.

He's leaving! she thought, terror gripping her.

The man who had set her free from her prison, from her torment. The man who had brought her safely under the Duke's protection and seen to her every need.

Why is he leaving?! And without even saying goodbye!

The ferry was already pulling away from the shore! Desperate now, she leaned out the window.

"Reggie!" she called. "Friend!"

But he did not hear her.

She spun back to her room and made for the door. She stopped, flustered.

No time! No time!

She hurried back to the window and leaned out once more. It was then a bird glided by, a starling or a sparrow, she could not tell which.

Aye! Of course! The bird! Take wing!

"Remember! Two months!" Cunninghim called, waving.

"Best of luck!" shouted Nightshade, mimicking the Duke. He watched in silence for a moment as the ferry headed closer to the opposite pier.

"There's a lot riding on him, you know," said the Earl, smiling for the officer's benefit. "What makes you so sure he won't run away the moment he's out of sight?"

"Where would he go?" replied Cunninghim, unperturbed. "Back to Bandidon? He has only the block waiting for him there. Beyond? I think of myself as a fair judge of character. You may believe me when I tell you our friend Reggie is no adventurer."

Cunninghim waved to the lieutenant, and cupping his hands around his mouth, he shouted, "May the Gods protect you!"

He waved again and watched for a moment, his ingratiating smile slowly changing into a smirk. "No, he'll do as he's been told. And then he'll return. Unless he winds up as the main course of some woolly-bully banquet."

They waited until he was safely on the other side, on his horse and cantering down the fire lane.

"Come," said Cunninghim in a rare good mood. "The plan has been set in motion. There is nothing more we can do. Let us pay a visit to our royal captive and see how she is faring."

They turned back to the castle and, much to their surprise, saw the princess on the path, flapping her arms as she hastened toward them.

"Oh, no," said Nightshade with a sigh. "She's gone off again."

"Where's he going," said MeAnne, rushing past them. "Call him back if you can. You must."

"My lady," said Nightshade, stepping quickly to collect her. "If you please, you're a bit too close to the water."

Indeed she was, for just then the monster broke the surface and headed toward them, only to turn away and submerge again once Nightshade had brought MeAnne a safe distance from the shore.

Later, after they had calmed her and brought her back to the room, Cunninghim and the Earl pulled her attendants aside and chided them for their carelessness.

"But m'lord," said Yamooka, who was quite dumbfounded that the Princess had somehow slipped by her. "There is always one of us on guard at the far end of the corridor. And as you know, there is no other way out of her room."

Yudini, also professing her innocence, added

quickly, "We would have seen her leaving. We would have stopped her immediately. I swear, m'lord."

"Then how did she get out?" said Cunninghim, giving them each a stony look.

Lowering her gaze to the floor, so he would not think her response flippant or defiant, Yamooka ventured, "Perhaps her window?"

"Don't be absurd," scoffed Nightshade. "That's a fifty foot drop to the ground."

"Even so, m'lord. Yudini and I were both on duty. There was no way she used the door."

"So what are you suggesting," said Cunninghim, fed up with their excuses. "That the girl can actually fly?!"

CHAPTER TWENTY SEVEN

Flashing lights within swirling shadows; muffled voices beneath rhythmic drums; slowly, slowly, the Prince clawed his way toward consciousness. In the millennium of his mind, countless images unfolded, vast castles and darkened keeps, fields of wind-blown heather and storm-tossed seas.

Faces, ghostly and translucent, appeared before him, speaking yet saying nothing; quickly born and lost again from memories old and new. And then, from the center of his dreamer's canvas came a light that grew in size and brilliance, and before he understood completely, his eyes were open and he was back from wherever he had traveled and basking in the sun.

"Where am I?" he said, squinting, his voice reverberating inside his head.

Sobbing, Malady dabbed his sweaty brow with a dry cloth. "In good hands, m' lord."

"Why do you cry?"

"Cause yer alive. 'Cause I thought I'd lost ya."

When his vision cleared and his eyes had adjusted to the light, he saw they were beneath a lush tree on the grassy bank of a large, placid lake. Beyond the shade of the tree, the sun was shining in a cloudless sky and birds circled playfully just above the water's edge.

"I'm cold," he said, shivering.

"That's from yer fever."

For the moment he said nothing more and watched her as she continued to dab his brow; and knowing he was watching her made the woman smile.

Soon the Prince found himself entranced, for there was something about the woman he had not recognized before. Perhaps it was the way the shadows accentuated her features, but just then she looked amazingly like MeAnne.

Suddenly, instead of her tattered shawl and kirtle, she wore a resplendent gown of gossamer with gold and silver inlays that sparkled when touched by the light.

"Where did you get that dress?" asked the Prince, confused.

"I had it made with my share o' th' diamonds, m'lord."

"Oh." He looked down at himself and discovered he wore only a loin cloth. "Where are my clothes?"

"They're hangin' out ta dry," said Malady in a motherly tone. "What's left o' them, that is. Nothin' but tatters n' rags, they are. It took me forever ta wash the dirt out."

He drew his arm across his chest, feeling suddenly self-conscious. Seeing this, Malady chuckled.

"There, there. No need ta be so bashful. I've had a husband, ya know. An' I can't tell ya how many times I've had ta wipe me boys' rear ends. Thank the Gods they're all grown up now."

He heard them laughing and shouting their usual taunts at one another. He turned in the direction of their voices. He blinked. For there, squabbling by the water's edge, instead of the children, stood two courtiers garbed in mail and tunics.

"Who are those young men?" asked Bryand, frowning.

Malady looked at him queerly. "My boys, o' course."

He became conscious of a throbbing pain in his right arm and shoulder. He ran his hand lightly across his breast, touching upon a bandage.

He frowned, and looking down, he found naught but a stump covered by bloodstained dressing. He gasped and turned to Malady, horror-stricken. "My arm! What's happened to my arm?!"

Cower was suddenly present, leaning over him, and in a tone that was matter-of-fact, the retainer said, "Fret not, my lord. We cut it off."

"You what?"

"We cut it off. There was nothing left of it. You see?" Cower presented the Prince with the charred limb and left it smouldering on his lap. "Be careful there, I believe it's still quite hot."

Bryand felt its scorching heat; felt the searing pain across his thighs. Revolted, shaken, he grabbed the limb and threw it, caring not if it burned his flesh.

"Boom-Shacka did that?" And with the mention of the demon's name, he reached for the charm around his neck.

It, too, was gone.

"My Charm!" said Bryand, frantic. "What have you done with it?"

"Oh, that ugly thing," said Malady with a perfunctory wave. "I threw it away."

"Threw it away!" He shrieked. "Do you know what you've done?"

A bank of ominous-looking clouds roiled across the sky at unnatural speed, blotting out the sunshine and throwing a dark shadow across the water and the shore. The breeze gave way to a savage wind that shrieked like a lunatic chorus and whipped the trees about in a chaotic dance.

There came a loud rumbling sound, though not from the storm clouds above, but rather from deep within the trembling ground. The lake, so calm and pleasing to the eye a moment before, now churned with large, sulfuric bubbles that broke the surface, spewing scores of dead fish into the air.

Bryand shot to his feet and looked on with fear. The boys were in the water, youngsters once more; splashing each other as they horsed about, completely unaware of the impending danger.

"Get out!" cried the Prince, rushing to the edge. "Get out, get out, get out!"

The sky was dark as night. The wind screamed like a wild palooka.

The earth quaked, throwing giant waves onto the shore; and with an explosion of steam and hot silt, Boom-Shacka sprang from the lake's depths with a triumphant roar.

"Quickly," shouted Bryand, whirling to Cower. "Give me my sword!"

"What for?" asked the retainer calmly. "You're right-handed. You've always been right-handed."

The demon sloshed through the frothing water, steam rising from his fiery body; and with his eyes locked upon the Prince, he proclaimed, "I warned you, mortal, but you paid me no heed! So impudent then; so arrogant! But now you will squirm and grovel! And then you will scream as you cook."

He chortled thunderously. "You are mine now, mortal, mine!"

Bryand turned to the others, who stood idly by. "Run for your lives!"

"Why?" asked Noim simply. "He doesn't want us."

Finding himself alone and unprotected, Bryand's courage withered, and he darted for a cluster of trees and shrank against a thick trunk.

But the demon saw him enter and started ripping the trees apart. "There is no place to hide, mortal. You are doomed!"

Flaming leaves and branches rained down upon him. And with his position now untenable, he retreated into the open, hoping to out-run the demon.

His feet were like stone weights and the air itself like a clinging web, and no matter how hard he tried, he could not move from where he stood.

The ground shook violently, and before the Prince could react, Boom-Shacka's throne rose out of the ground beneath him. Bryand found himself lying on the seat, whereupon a horde of shadows fell upon him and held him prisoner there.

He struggled desperately to free himself, marshaling all his strength. Still, the shadows held him in an adoring embrace, all the while destroying his will.

And then Boom-Shacka was upon him, snuffing out the daylight, thrusting his hideous visage an inch above the Prince's face.

"No one escapes me," he whispered, his breath like a blistering desert wind. "I am eternal. I am darkness. And for you, I am death."

The demon's hands came round him; his flesh began to sizzle, and as Boom-Shacka bellowed with laughter, Bryand screamed in agony above the roar of the flames, "No! No! This cannot beeeeee!"

He awoke with a start, his body soaked with perspiration, his chest heaving.

"His fever's broken," said Cower, sounding much relieved.

"Where am I?" rasped the Prince.

"In good hands, m'lord," said Malady, dabbing his brow with a dry cloth.

He glanced about, and unlike his dream, he saw

they were in a small chamber bare of furniture, save for a few stools and the cot upon which he lay.

"I'm cold," he muttered.

"That's from yer fever."

He glanced at her, at her moldy hair, and she smiled in the same way she had in his dream.

A shiver run through him. Desperate now, he reached for his arm, found it in place, then groped for the charm that hung around his neck.

"Never take this off," commanded Bryand, clutching it firmly. "It goes to the pyre with me!"

She nodded quickly, startled by his vehemence. "Aye, m'lord. Whatever you say."

Bryand included Cower. "Do you understand!? To the pyre!"

He dropped to the cot, muttering, "No matter what."

At length his eyes closed and his voice trailed off and - with his hand still gripping the charm - he fell into a deep sleep.

Two days passed and the Prince still had not returned to consciousness. But on the morning of the third day, he began to stir; and when his eyes fluttered open at last, he found Cower sitting on the stool beside him, smiling.

"Feeling better, my lord?"

"Aye," said the Prince hoarsely. He tried to raise himself.

"No, no; just rest." Cower brought a cup of water to the Prince's lips and held it while he sipped. "You're still very weak."

"How long have I been unconscious?"

The retainer wiped his mouth. "It's been five days."

Bryand looked at him, aghast. "Five days?"

"Aye, my lord. Since your last fever fit. Altogether, you've been out of touch, so to speak, for almost twice that."

Bryand closed his eyes, his emotions suddenly at war inside him. Ten more days gone. Stolen from him. So deep and complete was his sleep, he might just as well have been dead.

It was then, the door to the chamber creaked open, and Malady poked her head inside. When she saw the Prince awake and gazing at her, she smiled.

"Good morrow to ya, m'lord. Welcome back to the world of the livin'."

"Good morrow," he replied. "It's nice to be back."

"Are ya hungry? You should eat somethin' if ya can."

"Aye," he said, feeling suddenly hungry. "I could do with some food. Lots of it. I don't suppose you've a roast pig hiding behind your back?"

Pleased, the woman snorted, then left to find some food.

Bryand stared at the room, taking in the drab mud walls and the split timbers that ran overhead. "Where are we? And what is that terrible smell?"

"We are just east of Anapest," replied Cower. "And that should answer your second question as well."

The Prince nodded. "Ah, the manure depository-- . I toured the place once; with father. He kept gagging but, out of respect for the townsfolk, he refused to vomit. Not even upon their insistence."

He paused to collect his thoughts. "How did we get here?"

"Well, that's a long story, my lord," said Cower with a smile. "What's the last thing you remember?"

Bryand thought for a moment, then suddenly the fearsome image of Boom-Shacka in all his wickedness, loomed menacingly in his mind.

Shuddering, Bryand clutched the charm at his throat. To his surprise, it was warm.

"Tell me -- ," said the Prince with difficulty. "Did what I think happened-- ."

"Aye, my lord," said Cower gravely, sensing what was on the Prince's mind. "It happened."

"That face," said Bryand, grimacing. He paused, and a shiver ran up his spine.

"For the first time in my life, I was truly afraid." He looked at Cower for reassurance. "I still am."

"No one is impervious to fear, my lord," said the retainer reassuringly. "We all hide from something. And admitting it doesn't make you any less of a man. Or a king. In fact, I dare say it makes you a better one on both accounts."

"How so?"

"If you keep in mind that all men are afraid of something, then you will fear no man. And that will give you an advantage over the worst of them, and respect from the best of them."

For a moment, he was silent, weighing Cower's words.

Soon the door opened, and the boys entered. They stopped just past the threshhold to stare at Bryand intently.

"Are you gonna live?" ventured Donoim at length.

Bryand surfaced from his thoughts. "I believe so."

The boy scowled and turned to Noim. "Oh, well. I guess you win."

Malady reappeared, carrying hot porridge, which she fed to the Prince. In the meantime, Cower, in a very dramatic tone of voice, related the events that occurred after their encounter with Boom-Shacka and the demon worshipers.

"Leaving Malady and the boys safely hidden, I sneaked back to the clearing and-- ."

"You mean, you disobeyed my command?" interrupted the Prince.

"Aye, my lord. And you can be thankful that I did. Now eat your porridge. Anyway, by the time I returned, you were alone and unconscious; and though you were burning up with fever, I thanked the Gods that you were still alive. So, I dragged you out of the clearing and rejoined Malady and the lads; and together we stumbled through the darkness, working our way down the hill, until we reached that Gods-forsaken village.

"There was quite a lot of confusion there," said Malady as she spooned some porridge into Bryand's mouth.

"Villagers rushin' everywhere," said Noim. "This way 'n that."

Cower picked up the story once more. "It seems Boom-Shacka, their precious lord of darkness, wasn't very pleased with them and had set their houses burning including a slow-moving worshiper or two."

"That's very interesting," said Bryand through a mouthful of porridge. "I can't wait to hear what happened next."

"Don't talk with your mouth full," said Noim, taking the opportunity to play the parent.

"Yeah," added Donoim. "Yer spittin' porridge everywhere. Hey, mum, wipe his chin."

"May I continue?" Cower interjected.

Unperturbed, the little one looked at him and said, "be my guest."

Cower purposely cleared his throat. "Well, we found the horses, and a wagon to hitch them to-- "

"Another wagon?" asked Bryand, incredulous.

"That makes three, don't it?" Donoim chimed in.

"Doesn't it," replied the retainer.

"Doesn't what?"

The retainer shot him a withering glance. "Where was I?"

"Wagon number three," stated Donoim.

"Aye, the wagon. So we hitched the horses to it and

placed you inside."

"I was in the back with ya," Malady interrupted, no longer able to contain her excitement. "But then, what do ya think should happen?"

Cower frowned. "Here now, this is my story."

"We was attacked," said the woman, ignoring the retainer.

"Aye, we was attacked," Noim repeated. "But using my sword, the one you gave me, I-- . "

"He cut down one o' them demon worshippers!" shouted the little one exuberantly.

"And another," added Noim.

"They were all around us," Cower continued, his voice raised purposely to silence the others. "Somehow I managed to fend off their blows."

"'Cept fer the fella what knocked ya off the wagon," smirked Donoim.

"I was coming to him."

Donoim stepped close to the bed, a look of glee upon his face. "That one, I took care of."

"You?" asked the Prince, surprised.

"Wiv this," replied the boy, producing the ceremonial dagger. "So whadduya think?"

Bryand's smile faded somewhat.

He knew now that the dagger had once been Boom-Shacka's taloned finger, and he wondered with abhorrence just how many unsuspecting lives it had taken over the centuries.

His eyes went back to the boy. Donoim was waiting eagerly for him to respond.

The Prince placed his hand on the boy's shoulder and said, "I'm very impressed. That took great courage."

Donoim puffed out his chest. "Yeah. I guess it did." The boy held out the dagger to the Prince. "Here. Me 'n Noim want you ta have it."

"Noim and I," said Cower; it was second-nature

now.

Somewhat reluctantly, Bryand took the dagger and turned it over in his hands. "That's very kind of you, but wouldn't you prefer to keep it?"

"Uh-uh," said Noim somewhat too quickly. "We figured you might need it if Boom-Shacka ever caught ya without yer charm."

"Also," added Donoim candidly. "If that bugger ever d'cides he wants it back, we don't want him comin' ta us."

Cower related the rest of the story; how they had broken through the remaining attackers and galloped out of town.

At this point, Malady took up the narrative as she changed Bryand's dressing. "You was burnin' up with fever, you was. With yer skin all blistered and oozy as if ya had been out in th' sun too long. Luckily, we still had the leather pouch full of Aldina's skin balms, which I've been applying to yer lordship's skin ever since. The stuff's a blinkin' wonder. Why, I even tried it on my piles an' they've shrunk almost ta nothin'. Can ya beat that!?"

Bryand smiled, and attempting to be gracious, he replied, "I wouldn't even try."

She examined his chest, dabbing here and there. "You'll probably peel. But that's about all."

"I cannot thank you enough," said the Prince, patting her hand.

Malady blushed. Though for Malady this meant her cheeks took on a normal, healthy glow. "Anythin' fer you, m' lord."

"Someday I'll be able to repay your kindness. All of you," said the Prince, glancing about at the others. "You've been so loyal. Perhaps when we reach Pepperill there will be an opportunity for me to show you-- ."

His words trailed off, for at the mention of Pepperill, their smiles collapsed. "What is it?" asked Bryand, sensing trouble.

It took a moment before Cower found the words. "We were there a week ago," said Cower reluctantly.

The Prince braced himself for bad news. "And?"

"The village and the manor house have been destroyed."

Bryand's face took on a grave expression. "And Dwayne? What of him?"

Cower brightened somewhat. "He's alive, though no one knows just where. And so is Master Niles, who, we believe, is with him. Apparently, they were last seen heading in the direction of Torkelstone."

"Which is where we should be heading," said Bryand, pushing away the porridge. He attempted to rise, ignoring their protests.

"We've no time to waste. Torkelstone is our last hope of ever linking up with them."

"My lord," said Cower, suppressing a smile. "You've been unconscious for many days. You've had a close brush with death."

"Even so," replied Bryand, struggling to sit up. "We must away."

"My lord, we're a day outside of Torkelstone," Cower finally admitted. "And half a day more from Master Dillin's castle."

The Prince looked up, his mouth hanging open in surprise, which made the retainer want to laugh.

"Aye. And thanks to the good friars here, we've had food and shelter now for the past three days."

"Some shelter," said Donoim.

The Prince knitted his brow, perplexed by the boy's remark. But before anyone could explain further, there came a loud creaking sound from the rafters above their heads, followed by an urgent rapping on the door.

A portly man dressed in a friar's robe, whose name

Bryand later learned was Brother Lumpkin, poked his head inside without waiting to be admitted.

"We're evacuatin' again, folks," he said.

He was followed by three other friars who - all smiling congenially - approached the bed and carried the Prince out of the room, using the cot as a litter.

Bryand looked on, confused. But there was no time now to answer any of his questions, for the creaking had changed to a loud complaining groan, and the louder the groan became, the faster the friars moved.

"Quickly now, quickly now," came a voice from up ahead. "That's right. Don't crowd. Watch your step there."

As Bryand was carried through the front entrance, he caught sight of a friar standing by the door and shouting instructions to everyone about.

He would later introduce himself to the Prince as Father Fervor, the head of the order. But at the present, he was much too busy to exchange pleasantries.

He had silver hair and a clean-shaven face. When the man glanced Bryand's way and saw the Prince was awake, he smiled in a friendly manner while waving them on.

"Good morrow, young man; nice to see you up. Keep moving Brother Lumpkin. Faster children, you don't want to be beaned by a timber."

Fold upon fold of dark grey clouds blanketed the sky, and the rain fell in silvery sheets. Even so, they carried the Prince outside, across a well-kept lawn that was ringed by a flowerbed full of purple, white and fuchsia jump-jumps.

They stopped beneath a long canvas lean-to, where they watched in silence as first the side wall and then half the roof of the monastery caved in.

Bryand turned to Cower, confused, not knowing what to say or think. It was Donoim, however, who supplied him with at least one answer. "This is the second time that's happened since we been here."

"Let's get to work brothers," said Father Fervor, taking charge. And Ignoring the rain, the entire order, including the friars who had carried out the Prince, began the slow, laborious process of shoring up the walls.

Father Fervor, however, lingered a moment and called to the travelers, "Sorry about the inconvenience, folks, but hopefully, we'll all be back inside by nightfall. There's hot broth yonder."

He pointed to a nearby lean-to, a smaller version of the one they stood beneath, where a large cauldron had been set up over a smoky fire. "Now don't feel you're obliged to, but if your inclined to lend a hand, we'd certainly appreciate it. That is, except you, young man," said Father Fervor, pointing at Bryand. "You stay right where you are."

Despite what Father Fervor said, Bryand could not sit still. He and Malady took over dishing up the broth, while Cower and the boys hauled mud from a large pit behind the monastery.

As the hours passed, the Prince learned much about his benefactors. They were all pious members of the Order of Perpetual Reconstruction, called such for the monastery where they worked and prayed.

It was originally built from mud and stone and timbers. These were the only materials used.

Because of this, whenever it rained more heavily than a light drizzle, the walls had a tendency to wash away or, as Bryand had witnessed, the roof to collapse. (*with no disrespect intended, no one had ever figured out that cement might have been helpful in keeping things standing.*)

The monks in residence were forever repairing the place, and for this they were known for their patience, their diligence, *(but not particularly for their carpentry or masonry skills.)*

Each night, as the nobility of the land sat upon their cushioned seats, at cloth-covered tables laden with succulent foods, the monks of the order sat upon roughly-hewn benches, at tables bare but for the essentials - bread, broth, fruit and goat's cheese. It was a pasty diet and hard on the digestive system, but it sustained them in their faith.

Their days were divided between prayer and shoring up the walls, or the roof, whichever had fallen down last. And at night, after their meager repast, they would retire to their cubicles, furnished simply with a floor *(the one thing upon which they could always depend,)* a cot, and a candle by which to read the basic doctrines of the order or the building schedule for the following day.

It was a regimented life that few could tolerate. Those who joined could expect only hardship and deprivation; therefore not many did.

Father Fervor was the head of the order. According to Brother Lumpkin, he was a pious man who had devoted his life to helping those in need, providing them-with food and shelter, nursing their ills and illnesses alike.

For this, he was loved and respected by many. He was a vital man, full of strength and zeal, with a booming voice that could reach every corner of the grounds. And when he called, the monks stopped whatever they were doing and came running.

Sometimes he would call them just to watch them hastening across the lawns. Dressed in their clumsy habits and sandals, they looked like fatted geese, and this always made him laugh. Father Fervor was a man with a sense of humor, too.

If he had one fault, and this Brother Lumpkin had confided looking most concerned, it was his outspokenness and his lack of prudence in a time that demanded less of the former and more, much more of the latter.

But that was asking quite a lot from Father Fervor, who was not one to stand idly by while the weak were being exploited. Especially in the King's name.

He was forever writing letters of protest to the court and to the local magistrate. Brother Lumpkin was very afraid that, with the recent change of guards, Father Fervor was inviting serious trouble, and not just for himself but for the order, too.

When at length the Prince was able to question the man himself, Father Fervor's smile turned into a hard frown. "What was once a peaceful life has become a hideous nightmare. People are attacked on the road without provocation. Homes are broken into and men are murdered in their beds. Businesses have been confiscated, farms plundered; old taxes have been doubled and new taxes have been imposed. And for what? Do we see any benefits from all this money they collect?! Of course not. It does nothing but fill the King's coffers and make the man rich!"

Father Fervor was silent a moment, a sullen, brooding look upon his face. "This new ruler," said the man in a bitter tone. "I'm afraid he is nothing more than a fool dressed in King's clothing."

Brother Lumpkin cleared his throat. "Father," cautioned the man with a discreet nod in Bryand's direction, for, after all, he was a stranger. "Don't you think we should get back to work?"

Father Fervor ignored him. "What else would you call a man who plunders his own people? As far as I'm concerned, he doesn't deserve to rule; he's lost the right to be our King. And I for one, will not rest until I've done everything I can to depose him."

He looked at Bryand, noting the concerned expression upon his face. "Does that sound like treason to you? I'm sure it will to the local authorities, I've written them three times now."

"Aye," said the Prince candidly. At this, Father Fervor's face darkened. Bryand did not want the man to think wrongly of him, so he gripped the friar's arm and added quickly, "But it's a belief shared by many people these days. One, in particular, stands before you. Take courage, Father. Things will change soon. From here I go to Torkelstone, to join up with those who believe the same as you and I, and together it is our intention to raise an army and defeat the tyrant on the field."

"Who are you?" asked Father Fervor, intrigued.

But before the Prince could respond, the sound of galloping horses reached them, and then, from around a bend in the road, mud clods flying before them, a troop of guards appeared.

Father Fervor watched them carefully, waiting to see if they ignored the place or if they would ride onto the monastery grounds.

"Father Fervor," said Brother Lumpkin nervously, hastening to him. "What's to become of us?"

"Calm yourself, brother," replied the friar, staring past the man. "Do you remember what to do in the face of adversity?"

Lumpkin gazed at him and said almost hopefully, "Hide?"

"You're not thinking," Father Fervor chided.

Brother Lumpkin lowered his head and sulked. "It's not easy. Especially in the face of adversity."

"Of course not," said the friar, patting the man's shoulder. "But remember, brother, in the face of adversity, we always pull up our undergarments lest they are riding too low, adjust our habits, lift our chins, and stare adversity - that cowardly son-of-a-bitch - squarely in the face."

By then, the guards had wheeled their mounts onto the monastery grounds and had reined in before the gathering brothers.

Seeing where they had halted, Father Fervor, pushed his way through and strode purposely to the guard out in front. It was one-eye.

"Not in the flower beds! What's the matter with you! Get those horses out of there this minute!"

"Stay right where you are!" snapped one-eye to his men. He slipped his hand behind his tunic and produced some crumpled pieces of parchment. "Are you this Father Fervor who dares ta question the authority of the crown?"

"I am," he replied, unafraid.

"You're very bold sendin' these."

"I'm a bit surprised you could read them."

Father Fervor could not possibly have known just how bad a week one-eye was having. First, two mercenaries had dared to oppose him, stealing a cart of food he had stolen for himself. His ribs still ached from the encounter, and he had broken his front tooth, landing hard against his saddle as he tried to pursue them.

To add insult to injury, they had escaped into Sherman Oaks, where his men would not go, despite how violently he had threatened them. Since then he had been in constant pain, which he could not remedy, having long ago dispatched the local apothecary and sold the contents of his shop, and worse still, he had been summoned by the district commander and thrashed soundly for allowing one Father Fervor of the Order of Perpetual Reconstruction to spread sedition.

One-eye sneered at him from atop his horse, a look made fiercer by the fact that he had no upper lip. "You're a smart one, monk. Too smart. You've offended lotsa people around here includin' me."

"I speak my mind," said Father Fervor, unintimidated. "Tis my right as a free man. And I only offend those who need offending."

"Is that so? Perhaps you'll think differently when you've felt the bite of my whip across yer back. It's got a way of remindin' folks what shoot their mouths off and forget what their place is. Seize him!"

Two guards dismounted and wrestled Father Fervor to the ground. One-eye climbed down from his horse. He took hold of his whip, gripping the butt knot firmly as the rest uncoiled to the ground.

"Over there," he directed, pointing to the front door of the monastery. "Tie him ta the knocker."

One-eye strolled confidently to the door and leaned upon it, plying his whip in Father Fervor's face. "Know any prayers, friar?"

Father Fervor looked at him, a calm expression on his face. "You will not whip me. Not this day. Of that I am most certain."

"Oh, really," said one-eye smugly, leaning all his weight upon the door. "And why is that?"

"Because you've made two costly mistakes. The first was tying me to this door. The second was leaning upon it."

And just as Father Fervor predicted, there came a loud groan from the hinges and the door collapsed inward, sending one-eye sprawling into the monastery.

"See what I mean?" called Father Fervor, who had landed safely atop the door.

The guard stood quickly and dusted himself off. He was in a foul mood now, and he intended to make the friar pay dearly for it. He glanced about to see where his whip had landed, and he was just reaching for it when there came another loud groan.

One-eye looked up in time to see the rafter beams slipping from their joists. He turned, meaning to escape the hallway. But months of easy living and larders full of pastries had slowed his reflexes to a crawl. An avalanche of clay tiles and soggy timbers collapsed upon him as the front half of the roof caved in.

During this, the two guards who had tied Father Fervor to the door fell back to the exterior scaffold. They stood with mouths gaping open in utter amazement as stone and crumbled mortar collected at their feet.

Cower, who was standing behind them, found the opportunity presented to him irresistible. A subtle shove set the scaffolding rocking. Another shove and it pulled away from the wall.

Seeing this, Noim and Donoim immediately rushed to his side. Together, they toppled the temporary structure, dousing the guards with fresh mortar, buckets, poles and brushes and pinning them under a some heavy planking.

The remaining guards, two in number, having seen their comrades thus felled, sprang from their horses and rushed forward with their weapons drawn.

It was Brother Lumpkin's turn to improvise now. Shouting at the top of his voice, his face bright red from the exertion, he came barrelling from behind them and bowled them over like lawn pins.

At this point in the skirmish Bryand took command. He stepped out of the shadows of the lean-to, Slaybest in his hand. When the two guards saw him approaching, their whole attitude changed.

They had never faced an armed opponent, especially one looking so savagely intent upon cutting off their heads. So, they panicked, threw down their weapons and attempted to run away; one to his left and the other to his right; which put them only a step away from a head-on collision.

They realized this at the very last moment when each was in the other's face. But it was far too late to change course by then, and with a loud crack, proceeded only a second later by a loud "Oof!" they smacked into one another soundly and fell unconscious to the ground.

"You did it, Brother Lumpkin!" shouted Father Fervor, most exuberant now. "You faced adversity and spit squarely in its eye!"

"I did, didn't I," said Brother Lumpkin, breathless from the excitement. "Dear me, I've never been in a battle before."

"You were splendid!" shouted Father Fervor from where he lay. "All of you! I've never seen such courage! Such imagination! Now would someone be kind enough to set me free?"

They did so, congratulating one another as the rest of the friars of the order gathered around them and cheered.

"Perhaps we'd better do something with the guards before they wake up," the Prince suggested.

"A good idea, young man," said Father Fervor. "The Gods will tolerate one display of aggressive behavior. Any more than that, and they'll think we're enjoying ourselves too much."

They retrieved one-eye from the rubble, who was very dazed, and therefore most complacent as they tied his hands behind his back and shoved a gag into his mouth. Then they did the same to the other guards and rolled each of them in canvas like a rug in a carpet shop, piling them one atop the other by the side of the road for the local garbage company to pick up.

"You're dressed like a simple peasant," said Father Fervor to the Prince. "But from your bearing and the way you handle yourself, I'd venture to say you were a soldier. Perhaps even an officer. What's your name, lad?"

For a brief moment, Bryand considered revealing the truth about himself but changed his mind. "For your own safety, it's better you don't know. I've been cast outside the law of late, and remain a hunted man."

"He's the king," said Donoim, who had joined them after the skirmish.

"A king," said Father Fervor, indulging him. "My, my, isn't that grand."

"Not a king," replied the boy. "The king. The rightful one."

Before Donoim could say anything more, Cower was leading him away.

"What? Didn't I say that right?" asked the boy.

"We'll discuss it later. Let's go back to the guards. You can knock them unconscious if they start to wake up."

"That's a good idea!"

During this, Father Fervor, curious about what the boy had said, had been studying Bryand's face. "So, you're an outlaw. And a very educated one, if I had to guess."

The Prince nodded but refrained from saying anything more.

Father Fervor glanced about them and a sad note came into his voice. "I'm afraid we've rebuilt this place for the last time. As of this moment, the Order of Perpetual Reconstruction is changing its basic tenet. From now on we will be the Order of Perpetual Relocation. At least until the law grows tired of looking for us. We'd fair much better with a man like you traveling with us."

Bryand shook his head. "It would be an honor and a privilege. But you would suffer much pain from those who hunt me, if your name were linked in any way to mine."

"There's something you should know about me, young man, if I haven't already made it plain. I'm not someone who frightens easily, and when it comes to injustice, I'm like a macadamian wild cat. So keep your identity to yourself if you must, but know you this, I'm inclined to take the boy at his word. Though I know not why, I believe he was telling the truth, and the man standing before me now is indeed the rightful king."

Bryand studied his face for a long moment, and when he was convinced of the friar's sincerity, he said, "Very well then. I only hope you still believe the boy after what I've told you."

They strolled back and forth beneath the lean-to until, at length, Bryand had brought the friar up to date. And having spoken earnestly, and with such genuine passion, Father Fervor and the other friars who had gathered to listen, felt compelled to kneel before him with shouts of "Gods save the King."

"My lord," said the head of the order, his voice trembling, speaking sincerely for them all. "Were we of a different calling, we would follow you wherever you bade. But ours is not the way of the sword, no matter how justly it is wielded. Ours is the way of spiritual enlightenment and the enrichment of the soul. Yet, you can still counted us among your ablest supporters. Trust in me, sire, while you struggle to regain your kingdom upon the field of battle, we will travel the lengths of the empire, spreading the news of your brother's deception in such an honest and compelling way that all who hear will be truly swayed and join us in our cause."

"Thank you, Father Fervor," said Bryand, deeply moved, offering the friar his hand.

Father Fervor rose and shook it vigorously, and with a grin that stretched from ear to ear, he replied, "Fear not, your grace. We'll see you safely through Sherman Oaks. The thieves there will not attack such a large party, and by noon upon the following day, you will be reunited with your friends."

Then, motioning his followers to gather closer, he

said, "Come, brothers, come! Every minute counts! The Order of Perpetual Relocation leaves for Torkelstone just as soon as it can!"

But when no one moved, the friar knitted his brow, perplexed. "Is there a problem of which I am unaware?"

"No, Father Fervor," said Brother Lumpkin speaking for the rest.

"Then why aren't you preparing?"

"Father, we've nothing but the clothes on our backs, we're ready to leave right now."

In less than an hour they had started off, Father Fervor out in front setting a brisk pace, while Bryand and his companions, dressed in plain woolen habits, rode atop their wagon behind the other friars.

The sky above was dappled heavily with clouds. A cold wind laden with moisture gusted in their faces.

Yet the mood among the travelers was nowhere near as dreary as the day. For the first time in weeks, after so many disappointments, Bryand dared to think their journey was nearing its end.

Something told him he would see his friends soon, and though the struggle was only about to start, with the outcome still to be determined, at least he was done with all the setbacks, all the trials - he glanced at Malady and the boys - all the headaches.

No, he thought, that's not fair. They've kept up in every way. Perhaps with some complaints now and then, but as well as any soldier I've ever served with.

He chuckled to himself, feeling almost giddy. He was confident now; renewed; and ready to take command of his troops.

By early afternoon they had reached the edge of Sherman Oaks. Father Fervor fell out of line and waved the column on.

"Let's hop to it now, brothers. We've got to get beyond the woods before nightfall. That's right, that's right; pick up your pace. You've a healthy look to your cheeks Brother Lumpkin, keep it up."

As a response to Father Fervor's prompting, the brothers took up a chant, one they often sang while repairing the monastery:

Hop, hop, hop,
Never will I stop,
Not until I please the Gods,
Or I'm about to drop.

Flit, flit, flit,
Never will I quit,
This is how to please the Gods,
And not be called a twit.

Tread, tread, tread,
Never will I dread,
While singing praises to the Gods,
They cannot strike me dead.

They traveled nearly the entire width of the woods without incident, except for the time Malady needed to relieve herself. While squatting with her dress collected above her waist, she was bitten by something that made her scream so violently that the entire column, concerned for her safety, came blundering into the thicket she had chosen for her privy.

A quick examination by Father Fervor, the one and only person she would allow to look at her naked posterior, revealed she had been stung by a flying ant. The friar rid her buttock of the insect with a quick flick of his finger and the travelers were able to proceed once more.

The light was beginning to wane as they approached the far edge of the woods; and it was here, just as they were breathing easier, their journey was halted by the appearance of a dozen rough-looking men dressed in brown and dark green jerkins, bearing an assortment of weapons.

One brute was built much larger than the rest, a map of scars upon his face. He strode to the middle of the road, all but blocking the column's path, and he stood with his massive arms akimbo.

It was Kussensuch.

"Awrigh, Awrigh, lizzen oop," shouted the guild representative. "This eear iz guiwd territouri, an' no onz allaud ta crooss guiwd territouri wivowt pian a toe. So cuff it oop, one gowd piez per man."

Father Fervor, despite his wealth of compassion and understanding for his fellow men, was never one to avoid a confrontation, and stepping boldly up to Kussensuch, he said, "Come again?"

Kussensuch scowled and motioned for his interpreter to join them. Assuming an arrogant pose, the man turned to Father Fervor and, with practiced disdain, proceeded to explain. "This is guild territory and no one is allowed to cross without paying a toll."

"A toll?" replied Father Fervor, half puzzled, half annoyed.

"Aye. That'll be one gold piece per man."

"But sir. We are kirtle friars sworn to a life of poverty. Satisfying your demands is simply beyond our means."

This time it was Kussensuch's turn to be confused, and with his mouth hanging open, he turned to the interpreter and said, "Huh?"

The interpreter rolled his eyes. "Now I see we must go both ways. Very well then, he means they're broke.

They can't pay."

Kussensuch turned back to the friar, his eyes narrowing. "Oh, yoo'll pie, awright."

His hands came up quickly and grabbed Father Fervor by the front of his habit. Using, no effort at all, Kussensuch lifted him off the ground. "'Coose if ya dent Awm goona smook ya in me pet."

Father Fervor looked to the interpreter to translate.

"Pay up or he'll smoke you in his pit."

No one threatened Father Fervor. "See here, you cursed brigand, unhand me or I'll doff this habit and pummel you soundly."

Kussensuch glanced at his interpreter once more. "Wassat?

"Listen up ya rotten thief," translated the man after an impatient sigh. "Let go o' me or I'll take off me robe and punch yer face in."

During this exchange, Bryand had climbed down from the wagon and was approaching the front of the column. He flexed his right hand and reached inside his robe for Slaybest's hilt, wondering if he had enough strength to withstand much of an attack.

He had not gone very far when he became aware of footfalls behind him, and glancing over his shoulder, he found Cower approaching fast.

"What are you doing?" asked the Prince.

Cower maintained a humble attitude. "In a situation such as this, I believe two swords would be better than one. Besides, my lord, you're in no shape to challenge these men by yourself."

The Prince continued looking at him as they walked farther on. He realized their journey had changed many things about Cower, the least of which being the set of lean, hard muscles the retainer had acquired.

"Very well then," said Bryand, duly impressed. "But run if you find yourself in over your head."

"A good suggestion, my lord. One which I hope you yourself will heed should the need arise."

Bryand looked askance at the cutthroats, assessing their worth as fighters. Luckily, the biggest of them was already engaged holding Father Fervor and, therefore, not an immediate threat. The Prince determined he could surprise and drop at least two before he would have to contend with the rest.

But he never had the opportunity, for just as he was about to remove Slaybest from its scabbard, two men stepped from the shadowy woods behind the robbers, and made ready to attack.

"Put that man down!" one of them shouted in an angry tone. He hefted a medium-sized crossbow armed with a hunting quarrel, while the other stood a whole head taller than him, brandished a menacing-looking war staff.

Bryand stopped in his tracks and his heart leaped into his throat. For he recognized the voice, and judging by the stature of the man's companion, he knew immediately they were Niles and Dwayne.

Kussensuch disregarded the command. Instead, he turned, keeping his hold firmly upon Father Fervor. But when he saw Niles, he lowered the friar to the ground. "Whoot're yoo dooinere? An' why ain'ts yooo did?"

"Aye," said the interpreter, amazed. "What are you doing here and why aren't you dead?"

At any other time, Niles would have responded with a sarcastic remark or a witticism. But not today.

Deadly earnest, he replied, "We've a score to settle, Kussensuch. That should answer both your questions."

"Whoot scoor?" asked the giant, his eyes narrowing.

The interpreter opened his mouth, prepared to interpret, but Niles raised his hand. "I understood the question."

He looked at Kussensuch and sneered. "We're not happy with our current representation. You took a large initiation fee from us, and by that I mean a cart full of food, yet we've seen no benefits. To be perfectly frank we think your guild's a sham."

Kussensuch cast a dumb look toward his interpreter.

"He thinks yer a crook."

"Dooya nauw," said the leader, seething.

"Aye, I do." Niles tossed Dwayne his crossbow and unsheathed his sword. "And we've decided to make these woods an open shop."

That was a remark the guild representative could understand, and with a snarl, he drew his sword and rushed at Niles. His followers did the same, but they never expected to be attacked from the rear by Bryand, Cower, and Father Fervor, who jumped the interpreter and wrestled him to the ground.

"Here's something you won't need to translate," shouted the friar, and he proceeded to smack the man repeatedly in the face.

Bryand and Cower dispatched their foes easily, for most cutpurses were skilled in intimidation only. Sensing disaster, the remaining thieves broke off their attack. They dashed for the safety of the trees.

Kussensuch was in a furious state. Based on the sheer massiveness of the man and the difference in their weight, it seemed he would get the better of Niles.

But Niles was a knight and a veteran soldier who knew how to keep his head in a fight. Instead of matching blows with the guild representative, he avoided him, dodging this way and that, and in this way, gradually wore down the man's strength.

"Stend 'n faught lawks a men, ya bludy keward,"

raged Kussensuch. "How em ahh sooppozed ta kiews ya if ya wunt stend stuw!"

Though he had not understood every word the man had spoken, Niles caught the gist of it. Even so, he had no intention of obliging him.

He leaped aside a powerful swipe and pivoted to avoid a dangerous thrust. The strategy would have been completely successful had he not suddenly run out of room. Niles found himself between two thorny bushes with his back against a tree.

Thinking he had at last gained the upper hand, Kussensuch smiled menacingly. "Wew, now. Looky hayre. Sorta stuuck, are yee."

He did not wait for a reply, thrusting his sword toward the young man's throat. However, Niles, being a good two feet shorter than the man, ducked quickly and avoided the blade.

Most everything in Sherman Oaks was rotten; most particularly, the trees. Kussensuch's blade pierced the bark but did not stop there. It drove right through the body of the tree all the way to its hilt.

Kussensuch lost his balance. He fell forward onto Niles' sword. It entered his burly chest almost in the same way as the giant's sword had sunk into the tree.

He stared at Niles, his eyes wide with surprise. He shuddered. His knees buckled, then he slid off of Niles' blade and fell into a heap upon the ground.

"I believe this is mine," said Niles, pulling a capon leg from Kussensuch's belt.

"Blooody skeb," gurgled the guild representative, and he closed his eyes forever.

Niles stood over the guild representative's body, scowling. After a pause, he looked down at the capon leg in his hand, sneered, and let it fall.

Curious now, Niles started toward the three friars who had lent him their assistance. Were he not otherwise preoccupied, he would have thoroughly enjoyed watching them fight. Especially, the leader. He was quite a scrapper. And the tall one; he had handled himself well. Perhaps he had been a soldier before pursuing the monastic life.

"That was fine swordsmanship," said Niles as he approached them.

"Aye," added Dwayne, following close behind. "It was a good thing you were here."

"Well, you know what they say," said Bryand, pulling back his hood and revealing his face. "The Gods work in mysterious ways."

Niles froze in his tracks, and Dwayne's mouth fell open. For a moment neither spoke, causing the Prince to laugh.

"Daron!" said Niles finally, his voice filled with surprise. "What are you doing here of all places? Though, of all places, I'd say this one suits you best."

This left Bryand speechless. He had been so excited to see his friends that it never occurred to him that they might mistake him for his brother.

"No, Master Willowbrook," said Cower, answering for the Prince. The retainer pulled back his hood, revealing his face. "Not Daron, but your good friend, Bryand."

Instead of embracing him as Bryand had expected, Dwayne stood his ground and Niles presented him with a stony look.

"Friends!" blurted the Prince, finding his voice at last. "Don't mistrust your eyes. It is I! Bryand!"

And still they did not embrace him.

"What's the matter with you? Have you gone mad since last I saw you?"

Dwayne spoke solemnly. "Bryand, is it really you?"

"Aye!"

Niles sneered and shook his fists; no longer was he

able to contain the outrage pent up inside him. "First you banished us! Then you destroyed our homes and murdered our families! And now you dare to come within our reach like this? You'd best have an army secreted behind these trees, your majesty," added the young man in a scornful tone, "for if you've come alone, expecting our forgiveness, you've made a terrible mistake."

He drew his sword and advanced on the Prince.

"Hold!" said Bryand quickly, retreating a step or two. "I know you've suffered much these last few months, but not by my hand; never by my hand. This I swear, though I realize my word means nothing to you now. Please just allow me to explain."

Yet the hatred remained on the young man's face. "What explanation could you possibly have for betraying us the way you did?!"

"Much has happened to us all, Niles. Please, if our friendship meant anything to you in the past, allow me to explain."

"Keep your words. They mean nothing now!" shouted Niles, readying himself. "Not anymore!"

He lunged, his sword pointed at Bryand's heart. The Prince stepped clear, grabbed Niles' wrist and, using the young man's anger and momentum against him, sent Niles spilling to the ground.

"Niles, stop," shouted Dwayne coming forward.

But the young man did not listen to his friend, and renewed the attack.

Bryand parried a thrust and then another, all the while thinking of the irony of his recent past. He would not hurt his friend like this, but he could not allow himself to be hurt either.

Employing all his skills, the Prince pressed Niles back against the wagon, and with a feint and a quick swipe of his blade, tore Niles' sword from his hand.

Niles waited for Bryand to strike, not once looking away. But instead, the Prince sheathed Slaybest.

"We've known each other our whole lives. I was there when you rode your first horse. I was there when you were handed your first sword. I carried you home the day you broke your leg. I even helped set the bone. I dug trenches with you when the rains threatened to take your home and beat the locust from your fields the year of the blight. I've fought at your back. I've covered your retreat. And been grateful more than once for your having saved my life. After all that we have shared, do you think I could have done what you say?"

Niles weighed the Prince's words, then stared at the ground.

It was Dwayne who spoke next, after approaching them and placing a firm hand on Niles' arm. "Go on, Bryand. Tell us what happened."

So Bryand did just that, starting with the day his brother rendered him unconscious and stole his identity. And when at last he had finished, he picked up Nile's sword, and presented it to him hilt first.

Niles looked at the sword, looked at Bryand. He took it from him and walked down the road. A strangled cry escaped his lips and he swung his sword in a blind fury.

"Niles," said Bryand, concerned, and he started toward him.

Dwayne raised his hand. "Let him be."

He sliced at the air again and again, at war with an invisible enemy. At length, strength spent and out of breath, he doffed the weapon to the ground, whereupon he turned back to the Prince with a tortured look, then fell to his knees, weeping.

Bryand sat by him and embraced him, choking back his own tears. But they were tears of happiness as much as they were tears of sorrow, for he had found two of his friends alive, hurting but whole, and nothing would tear them apart again.

Wasting not a single moment more, they formed ranks and marched down the road, and by sunset they were well beyond the woods and on the grassy plains of Torkelstone County. Here they made camp and the Prince introduced his friends to Malady and the boys.

"Ya mean, he really is a prince?" said Noim. "He's not just crazy?"

"Well, lad," said Niles, a playful glint in his eye. "I can't account for his mental state. But, aye, he really is a prince."

Bryand laughed long and hard. It was good to laugh again! To boast, to squabble, to jest! Just being together was like a tonic to his spirits, and, oh, how his spirits soared.

He looked at his friends and a broad smile stretched his mouth as far as it would go. He had missed them so. Niles; his outspokenness; his cunning wit. And Dwayne, loyal Dwayne, with a heart to match his size. This might have been one of their overnight hunts or a royal excursion, so at peace was he.

Searching within himself, he discovered the pain and the heartache were gone. So quickly, he noted to himself, that they might never have existed at all.

He was half convinced that he would close his eyes and wake up the next morning in his bed chamber, with his father and mother awaiting his presence at the feasting table for their morning repast.

Oh, how he wanted it to be so! His parents alive again; the kingdom healthy and he and MeAnne sharing their days.

He had not dared to think of her for quite some

time. For whenever he did, his heart wrenched in his chest and he felt desolate.

Yet, now, on this night, surrounded by his friends, comforted by their good fellowship, he could think of her without despairing and of the day they would be together again.

"A dragon!" Dwayne exclaimed, a skeptical look upon his face. He and Niles were holding an earnest conversation with the boys. "I don't believe it. The last dragon was slain ages ago."

"I ain't lyin'," Donoim said, turning to his brother for support. "Am I Noim?"

"It weren't no dragon," the older boy admitted to the knights.

Donoim narrowed his eyes at him. "An' jus what would you call it?"

"A big ugly lizard."

Dwayne and Niles laughed, the boys laughed and even Malady snickered.

"An what would ya call the red-colored giant with the fuzzy bottom? The one what sprang at us from the ground?" said the little one haughtily.

"I dunno," laughed Noim.

"I do," offered Malady meekly.

They all turned to her.

"What, mom?" asked Donoim. "What would ya call it."

"Trouble," said the woman, suppressing a smile, which made the others laugh some more.

The conversation went on like this for awhile. But when the darkness was fully upon them, each in turn fell silent. For on the eastern horizon, they could see a bright glow, and above it, like a herald of doom, hung an ominous mass blacker than the night.

"What's that?" asked Malady curiously.

"Smoke. Something's on fire," answered Dwayne,

staring at the distant light.

Sobering, Bryand stared at the eastern sky. He knew at once what was the source - Torkelstone Castle was ablaze.

"Dillin's in trouble," said the Prince grimly. He looked about quickly, and his eyes fell upon the wagon team.

"The horses. Make ready to leave," said Bryand to his friends.

He took Father Fervor aside and when they were done conversing, the Prince turned to Malady and the boys and bid them gather around. Perhaps it was the look upon his face, for Malady started wringing her hands almost at once.

"This is hard for me to say," began the Prince, staring into their faces. And truly, it was, for he had grown attached to them. "We've shared so much over the past few weeks, I feel like we've become a family of sorts."

"Aye, that's true," said Malady, forcing a smile, though her stomach chose that moment to gurgle.

Bryand lowered his eyes, finding the words harder to say than he had expected. "But the time has come for us to part."

"I think I'm gonna be sick," said the woman, gagging.

Cower by now had learned the drill. He quickly lowered Malady's head below her waist. "Deep breath. Let it go. Deep breath. Let it go."

They leaned her against the wagon. Bryand gave her a long fond look. "I've spoken to Father Fervor and he has agreed to protect you until I return."

"You said you'd look after us," said Malady, distraught, and then, somewhat vehemently she added, "You promised Cleave."

Bryand nodded, agreeing with her. "And so I shall. But if I am to achieve the means to do that, I must travel fast from here on out. What lies ahead is far too dangerous, and I will not risk the lives of those I -- . Of those I care about."

"I've done well enough so far, ain't I? I mean, I come up against lotsa things what would make some other folks croak. An' I ain't had no seizures for a long time. I gone at least a whole week without even faintin'."

"You've been courageous." He glanced at the Noim and Donoim. "And so, too, have the boys. But I still must go on alone."

Malady's eyes filled with tears. She had hoped for so much. This ain't the way it was supposed ta be, she thought. I was gonna be a lady. I was gonna have servants an' treats.

But deep down inside her, she had always known it was never meant to be. A whole world of experiences separated them.

Apples n' juicy fruit, like me mum used ta say. Mix 'em and ya wind up with a stomach ache.

It's time, she thought, to say farewell, and by admitting this to herself, she accepted the hurt and found the strength to let him go.

She surfaced from her thoughts, realizing she was gripping the leather pouch, and remembering the skin balm, she reached inside and handed it to the Prince. "Apply it once a day," said the woman, wiping her nose with the back of her hand. "An' stay outa the sun fer awhile."

"I will," said the Prince, accepting the balm and the advice with an affectionate smile.

"When'll you come back fer us?" asked the little one, fretting.

"When I've won what is rightfully mine. Here," said Bryand, taking Malady's hand.

It was his turn to give her something, and he placed a small diamond on her palm. She looked at it and her mouth fell open. "It's all that's left. And if it weren't for blind luck, we'd have lost this stone, too."

"The villagers got them all when they emptied my purse," said Cower, smiling. "Save for that one that fell by accident into my boot."

Bryand looked at the stone, his last chance to buy arms and an army. "It's not as much as I'd hoped. But it's enough to pay your keep and much more should I-- ." He paused, wondering if it were wise to bring up the possibility of his death. He decided it was best to keep nothing from her. "Should I die somewhere along the way."

However, Malady was only half listening, so ecstatic was she over her newfound wealth. "Looky here, looky here," she twittered as she marveled at the stone in her hand. "I'm a duchess after all."

Bryand crouched in front of Donoim. "Mind your mother while I'm gone. And I don't want to hear you've given the friars any trouble."

"Says you," replied Donoim, his eyes downcast.

But then, much to Bryand's surprise, the boy gave him a strong hug, and as he returned it, the Prince found an unexpected lump in his throat. He tousled the boys hair, then stood and offered Noim his hand. "You're a brave lad. I couldn't have made it this far without your help."

Noim shook the Prince's hand. "Aw, it was nothin'." Then he added somewhat awkwardly, "M'lord."

Dwayne and Niles had already mounted one horse, leaving the other free for Bryand and Cower.

"Goodbye Father Fervor," called the Prince.

"Fear not, my lord," said the friar. "I'll spread the word. Your work will continue here no matter where you go."

The Prince swung himself up and waited for Cower to say his goodbyes.

"Remember, Donoim," said the retainer, staring

down his nose at the boy. "No watering lawns, it makes brown spots. And you," said Cower, clapping the other boy on his shoulder. "Keep in mind one thing: if you bathe, people will like you." He took Malady's outstretched hand. "Well..."

"Well," she replied, teary once again. "Don't forget ta take care of yerself while yer takin' care o' the Prince."

A smile threatened the corners of Cower's mouth. "I shall endeavor to keep that in mind. And you must promise to stay out of drafts once winter comes."

"Sure enough," said Malady, sniffling.

And then, to everyone's surprise, they hugged.

Leaving Malady with her arms around the boys, Cower said goodbye to Father Fervor and the other friars, then swung himself up behind the Prince.

"Strange," said the retainer, reflecting aloud. "I've dreamed of this moment, quite often I must admit, and now that it's here, I don't want to leave them behind."

Bryand nodded, unable to speak; surprised by the sadness in his own heart. Even so, he knew there could be no other way. If he had learned anything during the past few months, it was that there were many trials still ahead before taking his rightful place upon the throne.

He signaled Niles and Dwayne that he was ready to depart. He waved to Malady and the boys one last time, then, turning to the glow at the horizon, he spurred the horse to a gallop.

Toward Torkelstone, and whatever lay beyond.

CHAPTER TWENTY EIGHT

When Mortamour arrived at Torkelstone, he had found the town gates barred and its citizens armed and manning the ramparts ready to oppose him.

This surprised the henchman at first, for he had never come up against organized resistance. Angry now, (*which was, of course, his most preferable state of mind,*) he immediately ordered a guidon brought to him, to which he attached a white sash before approaching the gate alone.

"Who's in charge here?" called the henchman to the men above him. How he hated looking up at anything. Looking down on things was much more to his liking. "I would speak with the Master of Torkelstone."

"His son stands above you," called Dillin from his position just above the gate. He wore a loose coif of mail beneath a round-topped helm and a leather breastplate.

He leaned casually between two merlons. "Who wants to know?"

"I am Mortamour, Captain of the King's personal guard, and by his order I have come to place you both under arrest."

"Both," said Dillin in mock surprise. "Just what are my father and I accused of?"

"Treason," Mortamour replied.

"Treason," answered Dillin.

"I just said that."

"So you did. Are my father and I such a threat that the King must dispatch an entire army to arrest us? Or is it you who needs the support?"

Mortamour grinned. Insults like that one usually guaranteed a man a slow, painful death. "The King's justice is harsh at times. The whole town is to be punished for your crime."

"You mean destroyed. As were the villages of Willowbrook and Pepperill."

"Aye," said Mortamour, surprised. "But how did you know that?"

"Word travels fast when it spreads in fear."

"Perhaps. But it's more likely you were informed by the traitor you now harbor."

Dillin raised his eyebrows in mock surprise. "And who might that be?"

"The Prince, of course. Prince Daron."

Dillin stood erect and presented the man with a look that was deadly earnest. "You are mistaken. He has not sought refuge here. I, in fact, am the last person he would ever entreat. Prince Daron knows I am loyal to the King. Perhaps better than the King himself. If this is the reason for which I have been branded a traitor, you can tell his majesty, though I have lost his favor, I am still his faithful subject to command."

Mortamour shrugged. "Why you have been deemed a traitor is no concern of mine. I am but an instrument of the King's justice and nothing more. Therefore, save your declarations for him and waste no more of my time. Will you surrender?" Please thought the henchman. So I can be the one to spill your blood.

"If I do, will you still destroy the town?"

Mortamour nodded. "That, I'm afraid, is a foregone conclusion."

"Then I'll stay where I am, thank you, and may you do your worst."

Blistering irons, growled Mortamour to himself as he wheeled his horse about. Why are men with principals so difficult to subdue? Perhaps I should adopt a few myself.

Indeed, he had not a single one. But he quickly decided against it, for they were only a hinderance in his line of work. After all, who needed a conscience popping up just when you were about to slit someone's throat?

"Bring up the battering ram!" shouted the henchman to his troops. "Make ready the first wave of the assault!"

Dillin heard the officer's commands. From his position atop the gate, he watched the guards dispersing. So it begins, he thought, and he sighed deeply.

He stepped away from the wall and eyed first the line of men to his left and then the line to his right. Though they were close to a hundred in number, most of them were tradesmen and merchants.

Yet, when word had come of the guards' approach, they had rallied to his side. Some had come bearing pitchforks and shovels, while others had arrived in the weathered armor they had worn as younger men.

He knew them personally. Almost every one he could call by name. They were simple people, with simple lives, and he was proud to die among them.

He had always thought of himself as a practical person, preferring to approach things in a rational way. Because of this, he knew, unless circumstances changed drastically, he would be dead by the end of the day, as well as the men around him.

"Tweek," he called. A young man with very curly brown hair and a turned-up nose stepped out of the line. He was the castle's head page, or so he liked to call himself, being the oldest and most experienced of all the boys and girls.

Dillin guided him to the rampart steps. "Get you to the castle and have my father prepare to cover our retreat."

"Retreat?" queried the lad, his bushy eyebrows drawing together. "But the fight hasn't even begun."

A smile visited Dillin's mouth. He was very fond of the lad.

But now was not the time for explanations, and in a stern voice, he said, "If you want to train as a squire next year, you must first learn to obey a command."

"Aye, my lord," said the young man, snapping to attention.

"Then do as I say and go." He watched him take the stairs two at a time. "And stay at my father's side! I don't want to see you back here."

Dillin returned to the wall and watched in silence as Mortamour's men rolled up a heavy battering ram - a stout tree; one which he had watched them chop down, strip of all its branches and strap to a long wagon bed supported by four pairs of wheels.

He observed the soldiers drawing it, noting the way the sun shone on their backs and illuminated the colors of their tunics. Green and purple, he reflected. The royal colors; and this made him think of Bryand.

But not as a tyrant. Never as a tyrant. For he knew Bryand would not have dispatched an army to destroy his home. Not after all the years they had known each other and after all the things they had shared.

The news about Niles and Dwayne and the destruction of their holdings had been shattering. However, if nothing else, it had confirmed a suspicion that had been troubling Dillin since the day he and his father quit the court.

He knew of only one man capable of such deviousness. This was Daron's work. He was sure of it now. Somehow he'd taken Bryand's place and was killing off everyone capable of seeing through his deception.

Dillin shook his head, chiding himself. If only I'd discovered the plot sooner, while there was still time to organize something more than just this pitiful showing. Perhaps we all might have lived a little longer.

"Ready your arrows," he called. "Stand by with the boulders. And prepare to fall back on my command."

The attack began. The defenders kept the royal troops from scaling the wall for three hours. But by the end of that time, they had lost over thirty men. By the end of the fourth hour, they had been pushed off the wall and were fighting in the streets of the town.

At length, Dillin gave the order, and the remaining defenders retreated. They hastened up the main street, protected by a company of archers that had been held in reserve expressly for this purpose.

They loosed their arrows over the defenders' heads and into Mortamour's advancing troops. So accurately were their arrows delivered that the guards broke off their pursuit and fell back out of range.

The defenders retreated through the barbican gate and across the drawbridge, which was raised when the last of the archers filed into the courtyard. Dillin ordered the portcullis lowered. It was their final defense should Mortamour's troops gain access to the drawbridge and lower it.

Dillin knew it was a strong possibility, so he intended to make it a costly venture. Mortamour would lose many men during the attempt. But Mortamour did not strike him as someone who cared about the lives he wasted along the way to accomplishing a task.

◆ ◆ ◆

"Set fire to the town," growled the henchman, looking up the main street at the castle in the distance. He was not pleased with the progress he had made. The townspeople were far too stubborn in their thinking. Did they not understand it was time for them to die?

He had expected them to fight like the peasants they were. Instead, they had fought like demons. Now that the survivors were safe within the castle, he was no longer certain he would win the day.

That's all I need, he stewed. Another blemish on my record. Another 'next time.' But then he recalled the Duke's parting words, and he knew there would be no next time.

His face turned crimson. His hands curled into fists.

How dare he treat me that way, thought Mortamour, seething. I've killed a dozen men for him at least, and maimed dozens more. Well, I guess what they say is true after all - you're only as good as your last job.

"I want this place razed to the ground!" he shouted, grabbing a torch from a passing yeoman. "Leave nothing standing, do you hear!? Nothing!"

Mortamour joined the ensuing frenzy, setting ablaze anything that would burn. A pleasurable task at other times, but presently he was far too worried about his future.

Still, from time to time, the assassin paused to laugh out loud, or to shake his fist at the castle defenders while presenting them with a goading look. But this he did more for show than anything else.

Chapter three, paragraph two, of the Henchman's Handbook, clearly stated, "Always appear confident. Never show fear or doubt. Be bold, even flamboyant at times. This is crucial in gaining advantage over an enemy and is the fastest route to better employment offers; sometimes even a starring contract with a local theatre company."

Using the light in the eastern sky as their guide, the Prince and his friends rode through the night, pressing on despite the slick terrain. By dawn, they crested a hill and found the town in flames and the castle under siege. A black plume of smoke billowed up from a large gaping hole in the keep, ringing the castle battlements like a funeral wreath.

Yet it was obvious the fighting had not yet ceased, for they could see tiny glints about the walls as the fire's light was reflected on the defenders' steel, and even from as far away as they stood, they could hear the screams of dying men.

Please, Dillin, be alive, thought the Prince, staring at the battle in the distance. *Be alive and we'll make our stand together.*

Bryand kicked the horse into motion, its flanks already lathered white with sweat, and with each mile, the Prince's ire grew more intense.

By the time they reached the outer wall, the sun had cast off its pinkish hue and was shining unencumbered in a sky devoid of clouds for the first time in weeks. Yet, if the day was bright and cheerful elsewhere, a pall of dingy smoke lingered over the town.

They guided their horses through the main gate, past the main doors, which had been torn from their hinges and burned. There, they dismounted, not one of them saying a word.

The dead lay all around them, their bodies charred and blackened. The stink of burning coal oil hung upon the air and ashes like tainted snowflakes floated down to the scorched and blood-soaked ground.

Bryand's heart sank as he eyed the carnage, finding it almost impossible to comprehend. "This was not what I intended for my kingdom," he said before anyone else could speak. "War was to be a thing of the past; In my future there was only peace!"

Cower was the first to reply. "Hopefully, the Gods will help us to end things quickly. And then the rebuilding can begin."

The sorrowful look on Bryand's face changed to smouldering rage. "The Gods know I am grateful for whatever help they are willing to provide." He drew Slaybest from its scabbard. "But right now, they can help me most by staying out of my way."

He was off and running, slipping in and out of shadows, rushing from one rubble pile to the next, while the others did their best to match his pace.

They soon reached the large square that lay between the town and the castle's barbican. On most other days, it was filled with merchants selling their wares, with people laughing and conversing, musicians playing, and beggars weaving in and out.

On this day, only the Royal Guards were present, working catapults and other war machines, hurtling fiery boulders and massive spearheaded bolts at the castle's walls on the far side of the moat.

Further inspection revealed the barbican had already fallen. The drawbridge that connected it to the main castle had been lowered. Upon the drawbridge, soldiers had rolled a battering ram to tear down the castle's one remaining defense - the gatehouse portcullis.

Fighting there was most fierce. Between the open spaces between the portcullis' heavy iron bars, defending archers sent their arrows streaking. Spearmen threw their spears, and swordsmen stabbed any wounded enemy that unwittingly stumbled into range.

Archers from atop the castle walls loosed their arrows at the beleaguered guards upon the bridge. Those that had escaped being killed or wounded, had scrambled beneath the ram itself or retreated to the safety of the barbican vestibule and doorway.

"Do you think they'd open up if we knocked?" asked Niles, eyeing the slaughter.

Dwayne cuffed him on the arm. "Save your wit for another time. This is Dillin's home, remember?"

The Prince surveyed the scene, but with soldiers everywhere there seemed no way to gain access to the castle. "Speak up if you've an idea. As for me, nothing comes to mind."

"What is that?" asked Cower, pointing to a flotilla of logs spanning the moat by the south wall.

"A makeshift bridge," answered Niles, watching three pairs of guards hasten across it carrying long ladders over their heads. When Niles saw the skeptical look that Dwayne was giving him, he added, "I knew that even before I saw them cross."

Cower, who had not taken his eyes off the soldiers or their ladders, said, "That way appears quite conducive don't you think?" Bryand looked at him, not sure what the retainer had in mind. "Boldness, my lord. The one thing you could learn from your brother. How did he manage to steal your throne? By doing something no one else would dare to think."

"You mean, we simply walk across the moat and climb one of those ladders?"

Cower's eyes glowed with an intensity the Prince had never seen. "Exactly, my lord."

Weighing Cower's words, the Prince surveyed the activity in the square. "You know, it just might work."

"It better," commented Niles, staring at the ranks of soldiers ahead. "I doubt we'll get a do-over."

Bryand smiled at Cower. "Boldness you say." And then to the others, he added, "Let's go climb a ladder."

Dwayne dragged Niles to his feet. "Why must you always be so sarcastic?"

Niles shrugged. "I don't know. My mouth has a mind of its own sometimes."

"Aye," commented Dwayne. "To compensate for the one lacking in your head."

They caught up to the Prince and followed him into the square, past a catapult and its fiery ammunition, past the auxiliary troops, past the royal archers, and through the ranks of the men executing the assault. Though they wore plain shirts and leggings and looked most out of place, no one questioned their intentions or paid them any heed.

They crossed the float and took their places among the invaders and, when came their turn, they scaled the ladder quickly, first Bryand, then Cower, then the Masters of Pepperill and Willowbrook.

"B'Gods!" said Niles, looking up. "That rear of yours could blot out the sun!"

"Don't you start with me!" growled Dwayne, peering down. "Or I'll dust you off this ladder with my foot."

"Just as long as it's your foot and not your cauldron of a bottom."

Mortamour was barking at some men who were lagging behind in the fight. Suddenly his sixth sense barked almost as loudly. Something was wrong. He could feel it.

He turned and scanned the activity, thinking perhaps the defenders had rallied and somehow beaten back his troops. But such was not the case. He had gained possession of the barbican. One man had even swum the moat, climbed up the drawbridge, and cut it loose.

Brave chap, thought Mortamour with a slight nod. Definitely officer material; too bad he was crushed when the bridge descended.

Yet still he had the feeling that something was amiss. But what?

The catapults were hurling fireballs. His archers were loosing their arrows. The portcullis was being rammed, and his men at the south wall, had bridged the moat and were already scaling ladders.

He looked at each objective, just to insure that his assumptions were correct. All was indeed going as planned.

Funny, though, that his instincts should alert him. He was about to ignore the feeling and continue berating his troops when something at last caught his eye.

Those men, he thought, at that ladder there, peering at the four who were out of uniform and waiting to ascend.

Curious, he started forward, only slightly faster than his normal stride. It was then Bryand turned in his direction. Mortamour halted abruptly.

"Blistering irons!" shouted the henchman aloud. "It's him! It's the Prince!"

Like a loadstone being drawn to a metal object, Mortamour streaked toward the bridge. "Get them!" he screeched, waving his arms about madly. "Get them, I say!"

But the din of battle was far too loud for any of his soldiers to hear save for those nearest to him, and they, thinking Mortamour was vigorously cheering them on, merely grinned and waved back.

By this time the Prince and his followers had begun to climb and were about twelve feet off the ground. Mortamour grabbed a crossbow from one of his men. He took aim and fired. But the quarrel missed its mark and penetrated the thigh of the man just above the Prince.

Howling, the soldier grabbed his leg, lost his balance and fell to the ground, after which the Prince, (*though curious about what had just occurred,*) took advantage of the opening and climbed higher still.

Mortamour doffed the weapon to the ground and, with his teeth gnashed and bared, he bounded across the float, rending a path through the men waiting to climb.

"I'll catch you this time," he spat, shaking his fist at the Prince. "I swear on my mother's grave, I'll catch you!" (*This was quite a remarkable oath for him to use, for he had never known his mother.*)

He was still three or four paces from the ladder when a body landed directly in front of him. He stumbled over it. Before he could get to his feet, another hit the ground to his left. He heard screams from overhead. When the henchman looked up, he saw the ladder had been pushed away from the wall.

"Look out!" he cried, scrambling out of the way on his hands and knees.

The ladder caromed off the wall, breaking heads and spines when it and the men upon it landed on the rocks at the base of the wall.

"Get up," he snarled to those scattered about him. "Get that ladder back in place!"

But as he said this, Another fell, crushing the men on the flotilla.

"Get that back up!" Mortamour railed, the veins in his neck and face distended. "Do you hear me?! Before I murder you myself!"

It was then he turned and noticed the battering ram had gone askew while being rolled across the drawbridge. "Blistering irons! Can't any of you do anything right!?"

He caught sight of a sergeant. "Get these men climbing again or I'll have your head!"

Leaving the sergeant barking orders, Mortamour barreled across the float once more and headed toward the gate, ignoring the arrows that had been sent his way by the defenders still atop the castle walls.

By the time he reached the drawbridge gate he was sweating profusely and breathing hard. Yet still he found the strength to grab the officer he left in charge and throw him into the moat.

"Straighten this ram out!" commanded the henchman, ignoring the frightened looks from his men. "Get moving I say! Or I'll rip your livers out with my bare hands!"

The battering ram was extracted from the barbican entrance, then rolled forward again across the bridge on a straighter path. Mortamour took up one of its stations and shouted to the men around him, "Now put your backs into it! Get us in there! Or die out here with me!"

That was all the incentive they needed. The idea of dying alongside Mortamour and then appearing before the Gods, seemed even more ominous an end than any they had previously considered. In a moment, the ram was moving back and forth, pounding the portcullis with a devastating force each time it struck.

Niles was last to climb through the crenelation at the top of the wall. Once upon the wallwalk, he realized Bryand, Cower and Dwayne were engaged in sword fights with the soldiers who had scaled before them. But instead of joining the skirmish, he said, "Give me a shout if you need me!"

He positioned himself by the ladder and when the

next soldier came into view, Niles hit him squarely in the face. The soldier fell backwards, dislodging the man below him, and both plummeted to the ground below.

Encouraged by his success, Niles picked up a long pike and used it to push the ladder itself away from the wall.

"Going down!" he called, and, with one good shove, he sent, first one ladder and then another, toppling backwards along with all the invaders upon it.

Pleased with himself, he turned to the others with a smirk. "How's that for quick thinking?"

But from their grave expressions he realized something was terribly wrong.

"What?" asked Niles, puzzled. "What is it?"

It was then he saw Dillin's father lying on the wallwalk, his eyes staring blankly ahead. Draping the Master of Torkelstone's body, as if he had defended his lord until his very last breath, lay a young man dressed in a blood-spattered page's tunic.

"Come," said Bryand.

They worked their way along the wall attacking the remaining guards who were fighting the castle's defenders at the south turret.

It was not long before the two groups, Bryand and his friends on one side and the defenders on the other, had fought their way to the center of the fray.

But there was no time for shaking hands or pleasantries of any other kind. For the ladders had gone up again. More guards had already jumped from the crenellations to the wallwalk and were heading in their direction.

They met them fiercely, littering the walk with the dead. But more and more poured over the wall, and soon, Bryand and the others found themselves pushed back into the south turret. They slammed the door shut behind them, and braced it with their bodies, trying desperately to delay the attack long enough to catch their breath and bind their wounds.

Suddenly, they heard a loud thud that reverberated off the turret walls.

"What is that?" asked Cower, panting.

Bryand had recognized the sound. "The portcullis. It's being rammed."

Niles looked at Dwayne and snorted. "And here I thought it was the dinner bell."

Responding to Dwayne's peevish look, Niles quickly added, "It's the mouth again. I can't help it."

"Dwayne, the door," said Bryand with a jerk of his head. "You, too, Niles."

The two knights took over for the men holding it closed. Dwayne tossed a glance at Niles and saw the smirk upon his face.

"If you say anything about my bum right now, I'll crush you against this door."

"I was only thinking how glad I was you were here beside me. You and your bum."

Bryand turned to the others in the room. "Get to the courtyard. We'll hold them here as long as we can."

The defenders filed down the turret stairwell.

The moment the room was clear, Bryand and Cower made ready to meet their attackers.

"We keep them at the door," said the Prince quickly; determinedly. "Plug it with their dead. If they get through, we do the same at the stairwell and plug that too." Bryand turned to Cower. "Stay behind us."

"But, my lord-- ," Cower protested.

"Do as I say. If anyone gets past us, it will be up to you to stop him."

Cower said no more, but took his position and readied himself.

At the Prince's signal, Niles broke from the door, leaving Dwayne, using all his strength, to hold it shut.

"Now, Dwayne," came Bryand's voice from behind him.

Responding immediately, the knight hopped backwards, allowing the door to burst open. The troopers pressing from the other side fell forward at once, some all the way to the floor. These were either trampled by the men behind or pinned by bodies landing upon them.

Bryand and the knights closed in. One after the other, they rotated, maintaining a furious pace. In this way, they kept up a vicious attack and prevented the guards from breaking through. The doorway filled with bodies and became so difficult to access that the guards outside the turret, broke off and headed back along the wallwalk to find another way down.

"Come on," said Bryand, hastening to the turret stairs. The others followed close behind.

Emerging onto the courtyard through spiraling black smoke, the Prince found many defenders standing about, dazed and confused. He hurried to the center of the yard, and there he turned and faced them.

"Here," he called, his arms outstretched. "We form a defensive position here. Quickly now, on me; with archers behind us."

Cower rushed to the Prince's side while Dwayne and Niles, acting like master sergeants, organized the frightened defenders. Soon they had created a deadly skirmish line.

Over and over again, came the thud of the battering ram smashing against the castle portcullis, until at last it was answered with a terrible roar. A gust of wind momentarily cleared the courtyard of smoke.

In that brief moment, before the smoke closed over them once more, they saw the portcullis giving way, taking part of the overhanging structure with it. Stone and timber and screaming soldiers filled the castle entrance. The air was darkened again, this time with a cloud of mortar dust.

"Archers Ready!" Bryand cried, raising his hand as he watched the invaders swarm the gate. When it was choked with soldiers, he brought his hand down quickly and shouted at the top of his voice. "Loose your arrows! Loose now!"

Volley after volley streaked across the yard. A wall of dead was fast collecting, making entrance into the castle harder to achieve.

But quivers that had started half empty, soon held no more arrows to use. The archers tossed away their bows, drew their swords, and joined their comrades on the skirmish line.

Swords thrusting, axes swinging, they met the rushing invaders and broke their charge. Blood gushed and splattered in all directions. Bryand and the others pushed Mortamour's soldiers back through the entrance, which was now littered with dead.

But the defenders' numbers were fast dwindling against the onslaught of Mortamour's seemingly inexhaustible supply of troops. Soon, despite their valiant efforts, they had been pushed back to where they had originally formed their skirmish line.

"This is it," said Niles, grinning, his hands and face covered in blood. "At least I die with my sword swinging!"

"And I with one last fatal thrust!" Added Dwayne, hefting Stick.

"You're not dying," said the Prince, dispatching an attacker with a savage swipe. "Either of you."

Another soldier rushed forward, but before the Prince could engage him, Stick had pierced his throat.

"Thank you," Bryand said, nodding to Dwayne. "I want my throne. I can't claim it without your help. So, no heroics and no theatrics today. And by that I mean you, Niles."

"Me?!" said the Master of Willowbrook while engaged in a contest, nimbly dodging a powerful downward swing. "You must be thinking of someone else. I'm a pious, reverent fellow." And as if to punctuate his claim, he thrust his sword into his attacker's chest, "See you what I mean?"

The courtyard was filled with a sound much like that of a thousand smithies pounding their hammers against their anvils again and again. And above the clashing steel, came the shouts and grunts and cries of desperate men.

"Look, my lord," shouted Cower, pointing to their right. And it was then the Prince saw Dillin at the head of a dozen defenders. They had formed a flanking effort and were cutting deeply into Mortamour's ranks.

"Dillin," Bryand cried, but the din was far too loud for his friend to hear.

In an instant, the Prince was filled with more strength and purpose than he had known in many months. Before he knew it, he was fighting his way in Dillin's direction, meeting and dispatching one foe after the next.

"No heroics or theatrics, he said," called Niles to Cower and Dwayne. "What does he call that?!"

"Less talking and more doing," replied Dwayne, pushing Niles ahead.

They formed a triangle with Dwayne as the point, and in this way cut through to the Prince, who, with Slaybest dripping gore and blood, was fighting now like a man possessed.

There were perhaps five yards between Dillin and the Prince when a fresh, new wave of Mortamour's soldiers burst through the gate and strengthened their attack.

"Bryand," Dwayne shouted close to the Prince's ear.

"You'll never make it! There are too many of them to defend ourselves from here!"

"I will!" cried Bryand, sounding like a man possessed. He met an attacker. They locked hilts, and for a moment it was a contest of sheer strength. But the Prince was done with the delay. He grabbed the man's own dagger from his belt and deposited the blade in his eye.

"Inside!" Dillin's voice peeled above the din, as he pointed defenders toward the keep. "Quickly, men! Quickly! We'll make our stand inside!"

So pre-occupied was he with saving as many as he could, that Dillin did not know he had taken hold of Bryand's arm and was pulling him toward the keep. But before the Prince could speak, the knight was off to retrieve another man. Nor did he know it was Bryand who saved him, when a guard came from behind and nearly plunged his sword into Dillin's back.

Niles, Dwayne and Cower joined the Prince, and together they made one final push to halt the flood of invaders. In doing so, they gave Dillin as well as many others the time they needed to fall back into the keep.

"I believe it's our turn now," called Niles, fending off an attacker.

"Then what are you waiting for?" said Dwayne grabbing him by the back of his shirt and pulling him along.

"Cower!" The Prince cried at the door. "Cower where are you?"

"Here, my lord," said the retainer, already inside.

They slammed the heavy door shut, securing it with a thick oak beam and then a second that they hurriedly nailed into place.

So urgent and hard-fought was their retreat, that Bryand still had not made his presence known to Dillin. Unable to contain his joy any longer, he worked his way through the gathered defenders to where Dillin was pounding one last nail into the door.

Sweat and grime covered his face. There was a small cut directly below his right eye.

"Dillin," said the Prince in a voice choked with emotion, finding himself unable to say anything more.

Dillin turned and saw him, and for a moment he did not believe his eyes. "Bryand?"

"Aye," said the Prince, a joyous smile curling his lips.

They stared at each other. But only for a moment, before they were in each other's arms and hugging like they would never let go.

Tears sprang to the Prince's eyes. "I tried to make it here sooner. I really did try."

"I knew you hadn't betrayed me. I knew you'd come if you were still alive."

They held each other tightly for a moment more. Niles, Dwayne and Cower joined them. When Dillin saw his friends, his mouth fell open and he belched forth a hearty laugh. "Is that you, Niles? And Dwayne, are you here, too?!"

"Still as sharp as ever," said Niles, grinning.

"Thank the Gods!" shouted Dillin, hugging first one and then the other. "I thought I'd never see you again!" And to the Prince's retainer he added, "And you Master Cower. You are also a welcome sight, though I know not how you found your Prince again and kept yourselves alive."

"A retainer knows to trust his nose," said Cower, feeling a sense of pride. "Like a faithful dog, I simply picked up my master's scent."

Turning to Bryand, Dillin gripped his arms, and said, "It's Daron, isn't it? Somehow he found a way to betray you. After the tournament, I'd wager?"

"I've spoken those very words," Bryand answered,

overjoyed. "Yet it sounds so strange to hear them coming from another's lips."

Dillin hugged him briefly, then turned abruptly to his men. "We must make ready! Get the feasting tables and brace them against the door. Bring that sideboard, too! They'll be ramming us any time now."

When the barricade was finished, they gathered in the main hall and waited for the final assault. Their numbers were sorely lacking, being just under a score.

The air inside the keep was thick and pungent from the gray smoke that hung at the ceiling. Cower peered above him, taking note of the crackling sound coming from the second landing. Well, he thought, if a sword doesn't get me, the fire will.

The pounding began once again. The room reverberated with the sound. With each strike, the door's hinges pulled an inch or two more from the wall.

It will never hold, thought Bryand, staring at the door.

Dillin turned to him. "We have only minutes before the fighting starts again. If you die here, there will be no one left to stop Daron from destroying the rest of the kingdom."

"What are you saying," said Bryand, though he knew quite well what Dillin meant.

"There is still time for you to escape. The north side of the keep is not yet ablaze. You could climb out my window onto the wall in the same way we did when we were lads. But you must go now before they break through and cut off your escape."

Bryand scowled. "I haven't come all this way just to leave again."

Dillin cast a quick glance at the door. One or two more hits and it would be down. "Think of what your brother has done to the country, Bryand. Think of what he will do once there is no one left to stop him."

"The country can rot for all I care!" spat the Prince. "I'll not leave you here to die!"

It was then the door gave way, eliminating any further discussion.

◆ ◆ ◆

A triumphant cry rose up and Mortamour's men poured inside the keep.

But just as they funneled into the vestibule and were entering the main hall, the ceiling collapsed upon them, and they were buried by flaming timbers and scalding stones.

Tortured screams rose up. Wounded men staggered about. Smoke filled the room, and hot ashes drifted everywhere like fireflies.

A new wave poured in led by Mortamour himself.

"Where are you, my lord," he growled, squinting into the gloom. "I know you're still alive! Every instinct tells me you're still alive." And with his sword poised to strike, he plunged into the billowing smoke.

Dillin and his men took advantage of the confusion. They hurled themselves into the flames and smoke, and began a savage attack. Dwayne, in the meantime, stood his ground, Stick in hand, and, like a promontory in the face of a flood, met his attackers, broke their charge and sent them spilling backwards into their own ranks.

But not even such a fearsome fighter as Dwayne could stem their tide. Slowly, he was pushed back. He met an attacker and cracked his spine with a single blow. Another came at him, and he plunged Stick's sharp end into the man's chest. Still another fell upon him, and seeing he had no time to extract his weapon, he dodged the man's swipe, closed on him before he could regain his balance and broke his neck.

"This way!" shouted Dillin, appearing out of the smoke.

"Where are the others?" shouted Dwayne above the roar of the flames.

"Here!" cried Niles, joining them. Cower and the Prince followed, and they formed a line, fighting side by side until their backs were against the rear wall of the chamber.

Bryand met an attacker straight on, parried his thrust, and slashed him across the chest. The man fell, clutching his wound. Another guard appeared out of the smoke and occupied the Prince, while still another bore down upon him as well. Seeing this, Cower cried out and barreled into the man.

Steel bit into steel. Cower, surprising himself, met each blow. Boldness, that was it! Take the initiative! The retainer struck and struck again, pressing his adversary backwards.

"Cower!" Bryand called still occupied with his attacker. "Cower, stay back with us!"

"Fear not, my lord!" shouted Cower. "Be bold! Be brave!"

But just then the retainer's foot caught under the body of a dead man. He stumbled, and before he could recover, the soldier's sword cut deeply into his side just below his rib cage. Cower gasped from the pain. Yet he did not surrender to it.

Instead, he grabbed the soldier's sword arm and held it tight. Cower brought his own blade down with all his strength, cutting deeply into the man's shoulder by the base of his neck.

The soldier was dead before he hit the floor. Cower stood for a moment, staring blankly at the body. He realized the man's weapon was still in his side. He extracted it, convulsing from the pain, then stood and peered incredulously at the blood on his hands.

"Cower!" shouted the Prince, reaching him at last.

The retainer looked at Bryand, the shock still upon his face. "There's a lesson to be learned here, my Prince. "Never be too sure of your own prowess. Someone may come along and best you."

The retainer's eyes rolled up. His knees buckled, and he would have fallen had not the Prince grabbed him and dragged him back to the wall.

Mortamour swung his sword at any change in the smoke. His eyes stung. His cheeks were wet with tears.

Fire raged everywhere now, unchecked and unforgiving. Timbers exploded from the heat, sending flaming splinters through the air like fire arrows, only to be swallowed up by the gluttonous smoke.

"Where are you, my lord!?" the henchman shouted, his voice puny compared to the roar of the flames. "I know you're still alive!"

He saw a shadowy figure coming toward him and he struck at it with his blade. When he leaned down, he saw that he had killed one of his own men.

"Blast you for getting in my way!"

Just then there came a loud groan from directly overhead. Mortamour looked up. His eyes went agog, and he barely covered himself in time as a portion of the ceiling collapsed upon him and knocked him to the floor.

He shoved aside the smoldering debris and slapped out the fire that had caught upon his sleeve. He staggered to his feet and, like a man in a drunken stupor, stared at the cloud of glowing embers that hung in the air.

He heard men screaming. From somewhere ahead of him came the sound of weapons clashing. A soldier broke from the smoke and raced by him, his tunic all in flames.

"Instincts be hanged!" cursed the henchman. "No one could live through this!"

A gust of wind cleared the space around him just long enough for him to catch a glimpse of the hole that was once the keep's entrance. He struggled toward it, and soon found himself outside.

"Guardsmen!" he called behind him, panting. "Break off the attack! Let the fire finish the job!"

The five friends hugged the wall at the back of the room as taunting orange flames flicked at them through ramparts of oily black smoke.

"I've pictured myself dying in lots of ways," rasped Niles, covering his face with his forearm. "But I never expected to be roasted like a loin of pork."

The fire roared in triumph, blotting out all other sound, and the heat, like a vengeful foe, forced them to their knees.

But just when it seemed they had met their end, Dwayne, who was feeling the wall, happened upon a large metal ring. It burned his fingers when he touched it. But looking closer, he discovered it was the handle of a door.

He grabbed the ring. He face screwed into a grimace as his skin sizzled. Still, he did not let go and pulled open a door.

"Dillin! Where does this corridor lead?"

"Who cares!" cried Niles, "Any place would be better than this!"

They raced along the passage. Bryand and Dillin,

carrying Cower between them, lagged only a few feet behind.

Shortly, they came to another door, and opening it, they discovered they were at the kitchen. It too was on fire. A portion of the ceiling had already collapsed, and they could see the daylight vaguely through the smoke high overhead.

They entered just as the corridor behind them collapsed with a thunderous crash that sent thick smoke and hot embers roiling all around them. There seemed nowhere to go, and for one brief moment, they stood where they were, out of ideas and overcome by their fear.

"My, it's hot in here," Cower mumbled. "Someone's been doing a lot of baking."

"What was that?" said Bryand eagerly, giving the retainer his full attention.

"Baking, my lord."

At first, Bryand thought the retainer was losing his reason; that the pain from his wound was too much to bear. He held him closer, ignoring the blood that seeped through his fingers as he pressed his hand to Cower's wound.

"The oven, my lord. The oven."

He heard the retainer but had no idea what he was trying to convey. He looked about, frustrated, near panic. It was then, his eyes fell upon the castle oven, and he knew exactly what Cower meant.

"This way!" shouted the Prince above the roaring flames. And when they were at the oven, he left Cower in Dillin's arms, threw open the door, and struggled to pull out the iron bread racks.

"Stand aside!" said Dwayne, and he took over for the Prince, gripping the racks with his massive hands and yanking them free of the oven's walls. When he had pulled the last rack out, the brawny young man climbed in.

"Go," said Bryand to Niles, who stood rooted to the floor with his mouth agape. "Quickly!"

"Are you mad?" said Willowbrook. "We'll roast in there."

"We'll roast out here!" growled Dwayne, grabbing Niles by his shirt and pulling him inside.

"Excellent idea, my lord," said Cower weakly, once they were within the oven. "You have your grandfather's sense of ingenuity. Have I ever told you the story of the iron cap he made?"

"Save your strength, Cower," said the Prince, wiping the grime from the retainer's face.

"What's going to keep us from being roasted in here?" asked Niles anxiously, watching the Prince close the door.

"These walls," said Dillin from within the darkness. "They're three feet thick."

"True, but what if the fire ignites the stoker?"

"I wouldn't worry about the stoker," responded Bryand. "We'll smother long before that ever happens."

"And if we don't smother," added Dwayne. "There's always the chance that we'll be crushed by a collapsing wall."

Niles scowled, though in the darkness it was for no one's benefit other than his own. "Thank you all for assuaging my fears."

The air grew stifling, and as he drew it into his lungs, the Prince was reminded of his ordeal in the cavern and his narrow escape from the reptilian creature. Yet the heat was so enervating, he had not the strength to mention it.

Another time, he thought, wiping his sweaty brow. I'll tell them all about it another time.

He held Cower tighter. During all this time, the Prince had yet to remove his hand from the man's wound.

"Cower?"

"Aye, my lord," came his hoarse reply.

"We'll be out of this soon."

"Aye, my lord."

The walls became hot, but not unbearably so, and overcome with exhaustion, one by one they fell asleep. It was not until many hours later, when the sunlight peeked through the tiny vent in the oven door, that Bryand awoke and ventured a peek at the kitchen.

The fire had ceased its feasting and was now gnawing on what was left of the castle's bones.

The Prince emerged. He stretched his achy limbs, and surveyed the wreckage.

Everything that was wood had been reduced to smoldering coal and all that remained of the keep was its stone shell. Yet the smoke had cleared, or rather, was being cleared by the updraft that had been created by the collapse of the ceiling. The keep was now a giant flue.

One by one, the others crawled out of the oven and surveyed the wreckage. Then, Bryand and Dwayne lifted Cower carefully and placed him on the ground.

"I'll be right back," said the Prince to the retainer.

"I'll be right here," replied Cower in a breathy voice.

Staying low and out of sight, Bryand and Dillin worked their way from one mound of rubble to the next until they had reached the front of the keep. The battle was over and now there was only silence, the silence of the dead. Even Mortamour's men worked without speaking, gathering weapons and stores, piling corpses upon makeshift pyres and setting them alight.

The two men watched in silence, bruised and sore in body and in spirit. They had lost so much. In fact, they had little more than what they carried on them. Though neither of them admitted it, they were both feeling quite overwhelmed and confused about their futures. But they did not have time to dwell upon this for very long, because suddenly Niles was standing beside them.

"What is it?" asked Dillin, alerting at once.

Niles did not answer him. Instead he said in an anguished tone, "Bryand-- . You'd best come back to the kitchen."

When the Prince saw the grave expression on his face, terror rose inside him. He sprinted toward the rear of the keep unmindful of being seen. He scrambled over the scorched rubble, ignoring the heat and the pain.

"Don't take him from me," he said out loud for all the Gods to hear. "He's all I have! He's all you've left me!"

When he reached the kitchen, he found Dwayne standing apart from Cower. A tear ran down the knight's cheek.

Bryand fell before the retainer. "Cower?" said the Prince in a hopeful, almost pleading voice. He gently turned his face to him. "Friend?"

He looked into his eyes. But the light that was Cower's essence had left them, and despite all Bryand's pleading, coaxing, the retainer would not respond.

Cower was dead.

"I'm sorry, Bryand," said Dwayne, swallowing hard.

"I don't understand it," said Bryand, brushing Cower's cheek. "I always thought you invincible."

Dwayne placed his massive hand on Bryand's shoulder, gripping it, hoping to transfer to the Prince a measure of his strength. "He has an honored place awaiting him now. A chair by Himagain's throne, in the Hall of the Heavens."

Bryand nodded in agreement, his heart aching. But then, gazing at Cower, he was struck by a thought. "Knowing you," said the Prince tenderly, chuckling through his tears. "A chair by the fire with a padded footstool would be much more to your liking."

When Dillin and Niles returned, they found Bryand kneeling over the retainer's body. He did not even bother to wipe his tears away when he looked at them and said, "He needs a proper funeral."

The others peered at each other, confused.

"You mean, here?" ventured Niles, frowning. "Now?"

Bryand nodded. "Now."

Dillin shook his head. "Bryand, it's too dangerous, you can't risk-- ."

He clutched the retainer to him. "Go if you must. But I will not leave Cower here to burn without my standing by."

He lifted the retainer's body into his arms, and paying no heed to the cautions from his friends, the Prince carried Cower over the rubble to the outside of the keep.

He placed the retainer's body atop a pile of dead, whose spirits also waited patiently to be set free. He grabbed some coal oil from a passing laborer, and, fighting back his tears, spilled it over Cower's body, then found a smouldering coal among the ruins and set the pyre alight.

Dillin appeared, and then Dwayne, and then Niles. They stood beside the Prince, watching the crackling flames grow taller, each in his own way, saying his goodbye and sending Cower off with a silent prayer.

At length, casting a guarded look about them, Dillin said, "Please, Bryand. You court disaster. We must go now."

Bryand nodded, watching a wisp of smoke rise toward the Heavens, and they left in silence, knowing Cower, too, was well away.

CHAPTER TWENTY NINE

Mortamour stood by the castle gate, taking in the destruction. Torkelstone in ruins and the Prince and all his friends dispatched at last; a good day's work, he decided; the duke will be most pleased. Perhaps now he'll even allow me to take a little holiday.

He paused to think. What has it been? Two, no three years. Time for a well-deserved respite, he decided, and he started across the courtyard at a leisurely pace.

Where shall I go, he mused, scratching his beard as he approached the keep. He halted and pondered the question for a moment. The baths at Tapwater were supposed to be most rejuvenating. They had long been a favorite of the royal family. And there was no doubt his body could use a good soaking.

But when he gave it a little more thought, the idea of sitting around a pool with some aging men in loin cloths was not very appealing. No, thank you, he thought, frowning with distaste, Tapwater is definitely out.

He started climbing the rubble, working his way from mound to mound, feeling the heat rise up into the early morning air.

Wait, he thought, brightening. What about Lameduck? The hunting there was splendid.

Aye, he told himself, picking up a stick of charred wood and tossing it away. Now that's something more to my liking. He had always found blood sports to be invigorating and relaxing at the same time. Aye, Lame-duck it is, he decided, and with spirits high, he wiped the soot from his hands and jumped down from a tall pile of rubble.

By this time, he had reached the rear of the keep. Here much of the back wall remained, and he was casually glancing at it, when he noticed the oven. At first there seemed nothing unusual about it, but when he saw the racks and the way they had been torn from their fittings, his curiosity was aroused

He went to it, swung open the door, and stuck his head inside. His first impression was that, without the racks, the interior was quite large. Large enough even for a hiding place.

But it was not this observation that set his instincts clamoring again. Rather, it was the pool of dried blood he found upon the oven's floor. It was unmistakable. He had seen its like too many times before.

Alert now, his heart thumping in his chest, Mortamour scanned the ruins. Though, for what, he still was not exactly sure.

There were many footprints but none that was distinct. Searching further, He stepped over some fallen stones and charred timbers, and it was not long before he found a footprint perfectly preserved in the ashes. He studied it for familiar markings but soon determined he had not seen its like before.

He stepped over more stones, slid beneath a fallen buttress, climbed gingerly over a burned-out sideboard, whereupon he found another print that was the same. But there, just ahead of it, was a well-defined print of a different size and width.

He bent low, his nose just an inch away from the

impression. "Son of a whoremonger," he said beneath his breath.

For this print he had seen before, upon the bank of the Ankledeep River just above Themstall Falls.

He suddenly felt unnerved. He looked again, hoping he was mistaken. But, no. He recognized the markings; the slight depression on the outside of the heel.

There was no denying it. For he knew of no one else who could have been in both places. The Prince was still alive, and from the other footprints about so, too, were his friends.

"This can't be!" he shouted, jumping to his feet. "This can't be!" He tracked the footprints to a breach in the wall, scrambled over the broken stonework and dropped to the ground just short of the moat.

There he found more footprints in the muddy embankment leading to the water. He peered across the moat at the opposite embankment, and soon he located the trampled grass and broken reeds where the Prince and his friends had emerged. Anger surged in him unchecked; he kicked a pile of rubble, scattering some kindling into the air.

"Why can't I kill you?!" he cried aloud. "Haven't I tried hard enough?!" And then a new thought struck him, one than made him angrier still. "Blistering irons!" he shouted, his face turning purple with rage. "There goes my vacation!!"

He turned quickly, already dreading the scolding he'd receive when the Duke learned of the Prince's latest escape.

Why I put up with his abuse is beyond me, thought the henchman. If he didn't pay so well, I'd slit his throat.

His pace increased with every step. Gather a troop. Get to the horses. The Prince is on foot. He'll not have gotten far. "Damn you, your highness!" he shouted. "Damn you and your friends."

It was then, he stopped short in his tracks, his instincts screaming in a way he had not felt before. Odd, he thought, looking around. And to his astonishment, he saw Bryand a short distance away, standing alone and at the top of a large mound of stones.

"Sounds like I spoiled your day."

What a blasted fool, thought the henchman. Delivering himself to me like this.

Mortamour smiled and slowly, casually, he rested his hands on the buckle of his belt. "Spoil my day? Well, you did for awhile. But I have to say, no longer. In fact, it's now quite good."

"Glad to hear it," said Bryand with a charming smile. "Perhaps you'd return the favor and make my day just as good."

"And how would I do that," growled Mortamour, sneering, his eyes ticking back and forth.

"First, you can tell me if my father was murdered. And then, some other things as well."

Mortamour considered the question. "Well, honestly, before I answer that I'd need to know just who would shoulder the blame."

He took that moment to plant his feet firmly in spite of the heat beneath them. "See, between the man who conceives the plan, who supplies the means, and the one who does the deed, there's a lot of hairs that can be split."

"I see. So, if I understand you correctly, no matter who's to blame, my father did not die a natural death."

"Your understanding is correct."

"He was murdered."

"Aye, he was."

"And what of King Jasper?"

Mortamour smiled craftily. "Don't forget his family."

"Very well. Were they attacked by Woolly-Bullies

or were they murdered, too?"

"I really liked that Woolly-Bully ruse," said Mortamour, intending to provoke the Prince. "But, if it's truth we're speaking, then, aye, they were murdered, too."

"Thank you for your honesty."

"You're welcome, Prince Bryand."

He was surprised Mortamour knew his real name. All this time, he thought no one had any inkling of his brother's deception.

"You didn't expect that," said Mortamour, pleased with himself. "Oh, we've known pretty much from the start that Daron was on the throne. He's not a very clever fellow, at least not like you. Though, he doesn't know it yet, his days are numbered. His rule is coming to an end."

"You're hoping Cunninghim will replace him," said Bryand with a sober look.

"Not hoping, your highness, it's more like something I already know. The Duke's time has come. But don't let that trouble you none. You won't be around to see it."

"No? Where will I be?"

"With your father and King Jasper, of course. Say hello for me when you see them. It was I who disposed of them both. Your father was just a simple delivery but King Jasper," he said, very pleased with himself, "King Jasper was much more fun."

He pulled two small blades from behind his buckle and sent them flying toward the Prince. Bryand dodged the first and the second barely miss, cutting off a lock of his hair. Before he had completely recovered, Mortamour drew a dagger from his sleeve, and this he hurled at the Prince, who, in avoiding it, lost his footing, tottered backwards, and then fell out of sight.

Mortamour scrambled down the rubble, slipping

and sliding, kicking up embers as he went. "I hope I haven't killed you, your highness," he called, drawing his sword and starting up the pile of stones where Bryand had stood. "Or, perhaps I should clarify that remark and say, I hope you're not yet dead. I'm not real fond of long-range kills. There's nothing very satisfying about them. But bein' close, that's completely different. With close-kills, you get to watch the life leavin' from a person's eyes."

Once at the top, Mortamour looked down at what he expected to be the opposite slope. But, in fact, it was not. About three feet below him ran a narrow ledge, the remains of an interior wall. Below the ledge was a smoldering pit of coals and rubble and charred beams that were still burning.

"Smart of you, your highness," he said from where he stood, looking for any sign that would tell him which direction the Prince had fled. "To try to run away, that is. Although, it's not the bravest choice, I must admit, it's the one I would have chosen as well."

"And how about this?" came Bryand's voice from behind him. Mortamour turned and saw the Prince standing below him, hefting a rock in his hand, which at that precise moment, he hurled at the Assassin and struck him soundly in the chest.

It was almost as if he were imitating Bryand. For Mortamour lost his footing and tottered backward in almost exactly the same way. But after which, he differed slightly in one crucial respect. Instead of falling, Mortamour regained his balance, and with a mocking sneer, regained his footing as well.

"Too bad for you, your highness," he said adjusting the grip on his sword. "I mean, for things to have gone this way."

"I wouldn't count this over," said Bryand grimly, climbing toward him, his eyes never straying from the henchman. "Not by any means. You're not going anywhere until the bill has been fully paid."

The henchman chortled, enjoying himself. He truly is a fool. Why, he's even coming to me. How much easier could this be?

A moment later, they were facing one another and the contest had begun. Sword biting sword; parry and thrust; each of them gaining the advantage then having to relinquish it.

"Now that I think of it," said Bryand, disengaging for a beat. "I suppose it was you the day of the joust. The one who delivered the tainted cup."

"You've guessed right, your highness," said the henchman with glee, thrusting once, and then once again. "I have to admit, you've been hard to kill. I mean, till now, that is."

"I admit that you're good," replied the Prince, fending off his blows. "Better than most, I think."

"Thank you, my lord, and I must confess, you are not such a fool."

Quite suddenly, he disengaged, and in one quick move, produced a dagger from his boot. "Just one about to be dead."

Armed now with a weapon in each hand, Mortamour began a savage attack. Slash and cut; slash and cut; pushing the Prince up the mound until they had reached the crest.

The henchman grinned, and with each attack, the grin grew wider and wider until it was a malevolent sneer.

But the henchman had underestimated Bryand as an adversary. The Prince was not a pampered noble. He was a soldier and a master swordsman. He had trained his whole life for a situation like this.

After an exchange or two, Bryand feinted to his right, but quickly darted to his left, and with a quick swipe, dislodged the dagger from Mortamour's hand. The henchman tried to regain the initiative. He thrust his sword at Bryand's chest. But the Prince, emboldened now, stepped aside, pivoted quickly and cut deeply across the henchman's chest.

Mortamour dropped his sword. He clutched his wound and crumpled where he stood. His breathing came in labored spurts. Struggling through his pain, he looked up the Prince and sneered.

"So what now, your highness," said the henchman, almost as a dare. "Cut off my head? Run me through? What does that moral code of yours demand?"

He spit some blood in front of him, and as he did so, his eyes scanned the rubble for his sword. "Really, you've quite a decision to make. What does one do when there is no justice? No one in charge with the same integrity as you?"

"I am justice," said Bryand, barely controlling his wrath. "I am the rightful heir to the throne, and being such, in my father's name, I can and do sentence you to death."

He stepped closer and raised Slaybest over his head.

But at that same moment, the henchman, with all his nerve intact, presented him with a goading smile. "Tell me, my lord," said Mortamour, shifting his weight somewhat so he could lean closer to the Prince. "Are you in the least bit interested in what's become of the Lady MeAnne?"

"MeAnne?" said Bryand, surprised at the mention of her name. "What about MeAnne?!"

The smile on the henchman's face made room for an arrogant laugh to escape. "She's a prisoner in Nightshade's castle, my lord. And there, I'm afraid, she'll stay."

"Nightshade-- ," Bryand uttered, thinking of the castle on the lake and the fearsome creature within its depths. And then he pictured MeAnne's face.

In that brief moment, Mortamour saw the Prince had dropped his guard. The henchman sprang forward, using his head like a battering ram. He collided with the Prince, who did not expect the blow, and sent him spilling down the mound.

When Bryand came to rest, Slaybest was no longer in his hand. He saw Mortamour. The henchman had retrieved his sword and was now standing at the top of the rubble pile, staring down at him.

"Disappointing is it not? To have things go a different way than you expected? Although it would be more like your brother's nature, I'm sure you were hoping I'd be dead by now."

And then from where he did not expect it, came another's voice. "He might be disappointed. But rest assured, I am not."

Mortamour turned in the direction from which the voice had come. It was then he saw Niles, upon the opposite mound of rubble, standing exactly where he himself had originally stood.

His crossbow was armed and leveled, and with a snap of the trigger, the quarrel sailed through the air and struck the henchman in the throat.

Mortamour staggered and dropped his sword. He gripped the protruding quarrel shaft and tried desperately to pull it out.

He teetered for a moment longer, blood gurgling from his mouth. His legs buckled, and he fell backwards, glancing off the narrow landing and dropping into the glowing coals with enough force to set ablaze that which now encased him.

They heard his screams but not for long. By the time Niles joined the Prince at the top of the stones, all that rose from below was the crackling of the flames.

At length, Bryand looked at Niles. "What are you

doing here?"

He shrugged. "I knew you would need some help."

"I told you to stay with the others."

"I heard you. I came anyway."

"Someday, Niles, I'll be your king," said Bryand, somewhat annoyed.

"Fine," answered Niles, obliging him. " On that day, I'll start listening to you."

They had not traveled very far before they were joined by Dillin and Dwayne.

"Doesn't anyone obey my commands?" asked Bryand, now thoroughly vexed.

"Of Course we do," said Dillin, walking a pace behind him. "But sometimes, we must disobey, in order to keep you safe."

"I was never in danger," said Bryand defensively. "I was simply wearing him down."

"Hah!" chortled Niles from behind them. He was last in line.

Dwayne, with his massive strides, was two paces ahead of them all. "Well, I for one, will do nothing differently. No matter how much you complain. I pledge my life from here on out, wherever our path leads, to keeping you safe from all our foes and from whatever comes our way."

He pivoted on his heels and walked backwards for awhile without once breaking stride. "Each of us has lost what most people would consider everything. Our lands, our holdings, our stations. But I would lose them all again, and still have what matters most to me - our loyalty to each other, and the friendship that we share. As long as I have those, I am content. And know you now, if you don't already, I would give my life for any one of you."

"Really?" said Niles, at once sarcastic. "Even me?"

"Even you," answered Dwayne. "Though, in your

case, I'd have second thoughts."

EPILOGUE

The sun dipped below the horizon and twilight unfurled in a brilliant blend of orange, crimson, and finally, cobalt blue. Under the cover of darkness, they traveled south for many hours, with only a sliver of the moon to guide them.

At length, they reached a small knoll upon which stood a ring of low bushes.

It was there, protected by the foliage, they fell to the ground, exhausted from their journey and from the ordeal of the day before.

Bryand sat by himself just beyond the bushes, keeping watch while the others slept. Unlike his friends, he had no desire to sleep. He knew it would elude him; peaceful sleep, that is.

He looked into the darkness of the western sky and frowned. Bryand no longer cared for the dark. It reminded him of the suffering he had endured in his own dungeon.

He pictured himself lying in moldy straw, chained to the wall, and he recalled the fear he had felt, not knowing if he would ever again see the light of day.

But then he remembered it was Cower who had saved him from the dungeon.

Master Cower, he thought, and he pictured the retainer in his mind. A lump formed in his throat instantly and tears welled in his eyes.

Just a few days ago you were lecturing the children and arguing with Malady, and combing straw out of your hair.

This brought a smile to him. For one who prided himself on his grooming, you certainly were a mess. And this was not a criticism, but rather a tender observation.

So many goodbyes, thought the Prince, pulling up some blades of grass and tossing them into the wind. And for what? A throne that no one knows has been stolen from me.

It truly was a dilemma; one with many far-reaching complications. He knew that each would need to be addressed. But for the time being, he chose to concentrate on how exactly he was going to win back his throne.

He glanced at the three knights sleeping peacefully among the bushes.

So loyal, he thought. So undeserving of the pain and loss they had suffered. He thanked the Gods for their friendship. But even with all their strengths and abilities, they were only an army of three.

Where would he find the others he needed? It took money to build an army. Chests full. How was he going to buy arms and armor when he could not even buy a loaf of bread?

How utterly absurd, he thought, and the more he dwelled on the irony of the situation, the more it made him laugh inwardly. He wondered if his life could be any more foolish or foolhardy if it were a comedy written for the stage.

Look you. Here stands The Pauper Prince. Poorer than the poorest beggar in his brother's Kingdom. A man with no home; no country; not even a name that he can call his own.

He waited. But no laughter came in turn. No applause, either. The theater was empty and the stage was dark, and he was sitting by himself again atop the knoll.

He sighed and shook his head. The problems he faced seemed insurmountable. Perhaps it was best for everyone involved if he just disappeared.

He considered sneaking off. Now; before the sun had risen. But he knew there was not much sense in his doing so; with his sense of direction he would most likely wander aimlessly, or in a circle, and stumble upon his friends again just as they were waking up.

Thoroughly depressed, he stretched out upon the grass. His body all but sank into the earth. Not even the dew could restore him as it touched his cheek.

He felt weary down to his bones. In his mind he saw himself languishing at the bottom of a chasm, and he wondered if, in some prescient way, he was seeing his future residence.

"Come, my lord," spoke a familiar voice. "Another day has arrived and it is time you started off again."

Recognizing the voice at once, the Prince looked up and his mouth fell open in surprise. For there was Cower, alive and standing over him with his hands planted firmly upon his hips.

"On your feet, good sir," the retainer said in a quiet but resolute way. "No dilly-dallying; do you hear? I will have none of that from you."

The Prince gazed at the retainer, his mouth open, too stunned to speak or move.

"My you are a slugabed this morning. And a tight-lipped fellow, too. But you had better find your voice soon. The sun is almost ready to show its head. There is much to plan, and much to do."

"Cower," Bryand muttered at last. "But how-- ."

The retainer grinned and shook his head. "But how, but how. Is that all you can say? What is the plan of action?"

"Plan of action?" Bryand repeated.

"Aye, sir. That which you must do?"

Bryand frowned, thinking once more of his future. "I don't know any more, Cower. All I feel is lost."

A broad smile stretched across Cower's face. "Lost, you say? Since when has that stopped you?"

Bryand chose to ignore the jest. "I'm beaten, Cower," he said bitterly. "There's no one else to turn to and nowhere left to go."

The retainer sobered and knelt beside him. "Come now, my lord, have you not your strength? You instincts? Have you not your wits and your courage?"

"Aye," Bryand replied. "But-- ."

"Well, then, you are far from beaten. Nor shall you ever be, while you hold fast to the things that you believe in." He stood and placed his hands on his hips once more. "Now get up, my lord, and face the day."

"But Cower, I've no support, no resources. How can I hope to prevail against a whole kingdom?"

"You will find a way. In the meantime, you know what to do. The only thing a prince can do, especially one who would be a king."

"Cower, you don't understand," Bryand said, getting to his feet. Yet when he brushed himself off and looked for the man, he discovered he was alone. The Prince glanced about, confused. "Cower?"

"Are you all right?" Dillin said sleepily, sitting up.

Bryand scanned the surrounding area, still hoping to find his friend.

"Bryand? Is something wrong?"

At length, Bryand turned to him. "No."

"You were talking in your sleep."

"It was nothing. Rest awhile. The sun will be up in an hour."

The Prince wandered about the knoll, hoping he would find Cower. Soon, however, he realized that he had seen him only in a dream.

His heart ached. "I miss you, dear friend." A tear

skittered down his cheek.

He tried to think of something else; something less painful. He found his answer in the times they had shared. And the more he thought of these, the better he began to feel.

He remembered the man's gentleness and trustworthiness; his dry sense of humor. He thought of his quiet strength and of his character, and for the first time the Prince realized that what he prided most about himself, had been taught to him by Cower.

And with this new insight, suddenly the Prince understood what his dream was trying to tell him.

I must go on, he thought resolutely. I will go on.

It was what Cower had done facing the executioner's block, fighting the wolves, the flood, the creature, the tunnels, and so on during their whole confounded journey.

It was what Cower would do now if he were still alive; with the quiet but steadfast belief that someday all things would be set right.

He pictured the retainer in his mind's eye once more, the pleasant smile on his face, the one he wore each morning. Thinking of this made the Prince smile as well, and wiping away his tears he stood and inhaled a deep breath, no longer filled with gloom, but with hope and determination.

He strode through the break in the bushes and roused his friends. "Come," said Bryand. "Get yourselves up. We must be going."

"Where?" asked Niles, yawning.

The Prince scanned the surroundings. The sun had not yet appeared, but its heralds of light had already set forth upon their journey into the cloudless sky. All about them lay miles of rolling hills covered with fresh green grass, made lustrous by the morning dew.

"I have no idea," replied the Prince honestly. "And

seeing that I have no idea, I believe I should choose the way."

He paused, looked at each of his friends, and with a smile, he said, "After all, I'm the one with no sense of direction."

I must leave off now for a respite. I am suddenly experiencing a bad case of writer's cramp. Also, I am running out of ink and must squeeze more berries. I would ask Rolfo to do it for me, but, with food in short supply, I know he will eat them.

With the little ink I have left, I should note that the Prince was to have many more adventures, many more brushes with death. I know this to be true because I was there to witness them. In fact, just as soon as the feeling returns to my hand, I will begin to jot them down. Until then, however, I will wait.

And, I am sorry to say, so must you.

End of Book One

Made in the USA
Columbia, SC
12 November 2019

82972084R00372